Praise for *The Huntress*

"With magnificently audacious heroines who will haunt you long after the final page, *The Huntress* is a powerful and groundbreaking story of sisterhood that puts women back into history where they belong. Without a doubt, the best book I've read this year."

—Stephanie Dray, *New York Times* bestselling author

"Quinn deftly braids the stories of a female Russian bomber pilot, Nazi hunters, and a young Bostonian girl staring down evil in the most unthinkable of places. The result is a searing tale of predator and prey, transgression and redemption, and the immutable power of the truth. An utter triumph!"

—Pam Jenoff, *New York Times* bestselling author of *The Orphan's Tale*

"Prepare to be spellbound! *The Huntress* masterfully draws you in and doesn't let you go. Another brilliant work of historical fiction by the incomparable Kate Quinn."

—Susan Meissner, *USA Today* bestselling author of *As Bright as Heaven*

"*The Huntress* left me breathless with delight. . . . Kate Quinn has created nothing less than a masterpiece of historical fiction."

—Jennifer Robson, bestselling author of *Goodnight from London*

"*The Huntress* is a triumph of a novel! Nina Markova is a veritable force of nature who would have had the Night Witches themselves cackling with glee at her wild daring in this tale of revenge and justice, truth and secrets during the aftermath of the world's most devastating war."

—Stephanie Thornton, author of *American Princess*

"A thoroughly immersive page-turner, *The Huntress* captures readers from the first page, leading them on an explosive journey that shines a spotlight on the horrors of war and the legacy it leaves for those who survive. Impeccably written, richly detailed, tautly paced, and filled with compelling and intricate characters, Quinn's novel is both poignant and thrilling. This book will take hold of you and stay with you long after you have finished. You don't just read a Kate Quinn novel, you live it."

—Chanel Cleeton, author of *Next Year in Havana*

"An impressive historical novel sure to harness WWII-fiction fans' attention. . . . Laced with Russian folklore allusions and deliciously witty banter, Quinn's tale refreshingly avoids contrived situations while portraying three touching, unpredictable love stories; the suspenseful quest for justice; and the courage involved in confronting one's greatest fears."

—*Booklist* (starred review)

"Well-researched and vivid segments are interspersed detailing Nina's backstory as one of Russia's sizable force of female combat pilots (dubbed The Night Witches by the Germans), establishing her as a fierce yet vulnerable antecedent to Lisbeth Salander. Quinn's language is evocative of the period, and her characters are good literary company. With any luck, the Nazi hunting will go on for a sequel or two."

—*Kirkus Reviews*

"Quinn delivers a suspenseful WWII tale of murder and revenge. This exciting thriller vividly reveals how people face adversity and sacrifice while chasing justice and retribution."

—*Publishers Weekly*

THE
HUNTRESS

Also by Kate Quinn

The Alice Network

THE EMPRESS OF ROME SERIES
Lady of the Eternal City
The Three Fates (novella)
Empress of the Seven Hills
Daughters of Rome
Mistress of Rome

THE BORGIA CHRONICLES
The Lion and the Rose
The Serpent and the Pearl

COLLABORATIVE WORKS
A Day of Fire: A Novel of Pompeii
A Year of Ravens: A Novel of Boudica's Rebellion
A Song of War: A Novel of Troy

THE
HUNTRESS

A Novel

KATE
QUINN

wm

WILLIAM MORROW
An Imprint of HarperCollins*Publishers*

P.S.™ is a trademark of HarperCollins Publishers.

THE HUNTRESS. Copyright © 2019 by Kate Quinn. All rights reserved. Printed in the United States of America. No part of this book may be used or reproduced in any manner whatsoever without written permission except in the case of brief quotations embodied in critical articles and reviews. For information, address HarperCollins Publishers, 195 Broadway, New York, NY 10007.

HarperCollins books may be purchased for educational, business, or sales promotional use. For information, please email the Special Markets Department at SPsales @harpercollins.com.

FIRST EDITION

Designed by Diahann Sturge

Library of Congress Cataloging-in-Publication Data has been applied for.

ISBN 978-0-06-274037-3
ISBN 978-0-06-288434-3 (hardcover library edition)

19 20 21 22 23 LSC 10 9 8 7 6 5 4 3 2 1

For my father—
How I miss you!

Prologue

S he was not used to being hunted.

The lake stretched slate blue, glittering. The woman gazed over it, hands lying loose in her lap. A folded newspaper sat beside her on the bench. The headlines all trumpeted arrests, deaths, forthcoming trials. The trials would be held in Nuremberg, it seemed. She had never been to Nuremberg, but she knew the men who would be tried there. Some she knew by name only, others had touched champagne flutes to hers in friendship. They were all doomed. Crimes against peace. Crimes against humanity. War crimes.

By what law? she wanted to scream, beating her fists against the injustice of it. *By what right?* But the war was over, and the victors had won the right to decide what was a crime and what was not. What was humanity, and what was not.

It was *humanity,* she thought, *what I did. It was mercy.* But the victors would never accept that. They would pass judgment at Nuremberg and forever after, decreeing what acts committed in a lawful past would put a man's head in a noose.

Or a woman's.

She touched her own throat.

Run, she thought. *If they find you, if they realize what you've done, they will lay a rope around your neck.*

But where was there to go in this world that had taken every-thing she loved? This world of hunting wolves. She used to be the hunter, and now she was the prey.

So hide, she thought. *Hide in the shadows until they pass you by.*

She rose, walking aimlessly along the lake. It reminded her pain-fully of Lake Rusalka, her haven in Poland, now ruined and lost to her. She made herself keep moving, putting one foot after the other. She did not know where she was going, only that she refused to huddle here paralyzed by fear until she was scooped onto the scales of their false justice. Step by step the resolve hardened inside her.

Run.

Hide.

Or die.

THE HUNTRESS

BY IAN GRAHAM

APRIL 1946

SIX SHOTS.

She fired six times on the shore of Lake Rusalka, not attempting to hide what she did. Why would she? Hitler's dream of empire had yet to crumble and send her fleeing for the shadows. That night under a Polish moon, she could do whatever she wanted—and she murdered six souls in cold blood.

Six shots, six bullets, six bodies falling into the dark water of the lake.

They had been hiding by the water, shivering, eyes huge with fear—escapees from one of the eastbound trains, perhaps, or survivors fleeing one of the region's periodic purges. The dark-haired woman found them, comforted them, told them they were safe. She took them into her house by the lake and fed them a meal, smiling.

Then she led them back outside—and killed them.

Perhaps she lingered there, admiring the moon on the water, smelling gun smoke.

That nighttime slaughter of six at the height of the war was only one of her crimes. There were others. The hunting of Polish laborers through dense woods as a party game. The murder, near the war's end, of a young English prisoner of war escaped from his stalag. Who knows what other crimes lie on her conscience?

They called her *die Jägerin*—the Huntress. She was the young mistress of an SS officer in German-occupied Poland, the hostess of grand parties on the lake, a keen shot. Perhaps she was the *rusalka* the lake was named for—a lethal, malevolent water spirit.

I think of her as I sit among the ranks of journalists in the Palace of Justice in Nuremberg, watching the war crimes trials grind on. The wheel of justice turns;

the gray-faced men in the defendants' box will fall beneath it. But what about the smaller fish, who escape into the shadows as we aim our brilliant lights on this courtroom? What about the Huntress? She vanished at the war's end. She was not worth pursuing—a woman with the blood of only a dozen or so on her hands, when there were the murderers of millions to be found. There were many like her—small fish, not worth catching.

Where will they go?

Where did *she* go?

And will anyone take up the hunt?

PART I

Chapter 1

JORDAN

April 1946
Selkie Lake, three hours west of Boston

W ho is she, Dad?"

Jordan McBride had timed the question perfectly: her father jerked in surprise midcast, sending his fishing line flying not into the lake, but into the branch of the overhanging maple. Jordan's camera went *click* as his face settled into comic dismay. She laughed as her father said three or four words he then told her to forget.

"Yes, sir." She'd heard all his curse words before, of course. You did, when you were the only daughter of a widowed father who took you fishing on fine spring weekends instead of the son he didn't have. Jordan's father rose from the end of the little dock and tugged his fishing line free. Jordan raised the Leica for another shot of his dark silhouette, framed against the feathery movement of trees and water. She'd play with the image in the darkroom later, see if she could get a blurred effect on the leaves so they seemed like they were still *moving* in the photograph . . .

"Come on, Dad," she prompted. "Let's hear about the mystery woman."

He adjusted his faded Red Sox cap. "What mystery woman?"

"The one your clerk tells me you've been taking out to dinner, those nights you said you were working late." Jordan held her breath, hoping. She couldn't remember the last time her father had been on a date. Ladies were always fluttering their gloved fingers at him after Mass on the rare occasions he and Jordan went to church, but to Jordan's disappointment he never seemed interested.

"It's nothing, really . . ." He hemmed and hawed, but Jordan wasn't fooled for a minute. She and her father looked alike; she'd taken enough photographs to see the resemblance: straight noses, level brows, dark blond hair cut close under her father's cap and spilling out under Jordan's in a careless ponytail. They were even the same height now that she was nearly eighteen; medium for him and tall for a girl—but far beyond physical resemblance, Jordan *knew* her father. It had just been the two of them since she was seven years old and her mother died, and she knew when Dan McBride was working up to tell her something important.

"Dad," she broke in sternly. "*Spill.*"

"She's a widow," her father said at last. To Jordan's delight, he was blushing. "Mrs. Weber first came to the shop three months ago." During the week her father stood three-piece-suited and knowledgeable behind the counter of McBride's Antiques off Newbury Street. "She'd just come to Boston, selling her jewelry to get by. A few gold chains and lockets, nothing unusual, but she had a string of gray pearls, a beautiful piece. She held herself together until then, but she started crying when it came time to part with the pearls."

"Let me guess. You gave them back, very gallantly, then padded your price on her other pieces so she still walked out with the same amount."

He reeled in his fishing line. "She also walked out with an invitation for dinner."

"Look at you, Errol Flynn! Go on—"

"She's Austrian, but studied English at school so she speaks it almost perfectly. Her husband died in '43, fighting—"

"Which side?"

"That kind of thing shouldn't matter anymore, Jordan. The war's over." He fixed a new lure. "She got papers to come to Boston, but times have been hard. She has a little girl—"

"She *does*?"

"Ruth. Four years old, hardly says a word. Sweet little thing." Giving a tweak of Jordan's cap. "You'll love her."

"So it's already serious, then," Jordan said, startled. Her father wouldn't have met this woman's child if he wasn't serious. But *how* serious . . . ?

"Mrs. Weber's a fine woman." He cast his line out. "I want her to come to supper at the house next week, her and Ruth. All four of us."

He gave her a wary look, as if waiting for her to bristle. And part of her did just a tiny bit, Jordan admitted. Ten years of having it be just her and her dad, being *pals* with him the way so few of her girlfriends were with their fathers . . . But against that reflexive twinge of possessiveness was relief. He needed a woman in his life; Jordan had known that for years. Someone to talk to; someone to scold him into eating his spinach. Someone else to lean on.

If he has someone else in his life, maybe he won't be so stubborn about not letting you go to college, the thought whispered, but Jordan shoved it back. This was the moment to be happy for her father, not hoping things might change for her own benefit. Besides, she *was* happy for him. She'd been taking photographs of him for years, and no matter how wide he smiled at the lens, the lines of his face when they came up ghostlike out of the developing fluid said *lonely, lonely, lonely*.

"I can't wait to meet her," Jordan said sincerely.

"She'll bring Ruth next Wednesday, six o'clock." He looked innocent. "Invite Garrett, if you want. He's family too, or he could be—"

"Subtle as a train wreck, Dad."

"He's a fine boy. And his parents adore you."

"He's looking ahead toward college now. He might not have much time for high school girlfriends. Though you could send me to BU with him," Jordan began. "Their photography courses—"

"Nice try, missy." Her father looked out over the lake. "The fish aren't biting." And neither was he.

Taro, Jordan's black Labrador, raised her muzzle from where she'd been sunning on the dock as Jordan and her dad walked back to shore. Jordan snapped a shot of their side-by-side silhouettes thrown across the water-warped wood, wondering what *four* silhouettes would look like. *Please*, Jordan prayed, thinking of the unknown Mrs. Weber, *please let me like you.*

A SLIM HAND extended as blue eyes smiled. "How lovely to meet you at last."

Jordan shook hands with the woman her father had just ushered into the sitting room. Anneliese Weber was small and slender, dark hair swept into a glossy knot at her nape, a string of gray pearls her only jewelry. A dark floral dress, darned but spotless gloves, quiet elegance with touches of wear and tear. Her face was young—she was twenty-eight, according to Jordan's dad—but her eyes looked older. Of course they did; she was a war widow with a young child, starting over in a new country.

"Very pleased to meet you," Jordan said sincerely. "This must be Ruth!" The child at Anneliese Weber's side was darling; blond pigtails and a blue coat and a grave expression. Jordan extended a hand, but Ruth shrank back.

"She's shy," Anneliese apologized. Her voice was clear and low, almost no trace of a German accent. Just a little softness on the *V*'s. "Ruth's world has been very unsettled."

"I didn't like strangers at your age either," Jordan told Ruth. Not true, really, but something about Ruth's wary little face made Jordan long to put her at ease. She also longed to take Ruth's picture—those round cheeks and blond braids would just eat up the lens. Jordan's father took the coats, and Jordan dashed into the kitchen to check the meatloaf. By the time she came out, whipping off the towel she'd tucked around her waist to protect her green Sunday taffeta, her father had poured drinks. Ruth sat on the couch with a glass of milk, as Anneliese Weber sipped sherry and surveyed the room. "A lovely home. You're young to keep house for your father, Jordan, but you do it very well."

Nice of her to lie, Jordan approved. The McBride house always looked mussed: a narrow brownstone three stories up and down on the lace-curtain side of South Boston; the stairs steep, the couches worn and comfortable, the rugs always skidding askew. Anneliese Weber did not seem like the type who approved of anything being askew, with her spine ramrod straight and every hair in place, but she looked around the room with approval. "Did you take this?" She gestured to a photograph of the Boston Common, mist wrapped and tilted at an angle that made everything look otherworldly, a dream landscape. "Your father tells me you are quite a . . . What is the word? A snapper?"

"Yes." Jordan grinned. "Can I take your picture later?"

"Don't encourage her." Jordan's dad guided Anneliese to the couch with a reverent touch to the small of her back, smiling. "Jordan already spends too much time staring through a lens."

"Better than staring at a mirror or at a film screen," Anneliese replied unexpectedly. "Young girls should have more on their minds than lipstick and giggling, or they will grow from silly girls to sillier women. You take classes for it—picture-taking?"

"Wherever I can." Since Jordan was fourteen she'd been signing up for whatever photography classes she could pay for out of her allowance, and sneaking into college courses wherever she could find a professor willing to wink at the presence of a knock-kneed junior high schooler lurking in the back row. "I take classes, I study on my own, I practice—"

"One has to be serious about something in order to be good at it," Anneliese said, approving. A warm glow started in Jordan's chest. *Serious. Good.* Her father never saw Jordan's photography that way. "Messing about with a camera," he'd say, shaking his head. "Well, you'll grow out of it." *I'm not going to grow out of it*, Jordan had replied at fifteen. *I'm going to be the next Margaret Bourke-White.*

Margaret who? he'd responded, laughing. He laughed nicely, indulgently—but he'd still laughed.

Anneliese didn't laugh. She looked at Jordan's photograph and nodded approval. For the first time Jordan allowed herself to think the word: *Stepmother* . . . ?

At the dining room table Jordan had set with the Sunday china, Anneliese asked questions about the antiques shop as Jordan's father heaped her plate with the choicest cuts of everything. "I know an excellent treatment to make colored glass shine," she said as he talked about a set of Tiffany lamps acquired at an estate sale. She quietly corrected Ruth's grip on her fork as she listened to Jordan talk about her school's forthcoming dance. "Surely you have a date, a pretty girl like you."

"Garrett Byrne," Jordan's father said, forestalling her. "A nice young man, joined up to be a pilot at the end of the war. He never saw combat, though. Got a medical discharge when he broke his leg during training. You'll meet him Sunday, if you'd care to accompany us to Mass."

"I would like that. I've been trying so hard to make friends in Boston. You go every week?"

"Of course."

Jordan coughed into her napkin. She and her father hardly went to Mass more than twice a year, Easter and Christmas, but now he sat there at the head of the table positively radiating piety. Anneliese smiled, also radiating piety, and Jordan mused about courting couples on their best behavior. She saw it every day in the halls at school, and apparently the older generation was no different. Maybe there was a photo-essay in that: a series of comparison photographs, courting couples of all ages, highlighting the similarities that transcended age. With the right titles and captions, it might make a piece strong enough to submit to a magazine or newspaper . . .

Plates were cleared, coffee brought out. Jordan cut the Boston cream pie Anneliese had brought. "Though I don't know why you call it pie," she said, blue eyes sparkling. "It's cake, and don't tell an Austrian any differently. We know cake, in Austria."

"You speak such good English," Jordan ventured. She couldn't tell yet about Ruth, who hadn't spoken a word.

"I studied it at school. And my husband spoke it for business, so I practiced with him."

Jordan wanted to ask how Anneliese had lost her husband, but her father shot her a warning glance. He'd already given clear instructions: "You're not to ask Mrs. Weber about the war, or her husband. She's made it quite clear it was a painful time."

"But don't we want to know everything about her?" Much as Jordan wanted her father to have someone special in his life, it still had to be the *right* someone. "Why is that wrong?"

"Because people aren't obliged to drag out their old hurts or dirty laundry just because of your need to know," he answered. "No one wants to talk about a war after they've lived through it, Jordan McBride. So don't go prying where you'll be hurting feelings, and no wild stories either."

Jordan had flushed then. *Wild stories*—that was a bad habit going back ten years. When her barely remembered mother had gone into the hospital, seven-year-old Jordan had been packed off to stay with some well-meaning dimwit of an aunt who told her, *Your mother's gone away*, and then wouldn't say where. So Jordan made up a different story every day: *She's gone to get milk. She's gone to get her hair done.* Then when her mother still didn't come back, more fanciful stories: *She's gone to a ball like Cinderella. She's gone to California to be a movie star.* Until her father came home weeping to say, *Your mother's gone to the angels*, and Jordan didn't understand why his story got to be the real one, so she kept making up her own. "Jordan and her wild stories," her teacher had joked. "Why *does* she do it?"

Jordan could have said, *Because no one told me the truth. Because no one told me "She's sick and you can't see her because you might catch it" so I made up something better to fill the gap.*

Maybe that was why she'd latched so eagerly onto her first Kodak at age nine. There weren't *gaps* in photographs; there wasn't any need to fill them up with stories. If she had a camera, she didn't need to tell stories; she could tell the truth.

Taro lolloped into the dining room, breaking Jordan's thoughts. For the first time, she saw little Ruth grow animated. *"Hund!"*

"English, Ruth," her mother said, but Ruth was already on the floor holding out shy hands.

"Hund," she whispered, stroking Taro's ears. Jordan's heart melted completely. "I'm getting a picture," she said, slipping out of her own chair and going for the Leica on the hall table. When she came back in and started clicking, Ruth had Taro piled over her lap as Anneliese spoke softly. "If Ruth seems very quiet to you, or flinches, or acts odd—well, you should know that in Altaussee before we left Austria, we had a very upsetting encounter by the lake. A refugee woman who tried to rob us . . . It's made Ruth wary and strange around new people." That seemed to be all Anneliese was going to say. Jordan stamped down her questions before her dad could shoot her another glance. He was perfectly correct, after all, when he pointed out that Anneliese Weber wasn't the only person who didn't care to discuss the war—no one did now. First everyone had celebrated, and now all anyone wanted to do was forget. Jordan found it hard to believe that at this time last year there had still been wartime news and stars hanging in windows; victory gardens and boys at school talking about whether it would all be over before they got old enough to join up.

Anneliese smiled down at her daughter. "The dog likes you, Ruth."

"Her name is Taro," said Jordan, clicking away: the little girl with her small freckled nose against the dog's damp one.

"Taro." Anneliese tasted the word. "What kind of name is that?"

"After Gerda Taro—the first female photographer to cover the front lines of a war."

"And she died doing it, so that's enough about women taking pictures in war zones," Jordan's father said.

"Let me get a few shots of you two—"

"Please don't." Anneliese turned her face away with a camera-shy frown. "I hate having my picture taken."

"Just family snaps," Jordan reassured. She liked close-camera candids over formal shots. Tripods and lighting equipment made camera-shy people even more self-conscious; they put a mask on and then the photograph wasn't *real*. She preferred to hover unobtrusively until people forgot she was there, until they forgot the mask and relaxed into who they really were. There was no hiding the real you from a camera.

Anneliese rose to clear the table, Jordan's father assisting with the heavy dishes as Jordan quietly moved and snapped. Ruth was coaxed away from Taro to carry the butter dish, and Dad was soon describing their hunting cabin. "It's a lovely spot; my father built it. Jordan likes to snap the lake; I go for the fishing and the odd bit of shooting."

Anneliese half turned away from the sink. "You hunt?"

Jordan's father looked anxious. "Some women hate the noise and the mess—"

"Not at all . . ."

Jordan put down her camera and went to help with the washing up. Anneliese offered to dry, but Jordan turned her down so she'd have the chance to admire Daniel McBride's deftness with a dish towel. No woman could possibly fail to be charmed by a man who could properly dry Spode.

Anneliese said good-bye soon after. Jordan's father gave her a chaste kiss on the cheek, but his arm stole around her waist for just an instant, making Jordan smile. Anneliese then squeezed Jordan's hand warmly, and Ruth offered her fingers this time, well slimed by Taro's affectionate tongue. They descended the steep brownstone steps to the cool spring night, and Jordan's father shut the door. Before he could ask, Jordan came and kissed his cheek. "I like her, Dad. I really do."

BUT SHE COULDN'T SLEEP.

The tall narrow brownstone had a small basement with its own private entrance to the street. Jordan had to walk outside the house and then down the very steep outer stairs to the tiny door set below ground level under the stoop, but the privacy and the lack of light made it perfect for her purposes. When she was fourteen and learning to print her own negatives, her dad had allowed her to sweep out the rubbish and make herself a proper darkroom.

Jordan paused on the threshold, inhaling the familiar scents of chemicals and equipment. This was *her* room, much more than the cozy bedroom upstairs with its narrow bed and the desk for homework. This room was where she ceased being Jordan McBride with her messy ponytail and bag of schoolbooks, and became J. Bryde, professional photographer. J. Bryde was going to be her byline someday, when she became a professional like her idols whose faces looked down from the darkroom wall: Margaret Bourke-White kneeling with her camera on a massive decorative eagle's head sixty-one floors up on the Chrysler Building, impervious to the height; Gerda Taro crouched behind a Spanish soldier against a heap of rubble, peering for the best angle.

Normally Jordan would have taken a moment to salute her heroines, but something was gnawing at her. She wasn't sure what, so she just started laying out trays and chemicals with the speed of long practice.

She loaded the negatives for the pictures she'd taken at dinner, running the images onto the paper one at a time. Sliding them through the developer under the red glow of the safelight, Jordan watched the images come up through the fluid one by one, like ghosts. Ruth playing with the dog; Anneliese Weber turning away from the camera; Anneliese from behind, doing dishes . . . Jordan rotated the sheets through the stop bath, the fixer bath, gently agitating the liquids in their trays, transferring the prints to the little sink for washing, then clipping them up on the clothesline to dry. She walked down the line one by one.

"What are you looking for?" Jordan wondered aloud. She had a habit of talking to herself down here all alone; she wished she had a fellow photographer to share darkroom conversation with, ideally some smoldering Hungarian war correspondent. She walked the line of prints again. "What caught your eye, J. Bryde?" It wasn't the first time she'd had this niggling feeling about a shot before it had even been printed. It was like the camera saw something she didn't, nagging her until she saw it with her own eyes and not just through the lens.

Half the time, of course, that feeling was completely off base.

"That one," Jordan heard herself saying. The one of Anneliese Weber by the sink, half turned toward the lens. Jordan squinted, but the image was too small. She ran it again, enlarging it. Midnight. She didn't care, working away until the enlarged print hung on the line.

Jordan stood back, hands on hips, staring at it. "Objectively," she said aloud, "that is one of the best shots you've ever taken." The *click* of the Leica had captured Anneliese as she stood framed by the arch of the kitchen window, half turned toward the camera for once rather than away from it, the contrast between her dark hair and pale face beautifully rendered. But . . .

"Subjectively," Jordan continued, "that shot is goddamn spooky." She didn't often swear—her father didn't tolerate bad language— but if there was ever an occasion for a *goddamn*, this was it.

It was the expression on the Austrian woman's face. Jordan had sat across from that face all evening, and she'd seen nothing but pleasant interest and calm dignity, but in the photograph a different woman emerged. She wore a smile, but not a pleasant one. The eyes were narrowed, and her hands around the dish towel suddenly clenched in some reflexive death grip. All evening Anneliese had looked gentle and frail and ladylike, but she didn't look like that here. Here, she looked lovely and unsettling and—

"Cruel." The word popped out of Jordan's mouth before she knew she was thinking it, and she shook her head. Because *anyone* could take an unflattering photo: unlucky timing or lighting caught you midblink and you looked sly, caught you with your mouth open and you looked half-witted. Shoot Hedy Lamarr the wrong way, and she turned from Snow White to the Wicked Queen. Cameras didn't lie, but they could certainly mislead.

Jordan reached for the clothespins clipping the print, meeting that razor-edged gaze. "What were you saying, right at this minute?" Her father had been talking about the cabin . . .

You hunt?
Some women hate the noise and the mess—
Not at all . . .

Jordan shook her head again, moving to throw the print away. Her dad wouldn't like it; he'd think she was twisting the image to see something that wasn't there. *Jordan and her wild stories.*

But I didn't twist it, Jordan thought. *That's how she looked.*

She hesitated, then slipped the photograph into a drawer. Even if it was misleading, it was still one of the best pictures she'd ever taken. She couldn't quite bring herself to throw it away.

Chapter 2

IAN

April 1950
Cologne, Germany

About half the time, they tried to run.

For a moment Ian Graham's partner kept up with him, but though Tony was more than a decade younger than Ian he was half a head shorter, and Ian's longer stride pulled him ahead toward their quarry: a middle-aged man in a gray suit dodging desperately around a German family heading away from the swimming beach with wet towels. Ian put on a burst of speed, feeling his hat blow away, not bothering to shout at the man to stop. They never stopped. They'd sprint to the end of the earth to get away from the things they'd done.

The puzzled German family had halted, staring. The mother had an armful of beach toys—a shovel, a red bucket brimming with wet sand. Veering, Ian snatched the bucket out of her hand with a shouted "Pardon me—," slowed enough to aim, and slung it straight and hard at the running man's feet. The man stumbled, staggered, lurched back into motion, and by then Tony blew past Ian and took the man down in a flying tackle. Ian skidded to a halt as the two men rolled over, feeling his own chest heave like a bellows. He retrieved the bucket and handed it back to the astonished German mother with a bow and a half smile. "Your servant, ma'am." Turning back toward the prey, he saw the man curled on the path whimpering as Tony leaned over him.

"You'd better not have put a fist on him," Ian warned his partner.

"The weight of his sins caught up to him, not my fist." Tony Rodomovsky straightened: twenty-six years old with the olive-skinned, dark-eyed intensity of a European, and the untidy swagger of a Yank. Ian had first come across him after the war, a young sergeant with Polish-Hungarian blood and a Queens upbringing wearing the most carelessly ironed uniform Ian had ever had the misfortune to lay eyes on.

"Nice curveball with that bucket," Tony went on cheerfully. "Don't tell me you pitched for the Yankees."

"Bowled against Eton in the house match in '29." Ian retrieved his battered fedora, cramming it down over dark hair that had been salted with gray since Omaha Beach. "You have it from here?"

Tony looked at the man on the ground. "What do you say, sir? Shall we continue the conversation we were having before I brought up a certain forest in Estonia and your various activities there, and you decided to practice your fifty-yard dash?"

The man began to cry, and Ian looked at the blue sparkle of the lake, fighting his usual sense of anticlimax. The man dissolving in tears on the ground had been an SS Sturmbannführer in Einsatzgruppe D, who had ordered the shooting of a hundred and fifty men in Estonia in 1941. *More than that*, Ian thought. Those eastern death squads had put hundreds of thousands in the ground in shallow trenches. But one hundred and fifty was what he had the documentation for in his office back in Vienna: testimony from a shaky-handed, gray-faced pair of survivors who had managed to flee. One hundred and fifty was enough to bring the man to trial, perhaps put a rope around a monster's neck.

Moments like this should have been glorious, and they never were. The monsters always looked so ordinary and pathetic, in the flesh.

"I didn't do it," the man gulped through his tears. "Those things you said I did."

Ian just looked at him.

"I only did what the others did. What I was ordered to do. It was *legal*—"

Ian took a knee beside the man, raising his chin with one finger. Waited until those red-rimmed eyes met his own. "I have no interest in your orders," he said quietly. "I have no interest if it was legal at the time. I have no interest in your excuses. You're a cringing soulless trigger-pulling lackey, and I will see you face a judge."

The man flinched. Ian rose and turned away, swallowing the rage red and raw before it burst out of him and he beat the man to a pulp. It was always the damned line about *orders* that made him want to tear throats open. *They all say it, don't they?* That was when he wanted to sink his hands around their throats and stare into their bewildered eyes as they died choking on their excuses.

Judgment, thou art fled to brutish beasts, and men have lost their reason . . . Ian let out a slow, controlled breath. *But not me.* Control was what separated men from beasts, and *they* were the beasts.

"Sit on him until the arrest," he told Tony tersely, and he went back to their hotel to make a telephone call.

"Bauer," a voice rasped.

Ian crooked the receiver to his right ear, the one that wasn't faintly hearing-damaged from an unlucky air raid in Spain in '37, and switched to German, which he knew still had a wintry British tang despite all his years abroad. "We got him."

"Heh. I'll start putting pressure on the state prosecutor in Bonn, push to put the *Hurensohn* on trial."

"Put that prosecutor's feet to the fire, Fritz. I want this son of a bitch in front of the hardest judge in Bonn."

Fritz Bauer grunted. Ian envisioned his friend, sitting behind his desk in Braunschweig, puffs of gray hair around his balding head, smoking his perpetual cigarettes. He'd run from Germany to Denmark to Sweden during the war, steps ahead of having a yellow star slapped on his arm and being shipped east. He and Ian had met after the first of the Nuremberg trials—and a few years ago, when the official war crimes investigation teams were being shut down for lack of funding, and Ian had started his own operation with Tony, he'd turned to Bauer. "We find the guilty," Ian proposed over a tumbler of scotch and half a pack of cigarettes, "and you see them prosecuted."

"We won't make friends," Bauer had warned with a mirthless smile, and he was right. The man they'd caught today might see a prison cell for his crimes, he might get off with a slap, or he might never be tried at all. It was five years after the end of the war, and the world had moved on. Who cared anymore about punishing the guilty? "Let them alone," a judge had advised Ian not long ago. "The Nazis are beaten and done. Worry about the Russkies now, not the Germans."

"You worry about the next war," Ian had replied evenly. "Someone has to sweep up the muck of the last one."

"Who's next on your list?" Bauer asked now over the telephone.

Die Jägerin, Ian thought. *The huntress.* But there were no leads to her whereabouts, not for years. "There's a Sobibór guard I'm tracing. I'll update his file when I get back to Vienna."

"Your center is getting a reputation. Third arrest this year—"

"None of them big fish." Eichmann, Mengele, Stangl—the bigger names were far beyond Ian's limited reach, but that didn't bother him much. He couldn't put pressure on foreign governments, couldn't fight massive deportation battles, but what he *could* do was search for the lesser war criminals gone to ground in Europe. And there were so many of them, clerks and camp guards and functionaries who had played their part in the great machine of death during the war. They couldn't all be tried at Nuremberg; there hadn't been the manpower, the money, or even the *interest* in anything so huge in scale. So a few were put on trial—however many would fit on the bench, in some cases, which Ian found starkly, darkly ironic—and the rest just went home. Returned to their families after the war, hung up their uniforms, perhaps took a new name or moved to a new town if they were cautious . . . but still just went back to Germany and pretended it had all never happened.

People asked Ian sometimes why he'd left the gritty glamour of a war correspondent's work for this dogged, tedious slog after war criminals. A life spent chasing the next battle and the next story wherever it led, from Franco's rise in Spain to the fall of the Maginot Line to everything that followed—hammering out a column on deadline while hunched under a tarp that barely kept off the beating desert sun, playing poker in a bombed-out hotel waiting for transport to arrive, sitting up to his shins in seawater and vomit as a landing craft crammed with green-faced soldiers neared a stretch of beach . . . Terror to tedium, tedium to terror, forever vibrating between both for the sake of a byline.

He'd traded all that for a tiny office in Vienna piled with lists; for endless interviews with cagey witnesses and grieving refugees; for no byline at all. "Why?" Tony had asked soon after they began working together, gesturing around the four walls of their grim office. "Why go to this, from that?"

Ian had given a brief, slanted smile. "Because it's the same work, really. Telling the world that terrible things happened. But when I was hammering out columns during the war, what did all those words accomplish? Nothing."

"Hey, I knew plenty of boys in the ranks who lived for your column. Said it was the only one out there besides Ernie Pyle's that wrote for the dogface with boots on the ground and not the generals in tents."

Ian shrugged. "If I'd bought it on a bombing run over Berlin when I went out with a Lancaster crew, or got torpedoed on the way back from Egypt, there'd have been a hundred other scribblers to fill my place. People *want* to read about war. But there's no war now, and no one wants to hear about war criminals walking free." Ian made the same gesture at the four walls of the office. "We don't write headlines now, we *make* them, one arrest at a time. One grudging drop of newspaper ink at a time. And unlike all those columns I wrote about war, there aren't too many people queuing up behind us to do this work. What we do here? We accomplish something a good deal more important than anything I ever managed to say with a byline. Because no one wants to hear what we have to say, and someone has to make them listen."

"So why won't you write up any of our catches?" Tony had shot back. "More people might listen if they see your byline front and center."

"I'm done writing instead of doing." Ian hadn't written a word since the Nuremberg trials, even though he'd been a journalist since he was nineteen, a lanky boy storming out of his father's house shouting he was going to damned well work for a living and not spend his life sipping scotch at the club and droning about how the country was going to the dogs. More than fifteen years spent over a typewriter, honing and stropping his prose until it could cut like a razor's edge, and now Ian didn't think he'd ever put his name on an article again.

He blinked, realizing how long he'd been woolgathering with the telephone pressed to his ear. "What was that, Fritz?"

"I said, three arrests in a year is something to celebrate," Fritz Bauer repeated. "Get a drink and a good night's sleep."

"I haven't had a good night's sleep since the Blitz," Ian joked, and rang off.

The nightmares that night were particularly bad. Ian dreamed of twisting parachutes tangled in black trees, waking with a muffled shout in the hotel room's anonymous darkness. "No parachute," he said, hardly hearing himself over the hammering of his own heart. "No parachute. No parachute." He walked naked to the window, threw open the shutters to the night air, and lit a cigarette that tasted like a petrol can. He exhaled smoke, leaning against the sill to look out over a dark city. He was thirty-eight, he had chased two wars across half the globe, and he stood till dawn thinking in boundless rage-filled hunger of a woman standing on the shore of Lake Rusalka.

"YOU NEED TO get laid," Tony advised.

Ian ignored him, typing up a quick report for Bauer on the typewriter he'd carried since running around the desert after Patton's boys. They were back in Vienna, gray and bleak with its burned-out shell of the state opera house still bearing witness to the war's passing, but a vast improvement on Cologne, which had been bombed to rubble and was still little more than a building site around a chain of lakes.

Tony balled up a sheet of foolscap and threw it at Ian. "Are you listening to me?"

"No." Ian flung the ball back. "Chuck that in the bin, we haven't got a secretary to pick up after you." The Vienna Refugee Documentation Center on the Mariahilferstrasse didn't have a lot of things. The war crimes investigation teams Ian had worked with just after the war had called for officers, drivers, interrogators, linguists, pathologists, photographers, typists, legal experts—a team of at least twenty, well appointed, well budgeted. (Not that the teams ever *got* all those things, but at least they tried.) The center here had only Tony, who acted as driver, interrogator, and linguist, and Ian, who took the mantle of typist, clerk, and very poor photographer. Ian's annuity from his long-dead father barely covered rent and living expenses. *Two men and two desks, and we expect to move mountains*, Ian thought wryly.

"You're brooding again. You always do when we make an arrest. You go off in a Blue Period like a goddamn Picasso." Tony sorted through a stack of newspapers in German, French, English, and something Cyrillic Ian couldn't read. "Take a night off. I've got a redhead in Ottakring, and she has a knockout roommate. Take her out, tell her a few stories about throwing back shots with Hemingway and Steinbeck after Paris was liberated—"

"It wasn't nearly as picturesque as you make it sound."

"So? Talk it up! You've got glamour, boss. Women love 'em tall, dark, and tragic. You're six long-lean-and-mean feet of heroic war stories and unhappy past—"

"Oh, for God's sake—"

"—all buttoned up behind English starch and a thousand-yard stare of *you can't possibly understand the things that haunt me.* That's absolute catnip for the ladies, believe me—"

"Are you finished?" Ian drew the sheet out of the typewriter, tipping his chair back on two legs. "Go through the mail, then pull the file on the Bormann assistant."

"Fine, die a monk."

"Why do I put up with you?" Ian wondered. "Feckless cretinous Yank . . ."

"Joyless Limey bastard," Tony shot back, rummaging in the file cabinet. Ian hid a grin, knowing perfectly well why he put up with Tony. Ranging across three fronts of the war with a typewriter and notepad, Ian had met a thousand Tonys: achingly young men in rumpled uniforms, heading off into the mouth of the guns. American boys jammed on troopships and green with seasickness, English boys flying off in Hurricanes with a one in four chance of making it back . . . after a while Ian couldn't bear to look at any of them too closely, knowing better than they did what their chances were of getting out alive. It had been just after the war ended that he met Tony, slouching along as an interpreter in the entourage of an American general who clearly wanted him court-martialed and shot for insubordination and slovenliness. Ian sympathized with the feeling now that Sergeant A. Rodomovsky worked for him and not the United States Army, but Tony was the first young soldier Ian had been able to befriend. He was brash, a practical joker, and a complete nuisance, but when Ian shook his hand for the first time, he'd been able to think, *This one won't die.*

Unless I kill him, Ian thought now, *next time he gets on my nerves.* A distinct possibility.

He finished the report for Bauer and rose, stretching. "Get your earplugs," he advised, reaching for his violin case.

"You're aware you don't have a future as a concert violinist?" Tony leafed through the stack of mail that had accumulated in their absence.

"I play poorly yet with great lack of feeling." Ian brought the violin to his chin, starting a movement of Brahms. Playing helped him think, kept his hands busy as his brain sorted through the questions that rose with every new chase. *Who are you, what did you do, and where would you go to get away from it?* He was drawing out the last note as Tony let out a whistle.

"Boss," he called over his shoulder, "I've got news."

Ian lowered his bow. "New lead?"

"Yes." Tony's eyes sparked triumph. *"Die Jägerin."*

A trapdoor opened in Ian's stomach, a long drop over the bottomless pit of rage. He put the violin back in its case, slow controlled movements. "I didn't give you that file."

"It's the one at the back of the drawer you look at when you think I'm not paying attention," Tony said. "Believe me, I've read it."

"Then you know it's a cold trail. We know she was in Poznań as late as November '44, but that's all." Ian felt excitement starting to war with caution. "So what did you find?"

Tony grinned. "A witness who saw her later than November '44. After the war, in fact."

"What?" Ian had been pulling out his file on the woman who was his personal obsession; he nearly dropped it. "Who? Someone from the Poznań region, or Frank's staff?" It had been during the first Nuremberg trial that Ian caught *die Jägerin*'s scent, hearing a witness testify against Hans Frank—the governor general of Nazi-occupied Poland, whom Ian would later (as one of the few journalists admitted to the execution room) watch swing from a rope for war crimes. In the middle of the information about the Jews Frank was shipping east, the clerk had testified about a certain visit to Poznań. One of the high-ranking SS officers had thrown a party for Frank out by Lake Rusalka, at a big ocher-colored house . . .

Ian, at that point, had already had a very good reason to be searching for the woman who had lived in that house. And the clerk on the witness stand had been a guest at that party, where the SS officer's young mistress had played hostess.

"Who did you find?" Ian rapped out at Tony, mouth dry with sudden hope. "Someone who remembers her? A name, a bloody photograph—" It was the most frustrating dead end of this file: the clerk at Nuremberg had met the woman only once, and he'd been drunk through most of the party. He didn't remember her name, and all he could describe was a young woman, dark haired, blue eyed. Difficult to track a woman without knowing anything more than her nickname and her coloring. "What did you *find*?"

"Stop cutting me off, dammit, and I'll tell you." Tony tapped the file. "*Die Jägerin*'s lover fled to Altaussee in '45. No sign he took his mistress with him from Poznań—but now, it's looking like he did. Because I've located a girl in Altaussee whose sister worked a few doors down from the same house where our huntress's lover had holed up with the Eichmanns and the rest of that crowd in May '45. I haven't met the sister yet, but she apparently remembers a woman who looked like *die Jägerin*."

"That's all?" Ian's burst of hope ebbed as he recalled the pretty little spa town on a blue-green lake below the Alps, a bolt-hole for any number of high-ranking Nazis as the war ended. By May '45 it had been crawling with Americans making arrests. Some fugitives submitted to handcuffs, some managed to escape. *Die Jägerin*'s SS officer had died in a hail of bullets rather than be taken—and there had been no sign of his mistress. "I've already combed Altaussee looking for leads. Once I knew her lover had died there, I went looking—if she'd been there too, I would have found her trail."

"Look, you probably came on like some Hound of Hell from the Spanish Inquisition, and everyone clammed up in terror. Subtlety is not your strong suit. You come on like a wrecking ball that went to Eton."

"Harrow."

"Same thing." Tony fished for his cigarettes. "I've been doing some lighter digging. All that driving around Austria we did last December, looking for the Belsen guard who turned out to have gone to Argentina? I took weekends, went to Altaussee, asked questions. I'm good at that."

He was. Tony could talk to anyone, usually in their native language. It was what made him good at this job, which so often hinged on information eased lightly out of the suspicious and the wary. "Why did you put in all this effort on your own time?" Ian asked. "A cold case—"

"Because it's the case you *want*. She's your white whale. All these bastards"—Tony waved a hand at the filing cabinets crammed with documentation on war criminals—"you want to nab them all, but the one you *really* want is her."

He wasn't wrong. Ian felt his fingers tighten on the edge of the desk. "White whale," he managed to say, wryly. "Don't tell me you've read Melville?"

"Of course not. Nobody's read *Moby-Dick*; it just gets assigned by overzealous teachers. I went to a recruiter's office the day after Pearl Harbor; that's how I got out of reading *Moby-Dick*." Tony shook out a cigarette, black eyes unblinking. "What I want to know is, why *die Jägerin*?"

"You've read her file," Ian parried.

"Oh, she's a nasty piece of work, I'm not arguing that. That business about the six refugees she killed after feeding them a meal—"

"Children," Ian said quietly. "Six Polish children, somewhere between the ages of four and nine."

Tony stopped in the act of lighting his cigarette, visibly sickened. "Your clipping just said refugees."

"My editor considered the detail too gruesome to include in the article. But they were children, Tony." That had been one of the harder articles Ian had ever forced himself to write. "The clerk at Frank's trial said that, at the party where he met her, someone told the story about how she'd dispatched six children who had probably escaped being shipped east. An amusing little anecdote over hors d'oeuvres. They toasted her with champagne, calling her *the huntress*."

"Goddamn," Tony said, very softly.

Ian nodded, thinking not only of the six unknown children who had been her victims, but of two others. A fragile young woman in a hospital bed, all starved eyes and grief. A boy just seventeen years old, saying eagerly *I told them I was twenty-one, I ship out next week!* The woman and the boy, one gone now, the other dead. *You did that*, Ian thought to the nameless huntress who filled up his sleepless nights. *You did that, you Nazi bitch.*

Tony didn't know about them, the girl and the young soldier. Even now, years later, Ian found it difficult. He started marshaling the words, but Tony was already scribbling an address, moving from discussion to action. For now, Ian let it go, fingers easing their death grip on the desk's edge.

"That's where the girl in Altaussee lives, the one whose sister might have seen *die Jägerin*," Tony was saying. "I say it's worth going to talk in person."

Ian nodded. Any lead was worth running down. "When did you get her name?"

"A week ago."

"Bloody hell, a *week*?"

"We had the Cologne chase to wrap up. Besides, I was waiting for one more confirmation. I wanted to give you more good news, and now I can." Tony tapped the letter from their mail stack, scattering ash from his cigarette. "It arrived while we were in Cologne."

Ian scanned the letter, not recognizing the black scrawl. "Who's this woman and why is she coming to Vienna . . ." He got to the signature at the bottom, and the world stopped in its tracks.

"Our one witness who actually met *die Jägerin* face-to-face and lived," Tony said. "The Polish woman—I pulled her statement and details from the file."

"She emigrated to England, why did you—"

"The telephone number was noted. I left a message. Now she's coming to Vienna."

"You really shouldn't have contacted Nina," Ian said quietly.

"Why not? Besides this potential Altaussee lead, she's the only eyewitness we've got. Where'd you find her, anyway?"

"In Poznań after the German retreat in '45. She was in hospital when she gave me her statement, with all the details she could remember." Vividly Ian recalled the frail girl in the ward cot, limbs showing sticklike from a smock borrowed from the Polish Red Cross. "You shouldn't have dragged her halfway across Europe."

"It was her idea. I only wanted to talk by telephone, see if I could get any more detail about our mark. But if she's willing to come here, let's make use of her."

"She also happens to be—"

"What?"

Ian paused. His surprise and disquiet were fading, replaced by an unexpected flash of devilry. He so rarely got to see his partner nonplussed. *You spring a surprise like this on me*, Ian thought, *you deserve to have one sprung on you.* Ian wouldn't have chosen to yank the broken flower that was Nina Markova halfway across the continent, but she was already on the way, and there was no denying her presence would be useful for any number of reasons . . . including turning the tables on Tony, which Ian wasn't too proud to admit he enjoyed doing. Especially when his partner started messing about with cases behind Ian's back. Especially *this* case.

"She's what?" Tony asked.

"Nothing," Ian answered. Aside from pulling the ground out from under Tony, it might be good to see Nina. They did have matters to discuss that had nothing to do with the case, after all. "Just handle her carefully when she arrives," he added, that part nothing but truthful. "She had a bad war."

"I'll be gentle as a lamb."

FOUR DAYS PASSED, and a flood of refugee testimony came in that needed categorizing. Ian forgot all about their coming visitor, until an unholy screeching sounded in the corridor.

Tony looked up from the statement he was translating from Yiddish. "Our landlady getting her feathers ruffled again?" he said as Ian went to the office door.

His view down the corridor was blocked by Frau Hummel's impressive bulk in her flowered housedress, as she pointed to some muddy footprints on her floor. Ian got a bare impression of a considerably smaller woman beyond his landlady, and then Frau Hummel seized the mud-shod newcomer by the arm. Her bellows turned to shrieks as the smaller woman yanked a straight razor out of her boot and whipped it up in unmistakable warning. The newcomer's face was obscured by a tangle of bright blond hair; all Ian could really take in was the razor held in an appallingly determined fist.

"Ladies, please!" Tony tumbled into the hall.

"Kraut *suka* said she'd call police on me—" The newcomer was snarling.

"Big misunderstanding," Tony said brightly, backing Frau Hummel away and waving the strange woman toward Ian. "If you'll direct your concerns to my partner here, Fräulein—"

"This way." Ian motioned her toward his door, keeping a wary eye on the razor. Rarely did visitors enter quite this dramatically. "You have business with the Refugee Documentation Center, Fräulein?"

The woman folded up that lethally sharp razor and tucked it back into her boot. "Arrived an hour less ago," she said in hodgepodge English as Ian closed the office door. Her accent was strange, somewhere between English and something farther east than Vienna. It wasn't until she straightened and brushed her tangled hair from a pair of bright blue eyes that Ian's heart started to pound.

"Still don't know me from Tom, Dick, or Ivan?" she asked.

Bloody hell, Ian thought, frozen. *She's changed.*

Five years ago she'd lain half starved in a Red Cross hospital bed, all brittle silence and big blue eyes. Now she looked capable and compact in scuffed trousers and knee boots, swinging a disreputable-looking sealskin cap in one hand. The hair he remembered as dull brown was bright blond with dark roots, and her eyes had a cheery, wicked glitter.

Ian forced the words through numb lips. "Hello, Nina."

Tony came banging back in. "The *gnädige Frau's* feathers are duly smoothed down." He gave Nina a rather appreciative glance. "Who's our visitor?"

She looked annoyed. "I sent a letter. You didn't get?" *Her English has improved*, Ian thought. Five years ago they'd barely been able to converse; she spoke almost no English and he almost no Polish.

Their communication in between then and now had been strictly by telegram. His heart was still thudding. This was *Nina . . .* ?

"So you're—" Tony looked puzzled, doubtless thinking of Ian's description of a woman who needed gentle handling. "You aren't quite what I was expecting, Miss Markova."

"Not Miss Markova." Ian raked a hand through his hair, wishing he'd explained it all four days ago, wishing he hadn't had the impulse to turn the tables on his partner. Because if anyone in this room had had the tables turned on them, it was Ian. *Bloody hell.* "The file still lists her birth name. Tony Rodomovsky, allow me to introduce Nina Graham." The woman in the hospital bed, the woman who had seen *die Jägerin* face-to-face and lived, the woman now standing in the same room with him for the first time in five years, a razor in her boot and a cool smile on her lips. "My wife."

Chapter 3

NINA

Before the war
Lake Baikal, Siberia

She was born of lake water and madness.

To have the lake in her blood, that was to be expected. They all did, anyone born on the shore of Baikal, the vast rift lake at the eastern edge of the world. Any baby who came into the world beside that huge lake lying like a second sky across the taiga knew the iron tang of lake water before they ever knew the taste of mother's milk. But Nina Borisovna Markova's blood was banded with madness, like the deep striations of winter lake ice. Because the Markovs were all madmen, everyone knew that—every one of them swaggering and wild-eyed and savage as wolverines.

"I breed lunatics," Nina's father said when he was deep into the vodka he brewed in his hunting shack behind the house. "My sons are all criminals and my daughters are all whores—" and he'd lay about him with huge grimed fists, and his children hissed and darted out of the way like sharp-clawed little animals, and Nina might get an extra clout because she was the only tiny blue-eyed one in a litter of tall dark-eyed sisters and taller dark-eyed brothers. Her father's gaze narrowed whenever he looked at her. "Your mother was a *rusalka*," he'd growl, huddled in his shirt half covered by a clotted black beard.

"What's a *rusalka*?" Nina finally asked at ten.

"A lake witch who comes to shore trailing her long green hair, luring men to their deaths," her father replied, dealing a blow Nina ducked with liquid speed. It was the first thing a Markov child learned, to duck. Then you learned to steal, scrabbling for your own portion of watery borscht and hard bread, because no one shared, not ever. Then you learned to fight—when the other village boys were learning to net fish and hunt seals, and the girls were learning to cook and mend fishing nets, the Markov boys learned to fight and drink, and the Markova girls learned to fight and screw. That led to the last thing they learned, which was to leave.

"Get a man who will take you away," Nina's next-oldest sister told her. Olga was gathering her clothes: fifteen, her body rounding, eyes already trained west in the direction of Irkutsk, the nearest city, hours away beyond the Siberian horizon. Nina couldn't imagine what a *city* looked like. All she'd ever seen was the collection of ramshackle huts that could barely be called a village; fishing boats silvery and pungent with fish scales; the endless spread of the lake. "Get a man," Olga repeated, "because that's the only way you'll get out."

"I'll find a different way," Nina said. Olga gave her a spiteful scratch in farewell and was gone. None of Nina's siblings ever came back; it was everyone for themselves, and she didn't miss them until the last brother left, and it was just her and her father. "Little *rusalka* bitch"—he slung Nina around the hut as she hissed and scratched at the huge hand tangled in her wild hair—"I should give you back to the lake." He didn't frighten Nina much. Weren't all fathers like hers? He loomed as large in her world as the lake. In a way, he *was* the lake. The villagers sometimes called the lake "the Old Man." One Old Man stretched blue and rippling on the doorstep, and the other old man banged her around the hut.

He wasn't always wild. In mellow moods he sang old songs of Father Frost and Baba Yaga, stropping the straight razor that always swung at his belt. In those moods he'd show Nina how to tan a pelt from the seals he shot with the ancient rifle over the door; took her hunting with him and taught her how to move over the snow in perfect silence. Then he didn't call her a *rusalka*; he tugged her ear and called her a little huntress. "If I teach you anything," he whispered, "let it be how to move through the world without making a sound, Nina Borisovna. If they can't hear you coming, they'll never lay hands on you. They haven't caught me yet."

"Who, Papa?"

"Stalin's men," he spat. "The ones who stand you against a wall and shoot you for saying the truth—that Comrade Stalin is a lying, murdering pig who shits on the common man. They kill you for saying things like that, but only if they can find you. So keep silent feet and they'll never hunt you down. You'll hunt *them* down instead."

He'd go on like that for hours, until Nina dozed off. *Comrade Stalin is a Georgian swine, Comrade Stalin is a murdering sack of shit.* "Stop him saying those things," the old women who bartered clothes whispered to Nina when she came to trade. "We're not so far out on the edge of the world that the wrong ears can't hear us. That father of yours will get himself shot, and his neighbors."

"He says the tsar was a murdering sack of shit too," Nina pointed out. "And Jews, and the natives, and any seal hunters who leave carcasses on our section of shore. He thinks everything and everyone is shit."

"It's different to say it about Comrade Stalin!"

Nina shrugged. She wasn't afraid of anything. It was another curse in the Markov family; none of them feared blood or darkness or even the legend of Baba Yaga hiding in the trees. "Baba Yaga is afraid of *me*," Nina said to another village child when they were scrapping ferociously over a broken doll. "You'd better be afraid of me too." She got the doll, thrust at her by the child's mother who crossed herself in the old way, the way the people did before they learned that religion was the opiate of the masses.

"Fearlessness, heh," Nina's father said when he heard. "It's why my children will all die before me. You fear nothing, you get stupid. It's better to fear *one* thing, Nina Borisovna. Put all the terror into that, and it leaves you just careful enough."

Nina looked at her father wonderingly. He was so enormous, wild as a wolf; she could not imagine him afraid of anything. "What's your fear, Papa?"

He put his lips to her ear. "Comrade Stalin. Why else live on a lake the size of the sea, as far east in the world as you can go before falling off?"

"What's as far west as you can go before falling off?" The sun went west to die, and most of the world was west of here, but beyond that Nina hardly knew. There was only one schoolmaster in the village, and he was almost as ignorant as the children he taught. "What's *all* the way west?"

"America?" Nina's father shrugged. "Godless devils. Worse than Stalin. Stay clear of Americans."

"They'll never catch me." Tapping her toes. "Silent feet."

He toasted that with a swallow of vodka and one of his rare knife-edged smiles. A good day. His good days always came back to bad ones, but that never bothered her because she was fast and silent and feared nothing, and she could always keep out of reach.

Until the day she turned sixteen, when her father tried to drown her in the lake.

Nina was standing on the shore in a pure, cold twilight. The lake was frozen in a sheet of dark green glass, so clear you could see the bottom far below. When the surface ice warmed during the day, crevasses would open, crackling and booming as if the lake's *rusalki* were fighting a war in the depths. Close to shore, hummocks of turquoise-colored ice heaved up over each other in blocks taller than Nina, shoved onto the bank by the winter wind. A few years ago, those frozen waves had crawled so far ashore that Tankhoy Station had been entirely swallowed in wind-flung blue ice. Nina stood in her shabby winter coat, hands thrust into her pockets, wondering if she would still be here to see the lake freeze next year. She was sixteen years old; all her sisters had left home before they reached that age, mostly with swelling bellies. *All the same, Markov's daughters*, came the whisper in the village. *They all go bad.*

"I don't care if I go bad," Nina said aloud. "I just don't want a big belly." But there didn't seem to be anything else her father's daughters did, except grow up, start breeding, and run away. Nina kicked restlessly at the shore, and her father came lurching out of the hut, naked to the waist, oblivious to the cold. Clumsy inked dragons and serpents writhed over his arms, and his body steamed. He'd been on one of his binges, guzzling vodka and muttering mad things for days, but now he seemed lucid again. He gazed at her, seeing her for the first time all day, and his eyes had an odd gleam. "The Old Man wants you back," he said conversationally.

And he was after her like a wolf, though Nina got three sprinting strides toward the trees before the huge hand snatched at her hair and yanked her off her feet. She hit the ground so hard the world slipped sideways, and when it came to rights she was on her back, boots scrabbling on the ground as her father dragged her onto the glass-smooth lake.

The ice this time of year was thicker than a man was tall, but there were gaps where the ice thinned. The village schoolmaster, less ignorant about the lake than about most of the things he taught, said something about warmer water channels winding upward from the deeper rift, enough to make holes in the surface—and now, her father dragged her across the ice to one of the spring holes, dropped to his knees, broke the thin crust, and thrust her head under the freezing water.

Fear slapped Nina then, alien and spiky as new-forming frost. Even being dragged across the lake by the hair she had not been afraid; it had all happened too fast. But as the dark water swallowed her, terror descended like an avalanche. The water's cold gripped her; she could see the depths of the lake stretching away below, blue green and fathomless, and she opened her mouth to scream but the lake's iron fist punched into her mouth with another paralyzing burst of cold.

On the surface, her body thrashed against her father's grip in her hair. His stone-hard hand thrust her head down deeper, deeper, but she flailed a leg free and slammed one boot into his ribs. He brought her up with a curse, and Nina got one sobbing gasp of air that stabbed her lungs like hot knives. Her father cursed blurrily; he released Nina's sodden hair and flipped her onto her back, seizing her by the throat instead. "Go back to the lake," he whispered, "go home." Again her head went down under the water. This time she could see up through the ripples, up past her father to the twilight sky. *Get there*, she thought incoherently through another wash of fear, *just get up there*—and her hand stretched blindly . . . But it wasn't the sky her fingers brushed. It was the unfolded razor swinging at her father's belt.

She couldn't feel her fingers wrapping around the handle. The cold had her in its jaws, clamping down. But she watched herself move through the ripples of the lake that was drowning her, watched her hand jerk the razor free and bring it around in a savage swipe across her father's hand. Then he was gone, and Nina came roaring up out of the water, a shard of broken ice on the edge slicing along her throat, but she had the razor in her fist and she was free.

They lay gasping on opposite sides of the ice hole. Her father clutched his hand, which Nina had sliced nearly to the bone, sending curling ribbons of scarlet across the frozen lake. Nina huddled on her side, racked by bone-deep shudders of cold and terror, ice crystals already forming on her lashes and through her hair, a similar ribbon of blood winding down the side of her throat from the ice cut. She still held the razor extended toward her father.

"If you touch me again," she said through chattering teeth, "I'll kill you."

"You're a *rusalka*," he mumbled, looking bewildered at her fury. "The lake won't hurt you."

A violent shudder racked her. *I am no* rusalka, she wanted to scream. *I'll die before I ever let water close over my head again.* But all she said was, "I'll kill you, Papa. Believe it." And she managed to stumble back to the hut, where she bolted the door, peeled away her ice-crusted clothes, built up the fire, and crawled naked and shuddering under a pile of silver-gray seal pelts. Had it been deep winter the shock of the cold would have killed her, she realized later, but winter's bite was easing toward spring, and she managed not to die.

Her father slept it off in the hunting shack while Nina lay shivering under her furs, still gripping the razor, breaking into hiccuping little sobs whenever she thought of the water lapping over her face, filling her mouth and nose with its iron tang.

I have my one fear, she thought. From that day forward, as far as Nina Markova was concerned, if it wasn't death by drowning it wasn't worth being afraid of. *Get away from here,* she thought, unpeeling from the furs long enough to find her father's vodka and take several enormous gulps of the oily, peppery stuff. *Get out.* The thought pounded. *Go where? What is the opposite of a lake? What is the opposite of drowning? What lies* all *the way west?* Nonsensical questions. Nina realized she was half drunk. She crawled under the furs again, slept like the dead, and woke with a crust of blood on her throat where the lake's icy fingers had tried to kill her, and that one clear, cold thought.

Get out.

Chapter 4

JORDAN

Aaaaand it gets away! Line drive past the diving Johnny Pesky—"

"Garrett," Jordan told her boyfriend as groans rose around them across the stands of Fenway Park, "I know the line drive got past Johnny Pesky. I'm right here, watching the line drive get past Johnny Pesky. You don't need to give me the play-by-play."

It was a perfect spring day: the smell of outfield grass, the murmur and rush of the crowd, the scratch of pencils on scorecards. Garrett grinned. "Admit it, you missed our baseball dates when I was in training. Even my play-by-play." Jordan couldn't resist raising the Leica for a snap. With his dimples, his broad shoulders, and his Red Sox cap tipped down over short brown hair, Garrett looked about as all-American cute as a Coca-Cola ad. Or a recruitment poster: he'd enlisted at the end of his senior year, giving Jordan his class ring, but a badly broken leg during pilot training and the abrupt end of the war with Japan not long afterward had cut his stint in the army air force very short. She knew Garrett regretted that—he'd been dreaming of dogfights over the Pacific when he signed up, not of being cut loose on a medical discharge before even making it overseas.

"Sure, I missed our baseball dates," Jordan said playfully. "Maybe not as much as I missed having Ted Williams batting in the three-spot during the war, but—"

Garrett flicked a peanut shell into her ponytail. "Bet I looked better in an army air force uniform than Ted Williams."

"I'm sure you did, because Ted Williams was a marine."

"The marines were only invented so the army has someone to take to the prom."

"I wouldn't tell any marines that."

"Too dumb to get the joke."

The next Yankee came to bat, and Jordan raised the Leica. Only in the darkroom would she know if she missed the high point of the bat's swing. Flawless timing; every great photographer needed it.

"Come to lunch this Sunday?" Garrett rooted through his bag of peanuts. "My parents are dying to see you."

"Aren't they hoping you'll start dating some Boston University sorority girl in the fall?"

"Come on, you know they love you."

They did, and so did Garrett, which surprised Jordan. They'd been together since she was a junior, and from the start she'd been determined not to get her heart broken once he moved on. High school seniors went off to college or war, but either way they moved on. And that was just fine, because this business of getting married right after graduation to your high school sweetheart was ridiculous as far as Jordan was concerned (no matter what her dad said about it working perfectly well for *him*). No, Garrett Byrne would move on to a new girl at some point, and Jordan's heart was going to be a little bit broken but then she'd toss her head back, sling her Leica around her neck, and go work in European war zones and have affairs with Frenchmen.

But Garrett hadn't moved on. He'd come back from his medical discharge, still on crutches, and picked up their afternoon baseball dates and Sunday lunches with his parents, who beamed at Jordan as much as her dad beamed at Garrett. The knee-buckling weight of all that parental expectation made everything seem so firm, so *settled*, that a trip around European war zones taking pictures for *LIFE* seemed about as likely as a trip to the moon.

"C'mon." Garrett sneaked an arm around her waist, nuzzled her ear in that way that also made her knees buckle. "Sunday lunch. We can go for a drive afterward, park somewhere . . ."

"I can't," Jordan said, regretful. "Mass with Dad and Mrs. Weber."

"It must be serious." Garrett grinned again. "So, how is this Fräulein of your father's?"

"She's very nice." There had been another dinner, this time at Anneliese Weber's tiny spotless apartment; she had been warm and welcoming, and made crisp fried schnitzel and some kind of pink-iced Austrian cake soaked in rum. Jordan's father had gone all soft around the edges as Anneliese served him, and Jordan already adored little Ruth, who had asked in a whispery voice how *der Hund* was. It had all been fine, absolutely fine.

Jordan didn't know why, but she kept thinking back to that picture. Anneliese Weber looking by a strange twist of light and lens to be about as soft and welcoming as a straight razor.

"She's very nice," Jordan said again. The Sox went down 4–2, and soon Jordan and Garrett were streaming out of Fenway with the rest of the fans, crunching peanut shells and discarded score-cards underfoot. "It's our year," Jordan proclaimed. "This year we win it all, I can feel it. Walk me to the shop? I promised Dad I'd swing by."

Hand in hand, they made their way through the game crowd and finally turned onto Commonwealth, Jordan stretching her steps to match Garrett's, who still walked with a slight limp. It was *that day*, she thought, the sudden spring day coming at the end of a too-long winter. As they turned down the central mall on Commonwealth, it seemed like all Boston had tossed their heavy coats and come outside, winter-pale faces blissfully skyward as they stumbled along absolutely drunk on the warmth. It was why Jordan loved Boston— there was something about its citizens that was curiously welded together, more like a small town than a big city. Everyone seemed to know everyone else, their heartaches and their secrets. . . And that brought a frown to Jordan's face.

"I wish I knew more about her," she heard herself say.

"Who?" Garrett had been talking about the classes he'd take in the fall.

"Mrs. Weber." Jordan fiddled with the Leica's strap.

"What do you want to know?" Garrett asked reasonably. They were passing the Hotel Vendome, and Jordan nearly stepped in front of a Chevrolet coupe. Garrett pulled her back. "Careful—"

"That," Jordan said. "She's careful. She doesn't say much about herself. And I caught the strangest expression on her face when I took her picture . . ."

Garrett laughed. "You don't take a dislike to someone just because of a funny expression."

"Girls do it all the time. Sometimes you catch a boy looking at you in the hall at school, when he thinks you can't see him. I don't mean looking at girls the way all boys do," Jordan clarified. "I mean looking at you in a way that gives you the shivers. He doesn't mean for you to see, and maybe that expression only lasts a second, but it's enough to make you think, *I don't want to be alone with you.*"

"Girls think that?" Garrett sounded mystified.

"I don't know a single girl who hasn't had that thought," Jordan stated. "I'm just saying, sometimes you catch the wrong look on someone's face and it puts you off. It makes you not want to take chances, getting to know them."

"But this isn't a boy leering around the locker door at school. It's a woman your father is inviting home to dinner. You *have* to give her a chance."

"I know."

"Your dad's really serious about her." Garrett tweaked Jordan's ponytail. "Maybe that's the whole problem."

"I am *not* jealous," Jordan flashed. Then amended, "All right, maybe I am. A tiny, *tiny* bit. But I want Dad happy, I do. And Mrs. Weber is good for him. I can see that. But before I trust her with my father, I want to know more about her."

"So just ask her."

McBride's Antiques sat on the corner of Newbury and Clarendon—not the best shopping district in Boston, but distinguished enough. Every morning, as long as Jordan could remember, her father had walked the three miles from their home to the shop that had been *his* father's, mounting those worn stone steps toward the door with its ancient bronze knocker, unlocking the shutters to unveil the big gilt-lettered window. Jordan frowned at the window display as it came into view today, seeing that the tasseled lamps and Victorian hatstand from yesterday had been swapped for a tailor's dummy in a wedding dress of antique lace, and a display of cabochon rings sparkling on a velvet tray. Jordan mounted the steps ahead of Garrett, hearing the sweet tinkle of the bell as she pushed the door open. She wasn't really surprised to see her father beside the long counter, holding Anneliese Weber's hand with a proprietary air. "I've got wonderful news, missy!"

Jordan couldn't describe the mix of emotions that rose in her—why her heart squeezed in honest pleasure, seeing the happiness on her father's face as he looked down at the Austrian widow's left hand with its cluster of antique garnets and pearls . . . and why at the same time her stomach tightened as she came to give her soon-to-be stepmother a hug.

JUST ASK HER, Garrett had said. Jordan got her chance two days later, when Mrs. Weber invited her to go shopping for wedding clothes after she came home from school. As they sallied down Boylston Street, Jordan was still trying to find a casual segue into the questions she wanted to ask when Mrs. Weber took the initiative.

"Jordan, I hope you don't feel you must call me—well, not *Mutti*, I suppose for you it would be *Mother* or *Mama*." A smile at Jordan's expression. "At your age that seems silly."

"A little."

"Well, you certainly don't have to call me either. I don't mean to take the place of your mother. Your father has told me about her, and she sounds like a lovely woman."

"I don't remember her very well." *Just her absence once she got sick, really. And all the reasons why, which they wouldn't tell me, so I made them up for myself.* Jordan wished she remembered more than that. She looked sideways at Anneliese, gliding along in her blue spring coat, pocketbook in gloved hands, heels hardly clicking on the sidewalk. Jordan felt large and clumping beside her, naked without her camera.

"I thought we'd go to Priscilla of Boston," Anneliese suggested. "Usually I make up my own clothes, but for a wedding one needs something special. I don't know if your father discussed the plans with you, men can be so vague about wedding details. We thought a quiet day wedding three weeks from now, just the four of us at the chapel and a few of your father's friends."

"And on your side?"

"No one. I haven't been in Boston long enough to make friends."

"Really?" For a woman who'd said she was trying so hard to make friends in a new country—and whose English was so good—it seemed odd. "Not even a next-door neighbor, or someone at the beauty shop, or another mother at the park?"

"I find it hard, talking with strangers." A tentative smile. "I hoped you would be my maid of honor?"

"Of course." Though Jordan couldn't stop wondering. *Months in Boston, and you don't have one single acquaintance?*

"Your father and I planned for a honeymoon weekend in Concord," Anneliese continued, "if you could watch Ruth."

"Of course." Jordan's smile was unforced this time. "Ruth's a darling. I love her already."

"She has that effect on people," Anneliese agreed.

Jordan took a silent breath. "Does she get that beautiful fair hair from her father?"

A pause. "Yes, she does."

"What did you say his name was—Kurt?"

"Yes. What color do you fancy wearing for the wedding?" Anneliese turned through the doors of the boutique, moving through the ivory bridal gowns and floral bridesmaid dresses, waving away salesgirls. "This blue? So lovely with your skin."

She took off her gloves to test the fabric between her fingertips, and Jordan eyed her hands, naked of rings except for the engagement cluster of garnets. She tried to remember if she'd ever seen Anneliese wearing a wedding ring and was certain she had not. "You could wear your old ring, you know," she threw out, trying a new tack.

Anneliese looked startled. "What?"

"Dad would never mind if you kept wearing your husband's ring. He was a part of your life—I hope you don't feel we expect you to forget him."

"Kurt never gave me a wedding ring."

"Is it not customary in Austria?"

"No, it was, he—" Anneliese sounded almost flustered for a moment. "We were rather poor, that's all."

Or maybe you lied about being married, Jordan couldn't stop herself thinking. *Maybe it's not the only thing you've lied about either . . .*

Her father's voice, scolding: *Wild stories.*

"I think you're right about this dress." Jordan looked at the pale blue frock, full skirted and simple. "Ruth would look pretty in blue too, with her dark eyes. Most blondes have blue eyes like yours. She must have gotten her eyes from her father too."

"Yes." Anneliese fingered the sleeve of a pale pink suit, face smooth again.

"Well, it's very striking." Jordan tried to think where to tug the discussion next. It wasn't just Ruth or Anneliese's first husband she was interested in, it was everything—but something about the wedding ring had jarred Anneliese's poise. "Did Ruth ever know her father, or—"

"No, she doesn't remember him. He was very handsome, though. So is your young man. Would you like to bring Garrett to the wedding?"

"He'll be working if it's a day wedding—he's putting in hours for his father's boss until he starts at Boston University in the fall. His parents want him to join the business, though all he wants to do now is fly planes. Garrett never saw combat; he broke his leg too badly during training, and the war ended before he was anywhere near healed, so he was discharged early. Was your husband in the war?"

"Yes." Anneliese picked up a cream straw hat, examining its blue ribbon. Jordan tried a question about Anneliese's family next, but she didn't seem to hear it. "Do you plan to follow Garrett to Boston University this fall?" she asked instead.

"Well—" Jordan blinked, sidetracked. "I'd like to, but Dad isn't keen. With a business in the family, he doesn't think college is necessary." Especially for a girl. "He never went, and always says he didn't regret it."

"I'm sure he didn't. But you have your own path, like any young person. Perhaps we might try to change his mind, you and I. Even the best men sometimes require steering." Anneliese gave a conspiratorial smile, perching the hat on Jordan's head. "That's lovely. Why don't you try on the dress? For myself, I think this pink suit . . ."

Jordan slipped into a changing cubicle, diverted despite herself. She'd first thought of a stepmother as something wonderful for her father and his loneliness—then, given all she didn't know about this woman and her life even as she moved into theirs, as something to be uneasy about. It had never occurred to Jordan to think a stepmother could be . . . well, an ally. *Perhaps we might try to change his mind, you and I.* That made Jordan smile as she fastened up the blue dress with its snug waist and swirl of skirt, hearing the rustle of clothing as Anneliese changed on the other side of the wall. *Did you mean it?* Jordan wondered. *Or were you trying to derail me from asking about you?*

"Beautiful," Anneliese approved as Jordan came out. "Against that blue, your skin is pure American peaches and cream."

"You look lovely too," Jordan said honestly. Petite and elegant in a suit the color of baby roses, Anneliese revolved before the triple mirror. An assistant fluttered with pins, and Jordan moved closer, straightening Anneliese's sleeve. "Would you really help me with Dad, changing his mind about college? Most people tell me it's a silly thing to want, when I've got a nice boyfriend and a place in the shop waiting for me, and I'm already working the counter on weekends."

"Nonsense." Anneliese smoothed the jacket over her waist. "Clever girls like you—another dart here?—should be encouraged to want more, not less."

"Did you, at my age?" Jordan couldn't help the question that popped out next. "You said you went to college. Where was that?"

Anneliese's blue eyes met hers in the mirror for a thoughtful moment. "You don't entirely trust me, Jordan," she said at last in her very-faintly-accented English. "No, don't protest. It's quite all right. You love your father; you want the best for him. So do I."

"It's not that I—" Jordan felt her cheeks flame. *Why do you have to probe things?* she chastised herself. *Why can't you just flutter and squeal like a normal girl in a bridal shop?* "I don't *distrust* you—I just don't *know* you, and . . ."

Anneliese let her struggle into silence. "I'm not easy to know," she said at last. "The war was difficult for me. I don't enjoy talking about it. And we Germans are more reserved than Americans even at the best of times."

"I thought you were Austrian," Jordan said before she could stop herself.

"I am." Anneliese turned to examine the skirt hem in the mirror. "But I went to Heidelberg as a young girl—for university, to answer your question. I studied English there and met my husband." A smile. "Now you know something more about me, so shall we make our purchase and look for a dress for Ruth? There's a children's boutique not far away."

Jordan's cheeks stayed hot as they left the shop with their parcels. *I am a worm,* she thought, kicking herself, but Anneliese seemed to hold no grudge, swinging her handbag and tilting her nose up to the breeze. "My former husband would say this is hunting weather," she exclaimed, reminiscent. "I'm no good at hunting, but I always did like heading to the woods on such days. Spring breezes bringing every scent right to your nose . . ."

Jordan wondered why her stomach had tightened again, when Anneliese was chatting away in a perfectly forthcoming fashion. *Because you're jealous*, she told herself witheringly. *Because you don't want to share your father, and you resent her for it. That's a mean, nasty little feeling to have, Jordan McBride. And you're going to get over it, right now.*

Chapter 5

IAN

April 1950
Vienna

Y ou have a wife?" Tony dragged Ian into the corner for a quick, hissed discussion. "Since when?"

Ian contemplated the woman now sitting at his desk, boots propped on the blotter, crunching down biscuits straight from the tin. "It's complicated," he said eventually.

"No, it isn't. At some point you and this woman stood up together and said a lot of stuff about *to have and to hold*, and there was an *I do*. It's pretty definitive. And why didn't you tell me four days ago when I said she was coming here? Did you just *forget*?"

"Call it a sadly misplaced impulse to have a joke at your expense."

Tony glowered. "Was the part about her being such a fragile flower a joke too?"

No, that turned out to be a joke on me. Ian remembered Nina stumbling over the foreign words of the marriage service, swaying on her feet from weakness. The entire wedding had taken less than ten minutes: Ian had rushed through his own vows, pushed his signet ring onto Nina's fourth finger where it hung like a hoop, taken her back to her hospital bed, and promptly headed off to fill out paperwork and finish a column on the occupation of Poznań.

Now, five years later, he watched Nina suck biscuit crumbs off her fingertip and saw she was still wearing the ring. It fit much better. "I came across Nina in Poznań after the German retreat," Ian said, realizing his partner was waiting for answers. "The Polish Red Cross picked her up half dead from double pneumonia. She'd been living rough in the woods after her run-in with *die Jägerin*. She looked like a stiff breeze would kill her."

It hadn't just been her physical state either. Her eyes had been so haunted, she looked a step from shattering altogether. Logically, Ian understood she would have changed in five years, but he couldn't stop trying to reconcile the woman in his office with the frail girl of his memory.

Tony still looked unbelieving. "You fell in love at first sight with our Nazi huntress's only surviving victim?"

"I didn't—" Ian raked a hand through his hair, wondering where to begin. "I've seen Nina exactly four times. The day I found her, the day I proposed, the day we married, and the day I put her on a train toward England. She had nothing to her name and she was desperate to get as far from the war zone as she could." They'd hardly been able to communicate, but her desperation had needed no translator. It had tugged at Ian's heart despite himself. "The region was an utter mess, she had no identification, there were only so many strings I could pull to get her out of the limbo she was in. So I married her."

Tony eyed him. "Chivalrous of you."

"I owed her a debt. Besides, we intended to divorce once her British citizenship came through."

"So why didn't you? And how is it we've worked together several years, yet this is the first I'm hearing about a wife?"

"I said it was complicated."

"Whisper, whisper," Nina interrupted. "You're done?"

"Yes." Ian threw himself down in the chair opposite and looked her over, his wife. Mrs. Ian Graham. *Bloody hell.* "I thought you were working in Manchester," he said at last. Their last exchange of telegrams had been four months ago.

"Whoever do you work for?" Tony added, getting Nina a cup of tea. He still looked flummoxed, and Ian would have enjoyed that if he hadn't shared the feeling.

"I work for English pilot. He comes out of RAF, starts a little airfield. I help." Nina stirred her tea. "You have jam?" She wasn't precisely rude, Ian decided, just abrupt. She had to be what, thirty-two now?

Her eyes flicked at him. The blue eyes, he thought—*those* hadn't changed. Very, very watchful.

"Why are you here?" he asked quietly.

"The message." She tilted her head at Tony. "He asks me to help find your huntress. I help."

"You dropped everything and caught the nearest train across half Europe, all because you heard we might have a lead on *die Jägerin*?"

His wife looked at him as though he were an idiot. "Yes."

Tony fetched the jam pot, then leaned back against the desk. "I hope you'll tell me more about yourself, Mrs. Graham. Your devoted husband has not exactly been forthcoming."

"Just Nina. Mrs. Graham is only for passport."

"'Nina,' that's a pretty name. You're Polish?"

He switched languages, asking something. Nina answered, then switched back. "I do English now. Who are you again? I forget to write name down."

"Anton Rodomovsky." Tony took her hand that didn't have a teacup in it and bowed, all his charm coming to the fore. "Formerly Sergeant Rodomovsky of the United States Army, but both me and the US of A thought that was a failed experiment. Now I'm just Tony: interpreter, paper pusher, all around dogsbody."

Her eyes narrowed. "Interpreter?"

"Grow up in Queens with as many *babushka*s as I did, you pick up a few languages." Lazily. "Polish, German, Hungarian, French. Some Czech, Russian, Romanian . . ."

Nina transferred her gaze to Ian. "Interpreter," she said as if Tony wasn't there. "Is useful. When do we leave?"

"Pardon?" Ian was transfixed by the way she was dropping

heaping spoons of strawberry jam into her teacup. He'd never seen anyone do that to an innocent cup of tea in his life. Bloody hell, it was barbaric.

"I help look for the bitch," Nina said matter-of-factly. "When do we leave, and where do we go?"

"There's a witness in Altaussee who might have information on where *die Jägerin* went after the war," Tony said.

Nina drank off her jam-clotted tea in three long gulps, then rose and stretched like an untidy little alley cat. Ian rose too, feeling enormous; she barely came up to his shoulder. "We leave tomorrow," she said. "Where can I sleep?"

"Your husband lives upstairs," Tony said. "Shall I take up your things?" Ian shot him a withering look. "What, no passionate reunion?" he remarked, innocent.

"Very funny," Ian said, unamused. It had been the hardest thing to communicate to Nina five years ago when he proposed marriage—that he expected nothing from her, that he was honoring a debt and not looking to collect payment in return. The mere idea of pressing physical attentions on an illness-weakened, war-ravaged woman made him feel like a debaucher out of a Dickens novel. Nina had spent her wedding night in a hospital cot, and he'd spent his filling out paperwork in the name of *Nina Graham* so she could get to England as soon as she was released.

"I doubt our landlady will be too keen on you staying under this roof," Tony was saying. "I rent a room two blocks down from a nice little hausfrau. I'll walk you over, see if I can get you into her spare room."

Nina nodded, sauntering toward the door. For all her crumb scattering and sprawling limbs, she moved absolutely soundlessly—that too Ian remembered from five years ago; how his bride even while shaky with weakness had moved over a hospital floor silent as a winter fox.

Tony held the door for her, the speculative gleam back in his eye. "So tell me," he began as the door closed.

Ian turned, contemplating his office. One short visit had turned it to chaos: muddy footprints, rings of drying tea on the files, a sticky spoon staining the blotter. Ian shook his head, half irritated and half amused. *This is what you get for putting off the divorce paperwork, Graham.* The entire marriage should have been over within a year of the vows—he and Nina had agreed, in a combination of English, Polish, and hand gestures on the way back from the registry office, on a divorce as soon as her British citizenship was finalized. But that had taken so long, and he'd been heading out with the war crime investigation units, and Nina had been struggling to get used to ration-locked postwar England, and time had passed. Every six months or so Ian telegrammed to ask if she needed anything—he might not *know* his wife, but he'd felt a certain responsibility to make sure the frail woman he'd got out of Poland wasn't utterly lost in her new country. Yet she always refused help, and most of the time he forgot he was married at all. He certainly had no woman in his life with designs on Nina's place.

He had cleaned up the mess and gone back to his files by the time Tony returned. "You have an interesting wife," he said without preamble. "Please tell me you're aware she's not Polish."

Ian blinked. "What?"

"She's no native speaker. Her grammar's terrible and her accent's worse. Didn't you notice she swapped back to English the minute she could?"

Ian leaned back, hooking an elbow around the back of his chair and reevaluating everything all over again. How many surprises was this day going to lob at him? "If she isn't Polish, what is she?"

Tony looked ruminative. "You know how many grandmothers and great-aunts I had whacking me with wooden spoons when I was growing up? All these old ladies in shawls nagging their daughters and quarreling over goulash recipes?"

"Will you get to the point?"

"Hundreds, because the women in my family all live forever, and when you add in the godparents and in-laws—not just the Rodomovskys but the Rolskas and the Popas and the Nagys and all the rest—they came off the boat from *everywhere* east of the

Rhine. There was one particularly mean old cow, my grandmother's cousin by marriage, who talked about winter in Novosibirsk and put jam in her tea . . ." Tony shook his head. "I don't know what else your wife is lying about, but if she's from Poland, I'm a Red Sox fan. I know a Russian when I hear one."

Ian felt his eyebrows shoot up. "*Russian?*"

"*Da, tovarische.*"

Silence fell. Ian turned a pen over slowly between two fingers. "Perhaps it doesn't matter," he said more to himself than his partner. "She was a refugee when I met her in Poznań, and refugees are rarely fleeing happy pasts. I doubt her story is any prettier for starting in the Soviet Union than in Poland."

"Do you even know what her story is?"

"Not really." The language barrier had made it so difficult to exchange more than basic information, and besides, Nina hadn't been a source he'd been interrogating to get a story. She'd been a woman in trouble. "She was desperate, and I owed her a debt. It was that simple."

"What debt?" Tony asked. "You'd never met her before; how could you owe her anything?"

Ian took a long breath. "When I came to the Polish Red Cross, I was looking for someone else. His name was Sebastian." A boy in an ill-fitting uniform, seventeen the last time Ian had seen him. *I told them I was twenty-one, I ship out next week!* Even now, that memory made Ian catch his breath in pain. "Seb had been a prisoner of war since Dunkirk, held at the stalag near Poznań. I didn't find him, but I found Nina—she had his tags, his jacket. She knew him. She was able to tell me how he died."

"How do you know she told the truth about that?" Tony asked quietly. "She lied about being Soviet. She could have lied about anything else. *Everything* else."

Ian turned the pen over again. "I think I need to have a chat with my wife," he said at last.

Tony nodded. "After Altaussee?"

"Altaussee first." The witness, the hunt, *die Jägerin*. Nothing came before that.

"You didn't answer my question," Tony said eventually. "What debt did you owe Nina that you married her without a second's hesitation to get her to England?"

"Seb had promised to get her there. I kept his promise for him." Ian looked at his partner. "He was my little brother. The only family I had left. And Nina watched *die Jägerin* murder him at Lake Rusalka."

But the poisonous doubt had crept in. If she had lied about one thing, why not this? That night when Ian sat awake in his dark bedroom with his mind consumed by a woman, it wasn't the huntress. He leaned on his windowsill with a half-smoked cigarette, looking out over moonlit Vienna and wondering, *Who the hell did I marry?*

Chapter 6

NINA

May 1937
Lake Baikal, Siberia

Nina broke the rabbit's neck with a fast twist, feeling the last tremor of its heart under her fingertips. Spring had come to the lake, the air alive with the squeal and groan of ice as the lake's surface broke apart into rainbow shards. Icicles dripped and water lapped on the shore as the air warmed, but ice floes still drifted in the farther depths. The Old Man had control of the seasons here, and he kept a long grip on winter.

Nina reset the rabbit snare under the trees. She was nineteen now, her blue eyes wary under a shapeless rabbit-fur cap, razor never far from her hand. Her father was too drunk much of the time now to set snares or to stalk game, so Nina did it. The rabbit in her hand would go into the stewpot, and the pelt could line a pair of gloves or be traded. Hunting let her make a living without a man, but Nina still glowered restlessly across the lake. It had been three years since she lay gasping on the ice with her eyelashes freezing together, looking up into the vast sky thinking *Get out of here.* Three years of waking up with the choking feeling of cold water closing over her head, the terrible drowning sensation. But where was there for a girl like her to go, little and wolverine-mad

and knowing nothing except how to stalk and kill and move without a sound?

She didn't know, but she had to find it, or else she would die here.
Stay, and Nina knew the lake would take her in the end.

She stood swinging the dead rabbit by the ears and pondering
her useless questions as she'd done for so many mornings, and the
day might have ended as so many did: with her stamping back to
the house, and skirting her father as he lay snoring. But today, Nina
heard a rumble from the sky.

The gornaya? she wondered—but it was too early in the year for
the mountain-bred wind that could whirl out of the northwest from
a warm sky, whipping the lake into a frenzy and hurling waves three
times the height of a man across the shores. Besides, this was a droning mechanical sound that seemed to rise from everywhere. Nina
shaded her eyes, hunting for the strange buzz, and her jaw dropped
as a shape rose sleek and dark from the horizon and glided down
over the trees. *An airplane?* she thought. The village traders who
had been to Irkutsk claimed to have seen them, but she never had. It
might as well have been a firebird rising from myth.

She thought it would streak across the sky and be gone, but there
was a skipping sound in the drone of its engines. Nina had a moment's terror the machine would crash into the lake. But it banked
stiffly, descending below the tree line, and Nina began to run. For
once she didn't bother to move quietly, just crashed through underbrush and squelching mud. At some point she realized she had lost
the rabbit, but she didn't care.

The plane had touched down in a long clearing in the taiga. The
pilot was standing by the cockpit with a toolbox, cursing, and Nina
stared at him, mesmerized. He looked as tall as a god in his overalls
and flying cap. She didn't dare come closer, just sank to her heels in
a stand of brush and watched him work on the engine. She couldn't
stop looking at the plane, its long lines, its proud wings.

It took her a long time to work up the courage to approach.
But she moved out from the brush, slowly came forward. The pilot
turned and found Nina under his nose.

He jumped back, boots slipping in icy mud. "Fuck your mother, you scared me." His Russian was clipped, strangely accented. "Who are you?"

"Nina Borisovna," she said, dry mouthed. She raised a hand in greeting, and saw his eyes dance over the dried rabbit blood showing under her nails. "I live here."

"Who lives in a mud splat like this?" The pilot looked at her a little longer. "A real little savage, aren't you?" he said, turning back to his toolbox.

Nina shrugged.

"This isn't even Listvyanka, is it?"

"No." Even Listvyanka was bigger than her village.

The pilot swore some more. "Hours off course from Irkutsk . . ."

"Planes don't land here," Nina managed to say. "Where are you from?"

"Moscow," he grunted, slinging tools. "I fly the mail route, Moscow to Irkutsk. Longest route in the Motherland," he added, unbending. "Detoured past Irkutsk in the fog, had some engine trouble. Nothing serious. I could fly this girl home on one wing if I had to."

"What kind of—I mean—" Nina wished she could stop blushing and stammering. She could have eaten the local boys for breakfast, but here she was tripping over her words like a lovesick girl. Only she wasn't in love with a man, but a machine. "What kind of plane is this?"

"A Pe-5."

"She's beautiful," Nina whispered.

"She's a brick," the pilot said dismissively. "But a good Soviet brick. Eh, get back, little girl!" he barked as Nina reached toward the wing.

"I'm not a little girl," she flashed. "I'm nineteen."

He chuckled, went on working. Nina wished she understood what he was doing. She could have opened up a rabbit or a seal or a deer and known every organ and bone, but the Pe-5's innards were strange to her. Masses of wires and gears, the smell of oil. She breathed it in as though it were wildflowers. "Where did you learn to fly?"

"Air club."

"Where are there air clubs?"

"Everywhere from Moscow to Irkutsk, *coucoushka*! Everybody wants to fly. Even little girls." He winked. "Ever heard of Marina Raskova?"

"No."

"An aviatrix who just set the distance record. Moscow to . . . Well, somewhere. Comrade Stalin himself sent congratulations." Another wink. "Probably because she's pretty, Raskova is."

Nina nodded. Her heart had stopped its pitter-pat, settled to a purposeful rhythm. "Take me with you," she said when he finally shut up his toolbox and rose. She wasn't surprised when he guffawed. "Just an idea. I'm a good screw," she lied. She hadn't screwed a man before—most of the ones she knew were nervous around her, and anyway she was too wary of getting pregnant—but she'd do it right here in this clearing if it got her into that plane.

"A good screw?" The pilot looked at the blood under her fingernails. "Do you pick your teeth with a man's bones afterward?" He shook his head, stowing his tools. "Good luck, *coucoushka*. You'll need it, stuck out here on the edge of the world."

"I won't be stuck here much longer," Nina said, but he was swinging up into the cockpit and didn't hear. Before he could start up the engines, she darted close and laid her hand against the wing. It seemed warm to her, pulsing under her palm like a living thing. *Hello*, it seemed to say.

"Hello," Nina breathed back, and she darted away before the pilot could shout at her. She raced to the edge of the clearing as the deafening sound of the engines filled the air and sent birds spiraling up from the trees. Then she watched, delighted, as the plane slowly turned toward the long treeless edge, straightened, began to gather speed. Her breath caught when it lifted into the air, rising into the pool of blue that was the sky—aiming west. She stood there long after it had disappeared, crying a little, because at last she had answers.

What is the opposite of a lake?

The sky.

What is the opposite of drowning?

Flying. Because if you were soaring free in the air, water could never close over your head. You might fall, you might die, but you would never drown.

What lies all the way west?

An air club. Maybe it wasn't *all* the way west, but just a few hours west lay everything Nina had not known she needed.

She ran all the way home, feet already so light she could feel herself straining to take wing, and packed everything she owned—a few clothes, her identity cards, the razor—into a satchel. Without hesitation, she emptied every kopeck out of the jar her father kept as a money tin. "I've been making all the money anyway," she told her father, snoring on his filthy bed. "Besides, you tried to drown me in the lake."

She turned away to pick up her satchel. When she looked back, she saw one wolflike eye open a slit, regarding her silently.

"Where you going?" he slurred.

"Home," she heard herself say.

"The lake?"

Nina sighed. "I'm not a *rusalka*, Papa."

"Then where are you going?"

"The sky." *I never knew I could* have *the sky*, Nina thought. *But now I know.*

His snores started again. Nina almost leaned down and brushed her lips over his forehead, but instead, she took the half-empty jug of vodka from the kitchen table and set it by the bed. Then she flung her satchel over her shoulder, hiked to the station in Listvyanka, and slept on the platform waiting for the next train. The ride was cold and malodorous, dumping her into Irkutsk the following twilight. At any other time she might have gasped at the sheer grubby expanse that was a *city* and not a ramshackle village—there were more people visible here in the blink of an eye than she was used to seeing in the course of an entire week. But she was honed sharp and straight as her razor on only one thing. It took all night, but after being laughed at or shrugged off by half the people in Irkutsk, she found it: an ugly block building off the Angara River.

At dawn, the director of the Irkutsk air club came to work yawning and found someone had beaten him there. Bundled in her coat, blue eyes barely visible between rabbit-fur cap and scarf, Nina Markova sat curled in a ball on the top step. "Good morning," she said. "Is this where I learn to fly?"

Chapter 7

JORDAN

May 1946
Boston

Y ou deserve a grander honeymoon," Dan McBride objected.

"A weekend in Concord is all we need," Anneliese insisted. "It wouldn't be fair to leave the girls alone too long."

Jordan and Ruth were swiftly becoming *the girls*—Jordan could see her father's smile deepen every time he heard it. Anything was worth seeing him this happy. In truth, Jordan was happy too. She'd thrown herself into wedding preparations: clearing space in her dad's closet for Anneliese's things, pressing his wedding suit. Anneliese would stay the night before the wedding, sharing the guest room with Ruth, and then two different cabs would take them to the church the following morning. "You can't see your bride dressed for the wedding, Dad. You take the first cab, and Anneliese and Ruth and I will follow."

"Whatever you say, missy." He squeezed her cheek. "I'm proud of the way you handle things. There aren't many seventeen-year-old girls I'd trust with their new sister for a weekend alone." He twisted his old wedding ring, moved to his other hand. "I used to worry I hadn't done right by you, after your mother died. I didn't handle it as I should have."

"Dad—"

"I didn't. Little girl with a wild imagination, taking her mother's death hard—I worried I wasn't enough to raise you right." He took her in now, approvingly. "I don't know if I did anything right or if it was all you, but look at you now. All grown up with a good head on your shoulders."

I don't feel it, Jordan thought. Every time she met Anneliese's opaque blue eyes over the dinner table, speculation began raging inside, even as she chided herself. *This is ridiculous, J. Bryde. You like Anneliese.* (She did.) *She's lovely.* (She was.) *She didn't even tell Dad on you when you were rude enough to go prying about her past.* (She had not.) *So why are you still . . . ?*

Because you're still jealous, and still trying to find fault, Jordan told herself with a mental kick, and kept doing her level best to squash the feeling out of existence.

"You're so distracted," Garrett said a few days before the wedding, when Jordan's dad had all but ordered her to stop cleaning and go out for a date. "Do you even want to make out?"

"Not really," Jordan confessed, and Garrett sat up as Jordan finger-combed her hair back into place. Ten minutes of kissing in the backseat of his Chevrolet had pulled it out of its blue band. "Sorry."

"You're killing me," he said with big soulful eyes, but he hopped out of the backseat fishing for his keys. He wasn't one of those boys to keep pushing if a girl said no; he groaned, but he backed off. *Maybe this year we . . .* Jordan thought, trailing off.

"What's on your mind?" Garrett asked as they rearranged themselves in the front seat and he turned the car for home. "Wedding stuff?"

"It'll be easier when it's done," Jordan admitted. Surely it would. Anneliese Weber would be Anneliese McBride, her stepmother. They'd be a family. That would be that.

THE WEDDING MORNING dawned bright and beautiful. Jordan was up first, pressing her dad to swallow some toast. He looked so sweetly nervous as she slipped a white rosebud into his buttonhole, smiling from under those straight dark-blond brows just like her own. "I thought I'd be the one walking you down the aisle."

"Not for a while yet, Dad." She stood back. "There."

"You've been a brick, welcoming Anneliese like this. It means a lot."

"Better catch your cab," Jordan managed to say despite her choked-up throat. "If Father Harris shows up tipsy, pour some coffee into him. No postponing this wedding; I'm not stuffing you into this suit twice!"

She snapped a few shots off, then saw her father into his cab before dashing up to the guest room.

Ruth answered her knock, putting a smile on Jordan's face. "Ruthie, you look like a princess! Twirl for me?" Ruth twirled solemnly, blond hair brushed out over the lace collar of her new blue velvet dress. *I'm going to get a laugh out of you this weekend if it's the last thing I do*, Jordan vowed.

"There you are." Anneliese stood before the mirror patting her face and neck with a powder puff, perfectly composed in her pink suit and broad-brimmed cream hat, not a bridal nerve in sight. "We're almost ready."

"You're a vision," Jordan said. "Dad will be speechless."

"You look lovely too." Anneliese turned, looking Jordan over in her blue dress, and for once she seemed to speak impulsively. "I look forward to *making* you things, Jordan. I make all our day clothes, Ruth's and mine—I could run up a summer dress for you if you liked. Something not fussy, you aren't a fussy girl. Three-quarter length, nothing floral printed . . ." Anneliese stopped herself with a laugh, looking suddenly rueful. "*Du meine Güte*, I swore I wouldn't start offering to dress you, like you were a child! It's the opposite, you see—it would be a pleasure to make a dress for someone who *isn't* a child and wanting everything ruffled."

Jordan felt herself startled into genuine laughter. "It sounds like we'd better set up the sunroom for you as a sewing room, then. But first"—she reached into her blue clutch for something she'd meant to offer days ago but hadn't quite been able to manage—"I thought you might like to wear this today." She held out the gold bracelet her father had given her on her sixteenth birthday.

"I would be honored," Anneliese said quietly.

The last knot in Jordan's stomach melted away. "Now you have something borrowed—"

"Something old—" Anneliese patted the string of gray pearls around her neck.

"Something new—" Jordan fastened the bracelet around her soon-to-be stepmother's wrist. "Your pink suit—"

"And something blue," Anneliese finished, lifting her bouquet of creamy roses with stems wrapped in pale blue satin ribbon.

Jordan smiled. "The cab's waiting."

Anneliese straightened her hat and glided downstairs. She glided into the chapel with the same silent grace, and Jordan saw tears in her father's eyes. *This makes it all worth it*, she thought. Father Harris's voice rolled across the chapel, and it was done.

THERE WAS CAKE and champagne in the vestry afterward, corks popping as friends crowded around. Soon the newlyweds would take a cab to South Station and be off to their honeymoon; Jordan had already prepared little bags of rice to throw. Anneliese chatted with some neighbors, and Jordan's father swung Ruth up to his shoulder. "You want to hold your mama's bouquet?"

"Don't, she'll drop it," Anneliese began.

"She'll be careful, won't you, little missy?" He plucked Anneliese's bouquet from her hands and settled it into Ruth's. Jordan got an adorable snap of Ruth in his arms, burying her face in roses, looking cautiously thrilled with her new life.

More glasses being drained, more laughter. Jordan's father set Ruth down, hearing himself called over by a colleague. Ruth looked around, chewing her lip, and Jordan captured her hand. "What do you need, Ruthie? Oh—" As Ruth made a certain clamped-knees gesture. "Let me take you to the powder room." Ruth protested as Jordan took the bridal bouquet from her hands. "Mama said don't let go of it—"

"You can hardly take it into the toilet!" Ruth disappeared into the stall, and Jordan laid the roses down before the powder room mirror, snapping a close-up of the flowers. The pale blue satin ribbon was coming undone around the bouquet; Jordan started to rewrap it, but there was a hard little lump in among the stems. Some wedding charm for good luck? Jordan fished down into the roses and drew out the wedged object. The little piece of metal lay in her hand, glittering in the soft powder room light, and Jordan stood as if turned to ice.

A war medal. Not an American medal, but Jordan still recognized it. All through the war, Hollywood actors wore them if they were cast as the Nazi villain. An Iron Cross, black swastika gleaming.

She dropped it as though it were red hot. It lay among the bridal roses and loops of pale blue ribbon like a drop of poison. *Something old, something new,* Jordan thought, waves of bewildered horror crawling down her spine, *something Nazi, something blue.*

The toilet flushed; Ruth would be coming out. *Anneliese* could walk in at any moment. Hardly aware of what she was doing, Jordan raised the Leica. *Click*—the swastika lurking among the wedding flowers. What kind of woman walked down the aisle carrying a swastika? Why would she risk that? Swiftly, Jordan bundled the roses back together, burying the Iron Cross exactly where it had been before, then she rewrapped the ribbon. Her hands trembled.

Ruth came out, trotting to the sink to wash her hands. *Who is your mother?* Jordan thought, staring at the little girl. She put the roses back in Ruth's hands, looked at herself in the mirror, and saw the spots of color flushing in her cheeks. *Smile,* she told herself, *smile*—and went back outside.

"There you are!" Anneliese exclaimed, swiftly reclaiming her bouquet. "Ruth takes my flowers and just disappears. *Mäuschen,* I told you—"

Jordan gripped her father's sleeve, drawing him aside. "Dad—"

"Cab's here," he said, reaching for Anneliese's traveling case. "You have the telephone number of our hotel in Concord if there's any trouble. Though I don't see how much trouble my girls could get into in just two nights!"

I think we may be in a lot of trouble. "Dad," Jordan said, gripping his sleeve harder.

The crowd was already carrying them outside. He pulled Jordan along. "What is it?"

Jordan's tongue dried up. What on earth was she going to do, rip Anneliese's bouquet to bits on the church steps? What would that prove?

Anneliese's laughing voice exclaimed behind her: "Jordan, catch!"

Jordan turned at the top of the church steps, and the bridal bouquet came flying into her hands.

"For my maid of honor," Anneliese twinkled as guests clapped. "The train, Dan, we'll be late—" There was a whirl of luggage and flying skirts as he loaded the cab and Anneliese slid her pocketbook over her arm, and Jordan stood feeling frozen all over again. Because she could feel quite clearly that there was no hard little lump among the stems now. Anneliese must have slid the Iron Cross out before throwing the bouquet.

It must be something very precious, Jordan thought, *if she'd risk carrying it today, and only take it out at the last minute.*

Or it was never there at all, another thought whispered, and for one horrible moment Jordan thought she was going crazy. *Jordan and her wild stories.* She'd concocted the wildest theory imaginable out of thin air and jealousy, and this time her mind was furnishing evidence.

But the strap of the Leica reassured her. The Iron Cross *had* been there; she'd snapped a shot of it. She'd go down to the darkroom the minute she got home and look at the film. Already she was shivering, imagining the black arms of the swastika emerging skull-like through the developing fluid. Proof.

Of what? Jordan thought, staring at Anneliese as her father opened the cab door. *By itself, it's not proof of anything.*

Except that this woman was hiding something.

Ruth opened her bag of rice, flinging grains everywhere. A final flurry of hugs, and Jordan's father and his new wife slid into their taxi. Guests cheered as they rolled away, as confusion and horror swept over Jordan.

Dad, she thought, *oh, Dad, what have you brought into our family?*

Chapter 8

IAN

April 1950
Altaussee

Nina was not happy to be left behind in Vienna. "No. I go with you."

"I have to sweet-talk a girl in Altaussee," Tony said with his most persuasive smile. "How's it going to look if I've got another girl with me already?"

Nina shrugged. She had been filled in on most aspects of the chase ahead and was clearly eager to begin. Ian put his oar in the water. "We need someone to look after the office."

"You get to chase the huntress and I get to answer phone?" Nina said ominously. "Is horseshit."

"Yes," Ian stated. "But I am having a blunt conversation with you before I bring you along on the most important chase of my life, Nina, and since we don't have time for that conversation right now, you're staying in the bloody office."

Her blue eyes narrowed. He stared back unblinking, impatience pulsing through him. The train left in an hour.

"Okay," Nina finally said, still glowering. "I stay *this* time. Next time, you take me."

"Try not to burn down the building while we're gone." Ian

seized his battered fedora, ignoring Nina's dirty look, and a moment later he and Tony were speeding down the Mariahilferstrasse in a cab. Vienna slid past outside, war raked but still lovely. *A beautiful city*, Ian thought, *but not home*. He hadn't really had a home since Sebastian died. Home wasn't merely an address.

"Well," Tony said, speaking English so the driver wouldn't understand. "Another day, another hunt."

"This one is different," Ian said, still thinking of his little brother. Scabby-kneed, earnest, eleven years younger—with such an age difference they shouldn't have been close, yet they had been. Perhaps because their mother had died so soon after Seb was born, and the house had become such a mausoleum, their father interested in nothing but long lunches at the club and acting as if the Graham family still had money. "You're the only thing good about coming home for hols," the thirteen-year-old Seb had said frankly, back from school one summer. "You're the only reason I bother coming home for hols," Ian had replied, twenty-four himself, long moved out from under his father's roof. "Let's get out for some fishing before the old man starts going on about how I'd better not go to Spain and muck around with Reds and Dagos."

Ian *had* headed to Barcelona not long after that, packing a notebook and a typewriter to cover Franco's uprising, but even when he came back, sunburned and half a stone lighter, there had been time for his little brother. Teaching Seb to skip stones on a pond, Seb showing him bird calls. The two of them talking about the rumblings in Germany . . .

Sebastian dead in Poland, never to see the end of the war.

"This chase is different," Ian said again, and his yearning to catch *die Jägerin* was a hunger so vast it could have swallowed the world.

Tony flipped through the file on their target as the cab rumbled along. "You're lucky, you know."

"Lucky?" Ian looked at him. "My brother would be about your age now if he'd lived, but he didn't. I don't *have* a brother, Tony. That Nazi bitch took him away."

"You have a single person to blame. One." Tony looked Ian in the eye, meeting the flare of anger he could probably see there. "Lots of us don't have that."

"Us?"

"My mother had family in Kraków, whole flotillas of Jewish cousins and aunts and uncles who didn't emigrate when her parents did," Tony said. "I'd never met them in my life, but I promised my mother I'd look them up if I was ever in Poland. When I was de-mobbed, I went looking . . ." He blew out a long breath. "Gone. All of them."

Ian's flash of anger faded. "I see." He already knew Tony's background, of course; his partner had flung that at him the day they started working together. *I may be a born-and-raised Catholic boy from Queens, but my mother's side is Polish Jew. Is that going to be a problem, Graham?* "No," Ian had replied, and that was that. He'd always wondered if Tony lost family in the horror of the camps, but he had never asked. You didn't ask for information like that. You just listened, if someone decided to tell you. "I'm sorry," he said simply.

"The maw took them—the machine. There's no one person to find and accuse. All I can do is go after all of them, the thousands who staffed the machine, and there's no such thing as catching all the bastards." Tony smiled faintly. "But you, you're lucky. You know exactly who killed your brother. One person. And we have a lead where she is."

"You're right," Ian said. "That is lucky."

They fell into silence until the cab pulled up before the train station. A busy throng crowded the steps: Austrian businessmen in homburgs, mothers towing children in dirndls and lederhosen. *And us*, Ian thought, *on the trail of a murderess*. As much as he tried to avoid undue optimism, he was suddenly, absolutely certain. They were going to find her. Sebastian might be gone, but his story would be told within the passionless confines of a courtroom—his story, and the story of the children *die Jägerin* had murdered before she ever crossed Seb's path.

The world will know your name, Ian told her, going with lighter feet toward the first bread crumb Fate had thrown his way. *And that is a promise.*

THEY WERE TO meet Helga Ziegler and her sister on the southern shore of Lake Altaussee at noon. "Play the quasi-police angle," Tony said as they strolled the path, snow-capped mountains towering behind. "I've flirted with Helga and she likes me, but her sister might be more wary. It'll come across better if they think we're looking for witnesses to question, not war criminals to put in handcuffs. Austrians get so cagey if they think they're suspected as former Nazis—"

"Which none of them ever were, of course," Ian said dryly.

"If that's their line, we take it without batting an eye."

"I have done this before, you know." Many times, in fact. "Usual roles, Tony. You be charming, I'll be imposing."

"Right." Tony looked Ian over from the gray overcoat stirring at his knees to the wintry frown he always adopted for these moments. "You're so obviously an upstanding Brit on the side of the righteous, no one would dream of asking to see your credentials."

Ian slanted his hat at a more severe angle. "If they get the impression we're allied with the police, I shan't correct the notion." They'd played that card before many times, given the legal no-man's-land the center occupied: an independent service allied with no nations, given no government authority. Ian had connections inside police, law, and bureaucracy, but there was no legal way to force any witness to cooperate with the center's questioning. *And not being flush with cash,* he thought with a wry smile, *we can't exactly offer enormous rewards to loosen tongues either.*

They reached the appointed bench on the south shore, overlooking the flat sparkling expanse of lake. Tony pointed. "There they are."

Two women approached along the path. As they drew closer Ian saw the family resemblance: both blond and rosy, the younger in a pink dirndl and white blouse with a sparkle in her eye as she caught sight of Tony, the other taller and cooler in a green spring coat. She led a little boy by the hand, perhaps two years old, trundling along sturdily in short pants. Ian bowed as Tony made introductions with a few semi-misleading words about the center. Ian maintained an authoritative frown, flipping his wallet to show a meaningless bit of English identification that nevertheless looked tremendously official. "*Grüss Gott*, ladies."

"This is my sister," answered Helga, hand already looped through Tony's arm. "Klara Gruber."

The older woman met Ian's gaze. "What is it you wish to know, Herr Graham?"

Ian took a deep breath, seeing Tony's tiny nod at the corner of his eye. "May 1945. You worked as a maid for the family living at number three Fischerndorf?"

"Yes."

"Did you notice the family living at number eight?"

"Hard to avoid noticing them," Klara Gruber said tartly. "Americans tramping in and out."

Ian said what she was avoiding. "Making arrests?"

A nod as she smoothed her son's hair.

"After the arrests were done?"

"Most of the women went elsewhere, but Frau Liebl and her sons stayed on."

"You mean Frau Eichmann," Ian said quietly. Wife to Adolf Eichmann—he and an entire cabal of Nazi leadership had fled here in the chaos after Hitler's suicide. Among them, *die Jägerin*'s SS lover, Manfred von Altenbach, who had died resisting arrest. Some of his companions had submitted to handcuffs; some like Eichmann had managed to flee uncaught . . . But however the men ended up, they'd left a number of wives and girlfriends behind.

"Frau Liebl," Klara corrected. "She took her birth name back, after the war. So there wouldn't be talk."

"Is Frau Liebl still there?" Tony asked, tone casual.

"Yes." Helga shrugged. "Now that I have taken over Klara's job at number three, I see her sons running up and down every afternoon, playing."

"And their father?" Ian couldn't resist asking. Adolf Eichmann was a far, far bigger fish than those the center had the resources to chase, but if something could be learned here, perhaps in the future . . .

Head shakes from the two sisters. "You're not looking to bother Frau Liebl, are you? It all happened years ago."

A familiar flare of anger warmed Ian's chest. The excuses people were willing to make, the things they were willing to forget, all for the sake of *it happened years ago*. "I have no intention of bothering Frau Liebl," he said lightly, smiling. "It's someone else who interests me. I know that in '45, a group of women came to stay at number eight. One was blue eyed, dark haired, small, in her twenties. She had a scar on the back of her neck, reddened, fairly recent."

His heart pounded, and Ian thought what a slender thread this really was. How many women of that description did the world hold? Who could guarantee a scar would ever be seen?

"I remember her," Klara said. "I only talked with her once, but I noticed the scar. A pink line across the back of her neck, trailing under her collar."

"What was her name?" Ian's mouth had gone dry. Beside him he felt Tony coiled taut as wire.

"Frau Becker, she called herself." A little smile. "Not her real name, we all knew that."

Ian couldn't keep the sharpness out of his voice. "You never asked?"

"One didn't." She pulled her son closer, smoothing his collar. "Not during the war."

No name. Ian swallowed bitter disappointment, hearing Tony press on.

"Anything else you can tell us about her, *gnädige Frau*." He made a discreet gesture of reaching for his wallet. "It's important that we locate this woman. We would be *very* grateful."

Klara Gruber hesitated, eyeing the notes Tony had conjured. The center might not have the cash for large rewards, but Ian was perfectly willing to give up the week's supper budget to grease a few wheels. She nodded, whisking the money away as if it had never been there at all. "Frau Becker stayed at the Liebl household a few months after—well, everything." A vague gesture Ian took to mean *the arrests, the Americans, the end of the war*. The unpleasantness they could all pretend had not happened. "She kept to herself. I'd see her in the garden sometimes, on my way to market. I'd say hello, she'd smile." Pause. "I don't think Frau Liebl liked her."

"Why?"

A very female shrug. "Two women in one house, wartime shortages having to be shared. Everybody staring at them, knowing who their men were. I think Frau Liebl asked her to leave—she left Altaussee in the fall of '45. September, maybe."

The bitter taste came back to Ian's mouth. "Do you know where she went?"

"No."

He hadn't really thought she would.

"But Frau Becker asked me something, the day she left." Klara Gruber hoisted her fussing son to one hip. "She called me over to the yard at number eight as I came back from the market. She must have noticed me going by at the same time every morning, because she was waiting for me."

"What did she ask?"

"To deliver a letter for her in a few days. I asked why didn't she post it before she left, and she said she was leaving Austria, almost immediately." A pause. "That's why I think she and Frau Liebl didn't like each other. If they had, she wouldn't have given her letter to a maid down the street."

"A letter to whom?" Ian's heart thudded all over again; Tony had turned back into a stretched-taut wire.

"Her mother in Salzburg. Frau Becker said she'd pay me to deliver it myself, not put it in the post. She didn't trust the post." A shrug. "I needed the money. I took Frau Becker's letter, went to the address in Salzburg the week after she'd gone, put it under the door, and didn't think about it again."

"You didn't actually *see* her mother? Was there a name on the envelope, or—"

"No name. I was told to put it under the door, not knock." A hesitation. "She was being very careful, I suppose. But everyone was, Herr Graham."

Helga chimed in, defensive. "You don't know what it was like here in '45. Everyone looking for visas, papers, food. Everyone kept their business to themselves."

Because none of you wanted to know anything, Ian thought. That kind of thinking had made it quite easy for *die Jägerin* to cover her tracks.

Without hope, he asked, "I don't suppose you remember the address." Who would remember a strange address visited once five years ago?

"Number twelve, the Lindenplatz," Klara Gruber said.

Ian stared, could feel Tony staring. "How . . . ?"

She gave the first real smile of the interview. "When I came back into the square in front of the house, a young man on a bicycle knocked me down. He apologized and introduced himself—his name was Wolfgang Gruber. Four months later he took me back to that same spot when he proposed. That's how I remember the address."

Bloody hell, Ian thought. They had just got very, very lucky.

"Ladies," Tony said with a warm smile, pressing a few more notes on them, "you've been more helpful than you can possibly know." Helga blushed, but her older sister looked apprehensive.

"Are you going to make trouble for Frau Becker?" *Now you ask*, Ian thought, *after you pocket our cash*. "She couldn't have done anything wrong. Such a nice woman—"

"It's an inquiry related to someone else entirely," Tony said, his standard soothing reply when hearing the inevitable *He couldn't have hurt a flea* objection. But Ian looked down at Klara Gruber a long moment and asked, "What makes you so sure she was a nice woman?"

"Well, you know. She had a pretty way of speaking. She was a *lady*. And it's not a woman's fault, if her husband got involved with all that."

"Involved with what?" Ian said. "The Nazi Party?"

The sisters both squirmed. No one had said that word yet. He could feel Tony giving him a quelling look.

"No one in our family were party members," Helga said quickly. "We didn't know anyone like that."

"Of course not," Tony said with a smile of melting sincerity.

"Of course not," Ian echoed, stretching a hand toward Klara Gruber's young son. He gurgled, reaching out, and Ian felt the baby fingers curl warmly round his thumb. "He's a nice little chap, your boy. Frau Becker killed one not much older than him. Bullet to the back of the head. He was probably a nice little chap too."

The two women stared, no longer quite so rosy. Helga put a hand to her mouth. Klara pulled her child back, and Ian saw the flash in her eyes he'd seen many times before—a kind of sullen, stubborn anger. *Why did you make me know that?* her eyes asked. *I didn't want to know that.*

He smiled, tipping his hat. "Thank you again, ladies."

"YOU CAN BE a real bastard sometimes," Tony said conversationally.

Ian shrugged. "Their eyes are a little more open now."

They were walking back to the hotel where they'd taken rooms for the night. Ian would have headed for Salzburg at once, but Tony wanted to question Frau Liebl in the morning. Ian thought Adolf Eichmann's deserted wife would be far warier than a couple of former maidservants about talking to strange men, but Tony was right; they couldn't leave it unexplored. "I'll buy supper," he said, since Tony still looked disapproving.

"No, I've got to take Helga Ziegler out tonight, show her a good time. And she's in a sulk thanks to you, so it's going to take all my very considerable charm."

"Why take her out?"

"Spend weeks buttering up a girl only to drop her as soon as you have the information you need, and girls tend to feel used."

"That's because she *was* used, Tony. She was also paid."

"Still, no one likes to be fobbed off the minute they're not useful.

And she's not a bad sort. Her sister isn't either." Pause. "They aren't wrong, you know. Things were complicated during the war. Survival in occupied territories is never as black and white as you might think."

"Did they give aid to the resistance? Shelter refugees? Pass information to the Allies? Do *anything* to combat what was happening around them?" Ian paused. "If the answer is no, then as far as I'm concerned they have a measure of guilt. I'll be damned if I pretend otherwise."

"We don't know what they might have done to help. We can't assume."

"From the pattern of their squirming, we can assume quite a bit."

Tony snapped a mocking salute. "How pretty that worldview of yours must look, no shades of gray mucking anything up."

"You lost whole branches of your family, in large part because so many people—people like the Ziegler sisters—were willing to bury their heads in the sand," Ian shot back. "I find it hard to see shades of gray in that."

"Don't be such a hanging judge. We're standing in the ashes of a war like no other—if we don't try harder to see the shades of gray involved, we'll find ourselves in the thick of a new one."

"Call me a hanging judge if you like. I witnessed the hangings after Nuremberg and slept easy that night."

"You haven't slept too well since then, have you?" Tony parried.

"No, but it's got nothing to do with seeing right and wrong as matters of black and white," Ian said, getting off the last shot as they parted ways. He watched over his shoulder as Tony shook his head and strolled off, hands in pockets. They had their differences in opinion, Ian and his partner, but so far it hadn't prevented them working together. He wondered if it ever would.

Ian didn't go back to the hotel. He meandered until he stood across the street from 8 Fischerndorf. Five years ago, might he have seen *die Jägerin* standing on the doorstep? With an envelope in her hand, perhaps, waiting for the maid down the street to pass by?

I may not have your name, Ian thought to that long-gone figure, *but I have your mother's address in Salzburg. And if you sent your mother a letter before leaving Austria, surely you told her where you were going.* He'd caught more than one war criminal that way over the past few years—most found it difficult to cut ties with their families.

There was a little boy in the house's front yard, playing with pebbles. One of Adolf Eichmann's sons, perhaps ten years old. Seb had been a few years older when he went off to Harrow, skinny and nervous. It had fallen to Ian to take Seb and his trunk to the station; their father needed the world to know *My sons go to Harrow, chips off the old block!* but details like train schedules didn't interest him. "School is hell, but it's manageable," Ian had told Seb frankly. "Punch anyone who gives you guff, just like I showed you. And if the bigger boys have a go, I'll make a special trip just to drag them out behind the cricket pitch and give them a pasting."

"You can't beat up everybody who comes at me," Seb said forlornly.

"Yes, I can. Promise you'll write?" And Seb did write. Long screeds about bird-watching and eventually a passion for Pushkin chased Ian to Spain as he tramped after the International Brigade, scolding him to be more careful when an air raid near Málaga took the hearing from Ian's left ear for a week. Seb's letters had followed him to Paris afterward when he was writing articles about the coming conference in Munich, and a year later there had been the fortnight they spent together after their father died in a road accident. Sixteen-year-old Seb had got drunk for the first time, and Ian had to pour him into bed . . . then came the day not six months later when Seb turned up on Ian's doorstep in London, where he was writing about German U-boats sinking a British destroyer near Orkney, and said that he'd run away from school and enlisted.

"You *idiot*," Ian had shouted.

"Just because you can't fight doesn't mean I can't," Seb flared. Ian's hearing on the left side had mostly come back after Málaga, but not quite up to enlistment standards. Seb saw the look on Ian's face and muttered, "I'm sorry. I didn't mean that." The only quarrel that had ever erupted between them, over before it began.

"You're still an idiot for enlisting," Ian had retorted. "All your bird-watching left you bird-witted."

He wondered now if his little brother had looked for birds in the sky that May morning when he was captured, a few months later. If he'd wished for wings when his battalion was forced, outgunned and ill-equipped, to surrender on the Doullens–Arras road. Realizing, as he became a prisoner, that his war was over almost before it had begun—that he would sit out the rest of the fight in a cage, like any captive bird.

But you still fought, Ian thought. Sebastian Vincent Graham had escaped his stalag, had tried to escape occupied Poland, and he'd died doing it—died at *die Jägerin*'s hands. *And you made her pay.*

Seb had been the one to give her the scar on her neck.

So Nina had said, anyway, in her almost incomprehensible combination of broken English and hand gestures. Ian wasn't sure how she and Seb had met, how they'd stumbled across the huntress's ocher-walled house at Lake Rusalka—Nina couldn't explain it clearly—but there had been a struggle; there had been shots; there had been a blade. Seb had put up a heroic fight so Nina could get away.

If she told me the truth, Ian thought as he turned away from the Eichmann house.

"Let's have that talk now, Nina," he said aloud to the twilight.

Chapter 9

NINA

June 1941
Irkutsk, Siberia

W hen war came to the Soviet Union, Nina was putting a Polikarpov U-2 through its paces, riding a cloud-scented breeze high over Irkutsk. Not that a U-2 had many paces—a dual-cockpit biplane open to the sky, crafted of linen over wood, cruising along at a pace so sedate that newer, faster planes would have stalled trying to match speed. But the old bird was maneuverable; she could turn on a razor edge without cutting herself. Nina had been happy to take her up for a solo spin to check for the mechanics if the controls needed adjustment.

It had been in a U-2 that Nina took her first flight shortly after joining the air club. That liquid excitement when the instructor allowed her to take the stick and make her first gentle, banking turn; the plane's answering wobble as though aware of the uncertain new hands that guided it . . . She was four years past that first awkward turn now, an impressive number of flying hours under her belt, and she sent the U-2 looping and rolling among the clouds. The sky was Nina's lake. She'd felt that on her first flight as she dove into the air like a green-haired *rusalka* diving into a lake.

Diving not down but up, with a feeling of *I am home*. She had cried on that first flight, tears fogging her flight goggles.

It hadn't been easy, getting in the air. "It's going to take more than that, girl," the air club's director had sniffed when Nina pushed her application and birth record across his desk. "You'll need a medical certificate, education certificate, references from the Komsomol, and only then can you even submit to the credentials committee for consideration. Do you know anyone in Irkutsk?"

"No." Nina had no one who could pull strings for the paperwork and approvals she needed, but luckily, the head of the local Komsomol had taken a liking to her. "Here you see the epitome of proletarian spirit," he proclaimed after one look at Nina's hardscrabble background. "A girl who in tsarist days would have spilled the blood of her life in the field, now seeking the skies! The glorification of the state lies in the ability of its laborers to *rise*—" There had been a great many more slogans after that, and Nina was allowed to apply for the Komsomol with all its interviews and political literacy exams. She didn't know much about political history, but she knew to nod fervently whenever anyone asked if she wished to exalt the Motherland by participating in the recent aviation drive to match the aeronautics of the decadent West, and alongside that, she had impeccable peasant lineage. *The first time my father ever did me a favor*, Nina reflected. If he'd been a prosperous kulak or highbrow intelligentsia rather than a Siberian peasant with barely a kopeck to his name, the Komsomol would have turned up their nose. But an untutored peasant with ambition was looked on with enough approval for a membership card, and with that, a good many doors opened. Komsomol girls were sought after, presumed to be aspiring Communist Party members. Nina didn't care about policy or Party politics as long as she could get in the air.

And now here she was, dancing in the clouds.

Nina came out of her spiral, lining up the air club below. Nothing wrong with this old duck's flight controls. She began the descent, feeling no place where the plane left off and she began; it was as though her arms had lengthened into the span of the wings and her feet had stretched down into the wheels, the sun warming her hair the way it warmed the linen over the wooden struts.

She brought the U-2 down soft as a snowflake alighting on dark water—perfect three-point touchdown, not even a bounce— smiling as she felt the tail skid brake them to a halt. Maybe that was another reason Nina liked the U-2, because it had been designed without brakes. *So was I.* She hoisted herself out of the cockpit, sitting on the rim atop the plane as she unbuckled her half-bald rabbit-fur cap. Nina Borisovna Markova was twenty-three now, still small, compact, and sturdy as a gymnast; she had engine grease under her nails instead of blood, and she breathed exhaust fumes instead of lake water. She might still be a little crazy, she acknowledged, because all Markovs were, but at least she'd won a place for herself in this world, on her wings and not on her back. She knew what she loved, she knew what she feared, and what she feared didn't matter because there was no lake anywhere nearby to drown in. Nina sat atop her plane a moment longer, tilting her face up to the sun, then slid to the wing and down to the ground in one easy motion.

Looking around, she saw that something was wrong.

The runway should have bustled with students, mechanics, pilots. Even in Irkutsk, flying was such a craze that the air club was always busy. But Nina saw no one, and even the bustle of the city beyond—the noise of the streets, the sound of raised voices and feet in mass-produced boots trudging back and forth from work—seemed muted. Puzzled, she secured her plane—the process of checking her switches and mags, securing her flight controls, and taking care of the tie-downs all as automatic now as breathing—and headed for the nearest hangar. The sun stood directly overhead—high noon on a perfect June Sunday.

She found a silent crowd inside. Pilots, students, fellow instructors, all crowded together with faces lifted toward the loudspeaker high on the wall. Flying goggles and oilcans dangled from hands, and no one so much as cleared their throat. Everyone listened to the flat drone of the words coming from the radio.

"—*to the effect that the German government had decided to launch war against the U.S.S.R.—*"

Nina sucked in her breath. Coming to the fringe of the crowd, she saw the coal-black hair of Vladimir Ilyich and pushed up beside him—he was the best pilot in the air club besides Nina; they slept together sometimes. "Was there an attack?" she breathed.

"Fucking Fritzes bombed Kiev, Sebastopol, Kaunas—"

Someone shushed him. Nina pointed at the loudspeaker, the flat cadences of whoever was speaking. Vladimir mouthed back *Comrade Molotov.*

The public address continued. "—*now that the attack on the Soviet Union has already been committed, the Soviet government has ordered our troops to repulse the predatory assault and to drive German troops from the territory of our country . . .*"

So much for the Soviet-German pact, Nina thought. In truth she wasn't surprised. War had been hovering in the air for months like the smell of dynamite. Now, war was here. Everyone knew Hitler and his fascists were crazy, but crazy enough to take on Comrade Stalin?

"—*government of the Soviet Union expresses its unshakable confidence that our valiant army and navy and brave falcons of the Soviet Air Force will acquit themselves with honor—*"

The Soviet Air Force. Nina did a rapid calculation. She had more flying hours than almost any pilot at the club; she'd scraped through two years of advanced training at the nearest pilot school and had been sent back as an aviation instructor. Already there were rumors of new fighter planes coming off the lines; to get in the cockpit of one of those . . .

"—*This is not the first time that our people have had to deal with an attack of an arrogant foe. At the time of Napoleon's invasion of Russia—*" Hoots and cheers momentarily drowned out Comrade Molotov. Nina tried to imagine Hitler's swastika being unfurled over the Old Man on the far edge of the world and shook her head in amused contempt. This land was too much for outsiders; Napoleon could tell you that. Too cold, too vast, and too unforgiving for anyone not seasoned to it from birth. A little fascist with a scrubbing-brush mustache thought he'd march on Moscow? He'd have better luck emptying Baikal with a pail.

Comrade Molotov evidently agreed with her, blaring on through the loudspeaker. "*It will be the same with Hitler, who in his arrogance has proclaimed a new crusade against our country. The Red Army and our whole people will again wage victorious war for the Motherland—*" Cheers rose again, until Nina could barely hear his final "*The enemy shall be defeated. Victory will be ours.*"

The crowd erupted, some racing across the airfield to take the news to others, some flinging arms around each other. Maybe in the streets there were tears and dread, Nina thought, but this was the air club—if war was here, they'd all be in the air, and there was nowhere any of them would rather be. Vladimir Ilyich turned with a fierce smile, and Nina kissed him so hard their teeth clashed. "I'm going to enlist tomorrow," he said when they came up for air.

"So am I." Her blood was running hot as gasoline; she couldn't close her eyes even after she and Vladimir went back to his room and spent the night drinking vodka and rolling around his old sheets. She lay there with Vladimir's arm across her middle, staring through the dark, hearing a couple arguing on the other side of the wall, imagining a chain of ice floes drifting across the surface of the Old Man, one after the other leading over the blue horizon. The train from her village to Irkutsk had been the step from shore to the first floe as she thought *I can fly.* Now here was a step to the second floe, as she thought *I can fight Germans.*

"War isn't a game," Nina's roommate, Tania, said when Nina came home in the morning long enough to change her shirt. They'd been assigned to each other as roommates, sharing an eleven-square-meter room in a communal apartment with eight other apartment-mates. Nina thought it was a hole, but Tania said they'd been lucky to get it. "You shouldn't be smiling and humming like you're going to a dance."

Nina shrugged. Tania was an aspiring Party member, a staunch believer in order and virtue and the state; the only thing she and

Nina had in common was a room. "Wars are terrible, but they need people like me."

"'People like you.'" Tania picked up her pocketbook, ready for her shift as a blast-furnace operator. "You're an individualist."

"What does that even mean?"

"You don't volunteer for outside work." Tania was forever volunteering—collecting state procurement quotas from the collective farms, carrying out exercises to improve labor discipline in factories. "You don't participate in Komsomol meetings—I see you sitting there doing your navigation figuring! You don't make an effort to participate in proletarian life—"

"It's not worth the effort."

"See? The state has no use for individualism. Try to enlist, and they won't take you," Tania said with a certain satisfaction.

"Yes, they will." Nina grinned in that way she knew unsettled her roommate. "They need people who are a little bit crazy. Because crazy people do well in wars." Her father had said that, whenever he whispered tales of the tsarists he'd killed in the revolution. It was the first time she'd thought of her father in a while—she hadn't seen him since she left home. She'd wondered often if leaving him meant killing him, if he'd pickle to death in rotgut vodka without someone to bring home game for the stewpot. That had given Nina a twinge of guilt, but she wasn't going home, not ever, not for a father who tried to drown her. Yet she still wondered from time to time how he was, if he was alive. *I hope you are*, she thought, *because if the Hitlerites get past me in my plane—if they get all the way to the Old Man—then you're just the old man to bring them to a halt.* She could see her father slipping through the trees with his rifle, his knives, his sharp-toothed grin that was just like Nina's, cutting German throats in utter silence.

"Not just an individualist but a slut," Tania muttered, stamping out. "I know you were out with Vladimir Ilyich again last night—"

"Do you want to join us next time?" Nina called after her as the door slammed. She was out that door herself a few minutes later, meeting Vladimir and two of their fellow air club pilots. They sang as they trooped down the street, bellowing an old worker's march that Nina had never learned as a child. There was so much she had never learned, growing up in near-total isolation out by the lake. It was the kind of thing that still put a distance between her and most of the people she knew. It was better at the air club than among the Komsomol girls like Tania; at least at the club there was the unifying passion for flight. Even so, people like Vladimir and his friends had grown up knowing what a city looked like; they knew Party history and could recite Comrade Stalin's most famous speeches because they'd studied all the right state-mandated subjects. Growing up a peasant was a bonus, but growing up a complete savage, Nina thought not for the first time, had its disadvantages.

Not anymore. As Nina and the others joined the line outside the recruitment office, which already stretched down the street, she could feel that sense of distance draining away. The four of them talked eagerly about the new planes coming, the fighters that would put Hitler's Messerschmitts and Fokkers into the ground, and Nina *belonged*. She couldn't stop smiling.

But when the four of them emerged from their turn in the office, her smile was gone. Vladimir put a hand on her arm. "You can still do your part—"

"Not as a pilot!" The officer who had taken their applications had been brusque: no women to be taken in aviation units. "I have more flight hours than any of them!" Nina had protested, waving at Vladimir and the others.

"Your enthusiasm to serve the state will not go unassuaged. We have need of nurses, communications operators, antiaircraft gunners—"

"Why can't I be a *pilot*?" Fumbling for arguments, Nina fell back on Stalin. No one argued with the Boss. "Comrade Stalin himself has commended the drive of women pilots. I have been a flight instructor for—"

"Then do your job, girl," the officer said sternly. "There will be plenty of training work for you." And he moved to the next in line.

Vladimir tried now to sneak an arm around Nina's waist. "Don't be sour, *dousha*. Come celebrate with us!" Nina just glowered, slipping back to her shared room where she had taped a single three-year-old newspaper clipping to the mirror: Marina Raskova, Polina Osipenko, and Valentina Grizodubova standing in front of their twin-engine Tupolev ANT-37, grinning like fiends because they had just set the distance record. Nearly six thousand five hundred kilometers in twenty-six hours and twenty-nine minutes. Nina's heroines, everyone's heroines—even Comrade Stalin's, because he'd bestowed the Hero of the Soviet Union award on them all and said "today these women have avenged the heavy centuries of the oppression of women."

I'm not avenging the heavy centuries of anything *by being a damn nurse*, Nina thought. But none of the other girls who flew at the air club were taken as pilots either, even as the men were snapped up down to the last spotty boy.

"What did you expect, Ninochka?" Vladimir shrugged. "Only one in four flying at the club is a girl anyway."

"But I'm better than any of the men they took," Nina said bluntly. "I'm better than you."

She said it as a simple statement of fact, not an insult, but he looked offended. "Keep talking like that, *dousha*, and I won't offer to marry you before I go."

Nina blinked. "Since when do you want to marry me?"

"Every man wants a woman to wave good-bye when he goes to war. We could go down to the office, it would be easy." He flung a careless arm around her waist. "Don't you love me?"

"You're a great lay, Vlodya, and you're a good pilot but you're not better than me," Nina said. "I'd only fall in love with someone who can fly better than me."

"Bitch," he said, and stamped off to spend his last few nights in some other bed than Nina's.

All through the summer, the ranks at the air club thinned. The days marched toward fall and newspapers reported Hitler's barbaric swastika-clad army murdering babies and torturing Soviet women on the western front. Even as far east as Irkutsk the tide of patriotism swelled, war news traded with relish if it was a Soviet victory or fury if it was a treacherous German advance, and Nina's frustration ate her alive. There wasn't an aviation unit that would have her; there wasn't a commanding officer who would give her a plane; there wasn't a use for what Nina did best—she spent her days training seventeen-year-old boys who barely listened long enough to get a handful of flight hours before they were off to enlist. All the fine talk on the radio and in Comrade Stalin's speeches about the women of the Motherland proving their worth—what did it come down to? Be a nurse, or train the men.

And then it was September; Hitler's forces still advancing implacably east, and Nina walked the Angara River, looking over the railings across that swift blue ribbon that threaded the city. Mentally she was flying high in one of the new fighters, screaming through the clouds at a speed to make her ears bleed . . . All at once the skin between her shoulder blades twitched, and she knew she was being tracked. She stopped to fiddle with her boot, slipping her razor up into her hand, and unfolding it inside her sleeve before turning with a mild expression, ready for anything. Anything, that is, but the knife-edged smile that greeted her.

"Careless, little huntress," her father said. "I tracked you all the way from the air club."

THEY STOOD LEANING against the railing with their backs to the river, regarding each other. Nina left enough space between them to dodge, though his eyes didn't have the lunatic gleam they'd had the last time he tried to kill her. Still, she kept the razor between her fingers. Her father smiled again when he saw it.

"Mine," he said.

"Mine now. What are you doing in Irkutsk?"

He indicated a bundle at his feet. "A good hunting year. Prize pelts fetch more in the city."

"How did you find me?"

"I can track wolverines, girl. You think I can't track my lake witch of a daughter?"

"Sky witch now," Nina retorted.

"I heard. They let girls fly?"

"Three *girls* set the long-distance record." Nina studied her father, who seemed steady on his feet. "I thought you might be dead by now. Pickled in your own vodka."

A shrug. "It was easier letting you fill the stewpot when you were home—girls are supposed to look after their fathers. But that doesn't mean I can't do it myself."

"I'm not sorry for leaving."

A wintry smile. "You stole every kopeck I had on your way out. Are you sorry for that?"

"No."

"Thieving little bitch." He said it with a kind of grim amusement, and Nina grinned. So strange to see him here; he looked as out of place as a wolf would have looked sauntering under the streetlamps.

"I'm glad you're not dead," Nina said, surprised to find she meant it. She could easily hate the man who tried to drown her. But she rather liked the man who had taught her to hunt and told her stories, and she felt a wary respect for the man seemingly too iron-hard to die. The feelings bobbed alongside each other separate and comfortable, no need to rank one over the other. If any feeling about her father came first, it was the urge not to turn her back on him.

Her father was saying something about the war now, regretting that he was too old to join up and kill fascists. "Wonder if they die easier than tsarists," he mused. "Did I ever tell you about that Muscovite son of a bitch whose liver I prised out with a spade?"

"Many times, Papa."

"You always liked that story." He looked at her from under shaggy brows. "I should have at least one child in this war killing Germans. Your brothers are all in prisons or gangs, and your sisters are all whores. Will you go?"

"They won't put women in aviation units."

"Do they think you're too soft?" He barked a laugh. "I saw women in the revolution who could saw a man's head off without batting an eye."

"Revolutions talk big about women being the same as men," Nina said. "Now when you ask permission to join up, they tell you to go be a nurse."

"There's your trouble. Asking." Her father leaned toward her, and Nina smelled the feral reek of his breath. "There'll be a chance, Nina Borisovna. Don't ask, when you see it. Just fucking *take it*."

"That shows a calculated antisocial disdain for the collectivist principle." Nina quoted the kind of rubbish Tania was always parroting. "Antithetical to the principles of proletarian life."

"Fuck proletarian life."

Despite herself, Nina winced. "Keep saying things like that on a city street and you'll be in trouble, you crazy bastard. You'll end up with a bullet in your ear."

"No, because I'm a Markov. Trouble always finds us, but we eat trouble alive." Her father rummaged in his pack, tossing her something soft and bulky. Nina caught it, surprised. A lake-seal pelt, and it was a beauty—steely gray with a sheen like new ice, soft as snow. "Make a new cap if you're going to go fly fighters," he said, twitching an eyebrow at her old rabbit-fur cap. "That one looks like shit."

Nina smiled. "Thank you, Papa."

He shouldered his pack. "Don't come back to the lake," he said in farewell. "Next time I get a skinful of vodka I'll drown you for good, little *rusalka*."

"Or I'll cut your throat this time and not your hand."

"Either way." He nodded at the razor's edge, still showing between her fingers. "Kill a German for me with that."

She waited till he was out of sight, that tall shaggy form sliding into the crowd as noiselessly as he vanished into the taiga around the Old Man. *Will I ever see you again?* she wondered, and somehow thought not. There was some relief in the thought, some regret, some pleasure. No need to rank one over the other.

She was sitting cross-legged on her bed that night, cutting carefully into the seal pelt to fashion herself a new cap, when Tania turned on the radio. "They're broadcasting a women's antifascist meeting in Moscow." Nina barely listened, cutting away at the seal-skin. A proper flying cap with flaps to tie down over the ears, just the thing for open-cockpit flights.

"*. . . The Soviet woman is the hundreds of drivers, tractor operators, and pilots who are ready at any moment to sit down in a combat machine and plunge into battle.*"

Nina paused. "Who's that?"

"Marina Raskova," Tania said. Nina glanced at the cutout newspaper photograph on her mirror. The woman on the right, dark hair, sparkling eyed, very easy and capable in front of her Tupolev ANT-37. Nina had devoured every word about Raskova, but never heard her speak. Her voice came through the radio warmly intimate, clear as crystal. Nina would have followed that voice off a cliff.

"*Dear sisters!*" Marina Raskova cried. "*The hour has come for harsh retribution! Stand in the ranks of the warriors for freedom!*"

Tell me how, Nina thought.

THE ANSWER CAME, not that night but in a matter of weeks, the day Soviet troops were driven back to the Mozhaisk Line only eighty kilometers from Moscow. The day another piece of news swept over the air club: Comrade Stalin had ordered the formation of three regiments to be trained for combat aviation under Marina Raskova, Hero of the Soviet Union.

Three regiments of *women*.

"The local Komsomols have been asked to screen and interview volunteers," Nina heard a fellow pilot saying. "I've submitted all my paperwork already. Only the best recruits will be sent to Moscow—"

How can I make them choose me? Nina thought. A little barbarian from the taiga with patched-together schooling and a record of individualism, when women everywhere would be clamoring to join—women with university backgrounds, impeccable records, Party connections.

There'll be a chance, Nina Borisovna, her father had said. *Don't ask, when you see it. Just fucking* take it.

She didn't bother filling out paperwork. Instead she went home to collect her essentials—passport, Komsomol membership card, certificates for completing pilot training and glider training—then crammed a few clothes into a bag, stuffed her hair into her new sealskin cap, and went running under an iron October sky for the train station. She threw every ruble she had onto the counter and said, "One way. Moscow."

Chapter 10

JORDAN

May 1946
Boston

The day after Jordan's father escorted Anneliese off on their honeymoon, Jordan took Ruth to the Public Garden. Nothing like ice cream and a swan boat ride to get a little girl smiling . . . and talking.

"Chocolate or strawberry?" Ruth chewed her lip in indecision. "Both," Jordan decided. "You deserve it." That got a shy smile from Ruth, who was still hanging on to Taro's leash like a safety harness, but who seemed to be unfolding into something like trust.

Which you're taking advantage of, Jordan thought grimly, but pushed that aside. *People aren't obliged to drag out their old hurts or dirty laundry just because of your need to know,* her father had told her not long ago, but he was off on his honeymoon with a woman who had carried a swastika down the aisle, and Jordan's *need to know* was burning her up.

Licking their ice creams, Jordan and Ruth wandered down to the duck pond, Taro wagging between them. The water reflected the summer tourists throwing bread down from the bridge, but for once Jordan had no impulse to capture the moment on film. "See that flicker, Ruth? That's a dragonfly. Did you see dragonflies at the lake in Altaussee?" Ruth looked puzzled. "That was where you were, wasn't it? Before you came here."

Nod.

"What else do you remember, cricket? I'd like to know more about you, now that you're my sister." Squeezing Ruth's hand. "What do you remember before coming to Boston?"

"The lake," Ruth said in her soft voice. Her trace of a German accent was already fading. With her blond braids and blue jumper, she could have been any little American girl. "Seeing the lake every day through the window."

"Every day?" Anneliese hadn't said they were in Altaussee very long. "How many days?"

Ruth shrugged.

"Do you remember your father? How he died?"

"Mama said he went east."

"Where east?"

Another shrug.

"What else do you remember?" Jordan asked as gently as she knew how.

"The violin," Ruth said even more softly. "Mama playing."

Jordan blinked. "But she doesn't play the violin."

"She did." Ruth's eyebrows pulled together, and she reached for Taro's soft back. "She did!"

"I believe you, Ruthie—"

"She *did*," Ruth said fiercely. "She played for me."

Never had Anneliese said she could play an instrument. She never asked to turn on the radio to listen to music either. And she didn't own any violin—Jordan had seen her things carried in to be unpacked after the honeymoon, and there was no instrument case. *Maybe she had to sell it?*

Jordan looked down at Ruth. "Your mama said there was an incident by the lake in Altaussee. A refugee woman who, um, wasn't very nice to you both."

"There was blood," Ruth whispered. "My nose bled."

Jordan paused, heart thumping. "Do you remember any more?"

Ruth dropped her melting ice cream, looking upset, and Jordan couldn't keep pushing. She just couldn't. She opened her arms and Ruth burrowed into them. "Never mind, cricket. You don't have to remember if you don't want to."

"That's what she said," Ruth mumbled into Jordan's middle.

"Who?"

A pause. Then, "Mama."

But her voice lifted as though she wasn't entirely certain, and her small shoulders hitched. Jordan bit her tongue on any further questions—what could she even *ask?*—and hugged her new sister tight. "Let's go for a swan boat ride. You'll love that."

"But I dropped my ice cream."

"You can have mine."

Ruth calmed down by the time they got to the boats with their paddle-operated swans. Jordan still felt like a monster. *Wasn't that productive?* she scolded herself. *You upset your brand-new little sister, all to learn that maybe Anneliese played the violin, and that a refugee woman made Ruth's nose bleed in Altaussee. That's proof of nothing, J. Bryde.*

Anneliese had brought very few belongings to the house, hardly suspicious for a woman fleeing the wreckage of a war. Jordan had already looked through her closet and drawers, guiltily, but there was nothing to be found. If the new Mrs. McBride had anything incriminating, it had gone on her honeymoon along with the Iron Cross.

Watch and wait. As much as she wanted to run to her father, Jordan knew she'd need more proof than two photographs, or he might just shake his head and say, *Jordan and her wild stories.*

By Monday the new Mr. and Mrs. McBride were back, laden with presents. Jordan couldn't help a shiver of relief to see her dad hale and hearty, although what had she been fearing? That the dainty Anneliese would do him harm? That was the wildest idea yet, surely.

"I missed my girls!" He swooped Ruth up in a hug, and Anneliese's smile for Jordan was so infectious Jordan couldn't help smiling back.

"Come help me unpack, Jordan. I'll show you the scarf I found in Concord, just your color." She was so warm and open, Jordan couldn't help but wonder if she'd imagined the Iron Cross altogether.

"I wondered," Jordan asked casually as they unpacked upstairs, shawls and lace handkerchiefs piled around the bed, "did you ever play the violin?"

"No, why?"

"No reason. Oh, that scarf *is* pretty, Anneliese—" She let her stepmother loop the fringed blue-sequined ends around her neck.

"*Anna*," corrected Anneliese, arranging the scarf across Jordan's shoulder. "Now that I'm a proper American housewife, I'd like a proper American name!"

Yes, let's just erase your past, Jordan thought, even as Anneliese tugged her to look in the mirror. *Because there's something there you don't want us to know.*

"WE HAVE A SUITE at the Copley Plaza Hotel," Ginny Reilly was saying. "My sister had her honeymoon there, it's gorgeous. So when I have my wedding night there, Sean will carry me across the threshold—"

"You should carry *him* across the threshold," Jordan observed, keeping one ear on the kitchen where Anneliese was clattering dishes. "Sean's a string bean."

"Shut up, it's my fantasy." Stifled laughter from the girls sitting around the parlor floor with a stack of magazines. "He opens the champagne while I change into a negligee. Bias-cut ivory satin—"

More suppressed laughter, up until Ginny finished with a whispered, "When the light goes out he just *rips* my negligee off . . ." They all exploded, Jordan laughing too.

She lifted the Leica and snapped her friends, mentally titling it *June 1946: A Study in Feminine Frustration*. Graduation had come and gone just after Jordan's eighteenth birthday, and now that school was done, she found herself sitting around with a good many friends who wanted to plan their fantasy weddings—and wedding nights. They were all good girls with lace-curtain-and-Sunday-lunch parents, so nobody here had Done It, but they *talked* about Doing It. What else was there to fantasize about now that school was done? Ginny worked at Filene's, and Susan was going to Boston College in the fall but had already said she'd only stay till she got engaged. And Jordan, who had yearned for high school to be done, now found herself wondering what the point was. Her father still wouldn't budge about the question of college, when she brought it up last week. "Let me talk to him later," Anneliese had whispered afterward, with a smile of friendly complicity that gave Jordan a guilty twinge.

"Your turn, Jor," Ginny laughed. "How does your first time go?"

Jordan gave up fretting for the moment. "All right, here it goes." This was all very silly, but it was their time to be silly, wasn't it? "We're at war with the Soviets, and I'm filming the bombing of Moscow. I meet a glamorous Frenchman working for Reuters, and after the bombing he drags me off to an abandoned tank—"

"You want to Do It in a *tank*?"

"There are bullets flying. It's very romantic. Then my photo of the bombing makes the cover of *TIME*—"

"If I had Garrett, I wouldn't be daydreaming about Frenchmen," Susan said. "Is he going to give you his college ring?"

"He won't have one until he starts this fall," Jordan evaded. But Garrett probably *would* offer it to her, and if she took it, everyone would expect her to wear it around her neck on a chain, because that was the next step. The trouble with steps was that the more you took in a certain direction, the more people assumed that you would continue on, which Jordan wasn't sure she wanted to do. She was barely eighteen; how was she supposed to know if Garrett Byrne was the One and Only? Jordan wasn't even sure she believed in the entire *idea* of the One and Only.

Anneliese glided in with a tray. "Would you girls like some cake?"

"Please, Mrs. McBride!" Jordan's friends chimed, and then when she had retreated: "Your stepmother is the best."

"So elegant—never a *hair* out of place. My mother always looks so frazzled."

"She's wonderful," Jordan said. *If I could be certain she wasn't a Nazi, she'd be absolutely perfect.*

"Just because she has an Iron Cross," Jordan argued to herself, down in the darkroom after her friends had left, "doesn't mean *she's* a Nazi." Trying to be fair, unbiased, like the level-headed J. Bryde who could always find truth in the middle of sensationalism. "Maybe Anneliese's husband was a Nazi, and the medal was his. She said he was in the war, but she's avoided saying if he followed Hitler or not. That's the kind of thing you would keep to yourself, if you moved to America."

Perfectly reasonable. Entirely possible.

"Even if he was a Nazi, it doesn't mean *she* was. She could have carried his old medal because it was a reminder of him, not because she's a fascist."

Also entirely possible.

"Moreover," Jordan went on, pacing the length of the darkroom, "maybe she's not even keeping this background of hers a secret. Just because she didn't tell me doesn't mean she hasn't told Dad. He might already know. A little secret between husband and wife."

So ask him, Jordan thought. But something gut-deep held her back. Anneliese made Jordan's father happy; she had seen that very clearly over the past weeks of watching and waiting. The cheery way he whistled when he shaved in the morning, the bounce in his step when he came home from work. And though Jordan had no urge to imagine what happened behind her father's bedroom door, *that* side of things was clearly going very well too. Last week Jordan had knocked on their bedroom door in the afternoon and come in to see Anneliese straightening the bedclothes as her husband fastened his cuffs—Jordan had seen the private smile that passed between them. Maybe she was just an eighteen-year-old high school graduate who had never gone further than taking off her blouse in her boyfriend's car, but it was perfectly clear that elegant Anneliese with her impeccable housekeeping and starched handkerchiefs had a less impeccable, less starched side, one that

Jordan's father was very happy with after so many years of sleeping alone. And *everyone* had multiple sides, really, so should she really worry like this about the various sides of Anneliese?

Jordan frowned, fighting the dread that she really was just making up wild stories again—that same part of her that had to fantasize about war-zone men and whistling bullets rather than honeymoon suites and bias-cut ivory satin.

"There you are." Anneliese looked up from her sewing machine as Jordan came into the upstairs sunroom, now a sewing room. "What do you think?" Shaking out a half-stitched lilac cotton dress for Ruth.

"More ruffles. Ruth always wants more ruffles." Anneliese had made Jordan's graduation dress in this room: green silk molded tight to the waist, a wide neckline, elbow sleeves; the most stunning dress in the graduating class. Jordan's father had mopped his eyes, and Anneliese had given her an armload of cream roses to carry. Jordan felt that squirm of guilt again and flopped down at the sewing table with a sigh.

"Restless?" Anneliese smiled. "It's a hard time in a girl's life, out of school but not moved to the next stage yet."

"Are you going to tell me to stop moping around and get engaged?" Because Jordan's father was thinking it, she could tell.

"No, because the last thing a girl your age needs is to be—what's the word? *Bossed*." Anneliese pronounced it with precision; her quest to conquer American slang was unceasing. "My mother lectured me day and night when I was your age, and it just made me stubborn and resentful."

"You're so nice to me," Jordan couldn't help saying. *Strategy, or because you really* are *as good as you seem?*

Anneliese bit off a thread, eyes sparkling. "I have *no* wish to be a wicked stepmother."

I keep watching you, Jordan thought desperately, *and you don't give me anything to see. Nothing but reasons to like you.*

Until the afternoon months later, on Selkie Lake.

Chapter 11

IAN

April 1950
Vienna

That bitch," Tony fumed, kicking the legs of their bench on the railway station. "That goddamn Nazi bitch. I *know* she knew something."

"Agreed," Ian said, scanning his newspaper. "I'd be willing to wager she knew quite a lot."

The morning expedition to 8 Fischerndorf had not gone well. No combination of plausible half-lies, Tony's charm, or money had pried anything useful from Vera Eichmann née Liebl. She didn't know any woman with dark hair and a scar on the neck. No such woman had stayed with her after the war. If the neighbors said so, she couldn't be responsible for what they thought. They were only too eager to make up evil things about a widow struggling to make ends meet. Yes, she considered herself a widow. She had not laid eyes on her husband in five years. She wished to be left alone. The door had then banged in their faces.

Ian hadn't expected it to go much better, so he remained sanguine, reading while his partner raged. At last Tony stopped pacing and dropped onto the bench. "What I'd have given to drag that woman into her own cellar and beat the truth out of her."

"You wouldn't do that, and you know it."

"Wouldn't I?" Tony raised an eyebrow. "I don't have a lot of chivalric feeling for a woman like that. It's not like trying to understand the compromises little people like the Ziegler sisters might have made to get through the war—Adolf Eichmann's wife was at the top level. She had to know *something* about how her husband was shipping Jews east by the million. Believe me, I could bounce her off a wall or two and still sleep well at night if it got us the information we needed."

"What if it didn't? Would you start to break bones? Threaten her children? Where does it stop?" Ian folded his newspaper, feeling the spring breeze ruffle his hair. "That's why we don't operate that way."

They'd had this same conversation the first week they worked together, on the trail of a Gauleiter responsible for a number of atrocities in occupied France. After one particularly unproductive interview, Tony had murmured, "Let me drag him into the back alley, I'll get him talking."

Ian had with great calm taken his new partner by the collar, applied a half twist that cut off the breath, and lifted him up onto his toes so they stood eye to eye. "Do I have your attention?" he said quietly and waited for Tony's nod. "Good. Because we do not beat up witnesses. Not now. Not ever. And if you can't wrap your mind around that, get out now. Am I in any way unclear?" He let Tony go, and the younger man shrugged, eyes wary. "Your call, boss."

Now, Tony looked at Ian with curiosity in those dark eyes. "I'm not saying we'd ever go at a man's nails with pliers. There are degrees. When all it would take is a good shaking and a few slaps—"

"Anyone who would spill that easily can be loosened up without violence."

"It doesn't always work that way, and you know it. Don't tell me you've never been tempted to make a witness cough up."

"Of course I've been tempted," Ian said flatly. "I've been tempted to degrees you would not believe. But it isn't just about catching war criminals. *How* we catch them—that matters."

"Does it?"

Ian rested his elbows on his knees, looking down the train tracks. "I worked with an American team not long after the war ended," he said at last. "Investigating cases where German civilians were suspected of murdering downed airmen. The Americans used to detain the local Burgermeister until he coughed up a list of witnesses, then stand the witnesses up against a wall and threaten to shoot them unless they talked. They always talked, we'd get our man, and no witness was ever shot. But I hated it." Ian looked at his colleague. "There are more war criminals out there than we will ever be able to find. If I have to let go of the ones that won't get found unless we turn into torturers, I'm at ease with that decision."

"Will you be at ease with it if you have to let go of *die Jägerin*?" Tony asked. "What if the woman who killed your brother and nearly killed your wife lies on the other side of beating the shit out of a witness?"

Ian thought in stark honesty, *I don't know.*

He breathed away the instinctive flare of defensive anger, saw an approaching plume of smoke, and rose. "Train's here." It was a long, silent ride back to Vienna.

"**YOU ARE EVICTED**," Frau Hummel greeted them at the door, crimson with rage. "You and that barbarian *Hure*—"

She continued to shout, but Ian pushed past and threw open the door to the center. "Bloody *hell* . . ."

In one day, the office had gone from an orderly oasis to an utter disaster. Files were scattered everywhere in heaps, paper drifted like snow across the desk, and empty cups sat on every surface. The air smelled like scalded tea, and the jam pot was attracting flies. The author of all this anarchy sat in Ian's chair, bare feet swinging, blond head bent over a file she was leafing with jam-sticky fingers.

"No more biscuits," Nina greeted them without looking up. "Or tea."

Ian gave his desecrated office another long stare. Tony surveyed the chaos too, eyes dancing. "Nina," Ian said eventually, waiting until she looked up. "Why are we being evicted, and *why are you wearing one of my shirts?*"

"Mine is hanging to dry." She pushed Ian's cuff up her arm, fanning the file in her hand. "This case, the Schleicher *mudak*—my reading isn't so good, but it looks like the wife is lying. Why didn't you threaten to cut her nose off?"

"Is Frau Hummel really evicting us?"

"She threatened." Nina tossed the file down, picked up another. "I tell her I cut *her* nose off."

"Wonderful." Ian suppressed the urge to throttle his wife where she sat. "Nina, you were only supposed to take care of the post, answer the telephone—"

"Is boring." Nina picked up her tea, looked around for a spoon, and stirred it with the end of Ian's fountain pen instead. "I review your old chases, see how you work. Useful, for when we go after *die Jägerin.*"

"Useful?" He folded his arms across his chest. "You unleashed chaos in my office, you little savage."

"Is my office too. Until target's bombed flat, what's mine is yours, and what's yours is mine." She gulped some tea, then rose and stretched, the hem of Ian's shirt falling nearly to her knees. "What do you find in Altaussee? Where do we go next?"

"Salzburg." Ian glared. "Give me my shirt back."

"*Nu, ladno.*" She shrugged, began unbuttoning.

"Bloody hell," he growled again and yanked open the door to the tiny washroom. It smelled of peroxide; evidently she'd used the sink to touch up her hair. An improvised laundry line had been hung with a rinsed-out blouse and a set of silky blue knickers. "Your blouse is dry," Ian said, ignoring the underwear.

"You're easy to shock, *luchik.* Is very funny." She patted his arm, amused, and closed the washroom door. Ian turned to find Tony chortling.

"She collectivized the office," he said. "Definitely a Russki."

Ian bit back a snort. The urge to throttle his wife was now warring with the urge to laugh. "Well, help me clear up my Soviet bride's mess."

"She was putting files away as she read. It's not that bad."

"Without order lies madness." Ian believed that in his bones. With order came peace and law; without it lay war and blood. He'd seen enough of both to know it was true.

He locked that thought away as Tony sat back on his heels and asked, "When do we head for Salzburg, and are we taking your Soviet bride?"

"I don't know." Ian paused. "What does *luchik* mean?"

Tony grinned. "'Little ray of sunshine.'"

"Does it bother you that she's a Soviet?" Ian knew how suspicious the Yanks were of the Reds these days. Five short years from the end of the war, and benevolent ally Uncle Joe had become *everyone's* enemy, but the Americans seemed more paranoid about the Communist Menace than anyone.

"She hasn't gone around quoting *Das Kapital*. She hasn't done anything except desecrate your tea and lie about her origins, and there are plenty of reasons for people to do the latter." Tony slid a cabinet drawer shut. "We listen to lies day in and day out, not just from war criminals. Refugees and good guys lie too. About whether they're Jewish or gentile, about their war record or their imprisonment record, about their health and their age and how they got their papers. Good reasons or bad, everybody lies."

"Maybe." Ian rose. "It's time I talked to Nina. Will you smooth Frau Hummel over, make sure we aren't being evicted?"

"Some glamour in this job," Tony groused amiably, slouching out. "Become a Nazi hunter for the thrills, and it's all paperwork and sweet-talking the landlady . . ."

Nina padded out of the washroom, tossing Ian's shirt at his desk and sending more papers to the floor in a shower. Ian ignored that, fixing his wife with a level stare.

"You aren't Polish. Let's dispense with that lie first. You're Russian."

Nina looked up at him, wariness falling across her face. Then she shrugged. "Yes."

Ian blinked, so braced for a denial that her acknowledgment caught him off guard. "You aren't denying it?"

"Why?"

"You told me you were Polish. In the Red Cross hospital—"

"No." Her eyes were as opaque and bottomless as two blue lakes. "You assumed. I let you."

He tried to remember. Nineteen forty-five, the steely hospital scent of antiseptic over blood. Nina still half starved and woozy from pneumonia, Ian desperate for answers about his brother. The language barrier, the chaos all around. *No*, Ian thought, *she* hadn't *said she was Polish.* A girl found near Poznań, with the name Nina, which was so common in Poland . . . everyone assumed. "Why did you let everyone think you were Polish?"

"Easier." She flopped into his chair, propping her disreputable boots on the desk. "I wasn't going home. I say I'm Soviet, is where they'd send me."

"Where is home, exactly?"

"Go east through Siberia until you fall off the world edge into a lake as big as the sky. All taiga and water witches and ice eating railway stations whole; everything needs you dead and everybody wants to leave." Amusement gleamed in her eyes. "Would you go back?"

"If my family were there." He'd cross Siberia barefoot if his brother were at the end of it.

"My family isn't." If there was pain in her eyes, it flickered by too fast for Ian to catch. "I spend my whole life going as far west as I can from that lake. Poland? Is just the next stop."

"Dangerous. You were nearly dead when the Red Cross found you."

"I'm hard to kill."

Ian pulled up a chair, gazing at Nina across the desk. She gazed back, unblinking. "Where were you trying to go after Poland?"

"As far west as I can without falling off *that* edge of the world.

You help me get to England, I look around and think *not bad*. It's ugly, there's rationing, but the ice in winter doesn't eat you alive."

"How does a Soviet girl end up in Poland in the first place?"

"Assigned to the front. Surprised? Soviets, they use women in their wars, not just for factory jobs or behind desks."

Ian knew something about that. One of his fellow war correspondents, a motherly-looking American woman with nerves of gunmetal, had written a pointed article for her paper about how Soviet women were employed as tank drivers and machine gunners, whereas the great and enlightened United States of America just told their women to plant Victory gardens, and be thrifty with their bacon grease. Ian looked at his wife from the Siberian wastes and wasn't terribly surprised to discover she had been assigned to the front. *No wonder we won the war.*

"So," he said at last, "you defected."

"Not so official as that, *luchik*." She grinned. "You think I go to an embassy, ask for asylum? I see chance in chaos, I take it."

"Not very patriotic," he couldn't help observing. "Walking away from your countrymen in the middle of a war."

Her smile disappeared. "My countrymen, they want to stand me against a wall and shoot me."

"Why?"

"Is Stalin's world, Stalin's rule. Who needs a why?"

"I do."

"Not your business."

"Yes, it is." He linked his hands behind his head, not backing down from their stare. "You're my wife. I gave you my name, you got your citizenship through me. You and your past and anything else I helped you bring to my country are very much my business."

Her lips remained sealed.

"Did my brother know?" Ian asked, changing tack. "When he promised he'd get you safe to England if you both lived, did he know you were a Soviet?"

"Yes." No hesitation there.

"Why would he make such a promise? Was it an affair? Love

in a time of war?" Ian held his breath, waiting. It wasn't the first time he'd heard of desperate women escaping war zones by finding a dead soldier's belongings and making up a tragic wartime romance when his grieving family came around. Only Ian knew that for his little brother, that was unlikely. He waited for Nina to step into the lie . . . hoping, he realized, that she wouldn't. So far she'd only misdirected him. Now, he realized just how badly he wanted his wife *not* to be a liar.

"Lovers, Seb and me?" Nina laughed outright, shaking her head. "No. He liked the boys."

Ian let out his breath. "Yes, he did." Seb had told him that the night their father died, so drunk he could hardly stand. It hadn't shocked Ian particularly. You didn't spend years in an English public school without knowing exactly what two males could do together if they had the inclination. *You don't look surprised*, Seb had slurred, not only drunk but in tears by then.

I'm not, Ian had answered. Chagrined, maybe—he knew full well how this would complicate and endanger his little brother's life—but not surprised. *I've never seen you even* look *at a girl, Seb.*

I don't know anything about girls. A hazy wave indicating the all-male household where they'd grown up, the all-boys' schools. *Maybe I'll grow out of it?*

Maybe you will. If you don't, well, you'll have to keep your head down and be careful, but it's more common than you think.

It is?

Ian had poured them both another measure of whiskey and delivered a blunt, mildly drunken lecture on all the various combinations of the sexes he had seen tearing at belt buckles in Spanish hospital supply closets or going at it under Hyde Park bushes during blackouts—any prudishness Ian had carried out of school had died as soon as he went to war. Seb had passed out from whiskey and relief not five minutes later.

I was the first one he told, Ian thought now, painfully. And Nina, if she spoke truly, was the last. "He really told you?"

Nod.

"Tell me how you two met, what happened." Ian's voice sounded rough to his own ears; he cleared his throat. "I didn't get much detail when we spoke of it five years ago. Difficult to get a lot of nuance from a conversation that's half pantomime."

"I'm in Poland, getting clear of Soviet lines." No hint how or why she'd done that, and from her barbed smile, Ian thought it was a sticking point she wouldn't give way on. For now he let it go. "I head into Polish forest, aim west. Avoid towns, people. Not far from Poznań, I run into Sebastian. He's just made a break out of POW camp." She shook her head. "City boy, stumbling around the trees. I take him on."

"Out of the goodness of your heart?" Ian didn't exactly see Nina swooning with pity for an English stranger.

"Two get by better than one. I know how to survive. He knows German, Polish—Russian too, is how we talk."

"How did he know Russian?"

"Some Soviets at his camp. Prisoners have long hours to fill; they talk." Nina's smile lost its edge, the affection unmistakable. "Trying to teach me English, Seb talks about birds. I only know how to kill birds, and he's asking if the lake where I grow up has puffins." She linked her thumbs together and flapped her fingers each in sequence. "Puffins! Is even a real bird?"

Ian nodded, throat suddenly thick at the memory of Seb at nine, fingers linked in exactly that gesture as he described a robin in mid-air. All children flapped their hands to mimic flight, but not quite like that. *You know he liked boys rather than girls, and you know his gestures,* Ian thought. *Yes, you must have known my brother. What's more, he must have trusted you.*

"Puffins." Nina sighed, and both affection and sadness were clear in that sigh. "Thought he was joking me. *Tvoyu mat,* that boy was a joker."

"Why didn't you tell me any of this before?" Ian asked. "It's been five years, Nina."

"When do I have chance? We marry, you put me on a train to England and say you'll be there in six months to start divorce. I think,

'I tell you then.' But you stay in Europe, I stay in England, we talk by telegram. When am I supposed to start this talk, over last five years?"

"Fair point," Ian admitted. "We should start up divorce proceedings, now that we're finally at the same table to discuss them."

She nodded, matter-of-fact. "Has been long enough. You want your ring back?"

"Keep it." His father's signet, gold and ornate like something an earl would wear. His father always liked to imply there were lords in the family line, but there weren't, just defunct English gentlemen who bankrupted themselves to mix with the right people and marry the right girls from other defunct English families. The ring somehow suited Nina's sun-browned workmanlike hand, and Ian smothered a moment's dark humor thinking how apoplectic his father would have been to see it on the finger of a Communist blonde from the wastes of Siberia.

"Tell me one more thing. Just one." Ian put his musing aside, looking at the puzzle that was his temporary wife. She stared back, blue eyes giving away nothing. "What happened with you and Seb and *die Jägerin*? How did you come across her? What—"

"*Nyet*," Nina said sharply.

"What?"

"No. Not for you. Is mine. And Seb's."

"Until the target is down, what's mine is yours and what's yours is mine." Ian shot her own words back at her. "I have a right to know what happened at Lake Rusalka."

"No. I lived it; I don't have to tell it all. Seb fights her, he cuts her, he saves me, she kills him. It happens fast. He dies a hero. That's enough."

"It is not enough." Ian heard his voice sinking toward a whisper. "This isn't just a man's right to hear how his brother died. You are helping us hunt down the woman who killed him. *Anything* you know about her could be essential."

"And I tell you already—what she looks like, how she moves, how she speaks English, all of it. I tell you anything about *her*. Not the rest. That's mine," Nina repeated.

"If you jeopardize this hunt by holding back something important—"

"I'm not. What you want from me is knowing her if I see her, yes? To bring me out when you have her in your sight, so I can say if we have the right one?" Ian gave a reluctant nod. "That I can do. I saw her. I know her face anywhere. I remember her till I die."

Ian looked at Nina, feeling anger flare. She stared back with a gaze like flint.

Seb saved you? he thought. *His life was worth twice yours. How dare you live and not him?* But he stamped that terrible thought down as hard as he could. It was not Nina's fault Sebastian had died; it was *die Jägerin*'s fault. Only hers.

"You find something in Altaussee," Nina said, dispensing with the duel of eyes. "What?"

Ian could have been as cagey with her as she'd been with him, but he suppressed the urge to be spiteful. "*Die Jägerin*'s mother lives in Salzburg, and we know where."

"We go to Salzburg, then. I go this time," Nina added. "I want the huntress dead."

"We don't do that." Ian thought of the train station conversation with Tony—that there were lines not to be crossed. *How close to those lines is this chase going to lead you?* the thought whispered. *Because you're already skirting a very high cliff.*

"If not dead, caught." Nina shrugged. "I come to Salzburg with you."

"All right. We'll settle on an approach, and you'll do things our way."

"Why?"

"Because we've been doing this for years, and that's how it goes. And if what's yours is mine, just as what's mine is now apparently yours, you get my rules as well as my tea."

Nina's eyes suddenly twinkled. She looked impish and young all of a sudden, cheeks creasing in an infectious smile. "'My rules, my tea.' Marina said something like that once."

"Who?"

Chapter 12

NINA

October 1941
Moscow

Marina Mikhailovna Raskova, Hero of the Soviet Union and most famous aviatrix of the Motherland, had dark hair and rosy cheeks and a gleaming white smile. Her blue eyes were like lakes, and Nina fell into them like she was drowning.

"So—" Raskova looked Nina up and down, visibly amused. "You're the girl who's been making Comrade Colonel Moriakin's life hell the past few days?"

Nina nodded, suddenly speechless. They stood in a borrowed office in Moscow's aviation headquarters, an ugly box of a room with the usual desk heaped with folders and the usual portrait of Comrade Stalin on the wall. Raskova had sauntered in with a tossed comment over her shoulder to someone unseen—"You don't mind if I take ten minutes, Seryosha?"—her voice as warm and crystalline as it had sounded over the radio. Nina followed that voice into the office every bit as blindly as she had followed it to Moscow in the first place, and now stood twisting her sealskin hat between her hands, desperately trying to summon the speech she had practiced all those long, monotonous hours on the train from Siberia to Moscow.

"You come from Irkutsk?" Raskova prompted when it became clear Nina wasn't going to speak first.

"Yes. No," Nina blushed. "Baikal. Then Irkutsk."

Raised eyebrows. "You've come a long way to see me."

More than four thousand kilometers. From train windows Nina had seen vast gold sunsets over stretches of taiga, followed by endless kilometers of towering dark trees where it was all too easy to imagine Baba Yaga's witch house moving along on stalky chicken legs. Country stations where women in flowered shawls herded goats off the tracks were followed by city stations where railway officials rushed about in brass-buttoned coats. Farmland and pastureland, factories and tenement blocks, horse carts and cars, all whisking past Nina's wide eyes.

"Your first time in Moscow?"

"Yes." Her first glimpse of the city had been so terrifying—the vast spread of boxlike buildings, the peaks of distant spires and domes from old imperialist palaces and cathedrals, the spread of Three Stations Square where trains fed their passengers into the city—that her overwhelming urge had been to leap back onto the railcar. *You do not belong here*, the panicky thought pounded, looking at the overwhelming crush of uniformed soldiers, kerchiefed women, and slab-booted men. It wasn't just the size and scale of it all, it was the pulsation of fear at being so much closer to the advancing enemy. Houses were draped with camouflage; flak guns crowned rooftops like long-legged cranes; streets were lined with barricades of welded railway girders. There was nothing like it in Irkutsk. *You don't belong here, go back east—*

But she wasn't going east again, not ever. *You don't belong* here, *Nina Borisovna*, she had told herself, pushing through the crowd. *You belong up* there, *in the sky. And if going through here is the only way there, then through here is where you'll go.* So she tunneled her vision, shut out Moscow, and stamped out into the sour-breathed cold-hunched press of humanity to find the aviation headquarters. "I didn't pay much attention to Moscow," she managed to tell Raskova. "I won't be here long enough to make it worthwhile."

"You won't?"

"I'll either join your new regiment, or go home." Though Nina had barely a ruble left in her pocket, so how she was going to manage fare back to Irkutsk if she was rejected, she had no idea.

Raskova laughed, the sound warm and easy. "Why didn't you apply through your Komsomol or your air club?"

"They would have said no. They were picking university girls, educated girls." Nina heard her voice coming stronger, but her hands still had a death grip around the sealskin hat. "So I came direct to you."

Raskova leaned against the edge of the desk, peeling off her gloves. She looked like she'd come right in from the airfield, still wearing boots and overalls. Her hands were fine and white, but she had oil smudges across her knuckles just like any pilot. "Colonel Moriakin says you camped in the chair outside his office for four days until he agreed to see you."

"It was the fastest way to get an appointment." Nina was surprised when Raskova burst out laughing. "He said I was crazy, but that I should talk to you, Comrade Raskova."

"You're not the first girl to come to me directly rather than through official channels." Raskova folded her arms. "How many flying hours do you have?"

Nina embellished her record by a few hundred hours, presenting her certificates and detailing her training. Raskova listened with warm attention, but her next words hit Nina in the gut.

"Good numbers. But do you know how many girls have applied with numbers just as good or better?"

Nina's hopes went into a tailspin, but she persisted. "I'm a born pilot. Made for the air."

"So are all the girls I've picked. So are many of the ones I've turned away."

Raskova was gearing up a gentle refusal; Nina could feel it. She stepped forward, pushing down the dread. "This is about more than a flying record." Fighting to find the right words. "The girls in your regiments won't be training students or flying mail routes. They'll be bombing fascists, making nighttime runs, dogfighting with Messerschmitts. Your girls need—" What was the word, the right word? "They need to be tougher than old boots," Nina finished.

"And you're tougher than old boots?"

"Yes. You are too, Comrade Raskova." Nina lifted her chin. "Three years ago, making the cross-country flight for the long-distance record, when your team couldn't find the final runway due to visibility, you parachuted out. You were separated from your pilot and copilot and spent ten days alone in the taiga. No emergency kit. No food."

"I made do." Raskova said it easily, well accustomed to gushing girls and their hero worship—but in a moment's sudden reminiscence, she wrinkled her nose. "I still remember the cold. Like sleeping cheek to cheek with Father Frost."

"I grew up in that taiga." Nina took another step. "You survived ten days there. I survived nineteen *years*. Cold, ice, a landscape that wants you dead—none of it scares me. Flying at night doesn't scare me either, or bombs exploding, or fascists trying to shoot me down. Nothing scares me. I am tougher than any university girl with a perfect record and a thousand hours of flying time."

"Are you?" Raskova studied her. "Think twice about what you're asking for, Nina Borisovna. Going to the front—it's a very hard thing. Many think it a waste, giving planes to girls when there are already more than enough men to fly them. I have told Comrade Stalin himself that my women will be better, and so they must be."

"I am better." Nina could feel her heart beating hard in her chest, like a propeller whipping up to speed. "Let me prove it."

Another long moment. Nina hung suspended in agony. *There'll be a chance*, her father had said. *Don't ask, when you see it. Just fucking take it.* But Marina Raskova was the end of her chance— beyond this room, there was nothing to seize. It either all ended here, or all began here—and drowning in Marina Raskova's blue eyes, Nina began to feel desolation choking her throat.

The most famous aviatrix in the Motherland rummaged through her colleague's desk, found a pen and some official-looking paper, began to scribble. "This is a pass to the Zhukovsky Air Force Academy. You'll have to follow the rules once you get there," she warned with a twinkle, "but at least there's tea to go with the rules."

Nina felt her wings lift. "What else is at the academy?"

"Aviation Group 122." Raskova pressed the pass into Nina's outstretched hand with one of her knee-buckling smiles. "Your sisters-in-arms."

NINA STOOD A MOMENT gaping at the academy's palatial redbrick facade and imposing gates before braving the steps. Inside she found a rushing mass of trainee pilots dashing everywhere: women in flying caps and overalls, girls with curled hair and heels as though they were going dancing, female officers with cigarettes and taut faces shouting orders. Nina showed her pass and identification to the nearest officer and received a grunt. "We leave for training in a few days. You'll be issued a uniform—"

"Where do I sleep?" Nina asked, but the officer had already turned away. Nina wandered for a while, having no idea where to go, still dazed with her triumph. She had done it; she was here. A bone-cracking yawn overtook her as she meandered down a vacant corridor; after sleeping four nights in a chair, she was desperate for a nap. Throwing her coat down beside an unlit heating stove, Nina curled up on it and dropped into sleep like falling into a black pit. It seemed only seconds later when a girl's laughing voice said, "You look lost, sleepyhead!"

Nina pried open her eyelids. She'd been having some hazy dream of dogfighting through piled clouds as Marina Raskova's voice whispered encouragement in her ear, and she said the first thing that came into her mind. "Are you my sister?"

"What?" The voice sounded even more amused.

Nina rubbed her eyes. The figure bent over her was a blur against the harsh corridor lights. "She said my sisters-in-arms were here."

"Comrade Raskova said the same to me." A hand grasped Nina's elbow. "Welcome, *sestra*."

It was the same word for "sister" that Nina had grown up

speaking, but the Moscow tang in the girl's voice made it different, a new kind of sister. *That's good*, Nina reflected, *since I didn't like any of my blood sisters.* She let herself be helped up, and the shadow resolved itself into a girl a year or two younger than Nina but half a head taller, porcelain skinned and smiling, ink-dark hair in a plait past her waist. "Yelena Vassilovna Vetsina," she said. "From Ukraine, but I came to Moscow at twelve. Glider school when I was sixteen, then air club. I was studying at the Moscow Aviation Institute when the call went up for the regiments." She rattled off a very impressive number of flying hours.

A pedigreed candidate, Nina thought. Educated, polished, impeccable record, probably a model Komsomol member. The kind whose application would have been stamped and moved to the top of the pile. A little warily, Nina nodded back. "Nina Borisovna Markova, from Baikal. Flight instructor at the Irkutsk air club."

A dimple appeared in Yelena's chin. "How many flying hours did you tell Raskova you had?"

"Three hundred more than I actually do."

"I improved mine by two hundred. I felt so guilty, but then I met the other girls here and realized we *all* embellished our records. A regiment of liars, that's what Raskova's getting. Good thing we can all fly like eagles." The dimple blossomed into an outright grin. "Did you faint, meeting Raskova? I swear I nearly swooned. She's been my hero since I was seventeen."

Nina couldn't help smiling back. "Mine too."

"Where are you classed for training, pilot, navigator, mechanic, or armorer?"

"Navigator." Nina had hoped for a pilot classification, but Raskova had explained that there were enough pilots already. Nina was disappointed, but she wasn't going to quibble. It was enough just to be *here*.

"Pilot for me. I can't wait to get my hands on the new Pe-2s." Yelena looked at Nina's old coat. "Have you got your uniform yet?"

"No—"

"I'll show you where. It's horrible, the same standard issue they give the men. The bigger girls are all right, but little ones like you are swimming. And we're all clumping around in the boots, even my new roommate who has feet like pontoons."

Nina's uniform came in a bulky packet, and she began to swear the minute she unfolded it. "Even men's *underwear*?" Unfolding a pair of vast blue briefs.

"Even men's underwear." Yelena laughed. "Wait till you've worn it for a few hours—"

"Or walked a runway in it in zero degrees," grumped another woman's voice. "You would not believe the chafing." Several more trainee pilots had gathered, looking interested. To a chorus of "Go on, get suited up!" Nina went into an empty storeroom and shuffled out shortly afterward. Even more girls had clustered in her absence, and they all went into a unison gale of laughter at the sight of Nina's massive trousers puddling over huge clumping boots.

For a moment Nina bristled. Normally when she heard female laughter it was unkind or it was uncomprehending: girls like Tania mocking her flyaway hair or provincial accent. But this laughter was merry, and looking around, Nina saw that a good many of the girls looked every bit as ridiculous in their own enormous uniforms.

"We can cuff and stitch the hems, but you are out of luck on the boots." Yelena shook her head. "Have you got some cloth to stuff into the toes?" Nina's scarf went into the right boot, as Yelena unwound her own.

"I can't take yours."

"Nonsense! What's mine is yours and what's yours is mine, Ninochka."

Another reflexive bristle—Nina never heard fond nicknames except from men trying to get her into bed. But Yelena had finished stuffing Nina's boots and was making introductions, and everyone seemed to be on a first name basis. "Lidia Litvyak, we call her Lilia . . . Serafima here is from Siberia like you—"

"Not as far off as the Old Man, though!" came the friendly reply. Cautiously, Nina smiled back. Yelena kept rattling off names, and Nina knew she would hardly remember any of them, but there was a similar *look* to these women Raskova had recruited, no matter how different they seemed on the surface. Some looked barely eighteen and some approached thirty; some were little like Nina, others tall and strapping; some had city accents and some had provincial burrs . . . But they all looked like they were used to the feel of engine grease under their nails, Nina thought as they crowded around her bright-eyed and friendly, welcoming her to the ranks.

Questions were pelting now, as they asked Nina how she had come to flying. "I saw my first plane, and I fell in love with it." Heads nodded.

"My father was furious when I went to pilot school in Kherson," one girl said. "The women in our family all work in the steel factory—"

"I told my mother I'd fly someday," another said. "She asked me 'Where, from the kitchen stove to the floor?'"

Something in Nina's chest expanded. *Sestra*, she thought, giving the plain word the twist that had made it something unique when she heard it in Yelena's voice. Nina had not felt this burgeoning warmth since the day she walked singing with Vladimir and the other pilots to enlist—the warm feeling of *belonging*. Only these women would not leave her behind.

Nina's fellow pilots hauled her off to find a meal then, talking away, and they were still talking three days later on the train platform, on their way out of Moscow. To some unknown airdrome for training, where the first female pilots of the Red Air Force would learn to be lethal.

Chapter 13

JORDAN

October 1946
Selkie Lake

The end of October meant autumn leaves and duck-hunting season, and Anneliese seemed enthusiastic when Jordan's father proposed a day at the cabin. Now Jordan watched her stepmother look at the red and gold trees reflecting in the surface of Selkie Lake, exclaiming, "Beautiful!"

"Our first time here as a family." Dan McBride fished out the big square key that locked the cabin. "I thought you'd like it."

"Don't count on me to bag anything," Anneliese warned. "I can't hit a target to save my life."

"Now, I don't believe that—"

"Would I lie?" She made a rueful face. "Kurt tried over and over to teach me, but I'm hopeless. You'll get far more ducks without me."

"Ducks?" Ruth's brows furrowed as she climbed out of the car after Taro. "*Dead* ducks?"

"You don't need to see them, Ruthie," Jordan reassured. "They can take the guns out to the far side of the lake, and you'll stay with me. The only thing we'll shoot is pictures."

Ruth looked relieved. Still too quiet for a little girl, Jordan thought, but after a summer's worth of diner sundaes and trips to the movies, at least she was talking and smiling at the dinner table.

"How lovely!" Anneliese was enthusing as her husband unlocked the hunting cabin his father had built on the shore. She went inside, looking at the stock of firewood, the narrow cots and blankets, the kerosene lamps. "Everything necessary if one needed to hide."

"Who needs to hide?" Jordan asked, following her inside.

A shrug. "It's the way someone who has been a refugee continues to think, even when danger is over. Wanting a place with a door that locks and something to protect oneself with." Nodding at the rack of hunting rifles on the wall. "I suppose those will need cleaning after a season on the wall. That's what Manfred always used to say."

"You mean Kurt?" Jordan said.

Pause. "Yes. My father was Manfred; he first took me out on the occasional hunt, before I ever met Kurt."

You call your father by his first name? Jordan wondered. *Or did you just make a slip?*

She wanted to follow her dad and Anneliese, but there was no way to do it with Ruth in tow. They went off with their guns broken over their arms, and Jordan took her sister out to the dock where they sat with their feet swinging above the water, watching Taro bark at the ducks. "You know you're going to be my real sister, cricket? Dad is going to adopt you. You'll have our name." Jordan had helped her father lay out the paperwork that would make it official: Ruth's birth certificate, and the various visas and other bits of paper that had allowed her into the country. "You'll be Ruth McBride." Ruth's broad smile was somehow breathless. *How can I love you so much*, Jordan wondered, *when I'm watching your mother like she's a criminal?*

In a few hours Jordan's father and Anneliese were back, cheeks red from cold. "I've been thoroughly outclassed," Anneliese said, laughing as Jordan and Ruth came down the dock. "I warned you all I was a terrible shot." How natural she looked here in the woods, Jordan thought. The dry leaves didn't even seem to crunch under her feet. "Did you have a nice time, *Mäuschen*?" Anneliese said to Ruth, stretching out a hand.

She had duck blood in a smear across her palm, not quite dry. Very clearly, Jordan saw Ruth's blind recoil.

"Mama," she said, but turned away from Anneliese, back toward Jordan.

"Ruth—" But Ruth was shivering, not listening to her mother. She just clung to Jordan, who stroked the smooth blond hair.

"The blood must have scared her." Jordan's dad swung the game bag over one arm. "I'll get this stowed away so she doesn't see any dead ducks, poor little missy." He went to the car, and Jordan looked up from Ruth's shaking shoulders to Anneliese. She didn't have the Leica to record it this time, but she heard the *click* very clearly in her mind as she snapped an image of her stepmother's expression. Not a mother's concern as she looked at her crying child, but eyes full of hard, cool consideration. Like a fisherman deciding whether an inferior catch should just be tossed back in the lake.

Then her usual warm smile came back, and she bent down to tug Ruth gently but firmly into her arms. "Poor *Mäuschen*. *Mutti ist hier*—" She went on murmuring in German, and gradually Ruth calmed, arms stealing about her mother again.

"What is she remembering?" Jordan asked quietly. "The refugee woman who tried to rob you in Altaussee?"

It was a shot in the dark, but Anneliese nodded. "Very upsetting," she said, clearly done with the subject. "Take Ruth to the car? We should be on our way."

Jordan acquiesced, settling Ruth in the backseat. "Here's your book, cricket. We'll just be a minute." Jordan's father was in the cabin stowing the rifles, as Anneliese scraped mud off her boots. Her face was placid, and Jordan saw in her mind's eye that other expression. Cool, considering, hard.

She had *not* imagined it.

"What happened at Altaussee?" Jordan spoke low and bluntly at her stepmother's side, persisting when Anneliese made a little retiring gesture. "I'm sorry to ask about something unpleasant, but I don't ever want to accidentally upset Ruth as happened today."

It was the first time she'd pushed so forthrightly, but watching and waiting hadn't worked. Jordan raised her eyebrows, making it clear she expected an answer.

"A woman attacked Ruth and me," Anneliese said at last. "We were sitting by the lake, passing time until our train that afternoon. A refugee woman struck up a conversation, and then she made a grab for our papers and train tickets. Ruth was knocked over, her nose bled everywhere. She hit her head very hard."

"Ruth said there was a knife." Ruth hadn't said any such thing, but Jordan wanted to know if Anneliese would agree with her. *If she does, I'll know she's lying.*

But Anneliese just shrugged. "I don't remember, it all happened so fast. The woman saw the blood from Ruth's nose and ran away. I suppose she was desperate. So many people were."

"You don't sound very concerned," Jordan probed.

"It was quite some time ago. I told Ruth to forget about it. Someday she will. Much better for her." Anneliese shaded her eyes, looking across the lake. "So beautiful here. Why is it called *Selkie Lake?*"

Not your best deflection, Jordan thought. *For once I surprised you. Or Ruth did.* She filed that away for later. "The name came from Scottish settlers. A selkie is some kind of Scottish water nymph. Like a mermaid, or—"

"A *rusalka?*"

Jordan tilted her head. Her stepmother, she noticed, had almost seemed to flinch. *I've never seen you flinch before, not once.* Of all the things to rattle Anneliese, why this? "What's a *rusalka?*"

"A lake spirit. A night witch that comes out of the water looking for blood." Anneliese waved a dismissive hand, but the gesture looked jerky. "A horrid old fairy tale, I can't imagine why I thought of it. Don't tell Ruth, or she'll never sleep again."

" . . . I won't."

"You're such a good sister to my *Mäuschen*, Jordan." Anneliese touched her cheek, this gesture coming easier. "Let's go home."

She smiled, went past Jordan toward the car. Jordan looked after her, no more uncertainty in her gut. She didn't know what all this meant—a struggle by an alpine lake, violins and water spirits and Iron Crosses. But Jordan had a sudden urge to shove her father into the car and drive like hell, rather than let Anneliese in with them.

Who are you? she thought for the thousandth time. In her mind's eye she saw Ruth recoiling at her mother's blood-smeared hand, and an answer whispered, full of conviction.

Someone dangerous.

GARRETT LOOKED UNEASY. "I don't know about this . . ."

"Just keep her distracted." Jordan glanced past his shoulder toward the kitchen where Anneliese was humming like a tuneful bee. She'd been cooking up a storm in preparation for Thanksgiving in a week's time—*my first Thanksgiving as a proper American!* as she said gaily. The house smelled of sage and sugar, and early snow fell past the curtains outside to complete the vision of holiday perfection. Jordan felt no warm holiday spirit; her stomach was churning.

Garrett raked a hand through his brown hair. "If you really need to ransack your stepmother's room—"

"I do." Because Jordan had spent the last weeks since Selkie Lake going out of her mind with conflicting theories, and enough was enough. She'd looked through Anneliese's things before, when she was on honeymoon, but had found nothing. This time she was going to find what she needed, no matter what it took. By keeping the Iron Cross, Anneliese had shown she wasn't above keeping mementos of her past. There had to be something to find.

Once Jordan would have had no trouble walking into her father's room and going through it with a dusting rag in hand as excuse, but Anneliese had put a stop to that. Jordan wasn't exactly forbidden in the room, it was just that Anneliese in her deft way had instituted lines that were not to be crossed. "I'd never dream of going into your room uninvited," she assured Jordan. "Every woman needs her privacy. Just as new-married couples need theirs!" That little hint of marital intimacy had made Jordan uncomfortable enough to drop the subject. Very convenient.

Something was in that bedroom. There was certainly nothing in the *rest* of the house; Jordan had spent the last few weeks covertly combing through all the other rooms under pretext of holiday cleaning: running her hands under mirrors, inside picture frames, behind bureau drawers. Nothing.

Garrett was still arguing. "At least wait till she's left the house—"

"I tried a few days ago, when she went shopping. I had to dive out again when she doubled back to get her gloves." Also convenient, Jordan thought. Maybe Anneliese was keeping an eye on her, every bit as much as she'd been keeping an eye on Anneliese. "Keep her distracted. I can't do this if I think she's going to sneak up behind me on those little cat feet."

"You're actually scared, aren't you?" Garrett sounded dubious. That stung, seeing he didn't trust her instinct, but if she was being honest, Jordan couldn't blame him. When she laid all her suspicions out, they sounded preposterous. *Jordan and her wild stories.*

"What if you *do* find something?" Garrett asked, but Jordan pretended she hadn't heard, just headed into the bedroom.

Put it all back exactly *as you found it*, she warned herself, lifting up the folded nylon slips in the first drawer with fingers like tweezers. Nothing in Anneliese's drawers, nothing in her lined-up shoes . . . Garrett's voice floated from the kitchen; he was telling Anneliese something about pilot training, how college classes were boring compared to flying. Anneliese responded, spoon clinking against the side of a mixing bowl, but Jordan's blood urged her to hurry.

Anneliese's dresses, her skirts and blouses on their hangers, her hatboxes. Jordan pinched hems for lumps, lifted each hat and sifted the tissue paper before putting it back at exactly the same angle, felt along the wardrobe's back. Anneliese's traveling cases; nothing in any of the pockets. The case knocked against the back of the wardrobe, making a soft thud, and Jordan was out of the bedroom and down the hall in a blink, listening with thudding heart for the sound of her stepmother's footsteps. *You really are scared.* She remembered Anneliese by Selkie Lake, face cool and considering.

Anneliese's voice down the corridor: "That's Linzer torte, Garrett. If you like it so much, I'll teach Jordan to make it. Ruth, cut him a nice big slice." She sounded so calm and motherly.

Yes, Jordan thought, *I'm scared.*

The wardrobe yielded nothing. She felt her way around the bed-side tables, the bases of the lamps, aware that time was ticking. There was only so long Garrett could eat cake and make small talk. Nothing in the lamps, the drawers of the bedside tables, between the pages of Anneliese's Bible.

The *cover* of the Bible, though . . .

Jordan nearly dropped it, fingers suddenly shaky. A quick crane of her neck toward the door; still the hum of voices from the kitchen. As delicately as she could, she peeled up the soft leather of the cover, where her fingers felt a straight edge of something slipped between decorative leather and the stiffer stock beneath. The leather peeled easily; it was used to being lifted.

A photograph, small and worn. Jordan brought it nearly to her nose. Definitely Anneliese, some years younger and considerably more carefree, trim figured and tousle haired in a bathing suit. Ankle deep in lapping water, the ripples of a pond or a lake stretching behind her, a man at her side. Considerably older than she, broad shouldered and smiling, also in a bathing suit, one arm raised as if to wave to someone in the distance. Anneliese's handwriting on the back, but all she had written was *März, 1942.*

A *vacation picture*, Jordan thought flatly. All this trouble and suspicion to find a picture of Anneliese and what was probably her first husband, on a lakeside vacation. *Well done, J. Bryde. You'll be getting a Pulitzer for this for sure.*

She began to slide the photograph back into its hiding place, disappointment bitter on her tongue, and paused. Took another good hard stare. The date. *März, 1942.*

März. March.

And something else, besides the date. Some sort of mark under the man's upraised arm . . . A memory scratched at the edge of Jordan's mind, and she peered closer. Definitely a mark. A tattoo? Hard to be certain.

Jordan laid the photograph on the bed where the light was strongest and took several careful shots with the Leica. A photograph of a photograph; the detail wouldn't be as good as she wanted, but she couldn't take the original. If Anneliese had hidden it in her bedside Bible, then she reached for it often, even if only to feel the picture's edge through the leather. So Jordan slid the photo back into place, pressed the leather back down, replaced the Bible, and ran a hasty search over the rest of the room. No sign of the Iron Cross; either it was gone or hidden elsewhere, but Jordan didn't dare stay longer. She slipped out of the bedroom, easing the door shut, and dashed into the bathroom, turning the lock and sinking back against the bathtub.

"Jordan?" Anneliese's voice down the hall.

"Just a moment!" Hastily she turned the taps on, dashing cold water on her cheeks, which she could see in the mirror were flaming. Not with shame, with triumph.

The voice came nearer. "I was going to ask Garrett to stay for supper."

"Of course," Jordan called back, patting the water off her face. In the mirror she let herself have one smile, hearing her stepmother's heels click away. A date, a mark on a man's arm, and a medal. Three things, but all caught on camera—and cameras didn't lie.

Chapter 14

IAN

April 1950
Salzburg

G retchen Vogt. Respectable, widowed, lived all her life in Salzburg." Tony summed up his discreet survey of the mail, the city records, and the neighbors at the Lindenplatz. "One daughter recorded, Lorelei Vogt, of the right age to be our girl."

"Any photographs?" Ian asked as the three of them cut through the formal gardens at Schloss Mirabell, a pretty little palace like a marble wedding cake surrounded by fountains.

"None I could find on public record."

"Lorelei Vogt." Ian tasted the name, wondering if it really was the woman they sought. *Die Jägerin.* She might have lied to the Ziegler girl who carried her letter here; there was no guarantee Gretchen Vogt really was her mother, but . . . "Even if it does turn out to be her birth name, it won't be much use—she'll have changed it to flee. Still, I'd like to have a name for her other than *the huntress.*" Take her down from a mythic villain to just another common *sieg-heiling Fräulein.*

"Names, they're powerful," Nina agreed. "Is why Comrade Stalin doesn't like being called *the Red Tsar.*" She stopped to pluck a red begonia from the nearest flower bed, sticking it through her lapel. *My wife, the Red Menace*, Ian thought with a grin.

"Let me tackle Gretchen Vogt alone," Tony proposed as they passed out of the gardens. The Vogt house lay across the toffee-colored Salzach River, near the Mozartplatz. "If you and I go in together against *die Jägerin*'s mother and get the stone wall, that's it. Let me try the carrot first—if I fail, you come in heavy with the stick."

"Agreed. You take first crack. The old inheritance trick?"

"How much money can we spare?"

Ian pulled a packet from inside his coat. Tony counted notes, eyebrows rising. It was the whole of Ian's monthly annuity, including the center's rent. Ian nodded. "Use it." He got the racing chill across his nerves he remembered from poker games with fellow war correspondents during Blitz attacks, throwing every shilling on the next hand because the bombs were getting closer and the odds were good the roof was coming down. Throw it all on the line, because this was it.

Don't be reckless, he warned himself. "If we both fail, and neither carrot nor stick works on Frau Vogt?"

"I cut her thumbs off," Nina said cheerfully, flicking her straight razor. "Then she talks. Carrot, then stick, then razor. Is simple."

"You had better be joking, because that is not how this works," Ian said. "That is not how *any* of this works." But Tony was tossing some gibe at Nina in Russian, and she answered with a rude gesture, so Ian lengthened his stride toward their quarry, amused and irritated at the same time. "Let's go."

The Lindenplatz was a small square around a statue of some obscure Austrian saint with a sour face, the expected line of lime trees green veiled with new leaves. An old, gracious neighborhood made for the prosperous and the well educated. Families here would attend church in immaculate Sunday hats, summer on the Salzkammergut, and have nothing to do with jazz music. Number twelve was a graceful white house: spacious walled garden, well-tended window boxes spilling pink geraniums. Tony stood on that scrubbed front step, hat in hand as he awaited an answer to his knock. Nina and Ian watched discreetly from the square's center, blocked from number twelve's view by the stone-carved saint. "Don't stare, Nina," Ian murmured. "Put your arm through mine, and look like a tourist." He had an old Baedeker guidebook in hand, saved for occasions when he had to loiter without looking suspicious. *Austria, Together with Budapest, Prague, Karlsbad, and Marienbad.*

"Saint . . ." Nina squinted at the statue's plaque.

"Liutberga." From the corner of his eye, Ian saw the door at number twelve opening.

"*Tvoyu mat*, what kind of name is that?"

"A very holy anchoress, circa 870. What does that mean, '*tvoyu mat*'?"

"'Fuck your mother.'"

"Bloody hell, the mouth on you—"

"I can't see, what's Antochka doing?"

"Someone's answered the door. Housewife, white apron. He's going into his speech now . . . What does *that* mean, 'Antochka'?"

"From Anton. In Russian, *Anton* would be nicknamed *Antochka*, not Tony. I don't see how you get *Tony* from *Anton*."

"I don't see how you get Antochka from Anton either," Ian couldn't help saying, eyes locked on his partner. "He's been invited in . . ."

"What now?" Nina whispered.

Ian looked at number twelve's innocuous door. "We wait."

"How long?"

"However long it takes."

"We stand here for hours? You, me, and Liutberga?"

"Chasing war criminals is a great deal of waiting and paperwork. No one will ever make a thrilling film out of it." Ian turned her away from the statue. "We'll meander awhile, admire the trees . . ."

"What is *meander*? I don't know this *meander*."

"Wander, dawdle. Play tourist. If he's very long inside, we'll—"

Nina tugged her hand from Ian's arm and strolled across the

square, around the side of number twelve. The stone wall enclosing the back garden came up to the side of the house; the ground-floor window was shut, and Nina stood studying it as though she had a perfect right to be there. Ian reached her in a few long strides, taking her arm and pointing at the window box as though they'd come to admire the geraniums. "Get away from here before someone sees you," he muttered through gritted teeth.

"No windows this side"—jerking her chin at the next house—"and no one in square to see but Liutberga. She won't tattle on us, dismal stone bitch."

"Get away from there—" Ian cut himself off, hearing the sound of a door opening on the other side of the high garden wall.

"—discuss your business outside, young man?" A woman's voice, middle-aged, accented with the lazy Austrian vowels. It had to be Frau Vogt. "It's such a lovely day."

Tony: "I would be delighted, *gnädige Frau*."

Ian hesitated, wanting to listen here under the wall, but someone might pass by and notice. He turned, ready to haul Nina back into the square, and that was when he saw that the window was open, and his wife's disreputable boots were disappearing with eel-like silence into the house.

He made a grab, but all he got was a fistful of lace curtain. *Get out of there*, he mouthed soundlessly, keeping his attention on the flow of niceties Tony was issuing on the other side of the wall. Inside the dark hallway Nina was only a shadow—all Ian could see was the gleam of her teeth as she crooked a finger, beckoning. Then she padded noiselessly down Frau Vogt's hall carpet and disappeared round a corner. Her smile seemed to hang disembodied in the air like that of Lewis Carroll's Cheshire Cat.

I'm going to kill my wife, Ian thought. *I'm going to kill her before I even get round to divorcing her.* He tucked the Baedeker away, wondering if *Austria, Together with Budapest, Prague, Karlsbad, and Marienbad* listed "house-breaking" on its page of recommended local activities. Then he took one final look for watchers, saw none, and shinned up through the window.

Nina was in the parlor, flicking through Frau Vogt's mail. "This is illegal entry," Ian snapped in a whisper.

"Antochka confirmed she lives alone. He has her busy out there. Let's see what we find."

This is not what we do, Ian wanted to say. *This is not what I do.* He should have been hauling Nina back out the window they'd unlawfully entered, yet that same reckless thrill was running along his nerves the way it had earlier. The urge to throw it all on the line. *Don't be reckless*, he'd already warned himself today, but the two of them were already here, inside the house . . . "Five minutes," he warned Nina, cursing himself. "Disturb nothing. I'll keep watch on the garden. Bloody hell, you're a bad influence—"

"No pictures of her. Not grown, anyway." Nina indicated the mantel, where a stiff wedding portrait had pride of place—Frau Vogt and her husband in the fashions of a generation past. Several smaller photographs of a little girl, all round cheeks and curly dark hair. Ian searched the childhood face of his brother's murderess, if it *was* she, but from the corner of his eye he saw movement at the back door. ". . . some coffee?" Frau Vogt said as the hinges creaked. Ian pulled Nina back behind the door, both of them freezing until the footfalls had retreated the other way, with more clattering of china. "And a slice of Linzer torte. I don't know a young man yet to say no to a slice of cake!"

Clearly Tony was softening the widow up nicely. Ian let out a long breath, realizing he was bathed in sweat, realizing that he was also grinning. Nina grinned back, then ghosted past him out of the parlor toward the stairs. He followed, taking the stairs two at a time.

Care had been taken downstairs to keep up the appearance of gracious living, but upstairs Ian saw chipped paint, dust, faded squares on the walls where pictures had hung. If Frau Vogt was living in straitened circumstances, that boded well for Tony's proposed bribe. Ian moved past Nina, who was examining the hall photographs, and went to the window overlooking the back garden. He could see a wedge of wicker table, a tray, Tony's dark head nodding,

Frau Vogt in three-quarter view: an apple-cheeked doll of a woman in her starched apron. Ian held his breath and eased the casement open a crack.

"... this business matter on my daughter's behalf, Herr Krauss. How well did you know her?"

Krauss? Nina mouthed. Ian mouthed back, *His favorite alias.* *Krauss* sounded so solidly German, turning Tony from an Eastern European undesirable to a good clean-cut Aryan boy—a role embraced with savage irony by Ian's Jewish partner.

"I confess I didn't know your daughter well, *gnädige Frau,*" Tony confessed with earnest deprecation. "We met only a few times. Do you know where she's settled now?"

"No." A hint of sharpness from Frau Vogt. "She thought it best not to come back to Salzburg; it would bring gossip. There was such talk when the Americans came through making arrests and accusations." Pause. Ian held his breath.

Frau Vogt went on. "I received a letter from her after the war, hand delivered. She wrote that it would be better for me if she stayed away."

Ian wanted to shout, dance, punch the air in triumph. The Ziegler girl had been paid to deliver that letter by one Lorelei Vogt. *We have a name. We have a name—*

Tony: "Did your daughter tell you where she was going?"

"She said she didn't want me to have to lie, if people asked questions. Naturally a mother misses her only child, but it was still most considerate of her. There has never been any *talk* about me, and for that I'm very grateful. I'm just a simple widow, living quietly. The war had nothing to do with me. My daughter made sure it stayed that way."

Disappointing. Ian leaned one elbow up against the window frame, keeping well out of sight, listening to Tony tack a new course.

"You know, your daughter and I talked of books once, at one of her parties in Posen? I think she sensed a young soldier like me was a long way from home, so she tried to put me at ease. She spoke such beautiful English—"

"Yes, she was always clever!" Frau Vogt's stiffness eased. "She studied literature at Heidelberg, her father insisted on an education for her . . ."

"Why isn't he pushing?" Nina whispered. "Where's the bribe?"

"She was getting defensive. He's smoothing her down, letting her ramble."

"This is carrot method? It takes too long." Nina padded down the hall, disappearing into the first bedroom where Ian heard the sound of drawers sliding. Below, Tony was talking of university between bites of Frau Vogt's cake.

". . . my dream to continue my studies, but the war . . . It was right from the HJ to the army for me, and then Poland." Tony hit just the right note of tacit awkwardness, his face anxious under the untidy hair he'd razor-parted and oiled back like a proper lad who'd grown up in the Hitler Youth. It wasn't the first time he'd presented himself as a former soldier for the Reich. It took more than a German name and details about a regiment. It was all in the things one *didn't* say, Ian thought. The veiled phrases that said *You know it wasn't my fault, don't you?* "You understand, of course," Tony said, all schoolboy earnestness. "The war didn't have anything to do with me either, not really. I just did my duty, I was very young."

"Those were difficult times," Frau Vogt said with the same tacit note in her voice. "People forget that now. Another piece of cake?"

"If you'll join me in an aperitif. Just a dash of brandy for your coffee—" Tony produced the flask he always carried to lubricate such interviews.

"Oh, I shouldn't . . ."

"Of course you should, Frau Vogt!" Tony scolded, and *die Jägerin*'s mother let him add a generous splash to her cup. He began admiring her china as she cut him a second slab, and he dug in with the kind of schoolboy enthusiasm that had made mothers all across Europe pinch his cheek fondly. Ian sensed Nina's soundless snort at his shoulder.

"He lies better than a Muscovite fishmonger," she whispered. "Help me look in her room now—"

"I may have broken into this house, but I will not ransack a stranger's bedroom."

"Just stand by while I do it," Nina said, amused. "You're a hypocrite, *luchik*."

Ian slanted an eyebrow. "I will cling nevertheless to my shreds of the moral high ground."

"Shreds are on the ground at your feet."

"Noted."

Frau Vogt was chattering freely below. Ian was willing to bet she hadn't had such an appreciative audience in a long time. Loneliness was as effective a tongue loosener as brandy. "My daughter studied English literature, though I hoped she'd prefer Schiller and Heine as I did. It was Heine where I got her name, of course! Lorelei the water nymph. The maiden on the rock."

"Your Lorelei was far from just a maiden on a rock to be rescued. What a wonderful shot she was—I remember a hunt at one party—"

"Yes, she was her father's daughter. *His* father was a Freiherr in Bavaria, you know—my husband was the younger son, he didn't inherit the family Wasserburg, but he used to hunt there as a young man. He taught Lorelei to shoot."

"I thought she was Diana herself. I admit I was quite starry-eyed!"

Frau Vogt sighed. "She should have brought a nice young man like you home from Heidelberg. I was not always approving of the choices she made." Another tacit silence, broken by a sniff. "Her Obergruppenführer was very dashing, but he was old enough to be her father, and not to mention, well . . ."

Married. Ian shared Frau Vogt's wish that he hadn't been, just as devoutly, because if *die Jägerin* had been Obergruppenführer von Altenbach's wife rather than his mistress, she would have been much easier to trace. Paperwork flew like confetti at SS weddings; her name and photograph would have been filed in a hundred places.

Tony allowed a tactful silence to fall, not saying a word about the daughter who had become a married man's mistress. He tipped a little more brandy into both coffee cups, murmuring instead,

"Obergruppenführer von Altenbach was much admired. His work in Poland was exemplary, and his generosity unmatched. In fact, that's what brings me here today, Frau Vogt." Straightening his tie; the young man of business at last coming to the matter in hand. "Before his death, the Obergruppenführer laid certain provisions in place, looking to the future. Financial provisions for friends and loved ones. And no one, of course, was more important to him than your daughter."

Ian's fingers tightened on the curtain's lace edge. Here it was . . .

"The Obergruppenführer set money aside for your daughter, *gnädige Frau*. So you see why I'm looking for her."

Silence below. Ian craned his gaze as far as he could, but all he could see was Frau Vogt's neat head, the sudden stillness of her shoulders. "Money," she said at last, and the prickles were back in her voice. "After five years?"

"You know how slowly legalities move." Tony sighed. "No one was even certain if Lorelei Vogt was alive, especially after the Obergruppenführer's . . . unfortunate end, in Altaussee. So many people disappearing, so many opportunists. There was a real danger of fraud, with no way to identify your daughter even if she could be found. Which is why it took so long to find someone who knew her." He gave a modest bow. "Naturally I am being compensated, but truly, it would make me most happy to know I could aid your daughter in claiming what is rightfully hers. She was once kind to a lonely young soldier when he was very far from home—if I can aid her to a life of comfort as the Obergruppenführer wished, it would be my pleasure."

It wasn't the first time Ian and Tony had used an inheritance as a lure. In the straitened aftermath of a war, everyone dreamed of unexpected money descending on their lives. The whisper of wealth from dead Nazis was especially potent because everyone had heard of the fortunes squirreled away by the powerful and the prescient high in the Reich. *Never mind that I never found a single war criminal living in luxury behind gold-gated estates*, Ian thought wryly. Everyone had still heard stories of secret Swiss accounts, priceless paintings down mine shafts, gold held in reserve for . . . someone.

Why not your daughter? Tony's confiding tone implied. *Why not you?*

Damn, but you're good at this, Ian thought with a flash of pride in his partner.

"I wouldn't expect you to take my word," Tony went on, slipping a card across the table. "The firm who hired me would be pleased to reassure you."

"A quick telephone call . . ." Her voice was a blend of caution and appeasement. She wanted to trust this nice young man and everything he was telling her . . . But she wasn't a stupid woman.

Tony smiled, sitting back. "I'm happy to wait."

Frau Vogt rose, bustling inside. Ian prepared to dive behind the nearest door if she came up, but the telephone was downstairs; he heard the muffled sound of her voice as she picked up. Outside, Ian saw Tony add another slug from his flask to his hostess's coffee, pour his own out in the flower bed, and replace it with undoctored coffee from the pot. Frau Vogt's voice fluttered, sounding reassured. Ian smothered a laugh, imagining Fritz Bauer's avuncular rasp on the other end—it wasn't the first time he'd backed them up if a story needed verification.

The receiver clicked below, and she came back out to the garden. "Thank you, Herr Krauss. I don't mean to imply you were trying to . . ."

"A lady's trust must be earned," Tony said with another boyish laugh. "I hope Herr Bauer was able to reassure you? There is also, of course, the matter of your compensation."

She'd been reaching for her coffee cup; her hand paused. "Mine?"

"Of course. The funds in trust can't be released to anyone but your daughter, but your time in helping us locate her would be valuable." An envelope slid across the table, containing almost every shilling to Ian's name. "Even the tiniest detail—one never knows what might be helpful. Is there anything you remember about where your daughter might have gone?"

Silence. Ian stood barely breathing, looking down at Frau Vogt's braced shoulders. He realized Nina was standing beside him, not breathing either. Frau Vogt took a long swallow of brandied coffee, fingertips sitting beside the envelope, and without meaning to, Ian's fingers linked through Nina's and squeezed fiercely.

"I don't know where Lorelei is," the woman below said slowly. "But she has started to write letters."

Nina squeezed back.

"Where do the letters come from?" Tony was all earnestness.

"And where are they now?" Nina muttered. "I find no letters here—"

"They're all posted from America, over the last year or so." Ian heard the distaste running through Frau Vogt's voice. "Lorelei wanted to get far away from Germany, from Austria. The postmarks are all different, I don't know the cities." Tony patted her hand as she swallowed the last of her spiked coffee. "Lorelei's last letter came just a month or so ago, from a place called *Ames*—she said she could bring me over. Not to Ames, to an antiques shop in Boston, wherever that is. *McCall Antiques.* Or maybe *McBain Antiques. Mc-something.* People like her and me can get papers there, identification, new names, and then they move on. But how do I move on? I've lived in Salzburg all my life; how am I supposed to go to *America*? All those Jews and Negroes—"

America. That kicked Ian in the stomach, a sickening blow. To feel he was getting close and find out there was still an ocean in the way . . . His hand clenched at his side, and he realized Nina had tugged free, fingers drumming against her leg.

"Boston!" Tony marveled, pouring more coffee, more brandy. "Where did your daughter go after Boston?"

"She said it would be better for me not to know."

"Do you know what name Lorelei uses?"

"She said it would be better for me not to know that either."

Grimly, Ian admired *die Jägerin*'s caution, even as he hated her for it. If all war criminals were so careful, the center would have collapsed in months.

"Even without knowing details, it must be a comfort to hear from her." Tony slid the envelope of money forward. "A great comfort."

"Not so much as you would think." Frau Vogt's voice was starting to blur around the edges. She clearly wasn't used to brandy in the afternoon. "She never says much except that she's safe, that she's well, and that I should burn the letter when I'm done. A mother—a mother would like to know more. My only child, I miss my *daughter*—"

Ian felt a stab of pity for her, but let it die. *I miss my brother too, but I don't have the comfort of knowing he's safe and well.* He wondered if Frau Vogt had any idea at all what her daughter had done.

"Did you burn all the letters?" Tony asked softly.

"Lorelei told me to. The letters, her old things, all the photographs of her as a grown woman."

"And did you?"

A pause. "My daughter is very sweet, Herr Krauss. But she can be very forceful. I don't . . . like to cross her." Another pause. "Yes, I burned everything."

"Liar."

Nina paused, looking at Ian. He hadn't realized he'd muttered it aloud.

"She's lying." He leaned down to whisper into Nina's ear, brushing her hair out of the way. "No parent would destroy *every* photograph of their only child."

"Mine would," Nina whispered back. "But he tried to drown me when I was sixteen, so . . ."

Ian barely heard her, pacing down the hall now despite himself. A photograph would be invaluable—they wouldn't be able to use it in any legal capacity, not if it was acquired through means like today's, but just for private identification so they weren't relying solely on Nina's memory of what their target looked like . . . "There has to be a photograph here somewhere."

"Isn't. I scoured." Nina was pacing too; they brushed past each other shoulder to shoulder and when he saw her look up, he did too.

On the hallway ceiling was a hatch. Very likely to an attic.

"Come on, *luchik*," Nina breathed. "Boost me—" But he had

already seized his wife around the waist and lifted her toward the ceiling. He heard her fumbling a latch, heard the hatch lift, and then Nina was wriggling up through his arms like a serpent, hoisting herself into the ceiling. *You cannot claim even a shred of moral high ground here*, Ian thought, and at the moment didn't greatly care. He was not leaving this house empty-handed.

A quick check at the window. Frau Vogt had tucked the envelope of money away. "I don't have anything else to tell you—"

"Two minutes," Ian called low-voiced into the hatch. Tony was rising from his chair, dripping reassurances. "Hear me, Nina?"

Her voice floated down along with the sound of rustling. "*Da, tovarische.*"

Frau Vogt appeared to be crying, overcome by brandy and memory. Tony was offering handkerchiefs . . .

Nina's booted legs appeared suddenly from the hatch. "Catch me."

Ian caught her sturdy little form as she wriggled down from the ceiling, held her up as she bolted the hatch behind her. His grip slipped and he nearly dropped her. "Clumsy," she snorted, landing cat light.

"You're not exactly a featherweight, comrade." He could see something under Nina's jacket, but there was no time to inquire what. Ian eased the window shut and they descended the stairs, freezing out of sight on the landing as Frau Vogt ushered Tony toward the front door.

"Kind of you to hear an old woman ramble, Herr Krauss," the voice floated out, definitely tipsy. "I do get very lonely." Ian and Nina crossed the back hall toward the window. Ian's heart hadn't pounded so hard since he'd parachuted out of that bomber in '45. Standing over the void, waiting to jump . . .

The front door shut. Tony was out of the house; Frau Vogt might be walking back. Nina was wriggling through the open window. Ian hoisted himself after her, feeling his shoes touch grass. The back of his shirt hooked on the casement.

"*Tvoyu mat*, hurry up," Nina hissed.

"Stop your goddamned swearing," Ian said, and ripped loose. Nina eased the casement down. Ian yanked her around the side of the house, where they banged into Tony.

"What the hell, you two? Never mind, let's get out—" They all set off at a clip considerably quicker than a meander.

"Nina," Ian said when they reached the river again and collapsed gratefully against its railing, "tell me you found something."

Nina's eyes had a wicked gleam. "The Frau may have burned the letters and most pictures, but she kept one album."

"Did you get—"

"Is not a recent picture, she throws those away. This is most recent one I see." From inside her jacket Nina produced a photograph clearly pried off an album page: Frau Vogt and a cluster of friends or relatives before church steps, dressed in their best. "Far right."

Ian's breath caught. The young woman on the right wore a floral print dress, standing with gloved hands folded. Hardly more than a girl, childhood plumpness clinging to her face and figure, a self-conscious smile. Serious, young, on the verge of beauty and adulthood. But already watchful, her gaze meeting the camera steady and distant. *"Die Jägerin?"*

Nina made a small sound like a cat pouncing. There was something disturbingly sensual about it, Ian thought, like the cat wasn't just relishing the pounce, but the rending and tearing that would follow. "Lorelei Vogt," Nina said.

"At least fifteen years younger than she is now." Tony frowned.

"Was thinner when I saw her than here," Nina agreed, tapping the picture. "Darker hair too."

"So how much help will this photograph be, identifying the real thing if we run across her? This girl could grow up to look like anyone."

"I know her," Nina stated. "I know that face till I die, however old it gets. Is the eyes."

Ian stared at Lorelei Vogt's eyes. Just eyes. It was pointless trying to find evil in a face. So often, evil sat invisible behind perfectly ordinary features. But still . . .

"Hunter eyes." Nina summed it up, giving the sweet serious face of their target a tap. "Calm and cold."

Chapter 15

NINA

October 1941
Moscow

The cold slapped Nina like an open hand. It was well below zero, the air so frozen in the dark night that it felt like winter lake water, but the women of Aviation Group 122 were bright-eyed with excitement as they made their way down the tracks. There might be panic all through Moscow that the Germans would be spilling into the city at any moment—but Nina and her sisters were on their way at last.

"Where are they sending us to train?" Yelena wondered, tripping over her oversize boots.

"Who knows?" Nina gave a hop, trying to see over the girls ahead. The railcars stood open; the first ranks were climbing in.

"It had better be warmer than it is in Moscow." Yelena's dark lashes glittered with ice; her eyes were watering and the tears had frosted to her eyelashes. "How can it be this cold in October?"

"This isn't cold," Nina lied, trying not to shiver. No Siberian was ever going to admit to a Muscovite that she was cold.

"Liar." Yelena's eyes laughed. "Your lips are blue."

"Well, it's still nothing compared to winter on the Old Man. The cold there comes rolling out over the lake and there's nothing to stop her, the icy bitch." Yelena wrinkled her nose. "What?"

"You'll think I'm a terrible prude."

"What?"

"I can't hear anyone swear." Yelena blushed. "My father wouldn't let anyone curse—he'd flick you on the nose hard enough to make your eyes water. Not just the one who said it, but any of us in earshot. So whenever I hear a bad word, I cringe and wait to get hit on the nose."

Nina laughed, as they pushed their way along to the next railcar. "Fuck your mother, Yelena Vassilovna!" Just to see that nose wrinkle again.

"Laugh away." Yelena sighed. "I'm a little Moscow goody, and I know it."

Nina grabbed the handle beside the railcar's open door, swinging herself up. "Little Moscow goodies don't have as many flying hours as you. Here, jump up!"

Yelena took Nina's outstretched hand. A freight car, not a passenger car, and so cold inside their breath came in white clouds. Nina tugged her sealskin hat farther over her ears as more girls piled in. "I won't swear," she heard herself saying to Yelena, "if you don't like it." It had never occurred to her to care what her fellow pilots thought of her, because she'd always flown alone. But she'd be navigator to one of these girls in the pilot class, responsible for keeping her safe and on course. They had to trust her; she had to trust them. Trust may have been simple for Yelena with her warm, easy ways, but for Nina it felt like flexing a muscle she had never used.

"Swear all you want, Ninochka!" Yelena laughed. "I have to toughen up. If I'm going to kill fascists, I can't wrinkle my nose at bad words."

Nina grinned, feeling that muscle flex a little easier. "So say, *it's fucking cold in here*."

"It's—" Yelena screwed up her face.

"Say it, say it!" Little Lilia Litvyak laughed from Nina's other side, overhearing.

"It really is exceptionally cold in here," Yelena said primly, red as a beet, and they nearly fell over laughing as the railcar shuddered into motion. Then the news passed back like a ripple over a field of grain: "Engels, we're going to *Engels*—"

"—the training airdrome on the Volga—"

"—Engels!"

NINE DAYS TO ENGELS. Nine slow, cold days: braced and swaying with the movement of the cars, gnawing on rations of bread and herring and swallowing bitter sugarless tea, standing on railway sidings stamping their feet to keep warm as the track was cleared for more urgent supply trains to push through. Talking, always talking, and it was Nina's turn to be astonished. *They know so much more than me.* A tall brunette from Leningrad had work calluses from digging tank traps and hauling sandbags, but she had a university degree and spoke four languages. A pink-cheeked girl two years younger than Nina studied children's education—"Very important to give children a system of structured play that will develop their cooperative instincts." Marina Raskova herself spent a morning traveling in their railcar, and when they begged her to talk of her record-setting flight on the *Rodina*, she said that was old news and told them instead how she had wanted to be an opera singer growing up, singing a bit of the chorus from *Eugene Onegin*. Voices joined in throughout the railcar, and Nina stared uncomprehendingly. She couldn't hum a note of Tchaikovsky; spoke no language but her native Russian; had never been herded along in structured play or honed a cooperative instinct in her life.

She'd felt a similar disconnect when she first came to Irkutsk at nineteen, but then she had been so focused on learning to fly that she had adopted Komsomol meetings and the other trappings of civilized life without ever giving them the slightest thought. Now she sat surrounded by hundreds of women for whom such things weren't trappings to be shrugged into as a grown woman, but truths they'd imbibed with their mothers' milk. They talked of Marxist lectures and hikes with the Young Pioneers, of trying to find shoes during the famine years that didn't fall apart after one wearing. They even talked in whispers of the black vans that might take you away if you were denounced. Yelena had a neighbor in Moscow who had been taken: "He'd been allotted a bigger room than his apartment mates, and they wanted it, so they reported him as a wrecker," she said matter-of-factly. "When he was taken, his parents denounced him too so they wouldn't be sent with him." No one asked where. They knew not to ask, just as they knew about shoe shortages and lectures, Tchaikovsky and Party songs. It was more than the difference between the country girls and the city girls, Nina thought, because there were both kinds here. This was the difference between growing up civilized, and growing up wild.

"You don't talk much, Ninochka," Yelena said at some point, stitching away at her uniform. They'd been passing needles and thread back and forth for days, cuffing up hems as they talked. "How did you grow up, out there on Baikal?"

"Not like you," honesty compelled Nina to say.

"How?"

"Living on the Old Man in a collection of huts too small to call a village . . ." Nina shrugged. "It's the end of nowhere. No one sends you away to the wilds, because you already live in the wilds. No one queues for shoes; if it's winter you go into the forest with a snare and you kill something and make shoes from the hide, and if it's summer you make sandals out of birchbark. There's no one to denounce your neighbors to if they have a bigger apartment. No one has an apartment. We barely have neighbors." There was no one to hear if your father regularly informed the world that Comrade Stalin was a swindling Georgian bastard, but Nina knew better than to confess that. "Maybe once in a lifetime someone might get to a Marxist lecture," she went on, "if they can get to the next town a hundred kilometers away, and then they talk about it until they're a hundred. There are old women half convinced the tsar is still alive." She looked at the curious eyes around her and flushed.

"You're not a savage," Yelena said, reading Nina's mind. "Rabbits aren't savage—" and that made them all laugh, because it had been just yesterday afternoon that they had all been waiting on a railway siding, hugging their rumbling bellies because the bread and herring were late, and Lilia Litvyak had gone sidling round the edge of the station and returned with arms full of green globes—raw cabbages from a food cache awaiting transport. Nina and the rest had fallen on those cabbages like chomping rabbits. "Whether from Moscow or Leningrad, Kiev or Baikal," Yelena had intoned, "we are all now rabbits."

It stuck.

At last they piled off at Engels in freezing damp. The town was blacked out, the sky spitting icy rain. Nina shouldered her pack, shambling along with the rest of the girls. Yelena scratched under her cap. "I have nits, I just know it—"

"Quit grousing, *sestra*," came floating down the line. More milling in the dark as Marina Raskova went to find the officer on duty, and by the time they were herded off to bunk down, Nina had fallen asleep on her feet, swaying like a horse dozing in its stall. The gymnasium had been made over into a dormitory, rows of cots laid out hospital ward fashion. Nina flopped onto the nearest one without even pulling off her boots. "What'sat yelling?"

"Raskova," someone said, laughing. "The commander tried to give her a room of her own with a double bed, and she's shouting she's going to bunk down in shared quarters just like us."

"I would die for Raskova." Nina yawned, eyelids sinking. "I would cut off my leg for her. Carve out a kidney."

"All of us would, *malyshka* . . ." Nina's last sensation that night was someone pulling off her boots.

A cold gray morning dawned, and the women of Aviation Group 122 were up with the pale sun, tumbling out of bed, pulling bedclothes tight. "When do we get our hands on the new fighters?" Men stared when the women trooped across the base in their uniforms. Nina returned the stares every bit as rudely, but the more well-bred girls hurried along with blushes rising in their cheeks.

"I'm not used to being gawked at," Yelena whispered. "Not like this."

Nina slowed her own steps to a swagger, staring down a mechanic smirking from the nearest aviation shed. "Get used to it."

The first order of the day was a mass visit to the garrison barbershop. "Those braids and curls are coming off, ladies! Raskova's orders, line up for a chair," an officer called as the women clustered rebelliously, fingering their long plaits and muttering. No one seemed eager to step forward; Lilia was already arguing with a barber. Nina tugged the razor out of her boot and unfolded it. She looked around, challenging, and when she had enough eyes, she gathered her hair up in one hand. It was tangled and dirty after ten days without a bath, and with one sawing swipe Nina sheared it off. She dropped the fistful of hair on the barbershop floor. "Come on, rabbits."

Yelena put her chin up, shaking her long dark braid over one shoulder, holding out a hand for Nina's razor. Nina slapped it into her palm, even as the other girls began filing grimly toward the barbershop chairs, and that was the moment it all ceased to matter—the differences that had made Nina tongue-tied on the train. Hundreds of women from hundreds of different worlds had unloaded at Engels, country girls and city girls, those with degrees and those who knew nothing . . . And now they were simply the recruits of Aviation Group 122, identically shorn, and all their worlds combined into one.

THIS WAR WILL be over before we're declared ready." Outside Engels the fight was passing them by—Nina chafed whenever she thought of the Fritzes rolling unopposed over all those carefully dug tank traps; thought of the barrage balloons hung in the air all over the Motherland and the trainloads of crying children being evacuated out of cities, half the time heading straight into the advancing German lines. Leningrad was slowly starving to death that winter, people murdering each other for ration cards and bread . . . But in Engels, the training was never-ending.

"You girls are lucky," Marina Raskova scolded them. "There

are boys being rushed out to the male regiments with only sixty-five flying hours, no better than machine-gun fodder. I didn't bring you here to be machine-gun fodder."

"But we've got better records walking through the door than those boys being rushed out through it," Nina objected. "Why are *we* the ones still sitting in Engels?"

"We can't afford to fail," replied sober-eyed Yevdokia Bershanskaia. She was older than most of them at nearly thirty, already tipped for command. Not that she wanted to lead; she wanted to fly fighters. *But everyone wants to fly fighters*, Nina thought, *so someone's going to be disappointed*. "We're the only female pilots going to the front. There are plenty saying it's foolish giving planes to little girls when there are more than enough male pilots to fly them. To keep our planes, we'll have to be perfect."

Perfection meant ten separate courses of study per day, plus another two hours of drilling, from classroom to airfield and back. At night they were rousted out of bed by the blare of a Klaxon to form up on the icy parade ground; Nina tried putting her coat over her nightshirt once to save time, but Raskova—always neat and bright-eyed no matter the hour—spotted the hem flapping above her boots and made her do laps about the airfield with the icy wind blowing through her bare legs. She tumbled back into bed, teeth chattering and the skin over her thighs marbled blue, and seemingly seconds later the Klaxon was sounding the dawn, calling the women of Aviation Group 122 to rise and take the old U-2s up for practice bombing runs over the treeless plain where the Engels airfield stretched flat and barren, catching every implacable puff of wind that blew off the Volga.

"Did you hear the men laughing at us this morning?" Yelena came back to the makeshift dormitory, sweat freezing to the shorn ends of her hair so it spiked in all directions. "They think we're a joke in these uniforms, they make fun of our marching—"

"They're just jealous because we're getting new planes and not the old crates." Nina sat stitching up a hole in her glove with thread borrowed from Yelena. They had cots side by side; they shared everything from socks to sewing needles. *What's mine is yours, and what's yours is mine*, as Yelena had said the first day in Moscow, and they all lived by it—on Nina's other side, Lilia was using Nina's razor to slice fraying edges off her coat sleeve. "Did you hear Raskova's trying for Pe-2s?" Nina said.

"I heard the Pe-2s are a bear to get off the ground," Lilia volunteered.

"Better than those Su-2s they have the pilot group in now. Those are a joke." Yelena stripped off her gloves, flexing stiff cold hands. "They smoke, they leak, they're slower than a cow on ice—"

"They're putting the navigators in TB-3s and R-5 trainers in the new year," Nina said. "After we take the oath. Lilia, you put a nick in my razor, I'm kicking you all the way back to Moscow . . ."

"Try it, you little Siberian runt."

"Runt, yourself!"

The military oath was taken in November, and Marina Raskova made one of her easy speeches in that intimate voice like she was talking to you alone in the whole crowd. "In our constitution, it is written that women have equal rights in all fields of activity. Today you took the military oath. So let's vow once more, together, to stand to our last breath in defense of our beloved homeland." They all cheered themselves hoarse, and Raskova pressed every hand that stretched toward hers, kissed every cold-flushed cheek within reach. As hard as they all worked, Raskova pushed harder. Nina came to make a report one afternoon in December and found her commander fast asleep across a table heaped with papers. "I'm awake," she said, when Nina tried to tiptoe out again, though her eyes were still closed. "Make your report."

Nina rattled it off. "Get some rest, Comrade Major," she finished.

"We'll rest when the war's over."

The year turned; flight training started for the navigators. Flying at night, getting used to the pulse of the blackness around them in the open-air cockpit, cruising under an icy sliver of moon and learning to land with no more aid than a few makeshift runway lights. Everyone knew Raskova would be sorting Aviation Group 122 into its three regiments soon: the day bombers, the night bombers, the fighters. Only the best would be in the fighters, and Nina already knew she wasn't going to be among them.

It was a strange thing, not to be the best—she'd been the best for so long, certainly the best female in the air club, but here there were hundreds of women who had all been the best in *their* air clubs. Three members of an aerobatic team had enlisted; they could flip and twirl a plane like birds of prey. Lilia was impervious to air pressure; she'd push her machine to its limit without ever getting dizzy. Yelena could land featherlight on the roughest field in the region. Nina couldn't match any of them, and she knew it. That hadn't been a very pleasant realization at first, if she was being honest—her mouth had been sour with envy, realizing she was outclassed. But it hadn't taken long for envy to fall away under the grinding stones of work and practicality. They were all fighting the damned Hitlerites in the end, if they ever got off this cheerless stretch of airfield by the Volga. When that happened, Nina wanted to fight wingtip to wingtip with fliers even better than she was.

"You're a high-flying eagle," Nina told Yelena, "and I'm a little hawk."

Yelena slid an arm through Nina's, giving the warm squeeze of reassurance that enchanted Nina every time. Maybe because she'd never really had a woman for a friend before. "You're no little hawk, Ninochka."

"I understand *how* the plane works—I pull the stick in a particular way, the plane moves a particular way. You understand *why*. Thrust, ratio, aerodynamics—you fly better for knowing all that." They were crossing the frozen airfield toward the canteen on a freezing January morning. A group of men in mechanics' overalls let out derisive whistles, but Nina ignored them. "For me, none of the science ever sinks in." Nina rapped her own forehead. "Hard Siberian skull."

One of the mechanics was shouting something at Yelena, grabbing his crotch. She still tended to blush when she heard the hoots and crude jokes, but for once she was distracted. "Don't say you're stupid, because you aren't."

"Maybe not, but I'll never understand what I do in the air. I just do it." Nina wriggled her fingers. "Magic."

Yelena laughed, but it *did* feel like magic: Nina had no idea why a propeller worked or what the flying wires did, but as soon as the wheels lifted from the ground, her whole body disappeared into the plane. Her arms became wings, her torso filled the cockpit, her feet disappeared into the wheels. The sensation only strengthened in night flying; her eyes disappeared altogether and she could no longer *see* that she hadn't become part of the plane. Flying through a midnight sky came as naturally to Nina as a *rusalka* swimming through her lake. She didn't have Yelena's grace or Lilia's reflexes, but she had no fear of the dark and moved in the air like it was home. It didn't make her the best, but it made her very good, and for Nina that was enough.

February came to Engels, bearing rumor and heartbreak on an icy wind. One of the navigators learned that her parents had starved to death in Leningrad; a girl in the armorer class had a brother fighting the German advance who swore in his letters that the Fritzes were decorating their tanks with Soviet heads. But even the most ghastly rumor couldn't dent the ferocious anticipation as the women received their assignments. Nina stood breathless as names were read off.

Aviation Group 122 was no more. There were only the 586th, the 587th, and the 588th. New minted Junior Lieutenant Nina Borisovna Markova would fly out with the 588th.

The night bombers.

Chapter 16

JORDAN

Thanksgiving 1946
Boston

J ordan." Anneliese came into the dining room and dropped the
bomb. "Have you been looking through my things?"

Jordan froze, hands full of silverware. She looked across
the expanse of dining room table that Anneliese had decorated for
Thanksgiving with the gold-rimmed china that only came out of the
cupboard a few times a year. Looked at her stepmother, who gazed
back at Jordan with quizzical innocence.

"What's that?" Jordan's father said, distracted. He was on hands
and knees at the sideboard, unearthing the turkey platter.

"I was asking Jordan if she'd been searching my things," Anneliese
said, still with that puzzled air. "Because I think she has been."

"I was cleaning." Jordan hitched her voice into use with a jerk
she hoped wasn't too audible. *How did you know?* "That's all."

"Then why were you looking through my Bible?"

The picture, Jordan thought. She'd thought she'd put it back exactly as she found it, but—

Her father rose, puzzled. "What's this about?"

It wasn't supposed to happen like this. It was Thanksgiving Day—
the house smelled of sage and turkey and fresh-baked rolls, sending

Taro into a tail-wagging shiver of canine delight. Ruth was laying out napkin rings, rosy cheeked at the idea of her *first Thanksgiving*. Within the hour, they should have been sitting down to eat. This was not when Jordan had planned to broach the subject of exactly who and what her stepmother might be. She was going to wait until the holiday was done and both Anneliese and Ruth were out of the house. Then she would lay her case before her dad alone, speaking calmly like an adult, not a child with a wild theory. She would convince him first, and then they could surprise Anneliese together.

But now Anneliese was the one who'd surprised her, and all the cards were up in the air.

"It's nothing, Dad." Jordan smiled, trying to slide past the moment. "Let's check the turkey."

But Anneliese was holding her ground, looking more and more hurt. "My Bible is *private*. Why would you—"

Jordan's father was folding his arms now. "What's going on, missy?"

He wasn't going to budge, she could tell.

So, then.

Jordan looked at her stepmother, frail and pretty in her powder-blue dress, pearls like congealed ash compressing her throat. Met those blue eyes square and didn't blink. Anneliese didn't either, but Jordan thought she saw surprise there—as if her stepmother had expected fluster, not calm.

"If you think this is the time to bring it up," Jordan said, "then by all means, let's talk about this." She laid down the silverware, aware her hands were sweating. "Ruth, will you take the dog into your room and play? Thanks, cricket." She was not getting into this within Ruth's earshot. Jordan waited until she heard the click of the bedroom door and then turned back to her stepmother.

"I don't know if Anneliese Weber is your real name," Jordan said without preamble. "I don't know if you were really born in Austria, or if you came to this country legally or were running from something. What I do know is that you're a liar. You're a Nazi. And you're not Ruth's mother."

The accusation hung in the suddenly electrified silence, crackling. Jordan felt as though she'd pushed all the air out of her lungs along with the words. She looked at Anneliese, standing there so decorative and pretty. She'd imagined her stepmother flinching or recoiling—maybe bursting into laughter or tears.

But not a muscle moved in Anneliese's face. Her blue eyes didn't widen even a fraction of an inch. "Goodness," she said at last. "Where has all this come from?"

Jordan's father was looking thunderous. "Jordan—"

"This isn't a wild story I've made up." She kept her voice calm, reasonable. This was no time to be shrill or defensive. "I have proof, Dad. Just look at it, that's all I ask." She'd been keeping the photographs tucked in the lining of her pocketbook, waiting for the right chance to show her father—she got them quickly, laid the first one down on the table before him. The photograph she'd snapped in the powder room after the wedding. "Anneliese's wedding bouquet. She tied an Iron Cross into it as a wedding charm. An *Iron Cross*, and it's not from the fourteen-eighteen war either. That's a swastika. It's a Third Reich medal." Swinging her eyes back to Anneliese. "I didn't find it in your room when I looked, so what did you do with it?"

Anneliese was silent. Dan McBride's gaze flicked over the photograph despite himself. Jordan rushed on, the words flowing like a river. *Lay it out. Make your case.*

"That's not all. Look at this." The second photograph, the copy of the vacation picture in Anneliese's Bible: the couple in bathing suits, standing by the lake waving to someone unseen. "Is that your husband, Anna?"

"Yes," she answered, still calm.

"Kurt? Or Manfred? Because I've heard you use both names. Kurt Weber is listed on Ruth's birth certificate as her father, so who's Manfred?"

Blue eyes flickered, then. Triumph stabbed Jordan. She was getting somewhere. *Yes.*

"The Iron Cross is his, isn't it?" she pressed. "Because he was a Nazi. And don't give me that utter *horseshit* about—"

"Jordan!" Her father barked, an automatic reproof for swearing, but he was still staring at the photograph. She pressed on.

"—about how being a member of the Nazi Party didn't make you one of the bad ones, Anna, because he wasn't just a Nazi. He was SS, wasn't he?" Jordan stabbed a finger down on the man in the photograph, his upraised arm. "He has a tattoo on the underside of his arm. You can just see it, there. Most SS officers had their blood types tattooed under the left arm." Jordan turned back to her father. "Mr. Sonnenstein told us that, remember? He helped identify the provenance of those paintings that came out of Hamburg right after the war; he told us how the owner selling them had been SS, trying to pass as a French art dealer. How he'd been identified by his tattoo." Looking back at Anneliese again. "Your husband was a decorated officer in the SS. And neither of you were Ruth's parents, because the date on that photograph says *März, 1942*. March. Ruth was born in April '42 according to her birth certificate, Anna, so why aren't you eight months pregnant in that photograph?"

This time the silence wasn't charged through with electricity. It blanketed the room like a weighted sheet. Jordan's father was standing as if he'd been turned to granite, gaze switching between the photographs on the table. Anneliese stood hands folded, looking at Jordan, and something in that gaze made Jordan's heart bang off her ribs in a sudden surge of fear. It was the look she'd captured in the very first picture, the night her father had brought Anneliese to dinner. The woman who looked so fragile and pretty, now somehow dangerous.

"It's more than just this." Jordan swept a hand at the pictures. "You spin a story about a refugee attacking Ruth at Altaussee, but it's *you* Ruth recoils from. She remembers her mother playing the violin, yet you told me you never played it. Who *are* you?" From the kitchen came the muffled chime of the timer to check the turkey, but no one moved. "Who are you?" Jordan repeated.

"You haven't made up your mind about that?" Anneliese said. "You seem very certain about everything else." Those cold blue eyes swam with tears, and Anneliese was suddenly shaking with sobs.

You are not going to fob this off with crying, Jordan thought, pressing her lips tight. But her dad took a confused, automatic step forward, and Anneliese turned in a helpless movement, turning her wet face against his shirt. "Don't say anything to Ruth," she whispered. "It was all to protect her."

"Stop *lying*," Jordan flared, but Anneliese's tears rolled even faster. Her husband's arm came around her shoulders, even though his face was still blank with shock.

"There, now," he muttered. "Let's all be calm—"

"Be calm?" Jordan cried. "Dad, we let a Nazi into our *family*. She could be anything, a murderer. Who knows how dangerous she—"

"Stop shouting. I can't hear myself think—"

"Don't be angry with Jordan." Anneliese lifted her face, flushed and dewy with tears. "Please don't be angry with her."

"Angry at *me*?" Jordan's voice scaled up despite herself. "I'm the one who found *you* out. You're the one who lied your way into our—"

"I did," Anneliese said simply. "I don't deny any of it."

Jordan felt as though she'd stepped down a step that wasn't there, teeth snapping shut on empty air. She'd expected tears, anger, evasions. She hadn't expected pure, bald-faced acceptance of all charges. "What do you have to say, then?" she rallied, and she cringed to hear how hectoring she sounded.

"Kurt was not my husband's name," Anneliese said quietly. "I was never married. The man in the photograph here is my father, and his name was Manfred. He was an officer in the SS, yes. I knew nothing of his work, what any of them did. He never discussed work with me, and it certainly wasn't my place to ask. I'm not a modern girl like you, Jordan. I went to university and I read English poetry, but my mother died and I came home to keep house for my father, to obey him while I lived under his roof. I wasn't political; I kept to the kitchen. I didn't hear the terrible things about the SS until after the war, after my father had already died. Can you imagine my horror? A man who had always been a kind, good father, discovered to be part of . . ."

Her eyes welled up again. She turned her head as if she wanted to bury her face back in her husband's shirtfront, but with a gigantic effort kept talking, smoothing her cheeks with her hands.

"I wanted no part of Germany or Austria after the war. I wanted a fresh start. Of course I didn't tell anyone about my family when I applied to come here. Who would? I wouldn't be accepted if people knew." Her voice trembled. "My first week in Boston, a boy threw a stone at me because I had a German accent. What would they do if they knew what my father had been?"

"If you're so innocent, why didn't you tell us?"

"I wanted to leave it all behind me, all that ugliness. The hatred. People throwing names and stones . . . I wasn't bringing that into your beautiful house." She made a little helpless gesture at the four walls, the festive Thanksgiving table. Gently, her hand came to rest atop her husband's. "I did carry my father's medal at the wedding. It was the only thing I had of his . . . and I wanted him to walk me down the aisle. Was that wrong?" Her drowned blue eyes turned back to Jordan. "You want to know why you couldn't find the medal, when you searched my room? I threw it into a pond on our honeymoon. Because that part of my life was finished."

Something cold and hideous was growing in Jordan's middle, knotting her stomach. She still had the sensation that she'd taken a wrong step, ended up in the wrong room. *Made the wrong accusation*, the thought whispered, but she braced herself with a deep breath. "And Ruth?" she asked, fighting to sound level, reasonable. Because Anneliese's creamy voice was reason itself. "Explain Ruth."

Anneliese went off into another torrent of tears, hands over her face. Jordan's dad stood helpless, looking between his wife and his daughter, and something in Jordan squeezed when he reached out and touched Anneliese's hair. "Sweetheart—" He never could stand to see a woman crying. And Anneliese was gripping his hand, pouring out words—to him, only him, not giving Jordan so much as a glance.

"God gave me Ruth. He gave us to each other in Altaussee. The war was over and I was walking beside the lake—I'd finally gotten my papers, my tickets here. I was thanking God for my good fortune, and I see a little girl crying on a bench. Filthy, thin, her papers pinned to her coat. Only three years old. She couldn't tell me anything, where her parents were. Who knows what happened to them. I waited hours with her. I didn't know what to do. That was when a half-crazed woman tried to attack us. Everyone was desperate for boat tickets, for money. I fought for Ruth like she was my own, and that was when I knew she'd been *sent* to me. I couldn't leave her." A long quivering breath. "So I washed the blood off her face where she'd been knocked down and took her with me when I left Altaussee, and by the time we landed in Boston she seemed to think I was her mother. Most of the time, *I* forget I'm not her mother. She was so young, and it all happened like a terrible dream . . ."

Another choked silence fell. Jordan's lips parted. She couldn't think what to say. "I don't believe that," she forced out finally. "It all sounds—theatrical."

"War is theatrical, Jordan. I don't expect you to understand that; you haven't lived it." Anneliese's voice was drained, lifeless. The cold pit in Jordan's stomach clenched again. "Those of us who survive are only alive because of some stroke of luck. Ruth's parents were struck down; she was left behind. My father was struck down; I was left behind. Any survivor's story is extraordinary. Death is everyday; survival is a theater trick."

Still Jordan's father wouldn't speak. His face was gray and sagging, but his hand lay under Anneliese's.

"Why did you lie about Ruth?" Jordan clutched after the certainty that had sheathed her like armor. "*Why?*"

"I thought you might not love her . . ." Looking up at her husband. "She's almost certainly a Jew. How many men would take a Jew into their homes, give her their name? I was afraid."

He flinched. "I would never have hesitated to—"

"I deceived you. I'm so sorry." Anneliese reached out, touching his cheek. "Perhaps you won't forgive me. But don't hold it against my poor Ruth."

"Dad, stop," Jordan said desperately. "How can we trust her?

She has lied about everything, you need to—" Her own thoughts circled in confusion. *What do you even think anymore?* "Your name isn't Anneliese Weber, is it?" Rounding on her stepmother. "That's Ruth's mother's name, it's on her birth certificate, so it can't be yours. You were lying about that too—"

"I gave up my name for Ruth, so no one could take her from me. I was so terrified she'd be taken away . . ." Anneliese wiped her eyes. "I didn't want my old name, anyway. My father's name felt tainted. *Weber* was easier for Americans to pronounce. The name was something I never lied about."

"You *did*—"

"No." It wasn't Anneliese who spoke this time; it was Jordan's father. "She told me the day we met that her name was different now, that she had wanted something easier for Americans to say. Something to give her a fresh start."

Jordan's heart knocked. "Dad—"

"Don't be angry with her," Anneliese interrupted, touching his cheek again. "She was only trying to protect her father."

I am still trying to protect him. Jordan clutched after that instinctive shiver of fear that had touched her at the beginning of these accusations, meeting Anneliese's eyes, but she couldn't find it, not even a trace. Anneliese didn't look dangerous. She looked like a broken doll.

"I'm sorry." Her eyes were swimming. "I'm so sorry. I should have told you."

Jordan's lips parted, but she couldn't speak.

"You should talk." Anneliese looked from her husband to Jordan. "If you don't wish me to—" Her voice broke. "*Du meine Güte*, I'm sorry—"

She rushed out of the room, shoulders hunched as though expecting a blow. The first sob came just before the sound of the bedroom door closing.

Jordan looked at her father numbly. He stood with his hands hanging at his sides, wearing the good shirt he'd donned for Thanksgiving dinner. The table's bright silver and holiday pumpkins looked like festive flags decorating a shipwreck. Jordan dragged a breath into her frozen lungs and realized she was smelling smoke from the kitchen. Their Thanksgiving dinner was burning.

Her father was staring at her. She took a step forward, eyes blurring. Not knowing what to say. Not knowing what to think, except that this had all gone horribly wrong: "Dad . . ."

Dad, I still don't know if I believe her or not. Dad, I was just trying to protect you . . .

But she couldn't get past that first word. Her throat stopped, choked up with tears and the smell of burned turkey and ruined Thanksgiving. Feebly, she gestured to the two photographs. "Pictures don't lie," she forced out. "I believed what I saw."

But the thought reverberated through her head like a tolling bell now:

You saw wrong.

Chapter 17

IAN

April 1950
Salzburg

It should have been a night to sleep happy and triumphant, a night to dream of *die Jägerin* in handcuffs, but the nightmare didn't care. Vaulted out of sleep by the familiar dream, Ian tried to be amused at the utter predictability of night terrors but he was shaking too much. "Why the parachute?" he asked aloud of his dark hotel room, needing to hear a voice even if only his own. "Why the bloody *parachute*?"

Fruitless question. A nightmare was a needle plunging through the net of human memory; it slipped past one strand and caught up another on its point, stitching up dark dreams out of the unlikeliest recollections. The parachute wasn't the worst thing he'd seen in his career by any means, so why dream of it? Why not Spain, that day in Teruel when he'd carried his notepad up shell-pocked stairs into the Republican-attacked Civil Governor's building, listening to the terrible single shots of men killing themselves? Why not that schoolhouse in Naples after the German retreat, the coffins heaped with flowers that didn't cover the dirty bare feet of the children in them? Why not dream about Omaha Beach, for God's sake? "That would be the obvious nightmare to have," Ian muttered, leaning on the open window to drag in a shaky breath of geranium-scented air. Clinging to wet sand, watching blood swirl past through shallow waves, deafened by German fire but feeling the impact through his bones as the shells hit all around him . . . he'd seen the first gray in his dark hair within a week of Omaha Beach. Surely *that* should have been the worst dream in his nighttime arsenal.

No. It was the parachute under the emerald-green trees, peacefully swaying, and the endless drop below.

Stop. Ian gave the fear a brutal kick. *There is no parachute, no fall. No bloody nightmare either, because you have no right to it. You were just a journalist. A goddamn writer, not a soldier. They carried guns; you carried pens. They fought, you didn't. They bled and died, you wrote and lived. You haven't* earned *the nightmares.*

He went back to bed, closed his eyes, pounded the pillow. Rolled on his back and stared at the ceiling. "Bloody hell," he muttered, rising again to pull a shirt over chilly sweat-slicked skin, and went downstairs to the hotel desk. After a protracted wrangle with the sleepy night clerk, Ian was finally put through to the only other man he could count on to be awake at this hour. "Bauer, what do you know about extradition law in America?"

"*Guten Morgen* to you too," Fritz Bauer rasped. "Don't tell me you're following a chase overseas."

Ian turned his back on the night clerk. "Perhaps." The staggering complications of that had only begun to register this evening, as he sat over the remains of a scrounged supper listening to Nina and Tony wrangle about how best to track *die Jägerin* now that they had a name, a photograph, and a destination. "What would we be in for?" He only knew in the most general terms; Bauer could be counted on for specifics.

"It would be hell," his friend said succinctly. Ian could imagine the flash of light off his glasses as he leaned back in his leather chair. "An ocean of paperwork, money, and time."

Which was, of course, why, Ian thought, the Refugee Documentation Center didn't pursue cases overseas. As little jurisdiction as they had in Europe, they'd have even less across the Atlantic. For a ramshackle one-room operation, the cases that led overseas became dead ends, sinkholes for money and time. Who could afford that when there was always someone else to pursue here in Europe? Ian rubbed his eyes, willing that voice of cold logic to go away, but it proceeded remorselessly. *To go to such marathon lengths for one target is pure, self-indulgent obsession. Even if she did kill your brother, and nearly kill your wife.*

Bauer's gruff voice again. "American extradition details—that will take digging. I have a friend or two over there; let me put in a few calls once their offices are open."

"Thank you." Ian rang off, but the cold voice of logic was still talking.

There are criminals in Germany whom you have a much better chance of catching than Lorelei Vogt in America. Shove them all aside for a long shot at her—a long shot that will probably eat up everything you have, including your center—then this impartial search for justice you're so proud of turns into ordinary, commonplace vengeance.

And if there was anything Ian Graham didn't believe in, it was vengeance.

What now? he thought, but the night had no answers. Only, eventually, more dreams.

"IS MORE TO FIND here in Europe before going to Boston," Nina was saying. She shared Ian's seat in the train compartment, sitting with her back to the window and her disreputable boots propped in his lap. He pushed them off periodically, but she just plopped them back—his wife apparently had no more sense of individual space than individual property. "School friends from Heidelberg days," Nina went on, flipping through their increasingly frayed file. "And her lover, the SS *mudak*, what about him? He's dead, but what about his wife? She might be willing to talk about her husband's whore—"

"Von Altenbach's wife is dead too," Tony answered. "She ran with high Reich society, childhood friends with Magda Goebbels back when she was Magda Ritschel. That was why von Altenbach couldn't divorce her for our girl Lorelei. He took her to Poznań and left the Frau in Berlin, and the Frau committed suicide at the war's end. One of the true believers who couldn't face the world without their Führer."

"Lorelei's friends in Germany." Ian focused through the gray blur of sleep deprivation, trying to match his companions' energy. "She might write to her friends as well as her mother; wouldn't that be considerate of her?" He answered their smiles with one of his own, but it was an effort. The difficulties ahead were piling up in his mind like storm clouds.

No storms in the sky above as they disembarked the train in Vienna, though. "*Tvoyu mat*," Nina breathed, stopping at the top of the train station steps. "I want to be up there—" She pointed at the huge sailing clouds overhead. "Up *high*!"

"I can't get you that high, but I can get you sixty-five meters up." Tony stuffed his hands in his pockets. "Ever ridden the Prater wheel, Nina?"

"What is it, this *Prater*?"

Ian smiled too. "Our famous Viennese amusement park, you miniature Soviet housebreaker."

"We had a lucky break in the case yesterday," Tony urged. "Let's celebrate. We can scrounge enough change between us for a trip to the Prater."

Ian looked down at Nina, pushing the looming extradition problem aside. "We never did have a honeymoon, you and I. Shall I show you a few Viennese sights before we divorce?"

They took a cab to the amusement park in the Leopoldstadt where the great Ferris wheel loomed and children were already shrieking with excitement, pursued by fond, exasperated mothers up and down the rows of food vendors and shooting galleries. Nina pushed toward the line for the wheel, Tony betting her she'd lose her nerve at the top. She laughed so hard she staggered into Ian's shoulder. "I don't lose nerve," she said, as Ian righted her with a hand at the elbow. "Not at sixty-five meters."

"What does make you lose your nerve?" Ian asked, wondering

again just what it was she'd been assigned to do at the Soviet front during the war. But Nina had come to the front of the line for the wheel, not hearing him, and Ian stepped to one side. "You two go. I'm no good with heights."

"You're coming along, *luchik*," Nina said, and somehow she and Tony had an arm each and were yanking Ian into the gondola. As it swayed under his feet, his vision swayed with it and he turned back, but the attendant was already slamming the door shut. They were the last to load, getting the gondola all to themselves—and before Ian could leap out, the wheel was lifting them skyward.

His mouth was suddenly dry as paper, and the world sounded as though it had retreated underwater. *Don't be a coward, Graham.* He hadn't always been petrified of high places, after all. But the day he acquired the nightmare about a parachute had been the day that changed. *Do not be a coward.*

The gondolas of the Prater were famous: compact cars with a center bench and windows all around to see the panoramic scope of Vienna's steep roofs and church domes, now shrinking to the size of dolls. Nina was wandering along the line of windows, as Tony pointed out landmarks. Bile rose in Ian's throat and he swallowed as the car rose higher. If they'd been climbing up the stairway of a tall cathedral or walking the parapet of a rooftop, he'd have been all right—put a solid rail or a steady floor between him and the void, and he was fine. But swaying along through the air in this flimsy shell . . .

Better than an airplane, he told himself, hands linking so tight he saw the knuckles whiten. *To think you once queued up for the privilege of jumping out of a bomber over Germany.* Now he'd rather be flayed alive.

". . . open these windows?" Nina was saying. "Is boring, sailing up and up like a sedate old kite."

"What are you going to do, climb on the roof?" Tony laughed, clearly not worried as she dropped the top sill of the observation window. Nina hauled herself up, hanging her head and shoulders out into the sky. She was just trying to get a better view, Ian knew that, but his nerves didn't. He imagined his wife falling from the gondola like a bird shot down in flight, glass shattering around her, and he lunged across the swaying floor. Seizing her around the waist, he wrenched her down so fast she almost flew across the gondola. She fell against the bench with a crash and came instantly to her feet, blue eyes flaring. Ian turned his back, shoving the window up with a violence that cracked the pane. A silver line ran in a sudden *ping* across the glass and he couldn't help flinching, seeing the crack and then the tilted view of Vienna beyond it. They were at the wheel's apex, sixty-five meters up, five times as high as the day he'd—

Ian turned away and threw up in the corner.

When he straightened, Nina and Tony were both staring at him. He pulled a handkerchief from his pocket and wiped his mouth, realizing with a flash of shame that his hands were shaking. His voice wasn't, though. "Parachute jump, '45," he said, as the gondola began its descent. "Ever since then, you might say I've had a little trouble with heights. So next time I tell you to leave me on the ground, *leave me on the goddamned ground*."

Tony cleared his throat. "I'm sorry, I didn't—"

"I know," Ian cut him off, wishing this ride was over, wishing they'd stop looking at him. Wishing he weren't a coward.

"I say go again," Nina said.

"What?"

"Is what I would do. Ride this wheel around a hundred more times. All day. All night. Till I wasn't afraid."

"No," Ian said. The thought of going round even one more time made him want to vomit all over again.

"You go down your list of fears." Her eyes had a distant compassion, as if she knew what he was thinking. "Stamp them out, one after other, till there's only one. Is good to have one fear, *luchik*, but just one. I think the fear you want to keep is the fear you never find *die Jägerin*, yes? So get rid of this one."

Ian stared at his wife. She was retying the scarf around her neck, a homemade white thing embroidered in blue stars. She smiled.

"Come," she challenged, patting the bench. "I ride with you, long as it takes. Let's kill a fear today."

"Get between me and the door when we finally stop," Ian said, "and I will pitch you through that bloody window."

He didn't know how long that ghastly ride lasted, but it passed in utter silence.

BY THE TIME they reached the Refugee Documentation Center it was midafternoon, the shakes were gone from Ian's hands, and the humiliation at his loss of control was subsiding. "Right," he said as they came into the stale-smelling office. "I have a call to make. Nina, if you'd be good enough to sort post; Tony, catalog and file anything new. We have a dozen other files open besides Lorelei Vogt's, after all." The office filled with the crackle of paper and the hiss of the kettle, and Ian picked up the telephone. "What do you have, Bauer?" *Let it be good news.*

"The United States naturally has no jurisdiction over crimes committed overseas, so if you found your huntress—proved who she was and what she'd done—she'd have to be extradited for trial." Ian heard the rustle of paper on Bauer's end. "To Austria, possibly, as her birth nation, or to Poland as that's where her crimes were largely committed."

Ian could well imagine a courtroom of vengeful Poles eager to levy justice against the woman who had hunted their citizens on the banks of Lake Rusalka. "What else?"

"Before you could even think of getting her a trial in Europe, she'd probably have to be tried in the United States in a civil court, and you'd need clear proof of her crimes."

"We have it. Witnesses." Nina, eyewitness to Sebastian's murder, and the clerk who had provided the statement at Nuremberg about *die Jägerin*'s execution of the Polish children.

"It would still be heavy lifting," Bauer warned, and he launched into a flurry of legal technicalities that lost Ian on the third turn. So many things this team needed, he thought—photographers, drivers, pathologists—but surely what they could have used most of all was more legal experts. Ian heard his friend sigh on the other end, aware he'd lost his audience. "The United States hasn't extradited a single Nazi for war crimes," Bauer finished bluntly. "Not one. Are they even aware they have any? Or perhaps the question is, do they care?"

The leaden feeling returned to Ian's stomach as he rang off. Tony's voice was quiet. "What's the bad news?"

"I am pondering the realities of American extradition law," Ian replied. *Die Jägerin.* Learning her real name hadn't brought her down to human size, after all. She remained the huntress, remote and uncatchable. Ian forced the words out. "It's time we faced facts. We aren't going to Boston."

Two sets of eyes regarded him, dismayed. Russian blue and Polish-American black.

"It's over." Ian looked back and forth between them. "She got away."

"No, she got to *Boston*," Tony said. "Who knows where from there?"

"It doesn't matter. She might as well have gone to the moon." Ian gestured at the four walls of the center, biting his words off. "We are three people in a one-room office with two desks and four filing cabinets. Even if we found her in America, we could not possibly get her extradited for trial. We lack the man power, the money, the influence, and the resources to mount an overseas search. It is impossible. I was hoping otherwise, but Bauer convinced me. We're finished."

"Bauer hasn't convinced me," Tony said. "We're not finished until we fail, and we haven't failed yet."

"We will, if we pursue this."

"I'll admit, it's a long shot. But we might pull it off if—"

"This is not a debate." Ian cut him off in a wintry voice. "I started this documentation center, Tony. I say how and where we choose our targets."

"And we both know you wouldn't get half your arrests if not for me. So let's not pretend my mingy salary makes you my boss." Tony folded his arms across his chest, and Ian realized he was angry too. "We *can* catch Lorelei Vogt."

"Drop your everlasting Yank optimism!" Ian's temper flared to match Tony's, sweeping disappointment away. Anger hurt, but at least it was a satisfying pain. "This tin-pot office stapled together with sweat and ink does not have the resources to—"

"So you're willing to give up?" Tony's eyes bored into him. "When she killed your brother?"

"A lot of brothers have been lost in this war," Ian clipped. "My loss is no more worthy of special consideration than anyone else's. And I'm not willing to burn up everything in my life for vengeance."

"You've already burned up everything in your life, Ian. You just didn't do it for vengeance; that's for commoners who never went to Harrow." Tony gave a thin, edged smile. "You burned up everything in your life for this office, that monk's cell you live in, and three arrests a year."

Ian took a shallow breath. He spread his hands on the surface of the desk, leaning forward. "This center may be ramshackle, but it means something. My handful of arrests every year means something. Even if just a handful of reminders to the world that the guilty will face justice for what they've done. To me, that is worth it." He gestured at the four walls again. "If I go overseas and throw everything into a fruitless hunt for *die Jägerin*, this center will probably collapse. So I'll stay here and go on with the cases I have some chance of winning. And I will do that with or without you."

Nina had been silent up till now, straddling the back of her chair, idly flicking her razor open and closed, watching them spit insults. Now she rose. "I say we go to Boston."

"Have you heard anything I've said?" Ian transferred his gaze to her. "Even if we find her, we cannot put her on trial—"

Nina shrugged. "So we kill her."

"No." Ian came around the desk, covering the ground between himself and his wife in one stride. "We are not a damned death squad. We are better than that. Dead men don't pay. They don't suffer. The world learns nothing from them. Without public justice, it's all pointless. *We do not kill targets.*"

"Okay," she said. "*We* don't kill her. *I* kill her. I have no problem with that."

"What the bloody hell is wrong with you?" Ian's voice rose to a shout. "If you'd kill Lorelei Vogt in cold blood, what makes you any different from her?"

"I don't do it for fun like her," Nina flared. "I do it because she tries to kill me. Because I see her kill your brother." Nina stepped closer, head tipped far back to nail her gaze to his. "Russians don't forget that like Englishmen."

Ian stared down at his wife, close enough to feel her contained fury blazing up at him. She stared back, eyes narrowed, hair a blond feral mane. "I will not seek justice for one ruthless killer of a woman by joining forces with another," he said at last. "Get the fuck out of my office."

Nina tilted one shoulder in a shrug and moved toward the door.

"Hey!" Tony protested, starting forward, but Ian whipped around.

"I have always said I won't work with anyone who advocates for vigilante justice, Tony. Do not even try to tell me she is joking."

"Am not joking," Nina said, taking her old jacket off the hook by the door.

"I know you're not," Tony replied. "You'd open *die Jägerin*'s throat ear to ear and walk away smiling. But so would *you*, Ian, if you ever let yourself admit it." Tony shook his head. "You might know more Latin than your wife here, but don't think that makes you better than she is. You've got a savage in there too, you just pretend he's never coming off the leash."

"He never is coming off the leash," Ian said evenly. "Because I happen to believe that principle should be stronger than the need for vengeance."

"Excuses certainly are," his partner bit back. "You know the real reason you won't follow Lorelei Vogt to Boston? I do. Because you'd rather let a murderess walk free than take the risk of your righteous white hat ever slipping off."

Nina looked over her shoulder in the doorway. "Is true," she said.

Maybe it is, Ian thought. *Which is why I will not risk it. Control is what separates men from beasts.*

"Send me a telegram when you get back to England," he told Nina finally. "So I know where to notify you of divorce proceedings. Feel free to follow her out, Tony. As long as I've known you, you'd follow a woman's arse and an easy argument before you'd ever follow what was right."

"I wondered my first day here how long it would take you to fire me." Tony reached for his hat. "So long, boss."

Chapter 18

NINA

May 1942
Engels

She was beautiful. Olive green with red-painted stars, proud and new. Nina laid a hand on the sun-warmed wood.

Who are you? the U-2 seemed to ask.

"A friend," Nina breathed back. All over the airdrome, the pilots and navigators of the 588th were examining their new planes. They would fly soon to join the Fourth Air Army on the southern front in the Donets Basin region. These planes would see combat.

Yelena stood back, hands in her pockets. Nina turned, still stroking the propeller blade like the nose of a dog. "I know you're disappointed it's not a fighter," she said, already feeling protective of the U-2. She wanted to cover its ears, make sure it didn't hear it hadn't been its pilot's first pick. "But this girl will do us fine."

"I know." Yelena's smile had a wistful edge as she came and patted the propeller. Nina hadn't expected to be picked for the fighters, but Yelena had wept disappointment upon learning that she too had been assigned to the night bombers. Secretly, Nina was relieved. The regiment of fighters had claimed tiny fiery Lilia and a good many others she was surprised to realize had become friends. At least she wasn't losing Yelena. The intensity of her own relief had startled Nina.

"Is it really so bad?" she ventured around an unexpected tightness in her throat. "Flying a U-2 with me?"

"I'd have liked to fly a Yak-1, but . . ." Yelena's smile faded. "I told you I was born in Ukraine, before my family came to Moscow?"

"Yes."

"My old village has been overrun by Germans," Yelena said softly, and Nina's hand fell from the propeller. "Mama had word from her sister. Everyone was fleeing, roads jammed with people carrying bundles, children screaming, dogs howling. And German planes flew along the roads, strafing the crowd. My grandparents are dead. My cousins, dead." She stopped, lashes dropping in a quick, fierce blink. Nina wanted to put an arm about Yelena's shoulders, but held back. "I don't care if I only fly a U-2 and not a Yak," Yelena finished. "I'd fly a *broom*, as long as I was able to fight the Fritzes."

"And you've got the best navigator in the 588th," Nina pointed out.

Yelena gave a watery smile. "The most modest too."

They were going to fly well together, Nina already knew that. Marina Raskova had assigned all the pairings herself, and Nina's heart lifted when she heard her assignment. Yelena was better but Nina was bolder; Yelena had sharper reflexes, Nina had keener eyes. They'd balance each other perfectly.

"So, Comrade Lieutenant Vetsina," Nina said. "From here, it's my job to keep you alive. You fly the plane and I fly you, so you have to do everything I say." She said it jokingly, but the flash of protectiveness that went through her was oddly fierce. Were all the other navigators already so worried about their pilots' safety?

"Don't worry, Comrade Lieutenant. I'm a nice steerable creature. Just like her." Yelena looked up at their U-2, slinging an arm about Nina's neck. Nina leaned her head against that warm, firm shoulder. "What shall we name her?"

"I think . . ." Nina blew out a thoughtful breath, smelling the soap Yelena had used to wash her short glossy hair, contemplating their plane. What beautiful words those were: *their plane.* "I think she'll tell us when she's ready, don't you?"

THEY FLEW OUT on a warm May morning, Raskova in the lead. She'd be taking command of the day bombers but had vowed to personally escort all the regiments to their front first. She rose into the air like an eagle, one hundred and twelve eaglets following her, red Soviet stars flashing in the May sunshine. They leveled off below the racing clouds, Yelena's head moving in the cockpit ahead of Nina's as she snugged their U-2 tight and swift into formation. Major Raskova waggled her wingtips as the last plane veered into line, and they all waved back, the ripple moving down the line of wings like laughter. Nina realized her eyes were streaming tears behind her goggles—she hadn't cried since the very first time she'd taken to the air at nineteen. Yelena took her hand off the stick and stretched it back over her shoulder, giving Nina a blind wave, and Nina waved back. Without even seeing her pilot's face, she knew Yelena had an ear-to-ear smile.

No one was smiling when they touched down at Morozovskaia. "Those bastards," Nina spat. An escort of fighters from the Fourth Air Army had risen up to escort the 588th in, only the men hadn't been content to fly escort; they'd flown attack patterns like advancing Messerschmitts.

"They're friendlies," Yelena had shouted back to Nina, who tensed as she saw the first attacking swoop. "They're just playing—" She held their course, but several of the younger pilots had got flustered and dove out of formation.

"Raskova's going to have their balls for earrings," Nina snarled once everyone was safe on the ground.

"They didn't mean any harm," Yelena argued. "It's just hazing. Everyone coming new to the front is in for some hazing."

"Especially if you're us," the argument shot back. "Comrade Stalin's pet project—"

"—because we're *girls*—"

"Well, don't show them any reaction," Yelena said as they fell into march exiting the airfield. "Heads high, ladies."

Nina kept her eyes narrowed and her chin lifted as they walked the gauntlet of smirking men in flight overalls. Some wag from the back called out, "What's the matter, girlies, can't you tell stars from swastikas when you see 'em on a wing?" Nina broke marching rhythm to throw him an obscene gesture.

"Enough," Major Raskova barked, all-seeing as ever. "You'll be based out of Trud Gorniaka, ladies, find your billets. Don't get comfortable. With the front so unstable we could be moving any day or any hour—"

"The Germans are close here," Dusia Nosal proclaimed—a girl with a taut, thin face, probably the best flier in the 588th besides Yelena. She'd lost her newborn baby in a German bombing raid at the beginning of the war. "You can almost smell the sauerkraut. If we don't get orders within the week . . ."

But the commander of the 218th who came for the following day's inspection had barely a glance for the regiment. "He called us *what*?" Nina hissed.

"*'I've received one hundred and twelve little princesses, just what am I supposed to do with them?'*" Dusia mimicked. "He was on the telephone to General Vershinin, or so I heard."

"He wouldn't say that to Raskova's face!"

But Raskova had flown back to Engels, and the 588th received their orders from Major Yevdokia Bershanskaia now. "Two weeks of additional training," Bershanskaia said over their groans. She had none of Raskova's blue-eyed glamour, but she was steady, quiet, all brisk maternal efficiency like a hen herding chicks, no patience for stragglers or whiners. She'd wanted to fly fighters, Nina knew, but now she was commander of the 588th, and if she was disappointed, she didn't show it. "You're all to be individually flight-tested by a male pilot."

"What do they think we've been doing all that time in Engels?" Nina demanded. "Buffing our nails? We can't be trusted until one of the men signs off that we know which end of the stick to hold?"

"Ninochka," Yelena said with a sigh, "shut up."

Nina, still smoldering, climbed stonily into her U-2 the following morning with a freckle-faced pilot who looked about twelve and threw her plane around the sky so violently that her inspector nearly threw up. "Pass," he said, green-faced. Yelena's examiner was a tall handsome Leningrader with a lazy smile, and Nina hated him on sight. "They make damned pretty pilots in Moscow," he said, laughing at Yelena's blush. "Virgin ears, *dousha*? Better toughen up, or you won't last a fucking minute against the Krauts—" He kept stringing profanities, clearly enjoying Yelena's bright red cheeks, and when he finally let her climb into the cockpit, Nina hailed him from the side of the runway.

"What is it, little one?" he asked, loping up with a disbelieving glance for Nina's head, which didn't even reach his shoulder. "Are you even tall enough to see out of the cockpit?"

He yelped then, feeling the keen edge of a stropped Siberian razor pressing against the inside of his thigh. Nina smiled, angling her body so no one would see the blade between her fingers. Yelena waved from the U-2, clearly wondering what the delay was.

"My pilot," Nina said sweetly, "doesn't care for your fucking language, you bonehead Leningrad mule. Keep your mouth clean around her, or I will slice off your balls and cram them up your fucking nose."

"Women in the air," he breathed. "World's gone crazy, giving planes to you bitches."

"Bitches like my pilot fly better than you will ever fly in your whole goddamned life." Nina gave another sweet smile. "So take her up there for a loop and keep your fucking language nice, and I won't jam a propeller up your shit-factory and crank until your asshole flaps like your mouth."

"He said I'm a skilled pilot and a credit to the Fourth Air Army," Yelena reported afterward.

"Did he, now?" Nina said placidly.

The Fritzes were grinding toward Stalingrad, reportedly advanced into the curve of the Don River, before the 588th received their orders. "First combat mission to be flown by three planes only." Bershanskaia's hand made its signature chop before a single groan went up. "Myself and both squadron commanders. Regard it as an exploratory sortie, girls."

"Let's not grudge her," Yelena said. "For the commanders it's going to be all paperwork from here on out. She should have the honor of flying the first mission."

"Don't be so everlastingly generous," Nina groaned. "Just admit that you'd walk over your own mother to get into a cockpit by now."

"I'd walk over my own mother to get into a cockpit by now," Yelena said immediately. "Just not a *sestra*."

A fine summer evening, warm and breezy. Impossible to think that the front was just kilometers away from this prosaic stretch of flat fields and hastily erected bunkers, torn-up roads dotted with trucks and ground personnel in overalls. The horizon showed plumes of smoke rising kilometers away—coal deposits on fire, someone whispered. There was still a little daylight left when the regiment gathered on the makeshift runway to watch Bershanskaia and the squadron commanders make their way to their planes. "They'll fly to the auxiliary airfield at the front lines," the whisper went around. "Arm there, fly their run, then back here."

Three planes took off into a darkening sky. Nina watched, hands stuffed in her pockets, physically aching. *Tomorrow*, she thought. From the taut, yearning faces all around her, the others were all thinking the same thing.

"Well," Yelena announced, "I'm not going to bed until they've come back. Let's have some music!"

A girl from Kiev began an ancient folk song, her voice hushed and lilting, and a few of the others took it up, braiding harmony around her soft alto. A Party march followed, brisk and tuneful, and more voices joined in as the stars came out in their thousands. The sky turned to black velvet, and Nina surprised herself by lifting her own voice in an ancient cradle song from the shores of the Old Man. She hadn't even known she remembered it, all those verses in the lake dialect so old it was barely Russian. The other girls listened raptly. "What was that?" Yelena asked. She sat with her back against the nearest shed, fiddling with a length of cloth across her lap.

"A song about the lake," Nina said. "All songs from Baikal are about the lake. Waves that rock the boats and the cradles, and the *rusalka*'s hand setting both into motion. Then something with the moon . . . It doesn't make a lot of sense, really."

"Nothing makes sense," Yelena said. "We're in the middle of a war, and a few short kilometers from here people are dying. But us—we've never been so happy."

"Yes," Nina agreed, watching the moon shine on Yelena's hair.

Dusia was singing now, her sad face smiling for once, and two of the other girls began to dance, swinging about arm in arm, laughter rising through the night. Someone beckoned Nina, but she flopped down by Yelena, tilting her head at the cloth in her pilot's lap. "Are you *sewing*?"

"Embroidering my flying scarf. Blue stars on white, what do you think?" Yelena tilted the cloth under the starlight for Nina's eyes.

"Where'd you get blue thread?"

"Unpicked it from those horrible men's briefs!" Yelena grinned, and Nina laughed. They were already flying high at the thought of being in the air tomorrow. The anticipation was so sweet it cut the mouth, like winter-cold water from the icy shore of the Old Man.

They were making plans for how they'd celebrate once they flew five hundred missions and were made Heroes of the Soviet Union— "Gold stars on our chests, just like Raskova!" "When you get a medal, I hear you have to drop it in a crystal glass, fill the glass with vodka, and drink a toast!"—when a sawing, droning buzz rose in the distance: the sound of a U-2's noisy little radial engine. As one, the girls of the 588th sprinted toward the runway.

One plane touched down, then a second. The tails descended to the grass, dragging both U-2s to a halt, and the ground crew on duty went running out to make postflight checks and tie down the wings. Nina saw Bershanskaia's compact form climbing out of her cockpit, stepping from the wing to the ground. The first squadron commander came after, stripping off her goggles. The regiment was already swarming around them, pouring laughter and congratulations, but Nina's feet slowed. The returning pilots had blank, stony faces. Nina tilted her face to the rush of stars overhead.

There was no chopping buzz in the air signaling a third plane.

"Where is Squadron Commander—" someone began, but Bershanskaia cut her off. She didn't say anything. She just shook her head.

The girls stared at each other. Not even one night active, Nina thought with a painful twist in her stomach, and the regiment had its first two losses.

Bershanskaia looked from pilot to pilot, finding the white-faced deputy commander of the second squadron. "The squadron is now yours, Mariya Smirnova." A silent nod. "Get some rest, ladies. Tomorrow you all take the air."

MOST OF THE GIRLS trailed back to their quarters, some pale and stunned, some crying. Yelena headed the opposite direction, toward the flat field where the rest of the U-2s waited. Nina fell in at her side, shock still rolling sickly inside her. Two women dead, two women she had known . . .

"You should go to bed," Yelena said.

"I'm not leaving my pilot." That surge of protectiveness overcame Nina again, laced this time with tenderness. "Navigator's first job."

She caught up, taking Yelena's hand, and the long fingers tangled through hers. Nina's throat caught. They made their way to their U-2, staring up at it silently. Just a black shape against the stars. No proper airdromes so close to the front; on a fine summer night like this the planes sat in silent camouflaged rows in the flattened grass. *Where will we be flying by winter?* Nina wondered. If the German army was still in full advance by then, would it mean Moscow had fallen? Probably Leningrad too, starving and encircled, and Stalingrad . . .

"What do you think tomorrow's targets will be?" Yelena's voice was soft in the dark.

"German depots or ammunition supplies," Nina guessed.

Yelena ran her hand along the bombing rack under the lower wing of their plane. "Not much firepower on a U-2."

"Enough to disrupt, pester. Like a mosquito—you know that."

"But we're just one mosquito in a big war."

"One mosquito in a cloud of mosquitoes," Nina corrected. "And a cloud of mosquitoes can drive a man or even a horse so mad with pain, it'll plunge into the lake and drown itself."

Yelena noticed Nina's involuntary shudder at her own words. "What?"

"Drowning. The one thing I'm afraid of." She took a steadying breath, for a moment tasting the iron tang of the lake, feeling her father's hand shoving her head under the ice. "What do you fear, Yelenushka?"

"Getting captured and tortured. Crashing . . ." Yelena shivered. "What if it's us tomorrow?"

Nina was silent. There was only faint starlight, but she had no trouble seeing Yelena's pale face. She saw it clear as day: the wide-set long-lashed eyes, the firm lips pressed into a line to keep from trembling, the dark hair that had grown from its training-day chop into short dark curls around her long neck. Nina reached up, taking hold of Yelena's flying scarf with its half-stitched blue stars, and tugged her down so they could see eye to eye. "It won't be us," she said, and she fit her mouth over Yelena's. Soft lips, soft cheeks, fingers sliding into Yelena's soft hair. A moment's stiffening, a surprised little sound like a startled cygnet disappearing into the warmth between them. Then there was a tentative parting of lips. A slender hand alighted on Nina's cheek, and her blood turned to quicksilver.

Yelena's eyes were wide when they pulled apart. Nina wanted to soar. She didn't need the U-2 to take flight, she could take a running leap and fling herself up among the stars. With one hand she patted the plane, and with the other she seized Yelena by the wrist. "This bird needs a name," she said. "Come on."

They rummaged in the temporary mechanic headquarters, begging a can of red paint and some brushes from the few mechanics still prowling among their planes, and carried it all back to their U-2, pulling aside just enough of the camouflage to get to work.

Yelena did the painting while Nina and her sharper nighttime eyes directed the placement of the letters. "That last word is wandering up—down, stick down! Does Raskova know she picked a pilot who doesn't know up from down?"

"Does Raskova know she picked a navigator who can't give the simplest of directions?" Yelena swiped Nina with the paintbrush.

Dawn was perhaps an hour away by the time they finished. The last mechanics had gone; Nina and Yelena were surely the only two not asleep in their quarters. They surveyed their work, Nina sitting on the U-2's lower wing feet swinging, Yelena standing at her side head tilted. Along the fuselage, neat red letters read *To Avenge Our Comrades* with the names of the regiment's first two losses. On the other side was the U-2's new name.

Rusalka.

"Silent and immortal," Yelena said. "I like that."

"So do I," said Nina and reached out to tug Yelena's mouth to hers again. Not surprising her this time, moving slow to give her a chance to tug away—*please don't tug away*—and she didn't. Her hands cupped Nina's face, her lips hungry and shy. Nina felt the swoop in her stomach that she always felt when she began spiraling nose-first into a stall. The weightless delirium of falling.

"I haven't—" Yelena said uncertainly, lips still brushing Nina's, her fingers wound tight through Nina's hair. "Why me?"

"Because you're the best flier I've ever seen," Nina said. "I've never seen anything so beautiful in the air as you."

"Girls don't—aren't supposed to—"

"I don't care about *aren't supposed to*," Nina said roughly, sliding off the wing to pull her pilot down to the ground. The shadow under the *Rusalka*'s wing was dark as a lake, the crushed grass sweet and soft. Fumbling around overalls—was anything less designed for lovemaking than overalls? Nina had enough coherence left to wonder. Everything felt unfamiliar, intoxicating. Yelena had such smooth skin, an endlessly curving spine like a string of pearls, what seemed like a kilometer of ivory-pale waist. It should have been awkward, a dance they didn't know, but it wasn't at all. They were a perfect pair in the sky, moving like one—they could move like one down here on the ground, with the protective shadow of the camouflaged U-2 hiding them from sight, and the distant noise of ground fire and antiaircraft guns hiding any stifled, curlew-soft sounds of pleasure. *My pilot*, Nina thought, her hand stroking over Yelena's hip. *Mine.*

"Dawn," Yelena whispered eventually. "We should get back."

"Don't want to." Nina yawned against Yelena's arm.

"We have to, rabbit." Kissing Nina's temple. "Tonight we fly."

Nina opened her eyes to the pinkness at the east. She already wanted stars again, wanted darkness, wanted night. Wanted the night to wrap up the three of them, herself and Yelena and the *Rusalka*, and send them to do what they'd been born to do. Nina sat up, feeling her lips curl in a smile. "I can't wait."

Chapter 19

JORDAN

Thanksgiving 1946
Boston

Jordan sat in the red glow of the safelight, flipping the Leica's shutter back and forth. Even the darkroom smelled of burned turkey. *I'm not crying*, she told herself. But her breath hitched from time to time, and even the familiar embrace of the darkroom was no comfort. Perhaps upstairs Anneliese was sobbing and Jordan's father was consoling her and Ruth was wondering why her very first Thanksgiving was not happening, after all. And at some point Dan McBride would come down here and say—

Jordan flinched. The crumpled look on Anneliese's face, the destroyed hunch in her shoulders as she fled the dining room . . .

I was right. So why do I feel I got it all wrong? Jordan's thoughts flickered back to the photographs, the Iron Cross, Anneliese's dead father and his tattoo and the incriminating date, then she caught herself looking back at the image of Anneliese fleeing the dining room, studying it clinically, for signs of lying. Of putting on an act. A bone-deep wince followed: *Haven't you done enough?*

Round and round. Photographs and so-called proof and a ruined holiday. The only thing she knew for certain was that she was no longer sure of the case she'd put together. No longer sure of anything at all.

Finally it came—the sound of the darkroom door opening. A light switch flicked, the red glow of the safelight drowned in the harsh glare of white overhead bulbs, and then there was her dad, coming down the steps. Jordan made herself face him, putting the Leica aside. She met his gaze, knowing her face was already twisting up, but she couldn't stop it. He didn't look angry. She might have braced herself against anger. He looked exhausted, sad, disappointed. A look that made her shrivel inside, because she'd rather die than disappoint her father.

"Anna's finally sleeping," he began. "I've scraped together some dinner for Ruth. Do you want any?"

"No." Jordan's stomach was roiling so hard, she didn't think she'd ever eat again.

"I don't know what to say." He sounded so weary, so defeated. "I don't know how to—fix this. I'm sorry I didn't tell you more about Anna, that she'd changed her name. It's my fault."

"It's not your fault. She's the one who lied, Dad," Jordan managed to say. "To you, and to me. Even if everything she said was true about *why* she did it, she still lied."

"She did. I won't say I'm not angry with her. It was very wrong. But she's *sorry*, Jordan. She was crying her eyes out upstairs, saying it over and over." His voice was thick. "People have reasons to lie, to hide things. Since the war I see refugees in my shop every week, selling their last antique brooch or bit of silver—men with names they've obviously changed, women holding children who don't look anything like them, people making excuses for their scars or their accents. Every week I see people who were ashamed of what they did in the war, or what their friends did. War makes *millions* of people like that. Yes, she was wrong to lie. But that doesn't mean I don't understand why she did it. That I don't still love her."

It wasn't like her dad to speak so frankly, so emotionally. *He's hurting*, Jordan thought. *He's hurting so much.* "So you believe her?"

He spread his hands, helpless. "What's more likely, missy? That she has a father and a name she's too ashamed to claim, and a child who isn't hers? Or that she's some kind of Nazi schemer out of a Nuremberg headline?"

"I never said that!"

"You said she was dangerous." He spoke gently. "You said she could be anything, a murderer. You say she lied to cover up something terrible; she says she lied to cover up something she was *ashamed* of. Now, we've lived with her for months. We know her. She's never been anything but good to you, and to me she's been everything I could possibly . . ." He paused, swallowing. "We *know* her, Jordan. So I ask you: Which explanation is more likely? That she's dangerous? Or just ashamed?"

Jordan's eyes spilled over then. She stood with tears streaming down her face, not even trying not to sob. Her father put an arm around her shoulders, pulled her against his side. He still sounded defeated. "I don't blame you for wanting answers. You were right to ask. I just wish you'd—come to Anna about it differently. Willing to listen, as well as question."

"I didn't mean it like that," Jordan managed to say. "I was just— following what I saw." *And you did see something*, she thought, *but so what?* Her dad was right; she'd looked immediately for the worst explanation possible.

Jordan and her wild imagination. Where had it gotten her? Here, watching her father struggle so painfully with his disappointment.

"Maybe I should have sent you to college, after all," he said. "Anna was all for it. She said it would help you grow up, get your head out of the clouds. But I was hoping so much that you'd want to take the shop over from me. You and Garrett both, maybe. It was only a curio junk-room when I took it over from your grandfather, I wanted to make it into something special for you. A real future . . ."

His voice trailed off, but not before Jordan heard the naked hurt. The note in his voice of *why isn't it good enough, what I made for you?* She felt like she'd been kicked in the stomach.

"I don't know how to fix this," he said again, and she could see he was close to tears. Her rock-solid father, who had never shed a tear before Jordan in his whole life.

"I'm the one who needs to fix it." She let her head drop on his shoulder. "I'll—I'll apologize to Anna when she wakes up. I'll make it right with her, I promise."

"She'll need to make it right with you too. She needs to be more forthcoming with you, and she and I will talk about that." He kissed the top of Jordan's head. "You're my girl, and you were looking out for your old dad. I know that." He turned away, toward the stairs. He wanted to hide the tears in his eyes, Jordan knew. He couldn't bear for her to see that. "I should put Ruth to bed."

As he tramped up the stairs, Jordan could see the first touches of gray in his hair.

GARRETT ANSWERED JORDAN'S KNOCK, framed by the doorway. Jordan's eye automatically composed the shot, but she had no camera, and anyway, his smile fell away when he saw her face. "What's wrong?"

"Everything." Jordan chafed her cold hands together; she'd run out of the darkroom straight into a cab, no coat or gloves. "I just needed to get away from home for a little while."

Garrett steered her in, past a dining room littered with pie plates. Jordan smelled pumpkin pie, cinnamon, coffee. Garrett's father was half asleep behind a newspaper; he bid a sleepy hello, and Garrett's mother came out of the kitchen wiping her hands on her apron.

"Jordan dear, you look like you've been crying. Family squabble? These things happen at holidays. Every Christmas I swear this is the year I'm going to scratch my cousin Kathy's eyes out if she makes one more condescending remark about my cranberry sauce. Let me get you some cocoa . . ."

Soon Jordan and Garrett were sitting with whipped-cream-topped mugs in his bedroom, door left ajar after Mrs. Byrne's habitual twinkling "Don't get into any trouble, you two!" Garrett swept the pieces of a half-finished model airplane out of the way.

"The Travel Air 4000," he said, self-conscious. "I know model kits are for kids, but it's the plane I learned to fly on when I joined up . . . What happened, Jor?"

"I've sent my stepmother into hysterics and possibly destroyed my father's marriage," Jordan said. "How's that for a Thanksgiving squabble? I'd rather have someone scratching my eyes out over cranberry sauce."

Garrett tugged her into his chest, and Jordan inhaled the comforting smell of cocoa and model airplane glue. He didn't interrupt while she blurted out the rest. Garrett never tried to offer advice when anyone was upset, just hugged and listened. "What are you going to do?" he asked when she was done.

"Grovel to Anna, hope she forgives me." Jordan wiped her eyes on his green sweater. "You never believed my crackpot theories about her, did you?"

"You're not one of those girls at school always making things up, Jor. You're not crazy. You saw clues. Maybe you were wrong about what they added up to, but that doesn't mean they weren't there."

"No, I *was* right—Anneliese was hiding something. But I was jealous when Dad wanted to bring her into the family, as much as I didn't want to admit it, and that made me more interested in my theory that she was dangerous than the possibility that there might be another explanation. A harmless explanation. So I ended up hurting everyone." The humiliation stung red-hot. *I haven't really come very far from that little girl who told herself her mother had gone away to become a movie star because that was a better story than the truth.*

"Look on the bright side," Garrett said. "Your stepmother isn't some sinister Nazi, just a nice lady who makes *punschkrapfen*."

"I was so stupid." Lurking around her darkroom linking up dramatic theories, thinking she was so clever and observant. Thinking she was J. Bryde, future Pulitzer winner—what a *joke*.

"It'll blow over," Garrett said, sounding helpless.

"I have a lot of making up to do." *And you'd better get started,* Jordan told herself. *Because face it: you're not going to be the next*

Margaret Bourke-White or Gerda Taro. You're just an idiot girl who thought you could see like a camera, and all you ended up doing was hurting everyone you love. But you have a good family, if you don't ruin things with them, and a good future. So go home, and start being grateful.

"I should get back," she said, setting aside her cold cocoa.

"I'll drive you."

But they ended up pulling over halfway there, Garrett pulling his Chevrolet coup up next to the river when he saw Jordan was crying again. Because she was remembering that first photograph of Anneliese, the photograph that had started everything, wondering how that feeling had been so wrong—that surge of swift, sure recognition, of *knowledge*. Knowing that she had taken one of the best pictures of her life, knowing that in it she had seen something hidden and true and important. But it was all wrong. She hadn't seen anything at all.

"Come here," Garret said, kissing her in the dark car by way of comfort, his warm lips tasting like cocoa. Jordan twined her hands tight around his neck, squeezing her eyes tight shut. In a few more minutes she'd have to go back home, face her dad again, start forming an apology for Anneliese, but not yet. Garrett was pulling her collar open; Jordan hesitated a moment, then slipped the buttons of her blouse all the way down, and pulled his hands around toward the clasp of her brassiere. She could feel his surprise—this was where they usually stopped—but Jordan pulled him close for another kiss, and he gave a soft groan and tugged her hands under his sweater. If it had been a warm summer night, Jordan thought, they probably would have gotten on with it, right there with the sound of the slow-moving Charles River going by outside. But it was November, freezing cold, and the honks of holiday traffic sounded nearby, and eventually they pulled apart, breathing hard.

"Um," Garrett said, fumbling to do up his belt. "I didn't mean to, um. Push you—"

"You didn't," Jordan said, even though it wasn't what girls were supposed to say. Boys pushed, and girls scolded them. "I'm the one who pushed," she added, though girls weren't supposed to say that either, much less *do* it. But she didn't feel guilty, sitting here doing up her brassiere in the front seat of Garrett's Chevrolet. She wished it were warm enough to just move to the backseat and keep going, keep kissing, keep putting off the moment where she'd have to go home. She looked out at the moonlight on the Charles and pushed away a surge of dread. "I should get back now."

"Yeah," said Garrett, and he dropped his head for another long kiss. He took Jordan's hand and guided it, not under his sweater this time, but to his other hand, where she could feel the hard, cool lump of his college ring. "I wish you'd wear it," he whispered. "You know I'm serious about you."

"Okay," Jordan heard herself say. Because why not? It was the next step. She'd wear his college ring for the next few years, a placeholder for the step after that: the real ring that would come at some point during his senior year, after which the next step was a June wedding. His parents would be delighted. Her dad would be delighted. *I was hoping so much that you'd want to take the shop over from me*, he had said. *You and Garrett both, maybe. A real future.*

"Okay," she said again, and it felt fine.

Chapter 20

IAN

May 1950
Vienna

On the first of May, Ian jogged down the stairs from his tiny apartment to the center office below, only to find his wife already sitting in his chair.

He stopped, still doing up the buttons on his shirt. "I locked the door."

Nina made jimmying motions, lowering the paperback she was reading. Something lurid called *Regency Buck*. Ian looked at the open door, handle now dangling loose. *She reads romance novels and breaks locks*, he thought. *Just what every man wants in a wife.* "What are you doing here?" he asked, turning back his cuffs and going to work on the door. It had been a few weeks since she and Tony stormed out, and Ian hadn't heard from either.

"Tony is sorry," Nina said. "He wants to apologize, the things he said."

"So why are you here and not him?"

"He says you are Achilles in your tent and he waits till you come out. I tell him he's a stupid *mudak* and I will come instead, and he says Agamemnon sends Briseis and maybe that does it. I don't know any of these people."

"He's off his bloody head. I'm not Achilles, he's not Agamemnon,

and you're nobody's prize getting sent anywhere." Ian jiggled the door
handle back into place. "If Homer gave Briseis a razor, Achilles would
have died a good deal sooner."

"Who is this Homer?"

"He didn't write *Regency Buck*. Why do you read that tosh?"
Ian wondered, diverted. Razors didn't seem to go with romances.

"I come to library my first month in Manchester—need books to
learn about England, practice my reading. The librarian, she says,
'Georgette Heyer *is* England.' Is not much like the England I see, but
maybe is the war?" Nina tucked *Regency Buck* back into her jacket.
"Anyway, I come because Tony is sorry."

"We both said things I imagine we regretted." Ian wasn't surprised at the relief that loosened his chest. He and Tony had worked
together for years, after all; had been friends as well as partners.
Perhaps we still are. "I notice *you* aren't offering any apologies," Ian
couldn't help but observe.

Nina merely gave a long blink. *I kill her,* his wife had said of
Lorelei Vogt, so matter-of-factly. She meant it, she wasn't sorry, and
he'd be damned if he apologized either for throwing her out of his
office because of it.

Her eyes glinted as if she was reading his mind, and the hostility of their last encounter sparked the air for a moment. It wouldn't
take much to get it going again.

But Nina changed the subject. "Tony and I, we went to Heidelberg
for a week. We look for *die Jägerin*'s old university friends, student
records." A shake of the head. "Dead ends."

Ian had managed to put *die Jägerin* out of his head, mostly by
working twenty-hour days. He was the only one in the office now;
he had to take up Tony's share of the load. "Do you believe me now,
that pursuing her is hopeless?"

"We go to Boston anyway," Nina said. "Tony and me. Come
with us."

"I meant what I said." Ian leaned against the desk, looking down
at her. "I won't work with a vengeance squad. I won't work beside
you as you plan to kill her."

"*Bozhe moi*, don't be dramatic." Nina glared. "I want her caught, punished, dead, I don't care which. Tony, he says you are good at finding them. Tony and I try alone, maybe we fail—I don't know America, I hunt seals and deer, not Nazis. If you come, I promise now: we find her, I don't try to kill her."

"How do I know I can trust you?" Ian asked quietly.

"*Poshol nakhui, govno.*" Nina seized Ian by the collar and yanked him down to eye level, her blue eyes all but spitting knives. "Am *not* just a savage from the taiga," she hissed. "I am Lieutenant N. B. Markova of the Red Air Force. I make a promise and I keep it. *Blyadt*," she spat for good measure, shoving him back so hard he staggered. "Fuck you."

She reads romance novels, she breaks locks, and she's a lieutenant in the Red Air Force, Ian thought. *Just what every man wants in a wife!* He felt the strangest urge to laugh, not because he thought she was lying, but because . . . "Bloody *hell*, Nina. When are you going to stop turning my world on its ear?"

She planted hands on hips, glaring. "You come with us, I promise I do things like you want. Carrot, stick, no razor." *How boring*, her eyes said.

Ian didn't bother quoting the odds against their succeeding. Nina clearly didn't care what the odds of extraditing Lorelei Vogt were, and neither did Tony. "I know how much this chase pulls at you," he said instead. "It does me too. Tony said Lorelei Vogt was my white whale, and he's not wrong. But in *Moby-Dick*, everyone who hunts the white whale dies."

"I'm hard to kill. So are you—Tony tells me about the places you go in the war. Come to Boston."

"I have other cases. They are just as important as—"

"*Ian*," his wife said, his name in her voice bringing him up short. "You want the huntress. For Seb and for the children, you want her. I want her for Seb and for the children and for me. Is not just vengeance, is also justice. Can be both. Is not wrong if it's both."

She put out her hand, and the burning chill of recklessness raced across Ian's nerves again. Throw everything down because the bombs were coming closer and who knew what the odds were? Throw it all on the line. *You bring this out in me*, he thought, looking at his wife. The reckless side that had made him go to war with a typewriter instead of a gun, that risked everything for the right story, the right column. The right hunt.

This hunt goes on whether you join it or not, the voice of reason said. The one that refused to beat suspects, or be party to vigilante justice. *One way or another, she'll follow* die Jägerin. *If you don't go with her, who knows how the chase could end?* Nina certainly wasn't going to be held by any promise of clean dealing if he wasn't there.

He couldn't tell what this hungry swoop in his stomach was, if he was talking himself onto the right path or onto the wrong one. But with a coppery hunger, it was whispering, *Call me Ishmael.*

"Boston." Nina's small hand was still extended. "In? Or out?"

PART II

PART II

Chapter 21

NINA

September 1942
North Caucasus front

Night had fallen, and with it, the chase.

Ahead of Nina, Yelena was sprinting. Arms pumping, legs flashing, head lowered as she poured every last drop of strength into getting ahead of the crowd behind. One boot hit the *Rusalka*'s lower wing, and Nina's pilot vaulted straight up to the side of the cockpit, fist punching up toward the sliver of moon. "Too slow, rabbits! *Rusalka* claims first place on the runway!"

She was utter magnificence, crouched atop their plane on boot toes and fingertips like a cat. Nina's heart squeezed, even as a chorus of groans rose up from the other pilots running to their own U-2s in Yelena's wake. "God rot you, Yelena Vassilovna," Dusia Nosal gasped, reaching her own plane. "Long-legged cow—"

"I love you too, Dushenka," Yelena cooed, blowing a kiss as she dropped into the *Rusalka*'s cockpit, and Nina grinned, jogging behind with the navigators. First pilot to her plane every night earned the right of first takeoff, and Yelena had the longest legs in the regiment. Unless someone tripped her off the line (Dusia wasn't above sticking a boot out), the *Rusalka* had first takeoff five nights out of seven.

By the time Nina threw herself down into the rear cockpit, Yelena was already belted in and running checks. "Start up!" the call came from the ground.

"Starting up!"

"Swing prop!"

The propeller swung, caught, bit. The noisy little radial engine started up, sneezing smoke. The *Rusalka* rumbled out even as Nina was checking her compass and map. They'd only been in the mountainous region a few weeks, but this was a world different from the summer nights they'd flown at the southern front. Here in the Caucasus the winds could come screaming out between the steep mountain peaks and fling a U-2 into a cliff face in a heartbeat. And if the winds didn't get you, the heavy, gluelike mists might. Two U-2s had collided in one of those lethal mists last week. Only one survivor.

The lights along the field flickered on, marking a makeshift runway. So close to the front line, Nina could hear the crackle of not-so-distant ground fire and tracer fire, yet as soon as they lifted off there would only be the midnight-blue horizon stretching ahead, the endless blanket of stars. No clouds tonight, just a sliver of moon—a perfect night for flying. *Not for sleeping*, Nina thought with a wolverine flash of teeth as the *Rusalka* began to pick up speed under Yelena's hands. Their target was troop bunkers, every one packed full of German soldiers freshly arrived at the front. "Let's give the new boys a warm welcome, ladies," Major Bershanskaia had said in briefing that afternoon. Nina had looked around to see every *sestra* wearing the same feral grin. *No one sleeps tonight.*

The U-2's undercarriage lifted off the crushed grass, and the *Rusalka* soared. Nina's heart soared with it—no matter how many dozens of times she'd done this, it was always the same liquid-sweet catch at her throat. She took a moment to savor the icy rush of the air, and then it was back to business. Yelena was waiting.

"East a hair . . . aim for the southwest pass . . ." The *Rusalka* twitched to each of Nina's directions as she scanned the surrounding mountains. Some navigators relied on flares, pitching them over the side and setting course by the falling red glow, but Nina scorned flares. Map and compass, moon and stars were enough for her.

The first bombing run always passed in a flash. It was thirty minutes' flying before reaching the target, but it seemed like only seconds passed before they were descending through a wisp of cloud like silver veiling. "One minute," Yelena called, leveling out, and Nina went marble still. It was teeth-chatteringly cold up so high, autumn winds biting cruel and sere in the open cockpit, but whenever they lined up for a run, Nina flushed as warm as though she stood before a roaring fire.

The *Rusalka* hit an updraft, steadied. Then the world fell away into stillness as Yelena cut the engine.

That was the moment Nina loved best, when the U-2's nose dropped and she began her weightless glide downward. Like a *rusalka* plunging down into the glassy dark of her lake, Nina thought, webbed fingers catching the currents of the water as Nina's gloved fingers caught the currents of the air . . . Silent, invisible, undetectable, until far, far too late. Those yawning German soldiers below had no idea what slid toward them out of the night. *You're on our ground now, you stupid little boys*, Nina thought. *You have your Führer and your Fatherland, but we have the Motherland and she has us.*

"Six hundred meters," Yelena called. Nina poised her hand. A buzzing drone filled the wind as Yelena kicked the engine back to life; they were low enough Nina could see lights below, dark shapes of dugouts, German trucks. The instant they began to rise, Nina flicked the release. Their payload of bombs dropped into the black velvet night, Yelena already veering away from the searchlight that stabbed the sky seconds after the bloom of explosions below. The light hunted for them like a blind white finger, but Yelena had already jinked out of reach, finding the new altitude. Not three minutes behind them the next U-2 would be lining up, Dusia Nosal with her hatred-tautened face relaxing as she dropped her load in turn. And the next, and the next, and by the time every U-2 in the regiment had finished its first run, Nina and Yelena would be back on their second.

"First away," Yelena called through the interphones, satisfaction in every word.

"Well done, rabbit."

The *Rusalka* had barely touched down on the flattened grass before the first wave of ground crew came swarming out to service her. Girls in overalls jogged over with cans of fuel, armorers staggered under the weight of thirty-two-kilo bombs, mechanics crawled over propeller and engine by flashlight. Yelena twisted in her cockpit, reaching a hand back to Nina. "No ground fire," she said. "But they'll be wide awake next time."

Nina shrugged. "We've been holed before." There had been fierce nights on the southern front when the *Rusalka* had been so peppered by bullets that her linen-covered wings looked like a cheese after the mice got at it, yet she was always ready to fly by the following twilight. "Bullets won't bring down a U-2 unless they hit both of us. Even then, this bird could probably land herself." Nina squeezed Yelena's fingertips, a stand-in for the kiss they couldn't exchange in public, and swung out of the cockpit to the ground. A pair of armorers hunched over a bomb, one girl holding a flashlight for the other who squatted with gloves clamped between her teeth as she attached the fuse with fingers gone blue-marbled with cold, and Nina veered around them to go make her report inside. Major Bershanskaia always heard the first round of reports herself. "Good, Comrade Lieutenant Markova. Carry on." Nina saluted, gulped some tea that tasted of engine grease, and hurried back with a cup for Yelena.

"Drink up," she ordered, stepping onto the wing over the armorer lugging a bomb along on her knees toward the rack. Yelena drained the cup in one gulp, scribbling her signature on the release form a petite mechanic was thrusting under her nose, and in minutes they were circling for takeoff again. Behind them, the mechanics and armorers were already clustered around Dusia's U-2 like worker bees round a hive queen as Dusia slumped back in her cockpit and her navigator went trotting inside to make her report and bring her pilot some tea . . .

"Let's break our record tonight," Nina said as the mechanic gave the prop a swing. "Ten runs?"

"Ten," Yelena agreed as the engine's drone rose, and Nina could hear the elation in her voice. By the sixth, seventh, eighth run her voice would be blurry with exhaustion, but for the first few runs everyone was still bright-eyed. Once again the *Rusalka* leaped up into the diamond-sewn night, heading for the front line.

Will anyone die tonight? Nina wondered. The 588th had already suffered losses. Three just last week in that midair collision . . . But it was no use thinking of tracer fire ripping up through the cockpit, or the spiraling terror of a crash. There was a job to do. The first week of flying back in June, Nina and Yelena had managed four bombing runs per night. Now with the nights getting longer, Nina reckoned ten would be possible. And when the endless white nights of deep winter arrived, the nights when dark fell greedily on the day and gobbled it up like Baba Yaga eating unwary children, who knew what they might accomplish?

"How long has it been?" Yelena wondered on their sixth touchdown, gnawing on the cold biscuit Nina had grabbed inside. "Since we first started on the southern front?"

Nina had to think. The nights blurred together, the days even more. "Three months."

Yelena gave a jaw-cracking yawn. "Feels longer."

Those early weeks had felt like being flung into the deepest part of the Old Man with rocks tied to their feet. They took off for the evening's first run with the fascist line so close that Nina wondered if the airfield would be in German hands by the time they landed. Bombing the rolling columns of German tanks as they advanced, the pilots flew over fields of grain ripe to be harvested and saw flames leap along the golden rows instead of scythes as billows of wheat were converted into billows of fire rather than be left to feed a single German soldier. Black clouds roiled into the sky, and the regiment's U-2s touched down with smoke-blackened wings and red-eyed pilots to the news that the Fritzes had seized another town, another river, another city, one after another gone under the swastika. Hearing Major Bershanskaia's grim voice reading aloud from Order No. 227, direct from Moscow: "'It is time to finish retreating. Not one step back.'"

Not one step back? Nina thought, weighed down by exhaustion as heavy as a lead blanket. *Try that for yourself, Comrade Stalin. See how much you feel like advancing through those fields of burning grain.* Or through those piercing searchlights surrounding the antiaircraft guns, that feeling of being pinned and exposed like a butterfly tacked to a board. The first time they had been caught in a searchlight the *Rusalka* had sheared sideways, falling into a stall, and for a dizzying moment Nina had not known where the horizon was, only that she was blind and shells were exploding all around them. When her internal compass righted itself, she found herself screaming, *Flip, Yelena, we're inverted, FLIP*—and blindly Yelena rolled them right side up and they were out of the searchlights and lurching toward home. Nina hadn't been able to get out of the cockpit when they landed. Her legs simply refused to work. She sat there until they worked again, not really knowing what else to do, and then dropped out of the cockpit like a sack of turnips to stagger out, vomit matter-of-factly beside the runway, then make her report.

Face a barrage of antiaircraft guns, Comrade Stalin, Nina had thought when she heard Order No. 227, when it was read out that soldiers caught retreating were to be shot. *Then we'll talk about* not one step back.

Yes, it felt like a great deal longer than three months. Every night you came back, you thought of the ones who hadn't, like the three who had died last week when their U-2s collided in a muffling mist and two planes had shredded apart and spiraled to earth in pieces. Petals of burning flowers drifting through the air.

And yet, Nina thought. *And yet . . .* Every twilight the pilots and navigators gathered bright-eyed, bouncing on their toes as they waited to take to their planes. All of them tugging for the sky.

By the time the *Rusalka* returned from its tenth run, pink streaks of dawn showed and Major Bershanskaia called the halt. "Back to base airdrome, ladies." The U-2s lifted off again in a tired line, wagging wingtips at one another, heading like a row of geese for home.

Annisovskaia was home for now: a tiny Caucasus village in the Grozny region where the local secondary school had been commandeered and crammed with foldout cots. The local village women looked at them warily at first, but they were used to female pilots now, and a squat *babushka* lifted her gnarled hand as Nina and the rest trudged past. "Kill many Germans, *dousha*?" she asked Nina as she did every night, showing near-toothless gums in a merciless grin, and Nina called back, "Almost enough, Grandmother."

They trooped into the canteen, groaning at the sight of breakfast. "Stale biscuits and beets," Yelena said with a sigh, grabbing a plate. "Someday they'll feed us something different and we'll all fall over dead from shock before we get a mouthful."

"Hot kasha with mushrooms," Dusia said mournfully. "That's what I miss most."

"Borscht absolutely heaped with sour cream . . ."

"Raw cabbage," Nina said, making little nibbling noises like a rabbit, and they all laughed. "Someone wake up Zoya, she's face-down in her beets again."

No one, Nina had observed, was able to fall asleep right away after a night of bombing runs. It didn't matter if you were so tired that you'd been dozing off over the stick on your last run—as soon as you returned from the canteen to your cot, eyelids that had been stone-heavy flew up like untied window shades, and girls who had trudged off the airfield in yawning silence were chattering like magpies.

"—fell into a stall, I swear my wing clipped a shrub before I pulled up—"

"—updraft tossed us halfway to Stalingrad before Irushka got us leveled out—"

Nina skinned out of her overalls, flinging herself down on her cot. "Boots, rabbit," she called to Yelena, sticking her feet out. "I can't bend over."

"Certainly." Yelena curtsied, taking hold of Nina's right boot. "Does the *tsaritsa* require anything else?"

Nina wriggled her toes as first one boot and then the other came off. "A bucket of vodka."

"At once, *tsaritsa*." Yelena sank down on the bed next to Nina's and held out her own feet. "Word is we'll be staying in Annisovskaia a few months. Till the new year, even."

"Good. I'm tired of moving around, sleeping in dugouts." Nina folded her star-embroidered flying scarf over the end of the cot, the same scarf Yelena had been embroidering the night of the first sortie. Nina's pilot was working on another now, getting out her needles and thread. On the next cot over, a brunette from Stalingrad was mending her stockings; another girl was scraping mud off her boots. At the other end of the schoolhouse, four pilots had lined up for a turn at the only sink. Someone was softly humming. Someone else was crying, almost soundlessly.

"There they go again." Yelena contemplated her long slender feet in their wool socks, jittering as though they were being run through by electric current. Her knees jittered too. "I wish I knew why they did that."

Nina shrugged. After a night of bombing runs, everyone showed different effects. Yelena jittered for hours. Dusia went totally silent, curling up on her side and staring at the wall. Some of the girls chattered until they suddenly fell asleep midsyllable. Some cried, some paced, some jumped at the slightest noise—night to night, it was always different.

"You're made of rock, Ninochka." Yelena flexed her twitching feet. "You don't get any effects."

"I do." Tapping her forehead. "Always a headache behind my left eye."

"But you never get moody or weepy or snappish."

"Because I'm not afraid."

A curious glance came from the girl polishing her boots. "Never?"

Nina shook her head, matter-of-fact. "Only of drowning. You see any lakes around?"

"You're crazy," Yelena admired. "A little Siberian lunatic."

"Probably." Nina sank back on her pillow. "Markovs are all

crazy, it's in the blood. But it makes me good at this, so I don't mind being crazy."

Whether jitters or pacing or headaches were the postflight reaction of the day, everyone spent their morning working it off. It was always like that, Nina thought, massaging her own forehead until the faint ache receded. Gradually the shakers stopped shaking and the talkers stopped talking, until the room filled with the sound of sleep. For maybe as long as three hours, before sheer exhaustion wore away and everyone began tossing and turning—because the other constant that Nina noticed was that they all slept like shit. Even Nina. *Being a little bit crazy and mostly fearless does not help with sleep.*

It was in that sweet spot of dead, pure slumber when the entire room lay still as corpses that Nina swung out of bed and padded for the door, tugging her boots back on. She sauntered off toward a storage shed at the edge of the village and slipped inside, waiting. Brilliant sunlight made fingers of light through cracks in the boards, as though a dozen tiny searchlights were trying to find a dozen tiny planes. Nina watched motes of dust dancing in the light, half hypnotized, half dozing. Dust motes dancing like Yak-1s . . .

The shed door creaked open, then shut. There was the rattle of a board dropping down, blocking the door, and then Yelena's arms slipped about her waist from behind, and in a second's notice Nina was wide awake.

"Hello, rabbit." She tipped her head back against Yelena's shoulder. "Nice flying tonight."

"I hate getting caught in those searchlights." A shiver went through Yelena, and she pressed her cheek against Nina's hair. "That instant when I don't know which is sky and which is ground . . ."

"Just listen to your trusty navigator." Nina raised Yelena's oil-smeared knuckles to her lips. "I can always find the sky."

"You're wasted as a navigator, Ninochka. Nerves like yours, you should be flying your own plane."

"Then who's going to keep *you* out of trouble, Miss Moscow Goody?"

"I'm not such a goody anymore!"

"Then say *I hate those shit searchlights*." Nina could *hear* Yelena blush. "Say it, Yelena Vassilovna."

"I dislike those searchlights very much," Yelena said primly, and they both shook with silent laughter. They stood still a moment, Nina's head tipped back against Yelena's shoulder, Yelena's arms about Nina's waist. Nina felt the weightless floating sensation she felt when the engines cut out and she was gliding free and silent through still, pure air. "You're still trembling," she said, running her fingers back and forth over Yelena's twitching ones.

"It'll wear off in another hour. It always does."

"I can make it wear off sooner." Nina turned, tugging Yelena's head down for a kiss, pushing her back toward the shadowed back wall where she'd already tossed down her coat. Some days they were too exhausted to trade anything but a few drowsy kisses, but this morning their hands were eager, Nina's fingers helping Yelena's shaky ones with buttons, stray shafts of sunlight painting Yelena's ivory skin—skin that flushed pink as the inside of a shell as soon as Nina's hands slid over it. Yelena's head tipped back as Nina's lips traveled the insides of her elbows, the space behind her earlobes, the skin over her hip bones, the inside of her knee up toward her thigh, all the tender places that took her to pieces. Nina felt her pilot shatter, quietly, biting down hard on the side of her own hand to keep silent, and the last tremor went through Yelena, leaving those jittering fingers peaceful and still. "There," Nina said softly, and Yelena sat up and caught her in fierce arms.

"Come here—"

Yelena kissed as fiercely as she flew, but at first she had been shy. Under the *Rusalka*'s wing that first night she had blushed so hard she nearly glowed in the dark. "I didn't know girls . . ." She trailed off. "Did you?"

Nina shrugged. "You hear things." Mostly it was about men who used each other if there were no women—there had been some like that where Nina grew up. Pretty young women weren't that common by the Old Man, at least not in a village so tiny; men made other arrangements. Looking at things from a new angle, it seemed reasonable to assume sometimes women did too.

Not that anyone would talk about it, men *or* women. For men, Nina knew, getting caught buggering meant prison. For women, well, she wasn't quite so sure, but it wouldn't be good. An asylum, maybe. Getting booted out of the 588th, certainly.

". . . Have you?" Yelena's cheek had burned like a brand against Nina's shoulder, when she asked that first time. "Before me, I mean. Did you ever . . ."

"Sure," Nina said. "A few men at the air club."

"I never wanted to. I guess now I know why." A sigh. "Men wanted me and I never wanted them. Was it like that with you?"

"No, I like men fine." She remembered Vladimir Ilyich back in Irkutsk. He was a bonehead, but between the blankets he had made her toes curl. "There were one or two I liked a lot."

"Better than me?" Yelena had sounded anxious.

"No." Kissing her soundly. "Because no one flies better than you."

"Is that all you think about, Ninochka?" Yelena laughed, still blushing. "You don't bother even looking at someone until you know if they can fly or not?"

"Until I see they can fly, and that they're brave." Nina had paused, considering. *Was* there anything else, any quality that could possibly be packaged in human flesh, that was worth falling head over heels for? Courage. Flying skill. Those were the things that made her weak in the knees; those were the things she'd been pulled toward every time she made a move at someone else. It had always been men before because most of the pilots in the Irkutsk air club had *been* men. There hadn't been another woman in the air with verve and skill and guts to match Nina's own, so she hadn't even looked at them.

So maybe falling for Yelena wasn't hard to understand, after all. She was fine and fierce, keen and courageous, the best flier in the regiment. With a roll call of qualities like that, Nina would have lost her head over Yelena whether she was woman, man, or plant. To Nina it was exactly that simple and not worthy of any further thought, but Yelena tended to worry even now—the *why* of what had pulled them toward each other. "It isn't natural. It can't be," she sometimes brooded, quoting some speech or book Nina had never read. "'Women, as fully fledged citizens of the freest country in the world, have received from Nature the gift of being mothers. Let them take care of this precious gift in order to bring Soviet heroes into the world.' We're supposed to marry and be mothers and workers, above all have children. So this can't be right, what we do. Is it just the war, turning our heads inside out?"

"Maybe." Nina had yawned. "Who cares?" It was war: day was night, life was death, sorrow was joy. Who cared about anything but the now?

When they'd been on the southern front, they'd met at the back of the shop where mechanics stashed spare tools, and it had been warm enough to laze afterward skin against skin. Here in Annisovskaia it was cold enough for their breath to puff in clouds inside the shed, and they dived quickly back into trousers and coats. "We won't be able to meet outside much longer," Yelena said. She sighed, wincing as her shirt went over her shoulders. "You scratch worse than any rabbit! I should call you *kitten* instead."

"Something more dangerous than a kitten," Nina retorted. "And I'll find someplace warmer to meet." It was easier to steal time together than either of them had anticipated. Everyone was too tired after a night's flying to care if a fellow pilot sneaked out. No one raised an eyebrow if Nina and Yelena clasped hands as they walked to the airfield either, or if Yelena embroidered Nina scarves or Nina dozed with her head in Yelena's lap. The entire regiment traded kisses and hugs whenever off duty; gave each other presents and pet names. Time was too short not to show your sisters-in-arms that you loved them. Nina had seen other pilots sneaking off discreetly, who knew where to—perhaps private rendezvous with fellow pilots, or with the male ground crew from neighboring regiments.

Still, the two of them were very careful.

"You slip out first," Nina told Yelena. "I'll wait three minutes and come after."

"Nag," Yelena teased. "You're as bad as a mother."

"I'm worse. Because your mother told you to find a nice boy and get married, not go to war and become a pilot, and you didn't listen. But I'm your navigator, Comrade Lieutenant Vetsina, and unlike your mother, you have to listen to me."

Yelena snapped a mock salute. Her short curls were rumpled, and her cheeks as rosy as the little pink orchids that bloomed wild around the Old Man, poking their slippered heads up when the snow melted. Nina could hardly breathe, looking at her. *I want to hold you*, she thought. *I would fight the world off for you, Yelena Vassilovna*. It was something new, this tremendous wave of protectiveness. It wasn't like anything Nina had ever felt in her life. It clutched at her with something almost like fear.

Maybe she was afraid of two things, now.

Yelena blew her a kiss, slipping out. Nina waited three minutes and then sauntered after. When she slipped back into the dormitory, she could hear Yelena's soft breath already slowing toward a deeper rhythm. She'd sleep like a baby now, maybe as much as four hours. Nina wasn't far behind, dropping off the edge of wakefulness like a stone falling off a cliff.

"Up, rabbits! The Hitlerites aren't going to bomb themselves!" Major Bershanskaia's voice, obscenely cheerful. "Up, up, up!"

"Fuck your mother," Nina mumbled. "Fuck your mother through seven gates." Peeling open eyelids that had apparently been glued together with cement. "Fuck your mother through seven gates *whistling*." Bershanskaia was already gone to the next building, waking the next round of pilots. "One of these days I will cut her throat for being so damned cheerful, and then I will be stood up against a wall and shot, and it will have been *worth it*," Nina announced, tugging her blankets to her chin.

"Don't get shot, Ninochka." Yelena was already up and halfway into her overalls, as the room filled with yawns and rustles, the rake of combs through sleep-tangled hair. "I don't want to break in a new navigator, not when you know exactly how I like my tea."

"Stone cold and tasting like motor oil?"

"Exactly." Yelena yanked back the blankets, making Nina yelp and fly out of bed. "Up, up, up!"

"I'll cut your throat too, Yelenushka," Nina warned, yanking her shirt over her head and tucking her razor's cord around her wrist. Yelena had a pistol in her cockpit like most pilots, but Nina never went into the sky without her razor.

Another monotonous meal, the sun tilting toward the ground. As they headed for briefing, Nina saw trucks being loaded with armament and cans of fuel. The trucks would rumble out toward the auxiliary airfield closer to the front lines, the U-2s following by air. The ladies of the 588th crammed together to hear Major Bershanskaia give the daily update. Tonight's target was a bridge used by the Germans to ferry supplies and wounded. Maps were passed out; Nina's fingers flew over the sketched terrain.

"Comrade Major," one of the pilots called when the briefing wrapped. "I stalled last night on the fourth run and practically scraped grass by the time the engine kicked in. It was low enough I heard shouts coming from the Germans as they ran for cover."

"What did they shout?" Nothing to Bershanskaia was unimportant; her eyes were the sharpest Nina had ever seen. Their stocky no-nonsense commander might not have Marina Raskova's heroic glitter, but Nina was fairly sure she'd cut off a leg for Bershanskaia too. Even if she did want to slit her throat every day for being so damned cheery in her wake-up calls. "What did they shout, Comrade Lieutenant?"

"'*Nachthexen*,'" the pilot quoted. "before the engine drowned them out."

Bershanskaia pronounced the word silently. So did Nina. *Nachthexen*. One of the other pilots spoke up, the one who had been a language teacher before the war.

"'Night Witches,'" she translated.

They were all still for a heartbeat. *Night Witches*. For some reason Nina thought of her father, drunk and furious out on the frozen banks of the Old Man.

What's a rusalka, *Papa?* a little girl had asked him, never dreaming that one day she'd be flying through the sky in a plane called by the same name.

A lake witch, her father had answered.

And later on the streets of Irkutsk: *I can track wolverines, girl. You think I can't track my lake witch of a daughter?*

Sky witch now, Nina had retorted.

Maybe not.

Not quite a sky witch, or even a water-bound lake witch. Something else. Something new. Nina looked around at the ladies of the 588th, all of them that made up something the world had never seen before, and saw smiles tugging lips, flashes of teeth showing in private, pleased grins. *Night Witches*.

"Well," one of the navigators said at last, "I like it."

A burst of laughter, and Major Bershanskaia clapped her hands. "To the field, ladies."

A line of U-2s took off into the darkening sky for the new airfield, little better than an old turnip patch. The pilots hopped out, making way for armorers and mechanics. Everyone bounced on their toes, eyes on the sky. Exhaustion forgotten, hunger forgotten, shakes and shivers and bad dreams forgotten. The moon was rising, a plumper crescent than last night. Nina sniffed the night wind, heady and mountain scented, setting her blood on fire like a river of gasoline. Yelena tensed, ready to run, eying the *Rusalka* across the field.

Bershanskaia gave the chop of her hand that silenced all conversation. "Ladies, to your planes," she usually said. But tonight it was "*Nachthexen*, to your planes."

And they were all sprinting for their lives, sprinting for their planes, laughter crossing the lines in a fierce ripple. Yelena rode the crest in front, and Nina was bursting a lung somewhere in the middle of the pack. Twenty-four hours had turned like a wheel and here they were, back on the conveyor belt. Somewhere up ahead Yelena cried, "*Too slow, rabbits!* Rusalka *first!*" A few heartbeats later, Nina caught the wing and went flying into her cockpit.

And one by one, the Night Witches took to the air.

Chapter 22

JORDAN

Jesus, Jor." Garrett laughed as he jumped down from the cockpit of the little biplane. "I thought you were going to try and climb *out*."

"I can't believe you trained for war in a plane like this. It's cloth and plywood!" Jordan swung a leg carefully over the edge of her own cockpit. "I wonder if any of my shots will turn out. Trying to focus through goggles and wind shear . . ."

"I haven't seen you snapping away like that in a while." Garrett lifted her down from the wing.

"I've been busy. And it's not like I'm going to make a career of it." That used to be a bitter thought, but Jordan supposed all dreams hurt when they finally withered up in the glare of real life. What was the point in toting a camera everywhere, taking classes, sinking hours into photo-essays that no one would buy? She had a shop to work in, a sister to help look after. A wedding to plan.

"Mom wants to talk to you about flowers for the church," Garrett said as though reading her mind, chocking the biplane's wheels. "She wondered what you thought about orchids."

"Um." Jordan didn't have any opinion about orchids, but as a bride-to-be, she supposed she'd have to acquire one. Last Christmas Garrett had replaced his college ring with the expected diamond—a pear-shaped stone on a gold band, dainty and pretty. The thought of a fall wedding after Garrett graduated had seemed safely distant, but the ring had been the first pebble in a landslide as plans started falling into place with alarming speed: a September ceremony, a honeymoon in New York, Ruth in pale pink gauze as flower girl. Jordan's little sister was ecstatic. Everyone was ecstatic.

Jordan pushed off thoughts of orchids and centerpieces and raised the Leica, snapping Garrett beside the plane. "We'd better get back. I'm opening up the shop at one." The little airfield sat northeast of Boston: a crumbling business that hung on, Garrett said, by renting out its small collection of outdated biplanes for flight instruction, crop-dusting, and joyrides. Jordan returned to the car, and as Garrett squared things away with the mechanic, she tried fluffing her hair in the rearview mirror. When she had turned twenty-one last June, she'd decided it was time to swap the schoolgirl ponytail for something more adult, but now she wasn't sure the hairdresser had done her any favors. "We'll take some of the length off," the woman enthused, "then curl the back. You'll look just like Rita Hayworth in *The Loves of Carmen*. Did you see that one, honey?" But the Rita Hayworth effect required a lot of pins and curlers, and however much Jordan twirled and tugged in the morning, a good breeze had the whole dark-blond mess lying limp as a dishrag.

Whack it all off and top it with a beret like Gerda Taro, the long-smothered voice of J. Bryde whispered—the part of Jordan that still had silly daydreams about trading her pin curls and crinolines for a sleek leather trench and heading for New York with the Leica over one shoulder. But Jordan put that thought back where it belonged, turning to Garrett as he jogged over. "When can we come back? This was fun."

"Whenever you want." He hopped in over the driver's-side door. "I've been working here, every other Saturday. Pat—Mr. Hatterson, he owns the place—he's on the ropes. I put in a couple days a month, give the weekend joyriders a few loops and spins, and Pat pays me in flying time." A quick glance. "It doesn't scare you, me flying? Mom says it gives her the shivers now that I have my license. She keeps saying I already broke one leg flying, and a man who's going to be married soon needs to think of his family."

"Fly all you want when we're married," Jordan proclaimed, using the word she usually managed to avoid. "It doesn't bother me a bit."

Garrett leaned over and gave her a good, long kiss. "You're quite a girl, you know that?"

"I do know that." Jordan leaned forward, murmuring into his ear. "Do you still have that blanket in your trunk?"

She should feel him grin against her cheek. "Yep."

"Anywhere around here a girl and her fella could get lost?"

"Yep."

Shortly after the college ring had been traded in for its half-carat cousin, Jordan had decided a different kind of trade-in was in order. *You once wanted to travel the world with a string of European lovers in tow*, she thought. *At the very least, you can graduate from making out in the backseat of a Chevrolet coup.*

It was with a certain amount of snickering now that they drove off in a spin of tires and dust, not back toward Boston but farther past the airfield, down a smaller dead-end road. Garrett got the blanket out of the truck, bowing elaborately toward the trees. "After you, miss."

"Do you have—" Jordan tried her best to be a woman of the world, but she wasn't quite past euphemisms when it came to what her girlfriends in school had always just called *those things*. "You know."

Garrett patted his wallet. "I was a Boy Scout, remember? *Be prepared*."

"I hope this wasn't in the Scouts' manual."

"If it had been, I would have paid a lot more attention to my Scoutmaster . . ."

They found a thick stand of trees and brush, well out of sight of the car, then spread out the blanket and tumbled onto it. The first time they'd ever done this (four months ago, in an apartment borrowed from a friend of Garrett's) Jordan had expended considerable thought on exactly how one got from fully dressed and kissing to naked. Given all the fastenings on everything that the New Look required for a woman to look fashionable, there didn't seem to be any graceful way to take everything off.

"Here's my sister's copy of *Forever Amber*," her friend Ginny had advised, handing over a dog-eared volume. "I took it from under her mattress. Ten descriptions of women undressing in front of men, according to the attorney general of Massachusetts."

"He was paying awfully close attention considering he said the book was obscene," Jordan had observed.

"He also noted there were seventy references to sexual intercourse. I only found sixty-two, but I was reading in a hurry before my sister missed it."

In the end, *Forever Amber* hadn't been terribly useful. Undressing hadn't been problematic, after all; there hadn't turned out to be any art to it, as long as clothes hit the floor as fast as possible. It had all been awkward, but even if there weren't any waves of bliss, there had been lots of laughing, enough to ease them both past anything uncomfortable. And it hadn't hurt horribly, which some of her girlfriends said was the case. Maybe neither books nor girlfriends should be relied on for sex advice, Jordan reflected now, squirming away from a twig poking her back through the blanket as Garrett stripped his shirt off. Girlfriends, if they knew more than you, said completely conflicting things ("Men just like it better than us" or "It's wonderful when you're in love!") and books either said nothing at all (the hero and heroine disappeared into some all-encompassing ellipses) or promised automatic, vaguely worded ecstasy.

Still, this had to be the seventh or eighth time, and she and Garrett had things nicely worked out. A lot of pleasant rolling about on the blanket, sunlight dappling Garret's hair as he lowered his head to kiss along her collarbone, then a brief fierce tangle of limbs and gasps and sweat, and they broke apart smiling.

Jordan sat up, reaching for her blouse. "Garrett," she said, laughing as she looked over one shoulder. "Do *not* fall asleep."

"I won't," he said, eyes closed, stretched out on the blanket.

"You are." She planted a kiss on his ear. "Put some clothes on! I've got to open up the shop."

He sat up, yawning. "Anything you say, Mrs. Byrne."

"Don't say that till September, it's bad luck." Jordan straightened the diamond sitting on her knuckle, watching it sparkle in the tree-filtered sunshine. It looked so dainty, but it was a heavy bit of rock. Who knew a half-carat ring could weigh down a hand like a boulder?

THE BELL OVER the shop door tinkled not ten minutes after Jordan flipped the sign to Open, ushering in a harried-looking woman blotting her forehead. "Welcome to McBride's Antiques, ma'am. May I offer you some refreshment?" She poured ice water into a long-stemmed Murano goblet, proffering lemon wafers on an Edwardian calling-card salver. During winter it was peppermint wafers and hot tea in flowered Minton cups. *Customers like to feel welcomed*, Anneliese had said. One of her quiet notions that had made its way into the shop to good effect, or at least Jordan assumed it was to good effect considering how much more stock her dad had been buying. "There's no reason you can't be the most prosperous antiques dealer in Boston," Jordan's stepmother often said.

"We do well enough as it is," he pointed out, but Anneliese kept quietly making suggestions, and neither Jordan nor her father could deny her instinct for the little things that turned a profit. She never took shifts behind the counter—Jordan's father was proud that his wife didn't have to work—but she had her own ways of helping.

The first customer walked out with a japanned tray and a Georgian table clock, and the bell tinkled again almost before the door closed behind her. Jordan's welcoming expression became a smile as Ruth raced in, blond plait bouncing on the back of her school jumper. "Hello, cricket."

Ruth flung her arms around Jordan in a hug—eight years old now and a little chatterbox, not the silent big-eyed scrap she'd been at four. *My sister*, Jordan thought with a squeeze of love, and it was true now: Ruth Weber had become Ruth McBride. "Can I look around?" The shop was Ruth's treasure box, her favorite place in the world.

"*May* I look around," Anneliese's voice sounded. "And yes, you may."

Jordan greeted her stepmother with a smile. The smiles between them had been awkward ones for a while—the Thanksgiving after that first horrible one had not exactly been a tension-free evening, everyone knowing exactly what everyone else was thinking as they chewed on their turkey, but thank goodness that was all in the past. Jordan hugged Anneliese now, inhaling her sweet lilac scent. "How do you always look so cool and collected?" she demanded, taking in the spotless gloves and the crisp cream linen suit that looked like it had come from the pages of *Vogue* and not Anneliese's Singer. "I'm as rumpled as an old mop."

"A young girl looks all the better for a little *dishabille*. Middle-aged matrons like me have to settle for being tidy and presentable." Anneliese fished in her pocketbook, producing a fabric sample. "Look at this lovely yellow cotton. I was thinking a sundress for you—"

"Better for you, I look like a cheese in yellow."

"You do not. When am I ever wrong about clothes?" Anneliese smiled. Three and a half years ago she'd received Jordan's flame-faced apology only to offer a teary one of her own—they'd cried a little on each other's shoulders, and never referred to it again. These days whenever Jordan thought about that Thanksgiving, she gave a deep, sincere flinch at her own stupidity and wondered, *What was I thinking?*

"What brings you in?" Jordan went on. "You never come to the shop during business hours."

"Dan wanted the auction catalog for his trip tomorrow. He marked a set of Hope chairs—"

"Maybe this will be the last buying trip for a while." Jordan's dad seemed to be whisking out the door every other week these days, off to New York or Connecticut in one of the crisp herring-bone suits Anneliese had chosen for him. He didn't put in many hours behind the shop counter anymore, or in the back room where the restoration work was done. Jordan now managed the counter on most days, and in the back room—

"Is Mr. Kolb working today?" Anneliese tucked the auction catalog into her pocketbook.

"Here, Frau McBride." The door to the back room opened and a frail-looking man with puffs of gray hair above his ears popped out—he always came in early, well before Jordan opened up. "I vas expecting you." Mr. Kolb's English was so thickly accented, it had taken Jordan weeks to understand him. "The Hepplewhite table, she needs varnish . . ." He launched into technicalities, mixing German and English. He'd come to the shop a year or so ago, another refugee with the waves arriving from Europe after the Displaced Persons Act, badly rumpled in a cheap suit and flinching visibly whenever a stranger addressed him.

"You won't find anyone better to help with restoration," An-neliese had told Jordan's father when she proposed they sponsor Kolb's entry to the United States. "Old books, old documents; those are his specialty. He had a shop in Salzburg when I was a child. I'm so glad I had the thought of looking him up."

"He can't take the counter, with his English so poor. And he's very jumpy."

"He had a bad time during the war, Dan. One of the camps . . ." Anneliese's voice had faded to a discreet murmur, and the little German had been ensconced in the back room ever since, always with a peppermint in his pocket for Ruth and a shy smile for Jordan.

"English, Mr. Kolb," Anneliese reminded him as he lapsed into German. "That dealer you told me about, the one who decided to settle in Ames . . . ?"

"Yes, Frau McBride. Final payment made."

"Excellent. Did he pass that letter along for me to Salzburg?"

"Yes, Frau McBride."

"For a woman I used to know there," Anneliese told Jordan. "I'm hoping she might consider coming to Boston. I was so lucky to get here, make a new life. I'd like to help others like me do the same." Her English was perfect now, no trace of German accent—if anything, she'd begun to drop her R's like a real Bostonian. She looked so delighted whenever anyone assumed she was born and raised here, she never corrected them. She'd even lopped the second syllable off *Anneliese* when she took American citizenship; Anna McBride was how she introduced herself now.

Jordan's father came in, looking cross. "New Yorkers," he muttered. "Clogging up the street, not knowing how to *park*—"

"How is it that all tourists who can't park are automatically New Yorkers?" Jordan teased.

"I know Yankee fans when I see them." He dropped his hat on the counter, looking dapper in the suit he'd wear to the train station this afternoon. "Anna, did you tell Jordan about—"

"I knew you'd want to." Anneliese smiled. "Ruth, come into the back while I talk to Mr. Kolb."

Jordan's little sister ignored her, standing transfixed by a brooch in the display cabinet—a little wrought-silver violin to be worn on some music-loving woman's lapel. "Can I have it?" she whispered.

"Certainly not, Ruth. It's far too old and valuable."

"But—"

"Don't be greedy, it's an unattractive quality in children." Anneliese bore Ruth off to the back, and Jordan looked back at her father.

"What is it, Dad?"

"Just some wedding plans. Anna wanted to take you shopping for a dress."

Jordan adjusted the diamond over her finger again. Picking a wedding dress . . . That seemed like a very large step. Very *final*. She blew out a breath. "I put myself entirely in her hands. We'll even take pictures at the fitting."

"Get a picture of her while you're at it. You know how she's always ducking the camera."

"Mmm," Jordan said. Unfortunately, the best picture she'd ever taken of Anneliese was still that first one, the shot in the kitchen with her head half turned and her eyes as sharp as razors.

"I wanted to talk to you about a wedding present." He fished a little box out of his pocket, turning pink around the ears. "To wear on the big day—'something old,' you know . . ."

"Oh, Dad." Jordan touched the earrings with a fingertip: gold-feathered art deco wings with big pearls swinging below.

"Lalique, 1932. Rose gold settings, freshwater pearls." He shuffled a bit. "Your birthstone. A good smart girl like you, who picked yourself out a good smart man and a good smart future—a daughter like that deserves pearls."

Jordan hugged him, throat thick as she inhaled his aftershave. "Thank you."

He squeezed her back. "All this wedding talk, flowers and dresses—we haven't talked about afterward, the important things. If you want to keep house for Garrett, or if you want to keep your hand in here at the shop."

Thinking about *after* the wedding was almost impossible, like the crest of a hill she couldn't see beyond. She knew Garrett's father had spoken to Garrett about helping them with an apartment and then a house; she knew her father had probably been part of that discussion too, though no one had talked to her. But exactly how life alongside Garrett was going to continue after the honeymoon was still in many ways a question mark. "I know I want to work," she said firmly.

"Well, take some time after the honeymoon. I'll put up a Help Wanted sign this week, look for another clerk. Some suave fellow or pretty girl to work the counter; Mr. Kolb hasn't got the English for that." Jordan's father hesitated, fingering his suit's lapel. "Anything ever strike you about Kolb, missy?"

"Like what?"

"I don't know. He always looks furtive anytime I come in to check on the restoration work. And with his English so patchy, I can't ask him anything but the simplest questions. Of course Anna translates anything tricky." A pause, looking toward the backroom door where Anneliese and Ruth and Mr. Kolb had vanished. "I just wondered what you thought, working around him more than I do."

The last thing Jordan was going to do was make wild speculations about *anyone*'s past. "I'm sure it's just his nerves, Dad. The war, you know."

"Does he bring people into the shop? Not customers, I mean bringing people into the back."

"Not that I've noticed. Why?" The afternoon sun was coming through the window strong and golden, highlighting her father beautifully. Jordan moved for her camera, stashed behind the door. "Stay right there—"

"I came up here one day and Kolb had another German fellow in the back room. Older, a Berliner, didn't speak a word of English. Kolb went off in a babble, I could just about get that it was a rare books expert he'd brought in to consult."

"He has experts in sometimes." Jordan checked her film, lifted the Leica. "Anna gave him permission." *Click.*

"That's what she said. I just wondered. You have to be careful in a business that attracts swindlers." A shrug. "Well, Kolb does free me up, even if he makes me twitch sometimes. I want to tell him to relax before he frets himself into a heart attack."

"You're the one who never relaxes!" Jordan lowered her camera. "You promised you'd take an afternoon's fishing at the lake this spring, and you haven't been once."

He laughed. "I'll go soon, missy. I promise."

The backroom door opened then, and Anneliese's dark head reappeared. "Does she like the earrings?"

"She does." Jordan grinned. "Did you help pick them?"

"Not a bit." Anneliese shut the door on Mr. Kolb in the back room, Ruth peering at the broken-spined book he was repairing. "I thought next Saturday we might shop for a wedding dress? I may be able to stitch up a chic sundress, but wedding gowns are beyond me. I saw one in the window at Priscilla of Boston, empire princess silhouette, seed pearls—"

"I think I've picked which weekend I'm going to the lake," Jordan's father decided. "Suddenly I fancy tramping after some spring turkey."

"You hunt turkey." Anneliese gave Jordan a woman-to-woman smile. "We ladies shall hunt French Chantilly and petal-drop caps. I for one know which hunt will be the more ruthless."

A week later, Jordan was standing in the lavish fitting room at Priscilla of Boston on Boylston Street when the news came. Swathed in ivory satin exploding into a huge bell of a skirt, turning her head to feel the Lalique pearls swinging as Anneliese waved away the salesgirl trying to suggest ruffles: "My stepdaughter is not a *ruffles* sort of bride." Turning to tease Anneliese with some *mother-of-the-bride* joke, thinking how glad she was that the two of them could laugh and tease each other now. That was when Jordan saw Anneliese's eyes go toward the door, where a man in a dark suit stepped forward.

"Mrs. Daniel McBride?" Waiting for Anneliese's nod. "The clerk at your shop said you could be found here. It's about your husband."

Jordan stepped off the dressmaker's dais, feeling ivory satin pool around her feet. Her eye was taking pictures in jerky little snaps. The man in the suit, looking uncomfortable—*click*. Anneliese frozen still, face draining of color, a Chantilly wedding veil dropping from her hands—*click*.

The man cleared his throat. "I'm afraid there's been an accident."

Chapter 23

IAN

May 1950
Aboard the SS *Conte Biancamano*

I t was the first leisure Ian had known in years. Sitting in the cinema
lounge of the great ocean liner, nothing to do but watch the parade
of passengers in dinner jackets and sequined evening gowns, cigarette smoke and jazz swirling together in idle seduction, dark water
of the Atlantic sliding past outside. *Enjoy it*, the ship seemed to
whisper. *A little lotus-eating time before the chase begins in Boston.*

"I'm so bloody bored I could jump over the rail," he said to his
companion.

She grinned: a tall lanky woman in her fifties, loose trousers and
boar-tusk ivory bracelets, a faint stammer, and mangled-looking
hands that drew stares. "Another d-drink?"

Ian inspected his tumbler. "No, thank you."

"What happened to the stories I heard about you drinking
Hemingway under the table?"

"It got rather old."

"So will you, and then w-what will you have to show for it?"

"Fewer hangovers, Eve. Fewer hangovers."

Ian frequently reflected that the greatest advantage from a life
spent hopping all over the map trying to catch the next war was that

he never knew where he'd meet an old friend last seen in a Spanish airdrome or a Tunisian bar or the deck of a French troopship. His last encounter with Eve Gardiner had been during the Blitz in London, seeing her shake glass slivers out of her hair in the middle of a bombed-out pub. Everyone else ran for an air-raid shelter when the alarm went off, but Eve kept right on reading the Dispatches from London column. "*It's their good humor that surprises me,*'" she read aloud as Ian trailed back in after the raid. "*How this city can paste a smile on its collective face and still get to work more or less on time*—' Miss Ruby Sutton writes a good column. You've got your work c-cut out for you, Graham. Try to live up to all this good press and trundle off to work with a smile, won't you?"

And now here they were drinking scotch in idle luxury, bound for the United States. Behind him was bleak, bombed Vienna with the temporarily closed-down center; ahead was the new chase. Here there was limbo, and an old friend met by chance.

"It's been good bumping into you, G-Graham." Eve finished her drink, rising. "I'd stay, but I've got a tall colonel in my c-cabin who keeps me from getting b-bored on ocean crossings."

"Is that the secret of surviving shipboard travel?" Ian rose, gave her a kiss on the cheek. "I should have packed an army officer."

"You packed a Russian anarchist." Eve nodded across the cinema lounge where Nina's blond head was coming through the crowd. "Is she a p-pilot?"

"I have no idea. Why?"

"I saw her check the sk-sky the moment she went on deck. All fliers do that. How do you not know if your w-w—your wife is a pilot?"

"It's complicated. Would you like an escort back to your cabin? I'd hate to think of you running into a drunken passenger on a dark deck."

"I have a Luger P08 at the small of my b-b-b—my back, Graham. If a drunken passenger gives me any trouble on a dark deck, I'll just sh-shoot him."

Eve disappeared into the throng. "Who is that?" Nina said, throwing herself into the chair Eve had vacated.

"An old friend." Ian looked at his wife, speculative. "She says you're a pilot, Lieutenant Markova."

"Yes." Nina's brows rose. In her patched trousers and boots she stuck out from the sleekly dressed crowd like a barnacle, but she didn't seem to care. "How does she know?"

"She used to do something unbelievably vague in British intelligence, and people like that are rather good at observing things. Tell them good morning, and they know your occupation, your birthday, your favorite novel, and how you take your tea. What *is* your birthday?"

"Why?"

"Because I know your occupation, Comrade Lieutenant Markova, and I know your vile predilection for jam in tea and historical romances, but I have no idea what your birthday is. On the marriage certificate, I believe I made something up."

"March 22. Born a year after the revolution."

She'd have turned thirty-two not long ago, then. "I owe you a birthday present, comrade."

"*Die Jägerin*'s heart on a stick?"

"I've heard marriage meant the surrender of hearts, but I didn't think quite so literally. And *no*," Ian added.

Nina snorted. "Is Antochka coming to join us?"

"That Milanese divorcée he cozied up to two nights ago still hasn't let him out of her cabin." It had made for easier sleeping arrangements: Nina kept the tiny cabin assigned to Mr. and Mrs. Graham while Ian bunked with Tony. Ian had wondered at first if that would be awkward, given the quarrel they'd had in the Vienna office, but Tony made no reference to it and they'd fallen back into the old camaraderie. Ian was still grateful when Tony began staying with the Italian blonde with her mink and her scarlet fingernails. The cabin class reservations that were all they were able to afford on the May installment of Ian's annuity were not roomy.

"Is your fault we waste time on this boat, you know," Nina was complaining. "If not for your damned fear of heights, we fly this distance, much shorter time. I fear water, but you hear me complain about this boat?"

"Yes," Ian said. "You've been complaining about this boat since Cannes."

"I still go on it. You can't get on a plane, you're too sensitive? Western milksop. No one in Soviet Union is *sensitive*."

"Clearly," Ian answered, grinning.

"*Mat tvoyu cherez sem'vorot s prisvistom.*"

"What does *that* mean?"

"'Fuck your mother through seven gates whistling.'"

"Bloody hell, woman. The mouth on you . . ."

They gave up their table and wandered out on deck. A cool night, faint light on the ocean from a waning quarter moon. Nina looked at it, glaring. "I hate quarter moon."

"That's rather random," Ian observed.

Silence. Her face had grown taut.

"Did you see the ceiling frieze in the great hall on this ship?" he asked, watching her. "Jason and the Argonauts, setting off for the golden fleece. The original no-chance-we'll-find-it hunt. But they found it. Perhaps we'll find our golden fleece too."

"I don't want to talk," Nina said abruptly.

"All right." Ian lit a cigarette and leaned on the rail, looking over the water. Slowly the crowd thinned, trailing off to bed. Nina's profile was bright against the darkness, rather lovely. *She's designed to be looked at by moonlight*, the thought went through his head. Normally he'd have brushed that bit of whimsy aside, but now he stood at the rail of the vast ship thinking that he had never kissed his wife and realizing in a sudden visceral tug that he wanted to. She was a Russian whirlwind who stole his shirts and put her boots on his desk, but under the stars she looked like she was made of silver.

Goddammit, Ian thought, half angry, half amused. He had no wish to be attracted to a woman he would soon be divorcing. Yet here he was, flicking his cigarette into the water below and saying, "Would you slit my throat if I were to kiss you?"

Nina's eyes came down from the quarter moon overhead, dark with some old remembered pain. It took her a moment to focus on Ian. "Never mind," he said quietly, and began to turn away, but she reached up, yanked him down to eye level, and nailed her mouth against his. It wasn't a kiss, it was a hurricane. Her strong fingers laced around the back of his neck, her ankle hooked his knee, and Ian found himself burying his hands in her hair and yanking her hard up against him. He felt her compact form almost climbing up his as her teeth scored his lip. He bit at her right back, drinking the taste of her like ice and salt and violence. His wife kissed like she was trying to drink his heart through his throat.

"Bloody hell, woman," he managed to say, heart pounding. "The mouth on you . . ."

She regarded him coolly, as if they hadn't just nearly ravaged each other against a deck railing. "I don't want to talk."

He could still taste her, like the icy burn of vodka electric in his throat. "I don't either."

They dragged each other back to the tiny cabin booked in the name of Mr. and Mrs. Graham, which Ian hadn't set foot in. *Is this a good idea?* he thought.

No, he answered himself promptly. *But I don't give a damn.* Banging the door shut, he picked up his wife and kissed her again.

"*Chyort,*" she muttered, wrenching at his shirt as they toppled onto the bed. "What are you doing?"

"Confiscating your weaponry." Ian tugged the razor out of her boot top. "I know better than to take an armed woman to bed."

"You have to fight me for it." She gave a mock snarl like a wolverine, her strong limbs coiling and twisting through his. She was half laughing and half angry, at herself or at him he didn't know, but she was nearly throwing off sparks of heat and fury as they kissed and struggled and clawed to get closer. There were enough buried sparks of his own anger to meet hers, the banked antagonism of the quarrel in his office flaring into a different kind of fire as he roped her hair around his hand and pulled it tight, and she left the marks of her teeth in his shoulder even as she wrapped her legs around his waist. The razor came partly unfolded and nicked Ian's arm before he got it away from her.

"I know how to fight, you Red Menace." Ian hurled the razor across the cabin and kissed her again, drinking down her bone-buckling taste of ice and arctic wind, blood and sweetness. Her nails raked his back, and he sank into her like he was sinking into a head-wind, blown and tossed and dizzied by chaos.

The first thing she said afterward was, "We still get divorce."

Ian burst out laughing. They were both still breathing hard, sweating, sheets and skin lightly dappled with blood from the cut on his arm, which he still didn't feel even remotely. "I'd say this rules out nonconsummation as grounds."

"This is—" Nina hunted for a word, muttered something in Russian. Squirming away from his side, she set her back against the foot of the bed facing him, scowling. Ian's flare of anger had burned out, but she was still crackling and sparkling, all wary prickles in the dark. "We're on the hunt. We search, we fight, the blood is up, we screw. Is all it is."

Ian leaned forward to run a hand over the smooth curve of her leg still tangled with his, down the strong arch of her calf. She had a tattoo on the sole of her foot, he saw with fascination; some spiky Cyrillic lettering. Шестьсот шестнадцать. The visceral tug toward his wife that he'd felt at the deck railing hadn't gone out, it had only gone deeper. He curved a hand around her ankle. "If that's how you want it, comrade."

"Is." She looked fierce, and he wondered what she was remembering. What memory she'd pushed down when she dragged her eyes away from that quarter moon and dragged him down for a kiss instead.

"Who were you thinking of when you kissed me?" he asked, running his thumb over the Cyrillic on her small foot.

She looked him in the eye. "No one."

Liar, Ian thought, even as he tugged her back toward him and kissed her scowling mouth. *What's going on in that head of yours, Nina? Who are you?* He still had no idea, only that the answer was growing more complicated rather than less.

Chapter 24

NINA

This makes thirteen," Yelena called on ascent. By now they were accustomed to deciphering each other's words through the tinny interphones. "Take the stick."

Nina took over, shivering even in furred overalls and mole-fur flight mask. Nothing kept you warm in an open cockpit under a frozen moon. *Better than the armorers*, Nina told herself. They worked bare-handed even in the dead of winter; they couldn't attach bomb fuses through bulky gloves. They were losing fingertips, laboring with blank, stoic faces and bandaged hands as blue as wild violets, but they weren't slowing down. With more than six months' practice under their belts, the regiment had turnaround down to an art: a U-2 could land, fuel, rearm, and take off again in less than ten minutes. "It's counter to regulations," Bershanskaia had admitted, "but it's our way and it works."

Nina saw Yelena's head loll in sleep, up in the front cockpit. In these long winter shifts where eight runs per night stretched to twelve or more, all the pilots and navigators had started sleeping in shifts. Generally Yelena dozed on the way out, and Nina on the way back. *Better that than risk us both dozing off at once.* Sleep was the enemy on the long winter nights; sleep the seducer luring you to doze off and fall out of the sky.

Nina battled yawns until the target showed below. "Wake up, rabbit," she called to Yelena, rapping gloved knuckles on her pilot's head. "Dusia's lining up." Bombing headquarter-designated buildings was always hell; the searchlights and the ground fire were twice as fierce.

"I'm awake." Yelena shook her head to clear the cobwebs, then took control again and dropped them neatly down behind Dusia's U-2. Nights like tonight they flew in pairs: Dusia would blaze through first, flinging herself sideways as shells ribboned into the sky in pursuit . . . and the *Rusalka* came floating silently behind while searchlights and guns were busy. Yelena slid the *Rusalka* neatly under the one questing searchlight that didn't dive after Dusia's U-2, lining them up in perfect darkness. Nina triggered the bombs, and Yelena looped around.

"Nod off, Ninochka," she called through the interphones. "I'll wake you on the descent—"

But she broke off as the plane rolled left, fighting her efforts to level out. Nina swore, leaning out over her cockpit and suddenly very, *very* awake. "Bring us around! There's still a twenty-five kilo on the rack."

All traces of weariness bottomed out of Yelena's voice. "Can you see it?"

"Yes. Last bomb didn't drop."

Yelena was already taking them back out wide, past the target into the darkness. Nina caught a flash glimpse of the next U-2 lining up to descend, pilot probably wondering if they'd lost their bearings. No time to worry about that. Nina toggled the bomb's release, but nothing dropped. "Stuck fast. Level out on the straight, and throttle back."

"Why?" Yelena called even as she fought the plane's left-leaning roll, applying opposite aileron and stick to take them flat and steady. Nina unclipped her safety harness. "Ninochka, what are you doing?"

"Giving it a push," Nina said reasonably and stood up.

"Nina Borisovna, get back in the plane!"

"Keep just over stall speed," Nina overrode her, "and *steady.*"
Then she slung a leg over the side.

The airstream was rigid and icy as a current of water, knifing down
her sides as she put one boot and then the other on the lower wing.
Her body locked in the chill of the wind, and her teeth set up a chatter.
Nina clung, gloved fingers clamped around the lip of the cockpit, for a
moment utterly unable to move. It wasn't fear, she was just frozen as
though swallowed in ice. The wind was a malevolent bitch, wanting
to scoop her off toward the ground floating past eight hundred meters
below. She'd spin turning and turning through the wisps of cloud, and
Yelena wouldn't be able to do anything but watch . . .

Move, night witch. Her father's voice. Nina clamped her clattering teeth, then slithered her body along the lower wing between
the wires. The *Rusalka* wobbled and for a moment Nina wondered
if she was going to slide into the void, but Yelena steadied them.
Inching along the wing, feeling the slipstream's icy lingering hands
run across her back, Nina swatted blindly below but couldn't feel
anything. Peeling one glove off with her teeth, she fumbled at the
bomb rack, bare fingers sticking painfully to the frozen metal. Naked skin at this altitude felt like it had been set on fire, not dipped in
ice. How long before her fingers stopped working altogether? Nina
yanked at the unseen rack, more imagining the bomb's release than
feeling it, the wing shuddering beneath her. If they hit a mountain
updraft while she was clinging here one-handed, she'd get flung off
like a fishing line sailing into a lake . . .

Something pinched her fingers and gave way. Nina saw the bomb
drop silently into the dark. Pity to waste it on what was probably
a barren hillside. She slid back along the wing, then levered herself
upright and tipped almost headfirst into her own cockpit. The wind
seemed to give a spiteful, cheated hiss when she dropped out of reach.
Yelena's voice squawked out of the interphones, and Nina clawed hers
back in place.

"We can turn around," she told her pilot through chattering
teeth, and then, "*D-dammit.*"

"*What?*" Yelena shouted.

"I dropped my glove."

"Is that all you have to *say*? Climb out on my wing again and I will tip you fucking *off*, you little Siberian lunatic!"

"You s-swore."

"What?" Yelena was bringing the plane around now.

"You swore, Miss Moscow Goody." Nina tucked her ungloved hand under her armpit. Her teeth were clacking, but she still managed a grin. "Yelena Vassilovna, you swore!"

"Go to hell," Yelena said. A second later, through the interphones, a stifled laugh.

Nina leaned back, sleep already cooing in her ear again, telling her to close her eyes. "Where are we?"

"South of target."

"Right." The sky was already lightening; it was nearly dawn. "Adjust north-northeast and we—"

The shots came from nowhere, ripping down through the U-2's wing with a flat brutal sound like steel punching cardboard. The dark shape zipped overhead even as Yelena yelled "*Messerschmitt*—" and hurled the plane down. Nina twisted in the cockpit, staring wildly past the *Rusalka*'s tail, mouth paper dry. They had never tangled with German fighters, only antiaircraft guns. It had disappeared into the dark, but the Messers were so fast—too fast to match a U-2, which sailed along so slowly that any fighter would stall out trying to match speed. It would have to keep making strafing runs.

Another screaming pass, another line of fire tearing down one wing. If Nina had still been lying along that wing trying to pry a bomb off the rack, she realized, she would have been stitched the length of her spine.

The *Rusalka* lurched as Yelena took her into a straight dive. Not enough cloud to hide in, Nina knew, and evasive maneuvering took fuel—at this point they'd burned too much while circling to drop the final bomb. *Land and scatter*, those were Bershanskaia's orders for such occasions. *Land and scatter, ladies; they won't pursue you on the ground.* Already the *Rusalka* was careening downward at two hundred meters.

Shot down, Nina thought with curious clarity, *we are being shot down*. Better than burning in the air as the fuel line ignited—better than crashing with so many broken bones that it was nothing but a slow death hanging in your cockpit. Having to land and scatter left you a chance. "Field," Nina heard herself shouting into the interphones. Where was the Messer? "Field, thirty degrees right—"

Yelena saw it and brought the nose around. *Shot down*. The others would set Nina's and Yelena's breakfast dishes out at their usual places, waiting for their return. It was what the 588th always did when a U-2 failed to come back. Two days, maybe three, and only then did the plates stop being set, when no one could pretend it was still likely you'd come limping in alive . . .

The Messer swept overhead like a dark kite, firing another burst. Yelena dropped the U-2 from two hundred meters to a hundred to fifty, the fastest, roughest landing Nina had ever seen her pull off. Another heartbeat and wheels bounced on frozen winter earth.

"OUT," Nina bellowed, kicking free of her safety harness for the second time this flight. Yelena was already clawing free of her cockpit, cheeks burning crimson; their boots hit the earth at the same time. Some kind of rough field, shadowed scrub all around. The day was coming cruelly fast, pale light flinging their shadows in front of them. A flat chopping sound rose and the Messerschmitt came back around, painted swastikas flashing like spiders.

They reversed and bolted for the scrub, Nina never feeling more like a rabbit sprinting for cover. Lines of bullets crossed the field, and Nina wasn't even aware she'd flung herself flat—she just found herself on the ground, arms clamped around her head as puffs of soil jumped around her. She had no idea if she'd been hit or not. She felt nothing but the roar in her blood.

The plane passed overhead. Nina's ears rang. She dragged herself up, heart flipping in sudden panic as she saw Yelena's long form stretched on the ground ahead of her, but then Yelena's head turned. "Ninochka—" she gasped, and they were both up, stumbling for the scrub. They crawled in, and when the sound of the Messer's engines droned overhead again they froze, clamped together, Nina's face buried in Yelena's shoulder, Yelena's in hers.

The Messer made another pass over the field.

"Wait," Nina breathed.

They muffled the cold cloud of their breath in star-covered scarves. Another droning pass, another stipple of bullets.

"If the Germans capture us," Yelena whispered, "promise you'll kill me."

"They're not going to capture us."

"If they do—"

"Stop!"

A third pass.

"You know what they do to women pilots. They'll rape us and murder us." Yelena's whisper rattled faster like hailstones on a roof. "And we'll be branded traitors for allowing ourselves to be taken—"

"We aren't traitors. We followed orders—"

"No one sees it that way if you're caught." Yelena's breath hitched. "I left my pistol in the cockpit."

"Sshh!"

"If they catch us, cut my throat with that razor, Ninochka. Promise."

Yelena's face, white as frost now with terror, the most precious thing in the world. "I love you," Nina whispered. She cupped her bare hand and her gloved hand around Yelena's cheeks. "I love you, and I will kill you before letting the Fritzes get you, if that is what you want." *Anything you want. I love you enough for anything, even that.*

Yelena squeezed her eyes shut, gulping. Nina pulled her closer. The drone of the Messerschmitt's engine retreated.

They waited.

"Your heart's beating steady as a drum," Yelena whispered. "You aren't even afraid, are you?"

"No. Because we're safe. No one ever catches a *rusalka*, much less a pair. We slip through their hands like water."

Yelena buried her face in Nina's fur overalls. Nina stroked her hair, looking at the sky overhead. Icy stars winking out with the coming day. *So cold.* She closed her eyes and saw the turquoise water of the Old Man rising up to meet her, and then her eyes flew open with a jerk.

"You started to doze," Yelena whispered. "Waiting to see if you would be strafed to death by a Messerschmitt, you actually *dozed off.*"

"It's been a long night." Nina stretched her hearing out as far as she could listen. No buzz of engines, no thump of bullets. "Can we risk it?"

"We'll have to. It's almost day."

"They could be lying in wait—"

"We'd have heard them land."

They made their way out of the brush. So strange to be on the ground, snow crunching underfoot, strange hills and jagged trees unfamiliar against the horizon. Up in a plane you forgot what it looked like down in the middle of things. Life was either a cockpit or a set of interchangeable airdromes and runways.

Yelena let out a long breath. "If the *Rusalka*'s wrecked, we'll have to walk back."

"Then we walk back, like Larisa Radchikova and her pilot last month." They'd bailed out in the neutral zone and made it back walking through the active line, both of them sliced head to toe by shrapnel.

Nina and Yelena held their breath as they came back to the *Rusalka*, canted drunkenly in the middle of the field. The wings were so holed they looked like a screen. Yelena went to inspect the engine, while Nina hopped up to look into the cockpits.

"Well, we still have an engine." Yelena's voice floated up as she poked her head among the wires. "And a propeller . . . most of it."

Nina surveyed the mass of splinters where the instrument panels used to be. "We have controls. Not much else, but we each have a stick."

"All a U-2 really needs is a stick, an engine, and a pilot." Yelena reclaimed her pistol, standing back. "I'd rather trust the *Rusalka* to get us home than try to walk it." They had no way of knowing if this was German territory or not; they could walk into their own troops or into a nest of Fritzes.

Nina joined her in staring at the propeller. A third of the blade was missing on one side. "Knock a third off the opposing blade to equalize it?" Nina said at last. "It's already bullet riddled; we could break the end off without tools."

Yelena looked a little white, but nodded.

Nina tugged her down to eye level. "Yelenushka. Are you all right?"

Her pilot managed another nod. Nina wasn't sure she believed her, but nodded back. They worked as fast as they could, bashing at the propeller blade until they could get it evened up with the shortened one; Nina gave the prop a swing to get it going as Yelena coaxed the engine to life, and fifteen minutes later they were airborne, rising sluggishly after a takeoff twice as long as their nimble little plane normally needed. "We need height," Nina called as they wobbled along. She felt naked, flying in daylight. At least it was deep winter, when dawn looked more like deep blue twilight. Yelena brought the *Rusalka* up, the engine groaning as though mortally wounded. *It's just a flesh wound*, Nina told her plane. *A few days in repairs, and you'll be good as new.*

"I meant what I said." Yelena's voice sounded tinny, and Nina didn't think it was the interphones. "If we ever get shot down, I'd rather you kill me than be taken captive."

"No one's getting shot down. We're almost home." Twenty minutes at most.

"He could still be back there. The Messerschmitt."

"He's not back there."

"He might have lain in wait till we got back in the air—"

"He's not there!"

No reply. Nina could see Yelena's shoulders moving as she breathed in unsteady gulps. The *Rusalka* wobbled along, jolting

Nina back and forth in her cockpit like a nut jumping in a frying pan. *A frying pan full of hot oil*, she thought, and then thought at least the nut would be warm. She could still feel sleep hissing in her ear, that terrible urge to close her eyes and drift. *Go away, you dense night-slut*, Nina told sleep. *We're a hair from going down in a ball of flame.*

The dense fog of night was thinning. "Airdrome should be below," Nina called. "Correct fifteen degrees east—" The night's flying would long be over, but the girls would still be there, eyes on the sky. They always waited when a plane was late.

A flare blossomed, red and welcome: *Here is the runway*. Nina let out a long shaky breath in relief, and that was when Yelena shouted and threw the U-2 sideways.

The *Rusalka* shrieked as though she'd been gored. She shook so violently Nina thought the wings were going to shear off. "*Yelena*—"

"He's lining us up—" Yelena's voice came through the interphones, rising higher and higher. "I see him ahead—"

"It's just landing flares." Nina clawed free of her safety harness, the *third* time in the last hour. "No one's firing."

"He's firing on us—" The *Rusalka* gave a sickening shudder, nose dropping. "We're hit—"

"We are not *hit*. You're hallucinating." It had happened to other pilots; overstrain conjuring danger from nowhere, landing flares becoming enemy fire. Lunging forward over the broken remnants of windscreen, Nina grabbed for Yelena's hair where it escaped her flying cap. She yanked Yelena off the controls, bringing her head slamming back against her seat. "*Stop!*" Nina roared, grabbing with the other hand for her own stick. Her ungloved fingers were so numb she couldn't feel it. She gave a blind yank, and the engine sputtered. The *Rusalka* flattened out from her lurching spiral, fighting Nina with everything it had. She didn't dare let Yelena go; if her pilot clawed the stick back and sent them into one more spin, this poor wounded bird would stall out. Nina muscled the nose down, still standing in an awkward crouch half in and half out of her cockpit, one hand anchoring her pilot and one gripping the stick for dear life.

Her entire shoulder screamed with the effort of bracing the descent. The *Rusalka* dived toward the ground, bounced hard enough to rattle every tooth in Nina's head, then flung her forward over the shattered windscreen. A white-hot sliver of agony bolted through her forearm, but Nina didn't care, they were on the ground, rolling safe across frozen earth, and Yelena was all right. She was crying out—*I'm sorry, I'm so sorry*—and she wouldn't be saying that if she were still hallucinating in panic.

Nina sagged back in her seat, pain stabbing her arm, drenched in sweat, shivering all over because the sweat droplets were already freezing on her damp skin. She couldn't feel her right hand, and it wouldn't come loose from the stick, but that didn't matter. They were on the ground. Muzzily, Nina patted the U-2's shattered instrument panel. "Good girl." The world tilted.

In the thirty seconds it took for the flood of waiting pilots to reach the *Rusalka*, Nina was unconscious.

"WHO ARE THEY giving you to navigate?"

"Zoya Buzina," Yelena answered. "Her pilot's down with a bullet through the knee. Ground fire."

"Zoya Buzina?" Nina glowered up from her bed. "The redhead from Kiev with the buckteeth?"

"Don't sulk, she's good!"

"Not as good as me." Jealousy pricked Nina, seeing Yelena head off to fly with someone else while she lay in bed. Two weeks grounded, just because a shard of windscreen went through her forearm! "If she doesn't bring you back without a scratch, I'll knock her buckteeth down her throat."

That got a laugh from Yelena. The dormitory was empty besides the two of them—Nina fuming on her cot, arm in a sling, Yelena perched at the other end in her fur overalls. The others had trooped out for the evening's briefing. "Keep the hole in your arm warm," Dusia had said, ruffling Nina's hair. "Matches the hole in your head, you crazy rabbit." They all made jokes, but over sympathetic eyes. They all understood how much it hurt to be forbidden the air.

Yelena took a deep breath, and Nina braced herself. "I nearly killed us both—"

Nina leaned forward and kissed her, warm lips lingering in a cold room. "Stop that, Yelena Vassilovna."

"For an instant I thought the landing flares were lights from a Messer. I *knew* they weren't but it looked so real for a moment. I couldn't stop—" A shudder went through her. "If I'd thrown us into one more spin—"

"You didn't."

"Because you banged my head off the seat." Yelena tried to smile, but her eyes were more shadowed than ever in her narrow face. *When did you get so thin?* Nina wondered, a lurch in her stomach.

"You had a panic, Yelenushka. A hallucination. Everyone has them." Even the best pilots, the best navigators. It was just a question of whether a moment's panic was fatal or not.

Yesterday, for them, it was not. As far as Nina was concerned, that was an end to it.

"You didn't tell Bershanskaia," Yelena said. "If she'd known, she might have grounded me too."

"You need to get back in the air." Nina knew her pilot down to her fingertips, every last doubt and worry. "You stay on the ground even one night, you'll brood. Get in the air, fly ten good runs with no mishaps, and you'll be right as rain. Now go join the others, before Bershanskaia notices."

Another kiss butterfly light across Nina's lips, and Yelena was gone. Nina thumped back against the pillow, staring up at the ceiling. She closed her eyes, but all she saw was Yelena in a borrowed U-2, taking off into the night sky without her.

Are you sure she's all right to fly? the thought whispered.

NINA STRUGGLED OUT of her cot at dawn, making her way to the airfield past a notice for a Komsomol meeting (*Mutual Help in Combat Is the Komsomol Member's Law!*). The U-2s had returned; they were already being covered over with camouflage drapes. Nina grabbed the nearest of the ground crew. "Where's Yelena Vetsina?"

The girl turned, red-eyed, her lips trembling. Nina suddenly realized that the entire field was hushed, ground crew working with hunched shoulders. From somewhere, she heard the choked sound of someone weeping. The quarter moon above was disappearing into a beautiful dawn, but the world had telescoped into something nightmarish.

Nina heard her own voice and couldn't tell if it was a roar or a whisper. "What happened?"

Chapter 25

JORDAN

May 1950
Boston

To you, O Lord, *we commend the soul of Daniel, your servant . . ."*

Dan McBride's coffin was covered with lilacs and roses. It was the lilacs that smelled strongest, wafting up into the warm spring day like someone had smashed a bottle of perfume. Jordan's throat tightened in nausea. Who ordered a huge wreath of lilacs for a coffin, like a hoop of sickly purple tissue paper?

"In the sight of this world he is now dead; in your sight may he live forever . . ."

In fact, Jordan thought, eyes roving blankly over the flower-heaped coffin, over the bowed and black-hatted heads around the graveside—who decided flowers had to be heaped on a coffin in the first place? Her father's coffin should have been heaped with fishing lures, scorecards from Red Sox games, flasks of his favorite scotch. Jordan should have dragged down the Minton dishes that they had used for Sunday lunch as long as she could remember and lobbed each plate one by one to go *smash* on the coffin's lid . . .

"Forgive whatever sins he committed through human weakness, and in your goodness grant him everlasting peace . . ."

Peace, Jordan thought. *Peace*. What good was that to her dad when she didn't have it, when Ruth and Anneliese didn't have it? He was the hub of the family, the one who *brought* peace. They were still standing grouped together around the place where he should have stood: Anneliese a step away as though standing on his right arm, a slender column in black, a swathe of netting descending over her face from the brim of her black hat; Ruth trembling on what should have been his left side, hand in Jordan's. "It's almost over, cricket," she managed to whisper, as the priest intoned, *"We ask this through Christ our Lord"* and a ripple of *Amen*s echoed. Followed by a ripple of another kind as the coffin was lowered down into the earth.

I lied, Ruth, Jordan thought of telling her sister. *It's never going to be over. This day is going to last forever.* After this would be the graveside condolences, then the somber drive back to the house where cake and casseroles, whiskey and coffee would be served. More condolences and reminiscences and dabbing of handkerchiefs, everyone wanting to know *what happened*, everyone wanting the details, *such a tragedy*. How many times today were Jordan and Anneliese between them going to say it? *A hunting accident. No, no one's fault. His shotgun exploded . . .*

"Did your father look after his own weapon, miss?" the policeman had asked Jordan that day in the hospital corridor—Anneliese had been too upset for questions, frozen beside her husband's bed, listening to the rasp of his breath.

"Yes." As long as she'd gone to the lake with him, Jordan could remember him wiping down his shotgun, cleaning it carefully before hanging it back on the wall. "It was my grandfather's. He treasured it—he never let it go back on the wall in less than pristine condition. How did it—"

"The problem wasn't the shotgun, miss, it was the ammunition. It looks like he bought smokeless powder shells—with an old LC Smith twelve-gauge like he had, Damascus barrels, that soft old steel shreds apart if you use the newer ammunition. There are plenty who don't know that, I'm afraid. The rounds *look* alike, and people just don't realize. Did he buy his ammunition himself?"

"Always." Jordan fiddled with a crooked hook and eye at her waist. She'd torn herself out of that ivory bridal gown at the boutique and back into her summer dress so quickly, all the fastenings were crooked. "I don't shoot, and Anna doesn't either."

"Then he either bought the wrong variety or didn't realize the newer kind wouldn't suit his shotgun. I've certainly seen it happen before." A sympathetic glance. "I'm very sorry, miss."

Everyone was *very sorry*.

"*Eternal rest grant unto him, O Lord*," Father Harris finished at last. Jordan joined the unison reply. "*May his soul and the souls of all the faithful departed, through the mercy of God, rest in peace.*"

Amen.

"SUCH A TRAGEDY, Jordan dear. In the prime of his life too!"

"Yes." Jordan maintained her polite expression, her grip tight on the plate of German chocolate cake she hadn't touched. The woman was some distant cousin of her dad's; funerals always brought cousins out in hordes.

"How exactly *did* it happen, dear?"

"A hunting accident, no one's fault," Jordan recited. "His shotgun exploded when he was out at the lake hunting turkey. He was using the wrong ammunition."

"I've told my husband once if I've told him a hundred times, *always* check your ammunition. Do they listen, these menfolk of ours?"

The parlor at the house was jammed with people in black: helping themselves to casserole and cookies from the groaning table, sipping glasses of sherry or tumblers of whiskey. Anneliese stood by the mantel, about as lifelike as a waxwork. Jordan was never going to forget the sound that had come out of her when she saw her husband in the hospital bed—it was before bandages hid the full extent of his injuries, the missing fingers on his right hand, the wound to his neck, the horror that was the right side of his face. Anneliese had let out a choked whimper at the sight, like an animal in a trap. If Jordan had had even the remotest suspicion that Anneliese didn't love her father, that would have put paid to any doubts right there. She'd seen the tears overflowing Anneliese's eyes as the doctor went on and on about *extensive shrapnel damage to the mandible and teeth* and *destruction of the eye orbit and the zygomatic arch.* She didn't seem to have any tears left, now. She and Jordan both stood in the parlor dry and stiff as pillars of salt.

"At least your dear father didn't suffer," some well-meaning twit said.

"No," Jordan said through gritted teeth.

"How did it happen, dear?"

"A hunting accident, no one's fault," Jordan repeated, all the while wanting to scream *Of course he suffered! He hung on for two weeks after the accident, you think he didn't* suffer? The party of hunters who had found her father just after the accident might have saved him from bleeding out in the woods, but they hadn't saved him from *suffering.* The doctors had kept saying in jocular tones, "Your dad's a tough one!" as if that helped to see him lying in the hospital bed, looking more and more shrunken as the infection set in.

"At least his family was with him at the end."

"Yes." All those hours they sat stroking his hands, Anneliese on one side and Jordan on the other. *Can he hear us?* Jordan had asked the doctors, and they said something about blast injuries to the eardrum, which seemed to be their way of saying they weren't sure. He seemed to pass in and out of consciousness—he couldn't speak, not with the broken jaw and mangled tongue, but sometimes he tried to move. "He threw my hand away," Anneliese had cried once, and Jordan had climbed into the bed and put her arms around her father until he quieted. "I can't stand to see him in pain," Anneliese said, white as frost on a window. "Keep him asleep. As much sedation as he needs."

Only two weeks' worth, as it turned out.

The doorbell rang. Jordan went down, greeted more well-wishers, took another casserole into the kitchen. Every surface was already overflowing with casseroles and potato salad. *Go away, all of you, and take your food with you.* But these people were here for her father, she reminded herself. Rare book dealers and auction house owners; neighbors and church acquaintances; a cluster of fellow antiques dealers come from New York with hearty booms of "Fine fellow, Dan McBride. A thing like this happening, such a careful man . . ."

Garrett's voice in her ear as he wrapped her in a hug. "How are you?" *I don't want to be hugged,* Jordan wanted to cry, *I don't want to be asked how I'm feeling. I want to be left alone*—but that wasn't fair. She made herself hug him back, trying not to feel smothered.

"You poor dears," a neighbor clucked. "Jordan, you poor child, not having your father to give you away at your wedding—"

Jordan's hand stole up to the Lalique pearls at her ears. Given for a wedding, worn for a funeral. Garrett, seeing she wasn't going to speak up, said, "The wedding's been postponed till next spring."

A sudden explosion of tears at the other end of the parlor. Ruth's voice, so unexpected because Ruth never had tantrums. "—she wants to come *in*!" Pink-faced and tearful, wrenching at the door to the back bedroom where Taro whined and scratched, locked up for the afternoon. "I want my *dog*—" Her voice scaling up to a wail, as Anneliese cut swiftly through the crowd and took her by the wrist.

"It's time you went to your room, Ruth."

"Not without my *dog*," Ruth shrieked, yanking away.

Jordan shook off Garrett's arm and moved to scoop up her sister. "I'll put her to bed, Anna."

"Thank you," Anneliese said in a heartfelt murmur, heading off an incoming batch of neighbors as Jordan carried Ruth upstairs. Ruth was sobbing, flushed from heat and emotion.

"It's all right to cry, cricket. Just take off this heavy dress and climb in bed."

"C-can I have Taro?"

"You can have anything you want, Ruthie-pie."

Ruth and Taro were soon snuggled up together, Ruth's swollen lids drifting shut despite herself. "*Hund*," she whispered as Taro nuzzled her elbow. "*Hübscher Hund . . .*" Jordan paused as she pulled the bedroom curtains, disquieted. Ruth hadn't lapsed into German for years.

"Thank you," Anneliese said wearily as Jordan came back into the parlor. "I couldn't think what to do if she started screaming."

"She'll sleep now." Jordan rubbed at her eyes. "Ruth's the lucky one, getting some peace and quiet. How much longer do you think this will last?"

"Hours." Anneliese massaged her forehead. "Why don't you sneak out for a while? Walk around the block, have Garrett take you for a drive."

"I can't leave you with all this."

"Jordan." Anneliese's blue eyes were steady. "I would not have managed at the hospital those two weeks without you taking care of everything. Let me take care of this." A small smile. "It isn't so very hard, after all. Keep a handkerchief and a thank-you ready, and answer all questions with 'A hunting accident, no one's fault.'"

Jordan felt her eyes burn. "Anna—"

"Shoo." Giving a small shove. "Go find Garrett. I'll make excuses."

But Jordan didn't go find Garrett. She saw his broad shoulders across the room, and with a guilty glance she edged out of the parlor, grabbing her pocketbook as she wrenched the front door open. "Jordan dear," a plump motherly-looking neighbor clucked, black-gloved finger poised over the bell. "I brought some lemon meringue pie, your father's favorite—"

"Thank you so much, Mrs. Dunne. You'll find my stepmother upstairs."

"There was such a nice article in the paper about your father, what a pillar of the community he was. A pity they got his dates wrong—"

"Yes, I saw." It got her dad's age wrong, it said Anna McBride was born and raised in Boston and not that she and Dan had *met* in

Boston—"probably my fault," Anneliese had said. "I was in such a muddle when I was being asked for the details."

"You just take this pie, dearie, and I'll whisk on up!"

For a moment Jordan stood on the doorstep with the pie in her hands. She wanted to dash down to the darkroom and hide until everyone went away, but Garrett was sure to come looking if she went there, and Jordan didn't think she could take one more bear hug.

"You want a ride, miss?" The taxi driver who had dropped Mrs. Dunne on the doorstep leaned out the window of the cab.

"Yes," Jordan said, half stupefied. "Yes, I want a ride. Clarendon and Newbury."

IT WASN'T UNTIL halfway to the shop that she came out of her daze in the backseat and realized she was still holding a lemon meringue pie. She almost burst out laughing, or maybe burst out crying. *Dad's favorite.* Jordan scrounged enough change to pay the driver and climbed out in front of McBride's Antiques, pie dish still in hand.

The door had a black crepe bow on the knocker. Jordan tore it off, fishing her keys out of her pocketbook. The shop was dusty in the late-afternoon sunshine; it had been closed up nearly three weeks. Jordan flipped the sign to Open without thinking, setting the pie down on an antique ceramic birdbath, and wandered behind the counter. She traced her father's initials in the dust, biting back an almost irresistible urge to call out—*Dad?*—because surely that meant the backroom door would open, and she'd see him there, smiling as he said *What can I do for you, missy?* All she had to do was call out. It hadn't been him in the hospital bed. It was all a mistake.

The sob that broke out of her was huge and noisy, echoing in the tomb-silent shop. Jordan gripped the counter, welcoming the tears. "Jesus, Dad," she whispered. "Why didn't you buy the right shells? Why did you have to use that old gun instead of a new one that wouldn't blow up in your face?"

The bell over the shop door tinkled. "Excuse me . . ."

Jordan looked up from the counter, heaving a breath around the solid wall in her chest. "What?" Through the blur in her eyes she could see a young man in the doorway, hands in his pockets.

"Do you work here, miss?" He closed the door behind him with another jingle of the sweet-toned bell. Her father had polished that bell every week, keeping it bright. "I'm here about a job."

"Job?" Jordan echoed. She couldn't seem to focus. She blinked hard, once, twice. *Why did I come here?*

"There's a Help Wanted sign." The young man jerked his thumb at the window. "I saw a German fellow last week as he was coming in—"

"Mr. Kolb?"

"Right. But he said I'd have to speak with the owners."

Help Wanted. Her dad had put that sign up the week he died, looking for a clerk. *Some suave fellow or pretty girl to work the counter.* Jordan blinked again, focusing on the man standing on the other side of the counter now. Olive skinned, dark haired, lean, about Jordan's height, maybe four or five years older. Anneliese wouldn't like that loose collar, the rumpled dark hair without a hat. *Sloppy*, she'd say with that Germanic tut-tut.

"Anton Rodomovsky," he said, offering his hand. "Tony."

"Jordan McBride," she replied, shaking it automatically.

"What position are you looking to fill?" he asked after a moment's silence. "You've got your German fellow, what's he do?"

"Mr. Kolb does restoration work. My father—" Jordan stopped again.

"So you need a clerk, maybe?" Tony smiled, lean cheeks creasing. "I know absolutely nothing about the antiques business, Miss McBride, but I can work a register and I can sell ice to Eskimos."

"I don't—know if we're hiring. There's been a death. The owner—" Jordan stopped, looking down at the dusty counter. "Try back next week."

Tony looked at her a long moment, smile fading. "Your father?"

Jordan managed a nod.

"I'm sorry," he said. "I'm so sorry."

She nodded again. She couldn't seem to move, just stood like a pillar in her ugly black dress behind the counter.

"There's a pie in a birdbath over there," he said eventually.

"Everyone keeps bringing me pie," Jordan heard herself say. "Ever since he died. Like lemon meringue fixes anything."

He picked Mrs. Dunne's pie up out of the birdbath, deposited it on the glass counter, then went to a display case where a set of thirteen apostle spoons had been laid out in a fan. He brought back two spoons, offering one to Jordan.

Jordan's chest felt like it was about to burst. She dug a heaping spoonful out of the middle of the pie and jammed it into her mouth. It tasted like absolutely nothing. Ashes. Soap shavings. *My father is dead.* She ate another heaping spoonful.

Tony levered up a bite of his own. Chewed, swallowed. "This is—very good pie."

"You don't have to lie." Jordan kept eating. "It's terrible pie. Mrs. Dunne never uses enough sugar."

"Where can you get good pie in Boston, then? I'm new in town."

"Mike's Pastries is pretty good. The North End."

Tony jabbed the apostle spoon back into the meringue. "Looks like I'm going to Mike's Pastries to get you something decent."

"You don't have to—"

"I can't bring your father back. I can't make you feel anything but sad. I can at least make sure you don't have to eat lousy pie."

"I don't want any more goddamn pie," Jordan said and burst into tears. She stood there crying into Mrs. Dunne's crummy meringue, hiccuping and gulping. Tony Rodomovsky fished a handkerchief from his pocket and pushed it quietly across the counter, then went to turn the shop sign around from Open to Closed. Jordan wiped her streaming eyes, shoulders heaving. *My father is dead.*

"I'm very sorry to intrude, Miss McBride," Tony said. "I'll leave you alone now."

"Thank you." There was a fresh explosion of sobs building up in her chest, making its way through the chink in the bricks; all she wanted to do was cry it out. But she stamped it down for a moment, pushing her damp hair off her forehead and looking squarely at her Good Samaritan. "Come back Monday, Mr. Rodomovsky."

"Sorry?"

"My stepmother will want a proper application and some references," Jordan said, scrubbing at her eyes. "But as far as I'm concerned, you've got a job."

Chapter 26

IAN

May 1950
Boston

S uccess!" Tony burst through the door of their newly rented apartment. "I have officially made contact."

Ian grunted acknowledgment, stretched out on the floor between window and table, halfway through his daily set of one hundred press-ups. "How?" he pushed out between counting. *Ninety-two, ninety-three* . . . His shoulders were burning.

"What target?" Nina sat on the sill of the open window with her feet hanging out over a four-story drop, eating tinned sardines straight out of the tin.

"McBride's Antiques." Tony flung his jacket over a nail by the door, which was all they had for a hat rack. "Frau Vogt said the Boston shop dealing documents to war criminals under the counter was *McCall Antiques, McBain Antiques, Mc-Something*. The only remotely close match in the city is McBride's Antiques. You arc looking at their newest clerk."

Ian started to get up, but Nina swung her legs back inside the windowsill, dropping her boots on his back. "Seven more."

"Bugger off," he said, but lowered himself down toward the floor again. *Ninety-four . . . ninety-five . . .*

Tony flung himself down at the table, moving a paperback of Nina's called *The Spanish Bride.* "I'll need to supply references. Write me something glowing, boss?"

Ian finished the last press-up, shoved his wife's boots away, and flopped on his back on the floor. "What name?"

"Run 'em for my real name. Tony R, born and raised in Queens, enlisted right out of Grover Cleveland High School the day after Pearl Harbor—what's more trustworthy than that?" Tony struck a patriotic pose. "I can stake out the shop, and we can use the salary."

"Yes, we can." Between Ian's annuity and Tony's savings, they'd managed to rent a top-floor two-room apartment overlooking Scollay Square, which mostly seemed to be crammed with drunken university students pressing into Joe & Nemo's for hot dogs, and drunken sailors on leave pressing into the Half Dollar Bar. The apartment smelled like grease and shoe polish, but it was cheaper than a hotel and worth putting up with the broken door lock and the three-legged table whose corner sat on a nonfunctional radiator. Any income would, Ian had to admit, be welcome.

"That twitchy German clerk I ran into last week at the McBride shop?" Tony grabbed a pad, began scribbling notes. "I've got a name now, *Kolb.* I hate to play the game of *Let's automatically blame the Kraut*, but that Kraut was twitchy as hell. He does the shop's restoration work—"

"How you find that out?" Nina swung her legs back outside the windowsill. It made Ian queasy, watching her swing her boots over a four-story drop. "You don't start work yet."

"The owner's daughter told me, the one who offered the job. A man good at restoring antiques might mean one good with documents. This Kolb could have a sideline going under the table, hooking money out of war criminals. Lorelei Vogt's mother told us people like her daughter could get papers there, identification, new names."

"Why would they need new papers to begin with?" Ian rose, thinking aloud on something that had been nagging at him since this chase took its America-bound turn. "The United States is more obsessed with Communists than Nazis. There hasn't been a single extradited war criminal, and they've welcomed war refugees from Europe since '48—"

"As long as they aren't *Jewish* war refugees," Tony muttered. "Oh, no, we don't want the Yids here, anyone but them—"

"—so anyone who came here under their own name wouldn't need to bother with new papers."

"Smart ones would." Nina sounded matter-of-fact. "You keep your name, it's on file. If someone wants, they look you up, including your war record. Today, no one cares about looking. Tomorrow, who knows? Next year, five years, ten years—is still there, if anyone looks."

"My wife is a professional paranoid," Ian observed.

"I'm Soviet."

"Same thing, you teapot desecrator."

"A name gets on a list, it stays there forever in a drawer. Maybe nobody ever looks at it. Or maybe someone decides list matters. Then the black van rolls up for you." Nina shrugged. "If I leave my country with things to hide, I would change name, background, everything, to be safe."

You did leave your country with things to hide, Ian thought. He and his wife had spent most of the Atlantic crossing rolling around the sheets, but that didn't mean he knew much more about her. She wouldn't sleep next to him, looked wary at any sign of affection outside a bed, and was not interested in answering most of the questions he wanted to ask. Like why she'd left her homeland . . .

"Well, whatever McBride's Antiques might be dealing out of the back room to paranoid war criminals," Tony said, "I'll bet my next month's salary Kolb's the one dealing it."

"See what you can find out." Ian sat, tilting his chair back on two legs. "Check out the owners as well. They might be complicit, they might not."

"A peaches-and-cream Boston co-ed helped the huntress get a new identity and disappear?" Tony linked his hands behind his head. "I'm doubtful."

"You think girls of twenty-one can't be dangerous?" Nina drank off the last of the oil in the sardine tin. "In war I know plenty; call most of them *sestra*. Don't discount just because she's pretty."

"Who said she was pretty?" Tony countered. "I have no idea if she's pretty. She was crying her eyes out over her dad—I was passing her handkerchiefs, not eyeing her up and down like some street-corner lothario."

"But you already think she can't be involved. Is what you *want* to think." Nina looked at Ian. "Means she's pretty, yes?"

"Definitely," he said, pulling out the notes they'd made on the McBride family.

"I resent that," Tony remarked. "I am not some slavering GI who turns to jelly at the first pair of shapely female legs that walks by. I am perfectly capable of objectivity here."

"'Shapely,'" Nina said.

"Telling," Ian agreed.

"Now that you two are screwing, you gang up on me. Completely unfair." Tony flung a wadded-up scrap of paper at Ian. Nina bounced the sardine tin off his chest. "Fine. I'll keep an eye on the daughter."

"Look at the mother too." Ian's notes on the McBride widow were brief, coming from the obituary and the short newspaper article about the deceased antiques dealer and his family, including one Mrs. Anna McBride, born and raised in Boston. "And the shop files—there could be records of the others helped under the table. We know there are more besides *die Jägerin*."

"Would they be stupid enough to keep records for something illicit?" Tony kept scribbling.

"You always keep records," Nina said firmly. "Is not stupid, is something to *trade*. Someone to throw out of the sleigh for the wolves, if the police come knocking."

"More Stalinist paranoia . . ."

Despite all the banter, Ian could feel the crackle of energy whipping through the room now that the chase was underway. It was a

new office here, a new feeling in the air. In Vienna there had been
a separation between work and leisure: in the evening Tony went
home to his rented rooms, and Ian retired upstairs to his cot and
violin. Here in Boston, there was no separation; they were all underfoot from dawn to dusk. Once they'd exhausted the topic of Herr
Kolb and how to proceed, they elbowed the scribbled notes aside
and made room for bowls of soup heated up from tins and ate with
elbows knocking—and even then, the fierce concentration in the air
still hummed. Lorelei Vogt belonged equally to all three of them,
and now there was no ocean in the way.

We are going to find her, Ian thought. She is no match for the
three of us.

IT WAS NEARLY DAWN, and Nina was up on the roof.

Ian and Tony shared the one bedroom, which had two cots
against opposite walls; Nina insisted on the couch under the skylight in the sitting room. "I don't sleep next to anyone," she told Ian
when he offered her the other bedroom cot, rather hoping they could
push them together. Now it was four in the morning, the sitting room
was empty, and the skylight was open. Ian climbed onto the arm of
the couch. It would be a jump for Nina, but he grabbed the lip of the
skylight and levered himself skyward.

The rooftop was a flat barren square with a raised ledge running
around at knee height. The sky was still dark overhead, a creeping
edge of pink starting to outline the city horizon. Nina lay on her back
on the ledge, gazing up at the fading stars. Wearing, Ian saw with
amusement, her own patched trousers, one of Tony's old sweaters,
and a pair of Ian's socks.

"Will you stop collectivizing the laundry?" he demanded, not
moving toward her. He wasn't getting anywhere near the edge; his
stomach was already churning at the drop on Nina's other side.

"You have nicer socks than me."

"Harrods," Ian said. "The key to surviving most of the things
life throws at you is taking care of your feet. Something I learned

tramping around in Spanish mud in the thirties. You're going to fall off," he added as she stretched her feet up into the air. Her toes flexed and arched like a bird's tail fanning.

"No, I won't." Nina extended her arms out on either side, moving them dreamily up and down as if on air currents. Ian averted his eyes from the edge. The sounds of morning traffic drifted up: tires on pavement, the occasional shout from a drunk heading home, shouts back from respectable people heading for work. This was a young city, brash and confident, and Ian liked it.

Nina's eyes were still on the stars above. "*Tvoyu mat.*" She sighed. "I miss the night sky."

"From your pilot days?" Getting information out of Nina was like interviewing a porcupine, all prickles and defensively lashing tail, but he couldn't help probing anyway. The journalist's urge to ask questions, which hadn't died along with his urge to write articles. "You haven't said much about your flying days in the war."

"Was a navigator. I fly bombing runs in the 588th Night Bomber Regiment. Later known as Forty-Sixth Taman Guards Night Bomber Aviation Regiment." She sat up, slanting an eyebrow. "You look surprised."

"I am," he said honestly.

"What, you think girls don't fly?"

"I know perfectly well that women fly. I am surprised you were a *navigator*, because it's a job that relies on obedience, teamwork, and precision. Not exactly qualities that spring to mind when I look at you, you little anarchist."

"I was good navigator!" Nettled into reacting, as he hoped, she peeled off his socks, showing the tattoos on the soles of her feet—a red star across the arch of one, spiky lettering across the arch of the other. Ian had asked about them before, but received only a shrug. Now, she stretched out her left foot, placing it in his hands as he came closer, and translating the letters: шестьсот шестнадцать. "'Six hundred sixteen,'" Nina said. "Is how many bombing runs I flew in the war."

"You cannot be serious." English bomber pilots were considered lucky if they survived twenty runs.

"Six hundred sixteen." Nina smirked. "Us little Soviet girls worked harder than your English flyboys." Ian meditated a cutting retort—he'd devoted much newsprint ink to those English flyboys— but Nina pulled her foot out of his hands, replacing it with the foot that had the red star. "Order of the Red Star, awarded January '43."

Ian looked from his wife's tattooed foot up to her amused, knowing eyes. "I'm . . . impressed, comrade."

"The Hitlerites said a squadron of U-2s at night sounded like witches on broomsticks." Her sharp teeth showed in a smile as she pulled her foot out of his hands. "So they called us the *Nachthexen*."

"Night Witches? That sounds rather grandiose to have come from pragmatic German imaginations."

"We scared the piss out of them." She pretzeled her feet under her on the rooftop ledge, propping her elbows on her knees. She had a scar on her forearm, a knot of old scar tissue, like something had pierced all the way through her arm. Ian knew how to make her back arch if he ran his lips along that scar, but nothing else about it. "What about that?" he asked. "Since we're telling stories."

"Are we?"

"I certainly hope so, Scheherazade."

"Who's that?"

"The fascinating tale-telling wife of another fellow who didn't know what he was getting into when he married her."

Nina snorted, but inspected the scar. "Just a flying accident. Two weeks I wasn't allowed to fly. Also," she added, "the reason I met Comrade Stalin."

Chapter 27

NINA

January 1943
Moscow

They had all cried, weeping into one another's shoulders at the airdrome on the North Caucasus front. From Major Bershanskaia to the newest little mechanic, they wept.

"To Marina Mikhailovna Raskova," Bershanskaia said at last.

Wrung with grief, the regiment she had founded echoed the toast. "Marina Mikhailovna Raskova."

Dead at thirty-three, her Pe-2 crashing on its way to an airfield near Stalingrad. Surviving so much, only to die in a common aviation accident on the banks of the Volga.

"She will be buried in two days' time," Bershanskaia said later. "Full military honors in Red Square. The first state funeral of the war to be held in Moscow, awarded to *our* commander."

Three fierce nods answered her. Nina and two other regiment pilots grounded by injury had been summoned to Bershanskaia's office, and she was scribbling a set of passes. The Night Witches had flown off for tonight's target; a mission couldn't be put off just because their founder was dead. Raskova herself would have been outraged at the thought. Bershanskaia had no tears in her eyes now when she addressed Nina and the other two.

"An honor guard will stand watch over her remains during the vigil," Bershanskaia went on. "It is unthinkable that her regiments will not be represented. I will not pull active fliers from their duty, but the three injured officers with the best records are to be sent from each regiment. You three will depart tomorrow."

A new dress uniform landed on Nina's bed by dawn. She unfolded it and stared in horror. "Fuck your mother . . ." She was struggling into it, yanking at the stiff buttons, when the Night Witches trailed in exhausted and frost rimed. "What's this?" Yelena walked around Nina. "Are they finally giving us uniforms designed for *women*?" Smiles came out over tear-smudged faces as a dozen women in bulky overalls contemplated Nina in her dress uniform, complete with skirt and heels. Nina stared back at them in utter panic.

"I've never owned a pair of heels in my life," she wailed. "I'm going to fall on my face in the middle of *Red Square*!"

It brought the laugh they all needed so sorely. A watery laugh, but still a laugh. "Ninochka needs us, rabbits," Yelena announced, rummaging for her sewing needles. "It's time for the Night Witches to work some magic."

Dusia hemmed the too-long uniform skirt, bucktoothed Zoya transferred Nina's insignia and polished everything diamond bright, and a lanky navigator who had once been a hairdresser in Novgorod produced combs and towels. "We're doing something with this hair, Nina Borisovna." Fluffing the flyaway mane that had grown out to Nina's collar. "You aren't representing the 588th under a mouse-brown haystack. Irusha, I know you're stashing a bottle of peroxide, hand it over."

"Who cares about hair as long as it's tidy?" Nina demanded, wobbling on her new heels. But the girls had the bit between their teeth; their grief for Raskova too raw for more tears but demanding some kind of focus. "Let them fuss," Yelena advised. "They need some way to help, even if it's only hair." Nina surrendered, and by the time it came to depart she stood resplendent and steady in her heels, newly blond hair pinned in a swoop, lips reddened with a navigation pencil. Her two companions also assigned to the honor guard were just as splendid; the girls in their dormitory had been hard at work too.

"You three will do us proud," everyone said. "You'll do *her* proud." They loaded Nina and the others with dried flowers to lay with the wreaths a grateful Motherland would already be heaping up in Marina Raskova's memory.

"Bring me something from Moscow," Yelena said. "Anything, even a pebble. I miss it."

"Why?" Nina thought back to her haphazard glimpse of Moscow when she first came from Irkutsk. "It's ugly."

"You have to see it as what it *will* be, not what it is. It's a city on its way to glory. Our future home, after the war!"

Nina's stomach flipped. She couldn't look ahead past the next bombing run, and here Yelena was making plans for *after the war*. Nina tried out the words, experimentally. "After the war we're going to live in Moscow?"

"Where would anyone live but Moscow if they had the chance?"

"Somewhere that isn't a pit?"

Yelena swatted her. The train whistle was blowing. "You'll see Moscow in its full glory this time, all for Raskova. Promise me you'll love it." Nina opened her mouth to promise, but it was time to leave. A squeeze of the hand and Yelena was gone.

Nina intended to get a look at the countryside in between here and the city, but the exhaustion caught up with her and she slept almost the entire journey. All three of them did, cheeks pressed against glass compartment windows and slatted wooden partitions. Stumbling bleary-eyed into Three Stations Square in Moscow, Nina had the sensation that time was doubling back. She was getting off the train from Siberia, not the Caucasus front . . . the 588th had not even been formed yet, only Aviation Group 122 . . . Marina Raskova was up ahead somewhere, alive and well, waiting to give Nina her chance.

But Marina Raskova was nothing but a ceremonial urn filled with ashes, sitting in state in the great domed hall of the Civil

Aviation Club. And to Nina's eyes, Moscow still looked like a gray wreck.

"The doctor gave me these." One of her companions took out a bottle of tablets, seeing Nina yawn. "They'll keep us alert during the vigil. Coca-Cola pills—" Rolling the American slang.

Nina swallowed two and after that the world was both sparky and hazy, the events of the funeral jumbled like confetti tossed in the air. They made their way to some office only to be greeted by a flurry of gray-faced functionaries barking orders. Nina's arm throbbed in its sling as they were shepherded into the domed hall of the Civil Aviation Club, past the urn where Raskova's honor guard would stand watch, breathing in the stifling smell of roses from the massive bank of funeral wreaths. No time to exchange more than a fast murmur with the other women of the honor guard, women Nina hadn't seen since Engels. "Marina," they whispered to each other, a greeting and a toast all together.

Nina held herself rigid through the long vigil, keeping her eyes straight ahead as most of Moscow shuffled past: women with bent shoulders, bony children, men with boots held together by twine . . . Then came another confusing shuffle of functionaries and suits, and suddenly it was the next day, the world still sparking and floating as Nina took her place in the vast stately procession into Red Square, past draped bunting and more wreaths. The only face coming distinct among the masses was Raskova's, her dark hair and wide smile reproduced a hundred times over on photographs printed large and held aloft over the crowd, the way Nina's father said peasants used to hold up their icons.

The Coca-Cola buzz was wearing off by the time Raskova's ashes were laid to rest. Nina was swaying on her high heels as Lieutenant General Shcherbakov gave the funeral oration, echoing as he was broadcast across the land. Talking about *the highest standards of Soviet womanhood* and *credit to the Motherland*. Who were they even talking about? Speeches like this could be made at any funeral. Nina remembered the squadron commander who had died on the very first sortie; how the Night Witches had toasted her memory under the stars and sung soft songs that echoed across the airfield. That was how Raskova should have been remembered, not with rote rhetoric and the mournful broadcast beats of the "Internationale." It should have been women talking about Raskova today, not these old men.

Two down, Nina found herself thinking. First the squadron commander, then Raskova. *Who's next?* Which was stupid because the regiment had lost more besides those two. But the thought still echoed in Nina's brain: *Who's next?*

Yelena's face flashed before her eyes, along with a heart-stopping kick of terror.

Marina Raskova's ashes were formally interred in the Kremlin Wall. Banners dipped, officers held their salute, a single plane droned low and mournful over Red Square. It was done.

"RASKOVA'S EAGLETS."

At the sound of that famous voice, heard from so many broadcasts and radio speakers, Nina thought every *sestra* beside her was going to faint. Women who kept calm while being peppered by anti-aircraft guns were blushing and shuffling like schoolgirls, hardly able to look up at the great Comrade Stalin.

There had been endless receptions after the funeral; more suits, more droning; Nina had swallowed another trio of Coca-Cola tablets and now the world sparked bright colors again. They had all been lined up in some featureless anteroom, waiting over an hour—somewhere nearby, Nina could hear champagne corks popping. Suddenly a door opened and people flooded in, flashbulbs making everyone blink but Nina. *I'm used to enemy searchlights, I won't flinch at a camera.* She looked through the flash and there was Comrade Stalin emerging from his crowd of dignitaries like a wolf from the underbrush, hard fleshed as concrete in a glittering uniform.

More rustling as an aide droned. Marina Mikhailovna Raskova's honor guard would be honored themselves with the Order of the

Red Star; applause rippled. Nina gave an inward shrug. What did a medal matter? A dozen women in the 588th flying right now had better records; she was only getting this because she'd been grounded when Raskova died. She didn't think Comrade Stalin cared all that much about the medals he was giving out either; he stood scrawling at a notebook with a pencil stub. Making notes of the latest hundred thousand dead in Leningrad, maybe. How strange it was to lay eyes on a person who was so familiar, yet at the same time a stranger. Like peasants in the tsarist days getting a glimpse of God, only Comrade Stalin had more power than God.

Nine flashes rippled, camera clicking as each beaming woman stepped forward to be pinned with the five-pointed red-enameled star. The flash went off in Nina's eyes as the pin pricked through her uniform. *A little bit like stepping forward one by one to be shot.* If Comrade Stalin had decided to do that right here in this anteroom, stick a bullet instead of a medal into each woman's chest, no one would have stopped him.

Nina looked at the General Secretary over the shoulder of the aide pinning her. His mustache, grayer than it looked in all his portraits. Pockmarks on heavy cheeks. Teeth stained by pipe smoke. His eyes were lidded, almost sleepy as he watched them receive their medals. *But you aren't sleepy*, Nina thought. *Not at all.* Somewhere in the next room another champagne cork popped. Would everyone get champagne, or just Party members? Party members only, Nina guessed.

Comrade Stalin came forward to take each woman by the shoulders in hearty congratulation. "You do honor to the state." A kiss to each cheek, the peasant way, the proletarian way. Then the next in line. No one said anything in return; cheeks burned red as fire and eyes glowed. Nina looked past them to the aide who had taken Comrade Stalin's notebook and was now shuffling an armload of folders. The notebook fell faceup to the ground, and the aide picked it up but not before Nina caught a glimpse. The General Secretary with his important frown, scrawling away as though lives depended on every pencil stroke, had been doodling wolves. Wolves in red and black, slavering from the page.

Heavy hands grasped her shoulders. "You do honor to the state." The wiry stiffness of Comrade Stalin's mustache brushed her cheeks. With Nina in heels, they were almost the same height. *Such a giant in your portraits*, Nina thought, *and you're hardly taller than I am.* The thought made her smile in genuine amusement, and she saw an answering smile quirk under the graying mustache. "This one," the great man said to his aide. "This eaglet looks Comrade Stalin directly in the eyes!"

Comrade Stalin is a lying pig who shits on the common man, Nina's father commented inside her head, so loudly she wondered if the man breathing tobacco in her face could hear it. *Tell him he's a murdering sack of shit*, her father advised.

Not helpful, Papa, Nina thought.

The heavy hands still rested on her shoulders. "What makes you smile, Comrade Lieutenant Markova?"

This wolf could smell lies, of that she was certain. "My father spoke passionately and often of Comrade Stalin," she said with utter truth.

He liked that. "Your father was a great patriot?"

"He cut many tsarist throats, Comrade Stalin." Also utter truth.

"A good servant of the state, then." Comrade Stalin smiled. The whites of his eyes were yellowed, like Papa's. Nina thought of her father looking at her speculatively, right before he tried to drown her. Comrade Stalin's gaze was speculative too. "How many enemies of the state have you killed, Nina Borisovna?"

"Not enough, Comrade Stalin."

Fucking Georgian swine, her father hissed. *Drag him under, rusalka bitch.* And Nina couldn't help but think how easily she *could* kill the most powerful man in the Motherland right here and now. She had the razor in her sleeve; she never went anywhere without it. She could drop it into her palm, flick it open, and open that heavy throat with one slash. She smiled, amused by the thought.

"Good hunting, eaglet." Comrade Stalin kissed her again on

each cheek, then stepped back. His gaze withdrew from her like a needle; more cameras flashed. Then he was gone.

"**RED STARS!**" The cry went up at the barracks, and everyone curtsied as if three *tsarevnas* had come back to the regiment. "It's all due to you," Nina shouted over the tumult. "Comrade Stalin gave me a red star because he liked my new hair!"

"I like your new hair," Yelena admired in the shed afterward, as soon as they could sneak off alone. They lay spooned together in the back corner, Yelena's back against Nina's chest. Threaded through her collar was a drying rose plucked from one of the funeral wreaths behind Marina Raskova's urn—the only memento of Moscow Nina had had time to take home. "You belong as a blonde, Ninochka. It makes you stand out, and you *should* stand out."

"Then I'll keep it blond just for you." Nina tipped Yelena's head back for a lingering kiss. Their escaping breath puffed white in the frigid air. "Did you miss me?"

"Not a bit! Zoya never tries to climb out on the wing." Yelena grinned, and Nina swatted her. "You saw the girls from the other regiments—what's their news?"

"Both of the other regiments are integrated, did you know that? Men *and* women. Necessity, they said. The 588th is the only one still just us ladies."

"It'd better stay that way. The male pilots slack," Yelena said, scornful. "They actually go in for *meals* between bombing runs. When was the last time any of us had dinner outside of a cockpit? No wonder our numbers are so much higher." Squirming face-to-face so she could touch Nina's star, Yelena whispered, "So what was he like?"

No need to ask who *he* was. "Short. And he pretends he's such a big man!"

"It's the height of his soul, not his head." Yelena smiled. "I would have fainted if it had been me."

Nina had heard that kind of awe from the others, but Yelena had always been quick to smile at Party drolleries and contradictions.

"He's not God, Yelenushka. Just another sack of Party horseshit in a suit."

Yelena sat up straight. "Don't say that."

"I don't, not in public. I'm not stupid." Nina sat up too. "I don't want the black van coming to my door."

"But you actually *think* such things?" Yelena sounded horrified. "That the General Secretary is . . ."

"A pig-spawn schemer who stamps on the people?" Nina shrugged. "My father's been telling me that my whole life. Of course he said the same thing about the *tsar*, but—"

"Exactly. You said your father was as crazy as a vodka-mad boar. I didn't think you *agreed* with him about anything."

"Crazy doesn't mean wrong." It popped out of Nina's mouth. "I think Comrade Stalin's a fake."

Yelena drew her knees to her chest. "What do you mean?"

Nina thought of the city all decked out for Marina Raskova, who probably would have been happier with the sweet voices of her pilots harmonizing the peasants' chorus from *Eugene Onegin*, which she'd once sung with them on the way to Engels. "All the parades and the speeches—it's like a stage front, or . . ." Nina shrugged. "I don't know. I'm just a little navigator from the Old Man, I don't know anything."

"No. You don't." Yelena's voice was sharp. "Maybe it's all ice and taiga out on the lake and nothing ever changes, but I remember Moscow the way it was, growing up. And before that, the way my grandfather told me it was. Because of Comrade Stalin, things are different."

"Better?" Nina challenged. "Queuing at three in the morning to buy shoes, the way you told me your mother did when you were little?"

"It will be better. Comrade Stalin has a plan for it, for all of us. I look at Moscow and I can see it the way he sees it. The way it's going to be, after the war."

Nina stared at her. *He's a yellow-eyed wolf in a man's skin*, she wanted to throw at her lover, *and you look starry-eyed because the wolf decided to pin a medal on me rather than eat me?* "I missed you every moment I was gone," she said instead, speaking through stiff lips. "Are we really quarreling an hour after I get back?"

"No." Yelena sounded just as stiff. "You don't understand, that's all. You don't *see*. You grew up so differently—"

Uncivilized, Nina thought. *Just a little savage who doesn't understand anything.*

Silence fell.

"I wasn't really in any state to see things as you do," Nina offered finally. "Moscow *or* Comrade Stalin . . . I had double vision all through the funeral thanks to those pills." The tablets had given Nina a ferocious headache when they finally wore off. "Coca-Cola—if that's what Americans serve in diners, no wonder they're all crazy."

Yelena melted at once, as Nina had hoped she would. "I didn't mean to bite your head off." She unwrapped her arms from her knees, reached for Nina's hand. "I'm so tired, that's all. We've been flying such long nights. Fourteen runs, fifteen runs. They're moving us soon, did you know? Somewhere near Krasnodar." A sigh. "They say it will be even worse there."

She looked exhausted, tar-black circles under her eyes, the dried rose at her collar her only flash of color. *My Moscow rose*, Nina thought. "Is the *Rusalka* fighting fit again?"

"Yes, the mechanics finally cleared her." They talked easily then of the *Rusalka*, of flying, of the things they loved. *Is that why we never quarreled before?* Nina wondered. *Because we only talked of war and flying and each other?*

Well, they weren't going to quarrel again. It wasn't like Nina wanted to come back into the shed and talk Party politics. All she wanted to do was cuddle and laugh and make love. *Just give me Yelena and the* Rusalka, she thought. *That's all I need in this world.*

So which of you is next? came Comrade Stalin's amused voice. *Yelena? The* Rusalka? *Or you, little eaglet?*

Nina shivered as if a *rusalka*'s webbed green hand had wrapped wetly around her heart. *What did you see?* she wondered in the direction of the General Secretary, even as she and Yelena bundled up to creep out of the shed back to their beds. *What did you see?*

Maybe nothing. Maybe it was just the Coca-Cola pills, making her fearful.

Or maybe he saw that the last of Marina Raskova's eaglets didn't believe the horse-shit stories he wove for girls like Yelena, the stories about how the Motherland was on its way to a glorious future. Did he see that? Nina always wondered. He must have seen something, enough to remember her name. Maybe he'd jotted it as an afterthought into his notebook beside the running wolves. Because the investigation came within the year.

Chapter 28

JORDAN

June 1950
Boston

Jordan's father sat holding a piece of sandpaper, looking over one shoulder. The image shimmered through the fixer bath, ghostly in the red light. Jordan heard his voice from that afternoon, as clearly as if he were standing here in the darkroom. *What are you up to, missy?*

Pretend I'm not here, Jordan remembered answering. *I want a picture of you in the workshop.*

These were some of the last pictures of her dad she'd taken. Jordan felt a tear slide down her chin, wiped it away. She'd been crying on and off for the last hour, since she'd come banging down into the darkroom at eleven at night to develop the prints. Why not? She couldn't stand the thought of lying in bed staring at the ceiling. Couldn't bear to think about tomorrow, another day working in the shop now that it was open again, helping train the new clerk and coming home to one of the funeral casseroles Anneliese had pulled out for them to eat in total silence. Just three of them around the table, not four . . . Jordan blinked hard, standing back from her row of prints.

"That one." A low-angle shot of her father peering down at a tarnished card tray. "That's the real you." Daniel Sean McBride at work, the *essential* Daniel Sean McBride. It was him. It was good.

Jordan realized the tears were coming fast now. She let them fall, going on to the roll of shots she'd taken at the tiny airfield the day Garrett took her flying. She knew she should call Garrett; he'd been leaving messages. So had his mother, gentle hints about springtime dates for the rescheduled wedding. The thought of plunging back into wedding plans made Jordan want to shriek.

"I'll call you tomorrow." She sighed as she cleaned up her chemicals and trays.

As Jordan let herself back into the house, a slim pale figure moved out of the darkness at the foot of the hall stairs. "You couldn't sleep either?"

Jordan started violently at Anneliese's voice. "You scared me!"

"I'm sorry." Anneliese pulled the sash tighter on her pale blue dressing gown. "I was going to make some cocoa. Would you like some?"

"Sure. Did Ruth wake you up again?"

"Her night frights are getting worse." Anneliese moved into the kitchen on those soundless feet, pulling down two mugs. Taro padded in, keeping a watchful eye for any food that might hit the floor; Anneliese scratched her black ears fondly. "I don't know how to deal with Ruth when she's in such a state. She's always been so biddable, I don't know what to do with her when she's not."

"She just misses Dad." Jordan sighed. "Is she asleep now?"

"Yes, finally. Now I'm the one tossing and turning." Jordan's stepmother looked fragile in the bright kitchen light, dark hair loose for once, face naked without its smoothing of powder and lipstick. "No, sit down," she said as Jordan began to help with the stove. "You must be so tired, all those shifts you've been working at the shop."

"The new clerk will be ready to manage on his own soon. That will be a help." Jordan managed a smile, pulling out a chair at the kitchen table. "He told me he could sell ice to Eskimos, and he can."

"What's his name again?"

"Tony Rodomovsky." Jordan had thought she'd find it embarrassing, working with a man after he'd first encountered her sobbing into a lemon meringue pie, but it hadn't been. The new clerk had taken his handkerchief back the following week with light good humor, made no reference to her fit of weeping, and treated Jordan exactly as he treated everything else female he encountered in the shop—namely, he flirted with her. The kind of meaningless undemanding flirtation that was soothing. *How pretty you are*, his smile said. *Please, let me take care of the customers. In fact, let me take care of everything.* The female customers certainly responded to that smile. He knew next to nothing about antiques but he was so rueful about his own ignorance, it didn't seem to matter. "You know he actually got Mrs. Wills to buy something, not just spend an hour criticizing every piece?"

"That *is* a charmer. Have I met him?" Anneliese massaged her forehead. "It's all been such a whirl, I can't remember."

"Not yet. His references were excellent. Do you want to meet him before his trial period is up?"

"I'll look in soon." Anneliese sighed. "I don't even want to set foot in the shop. I had my little ideas here and there to help sales, but your father was so proud that his wife didn't have to work . . . Going there now seems like going against his wishes."

"I can take care of the shop, truly. You have Dad's other things to sort out." What to do with his clothes, his shoes, his belongings. Whether to move his shaving brush and razor in the bathroom. All the things to be decided after a death.

"He was very organized, thank goodness." Anneliese began warming the milk. "I don't want you to think we have to worry about money. There was insurance; we won't have to scrimp to make ends meet. I'm meeting with the lawyer about the will."

Jordan couldn't even begin to contemplate the official details. "If I can help . . ."

"Between the two of us, we can handle everything." Anneliese smiled over her shoulder, stirring the milk. "I'm so lucky you're such a capable girl, Jordan. More than a girl, really—I shouldn't keep calling you that. Having a grown woman at my side is a great comfort at a time like this."

The compliment warmed Jordan more than the cup of cocoa Anneliese placed in her hands. "Thank you." Anneliese sat in the chair opposite, pushing her hair back over her shoulders, and Jordan saw a faint pink line of a scar disappearing around the back of her neck below her collar. "Did you hurt yourself?" Jordan indicated the scar; she didn't think she'd seen it before.

"Childhood accident." Anneliese made a face. "I always thought it looked ugly, so I cover it up first thing in the morning. American makeup is a wonder!"

"It's *not* ugly. It's hardly noticeable."

"That's what your father said." Anneliese touched her mug to Jordan's. "To Dan."

"To Dad." Jordan savored the chocolaty warmth—Anneliese's cocoa was better than anyone's; something extra she put in it—and found herself appraising her stepmother across the table. "How are you, Anna? How are you *really*, I mean? You put on a very good face for the neighbors, but you're also drinking cocoa at one in the morning."

Anneliese massaged her temples. "There's a dream I've been having for years, since the war. It mostly went away when I came to live in this house, but now it's come back. Your father was a good antidote to bad dreams, very—" She paused, said a German word, tried to find its equivalent in English. "Very *of this earth*? I could wake up next to him, reassured. He was solid. Nothing could follow me out of a dream with him there."

Jordan felt her throat tighten, but it was a good tightness. "I remember him sitting on the edge of my bed when I was little, telling me the bats couldn't come out of the dream and get me."

"Is that what you dreamed of?" Anneliese smoothed a lock of hair back. "Bats aren't so bad."

"I was only Ruth's age, bats were bad enough. What's your nightmare?" Anneliese hesitated. "It can't hurt to tell me."

Her stepmother looked as if she wasn't going to speak, but her hand drifted up under the dark fall of her hair, rubbing the back of her neck, and the words started seemingly despite herself. "The dream always starts beside a lake. A woman is running, straight for me. She's small and ragged, and I see her hair flashing through the shadows, and I know she wants to kill me."

"Why?"

"I don't know why. You know dreams, they don't make sense. But she's filled with hatred." Anneliese shivered. "I chase the woman toward the lake, it's open there, she can't hide . . . But she does. She disappears into the lake—it swallows her up, pulls her in like it's helping her hide. I stand there on the edge, waiting for her to come for me."

Jordan shivered, herself. Anneliese's voice was slow, dreamy, as though she were half asleep.

"I wait for a long time, and finally I know it's all right. She's gone. I'm safe." Anneliese lifted her eyes. "And that's when she rises out of the lake, streaked with blood, and drifts across the water toward me. Her teeth are so sharp, and her nails glint like razors . . . And that's when I wake up. Before the night witch cuts my throat."

"That is *ghastly*," Jordan couldn't help saying.

"It is." Her stepmother lifted her cup, trying to smile. "Hence cocoa at one in the morning."

"Who's the woman in the nightmare?"

"No one I ever knew." Taro laid her long nose on Anneliese's knee; Anneliese stroked her and said something loving in German. "I think she comes from one of those gruesome fairy tales I heard too young. A *rusalka*."

"You said that word before." Jordan hunted for the memory. "When we first went to Selkie Lake."

"Yes, that's right." Anneliese's tone was lighter now. "A selkie comes from a lake too, but she's the Scottish version, not quite so malevolent. In Germany they have stories of a *lorelei*, who sits on a rock above the water, combing her hair. Go farther east, though, and she becomes much much more dangerous—a *rusalka*." Anneliese's blue eyes dropped to the table. "A *rusalka* only comes out in the night, dressed in the lake. And if you cross her, she will kill you."

A little silence fell. "Well," Jordan offered at last. "I feel lucky I only ever had bad dreams about bats. And about walking down the school hall in nothing but my brassiere, like a Maidenform ad."

"And now I've given you ideas about night witches! I'm sorry, Jordan. I should never have told you something so gruesome. At the witching hour too." Anneliese glanced at the clock, rueful. "I'm not myself after these dreams; they make me very fearful, and I babble. Very unlike me."

"Did it help?"

"I think it did." Anneliese drank off the rest of her cocoa. "I might be able to sleep now."

"Then I'm glad you told me." Jordan rose, collecting both mugs to put in the sink. "Can I just say . . ."

Her stepmother paused halfway to the kitchen door, Taro padding behind her. "Yes?"

"I'm so glad I have you." Jordan met those blue eyes square. "We didn't exactly get off on the right foot, thanks to my wild imagination. But I don't know what I'd do without you, now."

"You'd be just fine without me, Jordan." Anneliese reached out and touched her hair. "You're a tower of strength, just like your father."

They hugged fiercely. *Just us now*, Jordan thought. *Us two holding everything together for the sake of Ruth and a dog and a business.* The notion was perhaps not as frightening as it had been.

"Maybe you could walk me down the aisle next spring," Jordan said as they broke the hug. "What do you think, should we shatter tradition?"

"Of course, if you like." Anneliese's lips quirked. "There's only one small problem."

"What?"

"You have no desire at all to marry Garrett Byrne." Anneliese kissed Jordan's cheek good night. "There. I've given you something to dream about rather than night witches crawling out of lakes."

Chapter 29

IAN

June 1950
Boston

"Bad news, boss." Tony's voice reverberated at the other end of the phone like he was on the bottom of Nina's Siberian lake rather than a short distance away on Clarendon and Newbury.

Ian shifted the receiver from his bad ear to the good, still doing up the buttons of his shirt and wincing at the scratches Nina had left down his back. "Let's have it."

"Befriending Kolb has been a dead end. He won't get drawn in to talk. Just a grunt, and then some excuse to skitter away."

Disappointing, Ian thought, but not surprising. Tony's efforts to charm their suspect had been met by a stone wall for weeks now. Nina wandered in from the bedroom, wearing one of Ian's shirts and nothing else, and looked inquiring.

"I hate to admit failure," Tony concluded, "but the carrot approach has officially failed."

Nina stood on tiptoe so she could cock her own ear to the receiver. "Is our turn?"

"Have at it," Tony answered. "Right now Kolb thinks I'm just a dumb Yank too thick to notice I'm getting the cold shoulder, but if I keep on, he'll get suspicious. I'm down on strikes; you're up to bat."

Ian fumbled for a pencil stub. "Is that a baseball metaphor?"

"You're in the land of the brave and the home of the free now, boss, it's time to abandon cricket. I'll be here until closing; the pretty Miss McBride is bringing her stepmother to give me the nod of approval, but Kolb is off work this afternoon. Two more hours, if you want to take a run at him."

"Why not?" Ian looked down at Nina. "We don't have tickets for the symphony this evening, do we, darling?"

"Am not your darling, you capitalist *mudak*."

Ian grinned. "Give me Kolb's address." By the time he rang off, Nina had located her trousers in the trail of clothing that led toward the bedroom. Ian scrutinized them, patches and all. "Do you own anything that would make you look like a pinch-mouthed secretary?" She stared as though he were speaking Chinese. He sighed. "I suppose as a married man, this moment was inevitable."

Nina sounded suspicious. "What?"

"I'm taking you shopping."

"*BLYADT*," NINA BREATHED as they entered the spacious double doors of Filene's at Downtown Crossing. Ian could only imagine how strange it must look—how strange this whole, noisy, prosperous American city would look to a woman who had spent most of her life either on the far eastern edge of the world, in the Red Air Force, or in ration-locked war-torn England. She'd been astounded enough by the corner dime store off Scollay Square; now her eyes nearly glowed. "Everything just lying here? For sale, to anyone?"

"That's the idea."

"No lines out the door, no haggling, no rationing . . ." She stared at the perfume counter. "Even in England, is not like this. Shelves are empty, things are scarce. This is like . . ." She said a Russian word.

"Cornucopia?" Ian guessed. "Overflowing bounty?"

"Decadent industrialist filth. Everything my Komsomol meetings ever said, how the West is wasteful and corrupt. *Der'mo*, I wish I come sooner."

"Try not to comment on capitalist or socialist anything where anyone can hear you." Ian deposited his wife with a salesgirl in the ladies' department and grinned to watch an exceedingly dubious Nina hauled into a dressing room with an armload of skirts. "Men always think women take too long," the salesgirl twinkled, seeing him check his watch as she went off to find more clothes. Ian barely heard. Herr Kolb would be arriving home in two hours. If they could surprise him at his door, tired and off guard after a long day . . .

"Is what secretaries wear?" Nina came out of the dressing room in a flowered summer dress with a froth of crinoline.

"Definitely not. You need to look like a joyless soulless cow who hates everyone and everything, especially ungrateful little foreigners who lie about their war record. Surely you've met someone who—"

"My Komsomol leader from Irkutsk," she said at once.

"Perfect. Turn yourself into her."

"*Nu, ladno.*" Nina vanished back into the dressing room, her voice floating out. "Is another reason I like it here—no political meetings."

"I assure you the decadent West does have them, and they're every bit as boring. You've never been a cub journalist taking notes in the gallery as the MP for Upper Snelgrove drones on about combating district root rot."

The salesgirl bustled back with an armload of blouses. "She'll look ravishing in these—"

"No pink. No bows—" Ian rifled through the frilly stack. "Do you have anything in puce?"

"Your wife doesn't have the skin tone for puce, Mr. Graham. To be honest I don't think *any* woman has the skin tone for puce . . ." The salesgirl headed off shaking her head, and Nina came out in a flat brown skirt and short-sleeved blouse.

"Yes?"

"Longer sleeves. Something that covers up the fact that you spent years being strafed by Messerschmitts rather than taking stenography courses." Ian knew more of the history behind those scars now—Nina had been so entertained by his astonishment when she told him about meeting General Secretary Stalin, she'd unbent into telling a good many more stories up on the rooftop.

"I see other men in this store sitting outside dressing rooms." Nina vanished inside hers, already pulling the blouse over her head. "Is a thing American men do? Look annoyed while women try clothes?"

"Not so much an American thing as a marriage thing." Ian leaned against the wall, realizing how much he was enjoying himself. "Russian men don't wait for four hours as their wives try on dresses?"

"Russian men only wait four hours queuing for vodka." A snort. "At least is better vodka than here. You Westerners, you don't know how to drink."

"You have clearly never seen a roomful of war correspondents playing seven-card stud in Weymouth."

"Get some good vodka, and I drink you under the table, *luchik*."

"Make it scotch and you're welcome to try, you little Cossack."

Nina swept out in a navy-blue blouse, long sleeved and high necked. "Yes?"

She set hands on hips and face in a steely scowl, narrowing her eyes. "You look like an executioner who knows her shorthand," Ian admired.

"Is this hateful fucking blouse," she agreed, looking in the mirror. "Deserves to die in an arctic gulag, this blouse. Deserves to wrap fish guts on a whaler and filter gasoline into jerricans."

The salesgirl bustled up with something bright over one arm. "Are you sure you don't want something more colorful, Mrs. Graham?" She held up the dress by Nina's face. Red as a Soviet flag, and a hem that would show a lot of strong, curved leg. "Isn't she just born to wear red?"

"She certainly is," Ian said, straight-faced. "We'll take it."

Nina scowled. "Why?"

"Can't I buy my wife a dress?"

"We divorce, remember?"

"Wear the dress to the divorce," Ian said, and bought it. He couldn't afford it, but he didn't care.

Soon after, he and his pseudo-secretary were walking down Summer Street, looking for a cab. The street was wet and shiny; while they were inside, a shower of rain must have passed over in one of those fleeting summer storms so common in Boston. Nina noted the sky with her usual upward glance. "Good flying weather?" Ian asked.

"More rain coming, not good. But clouds for losing Messers, *very* good." She smiled. "What it is, is good hunting weather."

He offered his arm. "So let's go hunting."

WHEN HERR KOLB opened his door, Ian knew exactly what he saw, because a good many guilty men had seen the same thing over the past few years: a tall inquisitor in a knife-ironed suit, smiling with no humor whatsoever. Kolb did what most of them did when confronted by that man: took a nervous shuffle sideways as if he already wanted to hide.

Ian liked it when they did that. *I like it far too much*, he thought.

"*Kann ich*—can I help?" Kolb was a small man inside a suit that hung badly on thin shoulders; he blinked rapidly. They'd timed it well; he hadn't even had time to remove his jacket. "Sir?"

Ian let the silence stretch. They had to be nervous before he said a word. Too nervous to ask for identification, too nervous to think about whether he had authority to be here, too nervous to think about what their rights actually were.

"Jurgen Kolb?" he asked at last in his most superior English tone. His father's voice, the too-loud, too-confident drawl Ian had grown up hearing as a boy. The voice of a man who assumed the world was his oyster because he'd gone to the right schools and mixed with the right people; a man who knew the sun never set on the British Empire, and you had to make the Krauts and Wops and Dagos remember that, by God. "I'm Ian Graham of—" Ian rattled off a meaningless series of acronyms that he counted on Herr Kolb and his spotty English not absorbing and flashed his passport, which had enough seals and stamps to intimidate anyone with a guilty conscience.

Kolb's hand stretched out for the passport. "May I—"

Ian stared coldly. "I don't think that's necessary, do you?"

For a moment it hung in the balance. Kolb could have shut the door in their faces; he could have demanded to see proper credentials. But he folded, stepping back. Ian sauntered in, Nina following with a steely glare as if prepared to ship Kolb to a gulag on the spot. A rented apartment, stifling hot and smelling of cooking oil and rust, furnished with little more than a cot, a table, and an icebox.

"What is this?" Kolb summoned some indignation. "I haf done nothing wrong."

"We'll see about that." Ian took his time, strolling about hands in pockets. A bottle of cheap scotch on the table, a drink already poured. He'd poured a drink as soon as he got home, before even taking off his jacket . . . "I have a few questions for you, Fritz. Do be a good chap and cooperate."

"My name is not Fritz. *Ist* Jurgen, Jurgen Kolb—"

"No, it isn't," Ian said pleasantly. "You runty little Kraut."

"Ich verstehe nicht—"

"You *verstehe* just fine. Show me your identification."

Kolb slowly dug out his wallet, his passport, his various bits of paper. Ian flipped through, passing everything to Nina, who took notes as though copying down state secrets. "Good fakes," Ian said, admiring the passport. "Really top-class work." It was. Either *Kolb* was the man's real name, which Ian doubted, or his guess that the McBride shop clerk was some kind of documents expert was looking better and better.

"Ich verstehe nicht," Kolb repeated, sullen.

Ian dropped into his accented but fluent German, which made Kolb twitch miserably. "Your papers are false. You're a war criminal. You came to the United States without reporting your crimes in Europe, which imperils your legal status here."

The man stared at his lap. "No."

"Yes. You're helping other war criminals like yourself, probably in the back room of that antiques shop on Newbury and Clarendon."

Kolb's eyes flicked to the drink sitting on the table, then back down to his lap. "How'd you get the job, Fritzie?" Ian picked up the glass, swirling the scotch to draw Kolb's eyes to it. "Bamboozle the widowed mother into thinking you were a rare books expert? Take a backroom key out of the daughter's purse while she's off canoodling with her fiancé, so you can carve out a backdoor operation getting money out of your old National Socialist friends?" Ian shook his head. "Funny thing about Americans. They don't care much about ex-Nazis, they get more worked up these days about the Reds. But for all their fuss about *give me your huddled masses*, Yanks don't really like refugees, especially the kind who take advantage of widows and orphans." Pause. "Like you."

"It isn't true," Kolb muttered. Nina shook her head as if she'd never heard such lies.

"It is true. It's just a question of what I decide to do about it." Ian swallowed the scotch, grimacing. "Bloody hell, doesn't forgery pay well enough for single malt? Tell me who you've helped. Whom you've made papers for."

Kolb's chin jerked, but his lips stayed pressed shut.

"You don't seem to realize you're in luck today." Ian picked up the bottle, watching Kolb's eyes go to it. "I'm not really interested in you, Fritzie. Give me some names, and I'll forget I know yours."

The German moistened his lips. "I don't know any names. I come to start a new life. I wasn't a Nazi—"

"*Ich bin kein Nazi, ich bin kein Nazi.*" Ian looked at Nina, setting down the bottle. "They all say that, don't they?"

She nodded ominously, pencil flying.

"I was a member of the party," Kolb burst out in German, suddenly talkative. "But it wasn't like you make it sound. You had to be a party member just to get by. I was just doing my job."

Ah, the sweet sound of justifications. Once they started to justify themselves, you were getting somewhere. Ian sat back. "What job?"

"An assessor. Rare books, musical instruments. My advice was sought." Straightening his tie. "I examined antiques that had been gathered and sent to Austria, on the way to private collections in Berlin. That is all."

"*Gathered.* That's a nice word for *stolen.*"

"That wasn't my job." Stubbornly. "I only assessed items that came to me. Restoring anything damaged, seeing it crated for travel. I wasn't responsible for confiscations."

"That was someone else's job," Ian sympathized. "Of course. Well, a man who can spot a forgery usually isn't too bad at making them."

"I use my skills honestly to make a living, that's all."

"I want names. Who you helped. Where they are now." *Lorelei Vogt.* The name was on the tip of Ian's tongue, but he swallowed it. He didn't want Kolb knowing there was someone specific they were looking for, if there was even the remotest chance he might warn her. *He might warn her anyway that someone is sniffing for war criminals.* But that was a chance they'd have to take; without Kolb they had no lead at all.

The German moistened his lips again. "I helped no one. I am hiding nothing."

"Then you won't object if my secretary has a look around." Kolb opened his mouth, but Ian gave a freezing glare. "An innocent man would give his permission without hesitation."

Kolb shrugged, sullen. "There's nothing to find."

"All entirely cricket, eh?" Ian said as Nina slapped her notebook down and stamped into the bedroom. Kolb looked scared, but his eyes followed Ian, not his supposed secretary. Ian's hopes that Nina would find something incriminating began to sink.

"Have a drink," he said instead, pouring a splash of scotch into the glass. Just enough to wet the tongue, get a drunk's thirst really roaring, and from the eager way Kolb grabbed the glass, Ian suspected he was a thoroughgoing boozer. "Let's go over this again. Your real name, to start. Why hide it? It's not illegal here to take a new name. Normally you Jerries go for Smith or Jones, but I suppose given your pathetic English, you didn't see the point in trying to pretend you weren't German." Ian let contempt filter into his voice. "Or maybe you just shortened your real name? Was it Kolbaum, Kolbmann? There are a lot of Jews in the antiques business, are you a Jew? Helping out the Nazis to get yourself a pass—"

"I'm not a *Jew*." That pricked Kolb's Aryan outrage as Ian had thought it would. "I'm *Austrian*, pure descent!"

Even a small apartment like this one took a long time to search thoroughly. Nina checked every floorboard for loose nails, every cupboard for false backs, every bedspring and dinner plate and item of clothing, as Ian hammered at Kolb. He put a third of the bottle of scotch into the man, as he alternated between cutting sarcasm and a whip-snap roar that had Kolb cringing in his chair. Ian learned his real name was Gerhardt Schlitterbahn. Ian learned a tedious amount about the business Kolb had done in Austria for the Third Reich, assessing Blüthner pianofortes and first-edition volumes of Schiller confiscated from Jewish families. Ian learned how Kolb nearly starved after the war, how Daniel McBride had agreed to sponsor him in return for lending his expertise to the shop—and that was where the man clammed up.

It didn't matter if Ian threatened to come back with an arrest warrant, if he put money on the table, if he threatened to get Kolb sacked by informing his employers that the man they had sponsored was a Nazi. Kolb ignored both bribes and threats, mouth sealed shut. He was drenched in sweat, half drunk, sniffling and flinching whenever Ian came within arm's length, but he wouldn't admit he had aided any fellow Nazis, and he wouldn't list names.

Nina stood behind him, fists on hips, shaking her head. She'd torn this apartment apart with the kind of brutal efficiency Ian envisioned in secret police raids, and found nothing. If Kolb had incriminating lists or documents, they weren't here. Disappointment rose sharp and bitter in Ian's mouth.

Kolb gnawed his lip, eyes yearning for the scotch. *You know*, Ian thought. *You know where she is.* So much knowledge locked behind that clamped mouth.

"You're severely trying my patience, Fritz," he said at last.

"I have nothing to tell you." Kolb spoke in a righteous rising whine. So very hard done by. So *wronged*. "I've done nothing, nothing at all—"

Ian didn't mean to move. He didn't realize he'd risen until he swatted the bottle of scotch to the floor in a shower of glass, sank a hand into Kolb's collar, dragged him out of his chair, and hoisted him up against the wall. "You cataloged stolen books while the people who owned them were shipped off in cattle cars," Ian said. "Don't tell me you did nothing, you little Nazi shit."

Kolb squeaked, eyes huge. Ian hoisted him another inch, off the floor, so the man's face abruptly started turning purple. "Tell me who you helped get here." Ian heard the blood rushing in his ears. "Tell me who you're protecting."

Lorelei Vogt. Give her to me.

Kolb just stared, whimpering, and Ian had never wanted to hurt a man so badly in his life. Fling him to the ground and give his face a few good stamps, till he was spitting blood and tooth splinters out along with names.

He won't talk, the thought whispered. However much Ian scared him, Kolb feared something else more. Very possibly *die Jägerin. If I were a cringing paper pusher nursing a bottle of scotch, I'd be quite scared of what a woman like that could do to me—a woman who killed six children in cold blood.* Ian heard the thought come cool and ruthless. *You'll have to hurt him quite a lot to make him more afraid of you than her.*

At that point, though, information couldn't really be counted on. People in enough pain would say anything to make the pain stop.

But Ian didn't care. He wanted to do it anyway. He wanted to beat this man to a pulp.

He heard a *snick* behind him, and he didn't need to look back to know Nina had unfolded the razor from her sleeve. Anything he did, his wife wasn't going to stop him.

Ian took a long breath and lowered Kolb back onto his straining toes. He stepped back, fishing his handkerchief out and wiping his fingers clean of scotch splatters as Kolb sagged gasping against the wall.

"Maybe I believe you, Fritz." Ian fought to keep his voice light, conversational. "Maybe you're just a sad man left over from a bad war, trying to make his way in the world. You're lucky my colleagues"—waving a hand, implying hordes of faceless associates from the police department, the immigration bureau—"have other names more interesting than yours." Ian collected his hat, Nina her notebook. The razor had been stowed. Only the smell of liquor, the crunch of glass underfoot, and the fear in the little German's eyes gave away what had almost happened.

It still could happen, Ian thought. A fist to the gut, then when Kolb doubled over, bring the knee up and break his nose. The crunch would be glorious. "Do I need to mention that you shouldn't think of leaving Boston?" Ian asked instead.

"No," Kolb said at once.

"Good. Innocent men don't run. You run, I'll come after you. And I won't be so friendly next time." Ian clapped his fedora over his hair. The rage was draining, leaving a sick feeling in the gut. *Bloody hell, Graham, what did you almost do?*

"Have a good day," Ian managed to say, and fled.

Chapter 30

NINA

July 1943
Russian front near Taman Peninsula

D rink your Coca-Cola, rabbit." Nina yawned, stepping up onto the wing and passing Yelena a pair of stimulant tablets. "It'll be eight runs at least."

Eight runs over the Blue Line, the stretch of German fortifications between Novorossiysk and the Sea of Azov, a razor-edge thicket of searchlights, antiaircraft batteries, enemy airdromes, fighters on alert . . . The Night Witches had been hammering at the same stretch since they'd been transferred here in the spring. They'd been so jubilant, sweeping into their new post flushed with pride because by now everyone knew that they were pushing the Fritzes back. The swastikas were falling back before the red stars, and the 588th had their part to play.

The Forty-Sixth, Nina reminded herself as the *Rusalka* was cleared to take off. The 588th had been renamed the Forty-Sixth Taman Guards Night Bomber Aviation Regiment in February. "Five other regiments of U-2 fliers in our next division, ladies," Bershanskaia said with pride, "and not one has been named a Guards regiment."

"The men don't have our sortie numbers!" Nina had called from the back of the crowd, and even as Bershanskaia cut her hand downward to quell the resulting laughter, she smiled. Because they all knew it was true. The other regiments flew hard, but they didn't push their planes and themselves to the absolute limit. They hadn't fought to come to the front, only to be called *little princesses*.

It had been a very long time since anyone called a Night Witch a little princess, but Nina didn't think any of them had forgotten.

Yelena was saying something, Nina realized, pointing at the U-2 lined up ahead of them. ". . . worried about her," Yelena said, nodding at the other plane's pilot who was staring blankly out of her cockpit. "Irina hasn't been right since Dusia died."

"Irina didn't bring her pilot down alive," Nina said. In April, Dusia had taken a shot through the floor of her cockpit from a Focke-Wulf—clipped through the skull, dead in an instant. Her navigator Irina had had to land, stiff with shock, but she'd gone back to flying the next night. "She thinks she should be dead too, not sitting in her pilot's place."

"Don't tell me *you* think that!"

"No, but she does." Promotion from the rear cockpit to the front happened over the body of another pilot. You lost a *sestra*, you had to slot another into her seat and keep flying. Nina shivered, touching her star-embroidered scarf for luck.

A smooth ascent into the cloudless sky—tonight they took off fourth. Nina felt her pills kick in, giving the world its slowed-down razor-edged clarity, the glass-clear alertness. She'd pay for it later, jittering and blinking and unable to sleep, but it was worth it to feel this awake and alive, sliding immortal through the sky.

"Searchlights," Nina called through the interphones as they approached their target. Yelena had already seen those four searching columns, had already started her descent. Nina saw the lead plane in the cross-beams, a white spot bleached colorless—

And then it turned from white to red in a sudden burst of flame.

For a moment Nina thought her ears had burst, that she had gone deaf. *The guns*, she thought, *where are they?* There were no shells exploding in the air, the batteries below were silent, and yet a

U-2 was falling out of the sky in a shower of glowing red-and-gold fragments.

"*Drop!*" Yelena was screaming to the next plane in line, but strange flashes were already arrowing in, straight through the dark rather than from the ground. The second plane exploded, falling apart midair, and two more girls were dead. Bile crawled up the back of Nina's throat. "Night fighters," she heard herself shouting through the interphones, "they're lining us up with *night fighters*—" They had never been hit with that before; the tracer fire was setting the U-2s alight like dry kindling. The third U-2 in line should have been sideslipping, diving out of the line of flight, but it sailed straight into the lights, undeviating. Irina was in the cockpit, Nina thought, Irina who had brought Dusia's corpse down, then sat frozen for hours afterward. *She must be shock-frozen now*, Nina thought, shouting fruitlessly at the plane. Shock-frozen the way Yelena had been that time she imagined Messerschmitts where there were none—because Irina didn't even try to evade the tracer fire. She flew on, straight and slow as a stone lobbed gently into a river, and then she was burning in the air like a sheet of paper.

The next fighter to make its pass would target the *Rusalka*.

Yelena had already thrown them into a nosedive. "Get under the lights," Nina yelled through the interphones. They were sinking fast toward the ground, and from the corner of her eye she could see the flaming wreckage of Irina's plane—charred fuselage, half a wing, a horrendously bright flare that might have been burning hair on a dead woman's head—settle over the earth in glowing embers. The *Rusalka*'s altimeter fell, Yelena forcing them down under six hundred meters, five, four—"We're over the target!" Nina shouted, "keep straight—" Normally Nina would have released the bombs, but they were far too low. Two hundred meters now and still falling. Nina looked back and saw the U-2 behind them tumble out of the sky midway through its own evasive maneuvers, a burning propeller whirling into the night like a star, the navigator's flares going off in colored bursts even as the plane's wings broke apart. Nina saw the shape of a German night fighter for the first time, lit jaggedly by the green light of the flares.

"Under one hundred meters," Yelena called, bringing the engine back to life even as the altimeter needle scraped the bottom. The *Rusalka* roared, nose lifting as Yelena brought her around still hugging the ground. "I can't *see*—"

Nina struggled to get her bearing for the new heading, back to the airdrome. This mission was done. The searchlights were still stabbing the air, but the Night Witches had scattered to the wind, run for cloud cover, turned for home. The ground below glowed with burning fragments. *Four planes*, Nina thought numbly. They had never, ever lost so many at once. Losses came singly, a plane at a time, perhaps two. Not four.

She could hear Yelena crying in the front cockpit, even as she took them up to a safer height to jettison their bombs. "Tell me where to go," she was weeping, "tell me the heading. Take me *home*."

"HOW DID THE FRITZES know our target?"

"Even they get lucky. Who knows?"

Ten minutes. Eight girls. One moment they were immortal, the Night Witches descending on their targets. The next moment, burning like candles.

"I've been promoted to pilot." Nina mumbled the news into Yelena's hair, standing outside the schoolhouse that now served as their barracks. "Moved up with three other navigators." She should have been raging to be moved away from Yelena, but all rage had been drained out of her.

"It's where you belong," Yelena said valiantly. "The regiment needs you in a pilot's cockpit, not steering me around." But her face crumpled. Nina pulled her closer, openly kissed her wet eyes and her wet cheeks, not bothering to look for privacy. Ever since coming back to the barracks and seeing the eight folded cots against the wall that would not be filled that night, all the women were embracing, clinging, comforting each other. The most disastrous night in regiment history had bloomed into a beautiful summer morning, and they all knew they would be going up again tonight. The word had come down that they'd have night fighters of their own flying, if any German night fighters reared their snouts again.

"They've given you a U-2 already?" Yelena asked, wiping her eyes. "For tonight?"

Nina nodded. "Bershanskaia's pairing you with Zoya for navigator. She's good—you were right about that. She'll take care of you."

Not like I can. But she didn't say it; this was the time to fill her pilot with confidence.

"Who's your navigator?" Yelena asked.

"Galina Zelenko."

"Little Galya? How is that skinny prat supposed to keep you out of trouble?" Yelena sounded unaccustomedly savage. "She looks about twelve!"

"Eighteen, and terrified of me. Am I really that frightening?" Nina's attempt at levity fell flat. *I don't want to leave you*, she wanted to cry. *I can't fly with anyone but you.* But this was the way of things: lose a *sestra*, slot another into her cockpit, keep flying.

They stood in the sunlight, clinging to each other. "I just want this war to be *over*," Yelena whispered. "I want an apartment in Moscow overlooking the river, Ninochka. I want to sit at the window with a glass of tea, and hold your hand, and watch babies play on the floor. I want to sleep ten hours every night. I never want to kill even a spider again."

Peace and tea and sunlight. Nina tried to imagine it, an apartment with a wide gray river outside, children laughing, tea sweetened with cherry jam, but all she could see was planes falling through the night like burning flowers. *I want to kill Nazis*, Nina thought. *Whether this war ends tomorrow or in a hundred years, I don't think I will ever stop wanting to kill Nazis.*

"Aren't you tired of it, Nina? The dark, the jitters, the bad dreams?"

Never, Nina thought. She was heartsick and grief-sick and staggering with exhaustion; she had the usual postflight headache, and a ferocious crash coming when her Coca-Cola tablets wore off—but she already wanted to get back in the air.

Back to the hunt.

"HOW IS IT?" Galina asked anxiously, passing Nina her tea. She really did look about twelve.

"What do you mean *how is it*? It's airdrome tea; it's ice cold and tastes like gasoline." Nina signed off on the release the mechanic had stood on the wing to thrust under her nose.

"Can we give her a name?" Galina gave their U-2 a pat as she climbed into the navigator's seat. "Some pilots do."

"She's just a U-2. Take the stick when we reach altitude, we'll give you some practice—" and off they were, following Yelena and the *Rusalka* up into the clouds. "Light touch, don't yank . . ."

They were flying missions over the peninsula all that month, coming back to barracks near Krasnodar. Not even a repurposed shed this time but dugout trenches with plank beds, lines strung up so wet underwear and stockings could dry above the mud. Nina took to sleeping on the airfield under old plane covers, arm thrown over her eyes to block the light, hoping Yelena could join her. Long days and lack of proper barracks meant fewer places they could meet alone.

"I'm being sent out on detail," Yelena said in August, looking bleak. "Eight crews are joining the Black Sea Fleet battalions."

Nina's heart clutched. "When will you be back?"

"When we take Novorossiysk." Yelena kissed her, soft and reassuring, but Nina wasn't reassured. That was rough flying between sea and mountains, storms blowing off the water . . . she pulled Yelena to her fiercely, burying her face in that delicate collarbone. *Promise you'll come back*, she thought, but no one promised that. Yelena went off to Novorossiysk; Nina stayed on flying runs over the peninsula, the Crimea, the wave-shattered coast along the Sea of Azov.

"Nina Borisovna, you will assist the training squadron in your off hours," Bershanskaia informed her, scribbling at a stack of paperwork. The Forty-Sixth trained replacements within the regiment, pilots training their navigators, navigators training their mechanics, mechanics training their armorers. Any position could be filled within the regiment; they took pride in that. "Four mechanics have just moved up."

Nina saluted. "Get some sleep, Comrade Major." They were all frank-spoken with each other, regardless of rank. It shocked the officers from other regiments, but the Night Witches just shrugged.

Bershanskaia smiled, stubbing out her cigarette in an ashtray made of a flattened shell case. "We'll sleep when we're dead."

We're dying off fairly fast now, Nina thought. That night, it was almost her.

Galina read off the headings that evening, giving the night's target along the peninsula coast. Nina still felt strange to be the one listening to the headings rather than giving them. A night's uneventful flying, seven runs. "Very low overcast coming in off the water," Galina began as Nina made the wide returning turn on the last run.

"I see it." Nina dived down, but the gray masses of cloud snowballed before her eyes as the wind picked up. She pressed the U-2 lower through the dense cloud . . . lower . . .

"Correct course sixty degrees west." Galina sounded nervous. "We're pushing out too far—"

"I need to get under this cloud." The U-2 bounced like a ball in a chute. Three hundred meters, two hundred, and finally the plane bottomed out under the low hover of cloud. *Fuck your mother*, Nina thought in a sudden drench of panic. They were over the *sea*. Nina craned her head frantically but there was nothing in sight but lashing, roiling water, no land visible in this dense overhang. "Find me a heading. Find me *land*—"

"We came too far east, over the water instead of—"

"I don't care where the water *is*, just get me *off it*!"

The clouds whirled, shaking the U-2, pressing them down. Under a hundred meters, fifty . . . Nina watched the altimeter, hypnotized. *West*, Galina was shouting through the interphones, *set a heading west*—but the winds blew dead east, pushing them back as they strained forward, controls fighting Nina's grip. The U-2 sat almost motionless in the air, the forward kick of the engine canceled by the backward thrust of the wind, wobbling just to maintain altitude.

If we run out of fuel and fall into the sea, she thought in stark terror, *we'll sink and drown before we can fight out of our cockpits.*

Pull yourself together, rusalka *bitch,* her father growled. But all Nina could think was that she had run thousands of kilometers west to get away from the lake, had run clear into the *sky* to get away from the lake, and she was still going to die by drowning.

The altimeter needle lay flat at the bottom of the dial. *Eight meters,* she thought, *we are at eight meters' height.* Hovering just above the roiling dark water, roiling dark clouds pushing down from above, squeezed between a giant's palms—

"We're not going to drown," Galina shouted through the interphones. She had, Nina realized distantly, been shouting it for quite some time. "We're not going to drown."

Yes, we are, Nina thought. The bigger waves were splashing up and wetting their wings; she could actually *see* it.

"We're not going to drown."

Yes, we are. Her stick arm was a stiff screech of pain all the way up to the shoulder. It would be easier to stop fighting the wind, give the rudder a good hard yank to one side and plant them propeller first in the water. Do it hard enough and they'd both be unconscious before they drowned. Nina stared at the sea, hypnotized.

"We're not going to drown." Galina repeated it, a monotonous rhythmic chant. "*We'renotgoingtodrown.*" She repeated it until the ferocious tearing of the wind relented just a little, repeated it as Nina still sat frozen. It was Galina who bore the U-2 around into the teeth of the breeze and clawed some wobbling height, still chanting "We're not going to drown." She was still repeating it when Nina came out of her terrified daze and took the stick, bringing them down on the first available spot on the abandoned coast. They both sagged in their cockpits as the engine spun down, and finally Galina shut up. Nina clawed free of her safety harness and turned to look at her navigator. The girl was ghastly pale, head thrown back and eyes closed; her cockpit was spattered with vomit. "We didn't drown," Nina told her weakly.

No thanks to you, rusalka, her father said. Nina knew she deserved the contempt. Shivers of terror were still coursing through her, but that terrible deep freeze that had held her motionless and staring at the water was gone. She wondered if Yelena had felt like that when she'd hallucinated the Messerschmitt.

You had a panic. Everyone has them. Nina had been the one to tell Yelena that.

"Thank you," she told her new navigator now.

"Yelena Vassilovna said you hated flying over water," Galina said surprisingly. "She said if we ever got in a bad way over seas, I should tell you we wouldn't drown and be ready to jump on the stick."

"She told you that?"

"I asked her everything that would help me fly for you. You're my pilot," Galina said as though it were obvious.

Nina felt herself smiling. "What are you afraid of, Galya?" Calling her navigator by nickname for the first time.

A long pause. "The black vans."

Nina nodded. Normally one didn't speak of such things, but here on the barren edge of the sea there was no poisonous listening ear to hear and report. "They came for my uncle seven years ago," Galya went on. "His factory foreman denounced him as an agitator. He went to the Lubyanka and never came out. My aunt had to denounce him too or be taken herself. That's what I fear, the van stopping at my door."

"I can't protect you from that," Nina said. The van could come for anyone, for the smallest of reasons or no reason at all. "The van can't come for you in the air, Galya, so what do you fear up here?"

"Those new German shells, the ones with red and green and white tracers. When they split into dozens of little projectiles in the dark, I think of flowers . . ." Galya shuddered.

"Well, if we see flowers and you freeze, I'll get you out of it," Nina promised. "We stall out over water again, you'll get me out of it. In the meantime, *you* can fly home."

Galina brightened. They wobbled home, and it wasn't till they returned that they learned another U-2 had gone down in the sea, in the same low-rolling overhang of cloud.

Sixteen women died in all, over that summer and fall. Nina hoped all this territory was worth it, this unseen ground they were clawing back from the Germans. She couldn't even *see* the gains they were dying for, just that it was soaked in blood.

"Who are these new girls?" Yelena asked in bewilderment when she came back from Novorossiysk in October, looking around the barracks. "They're so young!"

"New arrivals." Girl volunteers to the front, every one of them round-eyed at the sight of the gaunt female pilots in their bulky overalls, more and more of which were pinned with Orders of the Red Banner and Orders of the Red Star. Nina and Yelena both had one of each now, and there were whispers that the first set of HSUs were going to be passed down—the gold stars of Hero of the Soviet Union, highest decoration in the Motherland.

"My pilot sleeps with a razor under her pillow and she knows Comrade Stalin," Nina overheard Galina bragging to one of the new recruits, who looked both terrified and impressed, and Nina would have laughed herself sick if she hadn't been already sick with worry over Yelena.

"You look terrible," she said frankly.

"That's a nice thing to tell a girl." Yelena made a face, teasing. She was skin and bone, her complexion ashy. The autumn dawn was icy, but cold was their friend; no one now lingered on the airfield when the night's flying was done. Everyone had retreated to the dugout, warming hands at the oil-drum fire, and Nina and Yelena drifted back out to the *Rusalka*, lying entwined under the wing. Always the *Rusalka*, never Nina's new nameless U-2. She was a nice plane, tough and reliable, but she wasn't *their* plane.

"Was it bad, flying over Novorossiysk?" Nina persisted, turning over so they lay nose to nose. Because Yelena's hands had a fine tremor they hadn't had two months ago.

"Not so bad. I heard things got rough here—"

"Nothing difficult," Nina said.

They smiled at each other. Both lying, Nina knew. *What else do we lie to each other about?* she thought, but pushed that away.

"The war will be done soon." Yelena sounded more certain than she had in the summertime. "And then we'll have it."

"What?"

"Us together in Moscow. I picture it whenever I need something to keep me on course. Don't you?" She nudged Nina. "Imagine us, sleeping at night again rather than during the day, chasing babies around the floor after breakfast . . ."

"Do I have to tell you how babies happen, Miss Moscow Goody? Because if you think anything *we* do is going to help on that front—" Tickling Yelena between the breasts.

Yelena laughed, swatting her hand away. "There'll be so many orphans after the war who need mothers. Don't you want children?" she asked as if it were the most natural thing in the world.

No, Nina thought. "I never thought about it," she hedged.

"I know what you're thinking—"

I doubt it.

"—you're thinking we won't be able to hide things out in real life. Hide *this*." A little swirling gesture encompassing the two of them, their private world under the *Rusalka*'s wing. "But we can, believe me. It's not like when men go together, people being suspicious. There will be so many widows living together after the war, pooling supplies and pensions—as long as we're raising children for the Motherland and we each have a story about a fiancé who died in the war, no one will look at us twice for sharing an apartment. We could be civil pilots, or teach aviation."

Her voice was eager, her cheeks pink. She'd been thinking about this a long time, Nina realized with a sinking stomach.

"It won't be like how we grew up, Ninochka—shortages, queuing for fuel, never being able to get shoes. The world's going to be different after the war, Moscow's going to be different—"

Worse, Nina thought. *After years of starvation and war, it's going to be worse.*

"—and we're not just air club fliers anymore. We're decorated officers of Marina Raskova's eaglets. You've met *Comrade Stalin*." That damned awe in Yelena's voice again. "We'll have no shortage of recommendations when we apply to join the Party, you'll see. Then we can pull strings for an apartment we don't have to share with three other families, get plush jobs at the Zhukovsky Academy or anywhere we like."

She was gabbling now, all hope. Such good, normal, *usual* things to want. Probably most of the women in the regiment cherished similar dreams for after this war was done.

"It's not too much to want, Ninochka. You, me, a home, a baby or two, a job flying civil routes instead of bombing runs." Yelena leaned forward, brushed her lips over Nina's. "All we have to do is survive the war, and we can *have* it."

"Maybe it isn't too much to want," Nina said. "But what if I want something else?"

"What?" Yelena smoothed her cheek. "Do you not want to live in Moscow? We don't have to, I know you don't like it—"

I don't like Moscow, or Irkutsk, or the Old Man, Nina thought. *I've come thousands of kilometers across Russia, and I haven't seen any part of it I liked except the skies*. She was happy flying over it, because then she didn't have to look at it: a land of implacable crowds and draped bunting, bread queues and the eternal droning of loudspeakers, ruled over by a wolf.

When the war is over, what do you want? Yelena was still waiting for her answer. Such a simple question, surely the simplest question of all for soldiers at war. Everyone dreamed of what came after the bloodshed was done. Everyone, apparently, but Nina, who could honestly say she'd never given it a single thought. Who had never thought at all beyond the present, beyond a night spent flying and a morning spent kissing Yelena. Who would take this strange, perilous, nighttime life in the regiment over any other in the world, even with all its griefs and its terrors.

What do I want, Yelenushka? Nina thought, looking at her lover's eager smile. *I want to fly missions, hunt Germans, and love you. And the only thing on both your list and mine is you.*

Chapter 31

JORDAN

June 1950
Boston

*Y*ou *have no desire at all to marry Garrett Byrne.* Anneliese's
wry comment still reverberated even as Jordan tried to busy
herself behind the shop counter.

Of course I want to marry Garrett, she told herself. *I've got a
half-carat's worth of sparkle on my left hand proving how much I
want to marry him.*

Ruth's voice drifted up from the nearest display case. "May I
hold the violin?"

"It's not a toy, cricket," Jordan said absently. "It's a late-
nineteenth-century copy of a Mayr."

"But it's small," Ruth begged. "It's *my* size."

"That's a half-size violin, Mr. Kolb says."

"Very pleased to meet you at last, Mrs. McBride." Tony Rodomovsky's voice issued from the front of the shop, where he stood with
Anneliese in her black suit. "My condolences for your recent loss . . ."

Anneliese murmured some reply as Jordan bent back over her
own work: trimming down one of the prints of her dad she'd made
late last night. It was a good portrait, very good—she could judge
her own work well enough to know that.

You could do something with that shot, the thought whispered. *Something professional.*

Like what? she answered herself. *You* aren't *a professional.* She was a girl with a nice job behind this counter, and an entertaining hobby in the basement. In spring she was going to be a wife with a nice husband going off to work every morning, and an entertaining hobby kept in the spare room.

"I've prepared the weekly report if you would like to see it, Mrs. McBride." Tony came back to the register behind Anneliese in her full black skirts, black jacket, and little black hat with the spotted net chicly angled over her eyes. "Just a moment."

"What do you think?" Jordan asked her stepmother as Tony vanished into the back room, remembering Anneliese had dropped by to give the new clerk a final look.

"He seems quite charming. If you're satisfied with his references, I see no reason not to keep him on; you're a good judge of character." Anneliese gave Ruth a quick hug and looked at the shop clock. "I'm meeting with your father's lawyer about the will; can you keep Ruth until closing? Oh, my—" Seeing the photograph of Dan McBride.

"Isn't it him to the life?"

Anneliese nodded, tears in her eyes. Jordan gave her black-gloved hand a squeeze across the counter. Tony came back with the report, and Anneliese took it distractedly. "We're glad you've joined us, Mr. Rodomovsky—" and she was gone in a waft of lilac scent.

"Phew," Tony said. "I was shaking."

"You were not. You think there isn't a lady on earth you can't charm, Mr. Rodomovsky."

"Tony," he said, as he usually did. "Every time you say *Mr. Rodomovsky*, I look around for my father and start counting up my most recent sins."

He was leaning on the counter giving Jordan the same smile he gave all the ladies who set foot in this shop—though it came, she had noticed, with variations. The boyish grin went to ladies over sixty, who pinched his cheek (then bought something). The roguish grin went to ladies over forty, who lidded their eyes speculatively (then bought something). The full grin included both the crinkled eyes *and* creases in the cheeks, and it went to ladies over twenty who blushed (then bought something). Even Anneliese had gotten the modified grin with the sympathetic edge, given her widow's weeds, and had responded to it. *Tony Rodomovsky probably flirts with a hat rack if there isn't anything else around*, Jordan thought with considerable amusement. She was glad Anneliese had approved him, because he was certainly good for business.

"Princess Ruth," Tony exclaimed as he saw the small nose press against the violin's glass case. "Are you to favor us with a recital?"

Ruth was usually shy with strange men, but Tony upon meeting her had gone down on one knee and intoned that it was well known that Princess Ruth of Bostonia spake not to her knights errant until they had earned her favor with supreme deeds of gallantry, and that he would fain ride to the ends of the earth to win her regard—whereupon Ruth had come out of her hair with a cautious smile. She let him kiss her hand now, then poised an imaginary violin and began to play. Jordan wondered where she had ever seen a violin played; she certainly had the stance right.

Her mother, Jordan answered her own question. *Her* real *mother*. Ruth must have seen her mother play—they'd never know how or where, young as Ruth had been. She'd seemed to forget about it for years, but here it was coming up again, making her gaze at the child-size violin as if mesmerized. Was Ruth remembering it now because the only man she'd ever known as a father was suddenly gone, the way her musical, mysterious mother had disappeared?

Jordan's gaze fell back to her dad's eyes in the picture. *He was solid*, Anneliese had said of him last night, over her cocoa. *Nothing could follow me out of a dream with him there.* Maybe that was why Ruth had bad dreams. The solid, four-square father who had anchored her world for the past few years was now gone.

"You're in a daze this afternoon, Miss McBride." Tony's gaze had turned serious. Jordan braced herself for the usual solicitous *Are you all right?* that she heard from neighbors and acquaintances and friends every day since her father died, and she mustered the usual bright *I'm just fine!*

"Would you like me to go away?" Tony asked instead. "I have a handkerchief or a listening ear if you want, but I can also leave you alone for some peace, quiet, and a good cry, in whatever order you need them. *Alone* being the important part."

Jordan couldn't help but laugh, startled. "I have . . . wanted that quite a lot, the last few weeks." That was why she kept drifting down into the darkroom. People didn't usually follow her down there.

"Right, then." Tony straightened. "Shall I bugger off?"

"'Bugger off'? Did you suddenly turn English?"

"I spent too many years working with a Limey." A quirk of a smile. "Here's an idea—why don't *you* bugger off, Miss McBride? Take Princess Ruth home early, have some time to yourself."

Jordan opened her mouth to refuse, but the bell jingled and Garrett's voice sounded. "Jor, there you are." He dropped his arm around her shoulders, giving a searching look as if to make sure she hadn't been crying. "Are you—"

"I'm just fine."

"I'm trying to persuade Miss McBride here to go home early," Tony broke in. "Maybe you'll have better luck, Mr.—"

"Byrne. Garrett Byrne." Offering a hand. "You're the new clerk?"

"Guilty. Tony Rodomovsky. You're the fiancé?"

"Guilty."

An exchange of handshakes. Jordan wondered if there were two young men anywhere on earth who could shake hands without the size-up that went with it: who had the stronger grip, who was taller. Garrett stretched to his full six two; Tony slouched against the counter looking amused.

"I can't go home early, Garrett," Jordan broke in before they could start on the next part of the ritual, which was to figure out who had been in the war and who hadn't. "Anna is seeing the lawyer, and I'll have to stay until closing."

"I can close up for you," Tony said unhelpfully.

"See?" Garrett reached down, tousled Ruth's hair. She ignored him, still playing her imaginary violin. "We could go to the movies, take Ruth. I've missed you."

"I've missed you too." *I have*, Jordan thought. *I have.*

"Mr. Kolb's already gone," Tony said. "There won't be much to do here."

Jordan hesitated. Her father wouldn't have left any new clerk alone in the shop until they had a good month under their belt and he was absolutely certain he hadn't hired a thief. But Tony had worked a flawless three weeks, and Anneliese had given her seal of approval. "You know how to close up," she told Tony, handing over the keys. "Come on, Ruthie. Want to go to the movies?"

Ruth's imaginary bow stopped midarc. She had been mesmerized by *Cinderella* early that year; she'd driven Anneliese mad begging for pet mice. "Cinderella?"

"Get your glass slippers, princess." Tony put her imaginary violin into a case with great care. "You just leave that with me, I'll keep it safe for your violin lessons . . ."

Garrett was holding the door, smiling, but Jordan paused, struck by a sudden idea.

"Don't forget this, Miss McBride." Tony held out the print of Jordan's father that she'd left on the counter, trimmed and ready for framing. He lingered a minute, looking at it. "Your father?"

"Yes." Jordan felt a lump in her throat. She could mention him with ease a hundred times, and on the hundred and first for no reason at all her throat would close up. She wished she understood it. Maybe it would hurt less. *Probably not.*

"It's a good picture." Tony passed it over. "You should keep it here."

"Why?"

"This was his shop." Nodding at the photograph. "In that, he looks like the quintessential antiques dealer at work."

"That's what he was," Jordan said, and *click*, there was another idea. Slowly, she smiled.

"Jor?" Garrett sounded puzzled.

"Miss McBride?" Tony cocked his head. "I like making a girl smile, but normally I've got some idea why."

If they hadn't had a counter between them, Jordan would have hugged him. She beamed instead, yanking her black straw hat off the stand and clapping it down over her hair. "Tony," she said, forgetting the *Mr. Rodomovsky*, "thank you. Twice!"

"ANNA, I'VE JUST HAD the *best* idea—" Jordan stopped, coming out onto the tiny balcony where her stepmother stood looking out at the street. "I didn't know you smoked."

"I used to like a cigarette before dinner." Anneliese took a drag, tilting her face up to the long summer twilight. She still wore the black suit she'd donned to visit the lawyer, but her pumps sat on the deck beside her handbag. "You know how your father felt about women who smoked, so I stopped. Would you like one?"

"Sure."

Anneliese took out a silver case and lit a fresh cigarette from her own. "Where is Ruth?"

"Playing with Taro upstairs. Garrett just dropped us off—he came to take us to the movies, but nothing was playing." Jordan inhaled smoke, coming to lean on the balcony railing. "I had an idea today, something Tony said. Let's get Ruth violin lessons."

For a moment Anneliese looked almost shocked. "Why?"

"She can't look at a violin without being mesmerized. It would make her so happy."

"A child who shrieks and lashes out doesn't need more indulging, she needs discipline. We've been too lax with Ruth."

"She's not spoiled," Jordan protested. "She's sad and angry, and she misses Dad. Why not try something different, something to remind her she can be happy?"

"Not the violin, though." Anneliese took another drag. "Whatever those memories of her mother are, they aren't pleasant. I don't want her even more stirred up. Better if she forgets about violins altogether."

"If she doesn't like it, we'd stop the lessons. But—"

"No, Jordan. I don't want her remembering more." Anneliese smiled, as if to apologize for her refusal. "Besides, it's a rather *Jewish* thing, isn't it, being obsessed with music? One of their nicer qualities, of course, they make fine musicians. But we don't want Ruth tarred with that brush. With a name like *Ruth Weber* she was undoubtedly Jewish. Thank goodness at least she doesn't have the looks."

"Anna, really!" Jordan exclaimed. "Every other little girl in Boston has piano lessons, music is hardly a *Jewish* thing. And even if it was—"

"Everyone sympathized with the Jews after the war, but that doesn't mean anyone wants to live next door to them. I don't want that for Ruth." Anneliese moved on, clearly done with the subject. "There's something else I should tell you, Jordan. You know I saw the lawyer today about your father's will. All in order—the shop to me for my lifetime or until I remarry, then to you and Ruth jointly."

"Yes." Her father's voice: *I wanted to make it into something special for you. A real future . . .* "What did you want to tell me?"

"That you don't have to want it."

Jordan looked up, startled. "What?"

"Fathers want to build something they can leave to their children. Sometimes they don't stop and think if what they've built is anything their children want to be saddled with." Anneliese's blue eyes were steady, sympathetic. "You've been such a dutiful daughter, working at that shop—but I know you never wanted it. You should have gone to college instead. I advocated for that, but your father didn't favor the idea, as you know. It wasn't right to contradict my husband, so I let the matter drop. But I thought he was wrong. I still do."

"He wasn't wrong," Jordan said, defensive. "I didn't need college. I had a future already, I had Garrett, I had . . ."

Anneliese waited for her to name everything else she already had. When Jordan trailed off, she went on. "I'll keep up the shop as your father would have wanted, don't fear. An income for me, an inheritance someday for you and Ruth." Lighting another cigarette. "But that doesn't mean it should burden you now, Jordan. You don't want to be stuck behind a counter selling apostle spoons to old ladies—I know you don't. What would you rather do?"

"I'm marrying Garrett in the spring." It came out of Jordan automatically.

Anneliese smiled. Jordan felt herself blushing.

"What about college?" Anneliese went on, gently ignoring both marriage and Garrett. "You could try for Radcliffe or Boston University, but I think a young woman benefits from leaving her hometown. You could go all the way to California, if it took your fantasy. A new school, a new state."

College. Jordan thought how much she'd wanted that at seventeen. "I don't . . . think I want that anymore," she said slowly. "I'm twenty-two. Starting next to all those eighteen-year-old girls, half of whom are just there to get engaged . . ."

Anneliese didn't look surprised. "You could go to New York, then. Get a job you enjoy, not a job you think you should enjoy."

Jordan felt her hands clench around the balcony rail. Was this conversation happening? Was it *really* happening?

"Don't think I'm trying to drive you away." Anneliese smiled. "This is your home. But you don't have to be tied here because of the shop and your father's wishes. I want you to be *happy*. Would it make you happy to go abroad? Find work as a photographer?"

"I don't know if I'm good enough for that," Jordan heard herself say.

"You won't know unless you try." Anneliese rested a black-sleeved arm next to the ashtray. "Take that camera of yours and find things to snap in Europe. It's another way to learn besides university courses."

"I can't leave." Jordan said it reflexively.

"Leave what? The shop?" Anneliese waved a hand. "You don't really want it to begin with, and it will run just fine without you. Leave Garrett? If he loves you, he'll wait. Leave Ruth? If you get married in the spring, she'll have to adjust to your being gone, anyway."

"But I'd still be in Boston, able to see her. Not a state away." *Or an ocean away.* "Ruth's already lost too many people."

"Ruth will adjust. Children do. She's your sister, not your daughter—you don't have to build your life around her." Pause. "And you don't have to feel disloyal for wanting something different than your father wanted for you."

I do, Jordan wanted to say. *I changed everything I wanted because of what he said.* But her imagination was already running far, far ahead of her. She thought of slinging the Leica over her shoulder and grabbing a bus for New York; walking into the big offices of *LIFE* and applying for a job as errand girl, darkroom assistant, anything at all to get her foot in those doors. She thought of trekking through Spain to see where Robert Capa had snapped his famous *Falling Soldier*. She thought of the project that had leaped into her mind just that afternoon after Tony's casual comment seeing the print of her father, the second idea for which she'd thanked him—the project drumming away inside her head in its urgency to be started. Taking the time to *do it*, not just tell herself she didn't have time because doing a big ambitious photo-essay was silly when the camera was *just a hobby*.

To never think the words *just a hobby* again.

"What I'm saying is that I can help you." Anneliese's voice went on warmly. "This is your inheritance, Jordan; you're entitled to it. Do you want to travel? I can give you an allowance. Do you want to take an apartment in New York, work as a photographer? I can help with expenses until you start earning a proper wage. It's not an offer I'd make to any twenty-two-year-old girl, but you're of age, and you have a good head on your shoulders. Leave the shop to me, leave Ruth to me, leave *Boston* to me—it's too small for you." Her stepmother faced her, smiling. "What do you want?"

Jordan opened her mouth to answer and instead burst into tears. She heard Anneliese stub out her cigarette and then move closer, slim arms folding around Jordan. She cried into that small shoulder as the sky darkened from twilight to night, a half-moon beginning to rise, and there was one final stab of resentment. That Anneliese, whom she had met at seventeen, knew her so well, and not her father who had known her her whole life.

What do you want?

For the first time in a long while, Jordan thought, *I want the world.*

Chapter 32

IAN

June 1950
Boston

How did it go with Kolb?" Tony's voice crackled through the pay phone.

"Nothing," Ian said flatly, watching the rising half-moon. In the time he and Nina had been inside Kolb's apartment, late afternoon had become full dark. "You finally met the McBride widow; anything of note?" They hadn't technically ruled out that the shop owners might be involved with Kolb's activities.

"Pleasant woman, blue eyes, dark hair, classic Boston clip on her *R*'s. No scar on the neck—hey, no harm checking. She was in and out with a few questions; no attempt to talk to the employees or customers. I'll keep an eye, see if Kolb makes any effort to speak with her or give her anything, but she seems to be hands-off with the shop, and my first guess is that she wouldn't know if he's got a racket going."

"He does," Ian said shortly. "We just can't prove it yet."

He hung up, returning to the diner on the corner where Nina already sat with a Coca-Cola, keeping watch through the window. Not much of a diner, empty except for an ancient waitress whose cigarette ash nearly fell into Ian's five-cent coffee. But the corner table by the window had an unobtrusive view of Kolb's building, and that same building didn't have a rear entrance besides an illegally defunct fire escape. Ian didn't see the aging forger swinging down from a fire escape by his hands, so the diner was where they settled to keep watch.

"You should go home," Ian told Nina. There was a part of him that was sorry—very sorry—that he hadn't beaten Kolb into a mass of blood and bone splinters: he wanted to sit here and drink bad coffee until that part was thoroughly strangled. "You did well tonight," he added. He'd worried her flair for chaos would spill into the work, but she'd cleaved to the plan, watched for cues, been useful.

"*Spasibo.*" Nina began taking out hairpins, shaking her hair out of its grim knot. "What if Kolb runs?"

"I'll follow, see who he meets. Watch him until he leads us to something or someone new."

Nina picked up the menu. "If he doesn't?"

"In cases past, we'd make the decision at some point to move on."

Her eyes narrowed. "Not here."

"No." There was an ocean in the way, not to mention an obsession. Ian took a sip of coffee, grimacing. "There are probably going to be a lot of hours spent in this booth."

"They have hamburgers. Is something, at least." Nina flagged the waitress. Ian knew she found hamburgers a miracle of American life far more compelling than freedom of speech. "Kolb runs, he maybe gets away for good," Nina said when the waitress plodded out of earshot. "New city, new name. He's a forger, maybe he make himself new papers."

Ian nodded, remembering various failed tail operations of the past. It wasn't easy for a tiny team to mount a comprehensive watch.

"Is only three of us," Nina said, reading his mind. "We can't sit on him every breath."

"We can try. I'll take him from dawn until he arrives at work." Ian hadn't been sleeping much anyway; he might as well come here at four in the morning and sit watching a door. "Tony will watch him at work. And you—"

"I take nights."

"Agreed, Night Witch." Ian felt the anger draining out of him, being replaced by shame. *You lost your temper. You threw a witness up against a wall and choked him.* He'd never done that before, no matter how much he was tempted.

Bloody hell, it had felt good.

Ian looked at his wife. "I believe I owe you an apology."

She raised her eyebrows.

"I threw you out of my office in Vienna because you said you'd take violence over legality. Yet I'm the one who just threw a man up against a wall simply because he made me angry. There's an analogy about pots and kettles that isn't making me particularly happy at the moment."

"Kettles? Kolb didn't have kettles."

"Never mind."

Nina's hamburger arrived. Ian watched her tear into it. The door of Kolb's building stayed closed. It was always even odds what a guilty man did after being accused: about half bolted in the first hour, and half decided to stay put and pretend they had nothing to hide. He would have bet Kolb for a bolter . . .

Ian sighed. It was going to be a long night, he could tell. One of the sleepless ones, where the parachute drifted at his shoulder.

"Is lake I dream about," Nina said.

Ian blinked. "What?"

"Lake. Drowning in it. Sometimes is my father holding me under, sometimes is *die Jägerin*. Always lake." She shrugged. "Your lake—what is it?"

"There's no lake. Like there's no kettle. Your English is very peculiar, comrade."

Nina took another huge bite of hamburger. "Is parachute?" she asked thickly.

His blood went ice-cold.

"Antochka says you mutter in your sleep. Something about parachute."

"It's nothing." That came out sharper than Ian intended.

"Is something," she replied. "Or else why is it your lake?"

He said nothing. Nina said nothing either, just looked at him.

"His name was Donald Luncey," Ian said, wondering why he was telling her. He hadn't told anyone. "GI from San Francisco, eighteen years old. He called me Gramps. I probably looked ancient to him. He looked about twelve to me."

"Sounds like my navigator after I was promoted to pilot." Nina smiled. "Little Galya looked like she should have been on Young Pioneer hikes, not flying runs over the Black Sea."

"What happened to her?" Ian asked.

Nina's smile vanished. "Dead."

"Donald Luncey too. March '45, American troops parachuting out into Germany. I begged permission to hitch a ride on the jump."

"Why?"

"It's what you do, if you want to be any good as a war correspondent." Ian tried to explain. "At the front, no one likes journalists. The brass worry you'll see something you shouldn't, make them look like idiots. The poor bastards in the ranks think you're a ghoul, sticking your notepad in their faces looking for a story as they're trying to stay alive. The only way they don't hate you is if you're in the thick of it too. Bunk with them, drink with them, jump out of planes with them, run into fire with them—you share the danger, they'll share their stories. It's the only way to do the job right."

Ian had chatted up Private Luncey when they lined up to jump. One of those narrow beaky faces, ears that stuck out like jug handles, a big smile. "We jumped," Ian went on. "The rest came down safely and went on to their mission, but Donald Luncey and I splatted off course. Hooked our rigs up in some German wood."

Another woman would have taken his hand. Ian's wife just looked at him steadily.

He'd snagged badly about twelve meters off the ground in the branches of a massive oak, hanging breathless and tangled under his lines. He'd had a knife, but the overhead angle was so awkward the blade slipped, spinning to the ground below before he could cut a single line. His straps were too badly knotted to slip out of without cutting. But he was lucky compared to Private Luncey, who had hit every branch on the way down through the tree that eventually snagged him up short. A shattered rib had pierced his lung, or at least Ian guessed that was what had happened. It killed him slowly over the course of seven hours, shredding his lung as he hung there screaming. Ian remembered every moment of those hours: first telling him to be still, not exacerbate the injury; then trying and failing to pendulum-swing close enough to help; finally just hanging there listening as the boy's voice ran out, from screams to the occasional monotone mutter of *Gramps . . .*

"By the time he died I was hallucinating," Ian managed to say. "Dehydration and shock—it turned Donald Luncey into my brother—into Seb. I knew it wasn't him, I knew Seb was sitting in a stalag in Poland, but it was still him, down to the last freckle. My little brother was hanging dead in the tree next to me." Hanging there for most of a day as Ian, mouth leather dry, shivering in the cold sweat of horror, stared at his corpse. Ian had tried to focus on the ground below instead, and that twelve meters under his swaying boots seemed to double, an impossibly long fall into darkness.

"Ah," Nina said. "Is why you have your thing, the thing about heights."

"Foolish, really. I didn't even *fall*. I was found soon after; they rigged me down safe. Quite lucky." Lucky, but maybe not entirely sane, Ian sometimes thought. It was five years after the war was done, yet still he had the dream and in the dream it was always Seb, right from the beginning. Donald Luncey wasn't even there; start to finish it was his brother he couldn't save.

"Don't brood, *luchik*." Nina upended ketchup over her hamburger like she was drowning it in blood. "Brooding is no good."

"You never brood, do you?" For all that she moved in such a cloud of anarchy, Nina was very even-keeled—rather remarkable, Ian thought, considering what she'd lived through. He wondered if flying in combat had drilled that into her, or if it had already been there—in her, and in her fellow Night Witches. "Most assume women have no place at the front lines, but after hearing about your friends in the regiment—"

"Women are good in combat," Nina said matter-of-factly. "We don't compete like the men do. Is all mission, no proving who is better with stupid stunts."

"You told me you once climbed out on a plane wing at eight hundred meters, you little Cossack. If you want to talk about stunts."

"Was necessary!" She smiled, but there was a shadow behind it. "My pilot yelled at me for that."

"Good for her." Ian studied Nina's lively face, suddenly gone still. "I can see how much you miss them. Your friends."

"*Sestry*," she said softly.

He could guess the word meant *sisters*. "Were they all like you?" She shrugged, and he imagined hundreds of Ninas, handed planes and set loose on the Führer's eastern front. Bloody hell. No wonder Hitler lost the war.

"No one ever did what we did before." Nina picked up her hamburger, dripping ketchup. "We pay for it, what we do. Dreams, twitches, headaches . . ."

"I know what you mean." Ian tapped his left ear. "It's never been quite right after that bombing run in Spain nearly did it for me."

"My ears too, not so good as they were. U-2 cockpit is noisy. And those years being awake all night every night—I still never sleep all night through."

"Don't be ashamed of it. You were a soldier." *Not like me with my pointless nightmares*, Ian thought, wry.

She seemed to catch his unspoken thought. "You went to war too, *luchik*. You go to war, you have a lake or a parachute after. Everyone does."

"Soldiers do. They've earned it. I wasn't a soldier. Nightmares are for those who fight, not those who scribble. Maybe I was at the front, but I could leave any time I wanted. They couldn't."

"So?" Nina asked. "Same risk for either soldier or hunter."

"Hunter?"

"Hunters," Nina said. "You. And me—well, I was soldier *and* hunter, but important part is hunter. Very different from soldier."

"I don't quite follow."

"Soldiers fight wars. It gives them nightmare—a lake, a parachute. It makes them want to stop, go home." The hamburger was gone; she sat spooning up ketchup by itself, like soup. "Hunters in war face same risks, same fight, so they get a lake or a parachute too. But we don't have the thing soldiers do, other people do—the thing that says *stop*. We have a nightmare, we hate it, but if war ends, soldiers go home while *we* need a new hunt."

Ian looked at her. "That does not make sense."

"Does." Calmly. "Soldiers get made. Hunters get born. You either need to track danger, or you don't."

"I don't *need* to track danger, Nina. Not all Englishmen go pounding over fields blasting shotguns."

Nina sighed, impatient. "Those boys you wrote about, GIs, airmen—what did they want?"

"They talked about home, like all soldiers. Films, backyard barbecues, going out for girls—"

"Then the war ends and they go back to that, yes?"

"The lucky ones." The unlucky ones ended up like Private Luncey. Like Seb.

"But some don't. Like Tony; he doesn't go home to get married, find work. He stays, finds a hunt. *You* don't go home either. Your war ends, you start tracking Hitlerites." Nina licked ketchup off her thumb. "The girls I fly with, they're mostly like your GIs. They dream of peace, babies, all the borscht they can eat. Their war ends, they get peace, they're happy. But me?" A grimace. "During the war, I have my bad nights, I dream the lake, but it never makes me want borscht and babies. My war finishes, you get me to England, I end up at the airfield in Manchester. Loops on old biplanes, no target, going crazy. Until I get the message about *die Jägerin*. Is good then; because I have target again." Nina pointed at Ian, then at Kolb's door. "You—in war you hunt stories, in peace you hunt men like him." Pointing at herself, then at Kolb's door. "Me—in war I hunt Nazis to bomb, in peace I hunt Nazis to make pay."

Ian shook his head. "If you and I are hunters, if we have the urge to chase down prey and we give in to it, that makes us no better than *die Jägerin*. And if *that* is the truth, then I will go home and put a bullet in my own brain."

"*Nyet*." Nina was very certain. "*Die Jägerin*, she's different kind of hunter. A killer who hunts things because she likes it. Maybe she has excuses—is orders from her Reich, is because her *mudak* of a lover tells her to—but is just excuses. She kills because she likes it, and she hunts what she thinks are easy targets—children, people on the run, those who can't fight her. Would you do that?"

"Bloody hell, Nina, no!"

"I don't either. We don't hunt the helpless, *luchik*. We hunt the killers. Is like villagers going after a wolf gone mad. Only when the wolf is dead, villagers go home and *we* find the next mad wolf. Because we can keep on. Others, they try keeping on, they just—" She mimed an explosion. "Is too much for them; they come to pieces. Not us. Hunters, they are different. We can't stop, not for bad sleep or parachute dreams or people who say we should want peace and babies instead. Is a world full of mad wolves, and we hunt them till we die."

It was the most thoughtful thing he'd ever heard her say. Ian sat back, looking her over. "I had no idea my wife was a philosopher."

"Is a Russian thing. Sit around, drink too much, talk about death." She pushed her empty plate away. "It makes us cheerful."

"Hunters chasing a huntress . . ." Ian rotated his cup of now-cold coffee. "This is your first chase, Nina—normally, our targets aren't terribly impressive. They may have done terrible things, but in the flesh they are pathetic men full of excuses, not unlike Kolb in there. *Die Jägerin* isn't. She had the nerve to hide in plain sight in Altaussee, even while it was being combed for Nazis. She managed to come to America on a new identity. She covered her tracks."

"And now she is target," Nina said.

"She's a very clever target," Ian stated bluntly. "It will not be easy to catch her."

"Hunters tracking a huntress?" Nina reached across the table, hooking what would be her trigger finger through his trigger finger. "I like our odds."

It was the first time she'd ever touched him outside a bedroom—normally Nina was prickly as a thornbush when it came to giving or receiving any sign of affection. Ian smiled. Fingers still linked, he fell into silence, watching Herr Kolb's unmoving doors. The moon was higher up the sky; they'd been sitting a long time in this diner.

"I think Kolb stays where he is tonight," Nina said, also watching the doors.

Ian agreed. "Go home. No sense for us both to be bored here."

"Isn't boring."

"Staring at a door? Draw comparisons all you like between flying bombing runs and tracking Nazis, but this kind of hunt involves a great deal more paperwork and waiting. I'm surprised you aren't bored stiff. Or"—an idea struck him—"is it that you like having a team again? Not like your regiment of *sestry*, of course. But you have Tony and me, and we all share a target. Is that what you—"

She jerked her hand away from his, something black bolting through her eyes too fast for him to follow. "Am not your *team*," she flung at him, every word like an ice bullet. "Is one hunt. One, only because of *die Jägerin*. We find her and is all finished. We divorce, I go home, is done."

"It doesn't have to be," Ian heard himself say. "Even after we divorce, you can still stay on at the center, Nina. You work well with Tony and me; you enjoy it. I know you do. Why not stay on?" He realized how much he wanted that. Under her recklessness she had a navigator's discipline and total dedication. And having a woman on the team, the places a woman could watch where a man couldn't—"Stay with us after we catch Lorelei Vogt," Ian urged, putting all the vehemence he could into the words. "Stay, Nina."

"No team," she repeated, eyes like stones, and stamped out of the diner.

Chapter 33

JORDAN

June 1950
Boston

Garrett looked back and forth between the two prints lying on the darkroom table. "You've been working all week on two pictures?"

"I finally got them right." A week's worth of slaving in the darkroom: developing, enlarging, cropping, like as not scrapping and starting all over again. Two prints. But two prints to be proud of.

"Huh." Garret looked back and forth between them. He'd come from the office, tall and pressed in a summer-weight suit. Jordan knew she looked like a complete wreck in comparison, hair tied up with a scrap of yarn, old shorts splashed with developer fluid. "They're nice," Garrett said, clearly hoping it was the right thing to say.

First a low-angle shot of her father in the workroom, holding up a silver card tray. She'd played with exposure and cropped the image till it showed just his hands, his forehead creased with concentration, the scrolled back of the tray, the outer edge of his smile. *An Antiques Dealer at Work*, she'd titled it with a quick pencil scrawl. "That's the essence of Dad at work, but it's also the essence of *any* antiques dealer at work. It's why I cropped the image to show just a sliver of his face. It's not just *him*; it's anyone in that job."

The second photograph was of Garrett at the airfield outside Boston, gesturing in front of the biplane. She'd cropped this image to its essence too; it wasn't her fiancé looking handsome for the flash, but a *pilot*, any pilot, every pilot: a wedge of image that showed Garrett's outward-stretching arm against the outward-stretching wing, Garrett's grin as man and machine alike yearned for the air. *A Pilot at Work.*

"Very nice," Garrett said again, looking lost.

Jordan looked at the two prints, for a moment wondering if she'd been wasting her time. *You're seeing things that aren't there*, the old critical voice scolded her, the one that told her not to dream wild things. But a cooler, more analytical voice said, *They're good*.

"The photo-essay will be called *Boston at Work*. A series of fifteen or twenty portraits, all pared-down close-ups." The idea had refined itself over the last week, since the evening on the balcony with Anneliese. *What do you want?* "I'm going to spend the entire summer on it."

Garrett scratched his jaw. "What about the shop?"

"Dad's old clerk Mrs. Weir offered after the funeral to come back to the shop if we needed help—Anneliese gave me leave to hire her full-time to replace me." Jordan was already teeming with ideas. People doing their jobs all over Boston, just waiting to be photographed—the bakers at Mike's Pastries in the North End, some pictorial slice of the flour and kneading fingers; Father Harris at Mass, the way his hands make a cradle as he elevates the host . . .

Garrett touched the biplane in the print of himself, looking wistful. "What's it for?"

"My portfolio. I don't have job experience yet, so I need solid work to show. I'm going to spend the summer photographing everything I can get my hands on." Jordan took a deep breath. "This fall I'm going to New York, to try to get work as a photographer."

"This fall?" Garrett looked puzzled. "But the wedding's next spring."

Jordan made herself look up, meet his eyes squarely. "I'd like to put the wedding off for a while."

She braced herself, but his face cleared. "It's just nerves," he reassured her. "My mother says bridal nerves are completely natural. She wants you to come over soon and choose flowers. She said something about petunias, or maybe it was phlox—"

"I'm not ready for phlox, Garrett. I'm not ready to set a date. I'm not *ready*." What a relief to say the words, not be forever squashing them down out of sight and out of mind. "I don't want to be married yet. I want to work. I want to be a photographer. I want to find out if I'm any good at all—"

Jordan ran out of breath before she ran out of all the things she had only realized this week that she wanted so badly. To go to France and snap the Eiffel Tower even if it was the most clichéd photograph in the world. To learn what it was like to work on a deadline over burning eyes and cold coffee, because some yet-to-be-found editor wanted something *done by eight sharp*. She wanted colleagues to bump around a darkroom with, sharing cigarettes and ideas. She wanted to see her name on a byline: *J. Bryde.*

Garrett was looking lost now. "We have so many plans . . ."

"Plans can change. Come with me," she said, linking her fingers through his. "Come to New York, have an adventure. Work for TWA instead of—"

"Come on, quit kidding."

"I'm not. Do you even *want* to work with your dad at the office? You're bored stiff there."

Garrett tugged his hand free, crossing his arms over his chest. "Are you calling this engagement off?"

"No. I am saying we should postpone—"

"We've been together five years. Mom's going to be heartbroken if we postpone again."

Jordan felt bad about that, she truly did, but she stamped the feeling down ruthlessly. She was not going to get pushed down the aisle because of guilt. "We're the ones getting married. Don't you want to be sure before we say *I do*?"

"I'm sure."

"Really?" Jordan paused. "You've never told me *I love you*."

He looked confused. "Yes, I have."

"When was the last time you looked me in the eyes and said *I love you* when we weren't in bed and in the middle of—"

"Lower your voice!"

"We're partway underground, there's no way Anna can hear us."

"And what's she have to say about this?" Scowling.

"Absolutely nothing." And what a glorious feeling that was. To make her own decisions, no input from adults who were absolutely certain they knew better than she did what to do with her life. "I'm getting an allowance, the same I'd have gotten if I went to college. And I have my own savings. I'll rent an apartment—" Jordan broke off. Too many details for Garrett, who was looking angry again.

"You know something?" He jabbed a finger at her. "You've never said *I love you* either."

Jordan leaned against the darkroom table, tracing its edge. Her pear-shaped diamond sparkled under the harsh lighting. "Were you faithful to me, Garrett?" she asked. "When you went off to war, you gave me your high school ring and made me promise not to go out with anyone else. Did *you*?"

He started to say something. Jordan raised her eyebrows. He cleared his throat.

"I didn't go on a date with anyone else," he mumbled.

She waited.

"But some of the guys, they said those of us who had come straight out of high school deserved a good time. So we wouldn't . . ."

Get shipped overseas and die without ever getting laid, Jordan supplied silently. "That's about what I thought."

"It was just the one time . . . Okay, it was twice. But I thought you'd be mad, so—"

"I'm not mad." Jordan sighed.

He brightened. "Really?"

"Garrett," Jordan said gently, "isn't it a problem that I don't mind? If I loved you madly, wouldn't I be a tiny bit hurt, or jealous, or *something*?"

Silence stretched.

"You like me a lot," Jordan went on. "I like baseball and we always had fun in the backseat of your car, and I didn't push for a ring or tell you to stop flying. You liked that." So many things had crystallized this week, down here in the red glare of the safelight as she worked. So many things. "I like you, Garrett. I really do. You're kind and sweet and you make me laugh, and you never told me I had to stop taking pictures . . . or thought I was a tramp because I liked rolling around in the backseat as much as you. But—"

"What are you getting at?" Garrett said.

"We're good together." Jordan made herself go on before she lost her nerve. "But is it love, or is it habit?"

A long silence. Jordan looked at him, steadily. Garrett looked at his folded arms. Finally he looked up.

"I'd like my ring back."

Well, Jordan thought, *that answers that*. She pried the diamond off her finger, feeling a lump in her throat. "I'm sorry," she began, but he turned around and started for the stairs, back straight and angry.

He stopped at the door, looking down from the top of the stairs. "I'll break it to my family if you break it to yours."

"Tell your mother I'm sorry. She's been wonderful to me, I—" Jordan stopped before guilty babbling set in. She looked away, down at *A Pilot at Work*. "Garrett . . ."

"What?" His voice was as stiff as his back.

"When you took me flying, you looked so happy." She pointed to the photograph of him. "That's the real Garrett Byrne. The one in the overalls, not the one standing in front of me now in a suit. You should go back to flying, not—"

"Take your advice and shove it," Garrett said and slammed out of the darkroom.

Jordan let out a long breath, looking down at her naked ring finger. Her eyes burned, and she wondered if she was going to cry. *Five years*, she thought. *Five years*.

"Back to work, J. Bryde," she said aloud, blotting her eyes. "This career isn't going to start itself."

Chapter 34

NINA

July 1944
Polish front

The Germans are falling back! Clear into Poland—" But the Fritzes fought, clawing for every step.

A frigid winter had gone by, teeth chattering behind mole-fur masks on night runs; Nina's navigator, Galya, lost a toe to frostbite, trying to laugh it off: "How are my dancing sandals going to look?" Yelena got clipped through the calf by ground fire soon after the year turned, and Nina's heart climbed up her throat to see her lover come limping off the field with one arm around her navigator Zoya's neck for support. "It's nothing," Yelena reassured even as Nina crashed to her knees and began running her fingers over the exit wound. "Straight through the muscle and out, stop fussing!"

Spring melted into summer, less flying, more sleep, but they all seemed to have lost their ability to sleep longer than a few hours at a stretch. "I get such headaches," Zoya cried, and Nina tried not to feel the prick of jealousy when Yelena hugged her tight and crooned reassurance. You were close to your navigator when you were a pilot; it was inevitable. You loved her. *Don't love her more than me, Yelenushka.* Red-haired Zoya, whose husband had died fighting in Stalingrad, who had two children in Moscow living with her mother—children whose pictures Yelena exclaimed over wistfully . . .

She doesn't love anyone more than you, Nina told herself. They still crept off to lie together under the *Rusalka*'s wing, kissing and talking nonsense. Nothing had changed.

Only because you don't bring up anything that might upset the balance.

They were flying over Poland by summer: a land of smoke and ruin and mud. A land that had been raped, Nina thought. The summer rains had churned the ground into a deep, malevolent glue that sucked on U-2 wheels and bogged fuel trucks. In their crude dugouts, the walls streamed water and the mud came up to the shin. "But look at this—" Yelena held out a fragile red flower. "Corn poppies. I found some blooming in the field behind the airdrome."

Touched almost to tears, Nina stared at the poppy already wilting on the stem. *I'm so tired.*

Does anyone care, rusalka? Nina's father sneered. So she kissed Yelena, threaded the poppy through her overall front, swallowed another Coca-Cola tablet, and kept going.

"IT SHOULD BE a crystal glass, not a soup can—"

"We don't *have* a crystal glass. We're lucky Bershanskaia let us have the vodka!"

The Night Witches laughed, oil smeared and radiant, exhaustion evaporated. The word had come down as they trooped into the canteen at dawn: Nina Markova and four other pilots were to be made Heroes of the Soviet Union.

It wouldn't be official until the ceremony, but that didn't mean they couldn't make the traditional toast. Yelena and four others had been the first to get their HSUs a few months back; now they jostled to the front and stripped off their stars. Yelena dropped hers with a *clink* into the small empty soup can in Nina's hands, and Nina's four fellow pilots held out soup cans to receive borrowed stars too. The entire regiment filed past grinning, everyone bearing a tin cup

with the daily two hundred grams of vodka allotted to pilots. Normally they let the alcohol go to the men, Bershanskaia's orders, but
today the Night Witches poured all their vodka into the cans of the
incipient Heroes, until the gold stars were covered to the rim.

"Drink, drink!" The cry went up, and Nina downed the canful
of vodka in one gulp, Yelena's gold star clicking against her teeth.
She surfaced dizzily, and Yelena and the other Heroes lifted cans of
their own, crying "Welcome, *sestra*!" and bolting down the rest of
the regiment's vodka. The others didn't grudge it, they all crowded
around cheering—Nina felt herself kissed so many times her cheeks
glowed. She was dizzy with vodka and love. *It's just a medal*, she
thought as she tried to press the star back into Yelena's hand, but
Yelena pinned it crookedly to the breast of her flight overalls, laughing. *Wear it for the day, get used to the weight!* Yelena looked so
beautiful with her cheeks flushed like corn poppies—"You're beautiful too," Yelena whispered back. Nina realized she must have said
it aloud . . .

When the alarm blared, she looked up almost sleepily, too warm
and content to be startled. But the canteen doors flung wide and
there were three panting ground crew shouting. "Fighters coming over the field, the U-2s haven't been camouflaged yet, get them
up—" and pilots and navigators alike jostled out of the canteen,
sprinting into the pink-streaked dawn. Nina dropped the soup can
and ran blindly after her pilot's flying dark hair. Yelena was already
in the cockpit and the *Rusalka*'s engine roaring when Nina toppled
herself nearly headfirst into the rear. Someone shouted, and the first
spider shape of a Messerschmitt appeared. A U-2 to their left took
off east over the nearest line of trees, another lifted to the north and
dived up for cloud cover, and then there were U-2s rising into the
sky in every direction. No orderly conveyor belt; everyone simply
flinging the planes into the air and escaping every which way. The
Rusalka rose like a bird, straight into the rising sun.

"Do we have the night's coordinates?" Nina nearly asked, sheer
rote habit, and blinked. Something wasn't right here. She fumbled
with the interphones.

"Whazzat?" Yelena sounded curiously fuzzy. The Messerschmitt passed over the airdrome; the strafing roar of its fire followed, and Yelena was yanking the *Rusalka* upward as fast as she could. "What?"

"Oh." Nina figured it out. "I'm in the wrong plane." Galya had headed for their U-2, but Nina had tracked blindly after Yelena and the *Rusalka*. It struck her as funny, and she giggled.

"Nina?"

Nina's ears buzzed. Was the plane weaving? "Fuck your mother," she called out. "I'm drunk." She'd always been able to hold her vodka like a Siberian, like a *Markov*, but she hadn't swallowed a drop in months. The whole world was slipping and sliding. "Are you drunk?"

"No," Yelena called back.

The *Rusalka* was definitely weaving. The airdrome had fallen away rapidly below, they were rising into tatters of pink cloud. Disappear in the sky and they'd be safe from any more Messers; they had the fuel to wait it out in the air, not like the time they were chased down. *Safe*, Nina thought as the airfield disappeared. "What heading are we on?"

Pause. "I don't know."

"The compass—"

"The compass is all blurry." Another pause. "I'm drunk," Yelena said, and suddenly they were both howling with laughter in their cockpits. A canful of vodka on an empty stomach after a long night's flying and no sleep . . . *We're drunk as polecats*, Nina thought, and that was even funnier. Flying with Yelena instead of Galya; flying in the day instead of the night; everything was upside-down. Then Nina realized they actually *were* upside-down; Yelena was looping over a tail of cloud. "Got it!" she whooped.

They were up above the cloud floor now, flying along in the rosy morning. Nina squinted over the side of her cockpit, wondering how long it would be before the Messers abandoned the attack. "'Nother U-2 below."

Yelena waggled their wingtips, and the plane below waved back.

Nina took the stick—why not, they had to burn some time before risking descent—and they played with the other U-2 for a while, chasing back and forth. The other plane always stayed below, rippling along the cloud floor . . . "Oh," Nina realized. "S'not another plane. It's our shadow."

They went off into gales of laughter again, and Nina fought her way out of the safety harness and half stood up, leaning into the rigid airstream. "Don't you climb on the wing again," Yelena shouted, but Nina stood up just enough to tug Yelena's hair back and kiss her dizzily, warmly, besottedly in the morning wind. "Let's land," she shouted back. "Because we're so drunk we'll end up over Berlin."

Yelena brought them down with a lurch, jouncing along the muddy runway to a halt. "Was that a landing?" Nina wondered, climbing out. "Or did a German shoot us down?"

"Shut up." Yelena giggled, sliding from her cockpit, and would have slid straight to the ground in a puddle if Nina hadn't caught her around the waist.

"Get up, rabbit!" Nina dragged Yelena down the runway as the ground crew hauled camouflage toward the *Rusalka*. "We can't go back to the canteen like this, I can't look Bershanskaia in the eye!" They managed to sign off what was necessary, then slunk off giggling behind the temporary airdrome.

"Poppies!" Yelena breathed. The field behind the airdrome was a weed patch, but red blooms had threaded themselves through. She bent over a patch of red flowers and staggered, toppling headfirst among the poppies and taking Nina with her. They couldn't think of a reason to get up so they just lay there in a patch of rye, twined up and kissing, Nina on her back staring up at the sky. Everything she had seen of Poland had been made hideous by mud and smoke and ruins, but here in this tiny frame of vision staring straight upward, it was beautiful. A pure blue sky, framed on either side by fronds of rye and waving poppies, Yelena's head resting heavy on her breast.

"We should get back," Yelena whispered eventually.

"Don't want to." Nina twined her fingers through Yelena's hair. "We have to, rabbit."

They disentangled and made their way back to the airdrome. The vodka had, for the most part, worn off. "I could sleep for a week," Nina said with a yawn, but before they could turn for the barracks, Nina heard herself being hailed. "Comrade Lieutenant Markova!"

She turned, saw the approaching figure of the regiment's deputy commander, saluted with a smile. The other woman did not smile back. She was grave at the best of times—Nina wouldn't have wanted to carry the burden of being deputy commander *and* chief of the commanding staff—but now she had a face like winter. Nina felt the last of her vodka euphoria drain away as cold tendrils of dread crawled along her veins.

"You're to see Comrade Major Bershanskaia at once."

"What's wrong?" Nina took a step forward. She couldn't think of anything that would cause such an expression but death: a U-2 crashed or missing. "Has someone not returned? Did Galya—"

"Report to Comrade Major Bershanskaia," the order was repeated. Nina was suddenly aware of eyes on her all over the airdrome. Heart suddenly pounding, Nina tugged her hand free of Yelena's puzzled arm and turned toward Bershanskaia's temporary office. Where she stood at attention in her flight overalls pinned with a borrowed gold star, crushed poppy petals still tangled in her hair, and learned that her world was at an end.

AT FIRST SHE DIDN'T KNOW what was happening. She stood baffled as Bershanskaia gazed down at her desk and talked in circles.

"I'm sure you understand that in times of war there is increased vigilance, Nina Borisovna. Enemies of the state uncovered every day."

Nina nodded, since a response seemed to be required.

"Enemies of the Motherland are found even in the most remote regions. Distance is no protection. We must all continually manifest the greatest vigilance"—she was clearly quoting someone, Nina didn't know who—"in relation to the enemies and spies that secretly penetrate into our ranks."

Pause. Nina nodded again, confusion mounting.

"Very recently there was a denunciation as far east as Baikal. A man denounced as an enemy of the state." Still, Bershanskaia would not meet Nina's gaze. "A tiny village not far from Listvyanka."

Alarms began blaring through Nina's skull. "Oh?"

"Perhaps you knew him." Bershanskaia lifted her head at last; her eyes bored into Nina. "I feel certain you do. Isn't everyone family in such small places?"

She emphasized *family* with nothing but a flare of her eyes. Nina stood gripping her sealskin cap as implications crashed like exploding shells. "Not everyone is related out by the Old Man," she managed to say. "It's a huge lake, after all. Many villages. Did the man have a wife, children?"

"Grown children, I'm told." Again that emphasis with the eyes. *Children.* "Though any children would be wise to distance themselves from a father accused of speaking anti-Communist rhetoric, and making inflammatory statements about Comrade Stalin."

Your father has been denounced. The words hung there, silent and hideous. *Papa*, Nina thought. So often he spoke up in her head, snarling and spitting. Now he was silent. *What did you say? Did the wrong someone finally overhear one of your rants?* Nina supposed, remotely, that he was lucky it had taken this long for his mouth to bring him down.

"A warrant has been issued for the man's arrest." Bershanskaia cleared her throat. "Enemies of the state must be punished with utmost severity."

"Is it—is it known who denounced the man?"

"No."

Was it my fault? Nina had met Comrade Stalin's eyes at Marina Raskova's funeral, had thought of cutting his throat, and he had paused. Not long—but he had paused. Had he noted her name in passing beside the running wolves sketched in his notebook? Or simply remembered that name when he saw it raised beside an award for a gold star? Was all of this happening simply because the General Secretary disliked the way the smallest of Raskova's eaglets had met his eyes? He'd ordered men killed for less . . .

Nina swept the thought away. *What does it matter* how *it had happened? It happened.* Whether from the Boss's intervention or a simple report from a neighbor, her father had been denounced. Nina's ears buzzed with the sound of that word, as though she'd been deafened by tracer fire. Bershanskaia's voice faded in and out.

". . . the innocent, of course, have nothing to fear at the hands of . . ."

Nina almost laughed. Innocence did not mean safety; everyone knew that. Her father was doomed; Bershanskaia knew it. And Nina's father *wasn't* innocent. Any of his ranting monologues over the years were bad enough to earn a bullet.

Papa—

"Where is he?" The words rasped out of Nina, cutting Bershanskaia off. "My—this enemy of the state." Speak no names, utter only vague generalities; that was how you talked of these things. A conversation could happen, and yet at the same time not happen at all.

Bershanskaia hesitated. "There are sometimes difficulties as enemies of the state seek to evade their due arrest and retribution."

Nina did laugh then, a one-note bark of laughter that hurt her throat. So they had not been able to scoop up her wolf of a father. He had probably melted into the taiga as soon as he saw it coming. Would they ever find him, those mass-produced men of the state with their blue caps and endless paperwork? *Run, Papa. Run like the wind.*

Her ears were still buzzing, but she could hear the drip of water from a leaky corner of the roof. *Drip, drip.* "What does this mean?" she managed to say. "For those—related?"

"You understand that in such cases warrants are frequently issued for the arrest of an enemy of the state's family." Bershanskaia's gaze bored into Nina again, unblinking. "Due to concerns that anti-Soviet attitudes may have taken root in the family unit."

"Would—would that be the case here?"

"Yes. Yes, it would."

Drip. Drip. Drip. The leak was slowing, and Nina stood frozen. A moment ago she had been wishing her father luck—now she thought, *I should have cut your throat before I left home.* Her father had eluded arrest, so they'd take his family instead. For the first time in years, Nina thought of her siblings. Scattered to the four winds, probably now being rounded up and lobbed into cells. She couldn't see a troika taking pity on the Markov brood, the feral offspring of an avowed enemy of the state. *Hooligans*: that was how they would all be categorized. The state was better off without hooligans.

"Children are not all like their father," she managed to say. "A war record would speak for itself, surely." Lieutenant N. B. Markova, Order of the Red Banner, Order of the Red Star, six hundred and fifteen successful bombing runs to her name, soon to be Hero of the Soviet Union. Surely it counted for something. "With a substantial record of service—"

But Bershanskaia was shaking her head. "The state does not take chances."

Well, then, Nina thought.

For a moment they looked at each other, then the major sighed, folding her hands on her desk. "Even a good Soviet citizen feels fear at the prospect of an arrest," she said, more conversational. "But a good Soviet citizen would know to bow to the will of the sentence, join in denouncing her father, and thus have a chance at saving herself."

"For what?" Nina asked. Instead of a bullet, getting ten or twenty years in a labor camp near Norilsk or Kolyma?

Bershanskaia switched tack. "We have been lucky to have sterling records among the regiment. If any of my pilots transgressed, I would not be able to speak for them." She didn't flinch from Nina's gaze. "Though it would grieve me."

Nina jerked a nod. The regiment came first. For any officer, it had to. Bershanskaia already had to be sick with worry over the regiment's future. Since the very beginning, the ladies of the Forty-Sixth had to justify their existence with every bombing run, had to be *perfect*—and now they had a rotten apple in their midst, the tainted daughter of an enemy of the state. What would it mean for the regiment? They no longer had Marina Raskova to speak for them as Comrade Stalin's favorite aviatrix. Nina nodded again without bitterness. Bershanskaia couldn't speak for her, not one word.

"Acquittal, of course, is entirely possible. You are not wrong that a sterling record of service will weigh in favor."

It doesn't matter, Nina thought. Even acquitted, she would never return to the Forty-Sixth—she'd be tainted by association with treason. She was finished here. She'd never fly again with Galya at her back; she'd never sip oily tea in the cockpit between runs; she'd never line up a target behind Yelena and the *Rusalka* . . .

That was when the agony hit her in the gut as though she'd been stabbed by an icicle. Yelena. What would *she* do when the van came for Nina? When would it come? It must be soon, if Bershanskaia had sniffed out advance notice of the arrest. It was always in the small hours of the night that enemies of the state were dealt with— the noise of the car stopping, the officious rap on a door. Yelena and the Night Witches would be halfway through a night's bombing runs at the time Nina was taken away with a guard on each side.

Dimly, she wondered how this was happening. How a day beginning with vodka and laughter and kisses in a pink dawn had come to this evasive recitation of horror and condemnation.

"For the regiment," Bershanskaia was saying in guarded tones, "things must happen . . . quietly. There mustn't be trouble."

The words triggered Nina in pure reflex. She felt her every muscle snap taut, felt the individual hairs on her head like hot wires. Her teeth locked down a feral hiss before it could escape. She remembered Comrade Stalin's *Not one step back*. The weight of her father's razor sat just inside her sleeve—a flick of the wrist would drop it into her hand. She didn't know what Bershanskaia saw on her face, but the major stiffened.

Nina forced the words out through the gate of her teeth. "I'm no good at *quiet*, Comrade Major."

But you are good at trouble, her father whispered in poisonous amusement, evidently deciding to speak up again. *You're a Markov. Trouble always finds us, but we eat trouble alive.* Nina was not going to sit meekly in lockup, grounded from flying, until her accusers arrived to take her away. The moment a thug in a blue cap came to take her by the arm, came to take her *east*, the razor would drop into her hand and she would paint the room red. They'd get her in the end—unlike her father she had nowhere to run—but it wasn't going to be easy, it wasn't going to be clean, it wasn't going to be quiet. Bershanskaia saw that very clearly; she exhaled behind her desk.

Nina stood there shaking, fury copper-bright in her mouth. *So,* she thought. *Haven't changed much, have you?* All the warmth and camaraderie of the Forty-Sixth, all the softening of Yelena's love . . . it still hadn't taken very much for Markov's daughter to come out, the *rusalka* bitch born in lake water and madness. Not very much at all.

Her knees gave out and she sat down abruptly in the chair before Bershanskaia's desk. Looking at the clock on the wall she was astounded to see it was late afternoon. Briefing would begin soon for the night's mission.

She exhaled a shaky breath. "This has been a very informative discussion, Comrade Major. I understand you have been interviewing *all* your pilots, to urge constant vigilance against saboteurs and enemies of the state."

"Of course." Bershanskaia's voice was cautious. "All of you."

"My navigator is having dizzy spells," Nina said. "Comrade Lieutenant Zelenko is unwell and would benefit from a night's rest." Nina raised her chin, looked Bershanskaia in the eyes. "As a former navigator, I am more than capable of flying tonight's runs alone."

Silence expanded around the words. Nina's mouth dried out, and suddenly her pulse was fluttering.

"You may fly alone tonight, Comrade Lieutenant Markova. Inform your navigator to report to the infirmary."

"Thank you, Comrade Major Bershanskaia," Nina said through numb lips. Saluted, for the last time.

Gravely, slowly, Bershanskaia saluted her back.

And Nina took her leave.

THE WORD HAD already spread.

No one approached Nina as she left Bershanskaia's office on feet that did not quite feel the Polish mud. Everyone watched in grave silence, eyes speaking volumes as she passed. No one reached out, no one spoke—until she came into the derelict barn that served as a barracks, and Yelena rose from Nina's cot with swollen eyes.

"Oh, Ninochka—"

The violent pressure of those strong arms nearly broke Nina in half. She sagged in Yelena's grip, gulping unsteadily as Yelena stroked her hair.

"The word already came out that Galya's grounded." Yelena clearly knew what that meant; her voice was filled with dread. "You're—you're going up alone?"

Nina nodded, not trusting herself to speak.

"Don't," Yelena whispered. "Fight the charges. It's all a mistake. They won't condemn a Hero of the Soviet Union! If you appeal—"

Of course Yelena with her shining belief in the system would think acquittal a simple matter of innocence. Nina just shook her head. "No."

"Why won't you—"

"I'm going up tonight, Yelenushka." Her six hundred sixteenth bombing run, Nina thought. Her last.

Yelena pulled away, eyes filled with tears. "Don't crash," she begged. "Don't throw your plane into those Fritz guns. Don't make me watch flames coming up from your wreckage—"

"I'm not going to crash," Nina said thickly.

She freed herself from Yelena's arms. No time to waste: forcing the chaos of her thoughts aside, she rummaged under the cot for her meager stash of possessions. A pilot at war needed so little—a pistol, a sack of emergency supplies in case of crashing. An old white scarf embroidered with blue stars . . . Nina stuffed everything into a knapsack, ransacking the barracks for all the food she could find. In Bershanskaia's office she'd been too stunned to form a plan; her thoughts stretched no further than the offer to fly alone. *Get off the ground*, that was all her instincts had told her—get into the sky before the shackles came.

Now what?

Despite herself, she envisioned aiming for a battery of antiaircraft guns, the white flare of the searchlight filling her world like a sun as she dived into it for once rather than away. The image crooned. Better to go, in fire and glory, to sleep.

I'm so tired.

But Nina pushed that vision away. She looked at Yelena, standing in her flying overalls trying not to weep, and opened her mouth. But she thought who might be listening and put a finger to her lips in warning. Shouldering her knapsack, Nina grabbed Yelena's arm and marched her wordlessly out, across the trampled field to the middle of the runway. The dying afternoon sun beat down, insects droned, and there was no one within fifty meters to hear anything they had to say to each other.

"I'm not going to crash my plane." Nina swung around at last, facing Yelena. "I'm going to run. I'm flying west."

The uncurling quiver of fierce affirmation inside her stomach was all she needed. West, not east. The dream of the girl growing up by the Old Man.

She looked at Yelena's wide eyes and cupped that much-loved face between her hands. "Come with me," Nina heard herself saying, heart beating in her throat. This was not planned either, but among the torrent of emotions running riot through her chest— shock at her own coming arrest, rage at her father, stark liquid grief for the loss of her regiment—something lighter joined the maelstrom: a feather touch of hope.

"Come with me," she repeated, and suddenly the words were spilling eager and blunt. No speaking in vague generalities now— here under the open sky, Nina was done with Party euphemisms.

"Wait until the last instant, then run for the navigator's cockpit. They won't be able to stop us. They'll report us both dead before the time my arrest warrant arrives, and we'll be free as birds with no disgrace attached to the regiment. How far west can we get, the two of us and a U-2 full of fuel?"

"Into Poland?" Yelena gestured at the ugly trampled ground around them, the smoke-smudged western horizon. "It's crawling with Germans—"

"Where else can I go? Anywhere behind our own lines, I'll be found. It's west for me, or it's propeller first into the nearest battery of guns."

Yelena winced, turning away from Nina's hands. "You don't have to go. You'll be acquitted—"

"No," Nina cut her off. "I flee now or I die later—a few days, a few weeks, even a few years, but I'll die. I can make my way through Poland, maybe even farther. To a new world." She had no idea what she was going to do, dropped into war-racked Poland, but she knew she and Yelena could survive together. "Come with me," she repeated, grasping Yelena's hands in both her own. "The *West*, Yelenushka. Where black vans don't come in the dead of night because your neighbor wants your apartment—"

"Don't *say* that!" Yelena cried in reflexive fear of eavesdroppers, but Nina threw her head back in defiance.

"Why not? They've already denounced me. They can't do it twice." The satisfaction of that was fierce. *Take me away from my regiment, my plane, my friends?* Nina thought to the vast barren country that had sired her. *I'll turn my back on you without a second glance, you frozen heartless bitch. And I'll take your finest Hero with me.* She and Yelena would be so much better, if only they could escape the Motherland and wait out the war. No arguments about Party politics or Comrade Stalin, nothing to divide them. *She'll see what this place is, if she sees it from the outside. I'll give her everything else she wants—an apartment by a river and babies playing on the floor.* Nina was ready to tear those things bare-handed out of the unknown capitalist world if she had to, tear them out and lay them at Yelena's feet if only she'd come west tonight.

But her heart seized, because Yelena's head was shaking back and forth.

"My mother is in Moscow," she said. "My aunts and uncles are in Ukraine. I can't leave them—they'll all be denounced and arrested in turn, if there's even a whisper I deserted."

"Bershanskaia will report us shot down, heroes who died fighting—"

"So I let them think I'm dead? Let them grieve? I'm the only child my mother has left."

I don't care about your family, Nina thought. *I only care about you*. But she didn't say it.

"It's not just my family," Yelena went on. "I can't leave the regiment."

"*I'm* leaving the regiment!" Nina lashed back. "Do you think that's easy?"

"No, no, I didn't—I meant—" Yelena's face contorted, tears shining in her dark lashes. "Ninochka, I can't *leave* them for you. I can't betray them. They need me."

"I need you." Nina wanted to shout, but it came out a whisper. Her hands were so cold, gripping Yelena's in the sunshine. "They'll fly on without you. None of us are irreplaceable. Slot another *sestra* into the cockpit and keep flying, that's the regiment's way. But you're irreplaceable to me."

Yelena tore her hands away. "You're asking too much," she cried. "Leave my family, my regiment, my oath, my *country*—"

"Your country is throwing me away," Nina yelled back. "Six hundred and fifteen successful bombing runs, and they're going to put a bullet in my head or work me to death in a gulag, all because my father is a drunk with a foul mouth. I don't *have* a family or a regiment or an oath, thanks to this country. You are *all* I have left."

Yelena was still shaking her head, but in blind stubbornness. "They won't shoot you. It's all a mistake."

"Wake up! This place is rotten—"

"How can you think that? You fought for the Motherland for more than two years—"

"Because it's all someone like me is good for." Nina realized she was shouting, but she couldn't stop. "I'm good in the air, I'm good on the hunt, and I'm good at surviving, so I gave it all to this regiment because of the women in it. I'd cut my heart out for any of them, but all I can do for them now is leave and let them tell the world I'm dead. I don't *care* about the Motherland, Yelena. She's a frozen mass of dirt, she was here long before I got here, and she'll be here long after I'm gone. She got two years of my service, but she's not getting my death. The Motherland and Comrade Stalin and all the rest can fuck themselves through seven gates whistling."

Her Moscow rose couldn't help recoiling. Nina seized Yelena's face between her hands, yanked her to eye level, and kissed her savagely.

"Come with me," she said again, against Yelena's trembling mouth. "Come with me and leave it all behind, or you will die here."

She put her whole heart into those words, everything she had, everything she was. She could feel her pulse thrumming like the *Rusalka*'s gallant little engine just starting to spool up for the fight. Yelena was going to burst into tears, she'd cry her heart out in Nina's arms, and after that it would be all right. There was time. They could go.

But though Yelena's long dark lashes were wet, not a tear fell. "Maybe it is all rotten," she said, so softly she was all but inaudible. "But if the good ones leave, who's here to make it better after the war?"

In Nina's chest, the engine died.

Yelena leaned down, touching her forehead to Nina's. "I know why you have to leave, Ninochka. It's leave or nothing. But I can't give up my homeland and my oath for love." She managed a small smile under swimming eyes. "That's the kind of thing that makes men say little princesses have no place at the front."

Silence stretched out between them, as vast and frozen as the Old Man. Nina's lips parted, but she had no more words. Not *Don't leave me.* Not *Go to hell.* Not *I love you.* Nothing. She took a stumbling step backward, tripping over a clod of earth.

Yelena steadied her with an outstretched arm, tried to pull her close. "Ninochka—"

Nina wrenched away. One more kiss, and the huge sob building in her chest would tear loose. One more kiss, and she'd be the one crying her heart out in Yelena's arms and vowing to stay, vowing to denounce her father, vowing to take ten years or twenty in a gulag if her pilot would only wait for her. One more kiss and she would be utterly undone. In the old stories a *rusalka* could bring a mortal to their knees, perishing in ecstasy after a single kiss that seared like ice.

Maybe Yelena had been the *rusalka* all along. Not small, shaken Nina Markova who felt like she was dying.

"Nina," Yelena said again, softly. Nina didn't look back. She stumbled to the edge of the airfield, tear-blind, lips sealed on her own pleas, standing there with her head bowed. She saw the gold star still pinned crookedly to her own breast—Yelena's HSU—and tore it off blindly, hurling it to the mud. The alarm went up to signal the briefing; pilots would be spilling out of canteen and barracks to hear the night's mission. Nina stayed rooted to the spot, eyes squeezed shut. She heard Yelena move past her, light footsteps in thick boots, and thought desperately, *Don't touch me. I will shatter if you touch me.*

A single in-drawn breath as Yelena stooped to retrieve her gold star, then she was gone. Nina stood at the edge of the airfield, watching the sun fade and a quarter moon began to rise as Bershanskaia delivered the evening's briefing somewhere inside. *I will shatter*, Nina kept thinking, the thought circling like a conveyor belt of U-2s. But she didn't shatter. She just stood numb, waiting for her heart to finish breaking, for that hateful quarter moon to finish rising, for her last flight as a Night Witch to begin.

Chapter 35

IAN

July 1950
Boston

Tony returned from his shift at McBride's Antiques looking like a cat who had got into the cream. "Good news."

"Did Kolb try to bunk?" Ian looked up from their paper-strewn table, hopeful. He'd had a week of diner coffee and was tired of it.

"Not that good, no. Kolb is headed home as usual, Nina ghosting along in his wake. Your little Soviet popsy is a natural tail."

My little Soviet popsy is at least speaking to me, Ian thought. Nina's temper seemed to be of the tinderbox variety, fast kindled and fast out—the morning after stamping out of the diner in a rage, she'd greeted him with her usual breeziness and showed no compunction about dragging him off to the couch when Tony left. Bloody hell, it was complicated having an affair with your own wife.

Ian brushed that aside, looking at Tony. "What did you find?"

"A *tattoo gun*. Tucked away very carefully in Kolb's workshop." Tony had been using his work shifts to discreetly search the premises for anything Kolb might have hidden. If he kept information on his former clients, and was cautious enough not to stash it at home, what better place than the McBride shop? "I've learned a fair amount about the antiques business in the last few weeks, and there is no reason why that workroom would need a tattoo gun."

"He's probably covering up blood-type tattoos." Someone paranoid enough to pay for a new name and background would be paranoid enough to cover a tattoo. "Something to hold over his head if we take another crack at him."

"When?"

"Not yet. I don't want him warning anyone, I just want him nervous." Nervous people made mistakes.

"Start on these while you're waiting." Tony fished some papers out of his pocket.

"Bloody hell, I haven't even got through your first batch—"

"Put your foot on the gas, boss." Lists were the main thing Tony was looking for, on his careful searches through the McBride files. *If I were hiding information in that shop on the location and identities of war criminals,* Ian had speculated last week, *I'd list the names and addresses as buyers, customers, or dealers. False names tucked among real names.* Lorelei Vogt's new name and address could very well be in one of those drawers, hiding in plain sight.

Tony slapped down a stack of lists copied over in his untidy scrawl. He never took the originals—if and when police became involved, Ian had no intention of seeing their evidence muddied up with accusations of theft. Tony asked permission every time he accessed the file cabinets and took nothing that wasn't put back. Gray territory, but they were used to working in those shadows. "Besides," Tony had pointed out, "if we need to act legally on any information we find, that's when we go to the McBride family, lay out everything, play on their civic duty in the apprehension of a criminal, and obtain full permission to act on the information we've found. My persuasiveness, your gravitas—always works like a charm."

Flipping through the new sets of lists, Ian reached for the telephone. Names of antiques sellers and customers: they'd all have to be cross-checked and confirmed that they were what the list said they were. So far all the names had checked out as legitimate, but they'd only been at it a week. The telephone bill was going to be astronomical. *Slow and steady*, Ian reminded himself. Most chases took months.

"I'm not combing any shop files further back than last year." Tony was trying to impose some order on the worktable, layered with maps and notes like an archaeological dig. "Kolb arrived in Boston with the early waves of refugees coming after the Displaced Persons Act; I slipped that out of Miss McBride. So it's doubtful he could have helped our huntress until early '49 at the soonest."

"According to Frau Vogt, her daughter left Europe late '45." Ian crossed off the name of an auction house in Dutchess County. "But if *die Jägerin* arrived in Boston before the Displaced Persons Act—"

"—it was probably something shady through Italy or the church routes," Tony finished. "No sponsor or family here, she'd have scrambled to establish herself."

"Unless she came with wads of cash, which isn't likely." Ian had never yet found a war criminal who had managed to flee his homeland and then set up in luxury. "So Lorelei Vogt spent some years getting by. Kolb came in late '48 or early '49; she found him and learned he could provide assistance . . ."

"Only then does she write urging her mother to join her. Do you think—no," Tony interrupted himself, leveling a finger at Ian. "Absolutely not."

Ian paused, reaching up to pin the latest list to the wall. "We're running out of room."

"Next it'll be taped-up photographs and colored string criss-crossing to connect different theories, and before you know it we're stuck in one of those god-awful flicks where some general is jabbing at a map saying 'The Yanks are here, the Limeys are here, and the Jerries are here.' No," Tony repeated, and Ian grinned.

"You take over the telephoning, then." It had been a while since Ian took out his violin, and playing helped his mind find its way through a thicket of possibilities. He pulled the instrument out, musing as Tony dialed a number and slid into practiced disarming patter. One of those names, listed innocuously under the heading of *Dutchess County antiques dealers* or *Becket, Massachusetts, china sellers*, might be a former war criminal, Ian thought. A camp guard fleeing a legacy of violence in Belsen, a paper pusher who had documented the roundup of Berlin's socialists . . . or *die Jägerin*. It was tedious and it might not turn up anything, but the chase had stalled while they waited for Kolb to lead them to something new, and the rule when a chase stalled was to sift through the ordinary and find something that didn't fit, then follow *that*.

Tony went from one call to the next as Ian began to play, trying to remember the song Nina had been singing on the rooftop two nights ago. He'd sat up there with her listening, leaned back on his elbows, wondering why she refused to think of staying with the center when she clearly liked the teamwork, knowing better than to ask. She couldn't storm off a four-story building like she'd stormed out of the diner, but she might just try.

Abandoning that question for now, he switched to Saint-Saëns. The music and Tony's telephone patter must have drowned out the sound of the door opening. When Ian drew out the final note and turned around, he saw a little girl in the doorway, bird boned and huge eyed.

Even as he lowered the bow in puzzlement and Tony turned around midcall, the blond child took a step into the room, gaze fixed on the violin as though hunting for where the music had gone. "Ruth!" A woman's voice called from outside, floating up the stairs, but the girl ignored it, looking at Ian. He looked back. The name he was hearing was *Ruth*, but the name imprinted in his mind was *Seb*.

"What was that?" the little girl said. Seven or eight years old, blond hair falling over a crisp blouse—Ian's dark-eyed dark-haired younger brother had looked nothing like her, so why the painful stab of familiarity?

Then Ian remembered Sebastian standing before their father one Christmas, looking stricken as he heard he was being sent away to school a year early, *aren't you a lucky chap!* That was the similarity:

both his brother and this little girl were two bandbox-neat children with well-shined shoes, yet the forlorn puzzlement in their eyes was like that of the war orphans Ian later saw in Naples, in London— children gripped in the throes of shock, huddled on hospital cots or in bombed-out buildings, eyes searching for their homes. Sebastian had looked up at their father, blurting out, *Can't I go live with Ian instead?* Seb got a clip on the ear for that, and a lecture about not letting down the side like a pansy.

I wish you could *live with me, Seb*, Ian had said. *But he's our father. Until you're of age, it's his roof.*

But it's not home, Seb had muttered.

The little girl in front of Ian now was staring at the violin as though she thought *it* was home. "What was the music?" she breathed.

"Saint-Saëns," Ian heard himself reply. "The Swan movement, from *Carnival of the Animals*. G major, six-four time. Who might you be?"

Someone who has already been failed in her rather short life, Ian couldn't help thinking, even though he knew nothing about this girl. He thought later that he was already predisposed in that moment, whatever Ruth McBride asked, to say yes.

Chapter 36

JORDAN

July 1950
Boston

Ruth beat Jordan to the door of Tony Rodomovsky's apartment, racing up the stairs as soon as she heard the faint strains of music. By the time Jordan made it to the top, Tony was standing in the doorway looking down at the little girl bemusedly. Behind him was a man Jordan didn't know, standing with a violin tucked under his chin. Jordan gave an apologetic smile for interrupting, turning to Tony. "I'm sorry to intrude—"

"Not at all. The lock on that door's so flimsy, it opens with a jiggle." He smiled, still puzzled.

"I was so busy bringing the shop manager up to date on my routine, I didn't see you'd left without your paycheck," Jordan said. "You're lucky I had your address on file, and didn't mind a detour on the way home." Handing the check over, she turned to call Ruth, mind already racing ahead to the open afternoon beckoning now that the capable Mrs. Weir had returned to manage the shop—not just today but for the rest of the summer. Jordan could finally sink into those rolls of film waiting to be developed, the bakers at Mike's Pastries, all those shots of white aprons and kneading hands . . . But then Jordan saw Ruth's face and stopped short.

How long has it been since you've smiled like that?

The older man had lowered his violin, clearly answering some question of Ruth's. His voice was deep, grave, crisply English. Ruth erupted into more questions, face alight. This was Ruth the happy chatterbox, Jordan thought, not the miserable, silent child she'd become since their father died. The child who woke up whimpering every other night muttering half-asleep fragments of German, refusing to be soothed. "I don't know about leaving in the fall," Jordan had confessed to Anneliese two nights ago, worrying. "Ruth's going to take it so hard." To which Anneliese in a burst of unusual frustration exclaimed, "Ruth will be fine. Make your plans and *go*, Jordan, it's best for both of you."

Jordan couldn't deny it was also what she wanted, more and more every day. But to leave Ruth so unhappy . . .

Ruth didn't look unhappy now, as she showered the stranger with questions.

Jordan caught her hand, caught at her manners too. "I'm sorry if my sister is bothering you, Mr. —?"

"Ian Graham—a friend of Tony's from Vienna; he's been good enough to put up my wife and me on a visit. I'd introduce my wife, but she's out." The Englishman shook hands: keen eyed, dark haired, lean as a whip, not quite forty. Jordan thought his name sounded familiar. Before she could place it, Ruth reached up—Ruth, so shy around strangers—and pointed at the bow in Mr. Graham's other hand.

"Please?"

Tony smiled. "Princess Ruth wants a tune."

"If you like," Mr. Graham said. "I warn you, I don't play particularly well." Lifting the violin to his chin, he played through the slow melody again. Ruth inched across the floor as if the music was pulling her, eyes fixed on his long fingers on the fingerboard, and Jordan's heart squeezed. She heard Tony moving some papers on the table behind her, but ignored the rustling, raising her Leica. *Click.* Her sister's small rapt face . . .

"I heard that on the radio," Ruth burst out as the final note sighed away. "It sounded different. Um—darker?"

"Quite right. That Saint-Saëns piece is written for a cello."

"Is that a bigger violin?"

"They're related, shall we say. Played between the knees rather than under the chin—" The Englishman demonstrated.

She mimicked him, babbling questions. Jordan took another snap, thrilled. Soon Ruth had Mr. Graham's large instrument in her small hands, and he was showing her how to tuck it under her chin and support it on her shoulder as he held her body steady. "You need a half-size violin, but try this anyway. A whole tone, A to B, like so—"

Tense with concentration, Ruth tried. "It doesn't sound right!"

He corrected her grip on the bow. "There. Now, first finger B, second finger C sharp on the A string . . ." He explained what those names meant, a tiny violin lesson in five minutes—Ruth barely blinked she was concentrating so hard. Jordan just stood there enjoying it.

"Ruthie," she said when the violin was finally handed back. "I'm finding you a teacher."

Ruth's eyes lit up as she looked up at the Englishman. "Him?"

"No, cricket. He was very kind to show you, but he's not a teacher."

"I want him," Ruth said.

"Ruth, that isn't polite. You don't know Mr. Graham—"

"I could give her a lesson or two, if you liked." The offer seemed to come out of the Englishman before he could consider it. He looked as surprised as Jordan.

"I couldn't possibly presume. You don't know me, or my sister."

"I don't mind showing her a few scales and basics. I'm no professional, mind." The Englishman looked down at Ruth, gazing covetously at his instrument, and grinned. His grin was something special, a quick flash of sunshine lightening that austere English face. "One does like to encourage the young toward culture."

Taking a favor from a complete stranger wasn't the kind of thing either Anneliese or Jordan's father would approve of. Jordan didn't care. Ruth never responded to new people like this—look at her tugging on the Englishman's cuff, spilling questions. For whatever reason, she liked this man. "Thank you so much, Mr. Graham." Beaming. "Of course I'll compensate you for your time."

"Never mind that. Can you get her a half-size violin?"

"Yes." Jordan thought of the instrument at the shop, the nineteenth-century copy of a Mayr. "It shouldn't leave the shop, but it's insured to be played." Anneliese would kill her for suggesting it, but Anneliese didn't have to know.

"The *Mayr*," Ruth breathed, thrilled. Mr. Graham raised an eyebrow, remarking, "You know Mozart played a Mayr?" By the time Jordan finished arranging a lesson and bid good-bye to the Englishman, Ruth was nearly levitating.

"I'll walk you out, Miss McBride." Tony followed, shutting the apartment door. On the other side, the violin started up again. Ruth's head turned, tracking the music, but all Jordan had to say was "Tuesday evening, that'll be you," and Ruth danced down the first flight of steps.

Jordan caught her hand. "Don't tell your mother, Ruthie." Anneliese meant well, but in this case she was wrong. "Our secret, all right?" Ruth was already nodding, smile flashing.

"I like to see her smile," Tony said. "You too, Miss McBride."

"Jordan." Impulsively. "I owe you a favor now, for introducing me to your friend. How did you meet?"

"Nothing too interesting . . ." They chatted about offices in Vienna and mountains of dull paperwork, as Ruth hopped from step to step, humming the Saint-Saëns melody in perfect tune.

"Why stay in Europe after you were out of the army?" Jordan wanted to know.

"Because I wasn't ready to hear my mother nag me about settling down with a nice girl. And because it's what I do—drift. I lack purpose, or at least that's what disapproving aunts and high school football coaches have always told me. I drifted out of the army without much purpose, I drifted around Vienna working for Ian, then I drifted home."

"Where you drifted into the antiques business?"

"Exactly. Who knows how long I'll drift along after you?"

Jordan grinned. "I'm moving too fast for anyone who just drifts."

"I can put on a pretty good burst of speed if I'm chasing something I want."

Her grin turned into a laugh as they came out into crowded Scollay Square. Jordan headed toward Tremont where she knew there'd be taxis, Tony sauntering along beside her, Ruth skipping between them. "You don't have to escort us all the way, Tony."

"But I'm being gallant," he protested. "I'm flirting with you, or didn't you notice?"

"Oh, I noticed." Now that she was without a fiancé for the first time in five years, Jordan was free to notice—and flirt back if she wanted. An enjoyable feeling. "You also flirt with every woman who walks through the shop door."

"I flirt with them because I want to sell them Ming urns. I flirt with you because I want to take you out to dinner tonight."

Regretfully, Jordan shook her head. "I have plans."

"Not with your Clark Kent boyfriend, I know that."

"He does not look like Clark Kent."

"Square jaw, Daddy's watch, backbone of the nation. I went to war with about a thousand of him."

"Don't be rude; Garrett was perfectly nice to you the one time you met."

"Nice boys are dull," Tony said. "Come out with me."

She slanted an eyebrow. "I am your employer, you know."

"And you said you owed me a favor . . ."

"Is that why you chimed in upstairs, telling Mr. Graham to play for Ruth? So you could maneuver me into a date?" Jordan certainly hoped so.

"I'm trying to maneuver you into a date because it's Friday night, and I'd rather spend it with you than with a sarcastic Brit complaining that Americans serve beer too cold." Tony caught Jordan's left hand suddenly, thumb sliding over her fourth finger. "And I couldn't help but notice you're about half a carat lighter than you were a week ago."

"Noticed that, did you?" His grip was hard and warm over hers, no nervous perspiration. Just his thumb passing over her ring finger.

"Noticed the next day, if I'm being honest." Tony released her hand before she could tug it free, raising his arm for a cab sailing toward them. "So dinner?"

"I'm only just out of a long engagement, Tony."

"That means you can't eat dinner?"

The cab rolled past, not stopping. "It means maybe it's a little soon to be going on dates."

"It doesn't have to be a date." His gaze was direct. "It can just be dinner."

Jordan looked at him, speculative. "Answer me one question first."

"Fire away."

"Do you cheer for the Yankees?"

"Best team in baseball."

Jordan smiled. "I don't go out to dinner with Yankee fans."

He clapped a hand to his heart. "I'm crushed."

"Like we're going to crush you in October?"

"Let me take you to Fenway and we'll lay a bet on that."

Jordan dropped her teasing. "I can't go to dinner *or* a game; I'm working. Three rolls of film; I'll be up till midnight." She liked bantering with him, liked that there didn't seem to be signs of a girl-friend in the apartment upstairs . . . but she wasn't throwing work aside for a date. The photo-essay *had* to get finished; there was so much to do and summer was slipping by so fast.

He didn't argue. "What about tomorrow?"

"Saturday movie night with Anna and the cricket here, then Sunday lunch the next day. Weekly tradition." Sunday was the day they all missed Dan McBride the most.

"Monday?"

"Working then too, sorry. I'm going to a ballet studio to get pictures of the dancers." She outlined her Boston-at-work idea. "You helped give me the idea, you know—something you said about my father looking like the quintessential antiques dealer."

"So that's what that was," Tony said. "That time you waltzed out of the shop with Clark Kent after giving me the biggest smile I've ever gotten in my life from a girl who was still vertical. I kept wondering what I'd done to prompt it."

"Mr. Rodomovsky!" Jordan said, pretending to be shocked. "Keep your mind out of the gutter if you please." She tried to keep a stern expression, but Tony quirked an eyebrow, and she burst out laughing.

He grinned. "Let me accompany you to the studio Monday. I'll carry your bag, hand you film. Don't you want a minion? I thought all photographers had assistants."

"Famous ones."

"I've seen your work. You're on your way."

He was flattering her, Jordan knew that. But warmth still spread in her stomach at the praise.

A cab finally pulled up. Tony opened the door, handing Ruth in with a flourish, and Jordan gave in to temptation. "Meet me at the studio," she said, giving him the address.

"I'll be there." He didn't try to squeeze her hand or touch her arm in farewell, just stood there hands in his pockets, smiling. Something a notch up from his automatic *you're-so-pretty* smile, something faintly, frankly wicked. Jordan was somewhat amused to feel a flutter in her stomach in response. *He doesn't mean anything by it*, she thought. *You could take a picture of charm spilling out of him like coins from a slot machine and title it* A Charmer at Work!

Well, so what? She had half a summer left here, and she was free to enjoy it with any charmer she pleased. "I'll see you Monday," Jordan said, and she made sure she didn't look over her shoulder as the cab rolled away.

"YOU'RE IN THE CLOUDS tonight," Anneliese said that evening after supper. "That's the second time I've asked for a dish towel."

"Sorry." Jordan passed it over, then reached into the sink of soapy water for another plate.

Anneliese studied her. "You look like you're thinking about a man."

Jordan bit back a smile.

"I knew it!" Anneliese laughed, sunlight from the kitchen window gleaming on her dark hair and her navy-blue dress. "Did he ask you on a date?"

"Yes." Jordan hesitated, plate in hand. "You don't think it's too fast, do you? For me to be thinking about someone new, when things just ended between Garrett and me . . ."

"And who ended them?" Anneliese asked. "Which one of you actually said the words?"

"Well, he did." Jordan hadn't told her the details before, merely that it was over. "I asked if we really loved each other or not, and Garrett asked for his ring back."

"So, *he* ended it. If your heart isn't smashed in pieces—and I'm glad it isn't—then why shouldn't you move on to someone new if you feel like it?"

"People call names if a girl gets around too quickly after breaking an engagement." Jordan knew exactly what those names were. She couldn't help thinking them herself this afternoon after leaving Tony's company, even as she told herself she was free now to see whom she liked. As much as Jordan wanted to be a woman of the world, it was hard to shake off the strictures of the Good Girl. "I don't want people thinking I'm a—"

"They won't think that of Garrett Byrne if he decides to get over you by dating every girl in Boston," Anneliese pointed out.

"Things are different for men, and you know it." Jordan added more soap to the dishwater. "Surely it was just the same in Austria when you were growing up."

"Yes." Anneliese leaned against the sink, thoughtful. "Perhaps your father wouldn't approve of you going out again so soon after ending a five-year engagement, but . . ."

"What about you? What do you think?" *Please don't disapprove*, Jordan thought. She hadn't realized just how much she valued Anneliese's good opinion.

Anneliese smiled, looking downright impish. "I think that if the end of a five-year engagement isn't the time for a frothy summer romance, then what *is*?"

Jordan laughed, relief and delight warming her cheeks. "You are wicked sometimes, Anna."

"And you're a grown woman of twenty-two who should enjoy her freedom. Sensibly," Anneliese added, lifting a rinsed-off saucer out of the dishwater. "I'm enough of a mother to ask that your frothy summer romance be conducted without throwing *every* caution to the winds."

Jordan sincerely hoped Anneliese wasn't going to initiate a chat about the facts of life—there were some things you did not want to discuss with your stepmother, no matter how marvelous and faintly wicked she might be—but Anneliese just dried the saucer and asked, "So this new young man who asked you on a date. Is he handsome like a movie star?"

Jordan thought of Tony's lean, cheerful face. "Not exactly."

"Tall?"

"No, my height."

"Did he save you heroically from being hit by a car or eaten by a dragon?"

"No, we met over a pie."

Another laugh. "He must have *something* special. Not just pie!"

Jordan considered. "He knows how to look. Really look, when a woman is talking."

"Ah." Her stepmother sighed. "Some men ogle, some men *look*. The first makes us bristle, and the second makes us melt, and men are at an utter loss knowing the difference. But we do, and we know it at once."

"Exactly." Jordan handed her a plate to dry. "Did Dad know how to look?"

"It was the first thing I noticed about him. He could admire a lady as though he were admiring a beautiful porcelain vase, without making her feel he was affixing a price tag."

"That's nice." As silent as Anneliese was about her early life, she would always talk about Jordan's father. It eased the hurt of missing him.

"Well, I wondered if it might be our new clerk with the black eyes who was making you dreamy, but surely you didn't meet *him* over pie." Anneliese turned to put away the gravy boat, missing Jordan's suppressed smile. "Just as well—that new clerk is Polish, isn't he? Poles are hard workers, but they're so emotional and untrustworthy in some ways."

Just when she seems like a woman of the world, Jordan thought, *she turns into Mr. Avery on the corner, warning everyone that Wops are slippery and Micks are lazy.* Jordan had always bit her tongue when it came to such comments from Anneliese, because her father chided, *It's rude to contradict your stepmother even if you disagree with her.* But he wasn't here anymore, and Jordan said tartly, "Anna, that opinion is ridiculous."

But Anneliese had already changed the subject, reaching for more soap and looking pensive. "I don't suppose your mystery admirer is English, is he? Mr. Kolb telephoned me about an Englishman who had asked him some questions . . . I wondered if you'd seen someone like that hanging about."

Jordan supposed it must have been Ian Graham dropping in to catch Tony at work—she'd offered to give him directions to the shop for Ruth's lesson, and he'd said he'd been before. "I'm not going on a date with any Englishmen. At least not that I know of!" Making a joke of it to dispense with the subject of Mr. Graham, considering she'd just hired him behind Anneliese's back.

"Well, perhaps Mr. Kolb was being needlessly fearful. Or," Anneliese added dryly, "drunk again."

"I've smelled his breath in the mornings," Jordan admitted. "I didn't want to say anything, considering it doesn't affect his work."

"He had a bad war. It makes some people drink, and it makes

others see trouble where there isn't any." Anneliese dried her hands on her apron, still thoughtful. "Do let me know, though, if anyone comes about asking questions. If Mr. Kolb is in some kind of trouble, I'd like to know."

Jordan blinked. "What kind of trouble would he be in?"

"A man who drinks can always find trouble."

Anneliese still looked pensive, warm kitchen light bathing her dark hair and dark dress. The shot distracted Jordan. "Stay like that and let me take your picture."

"You know I hate that!"

"*Please* let me snap you for my series. The essential you at work—"

"And what work would that be?"

Jordan paused. What did Anneliese do that summed up her essence? Cooking, as she whipped up her dense, delicious Linzer torte? Sewing, her quick fingers moving over a lace collar? Neither seemed quite right. In the rare photograph Anneliese allowed to be taken, she looked exactly the same: anonymous and pretty, face turned to the flash like a shield. What *was* the essential Anneliese? "I'll find out," Jordan promised.

Anneliese looked briefly amused, then the smile faded to something more somber. "Jordan, we've talked about you managing Ruth if I went on a buying trip for the shop . . ."

Jordan untied her apron. "I thought you wanted to hire someone to do the buying."

"After four years with your father, I think I can tell a good bit of china from the bad. I'd like to go to New York for a few auctions."

"I can watch Ruth. Especially now with Mrs. Weir holding down my end at the shop; she managed things for Dad years ago, so she'll keep it running like clockwork. You *should* go to New York, Anna." Jordan liked the idea of Anneliese heading off to take up the business reins. Maybe her stepmother too was eager to stretch her wings, be more than a housewife with her sewing room. *I'd like to see you try*, Jordan thought, not without a flash of guilt for her father. His love had been so all-encompassing, but it had also . . . confined. Jordan knew she wouldn't ever, ever voice that thought aloud, but she couldn't help *having* it.

"Then I'll plan a week or so in New York," Anneliese was saying, all crisp decision. "And if you don't mind watching Ruth, I'll take another two weeks in Concord after that."

Jordan paused, hanging up her apron. "Why Concord?"

"Because your father and I honeymooned there." Anneliese traced the counter with a fingertip. "I . . . want to say good-bye to that memory."

"Oh, Anna." Jordan touched her hand. Yes, there was guilt in Anneliese's blue gaze too. Perhaps she had also felt caged by Dan McBride's fond, firm hand over her life.

Anneliese gripped Jordan's fingers, eyelids lowered. "I'll have to be the strong one for Ruth once you're gone. Not short-tempered with her, the way I've been lately. If I can . . . get a little time to put myself in order, I'll be ready."

"Anything you need." Anneliese's hand was chilly in Jordan's. *Well done, J. Bryde. Too busy mooning about a prospective date to notice how worn-out your poor stepmother is.* Jordan gave Anneliese's cheek a remorseful kiss, told her to sit down with some sherry, and took Ruth and Taro out to enjoy the twilight. Reassuring Ruth that yes, her mother would be gone for a few weeks, but Jordan would be there for everything. And yes, the lesson next week really would happen; Mr. Graham wouldn't forget.

And how much easier it was going to be to get Ruth her music lessons if Anneliese wasn't there to sneak around.

Chapter 37

IAN

July 1950
Boston

Waking up this morning, I would not have bet that by nightfall you'd have a music student, and I'd have a date with a Red Sox fan." Tony came back into the apartment after putting Jordan McBride and her sister into a cab.

Ian tucked his violin back in its case. "I should have known you'd beeline for the first pretty girl to cross your path in this chase."

"I want her going home wondering if I'm going to steal a kiss Monday morning, not wondering why her clerk is shacked up with an inexplicable Limey and an even more inexplicable tableful of paperwork that was mostly, if she'd looked closer, copied from her shop." Tony flopped into a chair, propping his boots on the dead radiator.

"Yes, I saw you shuffling papers out of sight behind her as I was playing." That was the reason Ian had offered to play—well, partly. He shut the lid on the violin, still rather touched by Ruth McBride's intense reaction to it. Normally if anyone cried at his playing, it was because he was butchering the music. "Is that why you were nudging me with your eyebrows to take the little girl on as a pupil? So her sister wouldn't stop chatting and start looking about?"

"Partly." Tony linked his hands behind his head, studying Ian. "Though you surprised me by offering in the first place. Why did you?"

"I don't entirely know." That visceral reminder of Seb, as Ruth looked up with her stricken eyes . . . the offer had just tumbled out. "I tried showing Seb how to play at that age, but he preferred bird books and model trains." Ian smiled at the memory and Tony smiled too.

"Well, you made that little girl very happy."

The self-same song that found a path through the sad heart of Ruth, Ian thought, the old line of Keats springing to mind. *When, sick for home, she stood in tears amid the alien corn . . .* That first impression still lingered: *sick for home.* No, Ian didn't regret taking the time to make those eyes shine this afternoon. Even in the middle of tracking a murderess, one could take time to be kind to a child. Or else what was the bloody point of it all?

"I like Ruthie," Tony said. "Sad little thing, somehow. But don't turn down Jordan's money when she offers to pay you for teaching her. We are already looking at an enormous telephone bill."

Ian raised his eyebrows. "Since when is it *Jordan* and not *Miss McBride*?" Tony grinned. "Well, if you're taking her out, see if you can get anything new about Kolb. And don't step on any hearts in the name of information gathering." Though Tony seemed to walk that line very well, just light enough with women that they didn't seem to mind when he drifted away.

"You're now the expert in not breaking hearts?" Tony lifted the telephone receiver. "You get to flirt with the next girl in the line of duty, then."

"Certainly not." Ian skimmed down the next page of addresses. "I'm a married man."

"I thought you were divorcing."

"I am. We are. When there's time."

Tony paused, then put the telephone back down with a tilted smile. "Ian, has it entirely escaped you that you're falling for your wife?"

Ian glanced up. "Don't be ridiculous."

"Look, I was glad when you two started sharing more than just a name. You need something in your life besides war criminals and that violin, because whether you'll admit it or not, you're lonely as hell. And Nina's just your idea of a good time, because underneath that starched collar you like to live dangerously, and your wife is the most dangerous goddamned female you *or* I have ever met in the flesh. But it's more than just fun now, isn't it?" Tony paused. "Because after five years of forgetting you even had a wife, you're suddenly Mr. *I'm a Married Man.*"

Ian folded his arms across his chest, several replies warring. "I fail to see where any of this is your business," he said finally.

"Because you're my friend, you Limey bastard, and if your wife goes winging off into the clouds again when we're done here, is she going to leave you in pieces all over the floor?"

Chapter 38

NINA

August 1944
Polish front

A lone voice lifted up into the sky, hushed, wobbling. Yelena's voice from somewhere in the throng of pilots, singing the ancient cradle song from the shores of the Old Man, the song Nina had sung on the airfield that first night. Softly the other pilots took up the song, as Nina pressed her burning eyes shut. They knew. Whether by some whispered word of gossip or by the thread of communication that bound them like a shared radio channel, they all knew.

The quarter moon was still rising over the auxiliary airfield, the pilots awaiting the order to fly. Nina stood in the squelching Polish mud, sealskin cap dangling from one hand and knapsack from the other, a lump in her throat like a stone.

This cannot be happening, she thought.

The song trailed away.

With a huge effort, Nina looked up. Her fellow pilots had moved closer as they sang, as she stood head bowed denying the inevitable. They clustered tight around her, instinctively hiding the regiment's distress from any outside eyes who might have been watching. Many cried silently, faces turned to her like flowers: dark eyes and blue eyes, red-haired and brown-haired and fair-haired. Nina took a shaky breath, inhaling the scent of engine grease and clean sweat, mud and navigation pencils. The perfume that belonged to women who lived for the sky. She couldn't see Yelena, but in her mind she heard Yelena's voice. Not the implacable voice of an hour ago, crying out *You're asking too much!* The laughing voice of almost three years ago, as she grasped Nina's arm and said *Welcome,* sestra*!*

Then the memory was blotted out by Bershanskaia's quiet words. "To your planes, ladies."

Nina swallowed, pushed one foot forward and then the other. A wordless rustle rose through the throng, and for a moment all the Night Witches pressed closer. Silent fingers touched Nina's shoulder, her back, her hair as she moved through her sisters. Someone gave her hand a brief, fierce squeeze—she didn't know who.

"Tell Galya to keep a lighter hand on the stick," Nina said not too distinctly and set off across the airfield for her plane, first walking, then running. From the corner of her eye she saw Yelena for the last time, face contorted, bent almost double in red-haired Zoya's comforting arms, then the regiment lapped around her, hiding her from view before the wrong eyes could take notice of her grief, pulling her along in the mass of boots and overalls jogging for the line of U-2s. Nina's heart kicked, but she didn't look back. She was never going to look back, look east, look in the direction of the Old Man. To look back was to drown. To look forward was to fly.

She found herself stepping up onto the wing of the *Rusalka.* She hadn't consciously decided to take her old plane, but she should leave her own U-2 for her navigator—Galya was going to need every advantage a familiar plane could give her, now that she'd become pilot. Yelena wouldn't be fazed by an unfamiliar new plane, Yelena could fly anything . . . no protest rose behind her, so Nina dropped down into the *Rusalka*'s cockpit. It smelled like Yelena's soft hair, and Nina bit her lip until she tasted blood. She brought the engine to life, and agony subsided a little in that familiar thrum.

All around her, the other U-2s were awakening. No outsider would be able to say tomorrow that the regiment had deviated from routine: often they sang on the airfield, always they ran to their planes, and now the preflight checks proceeded exactly as usual. If someone asked questions later about tears and sad faces, Nina had no doubt Bershanskaia would bring forth a plausible story about the regiment being downcast because of recent losses outside Ostrołęka. The Night Witches would keep the secret.

Ground crew ran to light the runway, just a flicker to mark the point of liftoff. Nina remembered Yelena groaning last month, *Soon they'll be expecting us to land by the light of Bershanskaia's cigarette!*

Enough, Nina thought as the *Rusalka* was waved forward. *Enough.*

Stick forward. Speed gathering under the wheels. Nina took the air, feeling her arms disappear into the wings, her blood into the fuel line. Behind her the Night Witches followed, an arrow-straight line into the rising moon. Nina knew Yelena would be flying second right behind her.

Six hundred and sixteenth flight. The last flight.

Last time rising away from the airfield. Last time leveling off at altitude, skimming through silvery wisps of cloud. Last time descending toward the target. Last time cutting the engine, sinking down in a silent death glide. Nina took a deep breath, held it. Keyed the engines back up in a roar, felt the nose rise, and as the blinding white fingers of the searchlights stabbed the sky, triggered her bombs off the rack. She flung her U-2 on its wingtip and sailed on past the target, luring the ground fire and the lights to follow her and leave the ground dark in her wake, perfectly set for Yelena to ghost through with her own load of death. Nina felt the familiar blindness of the lights pinning her against the vault of the sky, heard the chain of explosions below, and saw shells blooming into red and green and white bursts.

Nina released her long breath, sinking down and down and down so the pilots behind her could truthfully witness that their lead pilot had failed to pull up and vanished on the descent. Twisting, she could see Yelena slip out of the lights, turning back. Nina leveled the *Rusalka* and kept flying low and straight into the blackness.

What lies west? a little girl had wondered on the frozen shore of a vast lake. *What lies* all *the way west?*

Like it or not, Nina was now going to find out.

As she climbed back above the clouds and dim moonlight filled the cockpit again, she saw the dried rose wedged into the instrument panel. The rose she'd plucked from one of Marina Raskova's funeral wreaths and brought back for Yelena, carefully dried out and tucked beside the altimeter. *My Moscow rose.*

The first choked sob burst out of Nina. She tore the rose away and pulverized it, raising her hand and letting the rigid wind stream carry away the shredded petals. She wept alone in her cockpit on her six hundred and sixteenth flight, soaring west, never looking back.

BY DAWN, wolf packs of Messerschmitts and Focke-Wulfs would be roaming this airspace. Until then, Nina had the advantage. *I am still a Night Witch.* As long as the dark lasted, she could hide from the whole world.

How long would it take to cross Poland? Beyond was Germany, the belly of the beast—would it be safer to turn south, aim for Czechoslovakia? Wherever she touched down, how was she going to find safety speaking no language but Russian, with no money to her name? She flew through a war-torn world filled with blood and barbed wire, and as soon as the fuel gave out and she had to put foot on the ground, she was quite probably dead. That conviction had shone in the tear-filled eyes of her fellow pilots: here was trouble even their crazy little Siberian couldn't fly free of.

On and on she flew in the murk of cloud, hunched over her controls. West and west and west. Below somewhere would be Warsaw in its dying spasms—then Warsaw was behind her, or she assumed it was. A malicious headwind kicked up, and the *Rusalka* labored. Nina eyed the fuel gauge. The altitude and the speed were already eating through her tank. The wind grew rougher, and her heart fell. A U-2 could cover more than six hundred kilometers on a full tank in good flying conditions, but in this spiteful headwind Nina wouldn't make four hundred.

"Fuck your mother," she muttered, but rage wouldn't get her farther west; nothing would but fuel, and she was nearly out. The night was far from over and the needle on the gauge scraping near empty when Nina brought the *Rusalka* down out of the clouds. No lights below of cities or towns, not even any scattered farmhouses. Nothing but a dark swath of forest, stretching as far as Nina's night-trained eyes could see. She brought her plane down until she was sailing along the treetops, looking for a clearing. A U-2 could land on a dinner plate, the saying went, but you still needed a dinner plate. She supposed remotely that if she couldn't find one, she'd crash among the pines and die spiked by branches or burning in her cockpit.

The engine quit. The fuel gauge stood at empty. The U-2 began to drop.

Nina glided down silently in her last bombing run, only this time there were no bombs to drop, no engine roar propelling her back up into the clouds. Just down and down and down between the treetops.

There—a clearing. Part of Nina was disappointed. The siren croon of oblivion hadn't entirely gone away; in the back of her mind it kept up its seductive whisper. But she couldn't take the coward's way out when a runway stretched in front of her. She lined up the *Rusalka* and brought her down in a perfect three-point landing, branches cracking as her wings brushed past walls of trees. Flying wires snapped. Something else broke with a judder like a spine cracking. Then at last they were still, and Nina sat in the cockpit with her breath coming in short gasps. She heard the rustle of leaves, smelled leaf rot and bark. Her nose had grown accustomed to harsher smells, gasoline and engine grease, but one breath of this tree-laced night and she was back in the vast woods around the Old Man, trailing after her father as he taught her to track through the taiga.

Nina climbed stiffly out of her cockpit and jumped to the ground. A little moonlight filtered down, enough to show that a blade of her propeller was gone. "That's it, then," she said aloud. Her half-formed hope of stealing some cans of gasoline from somewhere and fueling up the *Rusalka* again spun away. Without a machine shop there was no fixing a halved propeller. Nina had spent most of her waking hours in the sky since she was nineteen and had first slid into a cockpit, but now she'd have to content herself with this rickety human shape and its inadequate feet: the *Rusalka* would never fly again.

Get out, Nina thought, *get out of here*. Anyone—German patrols, Poles looking for enemies, fugitives sniffing out travelers to rob— could have heard the U-2 land; anyone could decide to investigate, and until proved wrong, Nina was going to assume everyone she met was an enemy. *Get out of here before anyone finds you*. But she couldn't move. Nina thought she'd already left everything behind that there was to leave—her regiment, her sisters, her lover—but there was one more thing, after all: her gallant *Rusalka* with its painted fuselage and assertive little engine, whose wings had carried her through so many missions, whose shadow had embraced her and Yelena in the grass on long summer days. The *Rusalka*, so alive to Nina's touch that she practically sang. Nina had thought there was no more pain left to feel tonight, but she embraced her plane, as much of its body as her arms could hold, and she wailed her agony into its frame.

Then she swiped at her burning eyes and began tearing at the U-2 with her bare hands, stripping cockpit and fuselage as if she were stripping flesh from bones, cannibalizing it of anything that might be useful. She stuffed her knapsack full to bulging, then went to the underbrush and filled her arms with dead leaves and twigs. The woods were damp and muddy from a recent rain, but even if they weren't, she didn't care about the risk of setting the trees alight. Grief was draining away to be replaced by white-hot Markov rage, her father's all-destroying fury that cared nothing for sense or self-preservation. Nina didn't care if she burned half of Poland and crisped her own bones to ash; she wasn't leaving the *Rusalka* to rot. Filling the cockpit with brush, she struck a match from her supplies and flung it into the tinder. The fire caught, kindled, leaped up. Nina stood back, watching the smoke boil. Only when the *Rusalka* was engulfed in flame, stiffened fabric curling away to reveal the skeletal wooden bones, did Nina turn away. She shouldered her knapsack and followed her own long leaping shadow west into the trees, as the *Rusalka* writhed and died on her funeral pyre.

A COMPASS. A loaded pistol. Matches. A sack of emergency supplies—sugared milk, a chocolate bar, the extra food she'd snatched from the barracks. The scarf embroidered with blue stars. A roll of stiffened cloth, struts, and wiring stripped from the *Rusalka*. The razor.

That was all.

Nina exhaled a shaky breath. "Not all," she said aloud. She had good boots and heavy overalls, her sealskin cap. She had warm summer weather. And she had everything learned growing up on the shores of the Old Man.

Nina walked until she heard the trickle of a stream, drank from her cupped hands, ate half a chocolate bar, then rigged a shelter from the *Rusalka*'s scavenged cloth and struts. She collapsed under it with the razor in one fist, sleep falling like an avalanche, only to wake in the night bathed in clammy sweat, agonizing cramps racking her legs, teeth chattering as though it were midwinter. Nina had never been ill a day in her life but she was ill now, nose and eyes watering, hands shaking too badly to light a campfire. She huddled under her shelter, trying to rub the cramps out of her thighs, smelling her own rank sweat, and when she looked up she saw her father gazing down at her with yellowed eyes.

"You're not here," she said through clattering teeth. "I'm dreaming."

He squatted down. "How long has it been since you had a Coca-Cola pill, little huntress?"

Two days—or more? Somehow another day had come and gone. Nina could have sworn it had only been an hour since the shakes woke her in the night, yet between one set of shivers and the next, she'd somehow lost a day. That made it at least three days since she'd swallowed one of those tablets that flooded her veins with quicksilver—and for months and months, she hadn't gone a day without them.

Her father snorted, scornful.

"Go away." Why did she have to hallucinate him of all people? "I don't want you. I want Yelena." She wanted Yelena so badly, her sparkling eyes and fierce kisses.

"You're stuck with me, *rusalka*," her father said. "That lily-livered bitch didn't want you."

"Go away," Nina cried, then cried out again from the pain of her muscle cramps. She closed her eyes for an instant, and when she opened them again it was bright midday. She'd never been so hungry in her life; she drank all the sugared milk and shivered to see how her food stores were all but gone. She managed to stagger downwind of her little shelter to lay a few game traps, hands shaking too much to fashion more than the simplest of snares out of plane wiring.

Time kept bending and melding. Her waking hours were full of cramping muscles and watery bowels, heading to the stream to drink and then back to her shelter to curl around her jittering limbs. Her sleeping hours were full of nightmares. Over and over she lost control of the *Rusalka* over the surface of the lake, sinking through aquamarine water with lungs bursting. She imagined footsteps outside the shelter and erupted screaming, squeezing the trigger of her pistol over and over as she aimed it into the darkness. Too late she realized no one was there, and she'd just wasted all her ammunition. She could have wept, but tears were no good; she crawled back into the shelter only to dream of Yelena dying, going down in a blossom of flame. *If she dies, you will never know it.* Yelena was gone; Nina was never going to know if she lived or died or fell in love with another. She succumbed to tears then, sobbing in the haunted night.

She had no idea how long she was ill—the days and nights seemed to flash past in cycles. At some point her father disappeared, and Nina's lethargy abated enough to strip off and wash her filthy overalls. Sitting naked on the stream bank waiting for her clothes to dry, she flexed her fingers in the sunlight. Grown thin, but they weren't shaking anymore. *That damned Coca-Cola*, she thought. Her dreams were still terrible, she was still racked with sudden illogical convictions that someone was sneaking up behind her, but the muscle cramps had mostly disappeared, and she was strong enough to set a fire and cook the rabbit she found in her snare.

"Time to move," she said aloud, because Nina Markova might want to die, but she was too stubborn to starve in a Polish forest. She climbed into her damp overalls, took down her shelter, began trekking west again.

And in the second week, she met Sebastian.

Chapter 39

JORDAN

July 1950
Boston

Dancers mirrored endlessly across a battered barre—*click*. Pointe shoes rubbing through the resin box—*click*. Quietly Jordan moved around the fringes of the Copley Dance Academy's advanced class. A taut-pulled bun coming loose midplié, a forehead leaned wearily against an arched foot. *Click. Click.*

"Did you get what you wanted?" Tony asked as they left the studio.

"I think so. I won't know for certain until I look at the negatives." Jordan slung the Leica's strap over her shoulder. "You were very helpful."

It surprised her just *how* helpful. Shooting pictures with Garrett had often left her annoyed; he kept sneaking kisses or else talking when she trying to concentrate. Tony had been different. He'd flirted outrageously, not with the dancers but with Madame Tamara, the eighty-year-old instructor who called him a naughty boy in Russian and ended up letting Jordan stay the entire class rather than shooing her out after ten minutes. Tony had gravely aped the dancers' pliés as they began, and they laughed so much they forgot Jordan was there; she'd been able to start clicking away without waiting for her subjects to relax. Tony had then faded quietly back against the wall, handing her film before she needed to ask for it. "You were an excellent assistant," Jordan said as they swung around the corner into Copley Square.

He smiled, lazing along hatless in the summer sunshine. Heat shimmered above the pavement, and through the square women blotted their palms inside sweaty gloves and men tugged at collars whose starch had gone limp. "Can we discuss my fee for the morning's work?"

"Oh, there's a fee, now?" Jordan adjusted her broad-brimmed summer straw. "What are you going to cost me?"

"A swan boat ride."

"No Bostonian would ever be caught dead on a swan boat unless you're being dragged by your little sister. It's for tourists."

"I'm a tourist, and my fee for hauling your bag and buttering up that old dame who claimed she was a White Russian countess who fled the Bolsheviks is a swan boat ride."

Jordan took his arm, turning toward the Public Garden a few blocks away. "White Russian countess?"

"Her accent was Ukrainian, but I was too much of a gentleman to call her a fibber."

"So you spoke Russian just now to Madame Tamara, and French to those Parisian tourists who came into the shop three weeks ago." Jordan tilted her head. "And I'm sure I've heard you speak German to Mr. Kolb . . ."

"He didn't like that much. Odd duck, that one. How did your father come across him?"

"He was coming overseas and needed a sponsor. He's twitchy," Jordan admitted, "but he had a bad war, or so Anna said."

"Is she a wicked stepmother, your Mrs. Anna? Poison apples, makes you sleep in the cinders?"

Jordan smiled. "No, she's wonderful."

"Too bad, I always liked stories about wicked stepmothers. My Hungarian grandmother told me ghoulish tales growing up, the kind where the wicked stepmother wins in the end, not Cinderella. The farther east from the Rhine, the darker the fairy tales."

"Hungarian now—really, how many languages *do* you speak?"

"Six or seven. Eight?" Tony shrugged. "My mother's parents were a Hungarian and a Pole, and my father's parents were a Romanian and a Kraut, and everybody came to Queens for a grab at the American dream. That's a lot of languages going back and forth over a dinner table when you're growing up."

"And you just picked it all up?"

"There are two ways to learn a language fast, and one of them is when you're under ten and have a pliable young brain."

"What's the other?"

He grinned. "Over a pillow."

Jordan slanted him a look. He doffed an imaginary hat in apology. "I apologize. *Es tut mir leid. Je suis désolé. Sajnálom. Imi pare rau. Przepraszam—*"

Jordan stopped, transfixed, assessing him.

He left off his multilingual flood of apologies. "Normally when a girl stares at my lips I think she wants a kiss. You're mentally composing a camera shot, aren't you?"

She raised her Leica. *"An Interpreter at Work."* A close-up shot of that smiling mouth midspeech, with the gesturing hand to frame . . .

Tony groaned, tugging her along into the Public Garden, where trees threw dappled shade over crisscrossing paths. "You cruel dasher of hopes, shooting me instead of kissing me . . ."

"I need a motion shot, so talk!" Jordan picked a bench near the entrance, some distance from the swan boats, where the tourists would be crowded. "Tell me something about yourself. Anything."

"I'd rather talk about you." He rested an elbow on the back of the bench. "When did you first pick up a camera?"

"I was nine, transfixed by winter trees and a little Kodak." He smiled, and she clicked three shots off, already knowing this would be a good roll. Tony Rodomovsky wasn't handsome, but he had a face that photographed well: dark coloring, bold nose, the kind of ink-dark lashes that were absolutely wasted on men who never had to pick up a mascara brush. "When did you join the army?"

"The day after Pearl Harbor. A walking cliché at seventeen, winking at the recruiter. *Yes, sir, I'm of age!* Then I got to war and found out that it was just as boring as high school. It was if you got stuck with interpreter duty, anyway. What was your war?"

"Scrap metal drives and emergency drills about what to do if the Japs invaded, as if the Japs were going to invade *Boston*, for God's sake." A shot of Tony listening; *click*. He listened very intently, backs of his fingers brushing her arm now and then. "Mostly, my war was daydreaming. I devoured stories about the women journalists and photographers going overseas—Margaret Bourke-White got torpedoed and had to ship off in a lifeboat, and I nearly died of envy. I absolutely longed to get torpedoed."

"As long as you got away with some good shots of it?"

"Which would then make the cover of *LIFE*, yes. That's exactly how the fantasy went. Then maybe I'd marry Ernest Hemingway and live a life of action and glamour." Jordan paused, as a connection drifted into place. The journalists and photographers she'd idolized, all dash and danger and war zones, the names she could rattle off like her friends rattled off movie stars. Capa and Taro, Martha Gellhorn and Slim Aarons and . . . "Graham. Is your English friend *the* Ian Graham?"

Tony looked amused. "In the flesh."

"And he offered to teach my little sister her scales?" Jordan shook her head. "I used to read his column during the war, after it was syndicated!"

"I'm going to be jealous, if you keep gushing about my boss."

"Why, can't a girl get a crush on an older man?" Jordan teased. "Especially a tall good-looking one with a devastating accent, who's been all the places she's ever wanted to go?"

"He's married, and besides, I'd rather you got a crush on me."

"So charm me. Tell me about being an interpreter at a documentation center." Lifting the Leica again.

"*Not* a life of action and glamour. A flood of refugees poured through Vienna—they told their stories to Ian, through me."

"Was he writing articles, or—"

"No, he says he's done with writing. Gave it up for practical refugee work and hasn't penned an article since the Nuremberg Trials."

"I can see it might wear your soul away," Jordan said, thoughtful. "Year after year, seeing human suffering and turning it into newspaper fodder. Was it like that for you, translating? Hearing war stories day in and day out, when the rest of the world only wants to leave the war behind?"

"No." Tony linked his hands between his knees, smile fading to something more pensive. "An interpreter tries to work a step removed. You're not really there, in a way. You're like a set of interphones; you make it possible for the two people on either side to hear each other. And that's everything, when you come down to it. That's it, in a nutshell: if people would just *hear* each other—"

Tony stopped. "They'd what?" Jordan asked quietly.

He gave a small, crooked smile. "Likely go right on killing each other in swaths."

Click. That's the shot, Jordan thought. Bitter cynicism from a mobile mouth, that same mouth curled in a smile that was still touched with hope even after all it had looked on. "It's not so different being a photographer," she found herself saying. "I'm no professional, not yet, but I've had a similar feeling to the one you're describing. The lens removes me from the scene I'm recording, in a sense. I'm a witness to it, but I'm not part of it."

"People think it makes you heartless. It doesn't." A boy walking a beagle on a leash went past; Tony stretched out a hand to the beagle, who lapped his fingers happily before moving on. "It makes you a better set of interphones."

"Or a better lens." Jordan tilted her head at Tony. Unexpected depths to her charming clerk—who would have guessed? "You were at war since Pearl Harbor, and then you stayed and did refugee work when everyone else went home. Why?"

"You know what my war was?" Tony smiled thinly. "Nothing. Four years of it. I never fired a shot in anger, never so much as got my boots wet. My entire war was spent in various tents and offices, translating acronyms between high brass of various armies who didn't speak each other's lingo."

"So you stayed on for a chance to do more," Jordan said. "Why come home this year? It doesn't sound to me like you're tired of it."

He took a long time answering, as if parsing out what to say. "I'm not tired of it," he said at last. "But I wouldn't mind doing something—different. Ian's an avenger, scales of justice in one hand and sword in the other. I want to do more."

"Like what?" A group of shopping-laden housewives fussed past, but Jordan ignored them.

"I don't know." Tony ruffled a hand through his hair. "Make a repository for all those stories, maybe? So they aren't forgotten and lost. No one likes to talk about their war, after it's fought. They want to forget. And what happens when they die, and they've taken all their memories with them? We've lost it all. And we can't."

You should talk to my stepmother, Jordan almost said. *Another refugee who only wants to forget.* But it was Anneliese's right, surely? Because her story wasn't just pain and loss, it was shame— the shame of the SS connection, what her father had been. "I'm an American now," she always said firmly if asked about her past.

"You know why I prefer pictures to words?" Jordan asked Tony instead. "People can't ignore them. Most find it easier to forget the things they read than the things they see. What's caught on film is *there*, it's what *is*. That's what makes pictures so wonderful, and so devastating. Catch someone or something at the right moment, you can learn everything about them. That's why I want to record every-thing I see. The beautiful, the ugly. The horrors, the dreams. All of it, as much as I can get a lens in front of."

"And how long have you known that's what you wanted?" Tony asked. "I'm guessing when you heard that little Kodak go *click* for the first time."

Jordan smiled. "How did you know?"

"Drive—you've got it in spades." His eyes went over her. "I don't have any, so I notice it when I see it."

Jordan returned his gaze, letting her eyes go over him just as frankly. "You're amusing when you flirt, Tony," she said at last. "But when you're being serious, you're downright riveting."

"That's too bad. I can't sustain *serious* for more than ten minutes."

"Maybe you should practice. You might get up to fifteen."

"My record is twelve. Who's going to kiss who?" he asked.

"Who said there's going to be kissing?"

"You're thinking it. I'm thinking it." His black eyes danced. "Who goes first? I'd hate to bump noses."

"Why do I need to kiss you? I just took half a roll of film of your mouth as you talked. By the time I'm done cropping and filtering the image, I'll know everything there is to know about it, without kissing you once."

"But what a waste that would be."

"Time in the darkroom is never wasted."

"That depends entirely on what you're doing down there."

"Working. And don't you dare say that all work and no play makes Jordan a dull girl," Jordan added. "I *hate* that saying. Mostly people use it because they want me doing things for them, not for myself."

"Besides which, they're wrong. Work doesn't make you a dull girl. Work makes you an absolutely fascinating girl." He lifted her hand from the camera and kissed the pad of her index finger, the one that spent most of its time lying against the Leica's button.

Click, went something in Jordan's middle.

"Swan boats?" he said eventually. "Or is paddling around on a pond too boring for you, Jordan McBride? I could be persuaded to waive my fee."

You just broke off a long engagement, a voice inside Jordan chided. *You shouldn't move too fast!* But she told that voice to hush, hooking her finger at the neck of Tony's shirt and tugging him toward her. "Maybe an alternative form of payment?"

A long, lazy, open kiss under the beating sun, Jordan's fingertips resting against his warm throat, his thumb stroking along the line of her cheekbone. He kissed with slow, shattering thoroughness, like he could do this all day and not get tired of it, like it could take him a year if that was what she wanted. Right now, she wanted.

"Is there anywhere you have to be?" Tony said eventually, kissing along the line of her jaw toward her ear. "Or can we do this all day?"

Oh, yes, please. Jordan cleared her throat, looking down at her watch to give her breath a chance to slow. Dammit, Anneliese would be packing by now for Concord and New York, rushed off her feet. "I promised I'd help at home. Then it's the darkroom for me—work."

Tony dropped a last kiss below her ear, then pulled back. "All right." No arguing that work could wait. Just assent, and that unwavering dark gaze. "I'll see you tomorrow, Ruth's lesson. Maybe we could go to the movies after."

"Yes," Jordan said without hesitation. How pleasant it was just to enjoy a man's company, his attention, his kisses without feeling the weight of expectation from parents and neighbors. *When are you going to settle down, Jordan? When will you two make it official, Jordan?*

How pleasant to enjoy a man who was *not* official, not in the slightest.

Chapter 40

IAN

I an was surprised how much he enjoyed showing Ruth how to handle her half-size instrument. Perhaps because she was so voracious, so *desperate* for everything he could show her. Weren't most children her age playing with dolls rather than begging to play scales? She hung rapt as he took her through positioning and stance, the basics. "Always tune to an A," Ian said, and Ruth sang a perfect A unprompted. "Very good. Remember that Saint-Saëns I was playing, how that began?" She hummed the opening in G major. Ian glanced at Jordan McBride, sitting behind the shop counter with a cup of tea. "I wouldn't be surprised if she has perfect pitch, Miss McBride."

Ruth's sister beamed. She'd brought the little girl into the shop just as Ian was hanging up his battered fedora on an antique umbrella stand and Tony was flipping the sign around to read Closed. Ian had been feeling a touch impatient with himself for making this offer when there was already so much to do, but Ruth's face had turned on the violin so eagerly and Jordan McBride's gaze followed her with such happiness, his misgivings faded into a wry smile. "Take your instrument, and dear God, do not drop it. To destroy a

Mayr, even a replica, would be a crime against art." Jordan puttered about preparing tea in Minton cups, and Tony leaned on the counter watching her do it.

"Enough for now," Ian said at last, after his pupil had wobbled through her first one-octave scales. Ruth begged "More, please!" but Jordan reached over the counter to take the violin.

"You'd keep us here all night, cricket, and Mr. Graham has other obligations. I'll bring you back tomorrow to practice."

Ruth sighed, watching the instrument go back behind glass. When her sister prompted, "What do you say to Mr. Graham now?," she fixed Ian with a direct stare and said, "When can you teach me more?"

"That wasn't what I meant," Jordan protested.

"When can you teach me more, sir?" Ruth amended.

Ian laughed out loud.

"You don't have to do this again," Jordan told him. "I don't wish to impose."

Ian opened his mouth to take the way out she'd given him. "I don't mind," he heard himself saying instead, and looked at Ruth. "Will Thursday do, cricket?"

Both McBride sisters burst into smiles like small suns. *Goddammit*, Ian thought. He liked them, and it made him wish he hadn't met them under slightly false pretenses.

"I hope I'm not too forward in asking." It burst out of Jordan like a dam breaking. "You were in Spain with Gerda Taro, Mr. Graham—she's such a hero of mine, you can't imagine. What was she like?"

"Gerda?" Ian recalled. "They used to call her *la paquena rubena*—the little red fox. She had a good deal of swagger as well as nerve." Jordan had stars in her eyes, and behind her Tony smiled. He'd warned Ian in advance that she'd recognized his name, and that surprised Ian as much as Ruth's passion for scales. Didn't young women gush over film stars, not journalists?

"You were at the liberation of Paris," Jordan was saying now. "I remember one of your columns—"

"Yes, I got my first draft down in the bar of the Hôtel Scribe, jammed in between a woman writing a piece for the *New Yorker*— Janet Flanner, I think it was—and John, who looked like he had the worst hangover in France."

"John who?" Jordan asked.

"Steinbeck." Ian saw Jordan's impressed expression, and hastened to add, "It wasn't as glamorous as it sounds. A roomful of exhausted press corps nursing blisters and griping about their deadlines."

She didn't look like she believed that. "And afterward?"

Ian leaned on the counter, drawn into the past despite himself. "There was a poker game played in the bed of a truck as we headed out of Paris . . ." He ended up telling one story and then another, through a second cup of tea as Jordan pressed him with questions.

"You tell these stories, and I can see everything unfold like I was there," she exclaimed. "But Tony says you've given up writing."

Ian shrugged. "See enough horrors, the words run out."

Jordan looked like she wanted to push a pen into his hands anyway, but Tony interjected. "Princess Ruth is getting restless." He nodded at Ruth, who sat drumming her heels. "And we've got a date, McBride."

That surprised Ian. "I thought you said she didn't know anything else useful about Kolb," he said when Jordan disappeared into the back room to put the teacups away.

"This isn't for work." Tony shrugged. "Nina has Kolb's tail until dawn, and it's too late to make more telephone calls. There's absolutely nothing else chase related I can turn my hand to, so I'm going to take a pretty girl to the movies."

"If you want a pretty girl to take out, wouldn't it be less complicated to pick one who *isn't* wrapped up in our chase?" Ian said mildly. "One you don't have to keep fibbing to?"

"I like her, that's all." Tony hesitated, looking unusually thoughtful. "She wants things, big things. I like that. She makes me think about wanting bigger things too. Not just coasting along on your train."

Ian tried to resist the gibe, but failed. "Has it entirely escaped you that you're falling for a witness?" he said straight-faced.

Tony shot him a dirty look. "This is not like you getting moony over our resident Soviet assassin—"

"Which is an absurd idea, and you can *drop it*—"

"—Jordan makes me laugh, that's all. I make her laugh. It's a bit of fun on both sides. What's the harm?"

"Is she going to laugh when she learns you had ulterior motives for asking her on a date to begin with?" Ian lifted an eyebrow. "I may not know everything there is to know about women, but I know they don't like to be deceived."

Jordan swept out of the back room. "I hope you don't mind Ruth coming to the movies, Tony? My stepmother's out of town."

"I can cover three tickets." Tony smiled at the tall blond girl in her yellow summer dress, she smiled at him, and Ian could see the heat there, plain as day.

Something about this chase, he thought. *It's throwing us all off-balance.* He went back disquieted, to take over the dawn watch on Kolb from Nina, then attack their list of telephone calls. But by the following afternoon when Tony came home from his shift at the antiques shop, disquiet was forgotten.

"CHEERS," IAN SAID to his team. "We've unraveled our first thread."

The three of them stood around the table, looking down at the list.

"Seven of these addresses are fakes," Ian said. "No pattern to it, they're mixed in with the real ones. But Riley Antiques in Pittsburgh, Huth & Sons in Woonsocket, Rhode Island . . ." He rattled off the rest. "Not one of them is real."

"What's on the other end when you dialed those numbers?" Tony asked.

"All private residences." Sometimes a woman had answered the telephone, sometimes a man, in one case a child's treble. But not one person at the end of the line had been anything other than puzzled when Ian asked about the business named on the list. "I heard at least three German accents, as well. And when I asked the operator to find me the number of the business, she told me there *was* no Huth & Sons in Woonsocket, Rhode Island, or anywhere else in Rhode Island for that matter. Same with the others. Those businesses do not exist." Ian could feel his heart clipping along in staccato pleasure, the thrill when tedious legwork finally produced a lead.

Tony gnawed a thumbnail. "Was anyone on the other end suspicious?"

"Some sounded flustered. One rang off on me. Mostly I pleaded a wrong number and rang off myself in a hurry."

Nina hadn't said anything at all. But her eyes glittered, and as Ian looked from her to Tony, he felt the same electric charge leaping between the three of them.

Seven addresses. *Die Jägerin* might be living at one of them.

"Car or train?" Ian asked. "We've got a few day-trips ahead of us."

"BLOODY HELL . . ." Ian looked around a sea of unfamiliar street signs, pulling over with a squeal of some very dodgy brakes. Tony had taken the train to Queens to see a cousin and come back in a rusty Ford on loan. "Hand me that map, Nina."

Nina rummaged for it, sharp white teeth crunching through the skin of a beet. She ate raw beets like apples, until her teeth were pink. Ian hoped they wouldn't be pulled over by any policemen questioning his tendency to drift to the correct (i.e., English) side of the road, because the woman at Ian's side looked like a small blond cannibal. "You're holding the map upside-down, comrade. Some navigator you are."

"I navigate skies filled with stars," Nina said huffily, "not places called Woonsocket."

"I am never getting in an airplane with you, so kindly start learning to navigate in two dimensions rather than three."

"Mat tvoyu cherez sem'vorot s prisvistom."

"Leave my mother out of this."

It had been a two-hour drive between Boston and their first tar-get, with Tony staying behind to cover the tail on Kolb. Nina had spent most of the drive telling Ian how she'd left the Soviet Union, flying into Poland two steps ahead of an arrest warrant before run-ning into Sebastian. American road maps might be a mystery, but Ian was getting a feel for how to navigate the minefield that was his wife: ask anything about Lake Rusalka or what happened there with *die Jägerin*, or display any sign of affection whatsoever, and she either lapsed into prickly silence or detonated outright. But she didn't mind telling him about Seb, and Ian stored her affectionate stories up like coins. New memories of his little brother, every one priceless . . . but now it was time to work.

The Ford soon coasted into a quiet suburb with green yards and bicycles lying in driveways. Number twelve was a small yellow house with a modest, lovingly tended garden. It most certainly wasn't an antiques shop named "Huth & Sons." Seeing it here, so plainly a residence and not a business, made Ian's pulse pick up. Someone who was not who they were supposed to be lived here.

Nina had fallen silent too, thrumming like a plucked wire. He drove past number twelve and parked around the corner. Nina slid out, back to severe respectability again today in the high-necked blouse she'd worn to interrogate Kolb, a broad summer hat shading her face. She took Ian's arm and they strolled up the street in per-fect propriety. As discussed, Nina released his elbow and continued wandering up the street, and Ian turned as if by impulse up the front stoop of number twelve.

Had there been no answer to his knock, Ian and Nina would have returned to the car to wait, but the door opened. A middle-aged man, stocky, hair parted and barbered with (Prussian?) precision. "Hullo," Ian said in his most drawling public school accents, remov-ing his fedora with a deprecating smile. "Terribly sorry to disturb you, but my wife and I are pondering moving to the neighborhood." He waved at Nina, standing one house down with the map raised close to her nose as if she were shortsighted. Critical to have her at a distance, in case it was indeed *die Jägerin* who answered the door, who might remember Nina's face as Nina remembered hers. Ian's wife gave a distracted wave back, deftly hiding most of her features between the map's edge and her big hat brim, but without looking like she was trying to hide. *Bloody hell, but you're good at this*, Ian thought in admiration.

"We're considering a house just a block over. Graham's the name." Ian extended a hand, banking as always on two things: that most people were incapable of refusing a handshake, and that most people instinctively trusted a plummy English accent. It worked, as it usually did: the other man shook hands, firm and unhesitating.

"Vernon Waggoner. My wife and I have lived here a year."

Definitely German, Ian thought. That unmistakable clip, the *W* like a *V*, the *V* like an *F*. Ian made pleasant small talk, asking if the neighbors were friendly, what schools there were for his nonexistent daughters. Did Mr. Waggoner have any children? No, just his wife and himself. Waggoner remained polite but formal.

"Your wife, does she like the neighborhood?" Ian asked. "Mine is most anxious to make friends here." It was entirely possible that *die Jägerin* might have settled down with a new husband; her options for work would have been few for a refugee. Ian wanted a good look at any woman who lived in this house, but there was only so long he could spin chitchat on the stoop.

"Vernon?" Another voice floated from the hall behind, and a woman appeared, drying her hands on a dish towel. "Do we have visitors?"

Her German accent was much heavier than her husband's. Ian's eyes raked her face even as he begged pardon for interrupting. Very plump, blond, blue eyes. About the right age for *die Jägerin*—it was entirely possible that the very young woman in their old photograph had put on weight and tinted her hair. Ian angled himself as he shook her hand, drawing her out on the stoop so Nina from her vantage point would have the best look possible. His heart thudded.

But Nina tucked the map under her arm and crossed the lawn to mount the steps, offering a gloved hand. Ian's hopes crashed.

Had she kept her distance, she would have been signaling *Yes, that's the one.*

"Do you hail from Austria or Germany, Mrs. Waggoner?" Ian continued, concealing his disappointment. "I spent some years in Vienna as a young man, I remember it fondly."

"From Weimar," Mrs. Waggoner said with a quick, relieved smile that a German accent was not going to be answered with a nasty look.

"I had a good friend from Weimar, actually . . . does the name Lorelei Vogt mean anything to you?"

They both looked blank, not even a tiny flinch of a reaction. Well, it had been a long shot. Even if they had met her, who knew under what name?

"I shan't take up any more of your time," Ian said, taking Nina's arm. She murmured something politely inaudible. "You've been most kind."

"Not at all," Waggoner said jovially enough, but it hadn't escaped Ian's attention that in this land of overwhelming friendliness, the man hadn't invited them in. He stood solid in the doorway, smiling a pleasant smile, eyes giving away nothing. *I wonder what you were,* Ian thought, *before you became Vernon Waggoner of Woonsocket, Rhode Island.*

"Thank you again," Ian said, and retreated down the stoop. Nina's hand in his elbow gripped like steel.

"Not her," she murmured.

"I know." They rounded the corner out of sight, and Ian opened the car door for her. "But he was someone. He has things he was nervous about hiding, enough to pay Kolb for a new name." Ian closed the door after Nina, slid in on his own side. "A camp clerk? A Gestapo guard? One of those Reich doctors who culled the unfit from the ranks of the master race?"

Ian heard his voice growing louder and halted himself. He'd wanted so badly for it to be Lorelei Vogt. He wanted that door to open and show him the woman who killed his brother.

"We come back for this *mudak* some other time," Nina said,

kicking off her heeled pumps. "We know where he is, what he looks like. Later, after *die Jägerin*, we get him. Whoever he is."

"He's a goddamned Nazi," Ian said. "But not the one we're looking for." He wasn't even aware of making a fist before he drove it hard into the wheel.

"Seven names on list," Nina said. "Six more chances."

He flexed his stinging fingers, and Nina made the gesture she'd made at the diner, hooking her trigger finger through his. Not a gesture intended to comfort—rather, it was a reminder. A promise that the hunters had yet to fire their shot. Ian looked down at her finger looped around his own, then at her calm blue eyes. Nina Markova, a hurricane in compact female form, outer chaos whirling around an eye of silent, startling serenity. He'd first felt that serenity when he realized they could sit across a diner table in wordless accord, and he felt it thrumming through his bones now despite the frustration of the hunt. He squeezed, and she squeezed back before pulling away and reaching for the maps, all business again.

I am falling for my wife, Ian thought. *Damn you, Tony . . .*

He put that revelation aside for later, with a gritting effort. They had work to do. "Hand me that list, comrade. Six more addresses, six more chances."

But Lorelei Vogt wasn't at the address in Maine either, or the one in New York or Connecticut or New Hampshire. At that point, two fruitless weeks having eaten almost every cent they had, Ian and Nina cursed and had to turn back toward Boston.

Chapter 41

NINA

September 1944
Western Poland

Time still had a tendency to shift and melt when Nina wasn't paying attention, so she wasn't sure if it was ten days or two weeks before she saw her first German.

She was back in the woods, after a tense series of days when the trees gave out and she had to move through open countryside, turning away from any signs that indicated towns, raiding isolated cottage gardens for carrots and turnips to augment the fire-roasted meat of whatever small animals she managed to snare. She'd considered knocking discreetly at one of those Polish cottages, seeing if she could trade game for bread, but Nina looked down at herself—dirty overalls, broken nails rimmed in dried blood. The first thing any Polish housewife would do if she saw Nina on her doorstep was scream, and who might come running then? A burly farmer with a pitchfork, or a German soldier? Nina was relieved when civilized fields melted back into woods. *Just keep away from people*, she thought—and that day, of course, she found five.

She was fighting her way up a bramble-choked slope when she heard a sharp cry and froze in place. That was no animal caught in a predator's jaws. That sound had come from a man's throat.

Another cry, a series of shouts, then a young man's voice panicked and distinct: *Nicht schiessen, nicht schiessen—*

"Don't shoot." Even Nina knew that much German. If you didn't manage to make your way back to friendly lines or kill yourself before you were captured, you raised your hands and said *Nicht schiessen*. Not that it would do much good, because everyone knew what the Germans did to prisoners.

Nina had been falling back the moment she heard human voices, but now that she knew a German with a gun was somewhere ahead of her, she stole forward. *All the missions I've flown,* she thought, *all the bombs I've dropped, and I've never seen a German face-to-face.* They'd been anonymous: the faceless pilots in the cockpits of Messerschmitts, the invisible fingers that triggered tracer fire into the sky.

Ahead of her, Nina heard a shot. A cry. The meaty thunk of a body hitting the ground.

She lowered her knapsack and sped forward, razor in one hand and pistol in the other, cursing herself for wasting her bullets driving off fever dreams, and went still behind a clump of underbrush. Held her breath, peering through.

Four men stood in the clearing. A fifth lay on the ground, thin arms outflung, drilled between the eyes by a bullet hole. His two companions stood behind him, hands raised, skinny as fence rails in uniforms Nina didn't recognize. Two Germans held them frozen in place, neatly barbered and uniformed, the one nearest Nina still lifting his pistol away from the dead man, the other with his weapon leveled at the two prisoners. Everyone shouting in German and some other language Nina didn't know, the younger dark-haired prisoner trying to plead, the larger towheaded one edging forward with some idea of attacking, the Fritzes clearly screaming at them to get back. Everyone shouting too loud to hear Nina emerge from the brush.

Her feet carried her forward before she even decided to move. She went straight for the nearest German, the one who had shot the man on the ground, and he didn't notice until he saw the younger prisoner's eyes spring wide at something behind him. The German whirled, and Nina caught a photographically clear flash of his face: young, dark haired, a well-fed throat pushing at his high collar. He backpedaled, bringing his pistol up, but it was too late, she was already on him like a wolf. For Nina he might as well have been every Hitlerite the Night Witches had ever faced. The night fighter who had shot eight women out of the sky, the Messerschmitt pilot who had chased the *Rusalka* down and holed her wings like a screen—this complacent German boy with the swastika clinging to his arm like a spider was all of them. Nina felt a rising howl tear out of her throat as she brought her razor around and laid his cheek open to the bone. Blood sprayed sudden and scarlet in the air. The German screamed, and a shot sounded somewhere as the second German lunged and the older prisoner went for his weapon, but Nina only saw flashes beyond the enemy in front of her. He went down, winnowed to the forest floor, and her arm never stopped swinging in wide scything cuts. By the time she looked up, he was a pulped mass on the pine needles and all was silent.

Slowly, Nina blinked blood out of her lashes. Her throat ached. The second German lay dead as well; the older prisoner, blond and bony, held his pistol. The young dark-haired prisoner had both palms clamped to his lower leg. Both stared at her with white around their eyes, and Nina realized the dripping razor still swung from one numbed hand. She tried to wipe it off on her sleeve and realized her overalls were drenched in blood. She leaned down, searching the German's body and finding an astoundingly pristine handkerchief. Cleaning off her razor and her face, she dropped the resulting red rag on the ruin of his throat, feeling her soul float back into her own body from somewhere remote. "Lieutenant N. B. Markova of the Forty-Sixth Taman Guards Night Bomber Aviation Regiment," she heard herself say distantly. "Hero of the Soviet Union, Order of the Red Banner, Order of the Red Star."

The two men stared at her, and Nina's remoteness disappeared under a wave of despair. Who knew if they were English or French, Dutch or American, but they didn't understand her—they might as well have been rocks for all the legible conversation that was going to happen in this blood-laced clearing. Nina wondered bleakly if she was ever going to have another conversation with a human being again—if she'd die the next time she encountered a German, with the last exchange of words to ever leave her lips being that terrible night on a muddy airdrome where Yelena broke her heart.

Then the younger prisoner limped forward, still clutching his lower leg—dark haired, skinny as a railway spike, a long serious face. "Gunner Sebastian Graham, Sixth Battalion Royal West Kents, lately of Stalag XXI-D in Posen," he said in slow, clear Russian. "Um . . . charmed to meet you."

"BILL AND SAM AND I blitzed out this morning. We were carted out on a work detail, road repair—we did a bunk straight into the trees. We've been stumbling around in circles for hours, trying to find train tracks so we could hitch a railway car. The goons eventually picked up our trail." Sebastian Graham shook his head. "Lucky thing for Bill and me, meeting you."

Bill—William Digby of a regiment and rank Nina didn't catch—grunted something in English that Nina would have bet was *Not so lucky for Sam.* The three of them hadn't lingered in the clearing among the carnage—Sebastian knotted a wad of rags around his leg where the second German's wild shot had clipped him, as Nina and the towheaded Bill stripped the two dead men of clothes, weapons, anything useful. Sebastian had to lurch along with his arm around Bill's shoulder as Nina hauled the overloaded pack, guiding them back to a quiet glade with a stream she had trekked past earlier that morning. They all collapsed panting, drinking their fill, and now Bill was wolfing down a bar of chocolate found on the second German as Sebastian rolled up his trouser leg to look at his wound, and Nina raked through the rest of the German spoils. This morning she had been one, and now she had become three. It was dizzying.

"Where *are* we?" she begged to know. It was the thing that maddened her most, after years of navigating by maps and coordinates—having no reference in this world of trees and Polish road signs except the points on a compass. "Are we still in Poland, or—"

"We're just outside Posen. That's what the Jerries rechristened Poznań. Fort Rauch in Stalag XXI-D—we're not even three hundred kilometers from Berlin." Sebastian Graham leaned forward eagerly. His leg had to be hurting him, but giddiness and freedom seemed to be blocking the pain. "Is the Red Army close? We had a camp wireless getting news of the eastern front, but if there's an advance arm nearer than we thought—"

"No. It's just me." Nina looked down at the pile of German loot—matchbooks, penknives, ammunition—and wondered how much to say about how she'd got here. "I flew off course and crashed," she simplified at last. "I had to abandon my plane."

Sebastian looked back at his bloodied leg. "Well, there goes my dream of being ushered to a Soviet hospital tent and receiving a liter of vodka."

"Be glad," Nina said. "Soviet doctors would give you the vodka, then cut that leg off." Her voice was hoarse, partly from screaming as she threw herself at the German, partly because she hadn't spoken to a soul for weeks. She'd had no idea how hungry she was for someone to talk to until this oddly bilingual English boy dropped out of nowhere. "How's that leg?" She peered closer, but Bill gave her a glare and a shooing motion, squatting over Sebastian's foot himself. "Your friend doesn't like me," Nina observed. The man had spent a while squatting beside his dead friend, only rising after a hissed argument that they did not have time to dig a grave. Nina suspected she was being blamed for not springing out of the bushes with her razor a few heartbeats sooner. *I helped save you two*, she thought, returning Bill's stare. *I could have kept walking and let all three of you be shot.*

"Don't blame him too much," Sebastian was saying. "Our compound was split down the middle between those of us hoping to see Uncle Joe coming over the hill to liberate the camp, and those who thought Uncle Joe and all his troops were barbarians."

"We are barbarians." Nina smiled in genuine amusement. "That's why we're beating the Fritzes."

Sebastian smiled back. He looked no more than sixteen or seventeen to Nina, scrawny and big-eyed with the barest scruff of stubble. So even the English were sending babies to the front by now. His Russian was slow, peppered with odd English slang she didn't understand, but his accent was surprisingly good. "Where did you learn Russian?"

"Before I came to the stalag in Posen, they bounced me through another camp, and there were Soviet prisoners in the compound next to ours. I was there a good long while, and there isn't much to do in the lockup besides play cards and listen to your stomach growl, so why not pay Piotr Ivanovich from Kiev a few cigarettes if he'll teach you his lingo? I always had a good ear for languages."

"What happened to Piotr Ivanovich?"

"Hanged for stealing." Sebastian grimaced, not from the water Bill was sluicing over his wound. "They left his body to rot. They always do that, with the Soviets." He gulped a breath. "It's no picnic being a Limey in German hands, believe me, but we have it better than you Russkies. Poor devils."

"In the Forty-Sixth, we all swore we'd put bullets in our heads before we'd be taken prisoner." Nina peered at Sebastian's wound. The shot had clipped straight through the calf. Not much to do with a wound like that but clean it, bandage it, and hope infection didn't spread. The flaxen-haired Bill was already ripping an undershirt from one of the Germans into strips; he began strapping it around Sebastian's leg, and the boy went gray. Nina reached in to help, but Bill swatted her away again, muttering something. "What?" Nina demanded.

"He doesn't believe you're a pilot. Says even the Reds aren't idiot enough to put women in bombers."

Nina raised her eyebrows. Stripping off her right boot, she reached into the heel and brought out her identification cards and insignia. "Tell him if he doubts me, I can take my red star and cram it down his throat till he's shitting red enamel."

Sebastian didn't translate that. Bill fingered Nina's identification, grudging, then tossed it down. Sebastian picked it up and handed it back more formally. "My friend isn't inclined to offer an apology, as he doesn't like being proved wrong, but I'll offer one on his behalf. We owe our lives to your intervention, Lieutenant Markova, and I offer our sincere gratitude."

Nina nearly laughed. Englishmen really were a different breed. How had *any* of them managed to survive this war, tripping over all those good manners? "I'd have slit that German's throat whether you were there to save, or not. But you're welcome."

Sebastian looked startled, but he turned and had another discussion in English with his companion. "Bill and I will make camp here for the night," the rejoinder came eventually. "Would you care to join us, or are you looking to continue east as quickly as possible?"

He thought she was aiming to rejoin her regiment, of course. "I'll stay tonight," she temporized, reluctant to leave the only person in this wilderness with whom she could hold a conversation.

Good thing you did stay, she thought a few hours later. *These two are useless.* They'd have used up every match they had trying to start a campfire if Nina hadn't showed them how to nurture the flicker of smoke into flame. They looked bemused when she brought out birchbark peelings and explained how they could be chewed for sustenance. And when Nina went out to hunt with the German's pistol and came back dragging a skinny young doe, Seb looked downright nauseated as Nina slit open the deer's belly and reached inside to pull out the innards. "You clean out the cavity and bury the guts," she explained, hauling out the slimy blue and red ropes. "Then butcher the usable meat. You've never hunted game?"

"Bill's from Cheapside," Sebastian said, "and I went to Harrow."

"Where's that?"

"Never mind." The boy looked at the slick pile of viscera. "All I've been able to think about for four years is food and suddenly I'm not hungry."

"Wait till you smell it cooking." Nina sat back on her heels, cleaning the razor. "Four years you've been a prisoner? How old were you when you enlisted, twelve?"

"Seventeen," he protested. "A few months later my unit got nabbed outside Doullens."

"You surrendered?" Nina couldn't help saying, remembering Comrade Stalin's *Not one step back* and the whispers about men shot by their own officers if they so much as edged backward, much less surrendered.

Sebastian's face showed a flash of shame, even four years after the fact. "It was hardly my decision." Stiffly. "I was just a gunner. We're supposed to be fighting a rearguard action, keeping the Fritzes off the Doullens–Arras road, and we've got one rifle and fifty rounds per man, and only eighteen Bren guns. Not much to do once the ammunition's gone and the tanks are rolling in." He looked around the tall dark woods, which were just starting to darken in twilight. "Four years behind barbed wire . . . and now I'm out."

His bony face was full of soft, dazed wonder, and Nina's heart squeezed despite herself. Four years locked in the flat stasis of fear and restlessness and hunger, and he was still capable of wonder. Nina couldn't decide if that was foolish or admirable.

Night fell, and the two Englishmen jumped at every noise from the woods as Nina cooked their dinner. Bill was still inclined to bristle whenever she gave him an order—English soldiers clearly weren't used to female lieutenants, Nina saw in amusement—but he stared at her when he thought she wasn't looking, and so did Sebastian. "I'm sorry," the younger boy apologized when Nina caught him watching her with that air of slight disbelief. "We don't mean to be rude. You can't imagine how strange it is, seeing a woman's face after forty-eight months of nothing but chaps."

Nina paused, rotating venison strips over the flames. "Am I going to have trouble with either of you?" she asked bluntly.

Sebastian's shoulders began to vibrate. Nina tensed, then realized he was shaking with laughter. "Lieutenant Markova," he said between gusts of mirth, "I was raised a gentleman. Now, my father's version of a gentleman pulls out chairs for ladies and otherwise doesn't think they're good for much, but my older brother's version pulls out chairs, asks a lady her opinion rather than assuming it, and never puts a hand where it isn't invited. But even if I weren't a gentleman, I'm not an utter idiot. And only the greatest idiot on earth would force *anything* on a woman he first met erupting from a bush to slash an armed man to ribbons with a razor."

His laughter was infectious, and Nina couldn't help smiling.

The three of them gorged on chunks of venison, charred on the outside and half raw inside, wolfing it till grease ran down their chins. "I don't care if I get nabbed and sent back," Sebastian said thickly, chewing through deer gristle. "This beats any kriegie meal I've had in four years. Is it true Warsaw is up in full rebellion?"

"Last I heard. Is it true Paris was liberated?"

They traded war news eagerly in two languages. After the food was gone, Sebastian tried to limp around the fire, but only managed a few lurching steps. "That tickles," he joked, lips thinned in pain, and Bill gave him a long look. Sebastian returned it, and the two men began a quiet discussion. Nina had a feeling she knew what they were deciding. She rose to check if her overalls were dry, hung over a nearby branch after being rinsed of as much of the German's blood as possible, and when she tugged them on over her unbloodied trousers and shirt and came back to the fire, Bill was going through the spoils from the dead soldiers.

"He's leaving you." Nina sat down by Sebastian. "Isn't he?"

"I told him he'll have a better crack at getting free if he's not dragging me and my gimpy pin. If he takes the Kraut uniform—the one not sopped in blood—he can head for the nearest train station, try to bluff on with the German's identification, aim for free France." Sebastian tossed a stick into the campfire. "I'd do the same if it were me."

"Would you?" Nina couldn't conceive of leaving a wounded *sestra* behind.

"It's what everybody does, planning escapes. You split up once you're outside the gates, to even the odds one of you gets clear." The English boy was trying to sound matter-of-fact, but he wasn't as good at hiding his emotions in Russian as he was hiding his accent. They watched Bill try on the German's uniform. It hung off his bony shoulders but wasn't a bad fit. Bill smiled for the first time and began tugging on the German's still-shiny boots.

"He'll be caught in a day," Nina said.

"Probably. Most of us are, when we blitz out—get noticed, get snatched, get thrown back in within a day or two. But some make it. Fellow named Wolfe in my unit, Allan Wolfe—he made it out on his third try, hasn't been seen since."

"Because he's probably lying in a ditch."

"Or he's back in England, free as a bird. Somebody has to get lucky." Sebastian turned a stick over in his bony hands. "If Allan Wolfe, why not Bill Digby?"

"He shouldn't leave you," Nina stated, watching the man going through the German's identity cards.

Silence from Sebastian. "I wasn't even supposed to be part of this blitz-out," he said after a while, softly. A curious conversation to be having in front of the oblivious Bill, but with the barrier of language, they might have been talking alone. "It was Bill and Sam, they were in it together, chums from Dunkirk. The Jerries threw me in with them at the last minute, doing roadwork in threes, and it was yank me along or scrap the plan. They thought I was a bit useless, and"—a shrug—"well, I got myself wounded while Bill killed one Kraut and you killed the other, so they weren't wrong, were they? Either way, I'm not Bill's responsibility."

Not now that Bill met me, Nina thought sourly. Westerners— show them an armed woman with a chestful of medals and six hundred sixteen bombing runs to her name, and what did they think? *Wonderful, a nurse!* Dump the wounded man on the woman and be on your way with a clear conscience, because naturally she'd take care of him.

Well, Lieutenant N. B. Markova wasn't taking care of anyone but herself. She was going west, no time to play nursemaid.

"Get some sleep," she told Sebastian Graham and retired to her own side of the fire. She heard an uneven hitching breath or two across the camp, but turned off her ears. *West.*

Bill took off at first light. Seb shook his hand and Nina gave him directions, tucking her compass back inside her shirt when she saw his eyes linger on it. They watched Bill tramp off through the trees, doubtless already dreaming of England, and Sebastian turned to Nina with an air of getting everything over with.

"I imagine you'll want to rejoin your regiment as soon as possible, Lieutenant," he said formally. "I shan't hinder you from making for Warsaw. I'll be picked up quite soon, I would guess. Back in time for a proper dinner of ersatz coffee and dehydrated-turnip soup." He tried to smile. "Frankly, all this was worth it just to get a belly full of venison and a night's sleep under the stars."

He stood there listing to one side, trying to hide the fact that his wound was hurting him. *Fuck your mother*, Nina thought. *Fuck—your—mother.* "Nina Borisovna," she said.

"What?"

"I'm not your lieutenant, call me Nina Borisovna. I'll stay with you awhile." She glared, stuffing her hands in her pockets. "Only until your leg's better. After that I head west."

"West?" He looked puzzled. "Why aren't you rejoining—"

"I can't rejoin my regiment, because I'll be arrested. I'm no deserter," she flared, seeing the flick of his eyes, "and I'm no coward either. My father spoke against Comrade Stalin, and my entire family was denounced."

She could see him doubting her. Anyone would. She hoped he'd do the cautious thing, tell her to leave him. Then she wouldn't be stuck nursing a green boy with a bad leg when all she wanted to do was run.

"I believe you," he said.

Nina almost groaned. "*Why?*"

"You killed that German and saved my life," he said simply. "You're no coward. And if you can't bring yourself to desert a stranger like me, you wouldn't desert your regiment unless you had to."

Nina did groan then. "I can't believe someone as trusting as you has managed to live this long, Englishman!"

He smiled. "My friends call me Seb."

Chapter 42

JORDAN

August 1950
Boston

Well, Jordan thought, *this is awkward*. In fact, you could take a snap of this group standing here on the airfield and caption it *Ex-Fiancés: A Study in Awkwardness*.

"Hello," she said as cordially as possible, considering she hadn't seen Garrett Byrne since she'd handed his diamond back and he'd told her to take her advice and shove it. And now they'd bumped into each other at the tiny airfield outside Boston where Garrett had first taken her flying, which wouldn't have been so bad had Jordan been alone, but she had Tony at her side, standing there with eyes that danced hilarity at all the things that weren't being said. For a man who had spent years interpreting the spoken word, Tony was remarkably good at interpreting the *unspoken* ones. "I didn't know you'd be here, Garrett."

Her former fiancé wore oil-stained coveralls, very different from the summer-weight suit he wore to work beside his father. "I work here full-time now, helping in the hangar and piloting the joyrides. I bought a part share," he emphasized. "I'm looking to make something of the place, eventually buy out Mr. Hatterson. Dad wasn't too happy at first, but he's come around some."

So you took my advice, after all, Jordan thought. Garrett looked far more natural in coveralls than in a suit. She managed not to say *I told you so!* but he could probably tell she was thinking it.

"What are you doing here?" Garrett folded his arms across his chest, eyes drifting to Tony, who had slung an arm around Jordan's waist. "We've met, haven't we? Timmy?"

"Tony. Rodomovsky. Nice to meet you again, Gary."

"Garrett. Byrne."

"Right."

Jordan shook Tony's arm off. Really, men. "I wanted to take some shots of the mechanics, if they're willing." *A Mechanic at Work*— her shots of the local boys at the Clancy family garage hadn't come out, there just wasn't much visual grandeur in car engines. "Would anyone mind if I went into the hangar and snapped a roll?"

Another man, she thought, might have been spiteful and said no. Garrett just gave a stiff nod, eyes drifting past Tony to the person hovering impatiently behind. "Are you going to introduce me to your other friend?"

Jordan opened her mouth, but Nina Graham ran right over her. "You have planes?" she asked in her strange accent, coming forward in a clack of boots. "Let's see."

Jordan had been rather startled to see a blond head in the backseat of Tony's Ford when he came by the house to pick Jordan up. "I'm sorry to say we have a third wheel," Tony said with a glare at his passenger. "Jordan McBride, may I introduce Nina Graham, Ian's wife. The moment she heard me mention this morning that I was driving you to an airfield, she invited herself along."

"Pleased to meet you, Mrs. Graham—" Jordan began, but an impatient flap of the hand cut her off.

"Nina. So you're the girl Antochka likes." She looked Jordan over, speculative, and Jordan murmured pleasantries even as she was thinking, *Rats*. A third wheel in the backseat—there was definitely not going to be any pulling over on the way to the airfield for kissing. With Anneliese still in Concord, Ruth gone every afternoon to a neighbor's house to play, the shop safe in the capable Mrs. Weir's hands, and with Ian Graham and his wife absent on some sort of driving tour for the past few weeks, Jordan and Tony had had the freedom for quite a lot of kissing. Jordan had been looking forward to more today, because Tony kissed like a man who actually enjoyed it, not a man who hurried through five minutes of it as a prelude to unbuttoning a girl's blouse. Only now there was this woman in the backseat who Jordan hadn't met before, though what she'd *heard* had certainly been interesting.

"Ian's Red war bride," Tony had said. "Don't ask."

Jordan had envisioned an exotic beauty in sables, not this compact bullet of a woman in shabby boots. Now, Nina Graham was shaking Garrett's hand in business-like fashion, firing off questions. "You have what, Travel Air 4000 there? What else? Stearman, Aeronca, Waco—"

"Mostly American craft." Garrett straightened, listing aircraft, and Jordan was amused to see his most charming smile wink on like a searchlight. "You're an enthusiast, Mrs. Graham?"

Nina smiled modestly. "I fly a little."

"Well, let me show you a few things while Jordan and Timmy here look around . . ."

"Holy hell," Tony whispered in Jordan's ear as Garrett sauntered off with Nina at his elbow, looking up earnestly as he expounded. "He's flirting with her."

"He's trying to make me jealous." Jordan smiled as she dug in her bag for film, relieved to realize she didn't *feel* jealous. The last bit of proof, if she'd needed it, that it had been right to call off the wedding.

Garrett's voice floated over. ". . . this Travel Air here, her name's *Olive*. Pilots like to name their planes, did you know that? I could take you up for a quick spin, go easy on you—"

Tony spluttered laughter. "She's going to eat him alive."

"Enjoy the show," Jordan said, laughing too. "I'm going to get my shots."

Tony carried her bag into the hangar, looked around for the mechanics, backed her unhurriedly into the shadow of a decrepit crop duster, and gave her a long kiss. "For later," he murmured, "when we lose the third wheel, after she's eaten Gary boots, bones, and coveralls."

Another kiss, even longer. Jordan pulled back eventually, trying to remember why she was here. *A Mechanic at Work*. Right.

She found the mechanics and introduced herself, chatted lightly, flattered them, and got them laughing—she'd picked up a few things from Tony, the way he got subjects to relax. She waved the mechanics back to work, asking admiring questions, scolding when they tried to meet the camera's eye, clicking away once they got absorbed. Two rolls of film, no fuss. *I'm getting better at this*, she thought, thanking her subjects. Her photo-essay was taking wonderful shape, the centerpiece of the work she'd have to show when she began job hunting in New York. Soon she'd have to begin thinking about an apartment, job interviews . . .

And breaking the news to Ruth that yes, her sister really *was* going away, but she'd be back every month to visit. Jordan grimaced. Ruth knew about the New York plan, but wouldn't acknowledge it—and lately, she was so obsessed with music that she barely noticed anything that wasn't violin shaped. Every evening, without Anneliese here to sneak around, Jordan took Ruth to practice at the closed shop; she'd play clear through supper if Jordan didn't drag her home. "Ruth's doing very well," Jordan said carefully over the telephone when Anneliese called from Concord.

"No nightmares?"

"Not lately, no." With practice every day and a lesson every time Mr. Graham could squeeze one in, Ruth was blossoming. "You'll want a proper teacher for her soon," Mr. Graham had said after the last lesson, just after he'd come back from his driving trip. "I can give her scales and simple melodies, but she's soaking it in like a little sponge. She's even trying to piece her way through tunes she's heard me play, or remembered from the radio."

If Ruth has music, Jordan thought, *she'll adjust just fine when I leave in the fall*. Which meant Anneliese had to be told. *Soon. Not yet*.

"Are you enjoying yourself?" Jordan had asked her stepmother over the telephone, hearing strain in Anneliese's voice.

"Making plans." Anneliese sighed. "It's been quite a summer for plans, hasn't it?"

And the summer was going so fast, Jordan thought, coming out onto the airfield. Soon fall would be in the air; she'd be packing for New York. No more evenings in the shop, watching a famous war correspondent teach her sister to play a simple, haunting lullaby from Siberia where Nina Graham had grown up. No more informal chats afterward as Mr. Graham made tea and told a story in his deadpan English baritone about how Maggie Bourke-White was so focused during her camera work that once her halter-neck shirt fell down around her waist and she didn't even notice. No more Tony . . .

He looked over his shoulder with a grin, pointing at the blue-and-cream biplane named *Olive* now rising from the runway into a slow loop around the field. Jordan couldn't stop her stomach from flipping at that grin, and she didn't try. *Enjoy it now, enjoy it all. Before summer ends.*

"Gary took Nina up for a spin." Tony was laughing. "He said she could take a turn on the student controls. This is going to be good."

Overhead, *Olive* came out of her sedate loop with a sudden swoop downward, took a screaming turn around the airfield, then flipped inverted and clawed up steep and fast. The plane nearly disappeared into the blue, then came roaring back a matter of feet over the hangar roof, painted belly flashing overhead seemingly close enough to touch. A final hammerhead turn, then Nina brought *Olive* down using about half the runway Garrett had used taking off.

Jordan looked at Tony. They both burst out laughing. She barely managed to get control of herself by the time Garrett climbed out of the instructor's cockpit, looking a little green around the gills. Nina hopped out in one lithe movement like a cat jumping from a roof, stripping off her flying cap. ". . . a little heavy on the controls," she was saying as Tony and Jordan approached. "But good little plane. Nice." Patting the wing, business-like. "You have anything faster?"

"Um. Well, not yet, we're a small operation—" Garrett pulled himself together, expression warring between chagrin and admiration. Admiration won out as he asked, "Could you show me a few things, Mrs. Graham?"

"SHE WAS A PILOT with the *Red Air Force*?" Tony had discreetly filled Jordan in on a few things after dropping Nina off at the Scollay Square apartment.

"Sure. We don't spread it around, not as Commie crazy as people are here." Tony pulled up in front of Jordan's house, hopped out of the car. "Here you go. I take it you're disappearing into the darkroom for a few hours to develop all that film?"

"How'd you guess?" But Jordan paused. Ruth was playing at a neighbor's house; it would be hours before she'd have to be picked up. *Hours*, Jordan thought, eyeing Tony.

He handed her out of the car, quirking an eyebrow at her considering gaze. "What's on your mind?"

Nothing at all proper, Jordan thought. *But the hell with proper.* She was tired of the stepping-stone path of dates and doorstep kisses and white-gloved visits to meet the parents; the sedate junior-league progression of approved stages that had made her feel so caged in with Garrett. She wanted something private and wicked and just for her, something absolutely, gloriously *improper*. She took a breath. "Would you like to see my darkroom?"

He gave his slow, eye-crinkling smile. "I'd be honored."

It was the first time Jordan had taken him—taken anyone outside the family, really—down these steep, separate steps under the front stoop to her private enclave. She threw the switch, pointing out Gerda and Margaret looking down from the wall, her equipment. Tony wandered around, looking at everything. "So this is where you spend all your best hours."

"Some bad hours too. Whenever I cry about Dad, it's always here." Not quite as often, now—grief was beginning to be overlaid by the first layer of skin and time. Jordan supposed that layer would get thicker and thicker, and in a way she was sorry. Grief cut, but it also made you remember. "Whether good or bad, everything that's important happens here," she said, inhaling the familiar smells.

Tony touched the long table, looked up at the lights. "I like it."

"I want something twice the size. I want printing assistants, I want other photographers to share it with." Jordan slipped out of her shoes. "There are so many things I want."

"I'd tell you I'd give them to you, but you want to earn them." Tony leaned against the wall. "Go ahead, get to work."

"I start working, I lose track of time," she warned.

"I've got time. Nina's taking over a shift of work from Ian, and he's hogging our only telephone. I've got nothing to do but watch you." Tony linked his hands behind his head. "And you are an unbelievably tempting sight when you are lost in work."

"Really, now." Jordan turned for the scrap of yarn she used to keep her hair out of her face. Lifting her hair off her neck, she felt his eyes on her nape like a kiss and looked back over one shoulder with a smile. "It's dull, watching film get developed. You'll be bored to tears."

"You nibble your lower lip when you're concentrating," Tony replied. "I can be happy for hours watching you do that."

"You're a charming liar, Tony Rodomovsky."

His smile faded. "I try not to be."

Part of Jordan wanted to cross the floor and drag his head down to hers on the spot. Part of her was enjoying the rising anticipation too much to hurry. "Well, let's see how well I can work with someone watching and thinking impure thoughts."

His grin returned. "*Very* impure thoughts."

She switched on the red safelight, pulled out her film, and got started, happily conscious of his eyes. Lifting the prints out and clipping them to the line one by one, she stood back.

"Verdict?" Tony asked behind her.

"That one, maybe. Possibly that one." Pointing. "I need to enlarge it, focus on just the hands against the propeller blade."

He wrapped his arms around her waist from behind, looking at the prints over her shoulder. "How do you know?"

"How does anyone know how to do anything?" Jordan caught her breath as his jaw scraped the side of her neck. "Classes. Practice. Years of hard work."

He nipped her earlobe. "Fair enough."

She tilted her head back against his. "Tell me a secret."

"Why?"

"Because we're in the dark, and people trade secrets in the dark."

"You first."

"I sometimes call myself J. Bryde. It's the name I want for my byline, but I talk to her like she's real, sometimes. The famous J. Bryde who travels the world with a camera and a revolver, men and Pulitzer Prizes falling at her feet."

"I'm no Pulitzer, but I'll fall at your feet."

He kissed the other side of her neck, and Jordan reached up to slide her hand through his soft hair.

"Your turn. What's your secret?"

He was still for a while, chin resting on her shoulder, arms tight around her waist. "There's one I want to tell you," he said slowly, "and can't."

"Why not?"

"Not mine to tell. Not yet."

"You have a wife and six children in Queens?"

"No wife. No girlfriends. No kids. That I promise."

"Prison record? Warrant out for your arrest?"

"No."

"All right, then." Jordan might usually have been curious, but in the dizzying warmth of this red-lit room, she didn't care. She wasn't bringing Tony home for inspection as a future husband to trot out his credentials. He could keep as many secrets as he liked; she had a few of her own. "Just tell me *a* secret then. If not *that* one."

"I'm Jewish," he said.

"Really?"

"Yes. Want me to leave?"

Jordan reached behind her and swatted him. "No!"

His voice had a guarded wariness. "Some people don't like hearing it."

"Was there a girl who didn't like hearing it?" Jordan guessed.

"A girl in England I thought was important for a while. She stopped returning my calls after I told her my mother's mother was a Jew off the boat from Kraków." A shrug. "I was raised Catholic, but one-fourth part Jewish is enough for plenty of people."

Jordan leaned back against him, the warm arms around her waist. "You're Tony Rodomovsky. I like all your parts . . . and don't you dare make that into a smutty joke."

"Wouldn't dream of it." They stood a moment, entwined and silent, then Tony kissed the slope of her shoulder and stood back. "You've got one more roll to develop."

"Yes," she managed to say.

The air had thickened. Jordan ran the second roll through, knowing she wasn't doing her usual meticulous job, not caring. She clipped her prints up and cleaned away her chemicals, feeling his gaze redoubled.

"Finished?" came Tony's voice behind her.

She shoved the last of the trays aside, turned around to meet his gaze, and felt the tilting sensation of utterly giving in. Not to stop and ask *Is this wise?* but to think *I don't care* and seize it. "Come here, you."

"Thank God. Another roll would have killed me." He came toward her in the red light, catching the end of the yarn tying back her hair and tugging it slowly free. She'd abandoned the Rita Hayworth pin curls long ago; Jordan felt her loosened hair slip straight and easy through his fingers.

"I'm going to New York in the fall," she said, getting it out before the talking stopped altogether. "Until then, I'm going to be working like a dog in this darkroom and looking after my sister—and hopefully, having a mad, passionate fling with you." Winding her arms around Tony's neck, she looked him in the eye. He had eyes to drown in. "How does that sound?"

His voice was rough. "Sounds like heaven."

Their mouths crashed together in the red glow of the safelight, hands pulling at buttons, shirttails tugging out of waistbands. Jordan reached behind, hoisted herself up to sit on the worktable, pulling him with her. Tony's shirt landed on the floor, then Jordan's blouse. "I always meant to put a cot in here for the nights I work late and get tired . . ." Jordan murmured between kisses. "I never got around to it."

"That is a serious oversight," he agreed, disposing of her brassiere and tossing her on her back.

"Do you—" Jordan stopped, gasped. He was kissing his way very slowly down the line of her ribs, and it was impeding her ability to speak. She'd had no idea the skin over her ribs was that sensitive. Then again, she'd never dated any male in her life, Garrett included, who had bothered paying attention to it. "Do you have any—"

"In my pocket." She felt Tony smile against her navel. "I've got no desire to be a daddy just yet."

"Good. Hurry up—" Reaching up to tug him closer.

"Nope." He pinned her wrists flat, giving that grin that made her stomach flip. "You had hours to work, J. Bryde. My turn."

Chapter 43

IAN

August 1950
Boston

F ive addresses, and nothing?" Fritz Bauer's cigarette rasp growled
in Ian's ear across the telephone line.

"Not *die Jägerin*, anyway." Ian would have bet good money
all five of the men who had answered his knock and listened to his
"moving to the neighborhood" story had a war record worth hiding.
"Nina managed to get snaps with a little Kodak, pretending to take
pictures of the neighborhood, getting our fellows at the edge of the
frame. Relatively clear shots—can you do some matching work with
your files, see if we can find names to go with the faces? If they're
identifiable war criminals—"

"What did I tell you about fighting an extradition battle in the
United States, Graham?"

"Someone has to fight it," Ian said with a grim smile. "I'll send
you the packet. I'm for Pennsylvania tomorrow."

Sixth address on the list, and the longest drive so far; more than
six hours. If *die Jägerin* wasn't there, their last chance was the address in Florida. *Let her be in Pennsylvania*, Ian prayed. He wasn't
sure the overstretched budget could take any more road trips. The

reason they were now into August—August!—with still two addresses left to check was because between the telephone, the rent, and the drives to the first five addresses, they had to wait for the next month of Ian's annuity to come in. *A search for a murderess halts dead in its tracks for the want of ten more dollars in the bank account.*

"Is it my imagination," he mused to Nina as they crossed the Pennsylvania state line, "or did Tony seem a trifle keen to see us on the road today?"

"He's getting laid," Nina said, matter-of-fact.

"Bloody hell," Ian said, thinking of his partner and Jordan McBride.

"You're shocked?" His wife sounded amused. "You think he should marry her first?"

"No, I'm no pot to go calling kettles black." He'd spent years in war zones where every day you survived meant a night seeing what you could drink and who you could take to bed, no one giving any thought to propriety or marriage. "But Tony had better not break that girl's heart," he added ominously.

"You like her."

"I like both the McBride girls." It surprised Ian just how much he'd been enjoying the half hour or so at the antiques shop after Ruth's lessons, when he made tea and Jordan begged for war stories and Tony told jokes. It had been a way to pass the time, waiting until he and Nina had the money to drive out and investigate the last addresses on their list, but it was more than that.

"I still don't imagine you teaching children, *luchik*," Nina observed, curling her legs under her catlike. She was never there for Ruth's lessons; evenings were always her shift following Kolb. "Is very—word? Tame? Domestic?"

"Ruth's a nice child. Children like her make me think about the future." Nina tilted her head, inquiring. Ian tried to elaborate, steering the Ford through a dilapidated suburb. "She was born during this last war, and thank God she had far better luck than those poor children Lorelei Vogt shot by the lake. She's alive to play music, grow up whole and healthy. Other children born when Ruth was will grow up to start more wars; that's the way of the human race, but Ruth won't be one of them. She'll bring music into the world instead. She's at least one thing that's right, going forward. Building a generation is like building a wall—one good well-made brick at a time, one good well-made child at a time. Enough good bricks, you have a good wall. Enough good children, you have a generation that won't start a world-enveloping war."

"A lot to think about a child who can play a few scales." Nina slanted him a look. "Is something you want? Children?"

"Good God, no. I find most children bloody annoying." A thought struck him. "You aren't trying to tell me something, are you?"

"*Der'mo*, no." Nina waved a hand, and Ian exhaled. They'd been careful, but accidents happened. "I don't want babies," Nina went on, matter-of-fact. "I never did. Is strange? It seemed every *sestra* in my regiment wanted babies."

"I think people like us do not make for good fathers and mothers. Always on the hunt—"

"And we prefer hunt to babies."

His wife had said *we*. Ian grinned.

A long exhausting drive, no answer at the house where they knocked, several more hours loitering around a Pennsylvania suburb waiting for the occupants to return . . . and then the shake of Nina's head as a stout balding man and his gray-haired wife returned to the house, hatted and respectable and probably bad customers, but not the bad customer Ian was looking for. They went through their little act anyway, so Nina could get her Kodak shot, but this was officially another useless road trip. Ian didn't punch the steering wheel this time when they got back into the car, but he did lean back and press his eyes closed in weariness. "Florida next," he said flatly. "I can't say it's ever been on my list of places to see before I die."

"*Tvoyu mat.*" Nina sighed.

"Indeed," Ian said, turning back for Boston. It would be pitch-dark by the time they returned, even with these long summer days. A day to sleep off the drive and then make a decision whether it would be cheaper to drive to Florida, or take the train. "Or we fly," Nina wheedled. "I borrow a plane from Garrett Byrne's little field, is easy flight."

"You can't just borrow a plane like borrowing a cup of sugar!"

"We lock him in closet," Nina said reasonably. "So he can't say no."

"Fuck your mother," Ian said, laughing despite himself. "*No.*"

The trouble didn't come until they stopped to eat. Twilight was falling in long purple shadows, and as they slid through the outskirts of a derelict mill town several hours outside Boston, Nina insisted on stopping. "I eat something or I eat steering wheel."

Ian parked at the nearest restaurant, an establishment named Bill's, which made the diner where they spent so much time watching Kolb's apartment look like a palace of haute cuisine. "Let's not linger," Ian murmured, eyeing the crowd of diners. There were a good many men with beers in front of them, shooting not terribly friendly looks at the newcomers.

The waitress gave a flat stare as she took the order, eyebrows rising at Nina's accent. "Where you from, ma'am?"

"Boston," Ian said at the same time Nina said, "Poland." The waitress stared some more. Ian stared back coolly. "Two hamburgers, extra ketchup," he repeated, and she took it down with another sidelong glance. Nina seemed more amused than anything, leaning past Ian to direct a long look at a beefy fellow giving her the eye.

"I wash up," she announced and rose to stroll unhurriedly between the grimy booths. Two men in steel-mill boots said something to her Ian couldn't hear, though he could well imagine. Nina laughed and said something long and staccato, accompanied by a hand gesture. The two men bristled, and she sauntered on into the washroom. One of them rose and lumbered over toward the seat Nina had vacated. Ian sat back, unfolding his arms across the back of the booth.

"Your wife talks funny," the man said without preamble.

"She's Polish," Ian said.

"I met plenty of Polacks during the war," he persisted. "They don't talk like that."

"You've traveled all over Poland, have you? Personally experienced the rich variety of regional dialects from Poznań to Warsaw?" Ian employed his most contemptuous drawl. "Do piss off."

The man's brows lowered. "Don't tell me to piss off."

Ian stared at him through half-lidded eyes. "Bugger off, then."

Nina's voice came behind him. "Is problem, *luchik*?"

"No," Ian said without shifting his gaze. "No problem at all, darling."

She slid past the beefy fellow into her seat, looking utterly relaxed. Ian supposed that when one had looked Joseph Stalin in the eye, belligerent drunks from western Massachusetts failed to impress. "We make Boston by midnight?" she asked as though their visitor were invisible. "Is very slow, driving these trips. I still say we borrow a plane."

"She don't sound like no Polack," the beefy man muttered, returning to his table with a dark look. Ian released his breath as their hamburgers arrived, staying on guard even as Mr. Beefy and his two friends rose and left. Nina was still getting odd looks—even in a prim blouse and skirt, she didn't quite look like the average tourist. Maybe it was the unblinking stare with which she returned those furtive looks, or maybe it was the way she ate hamburgers, which put Ian in mind of film reels about the eating habits of cannibal tribes in Fiji.

The waitress stiffed them on the bill when she made change, but Ian didn't quibble, grabbing his fedora and taking Nina's arm. They stepped outside into the street, now fully dark, and Ian wasn't surprised to see three figures step out of the shadows.

He tensed, shifting onto the balls of his feet. At his side he could feel his wife relax completely, body flowing into stillness. Ian saw she was smiling.

"Can I help you?" he asked the three men coldly.

"I met Russkies in the war too," the beefy man said, exhaling beer fumes. "She talks like them, not like a goddamn Polack. Is your wife there a Commie?"

"*Da, tovarische,*" Nina said, and everything happened at once. The beefy man moved toward her; Ian stepped into his path and threw a right hook against his jaw. The man yelled, his friend behind him yelled too, and lunged at Ian, taking him around the ribs in a bull's rush. Ian heard the unmistakable *snick* of Nina's straight razor unfolding.

"Don't kill anyone—" he managed to shout, before a fist smashed against his side and took his breath in a huff, and the beefy man threw a wild punch that glanced off his ear. Ian could see flashes of Nina struggling with the third man, who had got her in a bear hug and lifted her off her feet. Ice-cold fear and white-hot fury swamped Ian, even as he saw Nina's blond head snap forward and catch her attacker in the nose. An answering bellow split the night. Ian drove a boot into the beefy man's shin before he could wind up another punch, then slammed an elbow into the kidney of the man who had Ian around the ribs. Finally wrenching free, he saw Nina's razor hand whip round viciously fast, opening a slash through shirt and skin on the arm holding her off the ground. The man's bellow scaled upward into a shriek, and he dropped Nina in the gravel. She caught herself, pushing off the ground, and caught the man's backhand across the face.

Ian sprang on him and put a straight right into the man's Adam's apple, hooked a foot around his ankle, and yanked him off his feet, kicking him in the ribs twice for good measure. When he saw Nina was on her feet, he shouted, "To the *car!*"

She flew at his side, diving into the front seat even as Ian fumbled with keys and wrenched at the various start-up dials and settings. He heard a shout, felt the car shudder as a kick thumped the bumper, and then they were pulling away with a screech of tires, to the sound of Nina's wild laughter.

"You're insane," Ian shouted. "Goddammit, I lost my hat—"

"You can fight!" She was grinning. "You said you could, I didn't believe—"

"I've had that hat since before the Blitz," Ian complained, but he was smiling too. They were speeding out of this unsavory little hamlet into the darkness; the hand he'd punched with was killing him; he could feel blood trickle down the side of his face—and he couldn't stop grinning. He glanced at his wife. "Are you hurt?"

"I think maybe he breaks my nose?" She sounded unconcerned.

"Bloody hell." His smile disappeared. "I'm pulling over."

"Is not the first time. Papa broke my nose when I was eleven. I spilled a jug of vodka."

"Yes, you're hard as rock, you were raised by wolves, just let me look at it."

The side of the road was dark as pitch, sliced through by the Ford's headlights and then the light of the torch Ian pulled from the boot. Nina's feet crunched on pebbles as she slid out and let him examine her battle wounds beside the car. Her small nose was swelling rapidly and trickling blood, but despite her cursing as Ian pinched the nasal bones, nothing moved that shouldn't have. "Not broken. Next time perhaps don't taunt the drunks when they're squaring for a fight."

"What is fun in that?" She wiped the blood away with the side of her hand. "So, where does proper English stick like you learn gutter fighting?" She mimed the elbow he'd dropped on his second opponent.

"Every public school boy learns how to box. The elbow strikes and kidney shots I picked up from some guerrillas in Spain." Ian's blood was still pumping at twice its normal pace, the rush of excitement starting to drain. "I don't pick fights, but if anybody picks one with me, I'll be damned if I fight fair."

"I like this in you, *luchik*." Nina approved, blue eyes glinting in the dark. Ian envisioned the flash of her blond hair outside the restaurant as the man backhanded her. He pulled her suddenly into a rough, hard embrace. He wanted to go back and beat the bastard's head in.

"*Nu, ladno*—" Nina squirmed free, looking impatient. "Is fine, no one is hurt, we drive."

That's it, Ian thought, fighting back all his inner turmoil as he slid into the car. *I'm not letting you go. I don't know what I have to do to persuade you to stay, Nina Markova, but I'm going to find out.*

Chapter 44

NINA

September 1944
Outside Poznań

Nina folded her arms. "It's been two weeks. It healed clean."

Sebastian winced as he put his weight on his wounded leg. "It hurts to walk."

"You're faking," she stated.

The English boy sighed. He was just five years younger, twenty-one to Nina's twenty-six, but she couldn't help but think of him as a boy. There was something open and trusting about him; even his years in captivity hadn't dimmed it. "Can we sit down? Please."

Nina sat, glowering. Their camp looked considerably more lived in now that they'd been ensconced for a fortnight waiting for Seb to mend: stream-rinsed laundry hanging to dry, fire pit now lined with stones and rigged with a crude spit. Nina couldn't wait to leave it. "You know I want to head west."

"That's mad, Nina." He said it with embarrassment, hating to contradict her. "No destination, no plan—"

"I want out of Poland."

"You think *Germany* will be better? We have no papers, no clothes." Gesturing down at his dirty battle dress. "Odds are we'd get nabbed and then you'd be a kriegie right alongside me. Only you'd be the only woman in a camp full of men, and trust me, they aren't all gentlemen."

"We make our way west through the woods, then."

"You're going to take backwoods trails all the way across Germany, with no maps? What about when it gets cold?"

Nina laughed. "I'm from Siberia, *malysh*. It won't get cold enough to kill me."

"Don't call me *little boy*. All I want is not to get caught, and for *you* not to get caught." His long-lashed eyes held hers. "I owe you my life, Nina. If you hadn't come along, that German would have shot me, or if I'd got away from him, I'd have stumbled around in these trees till I died of thirst or some other Kraut scooped me. I owe you, and if we both get pinched, I can't ever pay you back."

Nina opened her mouth. *The little English snail is right about one thing*, her father remarked. *Your plan is mad.*

"We hide here," Seb persisted. "In the woods, something better than a camp clearing. Near enough to Posen to forage, keep our ear to the ground for news. Why move on? We won't find anywhere better to wait out the war."

"Wait out—!"

"It can't be long now," Seb rushed on. "A few months, maybe even before the end of the year, and this country is running over with Allied instead of German sentries—"

"Running over with Soviets, when our forces arrive. I won't wait for that."

"We'll tell everyone you're Polish instead. You lost your papers. The Red Cross will help, at the very least."

"What do we do until then? Sit around embroidering?" That brought Yelena painfully to mind, unpicking blue threads from state-issued men's briefs so she could embroider stars into a scarf.

"I've spent four years doing nothing but pass time. If we can stay warm, stay secret, and feed ourselves—"

"*We.*" Nina glared again. "You mean me." Two weeks in the

woods, and this city boy still couldn't light a fire without wasting half the kindling.

"Until the war ends, I need you," Seb acknowledged. "After the war, you'll need me."

Nina raised her eyebrows.

"I'm a British subject. Once the Germans are finished, I can get myself shipped back to England. I'll take you with me."

Nina blinked. "How?"

He shrugged. "My brother has connections everywhere; he can sponsor you. You could get British citizenship eventually. You just have to know people, and believe me, we Grahams know people. You keep me alive till the war ends," Sebastian Graham repeated, "and I'll get you to England and see you settled there. I owe you that."

Nina hesitated. What did she know about England except that it was full of fog and capitalists?

"England," Seb wheedled. "As far west as you can go without leaving Europe. Not to mention that we've got Piccadilly. The Egypt wing of the British Museum. Fish and chips—you haven't lived till you've had fish and chips, Nina. No Komsomols, no gulags, no collective apartments. A nice king with a stammer who doesn't go in for mass executions. It's a big improvement on the Soviet Union, believe me, and you can call it home. All we have to do is hunker down and stick together."

Nina had no idea what *fish and chips* was, or *Piccadilly*. Where her mind lingered was on the words *as far west as you can go without leaving Europe.*

"Survival now for citizenship later," Sebastian said. "What do you say?"

IT WAS A STRANGE THING, Nina reflected, to have nothing in the world but a single partner. She had lived so long among hundreds of women, then she had been alone among the trees with no company but hallucinations. Now she had Sebastian Graham, and could any alliance have been stranger?

"I wanted to join the RAF," Seb said. "Spitfires and glamour. But the recruiting bastard laughed in my face."

"Flying bombing runs isn't glamorous." Nina pushed a leaf across the flat stone between them. Seb was teaching her poker, having patiently marked up a variety of leaves with a charred stick to make a deck of cards. "Are oak leaves hearts or spades?"

"Spades." He cocked his head, listening. "That's a nuthatch."

"What?"

He imitated a birdcall.

"You don't know anything about the woods, but you know birds?" Nina pushed the oak leaf that was the queen of spades across the rock.

"I like birds." He linked his hands together, made a curious little gesture imitating flight. "My brother, Ian, gave me my first bird book. The other boys said it was sissy, until I punched them. Ian showed me how to punch the same day he gave me the book. He said I could like whatever I wanted, I'd just best be prepared to hit people if they gave me grief about it." Seb tilted his head back, listening for the chirrups and twitters coming from the trees. "So many birds here—nuthatches, starlings, bitterns . . . it seemed like at the camp, there were only those tattered hulking crows."

They were still at the same campsite for now. They'd need better shelter soon, but the weather was still mostly warm. Seb had no skill laying snares or tracking game, but he had a wiry toughness equal to hours of foraging as his leg healed, and his Polish was good enough to make him useful whenever they headed to the outskirts of one of the villages to trade game for bread. Nina managed to snag a pair of breeches and cap and jacket off a village clothesline, rough peasant wear that made Seb into a scruffy traveler rather than an escaped soldier. "We can't risk it too often," she warned the day they almost stepped out of the trees into a party of German sentries. "Never the same village twice, and never the bigger towns. They'll be crawling with Fritzes, not to mention hungry villagers looking to turn in suspicious travelers."

"You don't have much faith in humanity, do you, Nina?"

"Do you?" she asked, surprised. They were washing dirty clothes in the stream, Seb entirely willing to whack wet socks against a rock without complaining it was women's work the way most Russian men would. Maybe it was an English thing, Nina speculated, or maybe when you were already relying on a woman to gut game, there wasn't much of a case to be made about *women's work*.

"I've got quite a bit of faith in humanity, actually." Seb wrung out a wet sock. "The fellows at camp—they weren't all saints, but there were rules. You didn't steal. You shared food with your friends when you had it. And even the Jerries weren't all brutes. They had their rules too, and most tried to be fair." Seb laid the socks out to dry on the sunny rock. "There was a lot of generosity inside those walls. More than I ever saw at public school."

"What's this *public school*? Aren't all schools public?"

"It's not collective education, that's for sure." Seb snorted. "My father would have died of shame if a Graham ever rubbed shoulders at school with peasants."

"You're rubbing shoulders with a peasant now," Nina pointed out.

"And if my father were still alive, I'd bring you home to tea just to see the look on his face." Seb smiled at the thought. "Ian, now, he wouldn't blink even if you waved your razor at him over the tea sandwiches. Nothing shocks my big brother. But my father, cripes. One look at you and he'd choke on a scone." Seb's smile was rare and surprisingly sweet; paired with the dark hair now growing shaggy and those long lashes, he'd probably made a good many hearts flutter back on his foggy little island. Nina's heart didn't flutter in the slightest. He was a handsome boy, but he reminded her too much of Yelena. *I'm done loving sweet-souled long-lashed idealists who dream of flight*, Nina thought, wringing her own socks out viciously, *because those are the ones who scoop your heart out and take it with them when they fly away*. Like should stick to like. Let Seb and Yelena each find someone sweet and valiant to worship them all their days; Nina was done with love affairs. She'd sleep alone, or she'd find some clear-eyed hunter with a heart like a diamond; someone who would not carve out her soul and leave her hollow.

"Did you leave a girl behind?" Nina asked Seb, shaking her bleakness away. "Before you enlisted."

His eyes shifted away. "No."

"Boy?" Nina asked matter-of-factly and saw his face drain of color. "I don't *care*, I just wondered." If anything she was relieved, knowing he wasn't likely to try anything with her.

He didn't speak for almost an hour. Until Nina said into the silence, "I had someone. A girl. So . . ."

"Oh," said Seb.

"I thought it was usual for the English, boys and boys? That's what they tell us, that all the English bugger each other and that's why they can't fight."

"No." Seb's face had nearly regained its normal pallor. "They say it's a thing that happens at school, because you don't have girls. That you grow out of it."

"And you didn't?"

"No. I didn't have anyone, I just knew I didn't . . ." He trailed off. "I always thought once I got to *know* any women, it would be different. Growing up with just my father and brother, then school with nothing but boys, then the army, then four years as a kriegie . . ."

"You don't have to know anything about women to know if you want them in bed or not," Nina pointed out in some amusement.

"I suppose." Seb blushed. "Your girl, when did you know . . ."

"I don't talk about her," Nina said, and they were done with the entire subject.

Days grew shorter, an autumn note touching the air as September slid toward October. Laying snares, cleaning game, washing socks and shirts and their own grimy bodies in the stream. Nina still got bouts of the shakes, longing for her Coca-Cola pills, and she couldn't sleep longer than a few shallow hours at a time, but mostly she was bored. Seb had endless ways to pass the hours: poker with his leaf deck, practicing birdcalls, trying to teach her English. "You'll have to learn if you're coming to England."

"English is a stupid language."

"Take it slow. *God—save—the—King.*"

She parroted back, trying to imagine a life in a fogbank eating these strange things Seb called *pudding* and *scones*, drinking tea from a teapot and not a samovar. Perhaps she could get work at an airfield? But even if she could, there would be no women like the Night Witches. No mechanics singing as they passed wrenches, no armorers blowing on their blued fingertips, no pilots sprinting toward their planes, straining for the honor to be first.

Yelena's flying dark hair, her soft mouth.

Nina rose abruptly. "Forage?"

They always avoided busy roads and towns, waiting hidden in trees or crouched behind brush until there were solitary refugees or peasant women with baskets who could be approached. Seb had a story about how they'd fled Warsaw and were now living rough; there were all too many such stories. Every crossroads was strewn with the discarded detritus of refugees seeking safety: upended traveling cases, an empty handcart, ransacked bundles abandoned by travelers following signs to towns Nina had no desire to seek out. Few looked suspiciously at Seb and Nina when they came to barter essentials; Seb did the talking, and Nina kept her eyes open for trouble.

Seb held up the day's prize, a few mealy potatoes in a sack. "Tonight we feast. Better than trying to sneak past Berlin, eh?"

I don't know, Nina thought, trying to shake her superstition that this wrecked country was cursed. There was no rhyme or reason to be found in this bleak, wasted moonscape of a land where the passing hand of war had swept through, raked its sharp claws, and moved on. She raised her nose to the wind as they trudged back toward their camp, sniffing. "Winter's coming."

BY NOVEMBER, the cold had begun to wear Sebastian down. The trees stood stark branched, films of ice gleamed here and there in the darkest hollows, the earth was hardening, yet winter had only started to close its jaws. "This is nothing," Nina said, trying to bolster him. "You should see the winds come howling across the Old Man."

Seb was sitting huddled in every piece of clothing he had. He was thinner, his eyes shadowed. "Can we light a fire?"

"It's not even freezing. Save it for tonight when the temperature drops." He didn't complain—he never did; Nina liked that about him—but his mouth pressed into a straight line of frustration. "Weren't you used to being cold in that camp?" Nina said, her own frustration rising.

"Forty men sleeping in one hut warm the room with their breath. It's enclosed." Seb gestured at their shelter. They'd left their old camp, looking for something more shielded for the winter. Seb had argued they should make their way into Poznań itself, the wide forested swath that cut through the city to add a touch of the wild—calm lakes and thick woods—in the midst of civilization. *Closer to the Germans*, Nina argued back. *Close to the city means easier foraging*, he countered, and Nina reluctantly agreed, finding a good-size rock hollow in a tumble of boulders northeast of one of the artificial lakes, sheltered among pines and protected by an overhang on three sides. With a fire pit dug and all their laundry-line-pilfered blankets, it was as dry and snug a shelter as they were going to find. But it didn't keep out the cold. "I won't go so far as to say I miss my kriegie bunk," Seb said, trying to joke. "But at least it had a roof!"

Nina fought a wave of exasperation, thinking of Marina Raskova surviving ten days in the taiga without an emergency kit; Moscow-bred Yelena shrugging off the temperatures at Engels with jokes about the frost making her eyelashes look longer. But it wasn't Sebastian Graham's fault he was too civilized to know what real cold was. He was here, he was all she had, and Nina realized, looking at his hollowed face, how fond she'd grown of him.

"*Malysh*," she said quietly, taking his cloth-wrapped hand. "It's going to get worse. There will be snow. Our teeth will feel loose because I won't find enough greens or berries. We'll spend most of our time foraging for firewood, and even then it won't keep us warm. There will be times you want to die, but you won't, because I know how to survive a winter in the wild—and we aren't *in* the wild, Seb. We're in a tamed wood in Poznań, civilization just a few kilometers beyond the trees. We'll survive, we just won't enjoy it. You understand me?"

"Yes." He made an effort to smile. "I'm the one who persuaded you to camp through the winter, rather than push west. Stiff upper lip, I promise."

But from the way his smile fell away into silent brooding afterward, Nina still felt a pang of disquiet.

FORAGING THE FOLLOWING AFTERNOON, along the edge of the artificial lake. A long narrow body of water, edible reeds to be pulled, places to be marked for fishing if she could fashion hooks and lines . . . "What's that?" Seb pointed at an inlet a good distance down the shore. They'd never foraged this far before. "Something yellow."

Nina squinted, making out a peaked roof, glass windows. A house, and not a farmer's cottage either. "Some Fritz's lakeside retreat." Anything gracious or expansive in Poznań these days was owned by a German. At least for now; there were more and more rumors (whenever Nina and Seb found refugees with whom they dared trade news) about the possibility of a German retreat toward Berlin.

"A big house like that, they'll have a larder or cellar to raid."

"Too risky," Nina began.

"If there are too many people, we'll retreat," Seb cajoled. "Word of honor."

Nina fingered the razor in her overall pocket, the revolver at her waist. No more ammunition; that had long run out. But Seb was right; they didn't have to try. Only look.

Her stomach was growling as they set off along the lake's shore. Beaches scattered along the far shore; perhaps swimmers came here in the summer, but now all was quiet, nothing but the chatter of birds overhead. Seb knew them all and imitated their calls, color flushing his cheeks. Nina was glad to see it. By the time they reached the ocher-walled house, it was late afternoon. Long, low, mellow in the sunshine, the residence overlooked a sweeping view of water and trees, a dock stretching out before it into the blue expanse of lake. Nina looked away. Even a lake so blue and placid—as unlike the wind-whipped, ice-lashed Old Man as possible—gave her the shivers.

No one seemed to be moving around the house; the shutters were drawn, but smoke drifted from a tall chimney. Seb and Nina crept toward the rear, where the trees had been cleared and landscaped to frame the house like dark encircling arms. No livestock or chicken pens, no laundry lines, nothing easily foraged. They exchanged wordless glances; Nina shook her head. Seb rose from his squat to follow her back into the trees, and then a woman cleared her throat behind them.

How did she get so close without me hearing? The thought went through Nina like a bullet, even as she whirled around. There had been no sound on the leaf-strewn ground, yet there the woman stood: slim, dark haired, blue eyed, about Nina's age, warmly wrapped in a blue coat and checked scarf, placating hands held out. She smiled, but Nina's fingers stretched for her razor. *How did you get so close?*

She was speaking Polish in a low pleasant voice. Seb replied warily, his own Polish stumbling. The woman frowned, switched languages. English? Nina could cobble simple broken phrases together by now, but she was far from fluent. Seb started in surprise, switched languages too, talking too fast for Nina to follow. She kept her eyes fixed on the woman in blue, her quiet feet in their fine leather shoes, her calm eyes.

"She says this is Lake Rusalka," Seb broke off at last, switching back into Russian.

Rusalka. The word ran over Nina's skin like a rat. She took a step back. The woman smiled, took a step back too, empty hands raised. She said something else. Seb translated, face showing a cautious hope.

"She asks if we're hungry."

"Why?" Nina's every hackle was up.

"She wants to help." Seb's expression fought with itself, caution against hope, and hope was winning. "She says we have nothing to fear."

Chapter 45

JORDAN

August 1950
Boston

"A nna!" Jordan exclaimed, opening the door of the darkroom. "I thought you were going to be away another week."

"I missed my girls." Anneliese gave her a hug, all neat dark perfection in her chip hat and half veil, her black full-skirted coat. "Is Ruth playing over at the Dunnes'?"

"Yes." Jordan kept her eyes fixed scrupulously on her stepmother, letting out a quick cough to hide the sound of rustling from the darkroom below. "How was your buying trip?"

"Come upstairs; I'll fix some iced tea and tell you." Anneliese's brows lifted. "Unless I'm interrupting your work?"

"Not at all," Jordan said, very aware of Tony out of sight under the staircase below, buttoning up his shirt. "Give me ten minutes."

Anneliese's heels clicked off as Jordan shut and bolted the door. "Close call," she said with a laugh. "Are you decent?"

"Never." Tony came out shrugging into his suspenders, grinning. "You're going up for iced tea?"

"Yes, I should go be a good daughter." Tony caught Jordan around the waist as she came down the steps, and she wound her arms around his neck. "I've had weeks by myself to play, after all."

"I'll come over and play anytime." He kissed the side of her throat, then began looking for his shoes. "Want me to come up, be respectable with my hat in my hand?"

"No." Jordan found one of his shoes under the darkroom table—they'd been in a bit of a hurry this afternoon to get to the cot she'd prudently set up with spare blankets. "Absolutely not."

"Mothers like me, I promise. I know how to look like a nice clean-cut boy from Queens, not a shameless seducer lurking under darkroom stairs." He spoke with his usual teasing tone, but Jordan saw the wariness that sometimes came over him in a reflex. The wariness of his voice the first night here, when he'd told her about the girl who stopped returning his calls once she learned he was Jewish.

Jordan came closer, sliding her fingers through his. "You know why I don't want to introduce you upstairs?" she asked. "Not because Anna wouldn't like you. Not because you aren't the most charming, presentable gentleman I could hope to have on my arm anywhere. Because of Ruth."

"Princess Ruth loves me."

"Exactly. You call her Princess Ruth and applaud wildly every time she masters a new scale, and if you come up and start being charming over iced tea to her mother, she will be thrilled by the idea that you are my *young man*. And I'm not doing that to Ruth again, because she also adored Garrett and it broke her heart when I had to tell her he wasn't going to be her big brother, after all. I'm not letting her think anyone else is family unless I'm sure he's sticking around a long, *long* time." Jordan squeezed his fingers. "That is why I'm not taking you upstairs for iced tea."

That faint wariness disappeared. "I love iced tea," Tony said. "It might be worth sticking around a long, *long* time, if it's sufficiently good iced tea."

"I thought we were just having a mad summer fling."

"Modifications could be made to the original contract. A potential extension into a mad autumn fling, as per agreement by both parties."

"Maybe you'll be bored with me by autumn," Jordan parried.

"Not a chance, J. Bryde."

"Or maybe I'll be bored with you," she suggested. "I'll be in New York, meeting all kinds of fascinating men."

"It so happens I have family in New York. Lots of reasons to come visit . . . and no one ever gets bored with me."

"I don't know about sleeping with a Yankee fan past September. What happens when the Red Sox beat them in October and you're refusing to speak to me?"

"I'm a very gracious winner. I'll dry your tears, and you'll have the off-season to learn the error of your ways."

"Not a chance, Rodomovsky." She gave him a hard, swift kiss good-bye, let him extend one kiss into three, four, hard up against the nearest wall with her hands buried in his hair and his fingers slipping open the buttons she'd done up so hastily to answer Anneliese's knock. "No time," she murmured, but it still ended up being more like twenty minutes before she was upstairs in the kitchen with hastily combed hair, peeking out the front window to see Tony duck out of the darkroom.

I wouldn't mind having you for an autumn lover as well as a summer lover, Jordan thought, watching that lean form jog up the street as behind her Anneliese poured out iced tea. This wasn't like her times with Garrett, when it had been a little awkward if enjoyable, and there had been the feeling of being funneled inexorably toward the altar with every kiss. This was something looser and better fitting. They weren't *going steady*, they weren't *pinned*, they weren't *making it official*—they were just lovers, work and play and passion and friendship blending together into something so very easy.

"You have stars in your eyes." Anneliese handed her a cold glass, fending off Taro, whose tail was still lashing in delight at the lady of the house's return. "Who's put that glow in your cheeks?"

A man who makes my toes curl, Jordan thought, *who makes me laugh, who even helps me* work *better. And maybe it will only be a summer fling and he'll lose interest when I go away, or maybe I'll be the one to move on. But right now* . . . Jordan buried her smile in the iced tea. Possibly some nosy neighbor would tell Anneliese about a young man seen leaving the basement, but Jordan knew her stepmother wouldn't launch an inquisition. "What did you buy at the auctions?"

"Nothing," Anneliese said ruefully. "Not a thing. Your father made it look so easy; one look at a Queen Anne highboy and he just *knew* if it was a reproduction or an original, or if the restoration was good work or shoddy. It was foolish to think I had picked up enough to match him. I'll just have to let that go to someone more knowledgeable."

"At least you had a vacation." Jordan folded her hands around her glass. "And your week in Concord?"

Anneliese's face softened. "Your father was right there with me, I could have sworn. I even had the same room we had on our honeymoon. How have you and Ruth been?" Jordan filled her in, omitting for now the details of darkroom lovers and music lessons. "My photo-essay is almost done too. I have fourteen prints; I want fifteen."

"Then you should start thinking about a place to live in New York. I did a little apartment hunting while I was there. We can't have you sleeping in some flea-riddled bedroom with a toilet down the hall."

"It's still a bit soon to be apartment hunting."

"Why? Your project is almost done; what better time to look for work? And you did say you wanted to move in the fall. You'll need a chic suit for interviews—I found the perfect Butterick pattern . . ."

"I was going to wait till Ruth was settled back in school. It's going to be hard for her."

"Nonsense, she'll still have me and her friends and her dog. She shouldn't be the one holding you back. Unless"—Anneliese shot Jordan a shrewd, humorous look—"you have some other reason?"

Jordan laughed. "There is no getting anything by that sixth sense of yours, is there?" She should have known Anneliese was far too sharp not to discern the real reason for flushed cheeks and sparkling eyes.

"He must be quite something." Anneliese drew a fingertip around her glass. "But I'd hate to see you changing your plans for some young man, however special."

"He won't stop me leaving." However lovely things were with Tony, Jordan wasn't putting off a chance for work, real work. She wouldn't put that off for anyone . . . except one person. "I can't leave until Ruth's used to the idea, though. I just can't."

"Now, I really won't allow this," Anneliese scolded. "Let's set a *date*, Jordan. The date your new life begins; the day you go and start leading it. I don't want to let anything stand in your way."

"My way or your way?" Jordan smiled, joking. "If I didn't know better, I'd think you were trying to get rid of me!"

Anneliese's smile slipped for just a fraction of a second, showing a different expression, and in Jordan's lap, her camera finger twitched. *Click.*

"Well," Anneliese said quietly, "I certainly didn't mean it like that."

"Anna, I'm sorry." Reaching out to touch her stepmother's hand. "I didn't mean that the way it came out, not at all."

"Of course." Anneliese rose, took the glasses back to the kitchen. "Would you like more iced tea?"

"Yes." Jordan tried a smile. "Maybe we should look at apartment listings together. You really didn't have to do that for me when you were in New York."

Anneliese gave her usual warm smile over one shoulder. "It was my pleasure."

Especially if you really do *want me out as soon as possible*, the thought came.

But Jordan shoved that out of her head, because Anneliese was sitting down again looking entirely her friendly self, asking, "Your last photograph for the essay, what will it be?"

Jordan wasn't sure yet—Ruth at her violin, small fingers on the strings, the fierce line between her brows as she played with exquisite care through that simple Russian lullaby? But Jordan couldn't say that to Anneliese, so she said something about going to the nearest station to snap firemen at work, and Anneliese teased that perhaps it was a handsome fireman who'd been putting the roses in her cheeks. And even as Jordan teased back, another thought couldn't help but rise through her mind like the shadowy image of a print rising through the shimmer of developer fluid: When exactly had she started keeping so many secrets from Anneliese?

SHE MIGHT HAVE forgotten all about it, but four days later Jordan walked into the shop to find Anneliese and Mr. Kolb shouting at each other in German.

Or rather, Kolb was shouting—shambling back and forth, spitting German and brandy fumes. *Completely soused*, Jordan thought, recoiling from the anger on that usually affable face. Anneliese stood small and composed before him, answering in German that sliced the air. Both lapsed into silence at the sound of the bell, staring at Jordan standing there in the yellow summer dress her stepmother had whipped together in her sewing room.

"Jordan," Anneliese said at last, switching back to English. "I didn't expect you."

Jordan had dropped in to see Tony, but he was clearly on lunch break. She crossed to her stepmother's side, looking at Mr. Kolb. "Do we have a problem?"

He didn't look at Jordan, still staring at Anneliese. "Making you good money, good work—"

"You cannot come to work intoxicated, no matter how much good work you have done for me," Anneliese said icily. "Go home. Dry out. *Keep calm.*"

He said something else slushy and spiteful in German, and Anneliese cut him off with a rattling retort, eyes blazing. His mouth snapped shut, he looked at the ground. When he glanced back up, his shoulders had slumped.

"Get your coat," said Anneliese.

"I'll get it," Jordan said. She didn't want him lurching drunkenly through the back room with so many fragile things waiting to be knocked over. She found Kolb's coat hanging over the back chair, wrinkling her nose at the clink of what sounded like a bottle in the pocket, and turned around to find him right behind her, swaying. She jumped.

"So much money," he said. "That bitch—"

Jordan recoiled. "Do not speak about Mrs. McBride like—"

He cut her off, spitting more insults. *Hure, Scheissekopf, Jägerin,* swaying on his feet. He hardly seemed to know she was there.

Anneliese's voice snapped like a whip behind them. *"Herr Kolb."*

He flinched, and Jordan's tongue shriveled. She didn't think she'd ever seen a man look more afraid.

"I won't have you frightening my stepdaughter," Anneliese went on, evenly. "Go home."

Kolb snatched his coat and stumbled out. Anneliese opened the door for him, then shut it again. The shop bell rang tinnily in the sudden silence.

"Fire him," Jordan said, finding her tongue again.

"I can't afford to fire him." An acrid little smile. "He has made us a great deal of money, Jordan; he was quite correct about that. He's very good at his job."

"We can find someone else. Dad would *never* put up with that kind of talk."

"He wouldn't dare talk to your father that way. It is what it is, a woman owning a business." Anneliese shrugged. "Tomorrow he'll slink back apologizing. Drunks always do."

"That doesn't excuse what he called you." *Hure;* Jordan was fairly sure what that meant. *Scheissekopf, Jägerin;* she didn't know. "Bitch," well, that certainly didn't need any translation.

"Believe me, I take no pleasure in being insulted by clerks." Anneliese sighed. "For now, he's harmless."

"Are you sure?"

That curling smile returned. "I'm not afraid of a man like Herr Kolb."

No, Jordan thought. *He's the one terrified of you.* She'd seen his face, close enough to reach out and touch the beads of sweat.

Anneliese picked up her gloves. "Let's go home, shall we?"

SOMETHING WAS TUGGING at Jordan, like a pin stuck into the back of her mind. Something she couldn't quite get a grip on. Something Kolb said, something her *dad* had said . . . ? She barely ate any of Anneliese's excellent meatloaf that night, too perplexed by that niggle of a thought that refused to come out.

"You should go out," Anneliese told her. "Have your young man take you somewhere!"

The words echoed, all in Anneliese's voice.

You should go out.

He'll go when we can afford it.

The date your new life begins . . . go and start leading it!

Go.

But that was ridiculous. Anneliese wasn't trying to get rid of her, for God's sake.

Something else still niggled, even as Jordan looked into her stepmother's candid blue eyes. Making the excuse of film to develop, she took herself down to the darkroom, where she could smell the faint hint of Tony's aftershave. She wished he were here. He had a way of being able to find the question that somehow hooked the right answer from the mind's murk.

Slowly, Jordan flipped through her photo-essay. The airfield mechanic, the dancer. *What am I looking for?* The baker, the pilot. *What?* All the way back to the first: Dan McBride, his hands framing the card salver. Just the sliver of his eye, wise and amused.

It dropped into her head with a long, protracted click, like a heavy door creaking open ever so slowly, letting in the light a ray at a time.

Anything ever strike you about Kolb, missy?

Like what?

I don't know. He always looks furtive anytime I come in to check on the restoration work. And with his English so patchy, I can't ask him anything but the simplest questions. Of course Anna translates anything tricky.

Jordan's father, the day he'd given her the pearl earrings for her coming wedding. The wedding that never happened.

Does he bring people into the shop? Not customers, I mean bringing people into the back.

Not that I've noticed, Jordan remembered answering. *Why?*

I came up here one day and Kolb had another German fellow in the back room . . . Kolb went off in a babble.

He has experts in sometimes. Jordan remembered saying that too. *Anna gave him permission.*

That's what she said.

Jordan stood there, looking at the photograph of her father. She hadn't given that conversation a second thought, the day they had it. She'd been distracted by her upcoming wedding, rushing at her like a train. Her dad hadn't sounded worried, no note of alarm in his voice.

But if he was worried, would he have let you know it? The question answered itself, coolly. *No, he'd have told himself you shouldn't worry your head about it.*

And was it suspicious, really? Anneliese translating for Kolb, letting him bring in people to help in restoring badly worn books or chipped end tables?

Kolb today, angry. *Making you good money, good work. So much money. That bitch—*

"He has made money for us," Jordan said aloud. "Perfectly legally." Business had blossomed with Kolb to take over restoration work. Anneliese had been the one who suggested sponsoring him, her voice affectionate as she described his old shop in Salzburg, where he'd given her peppermints just as he now gave them to Ruth.

So why did he look so frightened when Anneliese told him to dry out and keep calm?

He had a bad war, Anneliese would say. A bad war could make a man flinching and fearful of anyone. Perfectly plausible.

Except that Jordan didn't quite believe it.

LOOKING AT THE CHECKBOOK the following day steadied Jordan's nerves. She'd always kept the family accounts; she knew to the dime what was in the bank. The neatly ruled lines showed no money that shouldn't have been there. A healthy balance, certainly, showing the kind of steady increase that any prospering business could be proud of. Nothing suspicious. But somehow the spike of relief wore off, and without quite examining her own thoughts, Jordan found herself reaching for her hat and pocketbook, and taking herself to the bank where her father had done business all his life.

"Jordan McBride!" the clerk exclaimed. A grandmotherly sort with ice-cream puffs of hair; Jordan had carefully waited until her line was free. Far better to try this with Miss Fenton, who had watched Jordan come in with her father since she was knee-high, than one of the new clerks who got stuffy about answering a girl's questions if she didn't have her father along. Jordan spent some minutes chatting across the desk—Is your niece really six already, Miss Fenton? Isn't she precious!—then trotted out a careful story about forgetting to note a deposit in the checkbook at home; had there been any large deposits made lately . . . Not in checking or savings accounts? What a relief. "I know Dad's gone, but I just wince thinking of him looking down at me and thinking I've been careless," Jordan said ruefully.

"God rest his soul, they broke the mold when they made Dan McBride."

"They certainly did . . . My stepmother's account, does that show any new deposits? Maybe that's the one I was thinking of." Jordan held her breath. Because Anneliese didn't *have* an account of her own. Jordan's father had given her housekeeping money whenever she liked, but the accounts had always been his alone.

"That account has been cashed out, dear."

"Oh," Jordan managed to say. "When?"

Miss Fenton squinted. "About a month ago."

Right before Anneliese had left for New York and Concord. "How much?" Jordan asked, holding her casual tone. It wasn't the kind of question a clerk should answer, not when her name wasn't on the account, but Miss Fenton never hesitated. She gave the number right away, and it was a number that made Jordan swallow. No fortune, perhaps, but a nest egg indeed.

"Mrs. McBride said it was an extra insurance policy of your father's," Miss Fenton twittered, oblivious. "Such a lovely woman, your stepmother! I've always wished I knew her better."

Mrs. Dunne had said the same thing once, when Jordan was dropping off Ruth to play. *I'm happy to help your stepmother! She should come to my sewing circle, all my friends would love to know her better . . .* Anneliese had been part of this neighborhood for years, yet how many people knew her well?

I do, Jordan couldn't help thinking. The woman who had kept agonized vigil at Dan McBride's hospital bed and had confessed her *rusalka* nightmare over nighttime cocoa. The woman who had put untold hours into sewing Jordan new skirts and sundresses and could laugh herself sick watching Taro run after a ball. The woman who had offered Jordan a cigarette and independence, affection and freedom. *I* know *her*, Jordan thought helplessly. *I know her and I love her.*

And yet. The fear on Kolb's face. This *money*, which perfectly well could be an additional insurance policy—except that Jordan didn't believe it.

And she wasn't really surprised later, after she said her good-byes to Miss Fenton and went home, checked the house to be sure Anneliese really *was* out doing the shopping, and put a call through to the country inn in Concord where her father had taken Anneliese for their honeymoon. The inn where Anneliese had stayed, in conjunction with her New York buying trip. "No Mrs. McBride has stayed here this past month, miss." Jordan described her carefully—*dark hair, blue eyes, in her early thirties, very chic and pretty.* "No one like that, miss."

It took longer, digging into her father's tooled-leather address book, to find telephone numbers for his colleagues in New York. Other shop owners, antiques dealers, bookbinders; men who had come to Dan McBride's funeral, with whom he dickered and talked shop at auctions like the ones Anneliese had just attended. Except that none of his colleagues, at least the ones Jordan could get on the telephone, remembered seeing her there. "I'd have noticed her," the co-owner of Chadwick & Black said, sounding mellow from what Jordan suspected was a two-martini lunch. "Your stepmother's quite a looker. Your father was a lucky man, God rest his soul."

"God rest his soul," Jordan echoed, replacing the receiver. So, Anneliese had not been in Concord *or* New York.

What did you do, Anneliese? Where did you go? What are you planning? Jordan shook her head in reflexive refusal, but she couldn't help it: the resurrection of every suspicion she'd ever harbored about Anneliese from the day she'd turned around from the kitchen sink with a soapy plate in her hand, asking Jordan's father *You hunt?* as the Leica's shutter snapped. Mysteries about names, dates, swastikas among roses.

Now, now, Jordan could almost hear her dad chiding. *No more of your wild stories, missy!* But he was dead, and there was nothing wild or imaginary about the fact that Anneliese had been lying about her recent travels, that there was something fishy between her and Kolb, and that she had a great deal of unexplained cash.

Swastikas. Jordan forced herself to think about them again. And all the rest.

What did you do, Anneliese?
Who are you, Anneliese?
Who?

Chapter 46

IAN

September 1950
Florida coast

K olb was sent home from work drunk yesterday, according to
Jordan," Tony said over a crackling line. "I think he might be
about to crack."

"Good." Ian rested an elbow against the door of the telephone
box, looking across the street where Nina was disappearing into a
beachside five-and-dime. The sun was falling fast. "Because our Florida lead was a fifty-two-year-old man who might have been a camp
clerk or a Nazi Party functionary but was definitely not Lorelei Vogt."
Tony swore, but Ian was fatalistic. "They were leads; we had to run
them out."

He and Nina had bitten the bullet and taken a bus down to the
tiny town outside Cocoa Beach, Florida, that was their final lead,
since bus tickets proved marginally cheaper and quicker than driving the rackety Ford, but the suspicion had already been growing
in Ian that with six addresses already scratched off the list, the last
name would be no more fruitful. "Who knows, maybe I'll be back
through here someday to help arrest that middle-aged fellow with
the Berlin vowels and the nervous look who opened his door to us
an hour ago," he said when his partner ran out of curses.

A pause on the other end, and then Tony's voice, more thoughtful. "Do you ever want to do more with the center than focus on arrests, boss?"

"Like what?"

"Making a repository. A museum, even, or maybe that isn't the right word. I don't know, but I've got ideas."

"Did Jordan McBride put them there?" Ian asked wryly.

"She makes me think. Makes me think a lot, actually." Tony took a breath. "What if we brought her into the chase?"

"What?"

"We have nothing to hide; we aren't doing anything shameful. She might even be able to help. She knows Kolb and the shop, after all. She might have some angle we don't know."

"Or maybe she'd fire you for lying to her, and there goes our access to Kolb's workplace," Ian pointed out.

Tony's voice was taut. "I hate lying to her."

"We'll talk about it." Ian ruffled a hand through his hair. "First item for discussion when Nina and I get back tomorrow." This Florida town was such a hamlet, there wouldn't be another bus until the morning.

Ian rang off as Nina came strolling out of the five-and-dime with a small package. The sun was down, night falling fast. "I suppose we should try to find a hotel, if they even *have* hotels." There wasn't much to this tiny hamlet except sticky heat and the sound of waves.

"Why bother with hotel?" Nina looked at the darkening sky. "Is nice night."

For any other woman, Ian thought, that would have meant there was a lovely sunset and a full moon, a night for romance. For Nina, it meant no clouds and only a sliver of moon—in other words, perfect weather to blow things up. "You want to pitch out on the sand all night?"

"Would save money, and we don't sleep anyway after a hunt. Too fizzed."

"True enough." Ian didn't know if there were two insomniacs alive worse than Nina and himself. On the road, economy dictated

sharing a room, and Ian was surprised how much better sleepless-
ness was when shared. He'd wake at one in the morning with a
parachute dream, steady his racheting heart by turning on the light
and reading (surreptitiously) one of his wife's Georgette Heyer
paperbacks balanced on Nina's bare shoulder as she slumbered.
Eventually he curled up around her and dropped back to sleep,
vaguely feeling her come awake an hour later and prowl out of bed
to sit at the hotel window and drink in the night air. When she came
back, she slid under the covers and started nipping his ear—"I'm
not sleepy, *luchik*, tire me out"—and after he'd obliged her, they
both usually managed to drowse past dawn, legs entangled, Nina's
arm thrown across Ian's ribs, his face buried in her hair.

I'm not giving that up, Ian thought. *If I can just figure out what
will make you want to stay.* How the hell did you woo a woman as
impervious as a bullet?

They ate hot dogs at a ramshackle beachside diner, and then
Nina found a public washroom and disappeared with the package
she'd bought from the five-and-dime. Ian waited outside, fanning
himself with the straw panama he'd picked up to replace his old
fedora, crumpling and bashing it until it sat on his head at the ap-
propriately battered angle. At last Nina came out with her hair lying
damp against her shoulders, smelling of peroxide. "Better," she said
contentedly, running fingers through her newly blond roots as they
set off in the direction of the beach.

"Why do you dye your hair?" Ian said curiously. "Not to be
rude, I like it. But considering that your only other nod to personal
adornment has been to tattoo your aviation record on the soles of
your feet . . ."

Nina shrugged. Another of those arbitrary questions she refused
to answer—Ian let it be, and they strolled on down the long deserted
beach, shoulders brushing. It was now full dark, just the faint glitter
of stars overhead and the gritty slide of sand beneath Ian's shoes.
Nina stopped and pulled off her sandals as they came to the edge
of the water. Her profile was bright against the darkness, and Ian
thought of the night on the ship rail. "Nina," he asked, "those five

years you spent in England before this . . . was there anyone for you? I wouldn't blame you if there were," he added, not entirely truthfully. Falling for his wife had brought out a possessive streak, he was finding, but that didn't mean he had to give in to it. "It wasn't precisely a real marriage."

"There were a few," Nina said matter-of-factly. "Was five years. You?"

"A few," Ian admitted. "No one lasting. Are any of your fellows waiting for you?" he made himself ask. If she said yes, he wouldn't say another word.

"No. Peter, he goes off to fly with aerobatic team. Simone, she's married—"

Ian stumbled in the sand. "*Simone?*"

"My boss at Manchester airfield, he brings a French wife home from the war. But he's in town every night with his mistress now, and Simone gets lonely. *Bozhe moi*, she could tire out a tiger. You ever need sleep," Nina advised, "get a Frenchwoman, forty-five, who wears *eau de violette* and hasn't had good roll in the hay in years."

Ian digested this. "Bloody hell, Nina—"

She chuckled. "I shock you?"

"A bit, yes." It wasn't as if he was unfamiliar with the idea of females who enjoyed female company. It was a little odd, however, to realize that his wife, like her razor, cut both ways.

"You're thinking now, this means I don't like you?" Nina grinned, tugging his head down for one of her voracious kisses. "I do."

"I have fairly compelling evidence by now that you like me, comrade." Ian returned the kiss, hand sliding through Nina's damp hair, then shrugged out of his jacket, flung it over the sand, and tossed her down on it. She wasn't wearing the willow for someone in Manchester, whether a British flyboy or a Frenchwoman who smelled of *eau de violette*, and that was enough to fill him with relief and hunger, setting his lips at Nina's throat and slowly kissing his way down. *Come on, comrade*, he thought. *There's starlight and sand and the smell of the sea, and there's me making love to*

you. Be moved by the goddamned romance of it all, would you?
Be moved, Nina. Give me a chance.

"Stay with me." He said it simply, in the moments afterward where they still lay twined up and breathing hard among the scatter of clothes, before his wife could get brisk and pull away. "I don't want to divorce you, Nina. Stay with me."

She stared at him, and he could feel her pulling away without moving a muscle.

"Give it a year," he said, drawing a thumb down her sharp cheekbone. "You like this work, you like the chase, you like me. Why not stay? Try it for a year, being my wife more than just in name. It wouldn't be like most marriages, children and Sunday lunches and peace. That would bore you, and it would bore me. We'd have this instead, the road and the hunt and a bed at the end of it. Give it a year." Ian put everything into the words. "Give it a year, and if you want to walk away at the end, we'll divorce. But why not try?"

Nina sat up, linking her arms around her knees, her face like a small obdurate shield. "I don't love," she said. "Is not what I do."

Go soft-eyed on her and she will bolt, Ian thought. "Love isn't the word," he said. "I'm not sure there's a word in the world for what you are to me, Nina. Maybe *comrade* says it best. Comrades who are husband and wife—why isn't that worth keeping?"

She shook her head sharply.

"Why?" Ian sat up too, trying to keep the anger out of his voice. "Tell me that. Tell me *something*. Don't just glower and prickle."

Nina glowered, prickling. He stared her down through the dark. She looked away, out at the long slow rollers of the Atlantic crashing under the night sky, and finally tugged at a strand of her damp hair. "You know why I dye it?" she said, carving the words off like ice chunks. "Yelenushka liked it—my pilot. I keep for her. Yelena Vassilovna Vetsina, senior lieutenant in the Forty-Sixth. Almost three years with her, and I love her till I die."

Ian saw the gleam of tears in his wife's eyes, even in the starlight. *Not a hard heart, after all*, he thought with a sinking feeling.

A broken one. "Yelena," he said, keeping his voice steady. "The Russian version of *Helen*, isn't it? What was she like?"

"Dark. Tall. Lashes to *here*. And *tvoyu mat*, she could fly. Nothing more beautiful in the air."

"What happened?"

Nina told him, tersely. Hard to imagine his tough, swaggering Nina as a brokenhearted girl sobbing her eyes out in a cockpit. He would have hugged her, but she would hate that. "Do you know what became of her?" Ian asked over the sound of the waves. "Your Helen of Troy."

"Yes," said Nina.

Ian waited. His wife stared out over the black waves. "After the war, was a little time you still get letters to the Motherland. Before everything shuts down and the West is forbidden. Is still like floating messages in bottles, trying to find people. I don't know where to find Yelenushka, but I find my old commander."

"Bershanska?"

"Bershanskaia. Is a relief, knowing she lived. The regiment, they got all the way to Berlin!" A flash of fierce, momentary pride sounded in Nina's voice. "Disbanded after, of course. No one wants little princesses in the air unless it's war and you really *need* them."

"Whoever decided that," Ian said, trying to lighten Nina's stony face and his own leaden heart, "can fuck themselves through seven gates whistling."

Nina smiled briefly, but it faded. "I can't write Bershanskaia as me, as Lieutenant N. B. Markova declared dead in Poland. I write as some cousin from Kiev now living in England, someone imaginary, and I put in details so Bershanskaia knows is me. I ask news of my *sestry*." A long breath. "I get one letter back."

The slow crash of waves, one, two, three. Rustle of fragrant vegetation overhead. *Mangroves, maybe*, Ian thought, stomach heavy as a stone.

"Bershanskaia lists the dead, ones who died after me." Ian didn't think that was a slip of the tongue; in a very real sense Lieutenant

N. B. Markova *had* died in that funeral pyre she'd made of her plane in the wet woods of Poland. "My navigator, poor Galya, she makes it to the end of the war and dies in crash outside Berlin. Others too—many bad nights, at the end."

Ian steeled himself. "Did your Yelena . . . ?"

"No. She lived."

That startled him. The grief in Nina's voice, he was certain her lover must have died.

"Hero of the Soviet Union, one of ten crews marching in Moscow Victory Parade on Air Force Day, June '45. I imagine her marching through Red Square, flowers falling on her hair." Another long silent moment; Nina seemed to have turned to ice. "Bershanskaia tells me she lives in Moscow, instructor pilot in civil aviation. She shares an apartment with navigator she had after me, Zoya. I always wonder, does she fall in love with Zoya? That bucktoothed *suka* has red hair, she's a widow, she has two babies. Always Yelena wanted babies. She falls in love with one navigator, maybe now two?" Sigh. "Or maybe she's just sharing apartment."

"I imagine she thinks of you," Ian said. "I can't imagine anyone *not* thinking of you." He had not one hope in the world now that his wife would stay with him. Astounding how much that hurt.

"Bershanskaia writes once," Nina finished. "Wishes me well, finishes *Don't write again.* Too dangerous, I know that. And soon there are no more letters allowed west to east, so doesn't matter." Pause. "I think Yelenushka's alive, teaching boys to fly, playing with Zoya's babies. Happy. Maybe is true. I won't know."

"What would you do," Ian made himself ask, "if you saw her coming along this beach toward you?"

"Kiss her till she can't breathe, ask her to stay. But she wouldn't."

"No?"

"She loves the Motherland, just enough more than me. Is all there is to say." Nina looked at Ian. "I love her, I lose her. I don't love anyone else. Is better."

For who? Ian wanted to lash back. But he stamped the anger down, and under it the pain. There was a dark-eyed Moscow rose in a training cockpit somewhere behind the Iron Curtain, and against her he stood no chance.

"I wouldn't have asked if I'd known," he said at last. "I'm sorry."

Nina nodded acknowledgment.

"I'll begin divorce proceedings," Ian went on, stripping his voice to a matter-of-fact flatness. "No sense waiting until this chase is over; it could drag on for months."

Another nod. "Is best."

Ian rose, shrugging into his clothes. Nina slid into her own. They didn't say another word.

Chapter 47

JORDAN

September 1950
Boston

J ordan hadn't intended to go to the Scollay Square apartment at
all. She'd been mindlessly walking the pathways on the Common all morning, forgetting her hat on a bench somewhere,
gripping the Leica like a lifeline. Gripping her pocketbook too, where
she'd hidden those long-ago photographs of Anneliese in the kitchen,
Anneliese's bouquet with its swastika, Anneliese with the man she
said was her father, because Jordan didn't dare leave them in the
darkroom. Anneliese never came down to the darkroom, or she said
she didn't, but Jordan wasn't sure of anything anymore. What did
Anneliese really do all day? Jordan was appalled at the speculations
that now prowled through her mind.

She'd managed to avoid facing her stepmother over the supper
table the last few nights, claiming work. "If I'm going to New York
so soon, I need to have everything ready—" and Anneliese was so
warmly encouraging of anything that advanced *that* plan. "I'll make
you some cocoa to take down." Jordan couldn't work after that, just
stare into the mug that Anneliese always topped with a dash of cinnamon, because she knew that was how Jordan liked it, and try to
make sense of it all.

"Look at this logically, J. Bryde," she had muttered aloud to the darkroom's silence. "Step by step. And get it right this time." She'd already gone down the path of suspicion before, after all, and it had blown up in her face. *I am not doing that again.*

So. An unexplained absence, not to Concord or New York but somewhere unknown. *Maybe Anna went to meet a man,* Jordan thought. *If she has her eye on someone new, so soon after Dad, she would hide that from me.* But a new suitor in her life didn't account for that strange scene with Kolb. *Some kind of fraud at the shop?* There were all kinds of swindles that could take place in the antiques business; perhaps Kolb had dragged her into something unsavory. *But I saw the look on his face; he's terrified of her. He wouldn't dare try to drag her into anything she didn't want.* Could Anneliese be the one who had initiated some shop swindle, and dragged Kolb along? *What financial trouble could she have that would make her risk everything for a little extra cash?* Risk the shop's reputation, risk legal charges, risk Jordan's father finding out?

Dad suspected, the cold thought whispered. *He told you he had his doubts about Kolb, and right afterward—*

But that thought stopped in its tracks, driving her out of the darkroom to walk the Common for the rest of the morning. *Anneliese was with me when Dad left for that hunting trip,* Jordan thought, aimlessly drifting toward the Common bandstand. *She was with me all morning as I tried on wedding dresses.*

That didn't silence the cold voice. What a terrible thing suspicion was, once you let it have full rein. Jordan didn't think she would ever be able to get this beast on a leash again, and she couldn't avoid Anneliese forever, ducking supper and hiding in the morning behind a newspaper. Sooner or later, Anneliese was going to realize something was wrong.

And what are you going to do, J. Bryde? You can't run to your father with your suspicions this time. Who are you going to tell? There's no one but you.

Jordan realized she'd stopped by the pillared marble bandstand. Tony had kissed her here on their third date. She ran her hand along the marble, wishing for him viscerally—not to kiss, not to cling to, but to *listen*. No one listened like him; under all the grins and jokes he missed nothing.

Tell Tony.

She felt a reflexive cringe at the thought of unpacking this unsavory family business with an outsider—even a lover she trusted. But Jordan hesitated only a moment before letting her feet take her toward his apartment.

She squeezed past a pair of gangly young men sitting on the grimy stairwell passing a bottle back and forth, edging up the last set of steps to knock on the door. No one answered. She rattled the door handle again, and it came open; Tony had said it was flimsy. She hesitated. Normally she'd never have invited herself inside, but Tony had said Mr. Graham and his wife were out of town—and Jordan didn't like the look of those men on the stairwell, talking too loudly as they passed their bottle. She went in and shut the door behind her. Tony wouldn't mind.

The room was hot, the broken table heaped with papers and tea mugs. Jordan reached for the nearest piece of paper and fanned herself with it. *Come home*, she thought to Tony, looking at the clock. She very badly wanted to talk to him.

The piece of paper in her hand slipped between sweaty fingertips, fluttered to the floor. Jordan picked it up again. Tony's writing, bold and spiky, some kind of list—the words *Chadwick & Black* jumped out. She'd telephoned that number just days ago. This was a list of antiques dealers, written in Tony's hand.

Puzzled, she looked at the papers piled on the table. More lists in Tony's handwriting. Maps, both American and European. Lists, all in Tony's hand, looking like they'd been hastily copied—list after list of names and businesses, many of which Jordan knew, on shop stationery. Copied out at the shop.

A slip of newsprint fluttered out of the bottom layer as she sifted, and Jordan bent to pick it up. Dan McBride's obituary, circled.

Jordan sat down, heart pounding, and began to sift through the layers. Scribbled notes in what looked like German and Polish.

Maps jotted all over with an upright script she recognized as Ian Graham's, having seen him write pieces of music down for Ruth to listen to. A thick file labeled *Die Jägerin/Lorelei Vogt*.

Jordan opened it. Clipped inside was a photograph of a family on church steps, the figure at one end circled in red.

Jordan looked closer. A young woman, gloved and folded hands, composed eyes over smiling lips. Jordan knew those eyes. Her ears roared, and she squeezed her eyes shut. Opened them again, brought the photograph closer.

Anneliese. Younger than Jordan was now, almost unrecogniz-able in her chubby, unformed youth, but not to Jordan, who knew her so well. It *was* Anneliese.

Jordan looked around the table with its heaped evidence of a long stakeout. "What is this?" she whispered aloud into the stale, silent air. Tony Rodomovsky turning up at the shop inquiring about a job. Ian Graham never quite saying what he was doing in Boston, except that he had all the time in the world to teach Ruth scales. His strange Soviet wife with her unmistakable edge of dan-ger. Anneliese's picture in a file with another woman's name . . .

Jordan pushed the photograph aside with shaking fingers and began to read.

Chapter 48

IAN

September 1950
Boston

Yﾟou two look like death warmed over," Tony yawned, picking Ian and Nina up at the bus station in the rattling Ford. "I'm the one running on about three hours of sleep, trailing Kolb all by myself."

"*Poshol nakhui*," Nina growled. "I spend two years straight on three hours of sleep, you can shut up."

"You can't trump a Russian when it comes to suffering," Tony grumbled, peeling into the Boston traffic. "They have *always* suffered more, and in minus-twenty-degree weather, and in a gulag to boot. You just can't win." He looked at both his passengers, Ian staring out one window, Nina the other. "Anything happen that I should—"

"No," Ian said around the stone in his throat, and the silence held as they trudged upstairs to the apartment. Normally Nina skipped backward up the steps just ahead of him until he told her to get out of his bloody way. Now she took the steps two at a time without looking back, uncharacteristically silent. *Better this way*, Ian thought, already eager to sink back into the grind of cross-checking and telephoning and diner stakeouts. Better the drudgery of a stalled chase than this tangle of pain and anger with which he had no time to deal.

At the top landing, Ian saw their door ajar. He reached out, twitched it open all the way, and every thought of Nina and her Moscow lover and the end of his hopes on a shadowy Florida beach disappeared.

Their worktable lay bare, papers and maps and pencils lying in a jumble across the floor as though someone had swept everything off in one violent heave. A woman's dusty footprint showed clearly on the back of a map, pointing out the door. On the empty table lay a torn sheet of paper and two photographs.

"*Der'mo*," Nina swore, and they were all rushing inside.

The photograph of a young Lorelei Vogt, yanked out of Ian's file with such force the corner had torn. Another photograph of a woman with a dish towel, standing beside a sink, looking back over one shoulder, eyes strangely alight.

Nina's breath caught in her throat, Ian heard it. He looked at her, mouth suddenly dry. "Is it—"

His wife stretched a fingertip toward the new photograph, eyes suddenly incandescent. "Is her." There was no doubt in her voice.

Ian picked up the sheet of paper beside the photographs. Jordan McBride's handwriting, Ian had seen it on shop paperwork. She had scribbled five words in pencil, nearly engraving the letters through the paper.

Lorelei Vogt is Anna McBride.

PART III

Chapter 49

JORDAN

September 1950
Boston

C an you drive faster?"

The cabbie sounded aggrieved. "Slow traffic, miss."

Jordan's heart was racing, her feet pressing against the cab's floor as though she could bodily push the car along. But horror sat cold and heavy in her stomach like a stone ball.

She'd wept in that Scollay Square apartment, choked sobs tearing out of her throat as she sat surrounded by the paper-trail bloodshed and horror of Anneliese's past. But only for a moment. There was no time to weep, no time to scream, no time to stay here and confront Tony when he returned. No time to fall on him and scream *why*, why had he been taking her to ballet studios and kissing her in the darkroom when upstairs a soft-spoken murderer sat humming at a sewing machine. Jordan had swallowed her sobs, swept the table clean with one violent motion, slapped down the photograph she hadn't dared leave in her darkroom anymore, wrote a note, and run for the stairs. The team didn't know who Anneliese was, that was plain from the file, and Jordan wasn't going to wait to tell them, as much as she wanted to. She burned to stay and demand answers, and goddammit, she was going to come back here and get them, but she had no idea when Tony and his friends would be back—and Ruth was at home *right now* with the murderess who had nested in their family like a poisonous spider. It didn't matter that Ruth had passed years in Anneliese's company unharmed; Jordan could not delay one minute before getting her sister out of the clutches of a woman who had murdered six children in cold blood.

Her breath left her in a harsh, guttural scrape. The cabbie glanced over his shoulder, but Jordan turned her face to the window. A beautiful summer morning was passing by outside, so many people out for a stroll—couples arm in arm, girls blowing along in giggling groups, men in checked shirts arguing about the Red Sox; none dreaming that there were monsters hiding in this American paradise they were so proud of. Jordan looked at the sunny street but saw instead the exquisite man-made lake in western Poland, conjured up so clearly in Ian Graham's flat, factual journalist's notes. Anneliese standing beside it, not much older than Jordan was now. The huddled children . . .

Jordan had read through the file of her stepmother's other crimes. Ian's murdered younger brother, a prisoner of war. The nameless Poles hunted for sport through the trees as a party game. But it was the children Jordan came back to. The children like Ruth.

Why didn't she kill you? Jordan wondered in numb horror. *She killed your mother. Why not you?*

The team's notes on Anneliese/Lorelei's time in Altaussee had been jotted colloquially in Tony's hand, as though he were musing aloud. *Our girl was living with Frau Eichmann after the war. No money, nowhere to go, lover dead. Frau Eichmann doesn't like her, tells her to leave autumn '45. Scared to apply for a visa in case name is flagged, terrified to be found/arrested. How does she get from Altaussee to America???*

I think I could tell you how, Jordan thought, remembering Anneliese's two very different stories about her time in Altaussee. After Thanksgiving, when she couldn't deny she hadn't given birth to Ruth, she came up with the story about finding her as an orphan abandoned beside the lake . . . but at first, when she was explaining

Ruth's nightmares, hadn't there been a story about how a refugee woman had attacked them on the lakeshore and frightened Ruth? Had Anneliese been telling the truth, as much of it as she could? It was the cleverest way to lie, after all.

She wasn't the one being attacked, Jordan thought. *She was the one who did the attacking.* Desperate to leave, desperate not to be caught, desperate to get away, she had met a woman by the lake—a woman named Anneliese Weber who had papers, boat tickets, refugee status, and a little girl. The answer to every prayer. *Just murder her and take it all.* Ruth—with her strained seeking eyes, her musicality, her sudden vacillation between laughter and fear, pulling toward Anneliese and then pulling away—had watched her mother murdered by the woman who then became her mother.

"Why did she take you?" Jordan whispered aloud. It would have been easier to travel unencumbered, surely. *And she had no qualms killing children before.*

Numbly, Jordan shook her head. The old admonishment rang in her brain of *Jordan and her wild imagination!* In the space of a single morning the world had turned into a wilder and more horrible place than her imagination could ever have conjured up.

"Here we are, miss."

Jordan shoved a handful of change at the driver and tumbled out of the cab. The car was here; Anneliese was home. Of course she was. Jordan drew in a shaky breath. *Pretend nothing has happened*, she thought. *Make up a story, get Ruth out of the house. Just do it.*

She squared her shoulders and went to face the huntress.

"DON'T CRY, JORDAN." Anneliese opened her arms, brows creasing. "He's not worth it."

No way to hide her reddened eyes, not from Anneliese's penetrating gaze, so Jordan hadn't even tried. The moment Anneliese came out of her sewing room with Taro wagging at her heels, Jordan released the sob hovering in her throat and exploded into tears, choking out as incoherently as possible that *he's broken my heart.*

"Your young man disappointed you?" Anneliese's embrace was

soft and lilac scented; Jordan managed not to shudder. "I thought he wasn't anyone serious."

"I got a lot fonder of him than I meant to," Jordan choked, realizing she was telling the truth. Somewhere in this welter of horror and fear there was a stab of betrayal all for Tony. Tony in the darkroom, arms about her waist, wire strong and wanting against her as she asked if he'd tell her a secret. *There's one I want to tell you and can't.* Letting her think that as long as there weren't wives or children or warrants to worry about, it was all *fine*. As all the while, he and his friends staked out her shop, her family, her life.

Use that, J. Bryde, Jordan told herself as she cried in her stepmother's arms. *Use the tears, use the anger, use it all*. She pulled back at last, wiping her eyes, tremulous smile not one bit faked. "I'm sorry to cry, Anna. You're right, he isn't worth it."

"You'll meet someone else in New York. Some dashing young man who brings you roses." Her brows were creased with worry. *You shot six children in cold blood*, Jordan thought. *Now you wring your hands over my boyfriend problems*. But she pushed that away, hard.

"I thought I'd go out for an ice cream, take Ruth with me. I need something sweet."

"A bruised heart definitely calls for ice cream. Ruth just got into her bath, but I'll hurry her out." Anneliese smiled, arm still about Jordan's shoulders, and Jordan's heart cracked because that smile was so warm and soothing that she still had the urge to trust it. Like Taro, who sat shoving an adoring black nose under Anneliese's free hand, Jordan felt the same instinctive surge of comfort as her stepmother's soft, murderous fingers stroked her hair.

First horror, then fear for Ruth had carried Jordan through the last hour of shocks. Now the third reaction rose, more terrible than the first two, and it was shame, because she couldn't help the reflexive leap of affection at Anneliese's touch. *She's a murderess. A Nazi murderess*—but there was still the urge to lean into that calming hand, to want to doubt the truth even after seeing all the evidence.

Because this was *Anneliese*, who had encouraged her to dream beyond Garrett Byrne and his pear-shaped diamond; who had admitted her own fears and listened to Jordan's; who adored the family
dog and made the best cocoa in Boston.

So much for dogs knowing good people from bad, Jordan
thought. *Or stepdaughters knowing a wicked stepmother in the
flesh.*

Except some part of her had suspected, right from the first. *If
only I'd convinced Dad—*

But she shoved that thought away hard too.

"Oh, Anna." Jordan squeezed that soft hand. "I don't know
what I'd do without you. I'll miss you when I leave for New York."

"We'll always be here, Ruth and Taro and me. New York isn't
so far away."

A prison cell is a lot farther, Jordan thought. Whoever Ian and
Tony and Nina really were, they were clearly looking to build some
kind of case against Anneliese. And with a sudden surge of implaca-
bility, Jordan brushed aside the fact that Tony had lied to her. If he'd
done it to put Anneliese in a cell, she was going to help.

"Ruth," Anneliese was calling up the stairs, "hurry out of the
bathtub, your sister is taking you for ice cream."

I love you, Anneliese, Jordan thought, looking at that serene
profile. *But I'm still taking you down.*

Chapter 50

IAN

September 1950
Boston

"Let's admit we're idiots." Tony broke the silence. "She was under our noses the entire time. I saw her with my own eyes, I *talked* with her—"

"She looks almost nothing like that picture we have," Ian said tersely. "It was too old to be useful. Only someone who knew that face very well would—goddammit, can't you make this car go faster?"

Tony had the Ford's gas pedal mashed to the floor, but the lunchtime traffic poured like slow honey. "I looked at her neck the day we met. There was no scar!" His hands were clenched around the wheel.

"She covers it," Nina guessed from the backseat. "Is makeup, maybe. *Blyadt*, how far is McBride house—"

Not far, but who knew how long ago Jordan had left Scollay Square? *She went for her sister*, Ian thought. *That's what I would do, if I learned my stepmother was a murderess.*

"I should have known when we spoke," Tony muttered. "That she wasn't a native speaker, the rhythms—"

"You said she had no accent, even dropped her *R*'s like a Bostonian."

"Still should have brought me in to check," Nina snapped. "I would have known her, more than you only seeing the old picture—"

Ian cut them both off. "We *all* could have done better, yes. But we had no reason to think Lorelei Vogt had stopped in Boston rather than passing through as all the others did; we had no reason to think Jordan's stepmother had connections to Europe—not with a name like Anna McBride, listed as born in Boston, no accent to give her away. There seemed nothing suspicious about her to investigate, and we had Kolb in front of us, looking suspicious as a rotting fish."

"And she kept her distance from the shop," Tony said. "Jordan said her father took pride that his wife didn't have to work, and I didn't think anything of it. But she kept her distance so if anyone took a second look for shady business, what they'd see was Kolb. And we did, damn us all—"

"Stop this. Stop it now." Ian pushed steel through his voice, slicing through the discussion. "We finally know *who* she is and *where* she is. Let's focus on that and assign blame later."

"Holy hell, I hope Jordan grabbed Ruthie and got out of that house," Tony muttered. "If she'd just waited—"

"Why should she?" Nina said. "Has no reason to trust us, or know what we do."

"We should have brought her in. Told her."

"We saw no reason to. We've never brought in outsiders before. Once and for all, stop the *what if*s and *should have*s." The last thing this team needed was to career into recrimination. But Ian's hands were clenched so tight around his panama that the brim had crumpled like paper, and the same tense fear was vibrating through the car between all of them, unspoken.

If Jordan or her sister came to harm because of this, the team was finished.

In a squeal of tires, Tony brought the car around the corner onto the street with the McBride house. "If Lorelei Vogt is there," Ian said, "we confront and apprehend on the spot."

"On whose authority? We have no warrant!"

Ian thought he could bluff around that. He was damned well going to try. This wasn't how they normally handled confrontations; usually there would be a careful plan laid and backing authorities notified. No time for that now. Ian looked at his partner and his wife, blood sparking in his veins. "Be on your guard every bloody minute. We've never confronted someone like this. Most of the men we find are no more dangerous without their Third Reich than field mice, but she is different. If she so much as lifts a finger toward herself or anyone else, stop her. By any means necessary."

Nina flicked her razor, and for once Ian was glad to see it.

They were spilling out of the car before it even stopped moving in front of the brownstone—and were greeted by the sight of an open door and an empty house.

Chapter 51

JORDAN

September 1950
Boston

*H*urry up, *Ruth,* Jordan prayed.

Her sister was finally out of her bath, calling "Can I get strawberry ice cream?" down the stairs as she trailed off towel wrapped to her room. Jordan couldn't rush her without looking suspicious, and she couldn't take another moment keeping her guard up with Anneliese, so she busied herself first in leashing up Taro—Jordan was no more leaving her dog in this house than her sister—and then muttered about getting something in the darkroom. "Go tear up any pictures you took of that young man," Anneliese advised. "It will make you feel better!"

Once down in the darkroom Jordan sagged against the door, realizing she was sweating as though she'd run a race. "Calm down, J. Bryde. Stay cool—" she told herself as she rummaged for a rag to pat her face. *Where are you going to go?* The thought hammered. *Where are you going to take Ruth?*

Back to Tony's apartment for some answers. That was a start.

She turned and nearly leaped out of her skin. Anneliese was standing at the top of the darkroom stairs, looking down with her warm smile. She'd made no sound at all.

"Anna, you startled me!" Jordan smiled, heart nearly leaping out of her chest. "Is Ruth ready?"

"Tying her shoes."

"I can't remember when you were last down here."

"It's always seemed very much your sanctum." Anneliese looked around at the equipment, the walls, the lights. She had her pocketbook over her arm. "I was thinking I'd come with you girls. It's been a long time since I had an ice cream cone."

"I thought you had to finish that skirt you were running up on the Singer." Jordan kept her smile in place.

"Hemming can always wait."

"Are you sure? I could bring a cone back for you—" Jordan cut herself off. Too suspicious to keep throwing up objections. "You know what, never mind. Anything I bring you will just melt in this sun. Come with us." She would sneak Ruth out when they got back.

"I'll just get my hat." But Anneliese didn't move, just stood looking thoughtful. "You know I went to the bank this morning? Miss Fenton said you were asking about the savings accounts."

Jordan kept her tone normal, relaxed. "I know you say there's no need to worry about money, but I still do. It was a relief to hear about that extra insurance policy."

"Miss Fenton said you looked a bit upset."

"I got a whiff of Dad's aftershave suddenly—one of the cashiers wearing the same brand. You know how it is . . . I left quickly before I started bawling."

"Mmm. Well, that sounds reasonable." Anneliese looked at the railing under her hand. "Do you know any tall Englishmen, Jordan? A man asking questions?"

"What? No, I told you that already." Jordan's heart started to speed. "Weeks ago."

"I know." Anneliese sounded apologetic. "But there is one, isn't there? Kolb was quite firm about that. He also seems to think he's been followed, and I was inclined to blame such paranoia on his liking for the bottle, but perhaps not. Then you turn up at the bank asking about my savings accounts, and here you are looking upset about a boyfriend, and you explain it all very nicely, Jordan, but it makes me uneasy. It really does."

"Why would it?" Jordan made herself look up, give a puzzled smile.

"Because when you've lived through a war," Anneliese said, "when you've been *hunted*, you pay attention to any little things out of the ordinary. However nicely they're explained away, they still . . . *ping*."

The silence fell between them as dark and heavy as lake water. Jordan stood, hands behind her gripping the edge of the work-table. Anneliese stood in her crisp black dress and dark chignon and perfectly painted lips. Jordan couldn't think what to do, except to look confused and innocent. Her heart hammered.

"*Scheisse*." Anneliese sighed. Setting her pocketbook down, she reached into it and pulled out a pistol in one firm, expert hand, and Jordan's mind went white with terror as a shot crashed out.

THE METAL TRAY at Jordan's right spun off the table in a clatter, even as she flinched back with a choked scream. It took her a moment to realize she hadn't been hurt. "Let's talk honestly now," Anneliese said, matter-of-fact.

Jordan's knees were pudding. She looked at Anneliese, at the pistol in her hand, and wanted to scream, but in this thick-walled space set below the ground, no one on the street was going to hear. She doubted anyone had heard the shot either. She opened her mouth.

"Whatever you're about to say, it had better not be a lie," Anneliese said. "I don't want to shoot you, Jordan, but I will if I have to."

"I believe you," Jordan said in a thin voice. "You murdered Ruth's mother in cold blood for her passport, you murdered a young English POW by a lake, and you murdered six Polish children after feeding them a meal, so no, I don't think you'll hesitate to kill me."

She expected Anneliese to deny it—weep, protest innocence, flow gently with emotion the way she had that Thanksgiving when she looked at the photograph of her SS lover and managed to convince Dan McBride and Jordan both that it was her father. But Anneliese merely moved down the staircase into the darkroom with a sigh. "I see you've learned a few things."

Jordan found herself trembling. "What *are* you?" She couldn't stop herself from asking the question, the great cry that had taken root in her mind since realizing the truth of it all . . . and even outside that primal cry was the cooler speculation: *If I can distract her, maybe I can get away. Or maybe someone will come.* It was not much of a hope, but staring down the barrel of a pistol, a slim chance looked better than none. "How could you do such things?"

Anneliese didn't answer. She just sighed again, a sound so mortally exhausted it seemed to have been dragged from the soles of her feet, and sat down on the edge of the rumpled darkroom cot. "I'm so tired of running . . ." Looking at Jordan, her mouth trembled. "Why couldn't you leave it alone?"

"Why couldn't—" Jordan pushed away from the table, only to freeze as the pistol's barrel came up.

"Sit down on the floor. Sit on your hands." Just like that, the tremble was gone. Anneliese's voice was weary, but her hand was steady.

Jordan sank down on the floor, tucking her hands under her, feeling the cold seep into her flesh. She expected Anneliese to rise and level the weapon, but she remained seated on the cot, seemingly too tired to move. Maybe she wouldn't run at all. Maybe she was ready to turn herself in. Jordan didn't really think so, but she tried a different tack.

"Whatever you do to me, don't hurt Ruth."

Anneliese looked surprised. "What reason would I have to do that?"

"She's not your daughter. Do you even love her?"

"My poor *Mäuschen*." Anneliese ran a finger along the cot's blanket. "I didn't mean to grow fond of her, you know. A Jewish child . . . I only took her with me because a mother with a beautiful little girl in her arms, well, no one suspects a woman like that. And she was so pretty. With that blond hair and none of the features one usually sees, the nose, the coarseness, perhaps there wasn't much Jewish taint. I thought I could raise her free of all that. A way to make amends."

"Amends," Jordan said. "For murdering her mother."

"I had no choice."

"You really believe that." Wonderingly. "You had *no choice* but to kill a woman and push her in a lake after robbing her of everything she owned? *No choice?*"

"You have no idea what cornered prey will do when desperate." Anneliese touched the gray pearls at her neck. "I was very sorry I had to do it. She didn't suffer, at least. I wear her pearls to remember her by."

For a moment Jordan thought she was going to vomit. "You aren't going to deny any of it," she managed to whisper.

"I don't see the point, really. You clearly know enough." Anneliese straightened. "How did you find out? Who's been telling you about me?" The barrel twitched on her knee. "Is someone coming?"

"Yes. A team of Nazi hunters who tracked you all the way from Austria." Jordan used the melodramatic term without hesitation. Anything to make Anneliese flinch. "You are never going to escape them, ever."

"Who are they? Do they have the police with them? Don't lie," Anneliese said as Jordan hesitated. "I know you very well, Jordan. I know when you're lying."

"An English journalist. His partners." Jordan was disgusted by the shake in her own voice. "They're coming for you."

"And what are they going to do, drag me before a jury? Extradite me?" Anneliese shook her head before Jordan could answer. "I suppose that doesn't matter. Whatever it is, I doubt I'd find it pleasant. People are such hanging judges over some things."

"Things like murdering children and prisoners of war?" Jordan shot back, shaking voice or not.

"I'm thirty-two years old, and my life is the sum of many moments. Why do some moments outweigh all the other, better moments? When is there enough running, enough punishment?"

"You think you've been punished?" Jordan nearly choked on a swell of incandescent fury. "You stole another woman's name and life and child, then nested yourself in my family so you could live every day in complete ease and comfort, and you think you've been *punished*?"

"Do you have any idea how much I've lost?" Anneliese returned. "A life I loved, a man I loved, contact with my mother except for the occasional cautious letter, which I don't even dare post myself. Every day I'm afraid and every night I dream." She shivered. "Strange how many nightmares I have in this house, where everything is so safe. My house on the lake in Posen, it was so isolated . . . no servants by the end of '44, everything falling to pieces, Manfred away for days at a time, yet I slept so soundly there. It was so beautiful. And I can never go back." Looking at Jordan. "You think that isn't punishment?"

Not enough. "So turn yourself in and fight the charges," Jordan said, switching tack. "Defend yourself. Whatever else you are, I never thought you were a coward."

She'd hoped that would sting, but Anneliese just gave a faint smile. "Cowardice doesn't exist, you know. Nor does bravery. Only nature. If you're the hunter, you stalk and if you're the prey, you run, and I am quite realistic enough to know that I have been the prey ever since the war ended and the victors decided I was a monster."

"You are a monster," Jordan said.

"Because of those children?" Anneliese shook her head. "It was an act of mercy. They were Poles, perhaps Jews, and the directive in Posen was to eliminate the Jews first, eventually the Poles."

"The war was ending, and you were losing. Why carry that directive out, with everything falling apart?"

"Because the executions and shipments were still proceeding.

Those children died far more kindly at my hands, fast and painless, with full bellies, than they would have fared starving to death in huts or dying of thirst on packed trains. I take no pleasure in suffering. If something must die, kill it cleanly."

Jordan thought she'd scream if she had to hear more of this, but she made herself continue. *Keep her talking.* "Why kill that young prisoner of war?" Sebastian Graham, Ian's younger brother, whose name she'd read in the file this morning. "There are rules about prisoners; you should have returned him to his camp alive. Why kill him?"

"Guards don't like it when prisoners escape. I likely saved him from a far more nasty death." Anneliese rose, business-like. *Don't lose her.*

"I loved you, you know." Jordan flung it down like a challenge. "I really did. And I thought you loved me. It was all lies, wasn't it?"

A look of surprise. "Why would you think that?"

"Ever since Dad died you've been trying to ship me off. To college, to work, to New York, anywhere, as long as you could get me out of the door."

"Only because I have to keep up my guard around you, all the time. I thought that would be easier if you were in another city. But it doesn't mean I'm not fond of you." The old smile, that woman-to-woman ease they'd had the last few months, relying on each other. "You're clever and levelheaded and gifted; you want things for yourself; you dream. I did too when I was your age. I wanted more than some Austrian *Advokat* husband no matter what my mother said, and you wanted more than that nice muttonhead Garrett Byrne no matter what your father said. I encouraged you to aim higher because I wanted to see you soar. It was a pleasure to watch."

"I don't believe you, Anna." Jordan said it defiantly, but inside she flinched. "Anna, Anneliese, Lorelei, whatever you call yourself."

"I hate that name." A shiver. "*Lorelei.* Like *rusalka.* Another water witch."

"Who really came out of that lake and gave you the *rusalka* nightmare?" Jordan pounced on the new angle of attack. "Someone who didn't agree with your definition of mercy?"

"I did tell you about that dream, didn't I?" A blink. "She was no one, really. Just a refugee woman in Posen."

"Did this one hurt you instead of the other way around?" *What does a monster fear?* "Is that why she makes you afraid? Why you dream of her?"

"I don't fear her. Why would I?" Anneliese's hand drifted up to her neck, unconsciously. *The old scar*, Jordan thought, hidden by makeup. "She's probably long dead."

But her face flickered, and Jordan knew it was fear. *I can read you too, you know.* Why had Anneliese told her the *rusalka* nightmare in the first place?

Because it was midnight, and she was frightened, and I was there. Because sometimes even monsters need to talk.

Jordan made her voice soft, as she gathered her feet beneath her. "Anna, won't you let me—"

The pistol rose again. "Sit back down." Jordan sat. "I'm aware you're trying to stall me," Anneliese said. "I confess it's tempting to sit here and wait until your friends arrive. I really am very tired of running. But that would be giving up, and it was my last promise to Manfred that I not give up. He died in a hail of bullets in Altaussee rather than let himself be taken; the least I can do is run." She looked at Jordan, very direct. "Don't look for me. You won't find me, not this time, and what harm can I do? I don't want to hurt anyone. I just want to live quietly."

"You don't want to hurt anyone, but you will if you think you're threatened. Dad suspected something at the shop, didn't he? He saw traces of your little scheme with Kolb. He just thought it was a swindle, not anything to do with war criminals, but he died before he found out more. How did that happen, Anna?" Jordan's eyes bored into her stepmother. "Did you murder my father?"

That was the other suspicion that had been growing like a monstrous flower in the back of her mind. Even in her frantic drive to get Ruth, some part of Jordan had been reflecting quietly that while Anna McBride knew nothing about firearms, a woman nicknamed the huntress surely would have known what kind of ammunition would make a twelve-gauge shotgun with soft steel Damascus barrels explode. Could have driven out to the lake cabin, slipped a handful of deadly rounds in among the innocent, then taken her stepdaughter shopping for a wedding dress when her husband next went on a turkey hunt . . . "Did you kill him?" Jordan asked, voice breaking. "Did you?"

Anna's face never moved, not so much as a flicker.

Oh, Dad. Jordan's mind in its iced-over horror stuttered. *Dad*—

"I was very fond of him, you know," Anneliese said at last. "If you hadn't pushed things—he never really trusted me after that first Thanksgiving. Not deep down. I'd catch him looking at me, in bed when he thought I was asleep . . . I suppose that's why he found it easy to be suspicious of Kolb, start asking questions." Anneliese shook her head. "I still wonder how you did it. Putting it all together, just seventeen . . . well, I did say you were clever, didn't I? I never dared keep anything in the house after that, for fear you'd sniff it out."

"Don't you dare tell me Dad's death was my fault," Jordan grated.

"I won't tell you anything. Go live your life, leave me to live mine. I just want to disappear with Ruth."

Terror swamped Jordan again in a wave. "You are not taking Ruth!"

"Of course I am. She's my responsibility—also my surety, Jordan. Because if I ever feel I'm being tracked again, I will shoot her and then I will shoot myself." Anneliese's gaze was candid, earnest. Jordan sat pinned by it, dry mouthed.

"Please—" she began, but Anneliese overrode her.

"I won't run a third time. I can't bear it. I'll take the easier way, and I'll take Ruth with me. One doesn't leave a child alone, that would be a great cruelty. So don't try to find me again, you and your friends. It will be much better for Ruth if you don't." Anneliese mounted the stairs, pistol glinting at her side. At the top of the staircase she looked over her shoulder. "I'll miss you, you know. Very much. I really wish you had left well enough alone."

The door clanged shut, the outside bolt screeched as it was turned, and footsteps retreated outside as Jordan flew up the stairs, flung herself against the locked door, and began to scream.

Chapter 52

IAN

September 1950
Boston

S he took nothing." Jordan was pawing through her stepmother's
closet. A floral, feminine bedroom, all Alpine landscapes and
arrangements of dried flowers. *Too late*, Ian kept thinking. *We
are too late.* "The only thing gone is Dad's car. Her traveling case
is still here, her clothes and underthings, even her checkbook and
driver's license—"

Because she's leaving it all behind, Ian thought. Lorelei Vogt had
shed Anna McBride and walked out to some new identity with nothing more than the clothes on her back. Rage swept him in a cold wave.
We did not come this far to start all over again at zero.

"She took nothing," Jordan repeated. She looked white and
wrecked, her rosy all-American prettiness drowned by shock. Ian had
never been so relieved in his life as when they'd wrenched back the
bolt of the darkroom door and she stumbled out—face tearstained
above an old red-checked shirt, blond hair wild, hands shaking, but
alive. Ian's relief was nothing to Tony's, whose olive-skinned face had
turned gray as the door came open. Jordan had pushed straight past
him, running inside calling her sister's name, and that was when they
realized Lorelei Vogt had taken something, after all.

Ruth.

"*Suka*," Nina muttered. She flipped her razor open and closed, yearning visibly for a throat to cut. Taro trailed after her, whining nervously. Ian managed not to pace, but he'd already left white fingernail crescents in his own palms.

"There has to be something to tell us where she's gone. Something—" Jordan was raking through her stepmother's handkerchiefs now, eyes flashing up to pin Ian and Tony with a stony gaze. "If you people had just *told me*—"

"I wanted to." Tony was searching the drawer beside hers; he reached out and touched her shoulder. "I've been wanting to bring you in. But we didn't know if your father might have been involved, and—"

She jerked away. "Dad would *never*—" Her voice choked. "Why did Anna even start these under-the-counter deals with Kolb, helping war criminals? If it hadn't been for that, *nothing* would have come to light for you to trace all the way to Boston. Why did she risk it?"

"Perhaps they were friends of hers," Tony suggested. "She wanted to bring her mother over too."

"She could have brought them legally, sponsored them as refugees. No one would have blinked at that."

"Money," Ian said tersely, starting to pace despite himself. "She wanted money of her own in case she ever needed to run again." *And now she has it*, he thought in another surge of ice-cold fury. Enough money to run a good long way.

No. You are not escaping us. You are not taking another innocent child. Not this time.

"I don't want you thinking my father was stupid for falling for her." The words burst out of Jordan even as she moved to search under her stepmother's bed. "She was so eager to lose her accent and join his church and be a proper American housewife. So proud to learn Boston slang, change her name from *Anneliese* to *Anna* when she got her citizenship. She fooled everyone."

"Not you." Tony rummaged among the linens. "Seventeen years old and you sniffed her from day one, which is more than the three of us professionals managed to do. You're a goddamn genius, J. Bryde."

"My father still died. I didn't make him realize—"

"Don't." Ian took her by the shoulders as she straightened from looking under the bed, nailing his eyes to hers. "Down that road lies madness, believe me. Put the blame where it belongs—on her." *Where did you go, where . . .*

"She cried for him, in the hospital. She was so devastated. I wonder what she would have done if he'd recovered from his injuries—"

"She had a plan for that," Nina stated without a shred of doubt in her voice.

Nothing was missing from Ruth's room either. Jordan rubbed helpless empty hands up and down her old blue jeans. "She didn't pack Ruth so much as a spare pair of shoes."

"Which means she has a bolt-hole somewhere." Tony was prowling the length of the cozy little bedroom. "She'll have stashed clothes, money from her closed-out savings account, new identification courtesy of Kolb."

"Yes." Jordan scrubbed a hand down the side of her face. "In the darkroom, she said she didn't dare keep anything in the house after I searched her room years ago."

"So where would she keep a bolt-hole?" Ian asked.

The four of them looked at one another.

"She went somewhere for a month, when she told me she was in Concord and New York," Jordan said at last. "She must have been setting something up. Making preparations to run, just in case she needed to."

"Must be somewhere close," Nina said. "Somewhere she could go, no one would ask questions. We have to catch her there, or—"

"Or she's gone," Jordan finished. "She and Ruth, off who knows where. She might not even stay in this country." Jordan's face collapsed. Tony pulled her into his arms. Nina and Ian just looked at each other, helpless and furious. *Ruth*, Ian kept thinking.

Poor little pilgrim stumbling through the alien corn. Lost forever, unless—

"Her bolt-hole would need to be somewhere close, but removed." Ian drummed his fingers on Ruth's bedpost. "A place to hide, change her appearance. A place no one could see her coming or going or have any reason to question her being there. Do you know of any—"

"Maybe our hunting cabin on Selkie Lake. It's more than three hours outside Boston, very remote, no swimming beaches or promenades. Just a big pond in the middle of the woods, really. We stopped going after Dad died, left it locked up. There's a big stiff old key . . ." Jordan flashed downstairs to her father's study, the others jostling behind, and began yanking desk drawers open. A cabin on a lake, framed by woods—Ian wondered if it might have reminded Lorelei Vogt of her precious house on Lake Rusalka where Seb had died.

Jordan rummaged every gaping drawer, looking up at last with cheeks blazing scarlet. "The key's gone. She went to the cabin." Lips trembling. "But she won't stay long. She'd *know* I'd remember it. And she's at least an hour and a half ahead."

We will never catch up. Ian heard his whole team think it.

Tony fumbled for the Ford's keys. "We'll try."

"We'll fail. We need to move faster." Ian knew how to make that happen, though everything in him turned to ice at the thought. "I'll tell you on the way, but first, Jordan—tell us about this *rusalka* dream your stepmother has. Every detail."

They headed for the door, Jordan recounting a surprisingly specific description of the lake-born nightmare from which *die Jägerin* apparently suffered. *So the huntress doesn't sleep well,* Ian thought in a surge of vicious satisfaction. *I'm glad.*

As Jordan finished, Ian looked at his wife as they came down the front steps outside. "Lorelei Vogt is afraid of the *rusalka*." Quietly. "That's you, isn't it?"

A tiny nod as Nina went to the car, head down. Tony and Jordan exchanged glances.

"We can use that," Ian went on, "if we know exactly what it is she's afraid of."

Nina reached for the door handle, her every invisible bristle showing to Ian's eyes, but he wasn't backing off this time.

"Spill, Nina." He dropped a hand over hers on the door handle before she could open it. "I know you don't want to say what happened on that lake, but we're out of time. Tell us."

Chapter 53

NINA

November 1944
Lake Rusalka

The soup was thick with potatoes and cream. The woman in the blue coat had brought two steaming bowls out behind the ocher-walled house, once Nina flatly refused the invitation to come into the kitchen. Sebastian took the bowl with barely contained eagerness, but Nina stood arms folded.

"Don't be rude," Seb whispered in Russian, his mouth thick with soup.

Nina's mouth watered, but she still didn't reach for the bowl. "She has a pleasure house on the lake and real cream for her stew." Looking at the slight blue-eyed woman. "That means she's a friend to the Germans."

"I told you, she's a widow. Her husband was German and died before the war began, so the Posen administration leaves her alone." Seb and the woman had had a lengthy conversation in English, which the woman apparently spoke. "She studied English in university, she's never had Reich sympathies."

"So she says." The woman looked so soft, her smile so warm. As if reading Nina's suspicion, she bent her head and sipped from the remaining soup bowl. She swallowed, holding it out again indulgently as if to say *See? No poison.*

Nina glowered, but took the bowl. The first spoonful nearly exploded her mouth with flavor, heat curling through her belly. She couldn't help bolting down the rest. The woman smiled, said something to Seb. There was another eager exchange.

"What?" Nina asked, swallowing the last drop from the bowl. "Thank her for the meal and let's be on our way."

"She's offering to let us stay the night." Seb's face glowed. "She says we can sleep in the kitchen, it's warm, she'll make up beds—"

Nina seized Seb's arm, dragged him a pace or two back away from the woman. "*No.*"

"Why not? Sleep under a roof for a change, under clean blankets—"

"Seb, no woman living alone would bring people who look like us into her house!" Gesturing at their filthy clothes. "Which means either she isn't alone, or that she'll telephone the Fritzes and turn us in as soon as—"

"Is it impossible to believe someone might take pity on us? Might offer help just to be kind?"

"Yes. That is impossible to believe. And we don't need her help."

"You don't trust anyone. That's your bloody problem." Seb's thin face flushed at the hunger-sharpened cheekbones. "And we *do* need help. We're hungry most of the time, running our bowels out eating nothing but game and roots. Why can't we accept help when it's offered?"

"Because if she's friendly, all we get is a night sleeping warm, but if she's not, we get *picked up by Germans.*"

"Maybe more than one night. Maybe she'd agree to hide us for a while." Stubbornness was falling over Seb's face in a wave. He wanted to believe so badly. Wanted to *trust.* "Not everyone in this war is only out for themselves. Try having a little faith in human nature for once."

"No," Nina said again.

He tried a different tack. "What could she do, one woman against two of us?"

Nina stared. "You know *me*, and you ask what one woman can do?"

"That's different."

Because I'm a savage, she thought. Because to an honorable young man like Sebastian Graham, well educated and well meaning and knowing nothing at all about the female sex, a small woman with smooth hair and buffed nails simply did not register as dangerous. Nina glanced over his shoulder at the woman in blue. She watched with a slight smile, content to let them hiss back and forth.

"I'm going back to our camp," Nina told Seb. "I'm not taking the chance."

He folded his arms. "I am."

Nina stood back a step, surprised at the stab of hurt. *I've fed you, hunted for you,* stayed *with you and now this?*

He flushed again. "Nina—"

"I'll meet you tomorrow at our campsite." Cutting him off. "If you don't come, I'll know you're on your way back to captivity in cuffs."

"Or I'm helping the good Frau about the garden in exchange for being allowed to hide in her cellar," he said quietly. "There are good people in the world, Nina. I trusted you, didn't I? When the only thing I knew was that you'd be shot if you went back to your regiment, I still trusted you."

Nina held up her razor. "I only trust this."

"Strange how much you remind me of my brother," Seb said. "Cool as ice and about as trusting."

"Smart man."

"Not a happy one."

"*Happy* doesn't matter. I'll settle for *alive*." Nina hesitated. "Come with me, Seb."

But he wouldn't. And Nina took off into the trees, too angry to look back and see him disappear into the ocher-yellow house.

HALF A KILOMETER'S FURIOUS HIKE down the shore, and Nina's steps slowed. Dusk was coming now, the dark of a new moon falling. *Good flying weather*, Nina thought. *Good hunting weather.* She stopped altogether, scuffing her worn boots through the dead leaves. Something was off, something was *wrong*, she had no idea what.

Yes, you do. That woman could be telephoning the Krauts now, telling them she has an escaped prisoner of war in her kitchen.

No. Something even more wrong than that. She could have turned him in without inviting him inside. Why did she do that?

Nina looked up at the sky. Blue dusk, blue eyes . . . that woman's eyes, no fear at all when she looked at the pair of ragged refugees turning up on her doorstep. Nina's matted hair, Seb's dark stubble, their dirty nails—anyone would have been wary, yet there had been no fear in her calm bearing. Anyone completely unafraid when standing outnumbered among filthy strangers in a war zone was either idiotic, saintly, or dangerous. The woman hadn't looked like an idiot. That left saintly or dangerous. Nina knew which Seb would have picked. *I know what I'd pick too.*

It was dark when she reached the house again. Light showed in a few of the unshuttered windows, throwing warm squares into the woods behind. Nina squatted in the shadow of a slender pine, watching. She'd half expected to see cars pulled up, German sentries posted to stand guard as the English prisoner was recaptured, but all was quiet.

It did not mean there wasn't a trap laid inside. Perhaps Seb had already been recaptured; the blue-eyed woman could have told the authorities that there was a woman at large as well. Nina watched another hour, listening to the sound of lake water lapping on the shore before the house, open razor in hand with its leather loop about her wrist. *Seb, where are you?*

Probably curled under a quilt before a banked fire, not giving Nina a thought.

She still didn't move. No moonlight, faint starlight silvering the lake. *Good hunting weather.* The thought kept echoing. *Good hunting weather . . .*

The door opened. Wavering light spilling across the darkness like wine, two figures silhouetted as they came into the night. Nina blinked, her night sight ruined, but she could recognize Seb's amble, his hair flopping on his forehead. The woman beside him moved lightly, hands in the pockets of her coat. She brought something out, and Nina rose fast from her crouch, but then there was the tiny scrape of a match, Seb leaning in gentleman-like to cup the flame, and the spark of a cigarette flared. The woman offered one to him, voices murmuring as they strolled toward the lake. Nina watched, still uneasy. Boards creaked as the pair stepped up onto the long dock that stretched out over the deeper water. Nina didn't trust anything that let you walk on a lake, whether pine boards or two solid meters of ice, but Seb strode along without hesitation, his belly full, a good night's sleep ahead, a civilized postdinner cigarette in hand, admiring starlight on calm water beside a woman who had been kind to him rather than hectoring him about keeping his boots dry and asking if he'd *ever* be able to tell which way was north.

Walk out there, Nina told herself, looking at the pair standing on the end of the dock. *Join them*. Maybe the woman really was just kind. Nina came out of the pine's shadow, moved to the dock, but she couldn't take the first step out over the water. She hesitated, flinching and cursing herself for flinching when the world was full of so many other things more terrifying . . . and at the end of the dock, as Seb tipped his head back to look at the night sky, Nina saw the woman flick her cigarette into the lake, reach into her coat pocket, and pull out something that glinted metallic in the starlight.

Nina launched herself onto the dock as the woman's arm straightened at an angle. Too late. The shot cracked flatly across the water.

Sebastian fell.

Inside her skull, Nina screamed.

On snow or bare ground, she would have been as silent as a U-2 gliding out of the sky. She'd have cut the blue-eyed woman's throat ear to ear before she realized there was anyone behind her at all. But the dock creaked under Nina's sprinting feet, and the woman was turning before the smoke from her shot cleared. Nina's night-trained eyes saw her in the faint starlight as though she stood under a noon sun: remote, calm, pitiless, gaze flaring only a little in the surprise of Nina's reappearance. The arm came up again, straight and unhesitating, the pistol's eye looking into Nina's. Another crack; at the same time Nina jinked left as if she'd been sideslipping out of ground fire and brought the razor around in a whipping slash. The woman twisted back, the keen edge slashing the side of her neck to the nape rather than opening her windpipe, and Nina did scream then, seeing those pitiless blue eyes fly open in shock. The woman clapped a hand to her neck, blood spilling dark between her fingers, but the pistol was coming up again, and Nina's sprint had carried her past Seb's body and out of slashing reach. At this distance the bitch couldn't miss and Nina couldn't duck, and the decision made itself in an icy drench of terror. Nina kept running, two more sprinting steps, and as the third shot tore into the night, she flung herself into the embrace of the lake.

THE COLD STABBED her through with a thousand tiny silver knives. The iron tang of lake water invaded her eyes, her ears, her nose. Panic clawed Nina almost blind, the sensation of water moving through her hair. She had not sunk herself under the surface of even a bathtub since the day she'd turned sixteen, lying half drowned on the frozen surface of the Old Man as her father slurred, *You're a* rusalka, *the lake won't hurt you.* Nina opened her mouth to scream—she couldn't help it—and the lake shoved its way down her throat like a claw of ice.

Panic and you drown, rusalka *bitch,* her father snarled, and somehow she got her limbs under control even as her mind melted with terror. She could swim—there wasn't a child who grew up on the Old Man who couldn't—and she pushed herself forward, wriggling like a lake seal. Up to the surface, lungs bursting, air searing fire-hot as she gulped it in.

The terrifying sound of another shot.

Nina dove under the surface again, not sure if she'd been hit or not—the fear held her in such an electric grip, there was no room for fresh pain to report. Bullet grazed or not, there was a stark choice in the middle of this thicket of horror: struggle out to the deeper lake, out of range, until the water numbed her limbs and she sank into exhaustion and cold, which would not take long . . . or thrash here in utter panic like a U-2 pinioned in the white glare of a searchlight and be shot at every time she surfaced. Or—

Nina jackknifed underwater, flipping before she could change her mind and kicking blindly back in the direction of the dock. Lungs almost exploding again, she slipped between the pilings, kicking up off the soft mud, surfacing in a silent sucking gasp for air. The dock was built low to the water; there wasn't even ten centimeters' clearance between the surface of the lake and the underside of the boards above. Nina clung to the piling, a splinter piercing her hand like a needle, head tilted back to keep her mouth above the water. Her limbs were already numbing. The pine boards creaked overhead, and there was the sound of metal clicking on metal.

She is standing right above me, Nina thought, *and she is reloading.* If she fired straight down between her feet into the dock, the bullet would take Nina through the eye.

Terror shattered her like new ice.

Let go, the lake whispered. *Sink into the blue. Let the* rusalka *have you.*

Disjointed images fluttered like bad film. Yelena's laughing face. Little Galya muttering in a terrified monotone, *We're not going to drown.* Her father, baring his yellowing teeth. Comrade Stalin, his mustache and his heavy feral scent . . . Nina tread water to keep her face above the frigid surface, listening to the blue-eyed huntress shift her feet just centimeters above as the lake continued to croon.

Let go, Ninochka.

She kept moving her legs, but she couldn't feel them.

Let go. Let the rusalka *have you. She's the first night witch, the one who comes from the lake with ice-cold arms and a kiss that kills.*

No, Nina thought. *I am the* rusalka. *Born from a lake to find home in the sky, come back to the lake.*

Then die here in your lake. Easier here than up above at her hands.

No, Nina thought again. *I may fear water, but to fight a Nazi in the dark of the moon holds no terror for me.*

She had no idea how long she hung there in the dark prism of Lake Rusalka, face tilted above the water, fingers fighting for a grip on the slimy pilings, numbed feet spasming to keep her afloat, as the blue-eyed huntress above kept watch. Only minutes, surely. It felt like hours.

Over the lapping of the water Nina heard the woman call out in German. Even Nina understood the three simple, desperate words.

"Where are you?"

Nina clamped her chattering teeth.

The woman's shoes shuffled. Her breath came unevenly. Nina heard the hiss of pain. *I cut her.* The red line opening across the nape of the neck, a kiss from the razor. The huntress would be bleeding, free hand clamped to her neck.

"Please be dead," the woman above muttered as if in prayer, her voice thick with fear. "Please be dead . . ."

A rusalka *cannot die,* Nina thought, cold making the thought stutter. *And you've been kissed by a* rusalka, *which means you're mine forever, you blue-eyed bitch.*

A long ragged breath from the woman overhead, another hiss of pain, and then footsteps retreated unsteadily down the dock toward the shore. The huntress must be dizzy from blood loss, Nina thought; she would have to go inside, bandage herself. Nina did not move, remained floating under the dock. The woman above her was coolheaded even if she was bleeding and afraid. She might retreat and wait in the shore's shadows, watching to see what came from the lake. It was what Nina would have done.

She hung there in the dark, in the lake, barely breathing.

Move now, her father said at last, *or you will freeze and drown.*

She might still be there, Nina thought. *Waiting.*

Move now.

Nina had almost no strength to haul herself from the lake onto the dock. She lay limp, trying to flex her fingers and toes, almost too stiff to move. She could have lain there forever, but she forced herself to her knees to look around. No waiting female form, no blue eyes watching. The ocher-walled house had gone dark. It would not stay dark. The huntress surely had friends; they would come to aid her.

Move.

But Nina couldn't. Sebastian Graham's body lay dark and silent on the dock. Still warm.

She knew it was hopeless, but she still crawled shivering to his side. The shot had taken him at point-blank range in the back of the head. He didn't have much face left. That handsome, chivalrous boy with his long lashes and high forehead, now turned to red ruin. "Poor *malysh*," Nina whispered through her frozen lips. "I should have gone in with you. I let you go, and I lost you." Guilt raked her soul, scarlet clawed, but she couldn't put her head back and howl under the stars the way she wanted to, she couldn't sink down on his dead chest and weep. She couldn't even bury him. Time was slipping past; who knew how long it would take the murderess to tend her bleeding neck and summon help, and though Nina thought she must have been in the water less than ten minutes, possibly not even five, she was soaked to the skin on a black autumn night and her limbs felt like they were made of ice. To her astonishment she still had her razor, swinging by its loop about her wrist—she kept that and her boots and trousers, but wrestled Seb's limp arms out of his jacket and his other layers, tossing her overalls into the lake and fumbling into Seb's blood-spattered but dry clothes. She flinched to leave him half naked under the stars, but without dry layers she would die. She made herself take his prisoner's tags, the ring on his hand. His older brother would want them. *Cool as ice*, Seb had said of him, *and about as trusting.*

"I'll tell him you died a hero," Nina told the boy who had been her friend for a few short, desperate months. "I'll tell him you saved my life, that you fought a Nazi murderess and made her bleed." She'd make him more than what he was, a warmhearted boy who died because he trusted that people were good.

No, she thought. *He died because he had the bad luck to meet you, Nina Markova. Because you fail every team you ever join, and then you lose them. You lost your regiment of two hundred* sestry, *and then you find Seb, and even though your team is now only one, you lose him too.*

Weeping, Nina kissed Seb's bloodied hair and lurched down the dock without looking back. She glanced once at the yellow house, feeling the primal desire to creep inside, track down that blue-eyed German bitch with her slashed neck, and finish what she'd started. But it would take everything she had just to get back to her campsite alive.

I am the rusalka *of the world's deepest lake at the world's farthest end*, she told herself, staggering delirious and blood light under the new moon. *I am a Night Witch of the Forty-Sixth Taman Guards Night Bomber Aviation Regiment. I do not fear Germans, or the night, or any lake in the world.* She did not think she would ever be afraid of drowning again.

She was afraid of something else now instead.

SHE ALMOST DROWNED in her own lungs by the end of winter, when the pneumonia settled in and shook her in bone-rattling spasms. But Nina Markova survived, coughing and emaciated, filthy and ravenous, until the Germans pulled away from Poznań in January of the new year—until she could emerge blinking and staggering from her forest into the sterile white arms of the Polish Red Cross pushing through the liberated camps and stalags. There were months of thermometers and medicines, months being moved from one hospital berth to another, tossing and turning as she dreamed of a blue-eyed huntress until she knew that face better than her own. Nina was thinking of that face as she sat upright in the latest hospital cot, deliriously tracing a star on the sole of one foot with a red navigation pencil and vowing to do it over in tattoo ink, when a whip-lean Englishman with desperate eyes came running at her with a torrent of questions, and she had been able to recite the first line of the story, the myth. Not *Your brother is dead because I failed him* but *Your brother died a hero.*

Chapter 54

IAN

September 1950
Boston

Nina avoided Ian's eyes. The woman who had stared down Comrade Stalin, Ian thought, now staring at her own interlocked hands to avoid *his* eyes. The Ford had wound its way out of Boston and was speeding northeast.

"I lie to you," Nina said, ignoring Jordan and Tony in the front seat, speaking only to Ian, her Russian accent thickening. "Is my fault Seb dies."

Ian didn't answer. Jordan and Tony exchanged glances, said nothing either.

"I should have stayed with him. *Die Jägerin*, she wouldn't catch me off guard. Or I should be faster, join him on the dock. I hesitate too long, is done." Nina sighed, and Ian heard the layers of guilt and pain in that sigh, the long nights she'd thought about this in the years after the war.

"You did your best," he managed to say.

"Not enough. Seb should have lived." Nina looked at him then, unblinking. "Is what you're thinking."

Part of Ian did think that. The unthinking rage of a brother too swamped by loss to be fair: *You knew how trusting he was, and you left him to be slaughtered.* Then the rage of a betrayed lover: *I slept beside you, I trusted you, I told you about the* parachute, *and you keep this from me?*

"I fail him," she said again, more softly. "Is what I do, when I have a team. I fail my regiment, I lose them. I fail Seb, I lose him. Is why I don't have a team anymore. I shouldn't have come, joined you . . ." Looking from Tony to Ian. "But I want to find the huntress. Since I have to stumble away from her by the lake, I want to find her again. It makes me selfish, so I join you. I shouldn't have."

That's your one fear now, Ian thought. Not lakes. Not drowning. To fail another *sestra,* another teammate, another comrade.

He drew a deep breath, shoved the shock and the anger away. Reached out with one hand and hooked his trigger finger through Nina's, looking into his wife's blue eyes that held such desperate sorrow behind their opaque shield.

"You didn't fail him, Nina. And you aren't going to fail us now. Believe that. This team will not save Ruth without you. This team cannot catch *die Jägerin* without you. If your one fear is losing another team, her one fear is you, and we are going to use that." Nina's eyes flared.

"We need to get there first, and we're at least an hour and a half behind," Tony said grimly behind the wheel.

Ian released Nina's finger with a fierce squeeze. "We're going to catch up."

The Ford stopped in a spray of gravel. Ian had never seen it before, but Tony had described it: the tiny ramshackle airfield where Nina had gone joyriding. Ian looked at a blue-and-cream biplane droning overhead, preparing to land, and felt a wave of pure terror. He shoved it down. "Jordan, can you persuade your former fiancé to do us a very large favor?"

GARRETT BYRNE LOOKED at them, dumbfounded. "You want to borrow a *plane?*"

"*Olive*," Nina said. "I like *Olive*."

"Ruth is in danger, Garrett," Jordan said. "It's for Ruth—"

"If she's in danger, contact the police and—"

"Brilliant idea, Gary," Tony snapped. "Telephone the police and report that a child is *with her mother*. That'll send them running, all right. Superb."

"I can't let an unlicensed pilot waltz off with one of my aircraft—"

"Tony, get his other arm." Ian came round the desk to take Garrett Byrne by the elbow. "We're locking him in the closet." *So much for the line we won't cross*, Ian thought. He wasn't just stepping over that line, he was vaulting across it, perfectly willing on Ruth's behalf to bolt Garrett Byrne in with the cleaning supplies. Garrett seemed to realize it.

"Jesus—" He yanked out of Ian's grip. "Jordan, is this true? You were right all along, your stepmother is . . ."

Jordan nodded, white faced.

"Jesus." He gulped it this time, looking at Nina. She gazed back, eyes slitted. "Mrs. Graham, you'd better bring *Olive* back without a scratch, or—" But Jordan was already flinging her arms around him in a violent thank-you, Nina was calling for maps, and Garrett pulled free and went jogging off to have the Travel Air 4000 fueled.

Tony looked at Ian. "Is this really going to work? Riding to the rescue in a biplane; this is something out of a serial where damsels get tied to railway tracks."

"It will work," Ian said with all the conviction he could muster.

"Only way to beat a car to the cabin," Nina said calmly, pawing through the maps. Her doubt and guilt had gone, Ian saw in relief—she had a mission to fly and the navigator in her had snapped to the fore, all business. "If I can land. Jordan, you say there is flat spot nearby, no trees? Show me—"

Soon they were all jogging for the runway, *Olive* standing proud in her blue-and-cream paint. Nina tugged flight goggles on. She could have been a ludicrous sight, goggles and boots and a Filene's summer dress, but she was all cool, hard competence. "Plane can take four. Two each cockpit."

"That's not safe," Garrett began.

Nina ignored him. "Is crowded but possible." She looked over her shoulder at Ian. "Jordan with Tony in front, you fly with me."

Ian had been afraid she would say something like that. "It would be far safer to fly with Tony, while Jordan and I follow in the car—"

"I fly four out of Taman once when U-2 behind me is chased down and the engine holed. Galya and I have to ferry the pilot and navigator. Was like flying a brick, but she stays up. Mostly." Tony was already settling into the passenger cockpit up front, Jordan scrambling after him. Nina crooked a finger at Ian, who fought a gripping wave of the deepest panic he'd ever felt in his life.

Nina felt the same panic when she threw herself into Lake Rusalka, he thought. *She could have let it take over, let herself sink, and then there would have been no one to bear witness to Seb's murder.*

Ian fought his stuttering heart down out of his throat and stepped up onto the wing. "Don't fail me, comrade," he said through gritted teeth, and dropped into the cockpit.

WHEN *OLIVE*'S WHEELS lifted from the ground and Ian saw the first terrifying glimpse of the earth falling away below, he wanted to shut his eyes and bury his face in his wife's hair. It was all scent and touch and noise up here in the tiny world of wind and metal, fabric and sky. It ravaged his ears.

The cockpit was so tiny it felt like being jammed inside a cartridge, Ian folded into the seat and Nina folded into him, her back against his chest, his arms welded around her waist, every limb in contact, every twitch of muscle shared. *We aren't nailed together this close when we're making love*, Ian thought. He had no idea how Nina was managing the controls, wedged up against them as she was, but she did it with complete confidence. Ian kept his eyes on her instead of the terrifying sky, his wife's hands moving over those strange dials and levers like a pianist, and felt a flash of terrified pride in her skill.

She shouted something he couldn't hear. How long the flight lasted, Ian had no idea. To him it lasted forever, then forever took on a new meaning as the engine died.

She's doing it on purpose. She knows what she's doing. Bringing them down toward Selkie Lake without the engine so that there would be no warning mechanical thrum to give their presence away. But all his instinct knew was that the engine was dead and they were dropping from the sky like a stone, and suddenly the world was full of terrible silence. Against the rush of the wind Ian heard Jordan's gasp, Tony's curse . . . and Nina laughing.

I married a bloody madwoman, Ian thought. As if she could hear him, Nina reached up behind her own head and touched his cheek. This time he heard her when she said, "We won't crash."

"Bloody hell we won't," Ian muttered into her hair. Nina stretched out her arms to the wind, back arching against him as if she could add her wings to the plane's, and Ian snatched her hands back inside. *Olive* was still dropping. "Hands on the controls, goddammit!"

She laughed again. Below the pines were rushing upward, and the silver flash of what must be Selkie Lake. Nina took the stick and for a moment, his wife's body twinned against his, Ian felt what she felt. *There is nowhere she leaves off and the plane begins*, he thought. *Woman and machine, masters of the air.* And one terrified man clinging to their tail feathers.

"Is there," Nina was saying, calm as water, "the treeless stretch. Is long enough."

Ian felt her hands moving, but he didn't look down to see the drop, just buried himself in the engine grease and north-wind scent of her hair as the biplane continued to fall out of the sky. He'd flung himself and the team into the void, and he'd trust his wife to bring them all down.

Don't fail me, comrade.

One final sickening lurch, and wheels bounced on ground. Every tooth in Ian's head rattled. *Bloody hell, we're alive.* He repeated it like an incantation, and then a different incantation: *Let* die Jägerin *be here.*

Chapter 55

JORDAN

September 1950
Selkie Lake

Nina saw the cabin first, its modest slanted roof showing between tree trunks, and at a gesture from her they all went silent. Jordan felt her own heart thumping as they crept closer, careful of the dried leaves underfoot. The silver expanse of lake opening wide between the trees, the short ribbon of the boat dock stretching out . . .

And sitting at its end, Ruth.

Relief washed violently over Jordan at the sight of that small figure. Ruth's feet swung over the water, and her blond head was bowed as she looked down into her lap. *Hang on, cricket. I'm coming for you.*

At Jordan's shoulder, Tony pointed. The sturdy old Ford belonging to Jordan's father was parked beside the cabin, trunk standing open. Even as they watched, the cabin door opened and Anneliese came out with a pair of traveling cases. A very different-looking Anneliese, Jordan saw. Much less the *Vogue* fashion plate in an old coat and trousers instead of skirts frothing with crinoline, hair now bleached a tired-out blond and lying damp on her shoulders. Jordan realized the rest of the team had gone utterly still at the sight of her—

Tony's gaze unblinking even as his fingers flexed, Ian turned to stone if stone could emanate waves of ferocity, Nina flowing into some strange relaxation, lips curving like a moon. Three profiles overlapping one another, devouring their first real sight of the woman they had been hunting.

"Ruth," they heard Anneliese call, closing the Ford's trunk on the cases and tossing the keys into the front seat. "We're leaving."

So close, Jordan thought. Even flying, they had barely got here in time. By car they would never have made it. A few fast-murmured plans flew, the first part of which was *Get Ruth*. Until Ruth was removed they could do nothing or Anneliese might kill her.

Nina slanted off toward the east, away from the cabin and the dock. Tony peeled left toward the cabin's far side where Jordan had told him about the back window. Ian and Jordan continued on straight, stopping well inside the tree line, where Ian cupped his hands around his mouth and gave a whistle: the haunting four-note opening of the simple Siberian lullaby he had learned from Nina and taught Ruth to play on her violin.

Anneliese, slamming the car door, didn't hear. At the end of the dock, Ruth looked up.

Ian whistled the opening bar again, low and calling. Jordan bit her lip, watching Ruth's eyes hunting for the music. Anneliese paused, clearly puzzled, but she didn't play the violin, she didn't know the ancient cradle song Ruth played so beautifully. Anneliese stepped onto the dock, her back to the cabin as she walked out over the lake. "Ruth, into the car. Stop sulking."

At the end of the dock, Ruth stood up. Jordan thought she could see the stubborn set of that fragile jaw all the way from here. Anneliese held out a hand, but Ruth brushed straight past her, breaking into a run. *That's it, cricket*, Jordan wanted to cheer as Ian whistled one more time and her sister pelted off the dock.

At that moment, Tony broke out of the cabin at a flat sprint, door banging open, something long in one hand. He scooped up Ruth like a football, tossing her over one shoulder and running for the car. Anneliese scrabbled in her coat pocket, but her pistol snagged for a split second and Tony was moving too fast. He yanked the car door and dove inside, pulling Ruth with him out of sight. Jordan could hear him urging Ruth down flat on the floor of the car, even as he slapped a long glinting shape down across the open driver's-side window: Dan McBride's spare shotgun, taken from the cabin and now leveled at Anneliese.

Jordan quivered inside like a plucked violin string, seeing Ruth disappear inside the car. Tony had sworn that if all went wrong he would drive away with Ruth, that he would make her safe first. The most precious pawn was off the board.

Now, staring across the chessboard, they faced only the queen.

Anneliese had frozen midway down the dock, pistol finally in hand, caught between lunging toward shore and firing from where she stood. Her back was to the trees as she stared at the car, and Jordan stepped out of cover onto the shore.

Ian strode arrow straight at her side. "Stay back," he said very low voiced. "This time she may shoot you."

"I know how to throw her off guard," Jordan murmured back, feeling the Leica about her neck on its strap. She'd snatched it on pure instinct when they left the house—perhaps the same instinct that made Ian stretch for his typewriter, Nina for a plane, Tony for his own nimble tongue. When preparing to level with an enemy, you readied your best weapon. "Anneliese doesn't really want to kill me, and after years of hiding, she's scared of the camera. I can use both against her. If I don't, she'll shoot *you*—you're the stranger; she'll aim right for your head."

Ian's stride didn't slow, sun glinting off his hair as he aimed for the dock. Jordan didn't stop either.

From inside the car, Tony was shouting at Anneliese in German and English, telling her to remain still or he'd shoot, keeping her gaze aimed at him. Jordan could see him from the corner of her eye. She didn't turn to look directly; neither did Ian. The world had narrowed to the two of them, and Anneliese. *It has to be us,*

Jordan thought. *The ones who have already gone against her and lost something—me, my father; Ian, his brother. Us.* The ones who refused to lose Ruth too.

Anneliese saw them as they stepped onto the dock, stiffening in a freeze of pure shock. She seemed to turn very slowly, or maybe it just seemed slow to Jordan through the Leica's lens as she lifted the camera—the flying strands of her hair, the blue of her eyes as they rounded, the knuckles whitening around her pistol. Watching it, something in Jordan telescoped, compressed, divided: there was the side of her that flinched in fear; the human side—and there was the lens that narrowed with perfect focus, the ruthless eye that put a lid on the chaos of emotions and simply watched Anneliese scrabble like a cowering animal chased out from under a bush. The cold inner lens that wanted nothing but to record what happened here and show it to the world.

"*Smile for the camera, Lorelei.*" It was Jordan who smiled as she took the picture.

Then the shot rang out.

Chapter 56

NINA

Nina crouched on the shore of Selkie Lake not eight hundred meters down from the cabin, yanking off her boots. She watched Tony snatch the child, saw Jordan and Ian come from the trees, saw the slim figure of the woman now frozen on the dock. *There you are*, Nina thought, yanking her summer dress over her head. The blue-eyed huntress with her Walther PPK and her scar. Half a decade and half a globe had had to be traveled, but the hunt went on. Only now, who was the huntress and who was the prey?

Ian was advancing down the dock now, implacable as granite, the American girl at his side just as steady. Tony worked the bolt action on the shotgun, the threat of it echoing across the lake, telling Lorelei Vogt not to run. *Your days of running are done.*

Nina straightened, naked except for her slip, the waters of Selkie Lake lapping at her toes, and unfolded her razor. Reaching carefully inside her mouth, she nicked the inside of her cheek. Spat blood.

Voices from the dock, more camera flashes. The huntress half frozen, half poised to pounce. *Don't kill anyone yet*, Nina thought to her enemy and her team both. *Wait for me.* She waded into the water, warmer by far than Lake Rusalka or the Old Man. The huntress's scar was calling her, the *rusalka*'s kiss. *You're still mine.*

A shot echoed into the perfect summer sky, and Nina was pierced by a bolt of pure, clawing, protective rage. *Oh, you blue-eyed bitch, if you killed my husband—*

And she dived into the arms of the lake.

Chapter 57

IAN

September 1950
Selkie Lake

The shot came from Tony. At the corner of Ian's eye he saw his partner had aimed into the sky, a flat report making the blue-eyed woman flinch and whirl even as she was still flinching from the flash of Jordan's camera. "*Smile, Anna*," Jordan called out again. *Click click click*. She'd said there was nothing her stepmother disliked more than having her picture taken, and she was right—Ian could see the woman flinch with every flash.

He took a deep breath, speaking up in his deepest, crispest tones of authority. "Lorelei Vogt, stay where you are."

She straightened at the sound of her name. He hoped she would lunge forward in a panic, let him get within arm's length and wrench the pistol away. But she stepped back instead, to the very end of the dock, face emptying of shock with frightening speed. Ian had never seen anyone knocked so off-balance recover their poise so fast. The pistol hung loose at her side, but he and Jordan still froze halfway down the dock before she could raise it. There was an odd moment of stillness where the sound of the shot faded and they regarded each other. Ian met the eyes of his brother's murderess for the first time, and every sound in the world—Ruth's muffled sobbing from the car,

Tony's voice soothing her, the monotonous slap of the lake against the pilings—faded to nothing.

Here you are, Ian thought, staring into those blue eyes in wonder. *Here you are.* For more than half a decade he'd thought of her every day, and here she was. Ian drank her in. He found her lovely. He found her obscene. He *found her.* "Here you are," he said aloud, and smiled.

"Who are you?" she asked, sounding genuinely puzzled, and it made Ian smile again. This woman had loomed over his life like a boulder, blotting out the sun, yet, of course, she had no idea who *he* was.

Ian didn't answer. Instead, he spoke words he'd dreamed of speaking for years. "Lorelei Vogt, you are charged with war crimes."

He expected excuses, the defensive shuffle, the whine that always seemed to begin *It was so long ago* or *I was just following orders* . . . Lorelei Vogt did none of those things. She merely shifted her gaze to Jordan at his side, steadily gazing through her camera lens. "How did you *get* here?" Genuinely curious. "Even if you got out of the darkroom at once, you couldn't—"

"Magic," Ian said. That was as good an explanation for Nina as any. *Nina, where are you?* Ian took a step closer, Jordan at his side.

Die Jägerin's pistol came up. "No closer."

Jordan clicked off another shot. Ian saw their target wince. "You really don't like having your picture taken, do you?" he observed. "I wouldn't like looking at myself either, if I'd done what you've done." *Click.*

Another flinch. "Jordan, stop."

"No." Jordan adjusted something on her Leica. "You and I have said everything that we needed to say to each other, Anna. I'm just doing my job, now. Recording the moment." *Click.* "The moment a murderess realizes she's going to pay for what she's done."

The woman's voice was calm. "You cannot arrest me."

"Yes, we can," Ian said. "For murdering Daniel McBride. You admitted as much to Jordan in the darkroom a few hours ago.

We can perform a citizen's arrest and bring you to the authorities. Murder is punishable by the electric chair in Massachusetts." Ian waited for the flicker of her eyes. "There's another option, of course."

"Murder me here, sink me in the lake?" The pistol lifted again.

"Don't tar me with your brush, you Nazi bitch. I have no intention of harming you." Ian felt no fear at all, only a humming tension running through him like wire. Was this how Nina felt on her bombing runs, when she cut the engine? He was gliding down now, falling very fast but very sure toward his target. "Put that pistol down, Lorelei Vogt. I know you can shoot either me or your stepdaughter between the eyes at this range, but be aware of this: the moment you do, my partner in the car back there will shoot you. And even if you get the drop on him"—Ian could see her eyes measuring it—"your time running is done. My article exposing you runs in the *Boston Globe* tomorrow. Page one above the fold, with photographs." Ian hadn't written a word in years, but he flung the lie at her with complete assurance. "There won't be a reader on the East Coast who doesn't know your face by the end of the week, and after that, the nationals will pick it up. There's nowhere you will be able to hide, not one corner of this huge country that will not know your face and recoil. That is a promise."

Click. Jordan snapped the shot right as the look of horror rolled across her stepmother's face. The pistol jerked in answer, not at Ian this time but at her. "*Stop.*"

Jordan took a step forward, blond hair blowing. "No." *Click.*

The shot deafened, echoing across the water. Ian lunged in front of Jordan, heart hammering, but the shot went wide into the water, a warning. Jordan never flinched, merely reached into her pocket and began calmly loading a new roll of film. Ian had seen photographers moving under shellfire on D-day in the same intense haze, the world narrowed to a lens that felt like a shield before them.

"You have Ruth." Lorelei Vogt's voice rose. "You have everything. Take it all and let me go—"

"No. That is not the choice in front of you." Ian's voice rose to a whiplash cut. "The choice in front of you is to be charged in Massachusetts for murdering Jordan's father, or be charged in Austria for war crimes. *That* is your choice, Lorelei Vogt. That is the only choice you have left in this life."

Click. Click. Click.

There was a moment he thought she was going to crack—a quiver across that smooth face, the even smoother gaze. Then resolve seemed to sheathe her in ice, chin lifting, pistol rising toward her own head, and Ian saw she was going to escape. She would escape justice and courtrooms and the world's hatred with a bullet, and he shouted without words because her death wasn't enough, it would never be enough, but even though he was running to close the distance between them, the barrel was already reaching the underside of her chin.

Then a rising shriek ripped the air, and they all saw what had just crawled out of the lake onto the end of the dock.

She crouched there for a moment like some giant spider, lake water sluicing off her skin. Ian knew perfectly well who she was— Nina Markova, his lover, his comrade in arms, his wife of five years—but as she uncoiled, she made even Ian's heart clutch in fear. She stood relaxed and reptilian, streaked with blood from the corners of her mouth down the sides of her throat, red lines curling down her soaked slip, down her arms, off the edge of the unfolded razor in her hand. She smiled, eyes glinting like winter ice, and her teeth were scarlet as though she'd been tearing at human flesh.

She rises out of the lake, streaked with blood, and drifts across the surface of the water toward me. Jordan had described her stepmother's nightmare in the huntress's own words. *And that's when I wake up. Before the night witch cuts my throat.*

There was no dream to wake from now, as Nina stalked down the dock.

Die Jägerin did not move. She stood wax white, quivering, a rabbit paralyzed by a snake's gaze, a Soviet biplane pinned to the sky by a German searchlight. Nina came remorselessly forward, razor outstretched. "*Mine,*" she was crooning, "*mine—*" And the woman who had murdered Ian's brother, and who knew how many others, backed up before her, twisting away in frantic horror. Ian saw none of her ferocious control this time as she brought the pistol back to her own head. Just fear—but he was still too far away to stop her from taking the bullet's escape.

Nina wasn't.

She flashed down on the huntress like a falling star, the razor coming around in a whistling arc. Lorelei Vogt screamed, staggering back with blood spilling from her arm this time rather than her neck. Red drops pattered on the dock, and Nina reached out contemptuously and pushed her down. Crouching slow and unhurried over the cringing woman, leaning so close they could have kissed, Nina plucked the Walther PPK from the nerveless fingers. "You don't get to die," she whispered to the woman who had shot at her across a lake half a world away, and dropped the pistol into the water.

Die Jägerin's face shattered. She crawled away, clutching her bleeding arm, scrabbling past Ian to Jordan, and she just stopped. Huddled against her stepdaughter, cringing from Nina, keening.

Slowly, Jordan bent down to embrace her.

Silence fell again over the frozen tableau. Nina came to Ian's side, never shifting her eyes from *die Jägerin.* Tony came out of the car on shore, shotgun cradled in one elbow, the other arm around Ruth, who clung white faced to his side. The only noise was the muffled sounds coming from the woman in Jordan's arms. Ian wondered if the children she shot had whimpered that way, as if snapped in half by terror. His heart resounded in his chest.

Nina had told him once, on the Prater Ferris wheel in Vienna, that one could kill a fear. She'd thrown herself into a lake today, to become a huntress's nightmare and protect her team. Ian had thrown himself into a plane. Lorelei Vogt, it seemed, could not kill her one fear when it crawled from her nightmares to look her in the eye.

Not yet, anyway, Ian thought. *So hit her hard before she recovers herself.*

Jordan said it before he could. "Anna," she said, her voice gentle, even though her face hadn't lost that distant look, the one that told Ian the world was still coming to her through a lens. Her hand rubbed her stepmother's shaking back in a soothing circle, even as her body remained stiff with revulsion. "You are going to make a choice now."

Chapter 58

JORDAN

September 1950
Selkie Lake

S he'll go?"

"She'll go." Jordan sat down next to Tony on the dock steps, where he sat with his sleeves pushed up and the shotgun still propped beside him. Anneliese was sitting just inside the cabin door some distance away, her arm bandaged, hands and ankles bound together, unmoving. Jordan looked away from her. "Where's Ruth?"

"In shock. I put her in the backseat of the car, covered her with blankets, let her cry herself to sleep."

She's going to have questions, Jordan thought. *What am I going to tell her?*

Maybe for now, *I'm here, and I'm never leaving* was enough. "Where are Ian and Nina?"

"Walking down the shore where Nina left her clothes. Our little Soviet popsy did a fine impersonation of a nightmare." Tony looked at Anneliese's huddled shape in the cabin doorway. Her shoulders were shaking. "Does she really fear Nina that much?"

"Nina is the one who got away. It haunted her." Jordan was maybe the only one who realized how much it haunted her. She hadn't hesitated to use it, telling her stepmother quietly that she could go to Austria and face trial for war crimes, or stay here and face trial for murdering her husband—but if she refused to go willingly down either path, Jordan would let Nina do the asking. "She chose Austria."

"Why?"

"Because I said Nina would never stay in Europe, that she hates it. Anneliese chose whatever continent would put an ocean between her and Nina." That was how terrified the huntress was of the *rusalka*.

Tony blew out a breath. "By letting her choose that, you know you're giving up the chance of justice for your father. Unless there's another messy extradition fight over her after her trial in Austria."

"If she was tried here for his murder—for which we have much less proof, only my word that she didn't deny it when I accused her—she might never face justice for Ian's brother and the Polish children. That isn't right either." Jordan still felt like she was floating somewhere very quiet. "So we do what we have to."

They sat in silence for a while, Jordan as hollow inside as a glass.

"We'll take her to Austria by boat." Tony rubbed his jaw. "Much harder to escape from the middle of the Atlantic, if she has thoughts of getting away. I'll see what's leaving Boston Harbor tomorrow or the next day. I don't care if it's a luxury liner or a raft with a paddle."

"I'll cover the tickets," Jordan said. "Whatever it costs to make it happen fast. I have Dad's insurance; if we can't use it for this—"

"It'll help."

"You'll have to watch her every minute," Jordan warned. "We have her tied now because she consented to it if it meant Nina would keep her distance, but she can't walk onto that ship tied up. Not when legally you don't have a warrant until you get to Austria. You'll have to be vigilant every second, until she's under arrest." *If an arrest order could be procured . . .* but Jordan refused to go down that rabbit hole. It was out of her hands; all she could do was trust Ian and his colleagues overseas. "I don't *think* Anna will try to run, not with Nina watching. But still . . ." Jordan thought of the woman on the dock with the pistol in her hand, a cornered animal ready to lash out at anyone, and shivered.

But then there was the woman who had encouraged Jordan to want the world, who had comforted her when she cried for her father . . . who had *murdered* her father. And none of those images seemed to have anything to do with the woman huddled in the cabin doorway now, clutching a towel to her bandaged arm and shivering.

"I pity her," Jordan said. "I hate that. I hate *her*, yet I still care for her. Why can't I turn it off, what I felt for her?"

Tony reached out, tugging Jordan against his shoulder. "I don't know."

"Don't tell Ian that I . . . For him it's so simple." Something had unwound in the tall Englishman the moment Anneliese had surrendered. "Do you want to go in with me?" Jordan had asked after leading the tied and shaking Anneliese to the cabin. "Ask her why she did it?"

"I know why she did it," he'd answered. "She did it because she wanted to, because she could. No matter what her other justifications might be. And I don't care to hear those."

I care, Jordan thought, staring at the cabin. She wished she didn't, but she did. Tony's hand rubbed the back of her neck under her hair, as if he were trying to massage the pain away. She brushed at her eyes. "Thank you, Tony."

"You don't need to thank me. I owe you."

"For what?" Jordan gave a half smile. "Using my weeping fit after Dad's funeral to infiltrate the shop, or sleeping with me?"

Tony was silent.

"You were tracking down a murderer." The anger she'd felt toward him initially had sunk and died under the tidal wave of today's shocks. It seemed like pretty small change now, his initial deception. "Getting the job out of me when we first met, that was a manipulation for the sake of your chase. But I have eyes, Tony. You weren't squiring me around ballet classes and airfields afterward just to get information out of me. You weren't getting *anything* out of me for the chase by then. As for what else you were getting, well, if all you wanted was an easy girl, I'm fairly certain you could have found one who didn't put you to work as a photographer's assistant first."

"I started tagging after you because I wanted to. No other reason." His black eyes were steady. "I'm still sorry for the lies. More sorry than I can say."

"And I still want to hit you, a little bit," Jordan tried to joke. "But I'll get over it."

"Hit me if you want, J. Bryde." Tony lifted her hand, kissed the pad of her index finger that pressed the Leica's button. "You were magnificent on that dock. Like you'd been striding through war zones with a Leica all your life."

"The eye took over." What a strange feeling it had been. Not the *right* feeling, maybe—surely it couldn't be right, for the eye with its obsession to capture the perfect shot, to take charge of that moment on the dock and overshadow the more natural things, the more *important* things: fear, love, worry for Ruth. Maybe it wasn't right, but Jordan had still felt it. *And I want to feel it again.*

Ian and Nina were striding back along the lakeshore, the Russian woman fully dressed and shaking out her wet hair, Ian strolling at her side hands in pockets. *They'll be gone tomorrow or the next day,* Jordan thought with a sudden wrench in her stomach. How much a part of her life they had all become, not just in banding together against Anneliese, but before: tea, jokes, reminiscences, the tender thread of Ruth's music. A brief, perfect friendship. And now, of course, they would be moving on. *Another hunt, another chase.* Looking at Tony, his black eyes fixed on Anneliese again. *Another girl.*

And I'll be here, Jordan thought, and the thoughts that had been submerged under the struggle of what to do about Anneliese broke free. No New York, no apartment, no interviews to see if she could sell her *Boston at Work.* At least not yet. Ruth would need her. The scandal was going to break, everyone was going to know what her mother had been. Everything would fall on Jordan now: the neighbors, the bills, the shop, the house, Ruth . . .

At least when Dad died I had Anneliese, Jordan found herself thinking, and that thought was so macabre, so terrible, so *true.* How long was it going to be before she stopped instinctively reaching for the quiet bulwark that had been Anneliese, always taking care of her in the background?

Now it's just you. Twenty-two years old, with a business and a house and an eight-year-old child. Looking down at the Leica, Jordan wondered how much time she'd have for it in the immediate future.

"Next question," Nina said, coming up to the dock, and paused to spit blood into the lake. "*Tvoyu mat,* one little nick in the cheek, it won't stop."

"Apparently I missed a vampire," Ian observed, looking at his wife's scarlet mouth. "What's your question, comrade?"

"I fly *Olive* home. Now we have two more people, so too many." Nodding at the car. "Who drives, who flies?"

"Drive," said Ian and Tony in unison. "With Anneliese," Tony added. "I'll take the shotgun and keep it on her the entire way."

"Fly," said Jordan. "Ruth can squeeze in with me." She'd be afraid, but better that than subject Ruth to ride in the same backseat as Anneliese.

"Good." Nina showed her teeth, still faintly red, in a grin. "Is a long time since I fly with a *sestra.*" For Nina it was simple too, Jordan thought: she'd caught the woman who tried to kill her; now was the time to rejoice.

"Just don't . . . turn *Olive* off midair this time," Jordan added. "If you don't mind."

"No fun," Nina grumbled, and Jordan found herself smiling. A weak smile, but a smile.

She didn't think the days ahead would bring too many of those.

BEFORE ANNELIESE DEPARTED the next day for the passenger liner that would take her back to Europe, she spoke only once.

She said nothing to Nina, sitting ceaseless and wakeful outside her locked door. She said nothing to Tony when he brought her meals on a tray. She did not even see Ian, who had taken over the typewriter in a fever of inspiration and begun hammering out the first article he'd written in years.

But when Jordan came into the bedroom with an armload of Anneliese's clothes for the voyage, watched from the doorway by Nina, Anneliese looked up from where she'd been sitting on the edge of the bed. Jordan stopped, clutching the pile of underclothes and dresses, pulse thumping.

"May I say good-bye to Ruth?" Anneliese asked.

"No," said Jordan.

Anneliese nodded. She stood, graceful again, hands clasped composedly before her, though she'd never look as composed as she used to—not when the first motion of her eyes was always a quick darting glance to find Nina. She flinched away from the gleam of Nina's teeth, looked back to Jordan. "When I am put on trial—" She stopped, the cords of her throat showing, and a trace of her old German accent crept back. "When I am put on trial, will you be there?"

"Yes," Jordan heard herself say. *Why?* But—"Yes," she repeated.

"Thank you." Anneliese reached out as if to touch Jordan's hand. Jordan stepped back. Anneliese gave a small sigh, took the armful of clothes, dressed herself in Jordan's and Nina's view to be sure she did not try to hide anything among the layers. Was escorted downstairs and out of the house, unbound yet enclosed by the triple gauntlet of Tony, Ian, and Nina. People were watching, across the street. Whispering. What on earth could be happening at the McBride house? *Keep an eye on the front page and wait*, Jordan thought, glad she had kept Ruth upstairs.

The taxi was waiting. Ian opened the door for Anneliese, like a courteous escort. Anneliese straightened her hat with an automatic gesture, looked at Jordan. Her lips parted.

Say it, Jordan thought. *Tell me you're sorry. Tell me why you did it. Tell me . . .* something.

Anneliese's soft lips closed. She sank into the cab; her gloved hand pulled the door behind her.

And they were all gone.

JORDAN DIDN'T MAKE the mistake her great-aunt did so long ago when her mother lay dying, saying *Your mother has gone away* in an effort to spare the truth. "Years ago, your mother did some bad things," Jordan told Ruth simply. "She's going back to Austria to answer questions about them."

"When will she come back?" Ruth whispered.

"She won't be coming back, Ruth."

Jordan braced herself, but Ruth didn't seem to want more information.

"Do we have to go back to the lake?" she wanted to know, fingers twined through Taro's collar.

"Never," said Jordan. "We're going to sell that cabin." Sell it or burn it like Nina had done with her U-2 in the forest, make a pyre of it for all the terrible things that had happened there.

Ruth said no more, her small face shuttered. Jordan didn't press her, only sent her to bed with a mug of cocoa and sat stroking the blond hair until Ruth sank into sleep. *You'll sleep, but you'll also dream*, Jordan thought, looking at her sister. Poor Ruth, confused all her life by nightmare fragments of memory. Sometimes pulling away from Anneliese, sometimes toward her. *I hope she never remembers what she saw. I very much hope that.*

But if she did, Jordan would tell her what happened. She'd tell Ruth everything she needed to know, as kindly and honestly as she could. "Good night, cricket," Jordan whispered at last, tiptoeing out.

It was the first time she'd been down to the darkroom since Anneliese had locked her in. She stopped at the top of the stairs for a moment, smelling her stepmother's faint lilac scent, then flicked the light and came down the steps. Only to be seized around the waist by a man's arms, and to hear a familiar voice in her ear: "Come here, J. Bryde."

Jordan shrieked, whirled, and smacked him all in the same

motion. "Tony Rodomovsky, I'm going to *kill you*—" Raining more smacks down on him where he stood at the foot of the stairs.

"I apologize." He offered himself up for the smacks, no resistance. "*Es tut mir leid. Je suis désolé. Sajnálom. Imi pare rau. Przepraszam*—"

"Shut up." Another smack. "You couldn't knock on the front door instead of—"

"I only just got back. Seeing the ship off, then settling things in Scollay Square. And I knew you'd be putting Ruth to bed, so I waited here."

Jordan stood back, palms stinging. "You're not on the boat," she managed to say, rather unsteadily.

"Brilliant deduction, Holmes. Why did you think I'd be *on* the boat?"

"You didn't say . . ." Jordan floundered. "It's done here. You're done. New chase, new hunt—"

He raised his eyebrows. "New girl?"

She kept her tone matter-of-fact. "We both said it was a summer fling."

"I thought we discussed modifications to the contract. A potential three-month extension into an autumn fling, as per agreement by both parties—"

"Don't tease," Jordan begged. "I watched my stepmother walk away in handcuffs, more or less. Soon it's going to be all over the front page—"

"Which is one reason I'm staying, at least for a while. Nina and Ian can handle the Austrian authorities without me. But there are going to be questions to answer here, especially when Ian's done with the story and it breaks." Tony's eyes were steady. "I said I'd stay to handle them."

That made Jordan weak with relief. She tried not to show it, but he reached out to push her hair back, smiling under the harsh light with an extra quirk of tenderness, and tugged her close for a slow, warm kiss, then another. Jordan felt her bones loosen in relief. "Oh, God, Tony. I'm so glad you came back."

She wished she hadn't said it—he was supposed to be a friend, a lover, not a rock to cling to. They'd only known each other for a summer. But his arms felt wonderfully rocklike and reassuring, and just for a moment she let herself cling.

"Are you *cuddling*?" He pulled back, felt her forehead with an anxious hand as if checking for a fever. "You never cuddle. Your idea of afterglow is developing six rolls of film."

Her laugh was watery, but it was a laugh.

"Now, that really is better." He pulled back, kissed the tip of her nose, and said with deliberate lightness, "Go swish prints around in trays. I'll cheer from the sidelines."

They were both silent in the red light as Jordan processed the most recent roll, comforted slowly by the familiar motions. One by one, she hung the prints, gave them a chance to drip as she cleaned up. She came back to the line, bracing herself, and Tony moved to stand at her elbow. Silently they looked from print to print.

"They're good," he said quietly.

Not all of them. Some were blurred, focused on people moving too fast. But that one . . . and *that* one . . . "Yes," Jordan said. "They're the best I've ever done."

She took down a shot of Anneliese leveling the pistol straight at the camera lens. Eyes like lake ice from Nina's frozen, unknowable home. Jordan knew where it belonged. Going to the folder with her photo-essay prints, she laid them all out in a line, starting with her father, ending with Anneliese and her cornered, merciless gaze. "I couldn't find the right image to finish it," Jordan said. "*A Killer at Work*."

Tony looked from print to print. "You'll sell it," he said. "You do know that?"

"Maybe." And she could even see this shot as the start of a new essay entirely focused on Anneliese, the progression of a demure bride to an ice-eyed murderess to a prisoner on trial. *Shades of a Murderess. Portraits of a Huntress.* Something like that might help Ruth understand the many faces of the woman who had stolen her and raised her and cared for her. But Jordan turned away from the worktable, rubbing her temples. "Ruth has to come first, now. I don't know how much time I'll have for this. I can't work the way I was planning to."

"Why not?"

"Because I'm all Ruth has." Once again Jordan felt the panic of that, the fear of failing her sister. "I'll have to do it all, now."

"As long as I'm in Boston, I'll help. Not because of you and me, because the team *owes* you, Jordan. This hunt blew your world to bits."

"That wasn't your fault," Jordan stated. "Dad was already gone before you even came here, and once you began tracking Anna, there were going to be other consequences no matter how she ended up caught. I'll gladly take them, if it means she's out of Ruth's life."

"That doesn't mean it sits right with me to swan off and leave you picking up the pieces. It won't sit right with Ian or Nina either."

"You'd help us?" The fierce common bond between them all had been Anneliese—what was left when that was gone?

Could it be Ruth?

Tony wrapped his arms around her waist. "Count on it, J. Bryde."

They stood for a long time, silent under the red light. Jordan's thoughts were a jumble, exhaustion and relief and cautious hope. The thought of going on entirely alone, carrying Ruth into the coming storm of the breaking scandal, had felt like that hair-raising moment when Nina cut the engine and the plane began to drop. Now it felt like Tony and his partners had reached around, flicked the switch, turned the engine back on. The plane had leveled.

Jordan twisted her head, kissed Tony lightly. "Come upstairs and stay the night."

"Are you sure? Nosy neighbors take note when gentlemen callers leave in the morning."

"My family is about to become notorious all through Boston." Jordan slung the Leica's strap over one shoulder and tugged him up the darkroom steps, switching on the overhead light. "I don't really care if the neighbors think I'm a hussy."

"Jordan?"

She half turned. *Click*. Standing two steps below, Tony lowered the little Kodak he'd taken out of his pocket, smiling. "I want a picture of my girl."

Sometimes you got great pictures with skill, Jordan later thought, and sometimes great pictures just *happened*. That cheap Kodak snap was the best picture of Jordan McBride ever taken, in its subject's opinion. Blue jeans and a ponytail, caught in motion halfway up a staircase, slinging the Leica casually over one shoulder as she looked back at the camera. A woman on the move, with a gleam in her eye like a lens.

It was the photo most used by J. Bryde, in her byline.

Chapter 59

IAN

October 1950
Vienna

The story was a razor in print form.

Ian had thought he'd never write again, that war had used up all his words. Now, sitting in a deck chair outside the locked third-class cabin where Lorelei Vogt would wait out the Atlantic crossing, he wrote the story of the capture, the story begun in Boston on Jordan's typewriter. Finishing it longhand on a notepad, he hammered it into shape: the article he was determined would make *die Jägerin* famous.

> *Lake Rusalka: a lake in Poland named for a creature of the night, and during the darkest years of the war, a woman lived on her shores far more fearful than any witch who crawled from a lake's depths.*

That was his lede, and in the paragraphs that followed Ian vivisected the woman born as Lorelei Vogt, reborn in murder as Anneliese Weber, rechristened in deception as Anna McBride, and identified by nature—primitive, primal nature red in tooth and claw—as a huntress. He knew every pulse point to push in those paragraphs, every emotional trigger to pull. Women would cry at this article; men would shake their heads; newspaper editors would see banknotes. Ian looked down at his final copy and thought, *Dynamite in ink.*

It felt good, not to be done with words, after all.

The ship stopped in New York before starting across the Atlantic. Ian took the chance to wire the story to Tony, told him to pitch it to every major newspaper in Boston, and promptly wrote a follow-up memorializing his brother and the Polish children and poor Daniel McBride. Ian barely slept and neither did Nina, one or the other of them on continuous watch outside Lorelei Vogt's door.

Not until the very end, after they'd left the ship behind in Cannes and boarded a series of trains that would take them to Vienna, did the huntress speak to him. Ian had been too tense for conversation or scribbling once they left the security of the ship, far too aware Lorelei Vogt could make a panicked run the moment his attention lapsed—but she passed through the train travel passive and silent as a wax doll. On the final train to Vienna, hearing the wheels slow beneath them, she looked at Ian suddenly as if realizing this limbo time of traveling was coming to an end. "I still don't know who you are, Mr. Graham."

Ian raised an eyebrow.

"I don't know you, so why did you come looking for me?" She sounded so puzzled. "You crossed half a world to catch me. What did I *do* to you?"

How many times had he envisioned sitting down with this woman and telling her in biting words what she'd taken from him? Telling her about a little brother who dreamed of flight and did not know what distrust was. How he'd yearned to do that. Yearned for something else too—for any memories she might have of Seb, the way he looked bolting his stew when she took him inside her ocher-walled house, the things they had talked about in her warm kitchen. The last look on his face before she shot him . . .

But Nina had recounted with quiet poignancy what the last look on Seb's face had been, had sketched him in the end as he stood in the moonlight warm and well fed, looking at the sky and never dreaming he was about to die. *I won't replace that memory with whatever poisoned image you might have,* Ian thought, looking at *die Jägerin*'s puzzled blue eyes. *I want to remember my brother through Nina's eyes, not yours. The eyes of a woman who saw a friend, not a murderer who saw prey.*

So Ian just gave a smile like his wife's razor. "You'll find out at the trial," he said. "If I am called to testify."

"You should have let me die," the huntress answered, low voiced. "You should have let me shoot myself."

"You don't get to die," Ian said. "I am not that merciful."

Lorelei Vogt bowed her head. It stayed bowed through the commotion and paperwork that greeted their arrival in Austria. Fritz Bauer came from Braunschweig in a whirl of suits and uniforms to witness the arrest. Bauer's greeting had been a fierce smile around his ever-present cigarette, but Ian hadn't been surprised to see the blend of curiosity and resentment their colleagues aimed at them.

"Sour faces," Nina commented, puzzled.

"No one wants to arrest Nazis anymore," Bauer said, not caring a jot for the glares. "Sweep it all under the rug, live and let live. Your girl may not get more than a few years in prison," he warned Ian. "Maybe even the case thrown out. Judges don't like locking up pretty young widows."

"I'll make her so famous they won't have a choice." Tony had said on Ian's last telephone call that the first story had exploded in Boston like a V-2 rocket. Ian already had the stories to follow it up, paced to land like a sequence of punches in a boxing ring. Once the nationals picked up the story, even the hidebound Austrians with their distaste for scandal wouldn't be able to slide away from their duty.

Ian watched *die Jägerin* walk away, disappearing into a cloud of homburgs and *Polizei* caps as she was finally taken off his hands. He supposed the next time he saw her it would be her trial. Jordan

McBride, he guessed, would be at his side, the lens of her eye poised behind the lens of her camera. *She needs answers more than I.* Or if she didn't, Ruth would someday, when she was old enough to ask the difficult questions about the woman who had raised her.

"I have a question for you, comrade." Ian looked down at Nina, strolling along at his side. They were staying at a hotel on the Graben, but he wasn't eager to return yet. They hadn't really talked, he and his wife, since the night on the beach in Florida. After that the chase had swamped them, and the tense need to watch their prey. "You could have killed Lorelei Vogt, out there on Selkie Lake. She had a pistol, she was moving to use it. You disarmed her rather than cutting her down. Why?" Nina's restraint had surprised him. Since when had she ever been restrained, in the matter of capture over vengeance?

"Dying, that is easier for her. She wants it, because justice is harder. So I don't cut her down. Is difficult," Nina conceded, a glint of fury in her blue eyes. "I think for a moment, when I dive into the lake and the shot goes off, that she's killed you."

Ian stopped. "And you wanted to cut her to ribbons to avenge me?" From Nina that was practically a valentine.

"But I don't," Nina said, virtuous. "I just disarm her. I think maybe you are right, *luchik*. Justice over vengeance."

"Bloody hell, woman, have I actually made a dent in you?"

She jabbed him in the ribs. "I make a few in you too."

Yes, you have, Ian thought. *And not just the fact that I am now addicted to your paperback Regency tosh.* He tugged her arm through his, and Nina let him. The beginning of autumn nipped the air, and a few chestnut sellers were out, but the city looked tired and gray. Ian missed the hum of energy from Boston, the brashness, even the accents.

"You go back to Boston soon?" Nina asked as if reading his mind.

"Yes." Not forever, perhaps, but there was no doubt his reception in Vienna was going to be cool for some time. He'd burned every favor he'd ever stored up ensuring Lorelei Vogt's arrest—it would be no bad thing to absent himself and pursue war criminals in America for a few years. Jordan had said on his last telephone call that he could have the workroom over the antiques shop rent-free, if he would just go on giving Ruth the occasional lesson. With a thrum of quiet delight Ian envisioned it: a bright space with a window over Newbury Street, the smells of beeswax and silver polish drifting from the workshop where Mr. Kolb no longer worked. Taking half an hour every day to stretch his back and teach Ruth a new tune when she was let out of school, drinking tea afterward with Tony and Jordan as they talked above the sound of scales, then back to work. Building a case, maybe, against Vernon Waggoner of Woonsocket, Rhode Island, who looked like he might have buried a few corpses in shallow graves back in his day. "Yes, I'm going back." Ian looked at Nina. "Are you?"

"Is nice place, the decadent West." Nina sounded noncommittal. "I like decadent."

"Come back, Nina. Stay with the team." Ian held up a hand before she could bristle. "I'm not asking you to stay married to me. I'm asking you to stay with the center. You belong with this team. You know you do."

"You want me?" She looked suddenly vulnerable, Nina who normally faced the world behind shields of serenity or prickliness, with the occasional switch to barbarism. "I think how I left Seb behind, think maybe you wouldn't want me to stay. Once huntress is caught."

That memory hurt, Ian couldn't deny it, but casting all the blame on Nina would be unjust. "My brother was a grown man. He made a decision, and you couldn't dissuade him from it. There it is."

She nodded. There was guilt there, and probably always would be, but overlaid by that Russian fatalism of hers. *Battered souls like ours*, Ian thought, *tramping out of the wreckage of wars, always have guilt. Ghosts. Lakes and parachutes.* They could both bear that weight, going on. "I want you on this team, Nina. On the hunt, wherever it leads. With me or not, but always on the hunt."

She considered that. "Then I come back to Boston."

Ian couldn't hide the grin that broke over his face. Nina almost grinned back, but scowled instead. "We still divorce," she warned.

"All right."

"Because after Yelena I don't—"

"Who asked you to love me?" Ian said lightly. "That's not what I'm saying at all, you Red Menace."

"What *do* you say?"

He had searched for what to tell her on the beach in Florida and got it wrong. But something tense and jealous had unspooled in him since *die Jägerin*'s capture, and there had been many hours to reflect on the Atlantic crossing, staring at the waves.

"I am only saying that I will find you mad wolves to hunt," Ian told his wife, "and that I will never break your heart." If part of that heart was always out of reach, that seemed entirely fair to Ian. You did not get a whole heart when you pinned yours to a splendid, battered, high-flying hawk like a Night Witch. Nina's soul would always in some deep place yearn to be soaring under a bomber's moon with her dark-eyed Moscow rose, and that was fine. Ian thought there was a chance, despite her prickles, that a bit of that remaining heart might thaw enough for him.

Or maybe I'm wrong, he thought. Maybe they'd divorce, after all. But he would still have a Night Witch on his team, and there wouldn't be a war criminal in the world out of their reach.

He was happy to wait as Nina decided what she wanted.

His wife was peering upward, smiling. He followed her gaze and saw she was looking at the silhouette of the great Prater wheel above the amusement park. "You want to go?" she challenged.

Sixty-five meters up. Ian had nearly come to pieces the last time he rode it. But he'd gone flying since then with a Hero of the Soviet Union, far higher than sixty-five meters. *With the bloody engine turned off.* Smiling, he shook his head.

"Why not?" Nina asked. "Kill the fear, *luchik*."

He slipped his trigger finger through hers and tugged her back in the direction of their hotel. "Already done, comrade."

Epilogue

NINA

April 1951
Fenway Park, Boston

Nina didn't understand baseball. "Why are they arguing?"

"The batter doesn't like the umpire's call," Jordan explained, ponytail swinging. "It's been a *very* generous strike zone."

"Strike zone? He hits him now?" This was a boring game, Nina had decided. Hitting people would liven it up.

"No, no. He's just arguing to make a point."

"Should hit him with the bat," Nina grumbled. "Why have a bat if you don't hit people?"

"I'll hit Kinder with a bat if he doesn't stop coming inside on the fastball. He nearly winged Rizzuto." On Jordan's other side, Tony glared down at the Red Sox pitcher. In between putting in hours for Ian and filling in behind the shop counter when Jordan needed it, Tony was signed up for classes at Boston University. *The center has always needed a legal expert, and I just happen to have the G.I. Bill on my side*, he'd said last Christmas with a gleam in his eye. *We can't keep burning up the telephone lines to Bauer for advice by the time it comes time to try our first extradition case.*

You, a lawyer? Nina had snorted.

I can sell ice to Alaskans and charm birds out of trees. It's either be a lawyer or a shoe salesman.

"Keep whining." Jordan laughed now, as Tony continued to grumble about the strike zone. "Your precious Yankees are down five runs."

"Not for long, J. Bryde . . ."

"This game is stupid," Nina told her husband.

"Agreed." Ian was stretched out long limbed and relaxed in his seat, hat cocked back, collar unbuttoned. The smell of mown grass and chalk rose from the field, and the crowd hummed with cheers and groans, cracking peanut shells, and scratching pencils on scorecards. It was a rare day off for all of them: the team was preparing a file on one Vernon Waggoner of Woonsocket, Rhode Island, cross-checking his identity against that of a clerk who had worked at Belsen, and Jordan (when she wasn't handling the team's photography) had been taking pictures for a tourism bureau. "Easy work, decent money," she said, snapping classic horizon shots all around Boston. "Brochure shots will buy the Sunday roasts until I sell *Boston at Work*." There was interest; her photographs accompanying Ian's articles on the capture of Lorelei Vogt/Anna McBride had received a certain degree of attention.

The ball went flying, which, to Nina's eye, made all the men in uniform run around in inexplicable ways and made Ruth bounce up and down in excitement. Nina squinted at the field. "You understand this, *malyshka?*"

Ruth had been chattering to Tony in mixed English and Yiddish, which he'd begun informally teaching her this winter. *Her real mother was Jewish—Ruth will never know her, but she can know something about her mother's people.* Ruth lapsed entirely back to English, telling Nina, "This is the infield fly rule," and going into far more detail than Nina wanted. Children could be very boring, Nina thought, even if you liked them. Ruth looked rosy in the sunshine, much less like the kind of scrawny chick a housewife wouldn't even bother to put in a pot. She'd had bad nightmares in the fall, something about a woman hiding in her closet at night to steal her away, and Jordan had fussed very unnecessarily. Nina had taken her razor, gone into the closet and banged around uttering some Baba Yaga screeches, nicked the pad of her finger so there would be blood on the razor, then walked out holding it up for Ruth's inspection, announcing, "Is dead now." Nightmares had been better ever since.

"Bloody hell, Nina, you ate all my peanuts." Ian rattled the empty bag.

"What's mine is yours, what's yours is mine."

"We're divorcing," he said. "So that's not true."

"I get more." She climbed out of her seat, up the park steps toward where the vendors hawked snacks, still marveling at the abundance of all the food on display.

Succumbing to capitalist greed, her father sneered, but Nina ignored him. She could buy a second bag of peanuts if she wanted them; she had sandals that weren't made out of birchbark or cheap factory-glued leather; she had a dress that had never been worn by someone else first: polished cotton as scarlet as the star on the *Rusalka*. The dress Ian had bought for her in Filene's last year, a dress that would have made Yelena's eyes dance with wicked intentions. If this was capitalist greed, Nina would take it.

Western whore, Papa grumbled, but his voice came more faintly now than it used to. Perhaps because she couldn't imagine him here in his wolfskins, eating peanuts and enjoying a lovely April day. Nina looked at the grassy outfield lapping up to the tall green wall in left field, and imagined April on the Old Man. The lake would still be frozen, the *rusalka* sleeping green haired and still below the ice, but the air would be freshening, looking ahead toward June when the ice would break into rainbow needles, turquoise blocks, shards sharp enough to cut a throat. Nina remembered standing on that frozen shore in seal-fur boots, hating it, asking furious questions of the world that had seemed so cold and closed in.

What is the opposite of a lake? What is the opposite of drowning? What lies all the way west?

Among Yelena and the Night Witches, she'd found the first two answers. But the third had tormented Nina in the bad years between Seb's death and Tony's call to hunt the huntress. Scrabbling to make a living in ruined, exhausted England, missing Yelena, telling herself never to get so close to anyone again. Thinking, as she trudged through rainy days on the ramshackle airfield, that this was all she deserved for failing first her regiment and then Seb. It was better to be alone; it didn't matter if the *all the way west* she had yearned for turned out to be a world not as cold but just as closed in as the one she'd fled.

No, Nina thought now, looking at the park, at the green grass and the men running in pointless squares. This *is all the way west.* She looked down the rows of seats and found Tony saying something to Ruth; Ruth listening as she unwrapped a piece of gum; Jordan snapping a picture of the field . . . and Ian lazily fanning himself with his battered panama.

"This is our year," the vendor who sold Nina her peanuts predicted. "We go all the way this year, I can feel it. This is our team."

"Yes," Nina agreed, smiling at the two blond heads below, the black head, and the dark with its salting of gray. Maybe they weren't Night Witches, they weren't a regiment, but—"Is our team."

She tore into the peanuts, wandering back down. Men on the field were running around again, people were on their feet shouting, who knew why. "Hit him with the bat!" Nina shouted, just to join in. Slid into her seat beside Ian, who had dropped his hat and pulled a paperback out from Nina's bag: *The Grand Sophy,* by Georgette Heyer. "You stole my book again, Vanya," Nina complained.

"Sophia Stanton-Lacy is being vexed by the spiteful Miss Wraxton, but I am confident she will prevail." Ian removed a bookmark. "And since when am I *Vanya*? We've moved on from *little ray of sunshine*?"

"Ian—in Russian, would be *Ivan.* Proper nickname for Ivan is *Vanya.*"

"Nicknames are to *shorten.* You don't shorten a three-letter name to a four-letter name to a five-letter name."

"You do in Russian," she said serenely.

He raised an eyebrow, studying her. "What are you thinking, comrade?"

"I think maybe we put off divorce for a year." She'd been turning those words over for a while, not sure about them. She followed them up with a glare. "Only a year. Then maybe . . ."

"Then maybe," he agreed, nonchalant. Englishmen, they couldn't do nonchalant. Or maybe just her Englishman. He was fighting the grin that tugged at his lips, the grin she'd liked from the start even when she couldn't understand a thing he was saying. It wasn't much like the grin that had scrunched Yelena's nose so sweetly, but there must have been something about it that was the same, because it had a similar effect on Nina's stomach.

"A year," he said again, as if he liked the sound of it. Nina liked it too. Not too confining, a year. It didn't make her want to bristle and retreat. It wouldn't stop her looking at a waning quarter moon and wanting Yelena back, missing her more than life—Nina didn't think that would ever leave her. But she could bear it.

Nina took Ian's panama and clapped it over her own head, tilting her face up to the sun, warmed through. "*Tvoyu mat*," she said, blinking at the blue sky above. "Good flying weather."

NAZI MURDERESS SENTENCED

BY IAN GRAHAM

OCTOBER 9, 1959

THE TRIAL OF Nazi war criminal Lorelei Vogt has played to its last act, as the woman known as *die Jägerin* stood yesterday in an Austrian courtroom to receive her sentence. Although she was first arrested in 1950, her trial would not commence until 1953 and proceeded to drag out for a further six years. Crowds gathered outside the courthouse to see the arrival of the defendant, made notorious by the award-winning photographic essay "Portraits in Evil" (J. Bryde) run in the October issue of *LIFE* magazine in 1956. Lorelei Vogt showed no emotion as her sentence was read: life imprisonment. So the wheel of justice turns.

Those hoping to read answers in her face were surely disappointed. The face of evil remains unknowable, and the questions remain: Who is she? What is she? How could she? Her victims are memorialized at the Rodomovsky Documentation Center in Boston, Massachusetts (director Anton Rodomovsky, human rights attorney), where the words over the center's doors read "The Living Forget. The Dead Remember."

The dead lie beyond any struggle, so we living must struggle for them. We must remember, because there are other wheels that turn besides the wheel of justice. Time is a wheel, vast and indifferent, and when time rolls on and men forget, we face the risk of circling back. We slouch yawning to a new horizon and find ourselves gazing at old hatreds seeded and watered by forgetfulness and flowering into new wars. New massacres. New monsters like *die Jägerin*.

Let this wheel stop.

Let us not forget this time.

Let us remember.

About the author

2 Meet Kate Quinn

About the book

3 Author's Note

14 Reading Group Questions

Insights,
Interviews
& More . . .

Read on

18 Further Reading

Meet Kate Quinn

© 2018 Laura Jucha Photography

KATE QUINN is a *New York Times* bestselling author of historical fiction. A lifelong history buff, she has written seven historical novels, including the bestselling *The Alice Network*, the Empress of Rome Saga, and the Borgia Chronicles. All have been translated into multiple languages. Kate and her husband now live in San Diego with two black dogs named Caesar and Calpurnia. ∿

Author's Note

"Does INS know of any Nazi war criminals living in the United States at this time?"

"Yes. Fifty-three."

That question was posed in 1973 by Democratic Congresswoman Elizabeth Holtzman in a routine subcommittee hearing, and the answer surprised her as much as it did me during my research for this novel. Had there really been known war criminals living in America since the end of the Second World War?

Yes. There just wasn't any funding or organization to investigate them. Holtzman later pushed for the creation of the Justice Department's Office of Special Investigations, but before the OSI, any Nazi war criminal who made it to the United States had a good chance of living in peace . . . including one woman upon whom I partly based *die Jägerin*.

Hermine Braunsteiner was a brutal female camp guard at Ravensbrück and Majdanek, who served a brief postwar prison sentence in Europe, then married an American and became a US citizen living in Queens, New York. Her neighbors were dumbfounded when she was tracked down in 1964 and accused of war crimes, and her astonished husband protested, "My wife wouldn't hurt a fly!" Anneliese Weber/Lorelei Vogt is a fictional composite of Hermine Braunsteiner and another woman, Erna Petri, an SS officer's wife who during the war found six escaped Jewish children near her home in Ukraine, brought them home to feed them a meal, then shot them. Petri was tried in 1962 and given a life sentence, and Braunsteiner became the first Nazi war criminal to be extradited from the United States. ▶

3

Author's Note (*continued*)

What moved these women to do such terrible things? The question is unanswerable. Petri was defensive, saying that she had been conditioned to Nazi racial laws and hardened by living among SS men who carried out frequent executions—she admitted wanting to show she could conduct herself like a man. Braunsteiner was self-pitying, weeping, "I was punished enough." Both women faced justice, but only after a long slog of legalities and paperwork: it took seventeen years for Braunsteiner to be extradited, tried, and sentenced to life in prison. I wanted *The Huntress* to have a swifter climax than a decades-long legal battle, and I certainly had no wish for my fictional characters take credit from the very real journalists and investigators who brought Petri and Braunsteiner to justice, so I made the decision to create a fictional female war criminal from both women's records.

Mention the term "Nazi hunter" out loud, and most real Nazi hunters will wince. The term conjures a Hollywood vision of pulse-pounding adventure, and the reality is very different. The first war crimes investigation teams were hard at work before the V-E Day champagne corks had even started popping; they took testimony from camp survivors and liberators, tracked the guilty down in POW camps and escape bolt-holes, and sought out the civilian murderers of downed Allied airmen and escaped prisoners as well as perpetrators of the Final Solution. Men like William Denson, US Army chief prosecutor at the Dachau trials, and Benjamin Ferencz, chief prosecutor in the trial of the Einsatzgruppen killers, were overworked heroes responsible for prosecuting hundreds.

But after the Nuremberg Trials there was an overwhelming public sense of "Well, now that's done" as far as Nazi war criminals were concerned. Even though only a tiny percentage of the guilty had been prosecuted, there wasn't much interest in further war crimes trials—the Soviet Union had become the enemy to fear, not the defunct Third Reich. By the seventies and eighties, as the Cold War waned and people realized time was running out as World War II veterans and witnesses aged, there was a surge of renewed interest in bringing Nazis to justice, but post-Nuremberg investigation teams had a real fight on their hands.

Such teams might be government funded, run through refugee documentation centers like those begun by Tuviah Friedman in Vienna and Simon Wiesenthal in Linz, or conducted privately. There was no common strategy or agreement on tactics, and such groups often disagreed (or even feuded!) Perpetually underfunded and overextended, they tracked war criminals through the tedious cross-checking of records, wary interviews with a suspect's neighbors or family who had no legal obligation to cooperate, and long hours following a suspect's friends and acquaintances, often attempting to make positive identifications with nothing more than old photographs and outdated witness testimony. Much depended on bribery, charm, guile—and patience, because most hunts took months or years.

Catching a war criminal was only the beginning. There was no guarantee an arrest would lead to a trial: in Europe, many former Nazis still held positions of power, and war crimes trials were stymied by everything from passive resistance to outright death threats. ▶

Author's Note (*continued*)

Pursuing criminals overseas was even more of a nightmare, and some teams resorted to illegal means in such cases: either a kidnapping job to circumvent extradition (Mossad's black-bag snatch of Adolf Eichmann, bringing him from Argentina to Israel where he was tried and executed), or outright assassination (the killing of Herberts Cukurs, called "the Eichmann of Latvia," in Brazil).

Ian and Nina Graham are fictional Nazi hunters, though they were inspired in part by the famous husband and wife team Serge and Beate Klarsfeld, whose partnership is both a moving postwar romance and an inspiring dedication to human justice—their most famous catch was Klaus Barbie, "the Butcher of Lyon," and they're still tirelessly dedicated to the fight against fascism although now in their eighties. Tony Rodomovsky is also fictional, as is his Boston center and Ian's Vienna-based one, though such centers were invaluable not just in hunting war criminals, but in documenting the testimony of Holocaust survivors. Without their work preserving witness statements and camp evidence, much information about Nazi atrocities would have been lost. Fritz Bauer, on the other hand, was a very real man: a Jewish refugee who returned to his homeland postwar and tirelessly prosecuted war criminals despite hostility from a West German government that wanted to forget its past crimes. Times have changed since those days, and in a modern Germany that has taken responsibility for its horrendous history, Fritz Bauer is now honored as one of the first Nazi hunters.

In writing *The Huntress*, I realized I needed a link between my team of Nazi hunters and their elusive quarry—and as soon as I

read about the Night Witches, I knew I had
found my link. The Soviet Union was the only
nation involved in the Second World War to
put women in the sky as fighter and bomber
pilots, and what women they were! Products
of the Soviet aviation drive of the 1930s, these
young fliers were championed by Marina
Raskova, the Amelia Earhart of the USSR.
The day bombers and the fighter pilots (among
the latter, Lilia Litviak, seen in cameo at the
Engels training camp, was killed in an aerial
dogfight during the war, but became history's
first female ace) eventually integrated with
male personnel . . . but the night bombers
remained all-female throughout their term
of service and were fiercely proud of this fact.

The ladies of the Forty-Sixth Taman
Guards Night Bomber Aviation Regiment
went to war in the outdated Polikarpov U-2,
an open-cockpit cloth-and-plywood biplane,
achingly slow and highly flammable, built
without radio, parachute, or brakes. (It was
redesignated the Po-2 after 1943; I was unable
to pinpoint an exact date for the change, and
continued to use the term U-2 for clarity.) The
women flew winter and summer, anywhere
from five to eighteen runs per night, relying
on stimulants that destroyed their ability to
rest once off-duty. They flew continuously
under these conditions for three years,
surviving on catnaps and camaraderie,
developing the conveyor belt land-and-
refuel routine that gave them a far more
efficient record than comparable night
bomber regiments. The women's relentless
efficiency waged ruthless psychological
warfare on the Germans below, who thought
their silent glide-down sounded like witches
on broomsticks, and awarded them the ▸

nickname "*die Nachthexen*." Such dedication took a toll: the regiment lost approximately 27 percent of its flying personnel to crashes and enemy fire. The Night Witches were also awarded a disproportionately higher percentage of Hero of the Soviet Union medals—the USSR's highest decoration.

Nina Markova is fictional, but not her exploits. Lieutenant Serafima Amosova-Taranenko was born in remote Siberia, saw a Pe-5 perform a forced landing, and swore to become a pilot. Senior Lieutenant Yevgeniya Zhigulenko finagled her way into the training group by pestering a random colonel in the aviation department until he gave her an appointment, then refusing to leave until he referred her to Raskova. Navigator Irina Kashirina successfully made a one-armed landing, taking the stick with one hand while holding her wounded pilot off the front-cockpit controls with the other. Captain Larisa Litvinova-Rozanova described the way pilot and navigator would trade naps to and from the target, as well as the horror of watching three planes before her and one plane behind her shot down by a night fighter (the regiment's worst night of losses). Major Mariya Smirnova was pushed out over the Sea of Azov by low cloud cover, and nearly drowned. Several Night Witches described such experiences as climbing out on a wing to knock off a bomb stuck on the rack, being chased down by pursuing German planes, singing and dancing and embroidering during airfield waits, hazing from the male pilots, and—worst of all!—the indignity of wearing mass-issued men's underwear.

Yelena is also a fictional character; it isn't known if there were any romantic relationships between women of the Forty-Sixth. In the oppressive atmosphere of the Soviet Union, no one would have spoken a word of any such liaison had it existed. Pilot memoirs and interviews are similarly close-lipped about criticism of the ruling regime—even after the fall of the Soviet Union, only one Night Witch openly admitted hating Stalin and his rule. Undoubtedly there were others who were less than ardent Communists even as they fought to defend their homeland, but like Nina, they would have remembered the listening ears of the secret police and kept quiet. There is no record that any woman of the Forty-Sixth defected on a bombing run, but the Red Air Force was evidently afraid such things could happen, since they made a point of refusing posthumous honors to any deceased pilot whose body was not recovered. Soviet superiors were clearly aware of the danger that some resourceful pilot might take his or her plane in the opposite direction to find a new life in the West.

Poland, where Nina crashes in August 1944, would have been a hellish place to survive. The doomed Warsaw rebellion was in full roar, the Soviet army pushing from the east as Nazis began to flee west. Poznań, renamed Posen by the Germans, was a place steeped in tragedy: many Polish citizens were displaced, arrested, and executed as German settlers moved in to make a new Aryan province. Lake Rusalka was created using Polish slave labor, and though there was no Huntress living in an ocher-walled mansion on its shores, the lake was the site of several massacres. Memorials to the dead stand today in silent witness among the trees around an otherwise beautiful nature spot. ▸

Author's Note (*continued*)

Poznań was also the site of a prisoner of war camp, Stalag XXI-D, home to many Allied prisoners sitting out the war in idle frustration. Many had been captured during the retreat to Dunkirk, including members of the Sixth Battalion Royal West Kents in whose ranks I placed the fictional Sebastian Graham. Escape attempts from behind stalag walls were common; most escapees were recaptured or killed, but at least one man—Allan Wolfe, referenced by Sebastian—walked to Czechoslovakia and managed to survive living rough in the countryside until the war's end, so survival in the wild was possible, if difficult.

The pretty spa town of Altaussee was a bolt-hole for any number of high-ranking Nazi officials in the war's immediate aftermath, including Adolf Eichmann. His wife continued to live at 8 Fischerndorf with their sons—in 1952, a few years after her fictional interview with Ian and his team in this book, the real Vera Eichmann quietly packed up her children and joined her husband in exile. Had anyone been keeping watch on her, Eichmann would likely have been caught years before his eventual capture in 1960.

As always, I have taken some liberties with the historical record to serve the story. I wasn't able to confirm if there was an air club at Irkutsk, though there were hundreds across the USSR by the time Nina learned to fly. It isn't known if representatives from the female aviation regiments were present at Marina Raskova's funeral in Red Square, or if Stalin himself was there—but given the deep affection in which both the "Boss" and the women pilots held Raskova, it seems likely. (Besides, I couldn't resist the opportunity of showing Stalin, along with his very real habit of doodling wolves on documents!) The occasion where the Night Witches had to scramble their planes into the sky when they had just sat down to breakfast happened in the Crimea rather than in Poland and is combined with a separate occasion recounted by Lieutenant Polina Gelman, who recalls getting extremely tipsy after an unaccustomed drink at a holiday dinner, then flying a bombing run while completely hammered.

Ian Graham is fictional, and so is his presence as a war correspondent at historic events such as Omaha Beach and the Nuremberg executions. He is based on several journalists like Ernie Pyle, Richard Dimbleby, and war photographer Robert Capa who spent the war jumping between the front line's hottest danger zones in search of the news. Such men might not have been soldiers, but they risked their lives parachute-jumping from bombers, running with guerrilla troops, and wading onto the beaches of Normandy armed with nothing but notepads and cameras. Their bravery was astounding, and after the war many suffered as badly from PTSD as any soldier. Among the male war correspondents and photographers were some truly heroic women as well, including Jordan McBride's heroes Margaret Bourke-White (star photographer of *LIFE* magazine), and Gerda Taro (the first female photographer to cover a war zone). Jordan is fictional, but her heroines are not, and deserve to be remembered.

The SS Conte Biancamano which brings Ian and his team to the United States was a real passenger liner running the Genoa- ▸

Author's Note *(continued)*

Naples-Cannes-New York route, but exact sailing dates have been adjusted for the story. Eve Gardiner, Ian's acquaintance from British Intelligence with whom he shares a drink on that voyage, might be recognizable to some who have read my novel *The Alice Network*. Ruby Sutton and her newspaper column, quoted by Eve during the Blitz, comes from Jennifer Robson's *Goodnight from London*, with permission of the author who was on tour with me at the time of writing.

Finally, a word about lakes and lake spirits. There is no Selkie Lake in Massachusetts, but Altaussee, Lake Rusalka, and Lake Baikal are all very real. This story began for me with the idea of lakes, the water nymphs rumored to inhabit them (some benevolent and some malevolent, depending on the folklore), and the three very different women who begin this story standing on vastly distant shores. It would take the tides of war plus one determined Englishman and his Jewish partner to find the connections between these women, and it leads them on perhaps a more pulse-pounding adventure than real Nazi hunters usually faced. But that's how the muse gave me the story, and I rarely argue with the muse. (Because I always lose!)

I owe heartfelt thanks to many people who helped in the writing and researching of this book. My mother and my husband, always my first readers and cheerleaders. My wonderful critique partners Stephanie Dray, Annalori Ferrell, Sophie Perinot, Aimie Runyan, and Stephanie Thornton, whose insightful red pens saved this book from being utter rubbish. My agent, Kevan Lyon, and editor, Tessa Woodward—thank you for giving me that extra month to finish;

you have the patience of saints. Brian Swift for his expert advice on firearms malfunctions, and Aaron Orkin for his expert advice on the kinds of wounds that result from firearms malfunctions—here's hoping we didn't all end up on FBI watch lists for those long email chains. Jennifer Robson for answering questions on the ins and outs of journalism, and her father, Stuart Robson, for his patience untangling complicated questions about World War II army rank and POW structure. Anne Hooper for her insights on children learning the violin, and Julie Alexander, Shelby Miksch, and Svetlana Libenson for their lessons in Russian slang (especially the swearing!). Huge thanks to Danielle Gibeault, and to Janene and Brian "Biggles" Shepherd of Fun Flights in San Diego for fact-checking all my aviation details and answering countless questions about flying. And finally, thank you to *Olive*—not just a fictional aircraft, but a very real WWII-era Travel Air 4000 who took me for a ride through the clouds above San Diego, with Biggles at the stick. *Olive* showed this ground-bound author exactly how thrilling flight can be! ∾

Reading Group Questions

1. All the characters begin the book standing on different lake shores—Nina at Lake Baikal, Anneliese at Altaussee, Jordan at Selkie Lake, and Ian at the lake in Cologne. Nina and the Huntress clash for the first time at Lake Rusalka in Poland, and everyone comes together ultimately at the lake in Massachusetts. Discuss how the idea of the lake, and the *rusalka* lake spirit, weaves through *The Huntress* as a theme.

2. Ian states that the life of a Nazi hunter is about patience, boredom, and fact-checking, not high-speed glamour and action. Do you agree with him? What preconceptions did you have about Nazi hunters?

3. Jordan's drive to become a photographer clashes with the expectations of her father—and almost everyone else she knows—that she will marry her high school boyfriend, work in the family business, and relegate picture-snapping to a hobby. How have expectations of career versus marriage changed for women since 1950?

4. The Night Witches earn their nickname from the Germans, who find their relentless drive on bombing runs terrifying, but the men on their own side haze them, mock them, and call them "little princesses." How does prejudice and misogyny drive the

women of the Forty-Sixth to succeed? Did you know anything about the Night Witches before reading *The Huntress*?

5. Nina calls herself a savage because of her early life in the wilds around the lake with her murderous, unpredictable father. How did her upbringing equip her to succeed, first as a bomber pilot and then as a fugitive on the run? Does her outsider status make her see Soviet oppression more clearly than Yelena, who accepts it as the way things should be?

6. When Jordan first brings up suspicions about her stepmother at Thanksgiving, her theories are quashed by Anneliese's plausible explanations. Did you believe Anneliese's story at Thanksgiving, or Jordan's instinct? When did you realize that Jordan's stepmother and *die Jägerin* were one and the same?

7. "The ends justify the means." Ian disagrees strongly, maintaining he will not use violence to pursue war criminals. Nina, on the other hand, has no problem employing violent methods to reach a target, and Tony stands somewhere between them on the ideological scale. How do their beliefs change as they work together? Who do you think is right?

8. Ian and Nina talk about lakes and parachutes, referencing the bad dreams and postwar baggage that inevitably come to those who have gone to war. ▶

How do Ian and Tony deal with their post-traumatic stress disorder and survivor guilt, as opposed to Nina and the Night Witches?

9. Throughout *The Huntress,* war criminals attempt to justify their crimes: Anneliese tells Jordan she killed as an act of mercy, and several witnesses tell Ian they were either acting under orders or ignorant of what was happening. Why do they feel the need to justify their actions, even if only to themselves? Do you think any of them are aware deep down that they committed evil acts, or are they all in denial?

10. Jordan sincerely comes to love Anneliese, who is not just her stepmother but her friend. After learning the truth about Anneliese's past, Jordan is perturbed that she cannot simply switch off her affection for the one person who encouraged her to chase her dreams. How do you think you would react if you found out a beloved family member was a murderer and a war criminal?

11. In the final confrontation at Selkie Lake, the team is able to capture Anna instead of killing her or allowing her to commit suicide, and she later faces a lifetime in prison for war crimes. Were you satisfied with her fate, or do you wish she had paid a higher price for her actions?

12. By the end of *The Huntress*, Jordan has
    found success as a photographer, Tony
    is a human rights attorney, and Ian and
    Nina are still hunting war criminals.
    Where do you see the team in ten years?
    Do you think Ian and Nina will remain
    married, or will Nina find a way back to
    Yelena, her first love? Do you think Jordan
    and Tony will stay together, or drift apart
    as friends? What about Ruth? ❧

Further Reading

FICTION

The Bear and the Nightingale by Katherine Arden
Night Witches by Kathryn Lasky
The Secrets of Flight by Maggie Leffler
Piece of Cake by Derek Robinson
Daughters of the Night Sky by Aimie K. Runyan
Rose Under Fire by Elizabeth E. Wein

NONFICTION

*In Enemy Hands: Canadian Prisoners of War,
    1939–45* by Daniel G. Dancocks
*For You the War Is Over: American Prisoners of
    War in Nazi Germany* by David A. Foy
*In the Shadow of Revolution: Life Stories of
    Russian Women from 1917 to the Second World
    War* edited by Sheila Fitzpatrick and Yuri
    Slezkine
*Stalin's Peasants: Resistance and Survival in the
    Russian Village After Collectivization* by Sheila
    Fitzpatrick
*Everyday Stalinism: Ordinary Life in Extraordinary
    Times: Soviet Russia in the 1930s* by Sheila
    Fitzpatrick
Margaret Bourke-White: A Biography by
    Vicki Goldberg
Hunting the Truth, a memoir by Beate and
    Serge Klarsfeld
The Polish Underground State by Stefan
    Korbonski
The Nazi Hunters by Andrew Nagorski
*A Dance with Death: Soviet Airwomen in World
    War II* by Anna Noggle
*Wings, Women, and War: Soviet Airwomen in
    World War II Combat* by Reina Pennington

Over Fields of Fire: Flying the Sturmovik in Action on the Eastern Front 1942–45 by Anna Timofeeva-Egorova
Red Phoenix: The Rise of Soviet Air Power, 1941–1945 by Von Hardesty
Hunting Evil: How the Nazi War Criminals Escaped and the Hunt to Bring Them to Justice by Guy Walters

Forgotten Holocaust: The Poles Under German Occupation 1939–1944 by Richard C. Lukas
Richard Dimbleby: A biography by Jonathan Dimbleby
Blood and Champagne: The Life and Times of Robert Capa by Alex Kershaw
Piece of Cake by Geoff Taylor ∾